The storm barreled down on Jikun, hurling his block of ice haphazardly across the foaming crests. A crack of lightning flashed in the sky and an image was briefly illuminated to his left—a pillar of stone jutting from the crashing waves, a ripped sail tangled across the jagged surface.

There came a sudden, fervent cry. "Jikun?!"

Another blaze of lightning and Jikun caught a glimpse of the pale skin of the Helven, his body gripping the debris of the ship. He vanished under a massive swell and reappeared in a frantic struggle for air.

"Over here!! Left!!" Jikun hollered. He swung his hand into the water, trying to propel himself forward. As though mocking him, a gentle wave knocked him farther away, and a ripple of thunder cascaded like laughter across the sky.

He saw Navon's head turn toward him, his hollow cheeks lit by a brilliant flare of light. His fingers were like bones clutching onto the cracks of the wood, his fingernails clawing at the surface.

A wave barreled into Navon from the side. With a terrified cry, his companion vanished beneath the water, swallowed with the remnants of the ship.

THE KINGS

Kings or Pawns

Heroes or Thieves

-UPCOMING-

Gods or Men

Princes or Paupers

HEROES OR THIEVES

THE KINGS: BOOK II

JJ SHERWOOD

EDITED BY ALEXANDRA BIRR

Heroes or Thieves

Cover art by Indah Sekarwangi
Cover design by J. Caleb Clark
Edited by Alexandra Birr
Map by J. J. Sherwood
First Printing June 2016
Library of Congress Catalog Card Number: 2016903983

Ebook ISBN: 978-0-9862877-3-2
Paperback ISBN: 978-0-9862877-4-9
Hardback ISBN: 978-0-9862877-5-6

Silver Helm
P.O. Box 54696
Cincinnati, OH 45245

(513) 400-4363 * SilverHelmPublishing@gmail.com

Visit the website at **www.StepsofPower.com**

Acknowledgements

When we authors fill our acknowledgement sections, we are often drawn first to the people who emotionally assisted the creation of our projects. In the case of *Heroes or Thieves*, no others come as prominently to mind as those who took the very product of their own hard work and generously offered it up to the series you hold.

So on that note, I would like to first and foremost thank the kindness, support, and humbling generosity of:

DENNY
ZACHARIAH BRADEN SELL
JESSICA AND PIPER BOZIK
ALEX HALBLEIB
JAMES CAMPBELL FERN
BOB AND ANNE BIRR

When we gather in that special place all adventurers do—that clamorous tavern that only mercenaries, soldiers, and that one town drunk seem to utilize—you eight would get the special table. Not the one that's lopsided. Not the one stuffed in the dark and dusty corner. Not the one where the seat is forever sticky no matter how hard that generously endowed barmaid scrubs.

The one reserved for the best of the best—inexplicably clean, polished, and already set with eight *clean* mugs topped with the best ale this side of the Windari Channel.

And finally, for the emotional support and advice we authors always need: Thank you, my family and friends. In particular, those who put in the special time to make *Heroes or Thieves* shine: Alexandra Birr, Bob Birr, Carol Bundy, Laura Peterson, and my wonderful husband, Mr. Sherwood.

PRONUNCIATION GUIDE

a – **r**a**ck**	e – **w**e**t**	i – **m**i**ss**	o – **l**o**ck**	u – **f**u**r**	ee – **s**ee**n**
ah – **f**a**r**	aw – **c**a**ll**	ey – **c**a**me**	ahy – **r**i**ght**	air – **f**a**re**	uh – **u**p
oo – **s**oo**n**	oh – **r**o**pe**				

Note: the "**h**" in all Sel'varian names is pronounced "breathlessly": ɦ
Note: the "**d**" in all Sel'varian is quick and almost "silent"
Note: **ʒ** is pronounced as a rolling J (*jsh*), as in the name "Jacques"

Aersophyla	air-soh-FAHY-luh
Adonis	A-duh-nis
Alvena	al-VEE-nuh
Cahsari	CAH-suh-ree
Darcarus	dahr-CAHR-uhs
Darival	DAIR-i-vawl
El'adorium	el-uh-DOHR-ee-uhm
Elarium	el-AHR-ee-uhm
Eldaeus	el-DEY-uhs
Elvorium	el-VOHR-ee-uhm
Emal'drathar	e-MAL-druh-thahr
Ephraim	EF-reym
Erallus	e-RAWL-luhs
Eraydon	e-REY-duhn
Esra	EZ-ruh
Fildor	FIL-dohr
Geldin	GEL-din
Hadoream	ɦAH-dawr-uhm
Hairem	ɦEY-rem
Hazamareth	hah-zuh-MAIR-eth
Heshellon	he-shel-LON
Ilrae	IL-ruh
Ilsevel	IL-se-vel
Itirel	AHY-ti-rel
Jerah	ʒAIR-uh
Jikun	ʒEE-koon
Kaivervi	KEY-ver-vahy
Kevus	KEY-vuhs
Kisacaela	ki-suh-CEYL-uh
Laeris	LEY-ris
Laethile	LEYTH-ahyl
Lardol	LAHR-duhl
Liadeltris	lee-uh-DEL-tris
Makados	MAH-kuh-dohs
Mikanum	mee-KAH-nuhm
Navon	nuh-VON
Noc'olari	no-koh-LAH-ree
Relstavum	rel-STAH-vuhm
Rulan	ROO-lahn
Ryekarayn	RAHY-kair-en
Saebellus	sey-BEL-luhs
Sairel	SEY-rel
Sanas	SAH-nes
Sel'ari	sel-AH-ree
Sellemar	SEL-le-mahr
Sevrigel	SEV-ri-gel
Taemrin	TEYM-reen
Thakish	THAH-kish
Tilarus	ti-LAIR-uhs
Tiras	TAHY-ruhs
Tsuki	SKEE
Turlondiel	tur-LON-dee-el
Turmazel	TOOR-muh-zel
Valdor	VAL-dohr
Vethru	VETH-roo
Wratherus	RA-thur-uhs

RACE PRONUNCIATION GUIDE

Darivalian	dair-i-VAWL-ee-en
Eph'ven	EF-ven
Eph'vi	EF-vahy
Faraven	FAIR-uh-ven
Faravi	FAIR-uh-vahy
Farvian	FAHR-vee-en
Galwen	GAHL-wen
Galweni	GAHL-wen-ee
Helven	HEL-ven
Helvari	hel-VAH-ree
Helvarian	hel-VAH-ree-en
Lithri	LITH-ree
Malraven	mal-RAH-ven
Malravi	mal-RAH-vee
Noc'olari	no-koh-LAH-ree
Noc'olarian	no-koh-LAH-ree-en
Ruljen	ROOL- ʒen
Ruljenari	rool- ʒe-NAH-ree
Ruljarian	rool- ʒAHR-ee-en
Sel'ven	SEL-ven
Sel'vi	SEL-vahy
Sel'varian	sel-VAH-ree-en

Glossary

Aersadore — the world on which Ryekarayn and Sevrigel reside.

Darcarus — second prince of the True Blood Sel'vi, purportedly a relentless troublemaker.

Darival — the freezing tundra of Sevrigel's north, recently besieged by an upsurge of the bestial white thakish. Home to General Jikun Taemrin.

El'adorium — the speaker of Elvorium's Council of Elves.

Elarium — Sevrigel's affluent capital of the south, site of the obliteration of General Jikun Taemrin's army by the warlord Saebellus.

Erallus — Hairem's personal guard and heir to the throne. He allowed himself to be surrendered by Sellemar to Ilsevel in order for Sellemar to gain the queen's favor.

Eraydon — the great hero of Aersadore who, 9000 years ago, sacrificed his life to vanquish the dragon god's forces.

Farvian massacre — the horrific slaughter of Sevrigel's entire Farvian population by their own Mad King.

Galway — the god of seafarers and water.

Hadoream — the third True Blood child of King Silandrus, remembered amongst Elvorium's palace servants for possessing a mischievous, kind, and free-spirited nature.

Halls of Horiembrig — Sevrigel's uninfluential capital of the West, which was captured by the warlord Saebellus during General Jikun Taemrin's occupation in the Sevilan Marshes.

Ilra — the neutral god of healing. A great number of his followers are the Noc'olari.

Ishkav — a dark god of death, worshiped by cult followers and fanatics.

Itirel — the tranquil, gifted Noc'olarian healer who assisted Sellemar in the rescue of Lady Ilsevel.

Kaivervi — a Darivalian hunter of great skill. Has romantic interest in Jikun and he in her, but due to Jikun's inability to commit, they remain apart.

Kamora — a goddess of beauty and nature, commonly worshiped by the Faravi and Sel'vi.

Lardol — the former head servant of Hairem's palace and Alvena's personal "tormentor." Helped Alvena escape after she witnessed Hairem's murder.

Madorana — the former head cook of Hairem's palace.

Malranus — the god of dragons, rival to Sel'ari. Worshipers are often secret in their religious practices for fear of persecution.

Murios — a powerful necromancer from Darival who prophesized the fall of a kingdom at the hands of a Lithri.

Necromancy — magic that harnesses the spirits of the dead to cleave living souls, animate dead corpses, or even resurrect dead mortals to life; its use on Sevrigel results in the death penalty.

Nilanis — Ilsevel's father and the previous El'adorium. Ilsevel had him executed as revenge for his secret murder of her brother, a loyalist to Saebellus.

Noctem — the god of the night and minor god of deception. Rival of Sel'ari. Worshiped primarily by the Noc'olari.

Phantom Isles — the islands to Ryekarayn's southwest, territory of monsters, demons, and all manner of bestial legends.

Royal Schism — the division 300 years past in which the True Bloods departed for Ryekarayn and the previous El'adorium, Liadeltris, ascended Sevrigel's throne.

Ryekarayn — the western continent of Aersadore; previous homeland of the elves before they departed to Sevrigel following the humans' betrayal of Eraydon. The continent is vastly untamed and now primarily civilized by humans and dwarves.

Sairel — king of the True Blood Sel'varian Realm upon Ryekarayn; commanding and studious in nature.

Sel'ari — the goddess of justice. She is a righteous, fierce warrior who brought the mighty dragon god, Malranus, down for her elven people. Primarily worshiped by the elves, especially the Sel'vi.

Sevilan Marshes — the swamp in which General Jikun Taemrin's army contracted the Marsh Plague while attempting to battle the centaurs.

Sevrigel — the eastern continent on Aersadore, home to all races of elves.

Silandrus — the traditional, devoted king of Sevrigel who abdicated his throne and established the True Blood realm on Ryekarayn.

Thakish — the ferocious beasts of Darival's icy tundra. They have three eyes, white fur, six legs, and fingerlike structures upon their backs. They hide within the snow and devour unsuspecting passersby.

Tiras — the most powerful necromancer Aersadore has ever seen and one of Eraydon's legendary companions. After being blinded in the Last Battle, he vanished, leaving behind a legacy of magic but only two written tomes.

True Blood — the elves (excluding the Faravi who were massacred prior to the event) who fought in Eraydon's battle and did not abandon Ryekarayn when their human allies turned on them.

Vale — Saebellus' crude and rowdy captain who Sellemar stabbed during his rescue of Lady Ilsevel.

Windari Channel — the channel separating the continents of Ryekarayn and Sevrigel.

Zephereus — god of the sun and glory. Righteous, but merciful, and primarily worshiped by humans.

RECAP

- An era of corruption reigns over the country of Sevrigel, led by the people's elected Council of Elves. After years of failing to cure the degradation, the True Blood King Silandrus departed the land with his three children and tens of thousands of followers. They established a new kingdom upon the continent of Ryekarayn that became known simply as the Sel'varian Realm. Until their former home purifies itself of its iniquities, they have refused interaction with Sevrigel.
- The previous leader of the Council of Elves, the El'adorium Liadeltris, ascended the Sevrigelian throne and became the first king of non-royal blood. However, after a 300-year reign and as a result of failing to appease corrupt wishes, he was assassinated by the very council who appointed him.
- Liadeltris' son, Hairem, was thenceforth crowned in a time of tumultuous politics and uncertain loyalties. Hairem was young and confident, but ultimately naïve; he held the belief that he could reform the council's policies.
- Hairem's visionary leadership quickly threatened to shift the balance of the council. In direct response, several of his loyal council members were assassinated. These attacks were secretly orchestrated by the new El'adorium, Nilanis, in order to retain a majority vote to support his policies.
- During the chaos of these brutal murders, General Jikun Taemrin returned from war to Sevrigel's capital of Elvorium. He had won yet another victory over the rebelling warlord and ex-general of the Sevrigelian army, Saebellus. While Saebellus had won no battles himself, his tactical genius and demonic beast persistently wreaked havoc on Jikun's army. In his first meeting with the newly appointed

King Hairem, Jikun believed the king's words that his priority was the military's success.

- But Jikun's success was not the priority of the council. Nilanis, attempting to gain further control over the king, invited Hairem to dine with his beautiful daughter, Ilsevel. While initially rebuffed by Nilanis' blatant attempt at matchmaking, Hairem soon believed Ilsevel to be a lady with fire and firm political opinions aligned with his own.
- While Hairem struggled with the council's attempts to control or ignore his wishes, Jikun returned north to visit his icy homeland of Darival. There he joined his comrades in a hunt of the predatory thakish, whose aggression had risen to unprecedented heights since his last visit. He expressed affection for his childhood friend Kaivervi, but was unwilling to commit to her.
- Jikun's trip was cut short by the council's demands. Upon their order, he moved his army south to the Sevilan Marshes, where the centaurs' burial grounds encroached upon the territory of the Sel'vi's phoenix. While King Hairem opposed this ruling to relocate the centaurs, he nonetheless complied with what he believed to be a wholly selfish decree. He furthermore denied Jikun's request to aid Darival against the thakish, stating that more troops could not be spared.
- While both internal and external conflict raged, a mysterious foreigner named Sellemar arrived in Elvorium. By night, he hunted the enemies of Sevrigel under the name of Ralaris, hoping to gather evidence to reveal the council's immorality.
- However, neither Hairem's disagreement with the council nor Sellemar's attempts to remove them had any effect on Jikun's fate. In the long weeks within the swamps, a plague swept through Jikun's ranks and devastated his soldiers. All military action ceased and the troops were forced to eat their own dead to survive. It was Jikun's first military defeat. The horrific event cost him the lives and health of a crippling portion of his troops.
- During the Marsh Plague, Hairem became engaged to Ilsevel. He swiftly used his new political leverage with her father to recall the army from the swamps.
- Due to Hairem's show of defiance—and in utter disregard for Nilanis' disagreement—the council ordered the assassin to kill the king. Hairem and his personal guard Erallus managed to fend the assassin

off and send him fleeing. Realizing the fragility of his own life and reign, Hairem named Erallus his heir in the event that he should die without a child.

- Finally receiving the order to return, Jikun surrendered to the centaurian leader. His army was forced to relinquish their armor and weapons. On the return journey to the capital, Jikun's defenseless division was attacked by Saebellus' Beast. Their survival was owed entirely to Captain Navon's forbidden use of necromancy.
- Upon their return—battered, ill, and near death—Jikun and his troops were quarantined outside the capital. This final indignity escalated Jikun's emotional distress and he attempted to strike the king. Mercifully, Hairem allowed the incident to pass unaddressed.
- While Hairem focused his new political hold on amending his errors, Ilsevel planned a visit to an ill relative outside the capital. During the journey, she staged her own capture by the warlord Saebellus. She used the encounter to express herself an ally and discuss with him the fall of the elven nation.
- Sellemar, hearing of Ilsevel's capture, revealed to the king and council his identity and close relationship with the True Bloods. He informed them that she was being held in the Halls of Horiembrig, an old city Saebellus had seized during Jikun's occupation in the swamps. After expressing his intent to rescue her, he was joined in his venture by Erallus.
- Along with Sellemar's mysterious companion Itirel, he and Erallus used the True Blood tunnels beneath the old eastern capital to retrieve Ilsevel and escape. During the venture, Sellemar both killed Saebellus' lieutenant, Kraesin, and severely wounded his captain, Vale.
- Meanwhile, Navon was attacked by Saebellus' Beast while praying in the temple of Sel'ari. He was forced to use his necromancy to compel the beast to retreat. Yet despite his triumph, Navon was imprisoned for the crime of using the forbidden magic and sentenced to execution.
- Shortly after Navon's imprisonment, Ilsevel was returned to the capital and wed Hairem. As she had planned with Saebellus, she offered intelligence of the warlord's movements toward the southern capital of Elarium.

- Hairem immediately sent Jikun to "thwart" Saebellus' victory. However, Jikun refused to lead the army without Navon, thus forcing Hairem to relent and pardon the captain for his crimes.
- Jikun consulted with Sellemar regarding the secret True Blood tunnels. The information led Jikun to believe that they had finally found a way to corner and defeat the warlord.
- Sellemar returned his attention to the council. Informed of his intent to reveal their crimes, the council made a grave miscalculation and sent the assassin to murder the warrior. Sellemar easily dispatched the human and threw his body into the canyon.
- Meanwhile at Elarium, Jikun found Saebellus' troops pinched between him and the city. After a careful scouting of the area, Jikun's army rained down upon Saebellus' seemingly unsuspecting troops.
- However, a large faction of Saebellus' army—soldiers Jikun believed to still be at the defense of Horiembrig—appeared suddenly and inexplicably from the previously scouted hillsides: leaving Jikun surrounded. Saebellus had formerly used the magic to vanish after every defeat, yet never once—in all their battles—had he chosen to demonstrate its power to appear. Stunned and unprepared, Jikun's troops were utterly defeated.
- Finding Jikun terrified on the battlefield, Captain Navon ordered his general to flee. When he discovered that Jikun was severely wounded, he pulled him from the bloodbath. Together they fled across the Windari Channel toward the human continent of Ryekarayn.
- Hairem received news of Jikun's defeat, yet he remained hopeful of Elvorium's success. He turned to Ilsevel for comfort—and she drew him close and slit his throat.
- Hairem's mute handmaiden, Alvena, witnessed the murder—a fact made known instantly to Ilsevel when Alvena, horrorstruck, burst into the room where Hairem lay dying.
- Alvena immediately fled and escaped the palace with the help of Erallus and the head servant, Lardol. She was taken to Sellemar's estate where he revealed yet another True Blood tunnel. With Sellemar's letter promising safe passage in hand, she travelled through, intent on reaching the True Bloods on Ryekarayn.
- Knowing Erallus would never ascend the throne, and with the heir's compliance, Sellemar turned the former guard over to Ilsevel in order to gain her favor.

- Days later, Saebellus arrived to the bridge of the capital. The council feared for its own safety and threw wide the gates for his arrival. Saebellus then gave the council an ultimatum: Ilsevel would marry him and make him king, or he would war with Elvorium and kill them all. Ilsevel feigned distress and accepted his terms in order to "save the people."
- They were immediately wed and Saebellus was crowned King of Sevrigel.
- The shroud of benevolence cast aside, Ilsevel's first act was to murder her father for his secret assassination of her brother, a male who had nearly tarnished their family name when he joined Saebellus' cause. She then informed the council that "the reign of kings has returned."

ÆNTARA
RYEKARAYN
GALESTRAM
ERAYDON CITY
RUSTALL
KARKADOS
DANESLAND
NORDEEP
AENID MOUNTAINS

N
DARIVAL
Kaivervale
Gulf of Saravi
Farvian Ruins
Widow's Peak
Elvorium
Galadorium
Raestra
Halls of Horiembrig
Velhar River
Scarlet Bay
SEVRIGEL
Windari Channel
Sevilan Marshes
Elarium
Selvarian Realm
Yislaval Mountains
Ironwatch
Dragon Wing
Hemskep
Sanae
Redbern Forest
Pass of the Dead
Dahel
Marilore
Makataj Desert

Prologue

The human drew closer, his body growing to fill the empty street with his every step. His breath was audible, heavy and thick, as though his lungs strained to expand within his hulking chest. Another boot thudded across the frozen earth—to Jikun's tensed ears, it fell like a distant toll of thunder, heralding the coming of a treacherous storm.

Jikun hovered one hand above the hilt of his sword while he lifted his other slightly in the air. He felt the faint tingle of ice, dull and throbbing, as it flitted across his fingertips.

A whisper of fabric grazed his skin, and he was abruptly aware of Navon's presence at his side. The Helven's pale face was shrouded in shadows, hollow and sunken in the dim moonlight. "Jikun, turn away from this," he pleaded. "The hour is not yet late—we can join the war and stop Saebellus! *Do not let your pride destroy you!*"

Their Sel'ven companion seized Navon by the shoulder, shoving the coward back into the darkness.

"*Silence!*" Jikun hissed again. The brand marking him as *cattle* seared across his arm in a reminder of the degradation of his current path. *Pathetic.*

The time for speech was at an end. Borin had reached the alley.

Jikun's fingers spread above the barren earth and a shaft of ice erupted from beneath, raining dirt and stone as it slammed into Borin's side and hurled the half-giant into the alleyway. Despite the speed and force with which he had been thrown, the man let out no more than a grunt as he careened past their bodies and sprawled into the dust.

"*Be still!*" Jikun snarled, sprinting forward. Cold water pulled from the soil and hardened, piercing the air to halt a hair's width from Borin's chest. Here, in the shadows of the alley, they were nigh-invisible daggers—poised to strike at the human's slightest movement.

As though grasping his situation for the first time, Borin's head jerked wildly up and around, absorbing the three elves surrounding him. His broad hand fell slowly to his side. "…What is this?" he growled as the silence settled. "An ambush?"

"Gods show mercy," Navon seethed. "*We should walk away from this!*"

Jikun stiffened and threw his shoulders back.

"Yes, this is an ambush," the Sel'ven interjected smoothly.

Jikun dislodged his captain's admonishment with a defiant strut forward; a crackle of ice glittered into being, forming a short barrier between the immense arms and Jikun's polished boots. "I want the information you withheld concerning Relstavum. And if I should find it less than I desire…" The ice lengthened and caressed the weathered leather strapped across the giant's breast.

Borin's nostrils flared. With startling speed, his fist flew outward, shattering the ice as though it were merely glass. He snagged the hem of Jikun's cloak, tearing it from his tall, lean frame.

"*WHO?!*" Then Borin's eyes widened with incredulous recognition. "I know who you are," he spat, flinging the cloak aside as Jikun hastened to restore his dominance upon the man. "You're the greedy elves from earlier today—the war criminals who figured they'd poke Balior with a stick. Twenty thousand in debt, aren't you? *Malranus' fire could not have burned you more thoroughly.*" He laughed then, a mocking, hollow laugh, as though the bodily threat to him—gleaming a mere fraction away—was gone. "You failed to defeat Saebellus with an army and now you want to face his forces without one? Relstavum is the man's *beast.*" His laugh intensified, threatening to reach Emal'drathar to mock Jikun with the gods.

But Relstavum was not Saebellus' Beast.

He was far worse.

"Silence!" Jikun snarled, the spears of ice diving through the man's rich clothes to prod beneath his bronze-hued flesh. He snatched his cloak from the earth, aware of the soft, white rays that exposed his unique features. It was too late to withdraw—he was too deep along his path. "I won't ask kindly again, human," he growled.

The Sel'ven gave a sharp, encouraging nod. *Do not forget what brought us to this place,* it said. He leaned forward, flicking a piece of rubble casually from Borin's shaven crown. "Answer the question, Borin," he repeated. The smooth nail left a streak across the silver stubble.

"You're fucking mad," the man swore, and the ice crackled once in warning. "Mad—!" But Borin's howls subsided, his chest quavering as it attempted to retract from the perilous daggers. "Your warlord has created an army within a single man: Relstavum is soul harnessing, though I'm certain none of you god-damn fools has any idea what in the Nine Realms that is. But you *should* know who *Tiras* is; Relstavum has *Tiras'* necromantic writings from Vise and he can *use* them. You can't have the mission because it's beyond your fucking abilities. Laeris has invested too much money in you to throw you to Saebellus' dog! Right now, there isn't a mercenary company alive that can contend with his might—and the man is only growing more dangerous. *This* is a matter for kings and armies! By Malranus Almighty, Relstavum levels *god-damn cities*."

The Sel'ven lurched forward without warning, slamming his foot against the slick ice bearing down upon the giant's shoulder. His hair had unraveled from its elegant braid, the strands swirling about his contorted lips. "And if this man continues to breathe, he will cost my brother his life and Aersadore her freedom. So *I'll ask you one more time, human!*"

The ice prickled as Jikun adjured, "Now, Borin!"

The half-giant bared his massive, grey teeth, etching a meager show of defiance across his insolent face. "You want to get yourself killed?—fine, *elf*," he jeered. "Relstavum was in Ironwatch two days ago, heading north. But you'd better vanish into the nearest god-damn mountains, because when I'm free of this, the Brotherhood will send mercenaries to hang you by your entrails whether or not you succeed. Who in the Brotherhood did you think you were questioning?" His voice was rising in fury and Jikun could almost feel the sound penetrating the nearby walls. "I'm not a god-damn commoner. I'm not a god-damn mercenary. I'm—"

'Laeris' Sword...' Jikun stilled, mind whirling at these new threats. His feet felt leaden, weighing him inescapably to the frosty earth. He had considered the torture. The necessity of using force to extract the withheld information. Even how the gargantuan man might retaliate with his own might. But Jikun had not reflected upon the *others* that existed beneath Borin's whip. How could he have forgotten that?

'You're slipping, Jikun.'

Borin's voice was mounting to a roar, now. "—Geldin Laeris' elite. I control every damn mercenary you could ever *think* to know. I have seen your face. *I know your kind.* If you think Relstavum is your enemy... You just opened the god-damn Gates. You won't get two cities from here before the Brotherhood will have blades in your back!"

Jikun's knees threatened to betray him and he clutched at the cloak in his pale hands.

"Even without our brand, your appearance is blood in the snow! If you think we won't find you before dawn, you—"

Navon interrupted with a vociferous cry. "Jikun, I advised you against this! *Soul-harnessing?!* Join the king's war—by Ramul, you are a soldier! Release him now and perhaps we can bart—"

Borin laughed, the sound a cavernous boom that rattled the icicles dangling from the nearby wooden eaves. "*Barter?* There is no bartering, elf! You will be *lucky* to die by Relstavum! The Brotherhood will hunt you down and we will *rip* retribution from your *bones until your screams deafen the god—*" His voice strangled off with a soft gurgle.

There was a suffocating silence. Navon uttered a choking gasp.

From the midst of the chunks of ice and earthen debris, the man's fist tightened once and then fell limp.

Jikun stared blankly at the daggers that had ruptured through the hulking human… that had pierced through his vital organs and crushed his burly throat.

Jikun's palm opened and the ice melted away, leaving the man sprawled across the earth.

With a casual hop, the Sel'ven freed himself from the proximity of the encroaching sludge. "…Well done. We have what we need."

"*Jikun, by Sel'ari, WHAT HAVE YOU DONE?!*" Navon finally managed to scream, his azure eyes wide with horror. He sprinted toward the corpse, as though there remained some hope that the human had endured. That he might yet be saved.

But Borin was dead.

His sacrifice was necessary.

This was Jikun's last chance to abolish Saebellus' tyranny before Ryekarayn was lost. And Sevrigel forever with her.

CHAPTER ONE

41 Days Earlier

A fire of red and orange ignited the western sky where the sun had descended below the horizon. Her flames seemed to lick the darkness that followed in her wake, bathing the underbellies of the clouds that had rolled in from the north. They were lighter now, their great weight of snow dropped on the mountain peaks in Arisfare—the continent's first snowfall of the winter. They would carry on to the south, relinquishing what remained as heavy showers. Then, as they reached the base of the Aenid Mountains on the edge of the Makataj Desert, they would fade entirely.

Into that sky's darkness, a great, winged silhouette rose above the Sel'varian Forest with two figures hunkered against its spine. Below them, upon the bed of an empty room, only the elegant handwriting on fresh parchment remained in explanation.

My dear father and brother,

I have seen the enemy swell in number these last few weeks, but today I have witnessed its effect upon my very blood. Darcarus' wound at the hands of these villains has opened my eyes, and I have realized we can no longer protect even those of our own royal family.

I am no fool. I am aware of the years Relstavum has labored to build a force that could contest with us. That would even dare to do so. Nor am I blind to Relstavum's ability to devastate this continent by his own hand.

We can no longer turn aside from the evil spreading in our land! In shunning the truth of our necessity to act, we have allowed Sevrigel to fall. What her people have tasted in defeat, we soon shall share. And while the conflict at our gates may be designed merely to lead us from the source of its command, its attacks shall cripple us all the same.

Thus, it is with clear conscience that I have resolved to act before more blood is spilt. I shall not let the land of our brethren be lost!

I urge you to join me. Sevrigel will never rebel against Saebellus to save herself, but behind your towering walls, you are not helpless: urge the humans' king to intervene. Or please, Father, break your stringent vow to never return, for the people are in dire need: end the separation between our worlds with our own military strength.

If you forbid Sairel to lead the force, Darcarus or I would gladly stand in his stead.

By the time this letter finds you, Darcarus and I shall be long gone. Do not fear for my safety for it is you I shall fret over every night. I shall miss you dearly.

Hadoream

Yet the dancers below the vanishing trio were wholly unaware of the farewell. Surrounding their flittering feet, a quick and jovial tune persisted, eloping with the cool breeze of the evening. It wound its way across the bustling gardens beyond where the dancers swept across the cobblestones and twisted about the gleaming fountain. The warm, yellow light of the garden orbs seemed to bob along with the melody, stretching and shrinking their merry shadows.

From the palace's tower high above them, King Sairel unfurled a small scroll of parchment, scrutinizing the tiny scribbles scrawled haphazardly across the page. His lips drew tight as he noted the dwarven seal embedded neatly at the bottom: the only legible mark on the page. He dropped it irritably to his left, licking his index finger to pull the next ivory sheet from the stack.

There was no time for gaiety and childish tunes. And yet, before he had the opportunity to dissect further legal contents, music drifted in from the courtyard below, determined to contaminate his quiet abode.

"'Dance!' cried the prince.
'I'll dance!' cried the tree,
And it danced and it cried
To the music's melody."

Sairel squinted irritably at the notice in his hands. Only when he had nearly blocked the ruckus out did a song seem to sweep all the more forcefully into the warm air of his vast office. And these words, imparted in the Common Tongue, grated with particular affliction upon his ears.

"A terrible, terrible, terrible lie.
As the mad king lives,
His people die."

Sairel rubbed a hand against his twitching eye and slid his chair back forcefully. The fire in the corner sparked, cracking as it bit into the newest log and showering the fireplace with orange, mutually annoyed sparks. *'They are going to give me an ulcer...'* Why ever the humans had contrived a *nursery rhyme* out of the slaughter of Sevrigel's Farvian people across the channel, he could not fathom. He stalked to the door of his study, pushing it open a crack.

The guard before him turned quickly at attention. "Is there something wrong, Your Majesty?"

"No." Sairel waved a hand dismissively. "Just order them to cease those dreadful human... *songs*, if that is what they indeed are."

The guard hesitated, sliding his palm anxiously across his helmet. "Yes, Your Majesty. It's the human's Winter Festival in the capital. Veacerel took the servants out today to see it. It—"

Sairel heaved a sigh, muttering below his breath. *'Sometimes Veacerel panders to the servants as though he may one day end up as one... Which he shall do if I keep hearing this song!'* he thought sourly. "Never mind, let them carry on. *Someone* should at least enjoy themselves while I labor." He closed the door before the guard's opening mouth, stepping briskly across the room to the balcony. He shut those doors as well, relieved that the melody was reduced to a low hum outside the thick glass.

The mahogany chair creaked as he settled back into it, and he slid the completed parchment to his left. He pulled the next one off his stack, scanning it and flourishing his name across the bottom. He pressed the seal of a phoenix into the corner and waved the parchment briefly in the air to dry. Then he discarded it to his left.

It was a brief glimpse of progress.

There was a hasty knock from the hall beyond and Sairel pursed his lips, throwing a hand into the air. He had just hushed the external ruckus and now the internal din was ready to be employed. "Can I not work?" he demanded.

"I'm sorry, Your Majesty." The door opened and closed promptly to admit a male dressed in dark greens and browns, a silver pin of office fastened to his breast. He was holding a small, cream-colored parchment. "I'm afraid you must read this…"

Sairel glanced sidelong at the teetering papers on his right and the mound growing on his left. "If I was offered a gold coin for every instance in which those words were uttered to me, I would be richer than all the dwarves of Ryekarayn. Combined." He waved a hand, beckoning his advisor forward. "Hand it over, Veacerel."

Veacerel strode briskly across the room and set the letter down, stamping his finger onto the unmarked and broken seal. "I whisked it away before your father could discover its arrival, but I'm afraid Darcarus seized it first. It's from Sellemar."

Sairel picked up the parchment immediately, flipping open the coarse paper. It was sweeter than Ryekarayn's, taken from the Maisprings along Sevrigel's coast. He could still catch the faint scent of the ocean rising from beneath the thin, scratched ink.

Sairel's heart tightened. The script lacked the usual elegance of the writer; instead it was swift and jagged, the ink bleeding heavily into the adjacent letters.

Hairem is dead. General Taemrin and his army have been annihilated. Saebellus has already seized the capital and he marches on his brothers at this hour. Ilsevel says "the reign of kings has returned," but what she intends to do is far from our True Blood cause.

All of Sevrigel has come to war. I fear, with Saebellus' tactics, you shall not be long to feel the ripple of their effects.

Sairel's annoyance faded. His grasp tightened as he reread the six short sentences. The words of the song drumming outside the pane clashed with striking relevance. "When did this arrive?"

"Not an hour past," Veacerel replied stiffly. "Magically relayed by Tilarus, I assume."

Sairel turned to the window. The night god was rising, cloaked in the endless mantle of stars. His eyes swept east, to where Noctem's darkness engulfed the narrow channel separating Ryekarayn from Sevrigel. "Tell Darcarus his lips are sealed or I shall seal them myself." He looked down, regarding the letter stoically, but beneath his impassive expression a sea of emotions roiled. It would have been hours—maybe a day—since the letter had been sent. Saebellus was still solidifying his grasp… Yet already Ryekarayn was buckling beneath the mere ripples of war.

The warlord's distractions for the human lands were well-formed—as cunning as his strategy that had produced Sevrigel's defeat: the elven nation would find no aid so long as such diversions remained unbroken.

Sairel's grip tightened on the parchment until his fingers grew white. "An empire is emerging from within the ashes of Sevrigel's ruin. I believe the struggles of Ryekarayn are now intertwined with our brethren's fate. Aersadore," he spoke gravely, "is at war."

Chapter Two

The war had been lost and Ilsevel had raised a dagger against Alvena's king. Raised a dagger against her king and slew him!

And Alvena had run. Beyond the palace. Beyond the city. Beyond even the canyon wall. The days had blurred together and she could not be sure a time had ever existed when she had *not* run.

She had left the slimy egress of the True Blood tunnel far behind, and somewhere within its gem-encrusted, gold-flaked walls, her urgency remained to gather dust. Now her ankles were raw; the sleeves torn from Lardol's shirt had held his large shoes to her tiny feet, but only just!—They popped and clicked away from her every weary step, dragging her further toward the cold, damp, dark of the forest floor where she might finally find respite.

'You need to stop. You need to rest,' she chastised herself. She certainly could not sustain this ridiculous pace all the way to the coast!

And to bestow further misery upon her tired and raw body, her hair was wet. A river had intersected her path and she had been forced to flounder her way across stark naked—her shoes and clothes stuffed beside the provisions in her oiled sack. Sellemar had said nothing of such an obstacle between her and the northern route. Admittedly, only the frogs nestled in the mud had spied her climbing awkwardly from the shore, but they would surely spend the whole night croaking about it!

'How could a seasoned warrior like Sellemar forget such a crucial detail!' Or perhaps it was *because* he was seasoned that the obstacle never even flitted across his mind.

The journey would be full of such unpredictable obstacles.

Alvena huffed. She dropped her sack beside a great oak and stubbornly wiped her eyes with the inside of her tiny wrist. *'So you have to be strong. Like him. And Hairem. And Erallus. And Lardol.'*

She raised her chin against the gloom of the canyon's forest floor, but nobody was present to admire her resolve. Abandoning pretenses, she instead shamelessly huddled down into the dirt at the tree's base and swept great piles of leaves over her body for warmth.

Those peeping frogs had to have a better idea for survival than she did.

Next she opened her sack, relieved to find the contents dry, her letter safe, and food with which to sate her ravenous hunger. Sellemar had said the nearest city was only a few days north, but her paltry reserve of provisions would not last that long!

She stuffed her mouth full—that was about the only thing her rationed meal would fill—and nestled her head into the crook of her arm. *'I wonder how many bugs are in these leaves?'* she found herself thinking as her eyes closed. *'How big are they? ...Are they beetles? Maybe some of them are spiders?'* Her eyes shot wide. *'Gods, they could be huge...!'* She promptly wiggled free of the leaves and dirt and hastily smacked the remnants from her nightdress. She shivered with cold and disgust. *'Ick ick ick!'* She stomped about the tree, taking deep and noisy breaths. *'Ick!'*

The chilled wind did not wait for her to finish.

'Alvena, you'll freeze!' she scolded herself as her skirt batted against her bare legs. She tried to picture Sellemar lying in the dirt, covering himself with leaves for warmth.

It was impossible to imagine.

'There has to be another way!' she thought angrily. Why had the gods made those creeping, scuttling creatures?! She shivered, hopping from foot to foot.

Still... She blew out her cheeks. Sellemar was probably not running about in the wilderness half-naked. She balled her hands into fists and lay back down in the leaves, trying to think about the saltiness of the meat she had just consumed and not the scratchiness of the bug-infested leaves.

Not long ago, she would have been sleeping with her head on feathers beneath sheets of silk. How fast life could change.

*

Alvena yawned, stretching her arms above her head. The sunlight was harsh this morning. It penetrated the chiffon curtains dangling delicately before her balcony doors, piercing straight through her eyelids. She nestled further into her covers, frowning slightly at their scratchy interior. Ugh, and her bed was really uncomfortable.

She sat up abruptly, her eyes flashing open. *'By Sel'ari! Hairem! Why didn't Lardol wake her up?! Hairem was probably wondering where she was—!'* An ancient tree came into focus above her and a chilly bead of dew rolled down her breast.

She tore her mind immediately from Hairem's visage, grabbing her sack and withdrawing her breakfast. *'The food is wonderful, almost as good as palace food. How generous of Sellemar. I love strawberries. I wonder what I'll have for lunch,'* she carried on to herself, but it was not long before her enthusiasm dwindled. Was that *mold* on her bread? How long had Sellemar kept these in his cupboards?! She stuffed it back into her bag. *'...Gods, I really have to pee...'* Her eyes flitted southward in concern. What if some elf with really really *really* good eyes looked down into the canyon's leafless canopy and saw her squatting behind a tree?

She clasped a hand to her mouth, mortified. *'Gods, I certainly hope not!'*

She made her business quickly, strutting away and hastily adjusting her nightdress. If *she* was an adventurer, she determined, she would make sure her party took routes that stopped at towns along the way and was not reduced to stooping behind bushes like common men. *'Unbelievable,'* she grumbled. How much longer did she have to endure this discomfort? Would Sellemar's letter truly barter for a ship away from all these trials?

Forgetting that the parchment had been moved to the sack, she patted her abdomen once.

"Stop that!" she heard a distant echo of the Common Tongue.

Alvena's hand dropped from her dress and she scuttled behind a tree. *'Who?! I wasn't doing anything!'* She peered wide-eyed out from around the trunk, her heart nearly leaping from her breast.

Only a pale, red leaf tumbled out into the surrounding crest of hills.

'Maybe a miner!' she considered warily. The journey north *had* brought her close to a new face of the canyon wall and she had heard stories of the excavation for the precious kisacaela housed within. The miners called it "elf's eye" when they sold it for exorbitant prices on Ryekarayn, claiming homeopathic remedies to every illness under the sun. Lardol used to talk about it. He had an enormous, polished stone in his room that Alvena used to sneak in to admire.

But perhaps that was why he was so old.

A musty breeze tugged Alvena's matted hair free to whip little, knotted twigs against her shoulders. In her paranoia, they felt like little gnarled fingers, tapping her dirty skin, urging her to look around. She snatched her hair and plastered it firmly against her head. She was not afraid. She had heard plenty about humans. *Humans* were the reason for all the corruption and vices in the world—all that her people valiantly struggled to remain above. But they were slow of wit and body, hardly more than taller, less malodorous dwarves.

The auburn leaf twirled once and alighted upon a mossy stone. *'Move along!—You can't stand here all day!'* She stepped slowly from around the tree and crept up the next hill.

To her initial relief and subsequent consternation, it was not humans that waited for her. *'Oh, great. Another river,'* she muttered as she trudged to the murky waters. *'That's your second offense, Sellemar.'*

And worse, this one was wider and teeming with little white crests that broke angrily against the shore. She paced down the shoreline, vehemently hoping for a bridge to manifest itself. Maybe the miners needed one to cross the river…

But a good march later, Alvena had nothing to show for her efforts. How could she reach the coast when she could not ferry herself across the damn river?! Anxiety clutched at her throat and a stinging tear rolled down her dirty cheek. She slapped the underbrush violently and gave the nearest bush an embittered kick. Nothing! Her short journey was an embarrassing—if not predictable—failure!

'Ouchchch!' she gasped as she tripped on a nearby log that snapped her toe askew. The pain released her well of emotions in full. *'Damn it! Why her?! Why Hairem?! Why were the gods punishing them?!'* She leaned down to clutch her throbbing toe.

And stopped.

A long, sturdy canoe peered out from under a bush, paddles resting in its belly. Alvena's face lit up. Sel'ari *was* looking out for her! *'Perhaps the miners use this?'* she pondered as she heaved it toward the shore with little grunts.

As the front end slid into the water, the boat twisted unexpectedly in the current and was nearly swept away. Alvena dove into the hull, clambering into the belly… and dropped one of the paddles into the water. *'Oh no! Did I need both?!'*

With a little bob along the waves, it nodded its goodbye and sailed down the river without her.

'...Oh well...' she initially dismissed, but the strenuous rowing quickly made her regret her clumsiness. By the time she reached the opposite shore, she wished she had done more at the palace than brush the king's hair and fold silken shirts. She tumbled onto the muddy shore and scrambled for the bow.

Her fingers grasped only air.

Relieved of her weight, the boat too had been wrenched askew in the current of the water. Bobbing its final farewell along the white crests, it sailed off to join the lonely paddle somewhere in the distance.

Alvena stood in the mud and looked down at the last paddle resting in her grimy hands. She dropped it into the water. It seemed appropriate that all the pieces go off together.

She turned around and started.

A short ways into the tree line, staring perplexedly back at her, were half a dozen tanned faces. Brawny... rugged... *hairy*... They could only be...

'Humans!' she realized, her spine stiffening.

"How's Dane an' Rulf suppos' t' get back now?" a grubby man at the front demanded, but he was quickly shoved into the back of the gawking horde.

Alvena found herself momentarily stunned, both in surprise and indomitable curiosity. Never had she seen such a variety of shapes and physiques! Some of the humans were lanky and muscular, some burly and broad, others squat and terribly disproportioned. But they all fashioned themselves in dirty cotton garments and thick-soled boots—not at all like the rich men who had stalked about the palace of the king.

A spindly man in the front struck a sudden grin, his eyes canvassing her slender body.

Alvena's curiosity withered.

'They're just harmless scavengers,' she assured herself, hastily averting her gaze as though her lack of vision would likewise inhibit theirs. She clutched the sack to her pounding chest and found her feet carrying her swiftly away. *'Don't run. Humans are like dogs, Lardol said—they'll chase you if you run.'*

A malicious voice pursued her, snapping at her heels. "That's a Sel'ven," it growled, and she imagined the lips curling into a venomous sneer.

"Damn bastards," another rejoined.

Alvena glanced over her shoulder to find that the humans had closed the distance. The icy wind flung itself urgently against her back and she quickened her pace. *Why were they coming closer?!*

"Where do you think you're going?!" a sweet voice rang.

But the rest of the men's faces had grown dark and hard.

Alvena's stomach dropped and she broke into a run. Her hair whipped behind her, the little twigs scratching frantically against her neck. *'Sel'ari protect me!'* she yearned to scream, the massive shoes flapping against her feet. Yet she didn't dare pause to fling them free. She had to run! She had to reach the coast—!

A large hand seized her by the shoulder, nearly yanking her off her feet. The humans were terrifyingly fast—not at all as the scholars had depicted them!

Alvena gave a cry, tugging desperately against his iron grasp. Tension had never been so high between their races that a human would dare lay hands upon an *elf!*

Yet the wide fingers tightened, digging into her flesh with jagged fingernails. "Stop your struggling, elf" the human snarled, drawing her close. His breath reeked of something smoked and greasy—concurrently sour and sweet—and Alvena envisioned a rotted carcass roasting over a flame. She tried to wrest her face free of the stench, but his hand swept into her tangled hair and squeezed. "Sel'ven bitch, *where do you think you're going?*"

'What do you want?!' Alvena shrieked, twisting her face into confusion. She struggled to elevate her skull to her tearing roots. *'Let me go, let me go, let me go!!'*

One of the gangly humans sauntered to their side, rubbing the flaking skin from a sun-burnt ear. "Let *this* be a personal message for your bastard king!" he raised his hand and brought it down across her face.

"And your bitch queen!" shouted another brute from the trees. A chorus of agreement rallied with his anger.

Alvena's lip burst and her eyes welled. *'Hairem?! What had Hairem— No...* Saebellus? *Saebellus? Why—?'*

A third human gnashed his teeth together furiously. "Don't look innocent," he spat. "We know what you are!"

'What I am?' Alvena panicked. *A fugitive?!*

The first man wrenched her upward, shaking her with violence. "And even if you aren't no spy—"

Even as Alvena's head snapped atop her spine, her fear fell away to bewilderment. *'Spy?!'*

"—you're just as guilty as every other fucking Sel'ven—just standing by while they hunt us down. As if right now we didn't have enough god-damn trouble in our homeland!"

And before Alvena could decipher his words, the second attacker lifted his fist again, slamming it down across her nose. She felt a rush of blood flood her face, running along the crack in her lips as she opened her mouth to wail. What spies?! *What laws?!* What hostility had Saebellus and Ilsevel bred in mere days?!

She tried to shake her head, opening her mouth to protest. *She had nothing to do with them!*

But the humans had deduced otherwise. The large man threw her savagely into the dirt, kicking out and catching her in the side. She tumbled across the damp leaves and mud, dashing her hip against a rock. She scrambled toward the water, tears streaming silently down her swollen cheeks, her ribs reeling from the blow.

'The coast... the coast! I have to make it—!' She plunged her hand into the water, grasping for anything to hang onto.

A hand caught her ankle, jerking her across the river sludge and flipping her viciously onto her back. The ruddy, bearded face loomed above her, pores gaping, scars snaking over his bulging veins. "You elves nipped the tail of a dragon. We *humans* aren't afraid to get our hands sullied with your holy, *righteous* blood."

'I didn't do anything!' she screamed, flailing wildly for the safety of the white crests. *'Nothing! Noth—!'* She stilled suddenly, feeling a hand catch the hem of her nightdress.

"I saw her first!" the second man growled, shoving the first aside.

Alvena grasped for her oiled sack, smashing the piddly contents into the human's sneering face. She kicked free, hurling herself toward the waters.

As she fell short of the icy waves, a thud struck the muck beside her throat. Alvena froze in horror, the arrow's brilliant plume of feathers grazing her neck.

'Gods...!'

Instantly, the two men fell on her, slamming her legs and arms aside, swearing and striking one another as they battled for the hem of her dress.

'STOP! STOP! HELP ME!!' she wailed. She caught a glimpse of the crowd gathered behind to *watch*, grinning like a horde of goblins.

The lean man was lobbed into the water and a roar of laughter split their party.

"Oh, Davon!"

"Show her, Gurnam!"

Alvena felt her dress rise up to her belly, her last grasp on the silk failing beneath the man's strength. *'Stop... '* she sobbed as he reached his hand up her thigh and trailed it along her pelvis.

A new voice ripped suddenly across the canyon. "GURNAM. WHAT IN ZEPHEREUS' NAME ARE YOU DOING?!"

Alvena's cries lodged in her throat as her hair was sharply released. She shot up, drawing her legs tightly against her chest, and heaved for each choking breath.

Gurnam lumbered to his feet, grunting out his disdain. Beside him, Davon had dragged himself from the river and retreated to the obscurity of the dense underbrush, highlighting the large human as the cause of the scene.

Alvena followed their gaze. The crowd had parted, casting themselves aside sheepishly as a dark-skinned man dressed in vibrant, dirt-spotted colors strode through their midst.

His hardened eyes locked upon her two attackers. "Didn't I order all of you to bathe? Is *this* bathing? In any way, shape, or form, *is this bathing?*" The new human advanced briskly to stop a nose-width before Gurnam, strands of his coarse, black hair breaking free from his slicked mane. His voice lowered into a dangerous timbre. "Get into that water and if you come out before you smell like a vase of Starfarian lilies, I'll drown you."

"Fuck you," Gurnam muttered as he swung about, wrenching his boots off and lugging them down beside Alvena.

She flinched, wrapping her arms tighter about herself.

"AND *the rest of you!*" the human bellowed.

"We found her," Davon dared to explain, wringing his soaked shirt into the mud. "She came steeled in Dane and Rulf's canoe... She probably killed them. We didn't take her from the city. We're not *stupid*, Sanas."

Sanas regarded him cynically through his narrowed, green eyes. "You think *that* killed Dane and Rulf? You think she's out here alone? A Sel'ven in the canyon, *alone?* In a *nightdress?* No, you're not *stupid*, Davon. You're a fucking imbecile." He reached down, grabbing her roughly by the forearm, and snapped her to her feet. "Where is your party, elf?"

Alvena wrapped her free arm across her breasts as the thin strap of her nightdress slid away. *'I don't have a party, I don't have a party, I don't have a party!'* she sobbed through her shaking breaths.

"You won't tell me?" Sanas demanded, his calloused hand tightening. "Do you want me to throw you back to these savages?"

Alvena's knees crumbled beneath her and she clutched at his shirt. *'No, please!'* She pointed to her mouth desperately as she opened and closed it soundlessly.

She felt his grip slacken. "...She's a mute." He regarded her for a moment in silence, wild strands of raven hair folding into the crease of his brow. "Tie her up. I don't know if there is a party of Sel'vi nearby, but we're not letting her run back to spread word of our location. When you're done bathing, Davon, go find the others. The rest of you: hurry up and finish the work on the cliff. We're moving out as soon as the crater is through." He whirled, pointing at two of the humans in the front of the group. "Watch her," he barked, shoving her toward them. "And don't touch her. Sel'ven women go for a hefty purse and I have to make back what I lost when Vethru ran off with half of our stash. If she gets away as well, you'll be begging Ishkav to smite you."

Alvena felt any remaining color drain away.

"And get her something to eat. It's a long way to the Noc'olari."

Alvena's ears twitched, the pain throbbing across her bruised face momentarily subsiding. The Noc'olari? What could her brethren have to do with these beasts?!

Sanas lifted a hand to rein in the loose strands of his greasy hair. "They're a lot more compassionate than your kind," he continued spitefully. And then, to her consternation, stepped past her, stalked through the group of solemn men, and vanished into the foliage.

'Don't leave me with them...' she whimpered, sinking to her knees.

The two humans lingering to fulfill Sanas' command strode to her side, both grumbling about their appointed task. "Tie her up but don't touch her," one of them muttered.

"He means don't *fuck* her, idiot," the other growled.

"I know that, you ass," the first retorted.

Alvena was hauled up and steadied on her feet before a sharp nudge directed her forward.

"Damn you, *walk*" the first man snorted. "We have a lot of work to do and I don't fancy being your wet-nurse."

Alvena dragged a foot, aware for the first time that Lardol's shoes had come loose in the scuffle. The mud was cold beneath her toes as she shuffled into the tree line amidst the venom-filled complaints of the throng around her.

"*Damn Sel'ven*," one hissed. "*Murderer*."

The walk to the encampment of the miners was brief—they had pitched their tents along the shoreline of the northern canyon's final channel. Alvena could see a half-dozen canoes, much like the one she had used and lost, bobbing gently in the water. The vessels offered easy access to a small mass of land just opposite, rich with kisacaela.

But here, on the southern side of the little river, there was no beauty. A dozen dirty tents were arranged in two rows in front of a smoking fire. The half-rotted carcass of her imagination was still strung up above it and a nearby line of damp clothes flapped balefully in the greasy breeze.

The taller human surveyed their encampment, mulling over the small selection of half-grown trees budding beneath the protection of the massive elder trunks. "Here is as good a place as any," the first human was saying as he crouched beside a scraggly trunk. He raised a coarse rope, pointing a gnarly finger in her direction. "Sit down, woman," he barked.

Alvena did not have the courage to resist, though she felt briefly ashamed at her compliance. But what *could* she do? She was weak. Just a handmaiden.

And so she sat, wiping a hand across her bloody face.

The second human pulled it down, pinning it beside her stinging hip. "Now tie her *tight*, Lukai." he ordered reproachfully.

"What do you mean, *Mobart?*" Lukai retorted. "Are you saying something?"

"You know what I'm saying," Mobart sniffed.

Lukai scoffed, wrapping the rope around her body and giving it a final jerk to pull it tight. Then he tramped behind the sapling to finish the knot. "Now if you have to piss, holler," he grunted, pushing off his knees. "*Stay there*."

'Holler…?'

Alvena watched as the two men sauntered toward the river, clambered into one of the canoes, and pushed off toward the canyon wall. Near its base, a small crater had marred the surreal surface. There, the cascading trail of blue gems, glittering in the dying light, was abruptly cut short by the humans' rampant greed. The valuables had been stripped and only a gaping hole of grey rock remained.

Valuables… Alvena started, head whipping about. What had she done with her sack?! *'Sellemar's letter!'* She looked up frantically, straining in Noctem's consuming darkness. There her bundle lay, discarded in a heap amongst the humans' dirty clothes.

No! They had it! Even if she broke free, she would never reach Ryekarayn without Sellemar's letter!

Chapter Three

The low creak of the door echoed softly through the cellar, causing Jerah to raise his head. Cutting through the silence was the sound of faint footsteps on the stone of the narrow, winding staircase. Gradually the sound grew louder as the elf descended to him with softly padded feet.

The torch swept into the room before the male and Jerah squinted his eyes against the foreign light.

"Good evening, Jerah," the male hailed as he settled the torch into its holder along the wall. A dozen spiders scuttled away from the sudden brightness and into the crevices of the stone. They were likewise blinded by the awful glare. As the elf approached, he stumbled slightly beneath the weight of the package he carried. "You look well," he offered vaguely, recovering himself.

Jerah held his hand up against the light, watching the shadows dance across the elf's face. He looked well? What did that mean—to look well? He had seen his own reflection once and thought he had looked quite unlike the elf. Perhaps the elf, then, was unwell. Perhaps he should mention just how unwell the elf looked.

He considered this as the elf dropped the package before him. It caught the chain connected to his wrist as it fell, jerking his hand from his eyes. He closed them, turning his head from the light. "You look unwell," he replied quietly.

The elf paused a moment and then let out a soft sound that was mimicked in an unsettling echo. "The proper response, *Jerah*, is 'thank you, my lord,' or 'and you as well, my lord,'" he replied, his tone reflecting his mild amusement.

And something else. Jerah did not know what to call it—this other tone that inevitably revealed itself whenever the elf spoke to him—but he had not heard the tone used on anyone else. Pieces of it lingered behind in the walls as it bounced about the little room. There was something about it that aggravated him—made his skin crawl with irritation and his strong jaw flex.

"Jerah!" the elf reprimanded him sharply.

Jerah's grip on his chain loosened and the metal fell with a loud clank to the dirty, stone floor beside him. The sound crushed the hunger of several nearby rats and they too vanished into the cracks along the wall. "I apologize, my lord."

The elf ignored him, sauntering through the darkness toward the back of the small, webbed cellar. "Where is your pail?" he asked, his hand tight across his nose and mouth. "Gods, does it reek of shit in here. Sometimes you hardly seem worth the effort." He was muttering to himself now, his free hand sweeping the darkness to repel any loose web strands.

Jerah shifted uncomfortably on the stone. His master must think him as pathetic as the humans of Ryekarayn. He seemed to curse them as much as himself, at least. His dark eyes followed his master as he bent down and, with a grunt, lifted his waste pail. Then his master jerked unexpectedly and released the handle, wiping his hand across his arm. "What in the name of the—"

"Water, my lord," Jerah informed him. "It leaks over there. That's the place that you said you would get fixed and that I should remind you of…"

"I said that? Yes… well, I've been very busy with the regime change, Jerah. But I've not forgotten about you—couldn't if I tried." He added the last words below his breath and Jerah felt an unpleasant feeling settle in his stomach at the tone. Then the elf continued at a normal volume. "Matters are changing. It's hard for Saebellus to find a use for you right now, but perhaps you'll be allowed out again." He left the torch as he moved slowly out of the cell. Then he vanished around the bend in the stairs to leave Jerah in his cold, damp quarters.

Sitting back, facing away from the light, Jerah settled down onto his rump. He leaned against the wall, rubbing his arms against the chill that spread from the stone and into his body. Then he opened his sagging package.

The first smell that greeted him was familiar: there were at least three pounds of dried meat. Jerah ate one as he picked up a long, white rag and a bar of soap. He set these aside hurriedly as the light caught the gentle curves of the last dozen items. These were round, smooth stones about half the size of his fist.

He picked them up one at a time, allowing the orange glow of the torch to play off of their shiny surfaces. There were hues of purples, blues, and greens on some, and oranges, yellows, and reds on others.

Something to occupy his long nights of loneliness.

By the time the last stone had been set aside, the pound of dried pork had been eaten. He reached a long nail into the space of his teeth, picking at it absentmindedly.

He made a face and raised his hands, narrowing his eyes against what now seemed a dimness of light. Still, he could distinguish the brown caked beneath his fingernails.

He reached for his white cloth, laying it in the puddle that had formed beneath the leaky ceiling. He wrung it once and then began to scrub beneath his nails, watching the brown stain grow rapidly across the cloth. *'I hate this part.'*

Dimmer and dimmer the light became until it vanished entirely. The cloth dropped from Jerah's hands and he wrapped his arms around himself, acutely aware of the silence that manifested in the darkness.

It would be dark for a long time now if his master no longer had a use for him. The cell would grow hot and sticky, freeze, and then repeat before Jerah might again see the white torch that shone in the void outside his cell.

CHAPTER FOUR

"Tie them up,"

The voice echoed from some crevice deep within Alvena's mind.

"*Now*."

Abruptly, Alvena sat up, nearly smacking her head on the bench of the canoe. How could she have forgotten about the abominable craft for even a moment? She felt as though she had wallowed in it for a lifetime. The travel with the humans had been a slow journey—from the day they had finished poking holes in the cliff face to the tedious bob of their canoes along the northern canyon river.

But if they were stopping, the Noc'olarian city had to be close! This was to be her first step toward freedom.

Or rather, it *had* been.

"Come on, hurry up!" Sanas yapped.

Her captors grumbled their complaints of sleep and food deprivation as they hoisted their supplies and hauled themselves across the dark shore. They were remarkably loud, snapping twigs under their feet and grunting about the treachery of the forest's root system. Alvena wondered why the Noc'olari bothered with the warning orbs floating atop the river when the humans made their whereabouts so easily known.

But then the trees broke away and her appalling captors were forgotten.

A massive, white tree stood in the center of the vast clearing: grander and larger than any tree Alvena had ever *dreamed* could exist—the tips of Elvorium's palace towers would have had to stretch to reach its mid branches! A dozen open doors were carved into its base and pearlescent staircases wound endlessly around and up into its lush, silver canopy. Blue-white orbs hung in the air all about it, casting the entire tree with a soft and iridescent glow.

'It's amazing,' Alvena breathed. Elves were majestic crafters, gifted with a surplus of age and magic, and this…

This embodied all of their experience and splendor.

Her toes curled, and she became aware of the warmth beneath her feet. Winter grass overlay the ground, dotted with white mushrooms and lilac flowers that glowed with an inner light. Clusters of these lined a wide, mossy path that branched into the great tree.

Marring the beautiful landscape, however, were countless white tents. But she did not see other humans. Instead she beheld the Noc'olari themselves. They were as majestic as she remembered—refined and pale, with skin that glowed in the moonlight. Their hair was as unique and as startling as their eyes: some touted bold hues of blues and purples, while some boasted vibrant silvers or teals. They were striking in their strange beauty, and yet blended seamlessly into the surreal colors and glow of their landscape. Ageless. Yet not one that Alvena could spy looked as young as she!

"More refugees," she heard a Noc'olarian female speak mournfully from nearby.

"Tragic…" another lamented, kissing the back of her thumb and lifting it to the star-speckled sky.

'These men are no tragedy,' Alvena quickly recalled, and scowled at her captors.

They merely shoved her deeper into their horde, blocking her view as they swept her toward the assembly of tents. "Move yer ass," Mobart growled.

The uncouth tongue drew the glare of a Noc'olarian male as he hastened across the mossy way. Alvena could see that one hand was covered in something dark while a clean, white linen was draped neatly over his arm.

Then he doubled back, rounding on them sharply. Incredulity rushed across his features as though he had not first absorbed what he had glimpsed.

"Wait," he ordered, reaching out and catching Sanas' sleeve. He was as tall as any of the humans and more powerfully built than any Sel'ven. Why, Alvena was quite certain he could fit two of her in the expanse of his regally rigid shoulders! Yet he was lean in his muscular physique. His skin reverberated in the moonlight, making the liquid on his withheld hand seem to shimmer.

The miners drew to a slow stop, looking to Sanas for direction.

Their leader cocked his head. "What is it?" he began cautiously, shifting his gem-filled sack. "You *are* still offering aid, aren't you?"

The Noc'olari ignored his question as he pushed the humans aside. Alvena found herself suddenly exposed before him, locked in his vivid, violet eyes. They gave her a swift and pointed scan. "What in Ilra's name are you doing with this girl?" he demanded, his accent almost fully concealed. But not well enough for Alvena to miss the similarities to Sellemar's.

She heard a chuckle sweep through the men about her, their response extenuated by a gust of wind. Sanas' slick hair slumped downward, quivering about his harsh, dark face. "This girl is a Sel'ven," he scoffed, rolling his shoulders as though the response was sufficient.

The Noc'olari was not swayed. He dropped Sanas' sleeve forcefully, then extended his clean hand out to her. "Come," he spoke in softer command.

Alvena took a hesitant step and the humans closed instantly in front of her, their barricade of backs nearly blocking the Noc'olari from view.

"Wait a minute there, elf. She is *ours*." Sanas grunted as Alvena punched his broad back furiously with her bound hands. He remained otherwise unfazed, but Mobart gave her a solid slap. "We found her scouting for her party of butchers in the canyon—and we never found the men whose canoe she stole. She deserves her fate. You worship Sel'ari, do you not?—this is Sel'ari's justice on their despicable crimes!"

The Noc'olari's chin tilted back as he laughed in disbelief. He wiped his hand on the white linen and Alvena could see a red stain left behind in the threads. "Scouting for a group of Saebellus' soldiers… *in a nightdress?*"

The humans exchanged an uneasy glance and once more turned to their flushed leader for a reaction. She saw his jowls quivering, his fist tightening, and she thought for sure he was about to strike the elf… But then he stilled, seeming to rethink his actions. Alvena wondered if he too had heard the tales of the Noc'olari's strange magics and ghoulish dances beneath the unseen moon. "Do not mock me, Noc'olari," he ventured through clenched teeth.

The Noc'olari's strong jaw hardened and he drew his body up before the herd. They shuffled back as he snapped a long, calloused finger toward the sky. Their eyes shifted upward, and Alvena was quite certain that some calamity was about to rain down from Emal'drathar. "I worship *Ilra*, human. If you want justice, you'll have to look somewhere else. Surrender the girl to me or you can find your own way off Sevrigel. Does my threat ring clear?"

It undoubtedly did. Sanas flung the rope from his hands as though it burned. "Her ugly face would have been lucky to be fed to a dog," he finished, jerking his head at the men about him. "Let's go."

Alvena looked down at her muddy feet and stained dress, but was too relieved to be offended by his remark. *'I'm safe!'* she breathed. Then her head snapped up and she pointed hurriedly at Sanas. *'My letter!'*

The Noc'olarian male followed her finger and his gaze set. "*I assume* you have something of hers. I will not ask twice."

Sanas' eyes narrowed and he sent his sack crashing to the ground at his feet. He reached down, undoing the leather tie and producing her now-crumpled and dirt-covered parchment. "Here—"

Before he could finish, Alvena darted forward and snatched Sellemar's letter with her still-bound hands. The men returned a single, dirty scowl before they stalked stiffly away.

Alvena hardly noticed. She had done it. She had reached the first city!—albeit a little unconventionally. The journey had certainly been more challenging than Sellemar had suggested, but perhaps the just and noble True Bloods were indeed on her horizon!

The Noc'olari crouched down and Alvena remembered the present. The male had drawn a silver blade from the side of his boot and ran it swiftly through the cord. "I am Itirel. You are?" He took her wrists, rubbing them gently with one hand as he gathered the broken cord in his other. She saw his eyes flicker across the parchment, a hint of curiosity barely concealed beneath.

Alvena opened her mouth and closed it, her grip on the letter tightening. *'Don't trust him, Alvena,'* she warned herself.

The Noc'olari smiled suddenly, as though in full understanding. "Ah, I see. If you can, try to forgive the humans. Death and fear can drive a man to do terrible things. I'm afraid the new decrees have been more than unfavorable toward them." He seemed to sense her confusion and continued, "Any humans found on Sevrigel are to be executed. My people are helping them leave... though between the famine, raids, and uprisings Saebellus has caused upon Ryekarayn, their homeland is hardly a safer place. The age is dark for many right now. You are not safe to travel alone."

Despite his infectious compassion, Alvena felt quite certain that such cruel barbarians did not deserve aid. He released her wrists and she was startlingly aware that the chaffing had vanished entirely. "You look terribly weary and I can see the hunger in your eyes." He straightened, gesturing to one of the nearby Noc'olarian females. "Yulasra," he called. "Will you see to this woman?"

Then he observed her once more and quietly spoke, "You are safe here. If you are in need of anything when she is through, write it down and I will endeavor to see that you have it." He briefly laid a hand upon her dirty shoulder, and then he was gone.

Before he vanished amongst the tents, Alvena wanted to reach out and cling to him for comfort. He was the first glimmer of hope that life outside the palace wasn't all suffering. He was soft-spoken. Bold. Kind… even to those who did not deserve it.

And he had saved her.

"Come, my dear. Let us get you cleaned," Yulasra prompted from her side. "Food, water, healed wounds, a warm bath… and something lovely to wear, shall we?"

*

Relief filled Alvena's chest as she stepped outside of the white tent, her hair braided over her shoulder, her skin clean and smooth. The injuries on her face had faded beneath the healing skills of the Noc'olarian female, and her stomach was heavy with satisfaction. Now *this* was the nature of the elves she knew! She sucked in the winter air and nestled beneath her thick, wool cloak. Even the weather could not remain bitter for long!

"Ah, you look much happier," chuckled a familiar accent.

Alvena started, looking over her shoulder.

Itirel, too, had changed. He now wore the purple robes of a Noc'olarian healer, the hue as dark and muted as his violet hair. With the blood on his hand cleaned and his disposition serene, it seemed laughable to imagine him as a wild elf of lore, chanting in the glow of some great fire in the obscurity of the new moon.

He followed her gaze and lifted his hand. "Unfortunately, he died," he lamented. "A merchant from a city Saebellus' army sacked. He prevailed in a journey here… but there was nothing that could be done for him." He stopped beside her, placing a hand beneath her chin and turning her face up to his. "You too seem to have had your trials. Here," he spoke gently, pressing two fingers to her lip.

For a moment, it flickered in pain and then abruptly, the throbbing was gone. As he drew his hand away, Alvena slid her tongue in search of the wound. Her eyes widened.

"Yes, it looks as new as on the day you were birthed. *It is*, let me clarify, wholly healed. A beautiful lady should not have to bear such an unnecessary scar." He took a step past her with his ever-present smile. "Have a pleasant—"

Alvena blinked. Whether he meant it or not, he had called her *beautiful.* No one had called her beautiful but Hairem! She took a swift step after him, causing him to halt.

He raised a violet-black brow. "...Do you want to come with me? I'm afraid I'm not at all doing anything pleasant."

'Has to be better than sitting around watching the moss grow,' Alvena countered. She gave a vigorous nod and slid closer. *'Please let the True Bloods be like him and Sellemar...'* She would *even* accept a liberal dose of Sellemar's arrogance.

Itirel shrugged his rugged shoulders. "I must make my last rounds before I retire for the evening. You are welcome to accompany me, but as I said, it is nothing pleasant."

'Carry on already!' She could not resist the urge to tap one of her new, shiny shoes in impatience. *'I clearly want to come!'*

"...Well, this way, then," Itirel beckoned, the corners of his lips twitching. His footsteps were silent as he glided over the mossy earth to the row of tents behind her own. She could hear an assortment of moans and wailing, and cries of anger and pain. Were they *all* humans? Why, surely such a refugee camp was treasonous against Ilsevel's intent! Her spine stiffened and she glanced at the drifting male. If he was surrounded by danger and chaos, he did not appear concerned. That accent... Was he from Ryekarayn?—Perhaps he did not fully grasp what had occurred in the capital.

No, he had to know.

She could feel the parchment scrape against her skin beneath her dress. How she wanted to share it with him! To hear him breathe words of comfort with such unshakeable courage...!

"That letter seems quite valuable to you," Itirel ventured as they made a slight turn on the narrowing path.

Alvena leapt. What? How...? She had just been thinking that!

"Judging by the unconventional attire in which you arrived, it seems safe to assume that you are a refugee as well. By what need have you to flee Elvorium?"

Rigidly Alvena marched onward, yet she felt as though he could hear her heart pounding her story beneath her breast.

"...You needn't tell me," he spoke after a moment. "My people will assist you regardless." He halted before the first tent, passing her a reassuring smile before leaning inside to the warm, amber glow.

Alvena felt her anxieties fade and poked her head in below his. A smile as easy as his own promptly donned her face. A human baby lay, fat and content, in the arms of a mountainous man. *'Ugly. And bald,'* she thought as she regarded the sleeping infant snug in its little blue shawl. How did anything so tiny grow up to be so barbaric? Her gaze shifted to the sleeping woman on the mat before them and she paled. The hollow face was tranquil and ashen, the body unnaturally still.

The Noc'olarian female inside gave a gentle shake of her silver hair as she gathered a pile of crimson rags. "I'm sorry, Itirel. I couldn't—"

"How long has she been dead?" Itirel interrupted. The warm smile was gone and Alvena was at once aware of the stinging wind.

"The lady passed away on the hour," the female began, tucking the last cloth beneath her arm with a reverent bow. "I preserved her as you directed."

Itirel's fluid gait became sharp and deliberate. He walked briskly into the tent and crouched down beside the woman, pressing his long, calloused fingers into her chest. Alvena watched in horror as the woman's body thrashed and danced as though she had been jolted with lightning.

"She's been dead too long!" the man behind him wept, his husky voice cracking. He dropped the baby into the crook of one arm as he reached out in a frenzy. "Just let her rest, gods damn you!"

The Noc'olarian female's rags scattered and she seized the flailing arm. "Sh!" she ordered. "May Ilra have mercy on her!"

And no sooner had the female invoked the god than the woman on the mat arched once and then fell flat, her chest rising and falling steadily beneath Itirel's hands.

In a terribly delay of reflexes, Alvena's feet finally sent her backward. Her hand snapped to the tent flap, holding it ajar just enough for her to glimpse the wonder inside. The human had been *dead*…!

Itirel withdrew, rising gracefully to his feet. "She will be perfectly well with a little further attention. Cisera can oversee her care."

Alvena let the tent flap drop, slowly tossing her head. What gift of healing did this male possess that the dead could return unchanged?! *'Incredible…'*

She could hear the human's sobs of gratitude as Itirel stepped outside, his face as impassive as before he had entered. She cocked her head. Was he not happy about what he had done? Or was he truly unaffected? She could not read him!

"It's a chilly evening, isn't it?" he began as though nothing at all had happened.

Alvena stared. He had just saved a long-dead human and he was bent on talking about the weather? The *weather* had not surprised her. *Bringing back the dead*, however…!

Her hair prickled at the nape of her neck. Was he a necromancer?!

No… No. She imagined necromancy must comprise something far more sinister. Dark magic: skulls and candles and sacrifices. Undoubtedly a torrent of blood. This male had done no more than touch the human…

What an *extraordinarily* gifted healer!

Through several tents, she bumbled behind in utter awe. When they reached the row's end, he paused, luminous eyes cast out over the encampment. She followed him, peering into the dark. Away along the forest line, she could detect a faint group of figures moving near the massive roots and she wondered if their smudges were any more distinct to him. He was an elf of the night… *'So he must see better in the dark!'*

"They're going to the coast," he informed her solemnly. "To Eraydon City." He stopped and Alvena could hear a thoughtful tone creeping into his voice. "And where are *you* going?"

Alvena opened her mouth and closed it, clutching one hand to her abdomen where the paper was still tucked safely away. No, she couldn't tell him. Yes, she had to get to Ryekarayn, but Sellemar had been very specific. He had said to show it to the ships bearing a blue phoenix. He had mentioned no one else. As much as she wanted to trust Itirel, this male was neither a ship *nor* a blue phoenix.

"There is a small wait to board, but you will arrive wherever it is you are going. Now, do not look so distressed—there is always hope. Our Lord, Kinraeus, has very close relations to the human king." And he left the knowledge there, as uselessly vague as though he had said nothing at all.

Alvena drummed her fingers along her crossed arms. *'Who is Kinraeus? How does he help save us?'*

Itirel smiled faintly. He was catching on quickly. "Sevrigel is unlikely to rebel, so our aid will have to come from Ryekarayn. The True Bloods are expected to remain neutral as the Royal Schism dictates, but the human king Joramon north of their borders is in dire need of help for his own people—he will seek aid. His kingdom is suffering a terrible famine, and Saebellus has recently ended the trade that helped to alleviate the shortage of food. Now he faces the threat of marauders who have taken advantage of his people's weakness. If our Lord Kinraeus can strike an alliance with King Joramon, he could offer economic stability in exchange for the king's royal forces—which would no longer be occupied by internal threats."

Alvena looked around eagerly in hopes of spotting this magnificent ambassador, but no one so splendid stood in sight. Still, her tension ebbed. If Itirel was right, perhaps she would no sooner arrive on Ryekarayn than find herself headed straight back for home!

A sudden shout hailed across the encampment. "Itirel!" Alvena heard footsteps racing toward them from their left, the sound muffled by the moss. "Itirel!"

Itirel stood tall and shot forth an indignant hand. "Sh!" he admonished. "There are many who are—"

The newcomer skidded to a halt, his glowing skin perspiring across his narrow brow, his lips parted as he heaved for breath. Despite his obvious exhaustion, his eyes were ablaze with excitement. He bounded forward and clutched Itirel's still-reprimanding hand.

Alvena retreated slightly, body tense once more. What was going on?

But the male ignored her entirely, shaking Itirel's hand in fierce exhilaration. Or perhaps in his eagerness he had not noticed her at all. "Yes!! *It's true!* He's come to Sevrigel! Rumors are spreading as fast as dragon fire, but we believe he just arrived in the south!"

She saw Itirel's composed expression alter abruptly. His face grew solemn, and yet, a flicker of mutual excitement seemed barely contained behind his eyes. "Are Saebellus and Ilsevel aware of this?! Of *him?*" he spoke almost breathlessly.

The elf shook his head, frizzy blue hair flying about his narrow shoulders and whacking Alvena in the eye as she anxiously leaned in for the details. "No, they do not know—not to my knowledge. Not *yet*, at least."

Itirel turned sharply to Alvena and she snapped back. Yet he barely seemed to see her as he spoke. "I had a wonderful evening with you, my lady. Be sure to inform the Noc'olari of anything you need. May Ilra bless you." And with that, he took rapid steps behind the new elf. She could hear his voice as he faded into the distance saying, "I will pack my belongings and find him *immediately*."

Alvena stared after them, now alone beneath the great white tree.

Her toes curled in the small leather shoes. *What* was so urgent?

Who had come to Sevrigel?

CHAPTER FIVE

Rain cascaded from Elvorium's sky in an unrelenting stream, the droplets so fine that they formed a fog of dreary inhospitality. Hardly a ray of sunlight managed to illuminate the golden rooftops, and still less fell to the cobbled streets. The afternoon marked the seventh day of King Saebellus' reign and the beginning of a bleak and miserable winter.

'You could have spared me the weather,' Sellemar begrudged his goddess as he hurried across the damp streets.

An upraised stone pocketed in the shadowed cobbles rebuked him sternly.

'Damn it,' he swore, and hobbled past the statues of Eraydon's company in the council's square. He spared them no glance of his usual affection; he had no doubt that half of their heroic faces would snigger at his plight.

He was late, and only so long as Ilsevel had not yet arrived in the Council Hall did he still possess some hope of surviving the day with all of his limbs attached.

Poverty was first to blame; if Sairel had the decency to spare the proper coin for his mission, he could afford a servant to at least make certain that he rose at a reasonable hour.

The sun had once been such an ally, but *apparently* Zephereus had more pressing concerns as of late.

Sellemar scowled once more toward Emal'drathar as he surmounted the stairs two at a time, then heaved the doors of the great hall wide. His dramatic entrance into the council chamber nearly three months before had been far more glorious than his current woebegone appearance availed; he was now disheveled, panting, and sufficiently soaked.

"Late, aren't we?" a male voice greeted him instantly from the far side of the room, bouncing off the walls in unison with the door's infernal creak.

It was difficult to decide which was more painful: Cahsari's voice or the agonizingly drawn-out, high-pitched screech resonating from the hinge.

A blessed silence then settled over the room and Sellemar was aware of the intrusive stares that accompanied it. Still, he managed a stiff smile and a generous, "Good morning," as he casually brushed the raindrops from his emerald, cotton clothes. In the presence of such despicable men, he could have been in a pauper's potato sack and still strode with equal confidence across the hall.

Cahsari followed his movement with a sneer and the beady gaze that so reminded Sellemar of a vulture eyeing its prey. Any day was infinitely worsened by the presence of the Helvarian creature, but Sel'ari *had* spared him some grief in his arrival: the queen was not yet present.

Sellemar pulled his damp shirt from his chest, dropping his voice to a mutter as he passed. "Imbecile."

Cahsari's eyes bulged and he leaned back in his chair with a strangled gasp. He gurgled at the nearby council members as though to demand their equal offense. "*What* did you call me?"

Sellemar wheeled and blinked once, slowly and deliberately. "Why ever would you think the word would refer to you?"

Which only seemed to enrage Cahsari further. His already narrowed eyes nearly vanished between their skeptical slits, and the newest wrinkles on the Helven's forehead did not help to distance him from the appearance of a vulture. Now Sellemar was quite certain he could never forget the unfortunate similarities.

He crossed the distance to his station and lowered himself into his elaborately carved chair, nestling his back against the painted blue phoenix. At once, the council decided he was of no further interest and subsided into a flutter of softly whispering voices—each member trying to keep his volume just low enough that the elf on one side could hear his words but the elf on the other side—of equal distance—could not.

Sellemar softly stroked his chin and regarded his fellow council members caustically: these were the trials he was now subjected to endure for his choice of espionage. He could have abdicated his position after Ilsevel revealed her true face—sailed across the channel to the safety of the Sel'varian Realm. After all, his venture to assist Sevrigel had been entirely voluntary of nature. Charity, as it were.

But now, he who had assisted the country to its fall was wholly responsible for undoing his mistake.

'But truly, Sel'ari, you could not have chosen worse company,' he griped. While Cahsari was most certainly dreadful, he was by no means unrivaled; the

Galwen, Fildor, held an equally distinct and callous expression only worsened by the thin line that materialized on his lips whenever their eyes met.

Beside him, the wiry Ruljen, Ilrae—although but recently appointed to his position—seemed as attached to Fildor and Cahsari as a babe to its mother's breasts.

In contrast, Mikanum managed a sympathetic response. He had grown thinner since the death of General Taemrin and what pressure he had received at the general's defeat could only have intensified by his own people's gradual silence and disappearance. Still, Sellemar knew his sympathies were undeserved: the Darivalian was as smooth and cunning as the most venomous of vipers.

And now the male had risen to his feet, his icy expression fixed grimly upon Sellemar. "El'adorium," he spoke politely, nodding his head toward Sellemar as though the distinction was needed. "As speaker, your timely arrival would be an example to us all. Granted, this is only your second meeting with us and—"

Sellemar's sympathies certainly did not extend to tolerating a rebuke. He interrupted the male in the most natural manner he could muster. "Thank you, Lord Mikanum. I shall be certain to arrive promptly to our next meeting."

To Mikanum's left side, a councilmember glanced up, his dark eyes rolling as he regarded the Darivalian's satisfied expression. *'What is his name again...?'* Sellemar squinted at the Eph'ven, as though this would help him recall the elusive knowledge. *'Helsheron... Heshanon...'* He frowned. Damn the Eph'vi and their impossible language!

The grand doors to the chamber swung open abruptly and Sellemar's regard of the council members vanished with the voices in the room. A single ray of sunlight pierced through from the outside, hastening to warn of the advent of the queen. *'Late again, Zephereus.'*

There was the soft clink of armor as the two guards at her front and back escorted her into the room. Between them, in the warm rays of light bouncing off their polished plates, Ilsevel stood. She radiated like Kamora herself, hair gleaming brilliant gold in the light, creamy flesh glowing and smooth.

Yet the power in that beauty only sickened Sellemar.

Hairem, Erallus, Lardol, Taemrin… her own father?—They were but the first casualties of her war.

The councilmember nearest the doors was the first to rise to his feet and bow. He was the only male Sellemar had not had time to scrutinize upon his arrival, but he had heard tales of the veteran of the Noc'olarian wars. "Your

Majesty," Lord Valdor said, his one eye sweeping across the queen and her company. "May Sel'ari bless this morning." His words, while respectful, dripped with discontent.

Yet none other than Sellemar seemed to note the tone; the council was scrambling into standing positions so that they could promptly mimic his greeting. With a painstaking humbling of pride, Sellemar forced himself to do the same. Then he straightened with a carefully neutral expression, eyes elevating to meet the queen's.

Hers were already upon him. She tilted her head and her lips curled into a tender, almost beckoning smile.

'Damn it.' It was as he had feared. He stiffened and willed his expression to remain vacant. He did not want the queen's affection—merely her *favor*… However, surrendering Erallus had procured him far more than he desired.

She halted before the jewel-encrusted throne of the king, pivoting unhurriedly to posture severely before her council. Yet when she spoke, her voice lilted as soft and tranquil as the chords of a harp. Deceptively docile. "His Majesty is unable to join us this morning. He has other matters that require his attention."

Sellemar sat, glancing at the empty chair beside her. *Saebellus*… He had not glimpsed the king since the wedding ceremony, but the warlord had far from disappeared. Swift in exercising his power and military genius, Saebellus was engaged in slaughtering any opposition to his recent rise to power. And that left Ilsevel to charm the populace with a pretty face.

But Sellemar was wise enough to infer more than that from the sly elf enthroned before them now. Ilsevel ruled from the inside, directing her dog whichever way she wished, while Elvorium clutched to her for safety lest Saebellus turn upon them next. A brilliant farce.

Ilsevel retained utter power.

Yet there she posed, folding her petite hands across her thigh. "First, I wish to welcome Sellemar into his new position." She inclined her head once more toward him, her smile extending with her regard. "I have no doubt that he shall bring more honor to the position of El'adorium than did Nilanis." Her smile persisted, but Sellemar could see a ripple of unease sweep through the council chamber.

What she had done would not be forgotten. For a thousand years after her demise, she would be immortalized as the queen who had heralded her ascent to power with the murder of her father.

And, gods willing, the murder of her husband.

"Now on to business," Ilsevel continued as the others settled behind their mahogany desks. Her face grew grim and what lines she had hidden creased unexpectedly. "Alvena has not been found."

Carefully composed, Sellemar merely blinked. *'Thank you, Sel'ari.'* Surely by now she had reached the Noc'olarian city!

Ilsevel drew his attention back with a sudden softening of her voice. "If there is anyone who possesses any knowledge of her whereabouts, he shall receive my..." her chest jutted forward and she awarded them a slow bat of her dark lashes. "*Utmost* gratitude."

The agitation in the room escalated. There emerged a very real threat, and yet she laughed, as though all their lives were but a game.

Wherever Alvena was could not be far enough.

Mikanum stood. "Your Majesty," he spoke with alacrity, his pale face flushing with eagerness to please. "I shall assist in finding the servant. I shall order half of my personal guards to scour the city and surrounding countryside for the fugitive."

Sellemar's nostrils flared in disgust. *'How desperate Mikanum has become.'*

Ilsevel's fingers twitched. "I am truly grateful. But do not waste your time outside Elvorium. She *must* be in the capital."

Sellemar dared not breathe for fear of betraying his relief. By the time Ilsevel realized Alvena was no longer in the city, Sairel would have her tucked safely behind his walls.

Another voice alighted in quick succession to join Mikanum's pandering. "I shall do the same," Cahsari declared, his palms clasping tighter together as though he was almost begging to throw himself at her feet.

"And I," Fildor and Ilrae announced in unison.

Sellemar watched as Ilsevel beamed at each of them, lingering to savor her hold upon her pets. Then a vein along her neck pulsed as her gratitude dissolved. "Lord Sellemar may have no troops, but what of you, Lord Valdor? Lord Heshellon? Shall you pledge your guards to find the little... witch?"

Sellemar saw the Eph'ven recoil. Gods, could none of his brethren retain some decency of composure?

Beside him, Valdor let out an audible grunt, plucking at the side of his patch. They had witnessed firsthand what she had done to her own flesh and blood—he had to know the danger he was in. And yet, the words that left his mouth shocked the room. "Your Majesty, if you will forgive my... *ignorance* of the situation... What exactly is the girl's crime?"

Sellemar's expression could remain fixed no longer; he felt his lips part, his eyes widen. *'Are you mad?!'* Even those that had submitted their aid sank low, seeming to will themselves to vanish lest her wrath fall to them as well.

Ilsevel's thick lips twisted crookedly. "Lord Valdor, I assume that you do not intend to assist?"

Unlike his fellow elves, Sellemar's shoulders remained tight, but his eyes flitted back and forth in warning. *'Silence!'* he willed. *'Do not question her!—Not about this!'* Ilsevel was as much a creature of deception as she was of pride—she had feigned such distress at Hairem's "assisted suicide," and now the criminal of her story had escaped her frantic search. No words would procure Alvena's safety now.

Valdor's bold eye flitted past his and landed in study upon the queen, his silence hovering like a heavy cloud above the room. Then his voice grasped at some semblance of humility and his head dipped. "Of course I shall assist Your Majesty in your search for the fugitive. You need only request my resources and they are yours."

As the attention of the room shifted to him, Heshellon retained somewhat more wit than his Noc'olarian ally. He averted his eyes swiftly to the floor. "…As are mine…"

Ilsevel tutted, waving a hand to dislodge the stifling gravity. She inhaled deeply, as though to savor the scent of rain hanging about the air.

But Sellemar knew it was victory she tasted.

"Well, that is enough about the witch," she exhaled with a smile. "I am certain you all have questions of your own." She snapped her fingers sharply, as though she had anything but their full attention. "When last we spoke," she continued, "I briefly mentioned our—that is, King Saebellus and my—intentions for the kingdom. As you well know, already the king has begun to eradicate the corruption in this land. And this shall progress until the elven nation holds one history of the past and one vision for the future. For those who are ready to return to the goddess' design, they shall be relocated to ensure the end of their entrenched minds and non-Sel'varian culture. Dissenters shall be put to the sword."

Sellemar grimaced. Relocation was a common and bloody military technique utilized to break resistance… for *humans*. It held no history in the world of *elves*.

Ilsevel's amusement had faded during her speech. Now her creamy face was grey, her full lips tight. "And what design is this, you may very well ask, as each of you has proven in turn that you believe yourselves above the moral law." Her eyes shifted in challenge to the males surrounding Sellemar.

Yet each one maintained a face of utmost innocence, instead glaring about to accuse his fellow councilmember in kind. Fildor dared even to glower in Sellemar's direction, as though he, Sellemar, who had never truly sat on the council before that day, was one of the sullied.

Sellemar scowled right back.

Ilsevel continued, wholly unaware of the insolence. "Sel'ari chose the Sel'vi as her first people and charged us with her tenets. Over time, the other races have infected us with their cultures. In the face of excessive dissimilarities, we have become confused as to the rights and wrongs—our virtue has become weakened and the people have thus fallen into moral complacency. And complacency breeds corruption. Now is the time for us to eliminate these impurities and conform under one culture and one law... *one people*. Our brethren must join the Sel'vi, or perish."

Sellemar grimaced. Where had she derived such a hostile notion of diversity? Before the battle that claimed Eraydon's life nine thousand years ago, the elves had been unified by their unique cultures. It was not until the Ryekarian humans—once staunch allies—betrayed them in battle that the elves felt compelled to abandon their homeland. Hence, their decline began.

No, the fault was not in their diversity, but rather in that the elves had forgotten their ancestors' way of life. When the elves came to Sevrigel following their desertion, they had experienced a period of unprecedented peace. For the first time in their history, they were not forced into constant unification to fend off foes. Idle and selfish living rushed in to fill the wiling hours. With no enemies to challenge their beliefs, the clarity of such things was lost. And the elves, once virtuous and pure, had no knowledge of how to fight the enemy within themselves.

And so, it was complacency that reigned.

Ilsevel's righteous conclusion merely became more impassioned. "In our victory we shall rise like a phoenix from the ashes and the world will once again know us as the pinnacle of virtue in this world!"

Silence enveloped the hall, and Sellemar wondered if the other lords were attempting to absorb the insanity of her words. Finally, one male dared to break the stillness. "Wise indeed, Your Majesty," Cahsari murmured, bowing his head. Sellemar could see his hands tense together as he spoke. Did he agree with her... or *this* time, was he merely afraid?

"Indeed, a just decree," Mikanum declared, pandering once more. "You are an inspiration to us all."

"As you will," Heshellon relinquished.

Ilsevel turned at once to Sellemar, leaning forward and placing her small chin into her palm. Sellemar's jaw tensed, but she did not seem to note his change of countenance. "You are a Sel'ven, my lord," she began, her voice shrill with enthusiasm. "What words of wisdom do you have for our brethren?"

Sellemar felt his stomach twist, his pride warring violently against his intelligence. *'Agree with her,'* he commanded himself, trying to take the advice he had so berated Valdor for almost ignoring. *'You will gain nothing through dissidence. You have a* charge*—you must rally the people!'*

There was a scrape of wood against marble and the room turned sharply at the unexpected sound.

"Madness is what this is. *Madness*." Valdor was standing, his white-knuckled fingers gripping his desk in an apparent attempt to quell his shaking. But his voice echoed boldly across the room, his pale eye set. A chill seized hold of the heavy air. "The Sel'vi are no greater than the rest of us. What has any culture ever done to *force* their beliefs upon your people? To what history do you refer where the goddess chose your kind above the others? The unity of the elves throughout the millennia has never placed one race above the next—not until we abandoned the homeland.

"While you speak of our vices, you ignore those your own race has engaged in. What of the whispered rumors of the Sel'varian heads that turned when warned that the mad Farvian king cultivated plans to *butcher* his entire people? Or the gates to Sheolra opened on the Phantom Isles so that the Sel'vi could employ demons to fight for them in The War of Dragons? Or the massacre called on the sirens for a few dozen murders spread across the eastern riverfront? These were all Sel'varian crimes! What you suggest is *genocide*."

Ilsevel's eyes were wild with anger behind her narrowed slits, but she did not stop the Noc'olari's tirade.

Sellemar shook his head at Valdor in disbelief. *'You fool...'*

Yet Valdor dared to continue, absentmindedly raising a hand to brush his eye patch while his one good eye fixed upon the queen. "How can you believe your own claims? And the rest of you? Standing here, nodding your agreement. Have you no pride? *No stand for your people?!* Sellemar, I expected more from you, at least!"

Sellemar felt heads turn to challenge his stance, but his expression remained carefully stoic. *'A stand here will accomplish nothing.'*

"What will happen to the Lithri in Darival for their refusal to join in this butchering—for we all know they, like so many other of the smaller races—will have nothing to do with this cause? What shall happen to the Darivalians for their failure to supply troops to fuel the capital's wars? Forgive me, Your Majesty, but you lost your good sense in the shock of Hairem's death. This, Your Majesty… This is *nothing* but *genocide*. I ask you to reconsider your actions."

At the conclusion of his words, no one moved. Sellemar could sense that the council members hardly dared to breathe. He could see Ilsevel shift from the corner of his eye, playing with a strand of hair as though she had grown bored with the elf's challenge.

She gave it a little twist. "Execute him."

A gasp swept through the room and Sellemar's jaw slacked.

Valdor drew himself up, his sensibilities apparently wholly lost. "Kill me, Your Majesty? For what? What is my crime?"

The guards on either side of the queen strode forward in solemn resolve, ascending the steps to Valdor's desk.

"What is my crime?" the Noc'olari demanded, shoving the nearest soldier away. "I demand to know my crime!"

Ilsevel stood, her face impassive, her eyes set like stone. Yet her voice rose in a cry that caused the window panes to hum with her fury. "*Execute him!*"

The soldiers recommitted their efforts, ignoring Valdor's second attempt to wrest away, and seized him firmly by the arms. Even as he swore in the Noc'olarian tongue and challenged their morality, they flung his arms behind his back and shoved him toward the center of the room.

Sellemar required every shred of control he could muster to remain where he sat, his chest burning at the sight of the helpless lord. *'Interfering will cost you everything!'* he warned himself. *'You cannot save him!'*

"WHAT IS MY CRIME?!" Valdor shouted all the louder, his one eye fixed upon Ilsevel. He was frantic, now. Death was rushing toward him and all the room stood still.

The queen raised her chin. The strand of hair that she had torn free of her braid stuck out, breaking her flawless composure. Yet she remained otherwise statuesque, watching the slow thud of the lord's feet dragging down the steps and across the marble tiles.

Sellemar could see his neck bulge, his limbs flail briefly. "*WHAT IS MY CRIME?!*"

A soldier near the door marched forward to assist. "Kneel, Lord Valdor," he demanded.

But the Noc'olari no longer resisted. He drooped in submission and even as he did so, the two elves on either side shoved and contorted his form until the pain alone prevented any revival.

Sellemar lurched to his feet, his hand clutching for his hilt, his mind racing to form a dozen plans of escape.

All futile.

"Your Majesty—"

Ilsevel raised her hand in command and the room fell silent.

Sellemar felt his breath catch.

"Lord Valdor, you are charged with treason for inciting rebellion."

Valdor's lips parted in disbelief. "*Genocide!*" he cried.

The soldier at his back inclined his head toward the queen. Then the room watched as his blade slid slowly from its hilt. Rose high into the air.

And then, with a swift and smooth stroke, it swept the air and sliced cleanly through the lord's neck. Blood sprayed across the floor. The body went limp. The head rolled to the side, Valdor's one eye staring at the queen in accusation.

Ilsevel flung her shoulders back, talons curling around the arm of her chair. "The Noc'olarian city in our north," she spoke calmly, "shall be removed first."

CHAPTER SIX

Jikun fought desperately upward, kicking violently, his heart racing against his breast. His hand flailed outward, grasping only empty waters.

"NAVON?!" he bellowed, breaking the surface and gasping for breath. "NAVON?!"

There was a brilliant flash of lightning and he frantically scanned the black waters, head whipping from left to right. There was no sign of the Helven.

"NAVON?!" His shout was reduced to a gurgle as a wave rolled over him, pounding his body into the ocean like the last leaf outside Elarium, tossing him easily toward the endless depths below.

Jikun extended a hand, feeling the rush of magic twisting about his raw fingers as ice formed in his palm. It grew, faster and wider, sucking his strength from him with every inch in its diameter. He grasped onto a small mast he formed in the center of the ice-raft and it bobbed to the surface, pulling him with.

Jikun sputtered and coughed, heaving deeply against the frozen surface as he clung in despair. "Navon?" he called weakly.

The storm barreled down on him, hurling his block of ice haphazardly across the foaming crests. A crack of lightning flashed in the sky and an image was briefly illuminated to his left—a pillar of stone jutting from the crashing waves, a ripped sail tangled across the jagged surface.

There came a sudden, fervent cry. "Jikun?!"

Another blaze of lightning and Jikun caught a glimpse of the pale skin of the Helven, his body gripping the debris of the ship. He vanished under a massive swell and reappeared in a frantic struggle for air.

"Over here!! Left!!" Jikun hollered. He swung his hand into the water, trying to propel himself forward. As though mocking him, a gentle wave knocked him farther away, and a ripple of thunder cascaded like laughter across the sky.

He saw Navon's head turn toward him, his hollow cheeks lit by a brilliant flare of light. His fingers were like bones clutching onto the cracks of the wood, his fingernails clawing at the surface.

A wave barreled into Navon from the side. With a terrified cry, his companion vanished beneath the water, swallowed with the remnants of the ship.

*

Jikun started, his heart racing, his eyes flashing open against a painful brilliance of sunlight.

Navon bobbed peacefully asleep in the water beside him, his cheek pressed against the ice of their raft.

Jikun let out a breath of relief, but it was stifled beneath a moan. He shook the vestiges of the nightmare from his mind. Sunlight. God-damn sunlight. And while silence surrounded them, thunder crashed through his skull—a feeling he could only liken to one too many drinks with a feisty and expensive woman.

But he had experienced no such fortune; the only mistress that had fondled him was the same vicious, black waves of the storm that had shattered their ship. His head ached and his joints groaned reproachfully with every motion. His stomach twisted and churned with fatigue. As a crackle accompanied his scant movements, he realized his white shirt had dried across his shoulder blades in stiff ripples formed by salt. A fine layer of the grains had dried across his eyelashes and sprinkled away as he squinted.

The waters arched and dipped about them, the waves having subsided into a gentle foam. They stroked their little raft, causing it to shrink in the warmth.

'Warmth...?' Jikun's intellect was slow to realize that the winter chill—which had stalked them for the week adrift in their shoddy vessel—had also dissolved. He lifted his head fully with a grimace, a spurt of pain rupturing from his wounded chest. Where… *were they?*

His heart stopped. His dried lips cracked as they opened to croak in elation, "Navon! *Navon* are you awake?!" All essence of his natural pessimism was drowned beneath his cry.

Across from him, the Helven groaned, face rising from the ice. "I can't feel my chee—"

"LAND!" Jikun gasped, almost breathless.

Clarity ruptured through the haze in Navon's eyes. "Land?!" He swung around in a frenzy, seeking confirmation. "Oh my gods… Jikun…" His voice rose, his lips curled. "BY SEL'ARI, WE MADE IT!!"

'We made it!' Even the goddess' name could not dampen his euphoria! Jikun kicked violently toward the bank, wishing his water-logged boots were not so much like an anchor. "Help me!" he ordered feverishly.

The glimmering shoreline grew until it stretched endlessly into the distance… They had nearly starved and drowned but this sight erased that trial! The frozen cuffs by which Jikun had anchored himself and Navon to the ice-formed raft melted away at his command, and the two elves sank into the rough sand of the shallow waters.

"Gods…" Navon panted, stumbling forward. "Gods, General… I didn't truly think we would make it…!" A glaze was forming over the Helven's eyes, his lips trembling with praise.

Jikun dragged his weak legs forward until the last wave of water broke over them… and then they buckled. He fell to his hands and knees, staring… *numbly*… ahead.

Sand. Endless ripples of golden sand.

And nothing else.

Jikun's fingers dug into the shore beneath him, his teeth clenching together until his jaw stung. His stomach now felt like a lump in his throat—his flicker of enthusiasm had been dashed against the coast and sunk into oblivion. "Damn the gods! *Damn Sel'ari!*" he erupted, spitting what little saliva his dry mouth had managed to conjure onto the earth. It failed to reflect his venom and so he followed with a fistful of hot sand.

It blew back into his face, ridiculing his fleeting hope.

"*Wipe* away that *fucking* smile, Navon. Do you know where we are?!—We're in a god-damn desert!" He made no endeavor to curb his tongue in the presence of his captain and rolled onto his back to shun the asinine optimism plastered to the male's face. He dropped a hand to his eyes in the event that the male repositioned. "We were supposed to land on the lush coast of Ryekarayn!—Grass! Forests! A damn morsel of edible food!" He slammed his free fist down, his chest shuddering. "We will die here the same as we would have done out there!" The failure and dishonor was more infuriating than tragic.

A shadow eclipsed him. For a moment, Jikun declined acknowledging the male, but when the Helven remained silent, he dared to let his hand fall away.

A mistake, of course.

Navon gazed upon him, sickeningly calm. "A lack of faith makes cowards of all men. You must not be so pessimistic, General." His words were slathered with morale, and he extended a hand toward Jikun as though his mood should reflect the same.

It did not.

* * *

A brief spasm of fear rattled Navon as his companion remained sprawled upon the earth, obdurate to his offer of assistance. The general had managed to retain some semblance of strength despite his injury and fatigue, but pessimism would certainly slay that resolve.

Navon steeled his gaze. *'Mesheck, Tiras, Eraydon...? No... Ephraim?'* He held no level of joy in impersonating the harsh character of Ephraim, but from all the ages of heroes and leaders, who better to perform when Jikun needed to be shown tenacity? At every misfortune since his defeat at the hands of the centaurs, his general had slipped further into a chasm of self-loathing and despair. Perhaps a nurturing leader would have most effectively soothed him, but Navon's dusty scrolls and own experiences offered no such figure to impersonate.

Ephraim would have to suffice.

Navon's extended hand tensed as the words and deeds of the old lion of The Seven welled inside of him. The words came to his mind and lips as though they were of his own character. "I will not wait here to die. Not after what I sacrificed to save you. Get on your feet!" he directed, his forceful tone certain to quench the general's wallowing.

But when Jikun merely knocked his palm aside, Navon detected the flicker of pain that hid beneath the fierce defiance. There was both a physical and emotional wound restraining his general's usual resolution. *'By Sel'ari,'* he determined, *'it is not a rebuke he requires.'*

And the thought banished Ephraim promptly from his mind in exchange for someone who channeled far more empathy with his resolve. *Eraydon.* "Come, Jikun," Navon began again, aware of the oddly stark contrast in tone. "We must be in the Makataj—Ryekarayn's desert." He extended his hand once more and offered what he hoped was a reassuring and apologetic smile. "We simply must travel north. I know Eph'vi live in the region. With a little luck, we will find them. *But* you must accept my help... And I, for one, require yours."

Jikun exhaled begrudgingly at Navon's altered approach. His icy blue eyes flicked out across the empty horizon and Navon had no doubt he was weighing the will of his pessimism against the genuineness of Navon's need.

A little manipulation would assure the desired conclusion. "…Or perhaps you may be right…" Navon lamented, tossing a hand with the dramatics induced by Mesheck. "This *is* hopeless." He squatted toward the sand and Jikun's head whipped sharply to him.

"Cease your complaints," the general barked, snatching his forearm for assistance. "Lead onward."

Navon heaved him upright. "As you command, General." He slung a triumphant step into the expanse of sand and Mesheck's internal applause faltered. For the first time, he absorbed the scalding temperature; it scourged his body from head to heel, with his naked feet bearing the brunt of the pain.

He had forgotten that more than his sword had been lost with the ship.

Jikun noted his change in countenance with a puffing of his wounded chest. "Here," he grunted, taking charge with the charisma of any great leader. "We have a long march ahead of us and this will serve you better than nothing." He tugged off his stiff shirt and flung the fabric; it was a dismal display of strength and landed a mere yard away. "…You will need your shirt for the other."

The skin of the northerner would certainly burn, but if Navon's feet failed him, so too would the rest of his body follow.

He wisely hid his admiration as he straightened from the binding of his feet. "Thank you. Now I have the pleasure of feeling as though my feet are in the soft confines of a portable oven," he laughed dismissively, sure to utilize the great healer Riphath's optimism in the face of such a physical trial.

His general's eyes glazed over. "If you laugh again at the gravity of our situation, I will stab you."

Navon's smile vanished. A definite overuse of optimism.

"Now," Jikun demanded impassively, rounding on the leagues of hazy grains. "Which way to the Eph'vi?"

Navon winced. "Remember the night I had to comb the entire Sagewood to find an antidote for your wound? I managed to find *that*, and in the dark, did I not? I reason I can certainly find the Eph'vi in a flat plain of sand."

Jikun followed his gaze outward. "I was nearly shitting out my intestines by the time you returned," he countered with a snort. "And dare I indicate that these events are *entirely* unrelated."

Navon struck his breast. "Stifle a little of that Darivalian cynicism and trust me."

"Trust..." Jikun relinquished with a sigh. "I *suppose* all your years of dedicated service earn you such a request, Captain." The title still left the general's lips without a flinch: the emotional dam was yet secure.

Navon had seen the effects of the Sevilan Marshes breaking free at Elarium. And now the dam the general must have built to repress *that* slaughter...? Gods knew a breach of that emotional trauma would be infinitely worse.

But he let none of his concern show. "Damn right I have earned it," he replied good-naturedly. He strutted forward, leading the general at his heels. *Forward* was the only direction in which he had determined to move. Into the heat. Into the sand. Away from the ocean. And he knew he required more than a staggering force of luck to find the Eph'vi before either of them expired. *'Sel'ari guide us,'* he prayed.

Yet his expression ever remained a beacon of positivity.

As they plodded on, the sun climbed higher and the warm, sandy surroundings became a searing span of scalding earth. The rays of the sun were like the touch of a brazier, sizzling against the bare flesh of their torsos and arms. Navon pressed a hand to his empty stomach, pushing it against the cavity in hopes of finding some form of relief from one of their trials. But the growl in his gut from days without sustenance had even ceased its once-persistent cries.

By the time Zephereus arrived at his zenith, Jikun's ability to draw water from the air had reached its final juncture. It was an honest wonder how the Darivalian yet managed to use any magic at all, and at the same time, it was a testament to the male's greatness. In his underfed, wounded, dehydrated, failing condition, he could still conjure strength for his underdeveloped talent.

Even if this misshapen creation was the final show of that might.

Jikun gave him a brief glare, as though he had detected an unsavory taste from Navon's sudden fixation of awe, and then returned to eyeing his little lump of ice. By the time it reached his mouth, it had all but evaporated.

Jikun scowled. "The air is drier than a cunt with no foreplay."

Navon's admiration clutched his chest once and expired. "Why must you be so terribly crass?"

"I no longer have to pretend I have a shaft up my ass, Navon. There isn't a god-damn Sel'ven—or anyone of note—for leagues."

And the heat was too intense for Navon to rejoin. It was moments like this when all the scrolls and old tomes in the world could not offer enough knowledge to survive. There was an expanding lack of hope. A mounting intensity of heat. Distant whispers of imminent death. Only Eraydon seemed viable to bear the weight of such trials, and Jikun's fading strength would soon be too great a burden to carry.

Hour drew into hour. The sun faded and the heat broke. The stagnation about them seemed to draw away. But before Navon could consider his relief, another danger cackled with the dusk. The dry air began to cool at an alarmingly unnatural rate, as though winter had swept across the Windari Channel and swallowed the night.

And through it all, the sand stretched endlessly into the distance.

Navon glanced sidelong at the ragged gait of his general. They would not survive another day in the heat. And they would possibly not last through a long, frigid night. If he did not find the Eph'vi soon, they would not find them at all. *'Sel'ari, I need you!'* Navon beseeched the stars above them. He wondered if, through the full moon of Noctem's presence, his message would prevail.

There was a sudden flicker in the darkness, faint and orange. Navon's body leapt and the words rushed from his cracked lips before he could fully grasp what he saw. "Jikun…!" he gasped. He snagged the male's cold shoulder, swinging his drooping body to the left. "Pray tell that you see it…!"

Westward, a faint twinkle of light gleamed, floating like a wisp of fire high above the sand.

Beneath his boney fingers, Navon felt Jikun's muscles stiffen. "What is it…?" he barely dared to speak, as though his breath might extinguish the tiny spark.

But Navon was already moving away, his blistered feet carrying him weightlessly over the earth. "Anything different is excellent!" he cried with a surge of relief. "The Eph'vi might reside that way! The light resembles fire, does it not?!"

Jikun ventured a single utterance of acknowledgment which Navon chose to interpret as budding optimism. "Maybe," his companion ceded.

Hope. Not just for Jikun, but for *him*.

Back across the Windari Channel, for a brief moment, Navon had allowed that single instance of his own character—not the scrolls or tomes, but *Navon*—to dominate his actions. Defying all that he had read, he had chosen to break tradition and honor. To pull his general from the battle at Elarium and ferry him across the channel.

None of the heroes would have been so selfish. He had chosen his affections for his friend over the lives of his troops. And he did not even have enough decency in his own character to feel guilt.

Pathetic.

They had been thrown off course into the cursed Makataj, but this glimmer of hope… What was this respite if not Sel'ari's forgiveness? What was this if not a second chance?!

Sel'ari had a plan for them yet!

Chapter Seven

The darkness around him was unlit, but Jerah could still see. The pounds of meat had long since been eaten, and his stomach gnawed at him pleadingly. "You are always hungry," he scolded himself, feeling much like he imagined his master felt. That was what his master always said to him, with the sort of tone Jerah often found made his jaw clench and his skin crawl. But in mimicking it so exactly, he found himself less aggravated toward his master than pleased with himself.

He had awoken just shortly before and completed his waking routine. Now it was time to pass the remaining hours of his day before he would sleep for the eighth time in his dripping room.

Jerah sat down against the cold wall with his stone balls on his right. He prodded the blue one forward to roll along the cracks in the floor toward the opposite wall. He smiled to himself, a crooked, hooked smile that his master had always worn when he seemed satisfied. Jerah found this expression to be useful in far more situations than his master apparently did, and used it often… *especially* when he was released. He had been surprised to find that it had the opposite effect on those witnessing it than on he himself making it—usually sending the viewer quickly in the other direction.

Jerah pondered this difference between satisfaction and flight, replaying the times of his release endlessly—like the twitching legs of a nearly dead cockroach. *Those beasts never died.*

His mind was pulled back into his little room as the red ball turned sharply over a bump in a raised stone and collided with the blue one, sending it twisting into the nearby wall.

Jerah left it there. It was all part of the game, he determined. Instead of simply seeing if a ball could roll farther than the others, now there was the additional challenge of avoiding running them into each other. He narrowed the imaginary alley in which they could move to enhance this challenge. Though perhaps not quite as tricky as catching the rats that crawled about his cell, the stones offered an interesting and new form of entertainment that lasted longer. The damn rats died within a day after he played with them. Stones, he was pleased to note, seemed to remain unchanged.

A distant voice made Jerah still. "—*didn't* actually believe Relstavum would amount. When Kraesin found him after the Phantom Isles, he took one look at him and wanted to use him as fodder for his hound. The poor bastard said, 'He won't succeed. Not in a century and certainly not in less.' But Saebellus' trust seems to have been well placed after all—look what the fucking madman did in a decade. Imagine if he really *had* worked for a century!" There was a chitter of soft sounds and then the distant voice continued, "If his success ever tempts him to turn, the beast will make a bloody mound of his allies."

Jerah promptly sat straighter. *The beast.* His master must have guests. He strained his ears to pick up the second voice, which was higher and quieter than the one before.

"Which I… the only… him."

Jerah's brow creased. He had missed most of those words. He stood, letting the orange stone drop from his hand, and raised his head toward the ceiling. He recognized the voices of both males. They were present most often when he awoke. The first voice was certainly his master, proclaiming boldly as he often did about *his* master's plans.

"Saebellus knows what he's doing. We're perfectly safe."

That was good. Jerah relaxed slightly, leaning against the wall. If his master was safe, then he was safe as well. That was what he always told him and Jerah had complete confidence in his words. After all, he had but to look at where he was now: safe.

There was silence for a few minutes and then voices emerged from further away, toward the back of Jerah's cell. He slid to them, his chains scraping across the floor. He hopped over the puddle on the ground and cocked his head toward the ceiling, his long, knotted hair falling away from his ear. There came a third voice now, strong and confident.

"Did you hear that the True Blood king invited Ilsevel and Saebellus all the way to Ryekarayn to dine with him and his brothers? Gods save us! As if Saebellus would accept any sort of diplomacy. He's come too far for that. I guess the uprisings are putting them on edge."

Someone made an unfamiliar sound… like… a series of fast, light grunts… or a gentle series of quick coughs… Jerah's brow knit as he imagined what this sound related to.

"It is NOT humorous," the higher voice growled, rebuking the third man.

Humorous? So that sound must relate to humorous. Jerah mimicked it quietly to himself as the conversation continued on, too soft for him to discern.

Finally, a few words became audible and Jerah fell silent again. "—since Saebellus took the port?"

Now, he knew what port was. He had drunk some himself once, on a celebratory occasion after he had been released a long time ago.

"Difficult," the third man replied. "I heard Relstavum is headed south to ensure the attempts at smuggling goods—or soldiers—between the channel dies. The Eph'vi will never see it coming."

This statement made little sense to Jerah, but he deduced that some ports would suffer and those smuggling ports were about to profit significantly. His master would certainly want in on that trade. He was a good male of business, after all. Especially with humans. His master always talked about how he made short work with them. Or of them.

Something like that.

"By Noctem, how the moon has risen! Saebellus is expecting me early tomorrow morning. I must sleep."

"I should be going as well. I have another operation," the third voice agreed. "Good night."

"My *wife* will be expecting me to make time for him tonight… Ow, Adonis!" his master replied. And with the heavy click of doors above him, the world fell silent once more.

Jerah sat down slowly, repeating the conversation in his head a few times. He had heard that name before: Relstavum. He was his master's master's plan. Another elf of the surface, Jerah imagined. He wondered, briefly, exactly how many people there were up above. He knew that the city had many elves in it, but if people were making port outside of his city, there must be a few more people there. And across the sea, on Ryekarayn, there were humans, which were fatter, shorter, and dumber elves. And then the things called dwarves, which were, apparently, the fattest, shortest, and dumbest elves. So if there were as many humans and dwarves as there were elves, then there must be enough of them to fill a few rooms the size of his quarters! And *then* there was the enemy general's army…!

But Master *had* said they had killed them all, so that meant there certainly were not as many surface-dwellers left.

He reached out to pick up his orange stone and stopped. It was no longer as it once was; instead, there were several pieces of varying sizes, sharp edged in the center and round on the outside. He picked up a chunk, turning it over slowly. This must have happened when he dropped it. He felt what he did when he was placed back in his chains—a cold, unpleasant feeling that allowed no room for a smile.

So, stones could change too.

CHAPTER EIGHT

Jikun sprinted toward the distant amber light, hardly daring to breathe. Beneath his lopsided gait, the sand was fading, ceding the ground to clumps of brown grass withered by the day's relentless heat. Yet the orange, floating light beckoned brighter and brighter until it had formed the shape of a fire burning high atop a taupe-colored tower.

'A tower... a watchtower...' Like the crystalline towers of Darival, this structure was a beacon of refuge in a long stretch of uninhabitable land.

"Sel'ari be praised!" Jikun heard Navon's latest debasement, but for once, he did not entirely despise the religious tribute.

The expanse revealed beyond the tower was indeed a fortune. Plains of inconceivably green grass blanketed the land beneath intertwining strands of glowing, swaying orbs. Charmingly squat homes emerged under the light, and surrounding them along the wide, dirt roads were colorful bazaars. These booths complemented the houses' simplicity with intricacies of design and vibrant colors.

The city was alive and bustling in the cold night air, packed with merchants and consumers. Living people. *Civilization.*

Jikun blinked hard once and dug his nails into his palm until he flinched. From the deepest reaches of the city, chimes rang out in greeting. "*Saved*," he whispered. He drifted across the lush earth and inhaled the heavy mist that hung in the air.

Beside him, Navon's gape signaled that he was equally as entranced. "I told you I would find aid."

"Are you alright?" came a sudden shout of alarm.

'Highstead—the Common Tongue!' The human language had never sounded more inviting, even from all the whores in the Port of Targados.

Several heads wrapped in scarves turned at once to spot the approaching strangers, and a horde of bodies dressed in thick wool and camel hide began to gather at the city's edge. They huddled together like a herd of curious livestock and Jikun immediately dismissed them as such. When he reached the crowd, he flung them aside in a frantic search for the food and water that was required to sustain them.

It was only when Navon stayed him with a restraining hand that his mind somewhat cleared. A rapidly advancing figure strode out of the throng of scrutinizing, caramel faces. A prickle of caution jolted down Jikun's spine and he lifted his hands from the shoulders of his next victim.

Dark skin… golden eyes… indeed, *Eph'vi*. Their practices had not before gnawed at every fiber of Jikun's tolerance, but in the face of his snarling gut and buckling knees, he could not think of a culture more revolting… even if it might be the only one that could deliver him.

The figure was approaching faster now, long legs striding purposely toward the pair.

Jikun recoiled. Eph'vi were not known for being particularly sympathetic—their crowning tenant made all but the most self-righteous squirm: fate aids and rewards those who have proven their worth; misfortune befalls those who have not. *'And gods be damned... in their eyes I would be the latter...'* Jikun concluded derisively, even as his memory struggled to deduce exactly *why* that whisper rang true…

Fear stabbed abruptly through his mind, screaming a warning of an… *incident...* to which he had given little allowance of thought. 'You *are contemptible:* you *broke your vows.* You *abandoned your soldiers. You are a traitor not just in the eyes of Sel'ari, but in the eyes of* all *elves!'* He staggered, shaking his head violently to shun the suggestion.

"My friend is in need of aid!" Navon called, placing a hand swiftly to Jikun's chest in a struggle to steady him.

The crowd had grown rigid and Jikun's chin dropped against his breast. Those judging eyes… *The battle had been lost...!* Surely Saebellus would still have slain his soldiers despite his sacrifice. *'My life... would have served nothing!'*

His hunger withered at the thought and he struggled to rebuke his weakness. *'You're making a fool of yourself and Navon.'* He pushed his friend aside. With the efficiency he had learned from masking the agonies of war, Elarium was pushed swiftly into the recesses of his mind, hidden somewhere beneath a pile of dead soldiers in a hazy swamp. All that remained was the veil of great military successes and personal triumphs.

The surrounding desert rushed back to Jikun's senses—as well as the craving for food, the need for water, the probing faces… and the figure that had broken through the throng to stand before them.

Navon took a single step toward the female, and Jikun noted that only the faintest trace of cautious sympathy could be seen in the creases of her dark, stoic face. *'Perhaps they deserve their trials,'* he could almost hear her condemnation.

"We are in need of aid," Navon repeated with a short bow that caused Jikun's rekindled pride to bristle.

The female's button nose curled at the scrawny, bent frame before her. "Hmph," she grunted. She pushed her thick scarf down to lick her darkened lips, and her accent followed thick as soldier's gruel. "What happened? Where have you come from? What aid do you seek from the city of Dahel?"

Jikun did not have to look down upon himself to imagine the visage of the shirtless, blood-stained, and fatigued male that he was. *'What aid do you* think *we need?'* he snapped internally, and a weak tremble coursed through his body at the effort. "We are survivors of a shipwreck off the southwestern coast." And that was the extent of his paltry creativity.

The female turned her apathetic gaze upon Navon, and the intensity of her inspection grew as though his very appearance—barefoot and deathly pale—offended her. "There is no charity for smugglers here."

'Smugglers?' Jikun's chest dared to swell, despite its sad state of sand and sash. "We are not smugglers—" he denied, but was undermined by his own voice as it cracked in the dryness of his throat.

"We are mercenaries," Navon interjected with a dashing smile. "Bastin of Alaris and Rulan of Venmore—I am certain you have heard of us."

The acerbity of the female's tone lessened, even as Jikun steadied himself pathetically against his captain's shoulder. "…The names are familiar," she mused.

Navon's expression became livelier, his posture straighter. "We were sailing from Elarium to Ryekarayn for business with Lord Thamos when our ship was destroyed in a storm. And as you can clearly see, all of our possessions were lost with it. We were most fortunate to escape with the flesh still strapped to our bones."

If Jikun's mind was any hazier, he may have believed the tale himself.

The female tossed her head at the small crowd peeking around her back, as though feeding off of their reaction. "Rulan and Bastin," she exhaled slowly, her features displaying an array of deliberating grimaces and wrinkles. Then her words became decidedly brisk. "Our charity rests with the tenets of Epherphese. I am Esra, one of fifty representatives on behalf of our council. In order to supply you and escort you from Dahel and out of the Makataj, I will need to convene with our Re'heshae." She tipped her chin at their tattered state. "They will devise your test. If you prove yourselves worthy, aid shall be given. Follow me."

She added nothing of if they failed.

Yet Jikun allowed himself the faintest smile as he fell into a deplorable limp beside Navon. He inclined his head. *'Swift thinking. Commendable work.'*

Navon grinned. Still, when he leaned over to speak, he did not address his own success. "Now is not the time or place to start whoring," he instead scolded.

Gods. And here Jikun had the audacity to believe they were sharing a sensible moment. His jaw snapped open in offense. "*Excuse me?*" he hissed as another sandy breeze swept past, making the little orbs of yellow light shake angrily along their cord. "I had intended to praise you for your quick mind. *Now*..." he trailed off. No, it was no use. Navon could read the lust in his eyes as plainly as if he had spoken his desire aloud. *'Shamefully predictable,'* he chastised himself. "Who are Rulan and Bastin, anyway?" he demanded gruffly. "I have never heard of them... but *you* were quick and confident in the use of their names."

* * *

Navon *had* been rather sagacious, but then, he had an ample supply of material to draw upon. Not only had wild tales of the iniquitous pair reached even moderately informed individuals on Sevrigel, but he had actually *met* Rulan and Bastin once before—and not so long ago. Unfortunately he had few others as his alternative; his focused readings did not offer him an extensive selection of unsavory characters to mimic, and impersonating a long-dead hero would likely *not* be terribly effective.

More importantly, evidence that this conurbation catered to seedy mercenaries was written plainly across the city.

As though his reasons should be obvious to his culturally inept companion, Navon gestured in a wide arc. He imagined Ephraim must have felt similarly when he had escorted the unrefined Eraydon into the folds of Sel'varian civilization. He watched as Jikun surveyed the easily recognizable Sel'varian intricacies of several vases and silken rugs displayed upon a table up ahead. Not far from them, Noc'olarian, Galvarian, and even *Farvian* artifacts were scattered with frequency amongst the merchants' wares and the balconies of nearby homes.

After Jikun had given the scenery an ample scan, Navon withdrew a few paces from the Eph'ven female. He spoke, careful to keep his voice hushed. "The Eph'vi are frequently involved with both human and elven smugglers," he intoned. "Rulan and Bastin are two mercenaries who are frequently bid upon in the business of procuring such items. I met them briefly when I acquired the book you eventually *stole* from me." He looked pointedly at his friend, a little surge of bitterness following the memory of the altercation inside his tent.

Jikun's brow merely furrowed. "So now we're black market mercenaries? Fantastic decision, Navon." He paused. "Wait. What book…?"

Anger and incredulity would have flared within Navon's breast, but who was he to fight the predictability of the self-centered hero? In fact, Jikun had probably had the audacity to stuff the tome beneath his bed under a pile of a whore's willfully abandoned lingerie.

"*The* book," Navon muttered. He could play as indignant as Ephraim or as furious as Tiras, but ultimately he had to admit that it was his own resentment that inflamed his offense now. All those diligent hours dedicated to his sole personal desire and Jikun did not even have the courtesy to remember! "How can you not recall that tome? It is not like you have stolen *multiple* volumes from me. In fact, if we were to eliminate your 'poetry book'—which I think is quite reasonable—it's the only one I've seen you touch in fifty years!"

Jikun blinked, as though struggling to recall what Navon could possibly be "complaining" about. "You mean that necro—*that* book?"

Navon heaved a sigh. "What *other* book could I be referring to?" he retorted, puffing out his chest.

Jikun cuffed him on the ear.

"Ouch! Damn you, Rulan!"

"Still have enough wits to maintain that lie, at least. I suggest you keep focused on your role lest I strike you again."

"Here we are," Esra interrupted as Navon withdrew his palm from his throbbing ear. She had stopped before a curtained doorway and was pushing the heavily ornate fabric aside, unaware of the spat behind her. "In here. My home. Wait. I'll see what I can do for the two of you."

"You have the mental capacity of a dwarf," Navon muttered.

"And you whine like a whore," Jikun jabbed back.

And then they ducked in truce beneath the curtain into Esra's quiet home.

The building was of simple stone and underdressed: a single vase on the low dining table was the sole decoration. *'So... empty,'* Navon reflected with an internal grimace. He had spent so long enfolded in the radiance of the Sel'vi that he had nearly forgotten that such baseness existed in most of the world. Like where he had been raised. Against the farthest wall a fire burned, fending off the chill of the night with an amber glow. It was also the only source of light in the otherwise darkened home. He shoved his own character aside, quick to shield his emotions with Riphath's stoicism.

"Wait," Navon heard Esra's distant command, and refocused in time to see her vanish into the street behind the curtain.

"Who do you think she is?" Jikun queried after a moment. "Not even a family name attached to her introduction."

"Someone you *cannot* bed," Navon reproached. "That you can even consider such a notion while in our circumstances—and in your condition in particular—*would* be impressive if it wasn't such a glaring problem."

Jikun returned a shameless smirk, and, rather than offer his usual caustic retort, surveyed the dimly lit kitchen.

Navon had already absorbed the sight of the worn cabinets. Empty counters. A spider web bridging the cracks of the un-swept corner. And there was no character to play—not even a self-assured Helven like Tiras—that could elevate Navon past his own resentment of the nakedness. If he had any affection for a life alone in squalor, he would never have left home.

The Sel'vi would certainly never demean themselves to such a state of oversimplification.

Across the kitchen, the uncultured general was settling in with ease. He slammed one cabinet door and flung wide another. "So we are sell-swords who procure items for the black market?" he was asking. "What do we know about ourselves? What's our family name? Are either of us wed? Are we related?—I hope not because we look as alike as a cavalier and his horse. Do we have children? Where do we live? Have we been here before?"

It was the last question that caused Navon to writhe past the jest. He watched as Jikun bent down to a drawer and slid it open to survey the contents. In tales, lying about one's identity never ended well; but by Jikun's relaxed approach, he clearly was not much of a scholar.

As though this instance was necessary to reveal such a truth.

Navon cleared his throat loudly. "We'll decide that information now," he informed as he knelt down on a large seat cushion at Esra's table. "I am Bastin of Alaris and you are Rulan of Venmore. We do business everywhere and so we aren't '*from*' anywhere; experience says people generally accept a mercenary's secrecy. I'm recently wed and you can't sit on one woman long enough to achieve that. I don't want children and at the rate you're whoring, you don't have a choice."

Jikun's eyes narrowed, unappreciative of Navon's wit, and he jerked open a second drawer.

Navon accepted his partial attention. "As for having been to… Dahel… There, we're just going to have to gamble. We must try not to sound committed on the matter. If someone recognizes us, we can feign memory loss caused by errant magic. It happens frequently enough when steali—*procuring* magical artifacts. A strike or two in the head—they're not going to condemn us on the mere grounds of suspicion… but *try* to not get carried away. And may I repeat myself once again, General: *NO* whoring—in your fits of ecstasy, who *knows* what information you might divulge."

Jikun pillaged noisily through the contents of the next drawer. "I'm impressed, Navon—you didn't need more than a moment to devise an entire slew of lies. *You* would make a *fine* sell-sword."

Navon huffed indignantly, feeling a score of his heroes gasp in offense. "You say it with such a negative connotation, and yet you are aware that Eraydon was a mercenary and the pinnacle of accomplishment. Just as with all matters, there are heroes amongst the thieves, Jikun. I would imagine we *both* can avoid devolving into the latter." Jikun snorted, and Navon snapped his fingers in a futile rebuke. "For now, we just happen to be *masking* as two *slightly* shady individuals."

"I'm fairly certain that you have branded us as thieves."

Navon paused, watching Jikun's hand surreptitiously slide from the drawer as though he was trying to hide his action from the Helven's perceptive gaze. "…What did you just take?"

Inconspicuousness foiled, Jikun raised a small kitchen knife and slid it snugly into the side of his boot.

Navon regarded him flatly. "*I* branded us as thieves?"

Jikun closed the drawer forcefully, startling Navon from his ease. "Let me be plain," he began sourly. "I did not exchange my army to do a novice's work. We can masquerade as these two miscreants for now, but if the Eph'vi refuse us aid, I am not taking chances that I am trapped as a groveling thug."

'And that little knife is our salvation?' Navon wanted to challenge, but he wisely held his tongue. His general's gaze had begun to shift deliberately about the room and there could be no doubt that the conversation had come to an end. Navon reprioritized. *'Food, water, clean wounds,'* he reminded himself, scanning the kitchen in hopes of uncovering any such assistance. His eyes bulged suddenly as a shimmer emanated from the table's single decoration.

Jikun spied the water at that same moment and as one, they sprang for the vase.

"I saw it first!" Navon cried, all semblance of sophistication and maturity lost in his frenzy to quench his thirst.

"Frozen tits," was the culturally vulgar response the Darivalian chose as he swung out to snatch the water.

Navon flung himself over the table, jerking the vase free of Jikun's grasping fingers. *'Frozen tits to* you,*'* he thought triumphantly as he tipped it back… but nothing flowed free to satiate his thirst. He lowered the stoneware and glowered contemptuously at the block of ice. Then he shot Jikun a defiant glare as he extended his tongue and slowly slid it across the surface.

"You think that will stop me?" Jikun leaned casually across the table and plucked the vase from his hands. "Thank *you.*"

Navon watched the vase leave his grasp with an impatient twitch. "You're so very welcome," he grumbled as the Darivalian gulped the contents down.

Jikun sank wearily into the comfort of the cushions across the table and passed him the remainder with a shameless belch.

"And you could turn away when you decide to act like a repugnant dwarf."

"Is there any other type?"

Somehow he had even forgotten that Jikun was his constant representative of the world's primitiveness. Navon rolled his eyes and drank until his thirst dissolved—but it passed only to be replaced by his still-existing trial. His scorched feet seared once more in pain and as though he had not already violated Esra's property enough, a thought entered unhesitatingly into his mind. There was still some clean water left. *'Jikun may be accurate about aid... We should clean our wounds in the event the Eph'vi do not offer any such assistance.'*

Riphath would insist so.

Navon slid to a sitting position upon the cushions and peeled the shirt from the blisters on his feet. The puss had oozed out and sealed the wounds to the salt-coated fabric. As Navon tore the bandage free, his loose skin ripped away with it.

"That looks severe."

Navon did not lift his eyes. "The appearance sells the suggestion."

Silence.

"Jikun," he began, trying to conceal Riphath's nagging, "you may be correct about the Eph'vi's lack of generosity. The kitchen knife is surely a worthy addition to our company, but might I suggest you focus on your more immediate care? Balior could take you any minute."

The male immediately prickled, wise to Navon's intent. "I'd like to see him try," he muttered, glowering once toward the sky in visible defiance.

Navon glanced up as well, seeing past the roof of auburn stone and starry sky, to the realm of Emal'drathar. He could imagine Sel'ari beholding their state with a stony gaze. Jikun was certainly not winning her or any of the deities' favor with his continual blasphemy. And yet here he stood. "I told you the gods have a plan for us. You will discover that we were wrecked upon this land for a reason," he countered as he rubbed a moistened hand across his foot to dislodge the flecks of sand. "But *not* if you don't tend to your wound."

Jikun groaned.

How could such a brilliant male be at the same time so foolish? "*General*," Navon barked sternly, giving way to Riphath's nagging. "You were nearly gutted back on Sevrigel and it's a miracle you have survived this long without proper care. At any moment, even *your* adrenaline shall perish and Esra will find you sprawled out on her kitchen floor."

Jikun patted the silken pillows once. "I've already planned to do the sprawling here," he laughed.

Navon smacked the table sharply. "Take your health seriously, damn it! You are not going to be able to survive on luck forever. We are on the human side of the world, Jikun, and it is *far* more savage."

Jikun gave a dramatic sigh. "Oh Mother, please stop fretting."

Navon snatched up a nearby pillow and hurled it at Jikun's face. "You're fortunate *I* was never the general on Sevrigel because I would have bled that Darivalian arrogance right out of you!"

Jikun caught the pillow and hurled it back, skirting the side of the vase and smacking Navon in the face. "Father will most certainly hear of this abuse."

Navon let the cushion fall aside, forgotten. His mouth opened and closed twice. "Good *gods*, General—your behavior would put the worst sprite to shame. You are a bloody *adult!*"

"*No*," Jikun feigned a gasp and struck his wrist dramatically across his forehead. "I *am?* What a *shocking* revelation!"

Navon pounded the vase several times in silent anger, the remnants of water sloshing about. "If you make me come over there and strip your shirt off—"

Jikun grabbed another cushion and chucked it at the male. "Control your lust—I'm not going to loiter with a bloody injury exposed. I'll take my chances with Lady Luck."

Navon shook the vase as though it were Jikun's neck. It offered him only paltry relief. "You had best start addressing your wound this very moment, General, or—"

"SH," Jikun hissed as a soft thud sounded from beyond the room. He leaned forward sharply to shove the vase toward Navon's lap.

Navon was forced to cut his words short as he hastened to balance the teetering stoneware. He had barely succeeded when the curtain slid aside and Esra stepped into the room. She paused, eyeing the churning vase and the two dirty males lounging about on her finely woven and scattered pillows.

* * *

Jikun awarded her with a subtle smile—one the women on Sevrigel would have paid to receive. It was worth the attempt.

He was half naked already, after all.

Perhaps the female had noticed his charming address or perhaps she had not, but if she indeed *had*, she was clearly not attracted to the opposite sex. She offered no reaction to his comment, or to her guests' intrusive behavior. "...I come with good news. Do not fret. The council is eager to grant you aid... *if* you can prove that you are who you claim you are. You shall do so by completing the task provided to you by the council tomorrow morning. Until then, you shall be housed at our community inn."

A community inn was squalor Jikun had never experienced the likes of before. And judging by the placement of Dahel in the scorching desert with naught but the sea for company, the general had no doubt that only smugglers would pile in for the nights—or weeks—their ships lay docked along the eastern coast.

The notion of a group of sex-deprived males crowding into a single room to while away their time was not exactly Jikun's preference.

Despite Jikun's outward misgivings—a curled lip, flared nostrils, and a deeply furrowed brow—Esra was predictably curt.

The captain shot him a warning glare.

"At my heels, minabi," she tutted at the door as Navon finished rebinding his feet.

Jikun briefly speculated what insult he had been thrown before he stepped onto the street behind her where his offense was promptly swallowed. *'What in the great tundra...?!'* Dozens of creatures of various species roamed and idled about the paths as though they were merely the adorable household wolf. But they each could have crushed Nazra beneath a single, massive paw.

"Beast taming is an innate skill found in all Eph'vi," Esra beamed as she strutted toward the center of Dahel. "You Darivalians have thakish you ride into the hunt, do you not?"

"Yes," Jikun lied. Responding with, 'Actually, the thakish hunt *us*' was mildly less impressive. He watched as a row of carefully painted vases and flickering evening lights were lost in the presence of several massive forms tromping alongside their tiny masters. Upon passing a blackened beast with glistening, scaled skin and lumpy, spiked hindquarters, the creature sucked itself into the nearest wall and grew as watery as its master's bloodshot eyes. When Jikun had hurried past, it fattened once more and the pair disappeared down the street.

"That was an agretha," Esra spoke as she noticed the subject of his gawking. "They are one of the most deadly. And my favorite."

Jikun's lips managed a slight twitch. "Delightful."

And she did not charm him again until they arrived at a long, flat building shimmering with an orange hue from the nearby lights. The exterior was seamless basalt, as though hued entirely from the face of a single, colossal stone.

This might have impressed Jikun if it was not ultimately a lump of rock.

"Here we are," Esra announced as she swept the curtain before the door aside. It was only slightly less gaudy than those that dangled before the windows. "On any given night, Keshal was bustling with foreign merchants. Since the arrival of the hel'onja, no one dares to travel from the coast." She ducked inside and continued in rough Highstead, "You shall have Keshal almost for yourself."

Jikun followed, ignoring the fact that she had brushed over an obviously sinister matter.

Navon, however, had curiosity to quench. "What is the hel'onja…?"

Esra trailed alongside the wall, past pillars carved of red sand and a slew of vividly painted murals. Her voice was softer in its reply, a hush not wholly formed by the distance. "The creature appeared two weeks ago, and since, travel to and from the city has stagnated," she began solemnly. "We call it 'hel'onja'—the black serpent—but it bears little resemblance to others of its species except in size. It is marked in strange symbols unfamiliar to our kind. It will not be controlled or pacified. It is a great bounty of luck that the two of you managed to arrive," she finished as she stopped before a mauve curtain at the far wall. "Someone must have need of you."

Navon smiled in his smug, little way and Jikun shoved an elbow staunchly in his side. "Contain your glee. We still have to get out of this damn desert."

"Esra, I am here," a new voice declared, and a male swept from behind the curtain with his arms spread wide. This Eph'ven was slightly shorter than the female—a rarity amongst males to be certain—with hazel eyes and a thin, dimpled smile. He was the very essence of an innocent elf, plucked straight from the pages of a Sel'varian children's story.

If he was of fairer skin, Jikun was quite certain his cheeks would have been rosy.

"This is Khatja," Esra spoke stoically. "He shall care for you until the council determines Epherphese's will."

The newcomer flounced into the large room with a generous bow, flashing the female a glamorous smile that signaled his eagerness to please. His gaze was disappointingly personal; it was quite possible he had already gotten his cock wet. "A deep pleasure to meet such distinguished males as yourselves," he began with a stupid grin. "I have heard a fair share of your adventures across the seas and, while I can in no way *condone* all of your actions, more than one item in my possession has been acquired from your work. Find a place to rest and I shall bring food, water, and aid to bear you 'til the dawn."

Jikun turned with the encompassing motion of his hand. *'Not as empty as suggested,'* he grouched as he inspected a large group of humans skulking along the left wall. The mass of them were drinking and eating and mumbling to one another in the Common Tongue.

Smugglers.

And along the rear curve of the wall was yet one more man. His solitude was distinguishing, and Jikun found his curiosity piqued enough to study him more closely. His skin was weathered, sun-beaten, and browned, but he appeared aged no further than his late thirties. He was exchanging a small bag of coin for a leather-bound book with one of the hairy crew members. *'An outcast smuggler, perhaps...?'* "And who is that? Part of that crew...?"

Esra cocked her head, as though baffled that she should have to explain. "No—the crew is from *The Ire*, unable to return to their ship because of the hel'onja."

Navon gave a nod, apparently familiar with yet another unsavory group.

"That man is Relstavum. *He* is a prestigious mercenary from the north, most famous for his work culling the bloodthirsters and lycanthropes."

On cue the man looked up, a leather-bound book in one hand, a heavy bag of coins in the other. His attention flicked across the room to meet Jikun's gaze, as though he had heard his name at that considerable distance; but as the mercenary was human, that was impossible. His eyes were dark, solid, and hollow, and yet they searched the Darivalian with unnatural intensity—a surveillance far too intrusive.

"He arrived two weeks ago. Fortunately, he is a master of ancient Farvian protection enchantments. He has been forging spells of warding against the hel'onja."

The human broke off his gaze as he muttered something to the smuggler. The coins were exchanged. The leather book vanished into his vest.

Jikun turned back to Esra.

"I bid you a good night," she was finishing as she strode to the entryway. "May Epherphese find you worthy tomorrow."

And without so much as a flicker of hesitation, she ducked out into the night, leaving the two shipwrecked males alone to enjoy a solitary night on the stony floor.

* * *

Navon swung to face the uncouth room. Someone in the midst of the smuggling scum belched and another man valiantly attempted to best it. Reflecting upon the termination of their once close friendship with these brutes, he was certain the Sel'vi had made a wise decision. Like any hero who had undergone arduous trials, Navon too was subject to misfortunes.

But for now, his displeasure was momentarily abated by the reappearance of Khatja, who brought them two wide cloaks, a dry, meager meal, and herbal bandages that emitted a questionable odor. Still, after a generous application of the remedy, Navon's feet felt practically ready to dance.

Beneath his dirty sash, even Jikun's wound was now exceptional. "Gods, that herbal oil reeks like shit," the general balked, as though he had not just skirted the edge of Balior's door.

His creaseless expression briefly faltered as he sank against the wall, and Navon was reminded of the caliber of his friend's masks.

"After we receive aid and are escorted from the Makataj," Jikun continued, recovering his command, "we will need to find honest work. I'm sure, with our skills, we can easily acquire such tasks in the human land. How far is Eraydon City from here?" The food had, at least, lifted his mood.

Navon could not resist a smile, even as he tilted his head in consideration. Eraydon City was the redeeming beacon of civilization on Ryekarayn. Not only was it the country's cultured capital, but it was also the birthplace of many of Navon's heroes. "At least a few weeks away... possibly more. But there are far more refined dwellings in the west—unlike Sevrigel, we will pass through a good number of settlements before we reach a major city. We may find opportunities for labor in any such place. All of the human lands have lords that claim certain regions—almost like... an elven councilmember, but only subordinate to King Joramon. Most of these men are free-reigning and very near kings themselves. True kings, may I stress, and not purely men who think themselves king—such powerful men will have much to offer."

Jikun snorted once in disapproval. "One king was bad enough," he huffed with a dismissive toss of his hand. "Where are you from? Is it nearby? Do you have connections there that we might find of use? Personally, I'd rather avoid the human lands. As much as I hate the Sel'vi, I imagine humans are even more loathsome."

Navon's pleasantry deflated and he stiffened. Before Tysis of Payne could rein him in, he uttered far too concisely, "No."

Inwardly, he groaned. There was no escaping the general now.

Jikun's eyes locked upon Navon's with all the endless persistence of the frozen tundra. "No?" he repeated, narrowing his lids against Navon's casual smile. "I suppose there is a story to this that somehow makes relations with the Helvari worse than serving humans?"

Navon attempted a dismissive shrug where it would have been preferable to lie. He was good at that. He likely could have woven a dozen historical stories together and Jikun would have been none the wiser.

But now his opportunity was lost. Jikun laughed and kicked out good-naturedly, catching Navon in the shin. "You nag the *shit* out of me like a lordling's wet nurse every step of my life, and I ask you one personal question and you think you get to decline? '*Jikun, is this your poetry? Jikun, how long will you be gone? Jikun, how do you feel? Jikun, don't strike the king.*'"

Navon rubbed his shin vigorously. Beneath the jest his friend *did* make an unfortunately valid point, but by Sel'ari, that *was* his role, was it not? He swallowed the discomfort rising in his belly as he struggled to reply nonchalantly. "It is not at all as exciting as *your* nagging seems to suggest. I was... I *am* a very... *dull* individual—there is nothing in my pages that would interest you, believe me, General."

Jikun was not dissuaded, nor—disappointingly—did he seem to catch the subtle jest at his diary. "Go on." Despite their distance from the elven nation, the Darivalian had not lost his commanding nature.

Navon thrust his own emotions aside and wrested the strength of Tiras to play his champion. "I am from the Æntara, in the far north, where all the Helvari are birthed. The land is the same as every mountain range inhabited by elves: there is a cluster of dwarves who claimed they arrived first and thus every so often, we must pound them back into the stone. Outside our territory, there live only brigands, goblins, and the cross between, all still grasping for dominion over the land the elves abandoned after the last True Bloods left. And when we are left to our own devices, we practice necromancy."

Jikun lurched forward, his eyes flickering intensely. "So did you ever kill one of these insolent dwarves? Hack a few goblins? Decapitate a throng of brigands?"

"...Many."

Jikun was clearly satisfied with the bounty of killings. "Good gods, Navon. I am so tired of killing skinny, towering elves I would sell my soul to kneel down and drive a blade through a fat gut."

"...Sometimes I question whether you are an elf at all."

Jikun sniffed dismissively and briefly rubbed his nose with disappointment. "Sounds like an untamed land... but you certainly do not reflect that. What did your father and mother think of you choosing the dress over the sword?"

Navon regarded him flatly, but even as he devised an equally scathing response, an immense and barren room devoured his amusement. The light of a single log danced across old necromantic symbols worn free of potency by their fragmented lines. Cobwebs fluttered in the breeze from the open door. The house was empty but for the small, male child that stood at its center, willing the broken lines to reform just long enough to swallow him.

"Navon?"

Navon shook the memories from his head, forcing Tiras onward to dull his emotions. But his good humor was lost. "My father was obsessed with necromancy… and when my mother could not endure his obsession any longer, she took my sister and left. Some of the elders said she made it north, to the Hatore region. But I don't believe she survived that long.

"Eventually, my father's necromancy even compelled *him* to leave, and he did, one day, to Sevrigel. I was… raised by the community, as no individual wanted to take responsibility for me getting gutted by the enemy. I was often sent to scout alone and fought in nearly all the skirmishes—my service was dutiful payment for their care. Primarily, however, I stayed in the mountains and studied. It has been such a long time and I was young: I would not remember anyone now and believe me, in a culture with far more pressing concerns, *no one* would remember me. As you like to point out, *I'm* not at all interesting."

Jikun's observation intensified on Navon's carefully composed expression in an attempt to infiltrate his captain's walls. But the general would find them equal to his own. "So you did not go with him," his companion clarified after a moment.

Navon felt his false smile falter. Tiras was not at all rising to his demands. "My father? No. He said he had to acquire Tiras' necromantic writings to his apprentice—they were the only two texts Tiras ever wrote before he left the Æntara and set out with Eraydon… Before he disappeared. And they contain the rarest collection of necromantic spells on the mortal plane. But you know this from your visit with Murios, don't you? And my father, like so many necromancers before him, lusted for both books. Ironically, years later, I heard that one of them was not far from our mountains in the possession of some great thane. Presumably, it is still in the king's archives in Vise. But my father never came back for it. For anything."

And before Navon had realized it, the image of the child before his eyes was collapsing, weighed down by the knowledge that all who he cherished in the world had left him there.

Navon grappled to return from the unwelcome vision. In all his years since he had left Ryekarayn, no one had ever questioned his origins—the Sel'vi just assumed that their world was that much greater.

And it was.

Of course it was Jikun, with his fervent love of family and homeland, who threatened Navon's walls now. *'Many great males had worse circumstances,'* he reminded the anguish, and quickly transferred his attention out across the room, searching for a distraction not only for himself, but for Jikun as well.

He found it in his single observer: Relstavum. The dark-skinned mercenary was gazing at them with striking intensity for a man that could not possibly hear across such distance. And still... Navon felt a sudden and unnatural tug toward the man.

There was something that he could glimpse through those eyes...

Jikun's words pulled him back into focus as he offered the rarest trait he had—empathy. "Your father strikes me as a bastard. But I don't understand... how did you come so far east as Sevrigel? And into the *army?* Not that I am protesting that excellent decision."

Navon knew far better than to respond with anything equally sentimental. "*So*," he began stoically, "I went searching for Tiras' book myself. Saved every coin. Crossed the channel. And then found that my father had been apprehended for practicing necromancy and was put to death years ago." He paused briefly and elevated his chin, his face remaining smooth. "...But I suppose that's what I should have expected."

Jikun's compassion had been exhausted. "Yes, you should have." He blew out his cheeks. "And then, after you learned the truth, you naturally joined the military, where reports of your discrepancies were likely to have you executed on the spot."

The male's inability to appropriately address—or express—vulnerable emotions was astounding. "I joined the army after spending years trying to hunt the book down and expending everything to do so," Navon replied patiently. "As a male who spent his entire life reading books and swinging a sword, not a great many talents present themselves as optional pathways for success." And he had to admit, in a heavily warring culture like the Æntara Helvari, not much else had been likely to cross his mind. "All we ever heard on Ryekarayn was of Sevrigel's 'unrivaled peace and beauty.' *Peace and beauty*. So the army seemed an ideal place to be paid for my skills while I studied. By the time the war with Saebellus intensified, I had already climbed the military chain—deserting did not really seem like an option."

Jikun's amused features relaxed into mild perplexity. "I've heard many motivations for why males join the army, but the belief of perpetual peace where you can bury your head in books is definitely new."

"When you have no place else to go and no greater skills to boast, it seems a fine place to be. Many of the greatest heroes served in a military capacity at one time or another."

"And that's what you want to be? Someone who history remembers?"

Ephraim's personality vied for a yes, but even Navon's own nature had sense enough to know better. "...No... I am wise enough to recognize that I am not that male. But I hoped to serve someone who would be."

Jikun was silent for a moment as Navon turned the focus of the conversation unexpectedly upon him. He cleared his throat gruffly. "So when you learned about Murios' book... Did you consider deserting then?"

"Yes..." Navon trailed off, but as Jikun's expression fell slightly, he smirked. "And then I realized, who would have wiped your ass?"

Jikun's offense was stilled by the moment of personal sentiment. Quiet settled about the tavern—even the smugglers had just finished some crass tune about the flexibility of large-boned women.

In that silence, they should have been able to hear a grain of sand hit the floor. And yet, a shadow fell over them suddenly. "Pardon my interruption," a smooth voice inquired beside them.

Navon jolted straight, caught off-guard by the abruptness of the human's appearance and too dumbstruck by his imperceptible movement to respond.

But the *feeling* that accompanied the man. Up close, Navon was certain of it... the look in the man's eyes—familiar. *Similar*. The pull he felt was that of two souls reaching out across a sea of indistinguishable whispers, both tattered and worn but uniquely distinct amongst the waves. Navon had felt this sensation many times amongst his own kind.

'He's a necromancer,' he realized.

Relstavum crouched down a foot away and smiled reassuringly, as though he knew the same about Navon. "I apologize for intruding. I would not normally involve myself with the Eph'vi and their customs, but I could not help but observe the severity of your state and overhear the grueling task you will face in the morning."

Navon saw Jikun give a short, blank nod—still too equally surprised by his own deficiency to speak.

"The struggles of the unfortunate involve me as well; I have been channeling Farvian warding to protect Dahel," Relstavum continued with a respectful incline of his head, as though he was a partner to their trial. "While the Eph'vi have done little to fully pay me for my efforts, still here I remain."

"So we were told," Jikun finally replied, and Navon could hear the instinctual caution and defense rise in his general.

'There is certainly no possibility that a polite and kind human is bearing any good,' Navon thought sarcastically. But after a moment he was certain: despite Jikun's sensitivity toward all mentions of necromancy and his instinctual pessimism toward the man, he was clueless as to Relstavum's use of the much-hated magic.

Relstavum reached within his vest and for half a heartbeat, Navon expected the leather-bound book. Instead, the man extended his hand and dropped a charm to dangle from a silver chain at his fingertips. The round, intricate design was beyond Jikun's understanding—as it should be. But there was something that struck Navon with familiarity. *Relief.* Something in its composition was not unlike those in the ancient necromantic tomes he had studied. But it was certainly Farvian in origin—the elven race that had long since been obliterated from the face of Aersadore. Navon, with his massive knowledge of manuscripts, could at least recognize the similarities to their dead language. "A Farvian ward of protection. This is the last one I have, but assuming it does its job, you can deliver it to me upon returning from your trial."

Navon could see Jikun look skeptically upon the gently swinging medallion. "If Farvian warding was so effective, why are there no Faravi left alive to testify to this?"

Navon flinched. *Why* did he have to keep such rude company? He bent apologetically and reached out to take the charm. *'From one necromancer to another...'* "Thank you."

Relstavum returned the same soft smile, then stood. There were no further words or exchanged expressions; Navon watched as he vanished from the inn, the ornate rug flapping gently in the icy breeze. He stared intently at the rippling fabric for a short time, irrationally hoping that the fellow necromancer would reappear to offer some semblance of comfort in the foreign land. But when it moved again, a new figure swept through, his face fully concealed deep beneath a drawn hood. Even with his body hidden beneath ample folds of similarly dirty, white silk, it was clear to Navon that he was leaner than Relstavum.

He sighed.

"It's all yours," Jikun spoke sharply, his words snapping Navon into focus. The Darivalian's eyes had narrowed, his usual cynicism fixating critically upon the charm.

Navon draped it around his neck and tucked it beneath his cloak, pressing a palm to the silver for that brief tie of solidarity. The acceptance of necromancy…? This was one side of Ryekarayn… one side of home he *had* missed. "It can't hurt," he smirked.

Beneath his coarse blanket, Jikun settled down across the sandy tiles. "Well I don't know enough about magic to get specific, but I'm guessing that statement is incorrect. I'm going to sleep. If our current misfortunes are any indication, we'll be facing the hel'onja in the morning. And I think *sleep* will do me more good than some old jewelry." He tugged at his blanket once. "On another note, the versatility of their same fabrics—rugs… curtains… doors… blankets… is admirable."

Navon chuckled and rested a few feet away, clutching the amulet as he closed his eyes beneath cloak and rug. "I'll see you in the morning."

"Yes… if one of these charming smugglers doesn't slit our throats while we sleep."

"…May dawn rise for you, Jikun."

CHAPTER NINE

Mist coiled in from the west, twisting through the bay as the old ships creaked and groaned. Not far to the east, a tumult of voices could be gleaned from the ruckus at the grimy human tavern, but here, only the gentle lap of water and the shifting suits of armor broke the night's silence.

A figure dropped from the rooftop and into the darkness. No sooner had he landed than mist rushed inward once more to bathe him in the shadows, concealing him from the Night's Watch. Only four males of the city guard were prowling about the Port of Targados that night. A sliver of moonlight penetrated the clouds and illuminated their presence in a flash of polished steel. For several minutes they patrolled up and down the length of the port.

And then, for only the span of a breath, the opportune moment presented itself: all eyes were cast away from the water, a weighty cloud masked the struggling moon, and a billow of heavy mist plumed between the bobbing ships. The figure leapt from concealment in a soundless sprint, crossing the cobblestones to leap with unrivaled grace onto the jutting stern of *The Black Queen*.

He landed with a thud too faint for human ears and too unremarkable for elves'. With strong fingers and well-placed footing, he sidled up the side and slipped over the railing.

"By Galway's arse, whattin I wouldn't sell to have a night with one o' 'em fine whores," a voice grumbled below the crow's nest, his lean shape swinging idly around the pole. The disgruntled sailor received a round of nods from four weathered companions, each man unaware of the shadow that had crept into position directly across from the mast.

The figure flicked a black oiled cloth from his belt loop and pressed it to his nose and mouth where it clung as tight as his own flesh. When the mask was secure, he withdrew a crystal vial, popped the cork, and let it roll across the weather-beaten planks. A single *thunk* signified that it had skidded down the upper level of the stern to nestle upon the main deck. The fog seemed to thicken, and then…

Bang!

A cloud of midnight blue gas erupted from the vial and the watchmen of *The Black Queen* dropped like stones to the floor, splayed and still as death.

Sellemar vaulted over the side of the ship, landing upon the deck just as the thick clouds lifted, a ray of intrusive light illuminating his face and dispelling him from the dark. *'Too late for that, Noctem,'* he thought with a smirk as he surveyed the unconscious figures.

And then he was gone, clearing the deck in moments to arrive at a heavy trapdoor, its old handles beckoning Sellemar to venture inside. A swift tug, a muted creak, and he descended into the belly of the rocking, amber vessel.

As he reached the base of the cargo hold, a series of growls and hisses heralded his arrival. There was a tremor of feet and a pounding of fists against iron bars.

Sellemar's eyes adjusted rapidly. The light emanated from a single lamp atop a decrepit wooden table. Its glow was hardly superior to the sliver of fogged moonlight from the world above, but it was consistent.

And it was enough to see that he had found his quarry.

The second bottle of Loedrin's Breath was at Sellemar's fingers in seconds, uncorked and sailing slowly through the air.

It bounced once. There was a furious growl. A soft hiss issued forth from an eruption of gas. And then the cargo hold from the Phantom Isles fell silent.

Sellemar felt his adrenaline level out as his prey became immobilized, and he strode forward as though the ship were his own.

And it was. With a lefry mask protecting him from the gas and a blade for defense in hand, he was the king of this shoddy vessel, unchallenged by the unconscious occupants sprawled out in their iron cells. Nonetheless, he maintained the same level of cautious preparation that had kept him alive for so many years—those creatures were only deceitfully peaceful now that the drug had rid their bodies of malice.

He contemplated the scene with impassive calculation. Rows of crates created small mountains before him, each marked with "Xs" of varying colors—whites, greens, reds, and blues. Their contents were a mystery, but given their origin, they were undoubtedly sinister in nature.

More important was the cargo of the iron cages—those beasts he had sent into a slumber. *These* were his prey. Bound in rusted chains, locked safely within their enclosures, were the demon spawn of Sheolra. They were brutal, soulless beasts, lacking sense of self and purpose. Violence. Bloodshed. Lust. It was all their kind knew, and all their kind could comprehend.

If the stories of Saebellus' Beast were true, then perhaps it too was one of them.

These particular beasts had been wrenched from their abode in the abyss to the mortal realm, then ferried across the sea to fill the gaps of losses in Saebellus' ranks. Already, Saebellus' personal Beast lurked somewhere within the capital. And to think—the warlord was about to acquire *more*.

Sellemar's lip twisted. It was a dangerous and sick desperation to use such animals of bloodlust.

He approached the bars of the first cage, drawing his sword and slicing in quickly and wholly painlessly. The beast was dead in seconds. He offered no prayer to ferry it onward as the demon possessed no soul for the gods to take.

On he progressed, dispatching the occupants of one cell after another with crisp efficiency. Soon the demons' blackened blood oozed with an overwhelming stench not unlike rust, leaking with flickers of essence as the corpses returned to the ether. The scent was nearly strong enough to send a conscious male's head spinning, but it was the sleeping that were stirred by the tangible call.

There was a sudden cry, a piercing howl that speared Sellemar's core and rattled his mind. He recoiled from the bars in a surge of fear, even as the creatures before him remained eerily still in the sudden explosion of noise. He whirled around, eyes wildly searching for the beast that had risen above the powerful drug.

The scent of blood must have aroused its hunger—its lust so intense that it had shattered the bonds of Loedrin's Breath with a crazed need.

There. From amidst the long shadows against the wall, one of the demons rose to its feet, its great mass trembling with fury. Its pale red eyes flicked and twitched, jerking about its enclosure in a frantic hope of finding a means to satiate its hunger.

It found Sellemar. Glee filled the demon's eyes, its face contorting into a mockery of elven emotions. Cracked skin peeled upward in a fanged snarl. Then the beast wrenched its body toward Sellemar, its bulk contained only by the thick chains and bars that separated them.

At that moment, it felt unsettlingly insufficient.

'By all the gods,' Sellemar breathed in sudden realization as the shadows beside the demons shifted.

Three demons beside it were stirring as well. Bloodlust and a cry that split Emal'drathar… They would not be the only ones to awaken!

Sellemar sheathed his blade and hefted his spear, the familiar weight reassuring as he strode forward to the awakened cage. He had to slay them before their howls captured the attention of the Night's Watch. "Damn Saebellus," he muttered. *'How determined must he be to ferry creatures from the demon realms?! Determined... and* daft.*'*

Acting concurrently with his thoughts, he saw one of the demons wrenching at his bonds and roaring to Ramul, his chest bulging as his shoulders popped and grated, as though *sensing* Sellemar's intent—and his confidence.

Then with one fierce yank, the chains at the demon's wrists snapped away like the rusted bits of metal they were.

Sellemar froze, confidence waning.

The three demons that had awoken beside the first grabbed the bars and howled, latching onto his hesitation with mad delight. A ripple coursed through the four—a tremor of rare racial solidarity in which the obstacle, source of food, and enemy were the same.

The first demon snapped the chains from the three awakened beasts behind him, building his force against their prey. Their snarls intensified as they watched Sellemar's swagger ebb away like the draining blood from his face. When the last demon in that particular cell did not stir, the largest of the four crushed its skull mercilessly beneath its heel. Essence and brain juice sprayed against the wall like the contents of a vomiting gut.

For the last time, its eyes met Sellemar's. And *it sneered.*

'Sel'ari guard me.'

With that, the iron bars separating him from the demons crumpled away like aged parchment and the demons tore into the amber glow of the rocking hold.

Sellemar leapt to the side, throwing his body behind a stack of crates to spin around into the shadowed alley behind him. He dashed into the darkness, his mind racing to calculate the differences in scent and vision, of his abilities versus theirs.

The cargo hold was vast, the many crates like a maze, and Sellemar darted and wove between them, low and out of sight. Before he had travelled even halfway down the expanse, one of the smaller demons found him. With a lurch and a cackle of triumph, its talons swept for the deep tissue of his breast.

Sellemar's spear lunged with greater speed. He thrust it clear through the demon's throat and in an unbroken motion, wrested the weapon free to leave the demon's essence dissolving on the beaten ground.

There was a sudden tap on the floor before him and a flash of shadow smeared the wall. A lean figure flitted just out of sight. *The other demon was on the prowl.*

'Damn it!' Sellemar hissed internally even as his breath remained calm. Only the tightening of his hand upon his weapon betrayed his fear.

The floor behind him gave the faintest creak and Sellemar whirled, leaping away on instinct, twisting his spear around to shield his narrow frame. The taloned hand shot from the darkness like a viper and raked down the shaft with a blow that knocked Sellemar clear off his feet.

But *he* was the hunter. Sellemar kicked the butt of his spear up even as he careened away, sending a wave of shock through the demon's body with a solid blow beneath the chin. The head snapped up to the cobwebbed rafters.

It was the last thing the beast saw before Sellemar regained his footing and shoved his spear through the creature's silver throat. It flailed once, its talons raking furiously for the nearby crates, and reared free in a final moment of crazed bloodlust. Sellemar immediately drove a second blow into the beast's naked breast and threw it to the floor. The thud boomed like thunder through the cargo hold, but the taloned hand could do no more damage.

Sellemar straightened, swallowing audibly as his eyes shifted across the cargo. There were two more demons loose, but the wooden crates were just as sinister. He reached out a hand, wiping it gently across the white "X" beside him. To Ramul if he knew what was in *this* one, but he had seen enough of the storage hold already to warn him that the contents were malevolent. *'More smuggled goods from the Phantom Isles. And nothing pleasurable to be sure.'* The Phantom Isles only betokened death and destruction, and the crates upon crates from the cursed lands were stacked nearly to the rafters. What was one demon to the mountain of these?!

And he had seen a drugged drake—large enough to rip a fully grown man to pieces in seconds—sprawled unconscious on the western side of the room. Gods forbid *that* wake as well!

The netted barrels of alchemic explosives around it brought him no further ease.

His breath returning, Sellemar crept past the body of the slain demon as though it might still lash out in death. His body tucked into the shadows as he moved, the shaft of his spear the only comfort in the darkness—his sword *and* shield against these bloodthirsty beasts.

The ship let out a heavy groan and Sellemar almost missed the soft creak of wood from somewhere nearby. He dropped like a stone into the shadows, hunkering beside a crate with breath held. He was fortunate enough to be able to driftwalk, but his body still carried a scent—noble though it was. Demonic olfactory perception was great enough to rival a dragon's, even in a weakened state. He could only hope that the lingering odor of Loedrin's Breath disrupted the demons' senses enough that they could not locate him.

At least, not at the same time.

That was hardly too much to pray for.

He jerked his head slightly as he once more stood, annoyed by the grease of the lefry skin pressed against his face.

'Damn it, Sellemar, you are playing too dangerous a game to lose your concentration now!' He stepped over the body of a sleeping human, the only watchman to be seen below deck. The rest of the six members of the night crew would continue to sleep like babes up above him. But even with that danger averted, the cries of the damn demons would surely bring the Night's Watch to arms in their stead—if they were not alerted already.

'Perhaps the greater olfactible sensitivity is causing the demons to be further affected.' And then a little jolt of pessimism to keep himself alert: *'Do not count on that.'*

And then he found himself tearing to the side, his body reacting on instinct before his mind had even absorbed the dark mass hurtling toward him. *'Damn it!!'* There was an audible rush of wind, a horrible crack. The crate with the white "X" was hurled with such force that it burst open against the wall behind him, sending a spray of white worms into the air. They narrowly missed Sellemar as he scrambled to his feet, but the others oozed free of the broken planks to wriggle with alacrity toward the unconscious body of the human. Sellemar leapt off the ground instantly, placing his feet against the side of the hull while he rested the bulk of his weight against the spear that held him up. He watched in horror as the worms swarmed past. Then he kicked off the wall, flipping clear of the scene below and landing neatly on a nearby barrel.

The worms swarmed into the body of the sleeping human and in seconds, the man's flesh withered and caved.

Maravian worms. He felt a convulsive shiver as he realized how close he had been to sharing the human's fate.

His balance had hardly settled on the barrel when his eyes snapped away from the repulsive sight. *'Sel'ari!'* The crate had not flown by itself!

But his distraction had cost him the ground. The two demons had emerged from the darkness, their bulging masses rushing across the crates behind him. The nearer one had vaulted from the floor before Sellemar could raise his spear. Wind whistled as the fist flew, smashing into the arm he had hurriedly raised before his face.

He tumbled from the barrel and slammed into the hull, the armor of the gauntlet saving him from an otherwise shattered forearm. His head struck the dense wood and left him dazed. *'Defend!'* was all the sense his mind could scream, and he spat the blood from his lip as he swept his spear out blindly.

He heard a yelp as the demon skirted the tip. A shape landed beside it, snarling and posturing its blurry form to terrifying height, threatening the lesser beast from poaching its prey.

The fog in his vision cleared and Sellemar lunged, driving his spear into the belly of the smaller demon. It wailed and bayed, flinging itself away into the nearby barrel. It toppled over the side to sprawl, momentarily stunned, across the floor.

Sellemar pulled himself up rapidly, ignoring the jolt through his spine. It was only the subtleness of the pin prick that abruptly sharpened his self-awareness, and he realized in horror that he had fallen by the edge of the mass of writhing worms. He scrambled back, drawing the blade from his hip as he did so and slicing unhesitatingly at the sting emanating from his shin. The maravian worm sloughed out in two as the wound burst open, and Sellemar cried out in pain and terror.

'Are their more? More?!' his mind frantically cried, searching the length of his body for the feeling of pins and needles, hardly perceptible above the dance of his spasming muscles. He ducked low, narrowly missing the fist of the last standing demon. *'No! No more! Focus!'* he commanded himself, even as his mind was racked with doubt. If the maravian worms did not kill him, this beast certainly would!

Its eyes were wild and bloodshot, its mouth gaping wide in a shrill scream of fury and delight. Blood. *Blood!* Sellemar's blood was flowing in a steady stream down his leg now, pooling into his boot and squishing as he shifted his weight. He lurched away from the multitude of worms. Around him, a barrage of yowls was joining in the frenzy, the fresh scent rousing the demons to consciousness. And all their bestial minds could comprehend in their unfamiliar surroundings was *blood.*

Sellemar's blood.

He could hear the beasts rattling against the bars of their iron cages, screaming and raging, yanking hysterically against their chains.

Sellemar scurried across the span of clear ground, spinning around the corner and dropping low. As the demon pitched around the side, Sellemar thrust his spear forward and through the creature's skull.

Its legs buckled and it slumped in a twitching heap.

'Damn it... I have to get out of here now...! I cannot finish...!' his thoughts were broken as a crate above him boomed and cracked—something had smashed against it from the other side. Something big. He leapt clear from showered debris as a slow trickle of worms began to crawl around the corner, seeking out his trail of blood.

Sellemar sprinted for the stairs to the upper deck, but was forced to reel back as another crate flew past and smashed into the planks at his feet. Sellemar's head whipped wildly to the side and he spotted the demon from before. The small beast heaved as its stomach pumped blood from its essence like a torrent of black ink. *'A resilient type... damn it!'* he deduced as the beast hounded him with growing speed, its wound merely driving its strength.

Sellemar leapt over the crate of green ooze, stifling a wretch as an overwhelming stench arose from within. A second and third crate followed in quick pursuit, splintered across the floor in a sea of obsidian shards and jellied tentacles—the latter of which flopped and twitched as though still connected to the body of the beast that had borne them.

And then came the barrel of alchemic explosives.

Sellemar saw the net sliced wide and the demon ripped a barrel from the stash, unaware of the deadly contents nestled within the ash buffer. Every ounce of Sellemar's muscles pulled now. He ran, lurching wildly past the wall lined with bellowing demons, and rushed single-mindedly for the stairs.

Then the barrel smashed into the iron cage behind him.

A thunderclap like the belly of a storm tore into the night sky. Sellemar was blasted off his feet and flung against the stairs in what he was sure was a dozen pieces. Darkness swallowed him and for an instant, his vision was lost. The roars of the creatures had ceased—only a keening ring wailed in his ears, and he felt even his faculty of touch failing him.

Then his chest sputtered and he coughed out a ball of ash. Blurred shapes twisted in the dim light. A faint trickle sounded from somewhere nearby. Muffled voices...

And then his senses smashed into him with the same force with which they had departed. He gasped and cried out, a wave of agony and sensation overwhelming him. The demons were yowling once more. The cage where the alchemic Hadavrae had exploded was a heap of broken iron and singed bodies. Several demons that had managed to survive the blast were clambering free… *of the water rushing into the punctured hull.*

A hole the size of the drake itself had been blown clear through the ship and the water rushed in with eager greed to join in the killing.

'By Sel'ari, the ship is sinking!' Sellemar realized in horror. He pulled himself to his feet, scrambling through his injury and up the stairs. Even as the ship around them groaned in warning, the demons clawed toward him in pursuit—not to save themselves, but in hopes of retrieving a swift and fresh meal.

Sellemar tossed himself through the open doors and onto the main deck. He spun around, eyes frantically sweeping the ship.

The five men still lay sprawled and unconscious. *'Damn it!'* Sellemar swore, running to one of their listless forms. He ripped the sword from the slacked grasp and shoved it between the handles of the storage hold.

It would not seal the way for long.

Sellemar was moving away instantly, his mind hastening to form a plan. He calculated how long he had to implement it before everyone was lost to sea with the beasts of the Phantom Isles. Sellemar had fair time to save himself, but the crew as well…? And worse still, the noise had surely brought the Night's Watch to the dock's shore! Even with the din of the beasts roaring behind him, he could hear shouts from somewhere beyond the bow of the ship.

Sellemar yanked his singed mask to cover his face.

"*Damn my sense!*" he swore as he rushed to the skiff at the side of the helm and lowered it swiftly until it was near level with the railing. He rushed to the farthest men, dragging them across the deck. "Going to your deaths sleeping is far more than you deserve," he growled resentfully. But it was not Sel'ari's way. He flung the five men into the small boat as rapidly as he could, praying fervently that the ship would stay afloat just long enough for him to get free as well.

Sel'ari heard his prayer and the ship did not capsize toward the stern until the skiff had dropped with a resounding splash into the water and the men bounced once within.

Cries of alarm rose louder from the Night's Watch on the docks. The sounds of hurried paddles hit the water as someone rowed out to meet the unconscious crew.

Sellemar stood upon the railing of the sinking vessel, his resolute silhouette briefly illuminated as another explosion rocked the ship from beneath. Then he kissed his thumb once and raised it to Emal'drathar. Tonight, he was glad for the darkness, for he too would vanish within it.

But what he had uncovered…? *That* would remain.

The warlord would not solidify his grip upon the elven nation. Instead, come dawn, he and his queen would behold their first taste of his Resistance.

CHAPTER TEN

A piercing scream rent the night air, penetrating Jikun's exhaustion and fatigue like a lance to the heart. He wrenched himself upward through his pain, at once fully aware of the world around him. The blanket dropped away from his pounding chest and he grasped for the kitchen knife. His eyes darted to the right for his companion—Navon was still there beside him, his stricken face illuminated in the glow of Keshal's dying fire. He had likewise risen to one elbow, his alarmed expression a confirmation that the sound had been more than a figment of Jikun's imagination.

Across the inn, the hearing-impaired humans were stirring and a white-cloaked man was already on his feet.

Jikun's mouth opened dryly. "What was—?"

But his words were culled into silence, drowned beneath a second scream of terror. No sooner had it begun to fade than a howl of cries pursued it across the city.

"W-what in Sel'ari's name?!" Navon stammered as he clambered to his feet beneath his cloak. He flattened his body against the wall as a maddened human barreled past him, frantic to escape the confines of the inn.

Jikun had experienced enough battles to recognize the sound. To *know* the sound. They were not merely screams of fear. Howls of warning. *These were the last cries of the living.*

His head snapped about Keshal's interior and he spotted the white-cloaked man leaning out of a curtained window. "What do you see?" he demanded. Deep within the recesses of his mind, military tents danced with blackened flames. *'What in Ramul is occurring?! We're in the middle of god-damn nowhere!'*

The man clenched the curtain, and for a moment, there was no response. Still, his breathing was audible from across the room—quickened and loud, made erratic by fear. "There is something moving in the darkness..." He hesitated. "But it looks like... smo...ke? What in the—?" The man flung himself from the frame, narrowly avoiding a dark shape hurtling through the window. It smashed into the fire in the center of the room, spewing a shower of sparks high into the dome.

Even if Jikun had not been riveted to the floor by the dim illusion of torched soldiers, it was too late to do more than watch as the scrambling humans fought to claw their way from the windows and door.

"Osin, don't let it touch you!"

"GAHHH!"

"Shit!"

"Zane!"

Emerging from the street beyond, tendrils of black smoke cracked like whips, twisting about the ankles of the thrashing, scampering men. As the bodies were tangled into the ethereal web, a host of gleeful skulls materialized in the cloud above.

"*Necromancy!*" Navon choked, reeling from the doorway.

Jikun's mind jolted. *'Necromancy? Here?! From whom?!'* He recoiled, for the first time conscious of the growing fog of sneering faces flooding into the inn.

Navon's nails dug into his cloaked shoulder, yanking him toward an adjacent window. The howls were escalating with a tumultuous wind, railing across the city and growing into a vociferous wail of terror and woe. "*We have to leave!*" he shrieked, flinging his hand straight against the billowing necromantic cloud. "While I have them restrained!" He tore the curtain aside and leapt through the open sill, turning back to extend a frantic hand. "JIKUN, NOW!"

The engulfed tents disintegrated suddenly, leaving Jikun naked in reality. *'Pull your mind together, damn it!'* he cursed, clasping Navon's hand and launching himself through the window. Behind him, a smuggler and the cloaked man were the last two who managed to escape before Keshal was consumed in a deafening roar.

Outside, Dahel was awash in equal chaos and blood. The streets were overrun with a churning mass of horrified and confused Eph'vi, who fled with smoke licking their heels.

Jikun's magic tore from his fingers before his fear could rally the resurgence of Sevrigel's screams. What little humidity graced the cold air was sucked from it, pooling at the feet of a scrambling Eph'ven and rushing toward the black sky as an impenetrable wall of jagged ice. The tendrils smashed furiously against the barrier and dissipated left and right, determined to seek a way around.

"Loedrin's Breath upon you, now is not the time to play heroics!" the man in white berated as the tendrils ceased their futile attempt, instead rounding upon the remaining victims.

Which now was them.

"*Damn you to Ramul!—RUN!*" the burly smuggler bellowed, his arms flailing as he pivoted and deserted them around the side of Keshal. There was an immediate, drowned cry; a spray of blood glittered once in the moonlight before it fell to the sandy street.

The man in white managed an impressively fast retreat and darted around the opposite side of Keshal's exterior. With a firm kick, he vaulted over the low wall of a nearby building and caught the edge of the roof, dissolving into the night beyond.

Navon snatched Jikun's arm, nearly ripping him off his feet. "We can't mimic that in our condition! Come! There must be another street this way!" His palm extended once more, forcing the necromancy to hiss and still as they plunged around the side of Keshal.

The intersecting street was little better than what lay behind, surging with trampling Eph'vi and the swarming, hideous skulls.

"It's everywhere!" Jikun shouted, watching as a male clawed crazily at the frame of his door in his final attempts to free his soul from its grasp. He shot a wall of ice behind the male and the Eph'ven sprang free—straight into the tendrils bursting from an adjacent alley.

A body dropped suddenly at their feet from the upper balcony. "Stay close, General!" Navon bellowed, and with renewed determination he broke into a sprint along the sandy streets, pausing only to make certain that Jikun was at his heels. Together, they wove and shoved through the stampeding throng, diving past crowded doorways and hurdling over mangled remains. Navon's driven commands to keep the mauling tendrils at bay ferried them to the path where Esra had guided them mere hours before.

It was nigh unrecognizable through the churning chaos and ravaged bazaar.

"We have to vacate the city!" Jikun cried, leaping over a lifeless, spread-eagled body.

To his right, a rug was torn from its hangings as an Eph'ven leapt through the now-open window. Before her feet could touch the earth, a writhing coil of smoke wrapped about her torso and wrenched her back inside, smashing her head against the frame as she went.

Navon averted his gaze from the congealed mess. "They're on their own, General! *You* are my responsibility!"

Jikun hurled a wall of ice before a surge of smoke, temporarily setting a child free from the trailing cloud. Instantly, a tendril launched from an open door and ripped the little girl inside. "*Gods damn it*," Jikun hissed, biting his lip.

"We're close!" Navon rallied above the wailing. "Just a little farther!"

Just a little farther. Jikun could glimpse the faint glow of auburn sand from up ahead as dawn's first light infused the grains with a hint of fire. "Just a little farther…!"

He clutched his hope fiercely as he passed the next familiar building. The curtains from the windows and doors were gone, revealing a bare home twisting with remnants of smoke about a shattered vase.

Something lashed against his ankle, burrowing a chill deep into his body. *'Come away, broken one. The flames cannot follow you here,'* a voice whispered. *'Here we pass no judgment.'*

But Jikun's adrenaline spurned the offer before the wall of his emotional dam could crack. *'Just a little farther… Just a little farther!!'*

And a moment later, they broke through the city line between Dahel and the endless desert, kicking up sand as their feet met the cold grains of salvation. Behind them, the necromancy yowled with rage. Eph'vi were still clawing to free themselves from the clouds of smoke rising like a thunderstorm from the sands.

A fierce tremor coursed through the earth. Jikun whirled, past the scatter of Eph'vi who had managed to escape Dahel. *'Gods, what now?!'* But before he could utter his confusion aloud, something hurtled across the orange sky… an enormous, sable mass that arched toward Emal'drathar before smashing violently into the earth.

"*By Sel'ari*," Navon wheezed in horror.

Jikun's grip tightened on the small kitchen knife. Was *that*…?!

The earth rumbled once more and Jikun spun toward the source, where a cluster of Eph'vi floundered in a struggle for balance. *'MOVE!'* his mind urged, but as his mouth opened to echo his cry, the sand caved in beneath the Eph'ven stragglers and they were engulfed within the monstrous shadow.

"What?!" Navon gasped, not daring to voice Jikun's fear.

And then the ground convulsed beneath them. Jikun staggered, feeling the sand writhe beneath him. Navon's arms soared outward for balance. "*It's coming!*" Jikun roared.

The earth rolled like a maravian worm beneath the flesh, rising and dipping in a fluid arc. The sand cascaded past their feet in a wave of gold. And to Jikun's alarm, it kept falling, collapsing into the earth as a great hole was torn wide below them.

There was a sudden flicker of red from beneath the golden grains, a forked tongue to their left and two great yellowed fangs to their right.

Jikun had no time to gather exactly what was transpiring, but he had observed enough of the vanishing Eph'vi to venture a guess. He lunged on instinct, grabbing Navon by the arm and flinging him away. As he extended his palm, a thick pillar of ice shot out from the water suddenly present around him. Jikun slammed it into the upper and lower jaw, reinforcing it long enough for him to kick off and catch the lip of the creature's mouth.

He had nearly been swallowed into the jaws of a reptilian monstrosity!

The hel'onja.

'It is huge*...!'* he heaved.

The strange symbols across the serpent's body bore an unsettling familiarity to those Jikun had seen scrawled in Navon's book. So *this* was the necromancer's assurance that no elf would leave Dahel alive. *'There is no chance by Lady Luck that we can outrun this beast... let alone kill it!'*

"JIKUN!" Navon yelled, catching him below the shoulder. He yanked him onto the sand as the jaws clamped shut, the broken pillar of ice left half-buried in its wake.

There was the briefest moment of stillness as though the earth had frozen... and then it roiled.

Jikun's throat constricted as the creature erupted from the sand to their right. The air outside the beast's mouth was dry... *useless!* And what little strength he had recovered at Keshal was almost spent... A scream in the distance threatened to coax his own to join, but it was culled too quickly by the swift flick of the serpent's tail.

Gods damn it, he had not left Sevrigel to be devoured by a fattened worm! Yet as Jikun glanced around himself into the flat, endless horizon he so despised, a chilling realization seized him.

He and Navon were the only remaining survivors outside of Dahel.

"Run!" Navon's voice rang as the serpent's tail lobbed high once more.

Jikun struggled to his feet, the escalating fire of the sand unfelt as he sprang away from the glistening scales. *'A plan... a plan...!'* his mind battled, but without his magic or soldiers, he could only flee helplessly.

"By the goddess almighty…!" Navon swore as the creature careened forward.

The serpent's nose dove into the ground beside Jikun as he scrabbled away. His toned soldier's body was faster than those of the citizens of Dahel, and yet the force was so great that he was thrown to the side like a child's toy. He bounced twice and rolled to his side. "Sh…it…" he groaned, black splotches dancing before his eyes. He felt a wave of nausea loosen his throat and he weakly attempted to lift himself upright.

And then a shadow swept over him.

'Dead.' It was the only concept his mind could grasp. Above him, the serpent reared, jaws loosening as the beast prepared to thrust down upon its dazed prey.

A form wavered at the edge of his vision and Jikun caught sight of the Helven: Navon's hollow face had grown ashen, his cracked lips parted as though struggling to breathe, his long fingers elevated as sable smoke billowed from the earth around him. It raced upward toward the creature in a storm of skull-like faces. A biting cold washed over the air as the smoke whisked past Jikun and over the creature's head.

This he knew. *This* he had just fled. As immense as the pillar Navon had hurled upon the Beast at the temple of Sel'ari, this torrent of souls was likewise filled with the hollow-eyed faces of the dead.

Necromancy.

There was a venomous hiss and a scraping like bone against bone, screeching out across the desert sands. Before the beast had reared away, Navon flew to Jikun's side, jerking him to his feet. "Go!" Navon commanded, tugging at his arm. "Can't you cast anything? Any spell at all?!"

Jikun felt his stomach lurch as he tried to draw moisture from the beast's distant body. "By Ramul, no," he heaved as he broke into a pathetic run. "All the water I could control outside a direct source went into that damn pillar! I missed a full night's rest…! But it looks like there is something up ahead… North!" He glanced behind him in time to see the serpent's tail disappear into the earth, diving free of the necromantic magic.

Navon's face contorted with every bandaged foot that struck the ground. "I have never contended with anything so large… I cast more souls than I ever did upon the Beast and I don't believe I did much except to—"

They vaulted away from each other, diving and rolling onto the sand on either side of the serpent's head as it ruptured through the earth between them. The thick scales over its ebony skull had been partially eaten away, revealing bloodied bone and flexing muscle. Its mandible swung low in a silent shriek, its eyes narrowing in enmity. Then they flared, locking onto Navon. Jikun was now nothing compared to the little beast that had dared wound it.

It lunged.

Navon flung his hand up in desperation, screaming in the ancient tongue as he frantically lurched toward the empty earth. But the hel'onja was faster—and with a triumphant snap, its jaws closed about his waist. In stunned horror, Jikun watched as Navon's body flailed in the beast's jaws and then went still.

His arm fell loose to dangle in the hot air beside him. *Lifeless.*

"Na…von…" Jikun whispered as the serpent tilted its head against the blazing sun to swallow the Helven like the countless Eph'vi before him.

Navon's head lolled to the side, staring blankly toward the earth, a thin trail of blood dripping from the corner of his mouth and catching in the ends of his raven hair. His last spell washed over the creature's skull as a billow of sable smoke, and for a moment, a face seemed to quiver in the darkness, its eyes bulging, its mouth gaping wide…

'Navon's face!'

"NAVON!!" Jikun screamed.

The cloud that surrounded the hel'onja's head was dissipating, taking the visage of Navon with it.

What in Ramul had happened?!

He threw his arm backward, tendons flexing. *'Cast something…'* he chastised his magic. *'Damn it, CAST SOMETHING!'* The air around him remained sickeningly dry and Jikun felt a wave of fatigue pulse from his wound as a small shard of ice began to crystallize in his palm. *'Useless!'* He bit his lip hard, flinging the ice aside.

If that would not avail him…!

But his resolve was shattered by a roar so bestial in nature and thunderous in power that his movements were smothered beneath a blanket of fear. In an uncontrollable response, his knees began to buckle, begging him to crumple to insignificance before the unseen source. Not even the Beast had invoked such terror! *'Damn coward!'* he swore at himself, and forced his trembling gaze upward in time to see a massive silhouette tearing out of the dawn sky. *'What in Emal'drathar is—?!'* was the last thought he managed. The shape smashed into the back of the serpent's head and the hel'onja was thrown toward the earth as though it were weightless.

Jikun's heart froze as the immense, winged silhouette lashed down yet again and peeled the serpent's scales back like paper.

A dragon. *A god-damn dragon in the middle of a wasteland.*

Navon's corpse slid past the serpent's slacked jaw, breaking Jikun's paralysis. His companion's body hit the ground, rolled once, and then... the Helven convulsed suddenly.

With that contortion, the face in the smoke disappeared. Navon's eyes shot open.

'Navon is alive?!' Jikun pushed off the sole of his boot, sprinting hysterically across the earth. Even at his distance, Jikun could hear the male gasp for breath. "Navon! Get up! Run!" he shouted, grappling to be heard over the rising wind. *'What in Ramul is going on?!'* A serpent had been enemy enough without the addition of legs and wings and god-damn fire! *'Fucking Ramul!'* His cloak whipped out, threatening to topple him. "Navon, GET UP!"

The Helven flipped onto his chest, scrambling to his feet despite his palpable confusion. Wild strands of his dark hair were still plastered to his face with blood, and his eyes searched frantically where the spectral fog had dissipated.

Jikun dared to look away, out across the sands. Any possible explanation for the dragon's origins was lost within the smoldering city; instead, his gaze immediately fell upon a figure racing past the base of a dune, eyes fixed upon the battle of the behemoths with surprising serenity. A man in white.

'He escaped...? Why is he coming this way...?!'

The serpent discerned the arrival at that same moment and with inexplicable vengeance, lashed its tail furiously toward the man. In an instant, the dragon struck its head, talons piercing into the skull. The blow left the tail to slam harmlessly into the sand beside the man. He gave a single shout before he slid down the rolling dune in a sprint directly toward Jikun and Navon.

Navon stirred suddenly into comprehension. "Is that a *dragon?*" he managed to croak.

But before Jikun could utter his weak conception of events, his words were drowned by the eruption of an otherworldly shriek. A charge blazed across the sky behind them, a tangle of red and grey light that writhed with hollow faces. *'NECROMANCY!'* His confusion had little opportunity to grow before the spell sliced clean through the dragon's leathery wings, sending the creature plummeting into the dunes below.

At the thunderous crash, the serpent lifted its head, shaking it to and fro in a daze. Its gaze wandered back to the little elves stupefied within its shadow.

"I don't know what in Ramul is happening! Just run—!" Jikun bellowed in panic, hooking Navon beneath the arm to shove him forward. To his left, the man in white had let out a horrified cry, skidding to a stop before the smoldering remains of the dragon. He swept his hand once and the beast vanished. Then, with a twist in his dirty white silk, the man was running once more.

'Who in the Nine Realms...?!' As though the rising necromantic winds demanded the same answer, the white hood was whipped back in a forceful gale.

A fair face ashen in discomfort and fury was revealed beneath. Not a man. An elf. A *Sel'ven*, no less! And through the chaos of the battle around Jikun, his mind was slow to comprehend the features lifted straight from Sel'varian paintings and murals and history books. A face even the Darivalians still taught.

He started with recognition. *'Darcarus? Darcarus?!'* What in the Nine Realms was the True Blood Prince doing in Dahel?!

And who had managed to slay his dragon?

There was a flicker of crimson light and Jikun's eyes shot past the prince, in the direction of the last necromantic surge; there was an enemy amongst the sands, far greater in power than the True Blood and his beast. Instantly Jikun spotted him—the sheen of the sun's glow was obscured by a torrent of sunken faces swarming back to the broad figure. The unnatural gust of wind caused the cream-colored mantle adorning the man's shoulders to whip away from the worn, leather vest below. A thick, powerful body; coarse, tanned hands; and a stern face with a command readied on his lips.

Relstavum.

Chapter Eleven

'What in Ramul is going on?!' But Jikun did not have long to consider the human: the necromancer who had ripped the souls from the city of Dahel. Whatever his plans, *they were not in their favor.*

As the human raised his arm above the sand, the serpent reared. Through its visible pain, clarity was returning.

"*Navon!*" Jikun roared.

The force of his shout dislodged the elf from his thoughts. Navon whirled, eyes meeting Jikun's, and a sudden wave of familiarity dawned over him. Whether or not he recalled the most recent events Jikun could not say, but upon seeing the serpent, Navon immediately sprang forward and propelled his legs into a run. *North.* All he knew was to flee north toward the silhouette of *something* exposed by the serpent's trail.

Yards away, the male in white—*Darcarus*—was sprinting in determination to reach their sides. *As though they could possibly offer him aid.* Before he managed another step, a booming voice filled the desert sands, conjuring tendrils of necromancy to surge from the ground beneath his feet. The True Blood pitched forward with an agonized scream, but Navon's fingers twisted into a countering symbol of his own. With a yowl of defiance, the tendrils were constrained once more into the earth.

'Relstavum is after the prince? The damn True Blood is going to get us killed!' Jikun thought, even as he reached out to yank the Sel'ven to their side. Hundreds of explanations and possibilities flitted through his mind in an instant, but answers to the chaos would have to wait. Jikun's movement became instinctual. *They had to escape the necromancer!*

He saw a blur from the corner of his vision—while he had paused to save the god-damn prince, the hel'onja had regained its senses and was now barreling toward them from the north. "RUN!" Jikun swung Navon away from his attempts to change direction and shoved him toward the serpent.

Navon had been in battle long enough to trust Jikun unquestioningly, and so he ran, the Sel'ven dogging their heels.

Jikun was at their side, his boots pounding against the sand, sinking in. Dragged down like a god-damn anchor yet again. *But he ran*. He felt an icy wisp of dark magic rush over his head, but he did not look back. Not even as his skin tightened—stretched against his bone, threatening to tear free of his body as though it were merely a loose fragment of clothing. He shrieked in pain…!

The serpent lunged.

Both of Jikun's hands extended. One took the Sel'ven by the arm, hurling him out of harm's way, and Jikun used the momentum to twist to the side. Still, it was not distant enough to fully avoid the serpent's dive. Its nose scraped past his ribs and he felt the crack of bone giving way beneath the force. One… two—he stopped counting and refocused. His fingers slid along the side of the beast's armored scales, calling upon the proximity of its internal moisture even as its eye smashed into his shoulder, tearing his arm free of its socket. He slowed, stumbled…

But his magic had already taken effect. The serpent's scales swelled and burst, great spires of ice erupting from the center of its body, spraying the hot sand with a sizzle of blood.

Jikun directed one such stalagmite south, toward where Relstavum still stood in his concentrated throes of necromancy. Surprise lit the man's face for an instant before he was forced to plunge into a nearby dune to avoid being skewered by the onslaught of ice.

Jikun did not cease running. He scanned the cursed, barren horizon. There was *nothing! Nothing* but that tiny ridge of exposed stone!

"Run for the rock!" Navon shouted.

Jikun's lungs were throbbing now—his breath emerged in short, agonized wheezes through his broken ribs. But even in his pain he could still jab, "Where else?!" He heard a low rumble from behind and swiveled in time to see the tip of the snake's tail disappear below the cursed surface. "This thing is fucking persistent!" *'Run, just run!'* he commanded himself, pushing his legs until they rebelled with exhaustion.

"What is it?!" Navon cried as the ridge before them began to take shape.

"It's a…!"

"It's a cave!" Darcarus exclaimed.

The grains before them rippled and Jikun vaulted to the side. "Go around!" he hollered as the serpent's head punctured the earth, showering them with sand. He swept his hand against the shimmering scales, now slick with blood, and sent a barrage of ice once more through its back. "Go!"

Salvation was nigh, but Jikun felt his heart plummet through his chest. The "cave" was no more than a small stone ridge, its opening hardly larger than a Darivalian pup.

They would never get through in time!

Darcarus tore the clasp from his throat and the excess fabric of his cloak fell away as he slid into the narrow crevice.

Jikun gave Navon a forceful thrust toward the hole. "In!" he commanded. Navon dropped obediently to the sand, rolling into the darkness.

As Jikun fell to his knees before the opening, he caught a fleeting glimpse of a series of strange markings etched across its surface, glowing oddly in the shadow of the beast behind him. *'What is that...?'*

Suddenly, a scream resounded from the dark and a hand flashed out to latch onto Jikun's cloak.

"Wha—?!" He gagged as the hand tightened, constricting his breathing. There was a tug at his neck and Jikun was wrenched into the void. Into the darkness. He felt a wall sweeping past him and smelled the rapid advancement of damp earth from below. His arms flailed, but already the nearness of soil was gone. Instead, a light appeared to his right.

Jikun's breath caught.

He was plummeting into a great dome of russet stone beneath the earth. A series of small holes pierced the top where dawn's light shone down in wide, gentle rays to illuminate the inner ground with a soft glow.

Jikun's attention was pulled from the sight as he noticed the cliffs directly below, just in time to twist his torso toward his feet. He landed with a twinge beside Navon.

* * *

Navon let out a similar moan. "We lost him! Thank Sel'ari!" And what a miraculous stroke of fortune that they had dropped safely to a ledge! He inspected the distant hole of the cavern through which they had fallen, five yards up. In his condition, the Darivalian would be of no assistance reaching the tunnel.

Navon grimaced as he turned away, at once aware of the waves of pain assaulting his body. Perhaps he was not as unharmed as he had first assumed…

He hastily released Jikun's cloak, which was still grasped white-knuckled in his palm. "Are you alright?" he queried, rocking back on his heels. "Gods! What in the Nine Realms was that?! I cannot believe we scraped by death yet again!" He tucked his hand against the warm wet of his side, trying to gauge the flow of blood without drawing Jikun's attention to the wound. "It's like something out of *A Dwarf's Tale*—like when Braisebin and his comrades plummeted through the roof of that old estate in Donsury, only to find—"

"*Gods*, you're such a savant," Jikun groaned. He had edged to the face of the grungy wall on their right to slam his shoulder against its craggy surface. There was an audible pop as the joint snapped back into its socket.

"…Savant is not an insult," Navon sighed, but trailed off from launching into a full rebuke. He had comprehended, for the first time, that they were not alone.

'Who…?'

He surveyed the male to their right with militaristic detail. The Sel'ven was perched on the tips of his expensive, yet heavily scuffed, leather boots as he considered the distance to the egress above. His hair was blond, layered with darker strands of gold, and loosely braided in a conservative fashion. His clothes—once exquisitely embellished cotton—were faded past their due. Yet even after the chaos, he remained strikingly elegant. His blue eyes were sharp and focused, emanating an intelligence that his youthful, scarless face failed to wholly display.

His words, however, were jarring. "You have got to be shitting me," he was muttering furiously to himself. "To Ramul with Lady Luck—no wonder he tried to kill you!"

Navon's jaw visibly dropped, but he could find no words to utter his conflicting emotions. Wealth, heritage, and refinement radiated from the male's lean and powerful figure, yet his words were dull and crass, of no greater wit than the Darivalian's beside him.

And to what in Emal'drathar was he referring?

Still… Navon *knew* this figure as well as he knew any legend from his books! *Every* elf could identify this male! "Prince Da… Da… Darcar—"

But before he could stammer out his disbelief—and admittedly feverish adoration of the apparition of a genuine True Blood—his vision of the male was obscured. Jikun's senses had finally cleared and he stepped between them, holding his rib cage gingerly and glaring down at Navon with the weight of all his conceivable threats combined.

A cuffing would be the least of these forms.

"What in Ramul happened up there?!" he roared, reaching out and smacking Navon's hand away from his side.

It had been foolish to imagine the veteran would not notice.

Jikun's eyes briefly assessed the wound for severity and when he seemed satisfied that Navon could take his beating, he pounced, ripping the amulet from the male's neck to fling it savagely over the side of the cliff.

Navon flinched. Yes, the dam with which his general had managed to contain his panic and fear was finally cracking.

"What I have gathered so far is that we have crashed, starved, fled Dahel half-naked, been nearly devoured by a snake, and, of course, been hunted and assaulted by a *necromancer!*" Jikun hissed, extending a finger. He jabbed over the cliff to what Navon could only fathom was the charm. "Protection *my ass*… There is a millennium-worth of things I want to say about your naïve trust in others, but I cannot pause to berate you fully without first addressing the chaos that took place back up there! I haven't forgotten: 'the GODS HAVE A PLAN FOR US!'" He let out a bellow of laughter that caused Navon's insides to fold. "Does that plan include *dying*, Captain? Because I have seen enough dead men to recognize the state, and *you... died!*"

The prince shifted into view at those words. His eyes slid back and forth between the two males, piercing with such familiarity that Navon could have no doubt. *'He knows who we are...* Of course *he knows who we are!'*

He tried expeditiously to pull himself up with some semblance of pride, but the snarl in his side refused to comply.

The prince's lips twitched empathetically. He opened his mouth in an attempt to insert information somewhere into Jikun's tirade. "Relstavum was—"

But Jikun rounded immediately on the male, his fist curling in warning. "*Shut up, you Sel'varian cunt.* Don't move, don't talk... don't even *breathe*…!—I will address you when I have *finished*."

The prince bristled, but Navon was unable to witness any further reaction as Jikun whirled around once more to grasp him by the front of his cloak. He jerked him close, locking eyes in challenge.

And yet Navon could read beneath Jikun's acrimony to that well-masked fear. Was it comradery, or terror in what the necromancy had done…?

Navon could not be certain.

"I died," he repeated solemnly, wise enough to agree—though he had not had time to consider for himself what had truly occurred. "I died…" And as he repeated the words, the darkness in his mind swelled, as though it was a physical entity merely waiting for an invitation. It forced the stoicism of Riphath aside and a vague memory washed in to replace the hero, rife with feelings he did not recognize. "Yes… I *think* I passed…" he trailed off as a cackle of mad laughter echoed somewhere in the recesses of his mind. *'Who…?'* But then it was gone and Navon doubted that it had ever been. He spoke aloud as his mind struggled to piece together the events. "I cast that last spell and then… I was standing in front of a gate."

His eyes widened. *That gate*. How had he forgotten such a place? It was so clear now…! An ancient, tarnished, bronze gate, rising toward a starless sky splashed with scarlet, luminous clouds. Ashen earth, as though an all-consuming fire had scorched any trace of life from it. An… unnatural place where the air was so dry it seemed palpably cracked.

And a breeze that tugged him, gently, forward…

Navon felt a chill sweep down his spine. He knew the place. He must have seen it countless times before… But he had never been so conscious or lingered so long.

The Realms of the Dead.

What words would Tiras use to expound such a place?! Navon struggled to wrest the ancient necromancer's thoughts and emotions to mind, but found them oddly distant. Hazy. *'What would Tiras…?'* But his mind faltered, realizing with unsettling anxiety that he could remember very little of the necromancer's character.

Ephraim? *Eraydon?*

But they too seemed lost. A bubble of anxiety rose in his gut. *'Calm, calm… there are a hundred more!'* And so he clung once more to Riphath, willing the intellectual and tranquil mind of the Noc'olari to dominate his personal fears.

With that unproblematic change, the words left Navon's lips with utter and sincere fascination. "There was unnatural light around me and yet the earth was dark. There was a giant before me… twenty feet tall… A tremendous, demonic beast wearing radiant armor… He said something…" Navon paused, remembering the pale face bearing down upon him, as smooth as a Sel'ven's, yet lacking all hints of life—the hair had dulled, the cheeks were grey, the eyes were sunken and had mislaid their shine. A serene voice had resounded in his mind.

"The Realms are prepared to ferry you home…" Navon repeated slowly. And the image was suddenly clear—not the darkness that swallowed him when he cast his spells upon the hel'onja, but a crisp, clean memory of a world not unlike the Æntara in its heavy scent of earth and putrid odor of decay. What had allowed him to remain so conscious?—So *present* in his magic?! "Like Tiras…!" he whispered. *'I was cognizant in the Realms, the same as Tiras!'*

And yet, even as he spoke those words, he could not recall the necromancer's personality to him.

"*Navon*," Jikun snarled.

Navon shook his head discernibly, swift to repress his own eager self that had boldly manifested in the absence of Tiras' personality. "A Guardian reached out and grasped my wrist. The gates unsealed and I pulled away. *I* freed myself." His voice was growing stronger now. Yes… he, *Navon*, had overpowered the direction of the Realms. What souls could he harness if he could learn to do so… *again? This* was the awareness required to pass the First Gate! This was not something any number of personas could replicate. This magic was *him*. *True* potential as he had boasted to Jikun time and time again!

"Then I was in the desert once more, staring at the serpent," he finished, even as Jikun's grip tightened. "*I* went consciously to the Realms and *back!*"

Jikun's fist swung at him, catching him in the chest before he could react. And the general's rage came with it, ready to crush any personal aspirations as easily as the Helven's ribs. "You *imbecile*," he growled. "Then you *were* dead! You god-damn *imbecile!* I ordered you not to touch necromancy, Navon! As if dying isn't punishment enough, you *know* Murios said that you might lose part of your soul—your *self*—if you botch your god-damn spells!"

'What sense of self do I have to lose?' Navon thought resentfully, but he was wise enough to keep the reflection to himself. He pressed his hand to his side and feigned an assault of pain to break his gaze.

Yet Jikun's words echoed to him. He had returned and yet… he could not retrieve the knowledge of the heroes he had once held so firmly.

"What did you cast? Five? Six spells and you *died?*" Jikun continued his rant. Despite Navon's act, he was far from relenting. "You are not as strong as Tiras. By Ramul, you are not even as strong as I imagined you were! You have been practicing your magic all these years against the Beast, but this demonstrates your vast inexperience. Gods know how many spells you'll be able to cast next time before that happens… before you *die*." He released Navon's shirt unexpectedly, digging his fingers over his bandaged breast.

"And if you cannot free yourself the next time, you come back *less* a soul, Navon, *if* you return *at all!*"

So it was *comradery* that drove the general's chastisement now.

Navon bowed his head, even as a new pit of personal greed boiled fresh inside him. At the consideration of success he had read about a thousand times but had never aspired for his own. With fewer champions of the past to suppress his character, the feeling eminently bore the weight of his own self.

His death in the jaws of the serpent had proven to be as much a success as a failure.

He saw Jikun's fingers tense, as though there was more than emotional distress beneath them.

Navon swiftly pushed his ambitions down. He, *Navon*, was nothing. Tysis of Payne was quick to agree. "You're right, of course, Jikun. You always are."

Jikun's lids narrowed. "...What's your ploy this time, Navon?"

"No, you are right. I shall be more careful."

If possible, his friend's eyes grew thinner, like two piercing slits, and Navon readied himself for the next blow, wishing it would fall somewhere other than his bruised ribs.

"More *careful?* You can't slither your way out of your error and *especially* believe that you would be allowed to cast another dangerous series of self-destructive—"

The general's emotions were peaking now, his face contorting between pain and fury. Navon knew far better than to argue: the male was already crumbling beneath the weight of their dismal luck and continual brushes with death. It was time to redirect his attention. "What do you think was the true purpose of Relstavum's actions?" he interrupted, noting the immediate change in his friend's countenance. "He hunted us down to kill us... and I have the sense that it was entirely premeditated."

"It wasn't," Prince Darcarus finally dared to speak again, his voice strong and decisive in that brief moment of silence.

* * *

Jikun rounded on the True Blood and fixed him with a critical eye. "Were *you* the reason we were nearly soul-raped?" he growled.

Darcarus' jaw slacked and he paused, taking a moment to consider the phrasing. "...Soul-*what?*"

Navon struck Jikun's foot with his fist and scrambled into an apologetic lump. "Forgive his language, Your Highness," he quickly gushed.

The groveling only flattened Jikun's regard. He was equally aware that this blustering heap was Prince Darcarus, second True Blood heir to the Sel'ven Realm on Ryekarayn and Sevrigel's epitome of perfection and grace. But he was *also* wise enough to know that the world of politics was perfidious in nature. As with the "just council," this gold-blooded prince held an equally deceitful inner disposition. Had Navon not endured enough trials from politicians to have learned his lesson? For a male who spent his life wrapped in historical scrolls, he was terribly slow to detect the pattern.

Darcarus continued, appearing mildly amused as he responded, "No, I am not the reason you were almost soul-raped. But then, you two are not from Ryekarayn, so I suppose I should forgive you for your accusations, General Jikun and… Captain Navon?" He paused, and his words settled like the silence before a terrible storm.

Something inside Jikun cracked. His breath sucked in and caught beneath his shattered ribs, drawing his emotions to it. He felt a rush of denial and pride. That this damned, spoiled brat would judge him! How dare an outsider blame him for his course! "It is not my fault," he hissed vehemently. "The council killed them. The council lost the battle. *The council* deserves punishment!" And yet he felt the color drain from his face, his lips growing numb. All semblance of his reassurance in his information dissolved with every word.

His breath could not escape, as though the truth was suffocating him, and he was vaguely aware of the buckling of his legs. The stone around him vanished to a murky swampland. *No*, a fiery battlefield. And dead soldiers… everywhere… everyone…!

A distant voice called outside his mind, but it was hollow and empty, ringing deafly on his ears. The world was rushing to envelop him. The True Bloods. The council. The battle he had fled…!

"Is he well?"

"*Jikun!* Are you alright?! Can you hear me?!"

There were hands on him. Two pairs of hands. *Restraining* hands. And the hold triggered a wild reaction within Jikun—a desperation to live. *His life was worth their sacrifice!*

His mind cleared, strength returning to his limbs. *'I will not die to the whims of politicians!'* He launched the two males away from him to find that he was lying prostrate on his back, unaware of how he had gotten there. He scrambled away in disorientation. *'Fuck the gods. Fuck the True Bloods. Fuck the coun—'*

Something jerked the cloak about his neck and his body was flung solidly into the earth. The breath fled from his lungs as his broken ribs contracted. Then two faces loomed above him, etched with concern.

Jikun swiftly raised his arm, threatening both away as a stab of pain clouded his emotions. In that moment of reprieve, he clutched at the apathy that emptiness offered, shoving his weakness within his walls.

"Are you alright?!" Navon demanded. "Jikun, can you hear me?!"

Jikun slowly sat up, his teeth clenched. He pressed a hand to his side. "You sound like a crying whore."

Navon exhaled audibly. "Thank Sel'ari—I think he is alright now."

Darcarus strutted away, dropping the end of Jikun's cloak. "Well that was damn close. I haven't seen anxiety like that since Sairel became king." He snorted derisively, tucking a golden lock snuggly behind his ear.

'Close?' Glancing away from Navon's uneasy smile, Jikun noted his proximity to the edge of the cliff. "Back up, both of you," he barked, sliding away. "I did not have a moment of anxiety. I'm just *fatigued*." He saw Navon glance up at Darcarus and immediately cuffed him. "*I said I did not panic*," he growled again.

Navon pressed a hand to his face, quick to avert his eyes from the prince in the event Jikun deduced the further passage of wordless information. "Alright! I heard you!" the Helven insisted.

And resorted to surreptitious glances.

Jikun calmly returned to his feet, gathering what dignity he retained to direct focus away from himself. "You never answered my question," he accused the prince, attempting to sweep a hand with equal nonchalance through his hair. He was hampered by an array of frizzy knots. "I asked you what Relstavum was after."

Darcarus hesitated, scanning Jikun's unsteady stance. They flitted once toward the cliff and then his lips twisted, as though he found Jikun's tone—in light of the near fall—amusing. "I responded that Relstavum was not seeking your blood. Or mine. At least, not at first: he likely changed targets *after* he saw Aersophyla bash his serpent's skull inward. But before that, he simply wanted Dahel… though it's possible his day of massacre was moved forward when he realized he had the enemies of his master within his grasp."

'His master…?' Jikun attempted something other than a blank stare.

When this failed, the prince scratched his scalp above the lock and grimaced. "Relstavum is the mastermind behind the troubles on Ryekarayn—the bandits, the uprisings… the massacres. As far as most are aware, he is just a mercenary—a bounty hunter for beasts. To the few informed, he is also an unparalleled necromancer. But the truth is, Relstavum hasn't done much in his own interest for the last decade—he's been employed for more crippling purposes." Arrogance briefly imbued his tone as he reveled in his knowledge. Jikun's lips soured, but the Sel'ven carried on, "Over the last ten years, Saebellus has established his influence over the land—political and criminal—through this agent. The Realm has always known Relstavum was a criminal, but not to this degree—he kept his relations with Saebellus a secret until the warlord's shift in power. Since Ilsevel was taken prisoner, his illicit activities have increased and now, with the changes on Sevrigel, the purpose of his actions has been revealed. I would not be astonished to find that even the *famine* is his doing. Relstavum is the most powerful of Saebellus' pawns—the end of every string being pulled in this country."

"Saebellus…" Jikun repeated, but was not truly certain he had voiced the warlord's name aloud. Relstavum was working for Saebellus…?

Darcarus gave no reaction to his numb utterance and merely continued in a pompous lilt, "And as of late, Relstavum has completely obliterated the last few villages he's visited—these attacks were further distractions to prevent the human king from meddling in Sevrigelian affairs. *Distractions* to keep the king's little mind and great army occupied. But I had no intimation that Relstavum had exacted Saebellus' plans as far south as Dahel. I certainly would have kept well out of the Makataj if I had known he was anywhere within leagues of the damnable place!" The prince laughed then, his apathy oddly cold in light of the recent events.

Yet everything the prince said rang empty of meaning. *'Because of the changes on Sevrigel…?'* Jikun's mind repeated the words, but could form no conclusion. Instead it shifted, freeing itself from the discomfort rising in his gut by turning his skepticism upon the prince.

The male was nothing like Hairem. *Nothing* like Hairem's father. And in Jikun's mind, the Darivalian had imagined the True Bloods to carry themselves with even more regality than their Sevrigelian successors. This male—slouched in comfort against a pile of rubble—was as rough on the inside as he was on the out. Jikun watched as the prince patted down the fraying edge of his shirt. He may have abandoned the dirty white silk on his way into the cavern, but the act had done little to redeem his dismal appearance.

The signet ring wrapped about the calloused finger was all that assured Jikun that he had not made some mistake of identity. He smoothed down his tattered sash, drawing himself up. "What *were* you doing in Dahel—and at the community inn of all places?" he demanded suspiciously.

Darcarus pried a dried beetle from a tattered hem and flicked it coolly at Jikun's brow. "I was helping my brother, of course," he replied calmly, his nose wrinkling at his own pauper-ish appearance. He glanced up once at Jikun and seemed to reevaluate his fortune. "The gods agree *I* have no reason to be down here. Hadoream sailed for Sevrigel several days ago and, after replenishing my supplies, I planned to depart in the morning. But we know what occurred instead. When that damn necromancer attacked, I would have kept flying straight out of the Makataj but for this insane moral plight that I ought to help the two of you. Now I'll be pulling sand off my valuables until I am a thousand."

Navon's expression—which had certainly begun with all the admiration and awe a typical True Blood "deserved"—had slowly deteriorated into confusion and perhaps, Jikun detected, mild disgust. This male was not, he imagined, at all what the Helven had long venerated.

And the subtle reference to his genitals had not helped.

He looked up from the withered beetle and tried to salvage some good from the prince. "You were helping your brother?" he inquired. "What does King Sairel want with Dahel?"

Darcarus seemed briefly confused, then laughed outright and regarded the Helven with visible scorn. "Why in Ramul would I help Sairel?" he huffed, dropping his foot abruptly down upon the bug's carcass. "Hadoream. I had to get *Hadoream* to Sevrigel. Gods know *Sairel* doesn't give a damn about anything that doesn't reside within the confines of his office."

Jikun wanted to enjoy further True Blood insults, but his face was forced lax with perplexity. "Hadoream is traveling from Dahel to Sevrigel? You must have ships on the coast of the Mythowood. Why come all the way down south through this bloodthirsty wasteland when…" he trailed off as Darcarus' amusement faded.

The prince tensed, removing himself from his slouch against the wall. "You don't know…" He casually slid the tip of his boot over the edge of Jikun's cloak as though to secure it.

But perhaps this time, Jikun sensed, it was necessary.

"I meant to say I supposed you would not have *all* the details, but… I assumed you would have *some* grasp of the events. Why do you think Ryekarayn is sinking toward Ramul?" Even before he continued, Jikun felt his stomach lurch. "When you lost the battle at Elarium, you lost the war. …Saebellus owns Sevrigel now. Saebellus, General Taemrin, is *king*."

Jikun's throat constricted. *'Have some control of your damn…'* But even his self-rebuke was lost as the words struck him again.

Saebellus owned Sevrigel.

Saebellus owned Sevrigel?

"What about Hairem?" Jikun stammered. "My remaining troops outside the capital? *The impenetrability of Elvorium?!* It's surrounded by a god-damn cliff on all sides! *What do you mean Saebellus owns Sevrigel?!*" His voice had risen to a thunderous bellow that shook the very dust from the cavern dome.

Navon shifted closer once more, poised to restrain him. Yet his face was deathly white.

Noting that the Helven might be of no help, Darcarus subtly leaned his full weight over the boot on Jikun's cloak. "Saebellus did not conquer Elvorium—the council delivered it to him. Control yourself! Upon your defeat, Hairem killed himself and the council surrendered Ilsevel to be his bride. *I* do not personally blame you for the loss and its results, but that does not change what has come to pass. As for the *rest* of your soldiers…" He met Jikun's eyes solidly, his lips growing tight. He did not need to speak the words.

Jikun's heart froze, too numb to react. He had been beaten mercilessly by the gods since crashing in the Makataj. The heat. The pain. The trial. The necromancy. *'This damn hole in the earth…'* But news of Saebellus' victory over the elven nation?

The walls surrounding his emotions redoubled. Grew and wrapped around them so tightly that he could not be certain that they were even within.

"So… Hadoream is on Sevrigel with another army…" Jikun barely managed to whisper. The True Blood royals were all trained generals, yet the image of the prince riding at the forefront of Sevrigel's salvation brought him little comfort.

To fully shatter the notion, Darcarus stiffly shook his head, his lock of hair once more slipping free to swing idly by his lips. "*You're not listening, Jikun.* Saebellus did not merely conquer Sevrigel, he *owns* the very essence of the nation. To ensure that no one prevents the solidification of his rule, he is on a brazen path to control Ryekarayn as well. In a few months' time, his grip on Sevrigel will be secure and there will be no stripping power from him. So by fucking Ramul, *no*. My little brother is on Sevrigel in *secret* for now. I can offer him no army while our Realm requires it for our own defense; that damn necromancer's bandits dare to lay hands even on *us* if we stray too far from our gates." Here he paused and gingerly touched his breast, as though he bore a wound from such an attack. "You saw the destruction Relstavum just reaped upon Dahel. Hadoream would have to be Cadorian-*Plague*-crazy to take the army from Sairel right now."

Jikun's arms swung limply at his side as he gave a delayed, emotionless nod. This side of the channel was no better off than the one from which he had fled. His defeat had crippled both continents…!

"Jikun!" Navon suddenly cried, and Jikun realized too late that he had pitched forward once more into the stone. He hit the earth in a numb daze. A wave of pain crushed his ribs, but he could not be certain if it was caused by the fall or the force of his quickening breaths.

"Shit," he heard Darcarus grunt, and the male's face swam foggily into view. "At least he is on the ledge."

"Do you think he can hear us?" Navon inquired, his worried expression floating in beside the Sel'ven's.

Jikun flipped over sharply to accommodate an unexpected wretch. What little contents his stomach had contained after his days of fatigue splashed out over Navon's blistered feet.

His companion barely flinched, but rather spun on the prince, his raven hair wild. "You cannot be so insensitive when you discuss the fate of Sevrigel! The place was his homeland! Those who passed were his brothers!"

"Makes me almost grateful I have Sairel," Darcarus muttered in reply, pressing a finger to the captain's balled fist and easing it away. He clapped his hands before Jikun's face, but the Darivalian did not react.

"They are all dead," Jikun whispered. He had *known* that, and yet having the reality confirmed… In the shadow of Hairem's suicide and Saebellus' kingship… What mad hope had he conjured?! What in all of Aersadore could he ever accomplish to atone for all the blood his cowardice had shed? "There is nothing I can do…" he mumbled. The cliff on his right or the sword at the prince's side—both seemed far too swift a punishment for his failures. Maybe dying slowly of trial after trial was exactly what the gods had designed for him.

And still less than he deserved.

"*Jikun*," Darcarus hissed, and by the level of his tone, he was repeating his call. "Jik—"

"What?"

Navon snapped to instant attention. "He's conscious! Jikun, it is as the writings of Shalah say: 'You cannot live in the past; the past is already gone.' What we did is something that will—"

But Darcarus shoved the Helven aside as though he were a disease. "Honor is for those who have nothing to lose. As I said before, General, I think you made the sensible choice—what good could you do with your head rolling across the earth? I was compelled to help you for a reason and now you are *alive*. I could use your experience. Not just use it, I *need* it. Of many thousands, *you* are the one who managed to escape Dahel's destruction. And if you had not assisted me in turn, Relstavum would have most certainly killed me. You saved my life. Now I offer you yours in return.

"You need to justify your decision, do you not?"

Jikun felt his mind stirring, a dull throbbing reawakening within his breast.

"You need to prove that you made the just decision at Elarium. Well, I believe the gods planned this encounter: what series of events must have taken place to lead us both here? Now we have a true chance to save Sevrigel through my brother. But he needs an army: the *army* Sairel currently requires to defend against Saebellus' machinations. But if Relstavum were *dead*…"

Jikun blinked, sharply aware of the stench of vomit and the pain in his chest… but also of the Sel'ven's intent.

The male was crouched beside him, breath cool on his ear. "If Relstavum… if the leader and mastermind behind the rebellions, genocide, and bandits were dead, those evils would die with him. We would be capable of redirecting our resources to combating Saebellus before he neutralizes the forces of resistance upon Sevrigel." He put a hand firmly on Jikun's shoulder. "General, I am not talking about saving one country or the other. If we kill Relstavum, *Aersadore* is saved. What more righteous path is there for any soul? You can condemn the lives of your soldiers to futility, or you can demonstrate that their sacrifice for your life was necessary to achieve Aersadore's freedom… That in itself is far greater than even the vast bounty that will be rewarded for Relstavum's death."

Jikun's mind churned. Darcarus was right. He had to lose the battle to win the war. And if he won the war, was his life not worth *all of theirs?*

Honor was for those who had nothing to lose.

Navon thrust back into view, his face twisted in disgust. "That plan is madness!" he accused the prince. "Do not try to justify our crimes! Sel'ari would never condone the murder of tens of thousands for two lives—no matter what those two lives would go on to accomplish. Failing to act is no different than wielding the blade. We need atonement, *not* justification!"

Darcarus tossed his long, blond hair, deliberating catching Navon with the end of his braid. He stepped between Jikun and Navon's outraged gape once more as though protecting Jikun from the plague-ridden words his captain was spewing. "You may sleep soundly with the deaths of thousands hovering above your head, but I believe Jikun has a dash more morality at heart."

Navon choked out a single laugh before he dropped his voice into a snarl. "This is not about morality. We forfeited our entire lives when we fled: we have no money, no future, no titles, and no weapons. We are *beggars* on the very brink of death. And now you dare suggest we aspire to be heroes?! You are a coward to take advantage of his weakened mind!"

"Hardly. I do not come without a sensible path. I am offering my *aid*—physically and monetarily," Darcarus replied succinctly. "Or do you intend to continue running from Saebellus?"

Navon drew level with the Sel'ven. "Even *if* we were to accept your aid, there must be other methods of combating Saebellus than contesting Relstavum ourselves—the male is clearly far more powerful than *all* of us," he spat. "You said that Relstavum is forming a rebellion against the king. We should join the force fighting that rebellion—the military will clothe us. Feed us. Provide us with an honest living. And if Relstavum loses that battle, it will shatter the faith of his allies which—assuming they've won no true victories—must be fragile. This rebellion may hold lofty aspirations for Saebellus, but it is an incredibly risky venture. We failed to defeat Saebellus in battle before—this is clearly Sel'ari's opportunity to atone!"

Darcarus stepped closer, until the two elves were practically feeding off one another's furious breaths. "How exactly does that signify that Jikun made the right choice at Elarium?—The humans will win or lose this war regardless of your assistance, *Captain*. Two paltry soldiers, no matter your questionable magical skill, will not grant the army victory."

"It takes every soldier to form an army, you insolent, arrogant pri—"

Darcarus twisted Navon's ear smartly and spat in his shocked face. "*Saebellus* has assigned Relstavum full responsibility in assuring that Ryekarayn remains uninvolved in Sevrigel's struggles. This last decade of work has been *Relstavum's* endeavor, and he holds the knowledge and commitment of all involved: these are *Relstavum's* plans, *Relstavum's* allies—if you remove the damn necromancer, you sever *everything* connected to him. Saebellus' fragile hold on Sevrigel does not allow him the ability to divide his attention between two continents—if he loses Relstavum, the last decade of his plans are gone. He does not have the resources *or* personal allies necessary to concoct a new scheme." He watched as Navon rubbed his cheek vigorously in an attempt to regain some semblance of dignity. "Only after Relstavum is defeated can Ryekarayn aid Sevrigel, you stupid, little—!"

"Silence!" Jikun roared. He groaned, his head drowning in too many damn emotions. He sucked in a breath. "I will do it."

Navon's hand fell away, leaving a red patch in its wake. "What?"

"I will do it," Jikun repeated for his companion's sake. "If Relstavum is the key to everything Saebellus could hope to gain on Ryekarayn, then he is the key to destroying everything as well."

"Relstavum obliterated a dragon and nearly killed us both with that undead serpent. We are objectively outmatched! A war needs soldiers—*that* is what we are!"

"*I* have made my decision," Jikun hissed. "You can join me, or you can go on alone."

He could almost hear Navon's heart still. There was utter silence in the cavern as the Helven digested those cutting words.

"So what is your plan?" Jikun spoke after a moment, raising his heavy head.

Darcarus grinned, extending a hand to offer assistance. "First, we get you back to health; flinging your corpse at the necromancer would be futile. Then, I would have bought you both gear worthy of kings… *but* my coin was in my cloak… If Relstavum is kind enough to leave it, we will have everything we need… If not, we will have to ask more of the Brotherhood than I had intended. But our course is to them either way: Geldin Laeris' mercenary organization should know Relstavum's whereabouts. Gods know there is nothing they *don't* have their hands in." He raised his palm sharply as though Jikun had even considered protesting.

Navon knocked Darcarus' hand down with a personal vengeance. "*Why* can you not return to your home for more coin when that seems the surest fix to all our woes?"

Darcarus' shoulders stiffened, his hand flexing into a responding fist. "You are slow, Helven. It should have been very clear that what I did in Dahel was in secret. I was not supposed to be here, helping ferry my brother to Sevrigel… Dare I add that *he* was not supposed to be here, *travelling* to Sevrigel. By Ramul, we weren't even supposed to be privy to what is occurring on Sevrigel!—That's three offenses against my father already. If I go back to the Realm without his *precious* baby *boy*, they'll surrender my bowels to the rats. And had I Hadoream at my side, I would still be beaten senseless for meddling in affairs unrelated to our *glorious* Realm." He laughed as he spoke, but there was venom lurking behind his words and his eyes shot to the northern end of the cavern, as though piercing his father with their spite. "So we will rely on the Brotherhood. They will direct us."

"*That's* what I'm afraid of."

"I said *enough*," Jikun growled. "I will warn you once more, Navon—you can come with, or you can go join that war *alone*."

Navon's fingers were interlocking in and out of symbols that Jikun was beginning to recognize. He displayed an expression the general did not know he was capable of directing toward one of Sel'ari's chosen. "I agree that we first need sustenance. There is food down below," he finally mumbled.

Jikun ignored the Sel'ven's offer of assistance, instead reaching out for his captain's hand. "Did you say *food?*"

Navon's muscles eased in Jikun's undivided attention. "Yes. I saw it when you nearly fell over the edge the first time." He gestured to the ledge and Jikun allowed himself to be assisted to its side. "Maybe it is connected to the oasis in Dahel…"

When Jikun dared to cast his gaze over the cliff, what he saw took his breath away. In the massive cavern below, water gurgled softly over the rounded grey stones of a stream that wound gently through thick, lush grass. Towering, flowered trees hung still in the damp air, tossing petals onto the wildflowers growing about their roots. Branches drooped heavily with an abundance of fruit. The land was flat except for a steeply sloped hill that climbed toward shafts of sunlight. They radiated down from the stone dome, breathing life but not heat into the world beneath.

And this was the paradise in which they now sat.

"Praise Lady Luck," Darcarus breathed as he came up beside them, slouching as though the tension was forgotten. "Would you look at that?!—Our fortune is coalescing! What did I tell you about the gods' plan?"

"Not you, too," Jikun muttered as he stretched his aching neck and tried unsuccessfully to once more smooth his gnarled hair. "An underground oasis…?" Far too much luck for his taste. "Looks too… *Sevrigelian*… Keep a keen eye." Those trees… those flowers… they were undoubtedly northern Sevrigelian in origin. But what was Sevrigelian foliage doing lost beneath Ryekarayn's desert sands?

Navon nodded once and Jikun could only imagine that a thousand prayers of thanks were racing about in his tiny brain.

"Is that fruit?" Darcarus exclaimed from his left. "On that tree?! Kamora fuck me senseless! We need to get down there *now!*"

Navon cringed.

'Kamora fuck me senseless...? How have I not sworn such before? That is one god I wouldn't *mind getting fucked by,'* Jikun thought, easing somewhat in the familiarity of the uncouth company.

Navon was still grumbling his offense as Jikun stepped gingerly around the edge of their stone platform. "There is a drop to another ledge here—three or five yards? ...And more after that!" The realization that the food beneath them could be reached, and without an exertion of magic he doubted he still possessed, evoked a surge of mindless hunger in Jikun's gut. Even the brilliance of the prince's blasphemy was forgotten.

Darcarus was already vaulting over the ledge, leaving Jikun and Navon to fend for themselves; it seemed his own base desires trumped even his rallying speech.

The three descended the series of massive, earthen steps until finally, with deep exhales of relief, they landed upon the moist grass of the cavern floor.

Jikun had hardly gathered his immediate surroundings when Navon let out an elated gasp. "*Fish?!*" he dashed past him, nearly sending Jikun toppling to the ground. "Jikun, there are fish!"

Jikun found himself scrambling after, his pain dismissed, his dry mouth struggling to salivate. "Fish? Fruit? Water?" he murmured in mutual disbelief.

"A godsend!"

As Darcarus stepped up beside them to the shore of the stream, he carried himself like a quintessential Sel'ven: as though he had a stick shoved up his ass. Jikun did not bother to gather any semblance of pride. He dipped his hands into the cool water, drew it to his lips, and sucked it down fervently. As a fish darted past, he shot a thin spear of ice from his palm to the stream's floor, pinning the silver ray through the center.

"I'll collect some fruit!" Navon added hungrily, vanishing into a cluster of trees behind them as Jikun speared another.

Darcarus was pursuing at his heels. "Wait right there, imbecile!" he hollered. "You should not go off alone! Gods, how were you ever a captain?!"

The hasty footfalls faded and were gone, leaving Jikun beneath the formidable weight of silence. His gut grew swiftly unsettled. An unfamiliar picture arose in his mind, an image he had barely gathered in that last, frantic moment of escape—strange, runic symbols that hung over the cave's entrance.

He paused, dropping the second fish beside the first, and leaned over into the earth beside the stream. "Navon, come translate this," he called out, trying not to let the unease alter his tone as he traced his finger through the mud.

Navon reappeared behind him, practically prancing as he laid the fruit down as delicately as though they were orbs of glass. He seemed to have momentarily forgotten his bitterness toward the prince and his plan—though his cheek was still smartly red.

"Translate what...? Oh..." Navon trailed off, setting the last fruit hesitantly beside the others. "...Why?"

Jikun pointed his muddy finger upward once, then wiped it on the hem of Navon's cloak. "There was something like this on the cave. Something like..." he gestured to the three vague symbols he had recalled. "Something like that."

Darcarus had reappeared on their right and swiftly wiped his boot across the soil. "That was ancient Farvian. Some variation of sealing magic," he replied gruffly, rolling his shoulders back to banish what Jikun suspected to be mutual disquiet.

Jikun slowly leaned back. "To keep something out... or to keep something in...?"

Navon raised a fruit to his lips, eyes still fixated on the smudged earth. He hesitated, considering Jikun's words. "Isn't that the question," he replied grimly. He dared to look to the prince, but the male merely shrugged.

"I gave little heed to my tutor," he replied. "That was for Sairel's indoctrinated mind."

'God-damn useless royalty,' Jikun scoffed as he studied the carefully composed face of the Helven. He knew that the directions of their thoughts were aligned.

Relstavum.

"This isn't what I saw in Dahel," Navon attempted to reassure him. "Or what was on that amulet."

Jikun stood, ears straining for even the most hushed sound. Wherever his eyes searched, their lush haven was peacefully serene, and he detected no sign of intelligent life. The cavern remained reticent, closely guarding whatever secret it possessed.

"Eat!" Darcarus barked as Jikun's eyes finally returned to the stream. He seized Jikun by the cloak and jerked him downward. "Your health!"

Jikun choked out a gasp as he spilled onto the ground, barely catching himself with his hands in time to prevent his nose from taking the brunt of the fall. "Damn it! Stop that!" he growled, rubbing his neck and huffing through his cracked ribs. He cuffed the prince for good measure. "This is not a damn leash! The next one of you who pulls this I will beat until he looks like an Apapian plum." His complaint was abruptly terminated as a fruit bounced off his forehead and rolled away beside him. He hurriedly snatched it from the earth, ravenously biting into its flesh. The runes… *the necromancer…* it was all momentarily pushed aside. He could not sustain his caution above his fatigue.

They devoured every bit of fruit and fish they had gathered, and when the meal was at last consumed, Jikun lay back and let his body sink into the thick grass. "It's been weeks since I've had a decent meal," he breathed softly.

"I can relate," Darcarus grunted. He had removed the braid, and his hair splayed about his freshly washed face. Like the Sel'vi in Jikun's army, Darcarus had prioritized cleanliness over even his fatigue. "You would not believe how ungenerous humans are in some parts. It's like damn *dwarven* hospitality right now. *Not* that the Eph'vi are much better."

But Jikun had stopped listening. His attention had drifted to Navon, and he briefly considered speaking some words of reassurance in his decision about hunting Relstavum. He would be a fool to join the war against the rebels and risk losing Sevrigel yet again. Yet it was clear by the steady rise and fall of the Helven's chest that his companion had already succumbed to sleep.

As his own eyes began to droop, Jikun forced them wide in one last scan of the cavern ceiling. He pushed his fingers against his ribs, using the pain to keep himself awake. But it would not last long; the agony was just as great as his fatigue and it would send him into far deeper throes of unconsciousness.

He dropped his hand and stared as long as he could sustain at the great dome. He could not erase the visage of the ancient elven magic from his mind—it was as though the symbols had been burned into his memory. *Sealing magic*.

A fissure as small as the entrance to the cavern would not need sealing magic to prevent the hel'onja from entering. Did other beasts prowl the desert that someone wished to keep out?

Or was the magic intended to imprison something within?

CHAPTER TWELVE

"Jikun. Jikun, wake up!" came a jarring, harsh whisper.

Jikun's eyes fluttered open, the memory of recent events rushing back to him. Immediately, his hand groped at his hip in search of his sword… then slowly drew away. His mind was groggy, but he had enough sense to remember that the gift from the Darivalian councilmember—his prize for his success in war—was gone. "I can get a better one," he mumbled.

"What?"

Jikun cleared his throat, pushing up onto his elbows despite his ribs' snarl of protest. "What is it?" he demanded. He blinked away the sleep, then squinted in confusion as Navon's face came into focus. His ashen pallor had faded, but what had replaced it was equally as chilling as the effects of the necromancy: runic symbols now spanned the breadth of the Helven's forehead, etched in a crimson liquid that shimmered in the dim cavern light.

Jikun had seen too much carnage to not recognize it as blood. "What in Ramul were you—?"

Navon waved his hand sharply. "You have them too," he spoke quietly, wiping the crook of his arm across his face.

"I look like a child's god-damn finger-painting venture," Darcarus groused beside the stream as he splashed water over his face.

Navon rolled his eyes, wiping the blood nonchalantly across his thigh. Jikun ignored his captain's subtle mutterings that followed, aware for the first time of a cool feeling on his cheeks and forehead. "Why in the name of—"

Navon refocused immediately as Jikun's voice echoed throughout the cavern. He slapped his palm across Jikun's mouth. "We are not alone!"

Jikun pried it off, tasting the bitter tang of blood on his lips. "That much is obvious," he spat, and staggered cautiously to his feet. "Do you still have my knife?"

Navon pulled the kitchen blade from the waistline of his pants, but did not surrender the weapon. "You are in no condition for combat." He warily scanned the trees in the distance. "I doubt they are hostile… They made no attempt to assault us in our sleep."

"Most would consider a stranger's blood smeared all over their face an assault," Darcarus countered as he withdrew from the shore. Undaunted by the Helven's growing disdain, he grabbed the end of Navon's cloak and attempted to dry his face on the hem.

"Hey, use your own!" Navon hissed.

"I lost mine in the desert," Darcarus retorted, wrestling to pat his face off before the Helven could struggle away.

"Enough, the both of you!" Jikun reprimanded as he scraped his hand across his face with abrasive force, smearing the symbols. The blood remained, but the runes, at least, were broken. "I swear you two have the attention span of a god-damn wolf pup. Now, I saw nothing living when we scouted the cavern from the cliff, but there is at least one madman running about down here."

Darcarus stood beside them as Navon finally managed to wrench the cloak away. "There *can't* be more than one—where would they hide? Navon and I walked the breadth of this place in search of food."

"Hardly." Navon gestured to a small cluster of trees with the knife. "For one, not in there."

The three were silent as they followed the point of his blade out toward the dark huddle of trees.

Darcarus caught the male's wrist swiftly and jerked it down. "Good gods, what in Ramul do you hope to do with that kitchen knife?" He drew his sword, advancing to the front of their little threesome. "It is probably watching us right now…"

Jikun stepped at his heels, Navon shaking the chastisement from his wrist as they went. Before him, the forest maintained a thick and eerie silence. He squinted into the gloom. "Do you think Relstavum…?"

"Greetings." Jikun's heart leapt in his chest as a male plunged suddenly through the branches of the tree directly in front of Darcarus, hanging by his knees from a gnarled branch. His lean body swung slightly back and forth above the grass as he regarded them in a wide-eyed gaze of attentiveness.

"Balior take me," Jikun gasped, reflexively raising a hand in preparation to cast magic. Yet it merely hung there, as Jikun found his attention riveted to the male in incredulous fascination.

This was not Relstavum. He was not even human.

'What elf...?' His fingers fell from their stiff and ready state. The male's hair was more vivid than his own—varying in shades of green and blue—with peacock feathers stuck securely in some unknown fashion. It trailed down from his head, brushing the grass with its tips. Countless runic symbols—such as those Jikun had seen on Navon's cheeks—were inked in blacks and jade across his face, neck, and hands. The male's brilliant green eyes flicked from one arrival to the next, and his long, slender face was turning a garish shade of red.

Darcarus, bearer of their weapon, merely stood stupefied.

Behind him, Navon reacted with a slightly more vigilant response. He retreated cautiously to regard the male in a mix of bafflement and wariness. "What are you… Who are… Why are you… What do you want?" he finally managed, his expression visibly perplexed. "Are you alone? Are you with Relstavum?"

The male raised a hand to the branch, gripping it tightly as he released his legs, and then dropped gently into the grass with the ease of someone well-versed in dangling and dropping. Darcarus finally lifted his damn sword, but otherwise remained dumbstruck by the colorful aberration. The elf's body jangled softly as numerous tiny, glass vials clinked together around his various leather belts. "I do not know who this Relstitum is," he replied in the Common Tongue, although his words were thick with an unfamiliar accent.

Still, that he was not associated with the crazy necromancer did not dismiss his own lunacy. What in Emal'drathar was in those vials…?—A peapod… hair… the foot of an animal, a clover, an acorn…Too baffled to even begin to ascertain a purpose for such trinkets, he instead caught the male with a sharp glare. "Who are you, then?" he insisted warily.

"And what did you write on us?" Darcarus added, pointing his sword at the male's gut.

The male sauntered forward, unperturbed by the threat, and patted Darcarus once on the breast as he passed. Then he extended his palm toward the kitchen knife, displaying a recently closed gash snaking up his arm. "Ohhh… Eph'ven craftsmanship. It has been long since I have seen such an item. Oh look, a bird!" He froze suddenly, fixated on the dome above them.

Jikun glanced up briefly, but then hastily refocused on the male. There was indeed a bird flying above them. It seemed worn out, careening back and forth across the ceiling in wavering dips toward the earth.

And then it landed with a soft thud at the male's feet. The stranger clasped his hands together, mouth forming a little circle of delight and surprise. "I was so growing tired of fish! What splendid luck! What splendid luck indeed!" He bent down and snatched the bird up by a single, scrawny leg.

Navon sidled to Jikun's side, grimacing. "Forget Relstavum, *this* male… is truly insane," he hissed.

"Truly," Darcarus rejoined.

Jikun glanced at the blade, disappointed that they only possessed the one. "Listen," he began, but the male had already hurried away, across the stream, toward the summit of the hill.

Navon's eye twitched after him. "…Do we… follow him?"

Jikun could only gape as he watched the elf scramble up the grassy mound and ignite a little fire at the top. "…What… is it?"

"Well, it is clearly an elf," Navon replied with a triumphant nod.

Jikun's expression flattened. "…Thank you," he replied, sarcasm breaking him out of his shock. He frowned as the elf rotated the bird above the fire on a stick.

Darcarus finally sheathed his blade. "Looks like some god got overly creative," he chuckled. "And did he just leave us to eat a dead bird?"

"Well, I don't think he's dangerous," Navon interjected with a sniff—as though the prince had been suggesting otherwise—and similarly sheathed his weapon into the waistline of his pants. "We can talk to it… him."

Jikun turned, surveying their surroundings once more. The cavern appeared to be otherwise empty. "Why in Ramul would I want to talk to him?"

Darcarus smiled weakly, rustling his hair. "Actually, it might not be the most terrible of ideas… We *would* benefit from knowing the way out of the Makataj…"

Jikun stilled, though he felt a strong urge to yank those pretty, carefully tousled locks. "What in Ramul are you talking about?—How in the Nine Realms did you get to Dahel?"

Darcarus blew out his cheeks, a few wild strands flapping out indignantly. "Aersophyla—my dragon. Outside the Aenid to the west, there *is* a Griffon outpost that travels to and from Dahel. But obviously, that does not help us anymore."

Jikun's head shook mindlessly in disbelief, his own knotted hair hanging dismally still. "So up on the ledge you spewed a plan with no idea how to actually get out of this damn wasteland? What about portal magic? Pray tell you can do more than summon dragons."

A look of sheer incredulity crossed the prince's face. "You are *unbelievably* difficult to please." But when Jikun said no more, he snorted his contempt. "Have you ever travelled through portal magic? It is—"

"Yes I have," Jikun interrupted stiffly. "I went from Elvorium to Darival many a time through such a method. And I dare say I rather like the efficiency."

Darcarus threw his hands into the air. "Then you saw that such a magic is maintained and controlled by *multiple* mages. And I am sure they warned you a dozen times what happens should the magic fail: you would end up only gods know where, never to be heard from again. It is *extremely* volatile magic. In all my years and all my studies—"

"—The ones you never paid attention to—"

"I have only known two males who can control portal magic outside of towers full of multiple, focused mages—mages who must *perpetually* maintain said magic. Both happen to be my brothers. And remarkably, Sairel is the only one I would trust. Hadoream... Well, on more than one occasion the things he sent through never returned. Wherever the Heart of Magic lies, that is where a stuffed bear, a one-eyed cat, and a jar full of buttons lie."

"...What?"

"He collected buttons."

Jikun massaged his temple. "I have heard enough. So what you are telling me is that our only recourse is..." he trailed off, glancing uneasily at the mad elf on the hill. "Just what I should expect from a politician—a promise without an actual plan."

Darcarus opened his mouth to retort, but his silver tongue failed him. Jikun pivoted and Navon fell into step beside him. Together, the three climbed their way to the top of the immense hill, where the temperature elevated in response to the summit's proximity to the desert sands above. Tiny grains sprinkled in with the occasional surface wind, shimmering in the sunlight as they settled into a layer of dust across the grass. That grass was worn and sparse, despite the ample sunlight, attesting to the male's frequent position atop the hill.

"Would you like some?" the male offered, continuing his conversation in Highstead as they halted several feet from his side. He lifted the stick, swinging the tiny bird about.

Jikun gazed in aversion as the bird's spindly legs flopped against its bulging breast. "No," he replied flatly, raising his hand to block the sight.

With a shrug, the male gave a violent thrust of the stick, staking it into the ground to cool. Beside Jikun, Navon jumped, his hand flitting to his knife hilt.

"I am Eldaeus," the male spoke abruptly. His tone had grown strangely solemn and he stared numbly at the bird.

Jikun glanced at Navon for an explanation to his change in countenance. "And I am Jikun. How—"

"Did the council send you?" Eldaeus prodded his fingers, eyes as round and pitiful as a Darivalian wolf pup when the hunters came to choose their mounts.

Jikun wrinkled his nose, momentarily distracted by the forlorn expression. And then he froze. "What council?" he demanded.

Eldaeus heaved a sigh of relief, his face breaking into a broad smile. He plucked the stick from the earth with glee and took a large bite of the bird, bones and all. It crunched as he bobbed his head from side to side to some unknown melody undoubtedly canvassing his mind. As though abruptly recalling that he had *more* guests, he pointed the stick accusingly at Navon and Darcarus. "You did not tell me *your* names. Did the council send *you?*"

Darcarus viewed the male skeptically. "I would not tell you my name if Sel'ari commanded it."

Jikun could not blame him. He tapped his foot in irritation. His life was improving: from the bloody defeat orchestrated by Saebellus to the near-gruesome demise at the command of his dog, *now* he was trapped in the desert with a madman.

Navon, however, was more than ready to pacify the elf with information, and Jikun half-wondered if it was not in a desire to contrast the prince. "I am Navon. And no, no council sent us… We came from Dahel."

Eldaeus cocked his head. "Dahel…?"

"Yes. Dahel. …The city to the south? …You can see it from here. I mean, when you are outside the entrance to this place."

Eldaeus' brows rose in delight. "They built a city nearby?" he exclaimed as he clasped his hands. "How fortunate!"

While Jikun was not overly familiar with Ryekarayn's cities, Dahel was certainly no recent enterprise for the Eph'vi. And to solidify Jikun's theory, Navon whispered from the corner of his mouth, "Dahel was established several millennia ago." He grimaced as he addressed the elf once again. "Can we… ask you some questions?"

Eldaeus rubbed his chin, contemplating his response. "You may ask me… three and a half questions."

Jikun narrowed his eyes. "Three and a ha—" He grunted as Navon stuck an elbow into his side. "Curse your mother's grave!—Those are broken, you bastard."

"Wonderful," Navon beamed, ignoring his comrade's complaint. "First, who are you?"

Eldaeus let himself fall onto his bottom, placing his hands on his knees. He wrote in the dirt in ancient elven, muttering to himself as he did so. "No title. No name. Those were taken from me," he spoke grimly. "So I am simply… Eldaeus. I am a Faraven of Sevrigel."

Navon's brows rose instantly and Jikun was too occupied with his stinging ribs to stop the Helven from his foolish rush of curiosity. "A Faraven? All the way from Sevrigel? Sel'ari, how long have you been here?!"

"Gods damn it, Navon! No wonder you lost the war," Darcarus barked, unable to resist the jab. "What in the Nine Realms are we going to do with *that* information?!"

Navon raised his chin and ignored the prince, but Jikun felt pain lance his heart. He forced the emotions to remain at bay. *'We lost the battle,* not *the war,'* his mind chanted in defense to Darcarus' careless comment.

Eldaeus threw his head back and began to laugh. Jikun could see tears forming at the corners of his eyes and he was torn whether they were induced by grief or amusement—either at the question, or at the subtle display of inner conflict between his guests.

"A very, very long time," Eldaeus finally breathed, his chin dropping to his breast as he wiped the moisture from his eyes. "A very, very long time."

Had the male lived before or after the slaughter of the Farvian people? As far as Jikun was aware, no True Blood survivors of the massacre still existed. He halted his own interest. What did it matter?! He shot Navon an internal rebuke. *'That is two wasted, you idiot,'* he thought.

Navon winced as he read Jikun's expression and paused, as though attempting to conceive a brilliant question. "How and why are you down here?" he finally asked.

Darcarus flung his hand into the air to curse something inaudible to the gods.

"We just discussed how we need a damn path out of the Makataj, Navon!" Jikun swore.

Curiosity: it could never be for anything *useful.*

Eldaeus looked up, not seeming to notice Darcarus' display, and merely squinted with reproach toward the sheepish Navon. "I suppose that is a one-

and-a-half question." He raised his hand up to the dome in a lamenting fashion. ...Clearly he had noticed the prince after all.

"I am trapped within this glorious cavern in punishment for crimes for which they could not kill me. By order of King Rel'estri and the council of Elvorium."

Darcarus lowered his arms. "Who is King Rel'estri?"

Emerald eyes flashed sharply to Darcarus. "You do not get to ask a question," Eldaeus pointed at him accusingly. "One left."

Jikun opened his mouth instinctively to inform the deranged elf that this would be, in fact, the fourth question, but held his tongue. After Navon's utter waste for information, an additional query was warranted.

Darcarus rounded on the Helven. "If you do not ask the right question, so help me I will find the nearest stick and shove it up your ass."

"Good gods, are you and Jikun related?!" Navon retorted. He pursed his lips to consider his next tactic. The Faraven was eyeing Jikun and Darcarus as though warning them against offering any suggestions. "How long would they lock me up for killing a Sel'varian prince?" Navon decided.

Jikun groaned. Darcarus spun away to fulfill his threat.

But Eldaeus ignored them both and cocked his head in true deliberation. "That is a very good question indeed," he began in refutation to their wordless rebukes. "Probably at least a few days." He trailed off and grinned unexpectedly, spinning about to face them. "Now it is my turn," he began, patting the ground beside him. "Tell me—"

Jikun cleared his throat loudly. "You will ask only three and a half questions and you do not get to ask *me* any."

For a moment, Eldaeus stared at him blankly. Then he laughed, sprawling into the grass with a broad smile. "I like you." He set the empty stick into the fire, dropping a hand across his marked forehead. "There *is* a way out of the desert on foot. I can lead you out... *if* you promise to take me in company."

Jikun pursed his lips and regarded the lolling elf cautiously. Did he have a choice? ...Not if he ever wanted to confront Saebellus in this lifetime. "Take you with...?" he repeated.

"I can fight!" Eldaeus grabbed the end of the stick still protruding from the flames and tossed it at him. "I will show you!" he announced as he scurried down the hill.

Jikun scrambled away from the smoldering stick, letting out a yelp. "Insane!"

"What a grasp of the obvious," Navon snickered.

Eldaeus reappeared swiftly at the crest, two sticks in hand. "Here. One for you. One for you. And…" he trailed off, looking at his empty hands. His head snapped down to where Jikun sat and he glared suspiciously. Then he snatched the stick from the general and snapped it over his knee. Jikun extended his hand for his new, equally pitiful weapon, but the maniacal elf was apparently not done with his task. Jikun could only watch dumbly as he rotated the three until he had the longest and Jikun and Navon were each left with half a stick.

Darcarus, who had returned with his promised and enormous branch, was ignored entirely.

"And one for me," Eldaeus finished. He thrust his weapon skyward, wasting no time. "I shall defeat you!" he declared loudly, voice echoing across the dome.

"Fine," Jikun grunted in exasperation, rising to his feet. To lose a battle to this male—even in his beaten body—would be a crime against a general's very essence.

"Wait, what is going on?" Darcarus demanded as he raised his shaft. "Why do you all have sticks?"

But there was no response. Jikun remained far above divulging anything about what he had idiotically agreed to.

Navon, however, seemed eager to begin. Perhaps he was covertly hopeful that his old general would be bested by this lunatic.

Jikun glowered.

"Can we use magic?—Er, can Jikun use magic?"

Darcarus waved his branch threateningly. "Gods damn you all, I was gone for a minute. What did I miss?!"

And as if he did not even exist, Eldaeus pranced about eagerly from foot to foot, nodding vigorously at Navon. "Use magic? Anything you like! Anything at all!"

Jikun sighed and dropped the stick. He flicked a finger and in an instant, the Faraven stood frozen in a block of ice, nothing but his head still free.

"Marvelous!" Eldaeus spoke in awe, attempting to wiggle free. "Truly marvelous!"

Jikun regarded him vacantly. All the theatrics and excitement for *this?* "That was it? That is all you can do?" He stepped back and stumbled suddenly, catching the side of the stick with his ankle as his other foot held it in place. He lurched backward and tumbled into the fire. "Fuck! Shit! Damn it!" he swore as he scrambled out of the flames, knocking his back against the considerable block of ice.

It teetered and lurched toward him, threatening to smash him beneath its several hundred pounds. Jikun swiftly commanded the ice to melt, but had only partially succeeded by the time it slammed him to the ground.

"...Gods..." Jikun groaned as the rest of the ice melted away.

Eldaeus promptly sat upon his back, pressing the stick to Jikun's neck. "Ta-da!"

"...You are delirious," Jikun croaked. "You didn't wi—"

He grunted as Eldaeus pushed off of him, raising the birch toward the stream as though to silent applause. "So, what say you?" he asked, pivoting to face the pair. "Will you have me?"

Darcarus gave a single clap of approval. "I don't know what in the Nine Realms just happened, but he is coming with us."

Navon reached down and helped Jikun to his feet. "Are you alright? *Really*," he attempted to query without revealing the chuckles slipping in beneath.

Jikun glowered, knocking the palm away. He was far too mortified to complain about his injuries *now*. "Of course I am alright." He viewed the Faraven cynically, brushing his chest off with mild indignation. "You really know a way out of the desert?"

Eldaeus' head flopped forward violently. "Of course I do. I was escorted here, remember? I recall the way out. The *only* way out!"

The unease in the humidity was suddenly tangible. Darcarus' complexion paled until it was hardly a shade darker than the tundra. "Are you talking about the *Pass?*"

Eldaeus flashed an innocent grin. "Yeeeeeeeeeeeeeeeeeeesssss I am, angry one! Come frolic amongst the grass and your pouting air will disappear!"

Darcarus reached out abruptly to strangle the male, but the elf leapt aside with a mad cackle. "You said you had a safe way out of the desert!" he growled. "We are going to leave you in this—"

"Wonderfully luscious cavern?" Jikun interrupted pointedly. "Not allow him to suffer and die like we are apparently about to do?"

Darcarus' mouth clamped shut briefly. "You are right." He hurled his branch away. "He deserves this fate."

Navon possessed too much curiosity to refuse communication with the True Blood now. "What fate are you suggesting? Surely it cannot be worse than your plan to fight Relstavum with our battered, broken company."

Eldaeus was a painting of pure elation. "There is no need to be so upset. The way is only teeming with the undead of the Lost Infantry Regiment from

The War of Dragons." He wiggled his fingers gleefully before their noses, and Jikun had half a mind to snap them like the skinny, little twigs they were. "They skulk and slink and sneak about the path, still honor-bound to their duty to defend the pass from Het's horde. You two do not look like dragons or Sel'vi, but they are only undead—I do not think they can tell the difference anymore."

"No one even knows where that path is because it is *suicide*." Darcarus gave the grass an angry kick.

Jikun knit his brow, watching the sand fly high and vanish into the darkness. He knew of the Lost Infantry Regiment—he had studied it in Darival's academies beneath the overbearing intellect of the institute's most prestigious scholar. Led by Captain Aritos to defend the pass through the Aenid Mountains from the horde of Het, every last male had been slaughtered by dragon fire. He could name every lieutenant. Every marshal. And the notion that the stories of his scrolls had come to life… He would have enjoyed a disbelieving laugh, but he feared encouraging the already manic Faraven. "You believe that tale of sprite whispers?"

As Eldaeus detected the disquiet, he emitted a shameless giggle. Then he dropped his voice to a whisper, one hardly audible over their own breath. "*The Pass of the Dead.*"

Jikun struck a palm across his brow. "Gods. *The Pass of the Dead?* From where in Ramul did you fashion that name?"

Darcarus remained staunchly unnerved. "This is not something Eldaeus contrived. The Eph'vi would never travel out of the northern mountain range on foot. The notion is utterly absurd. Certainly, there must be some amount of exaggeration to the tale, but that an entire race of people has avoided the Pass for millennia signifies that it must bear some *semblance* of truth."

"Yes. Like: it's a pass through the mountains and you're dead if you don't get your ass through it," Jikun muttered with a scoff. "The 'Pass of the Dead.' You all should be ashamed."

Navon winced.

"Oh please," Jikun carried on with an exaggerated moan. "How many times have *you*, Navon, a *necromancer*, seen a corpse running about on its own? I certainly have not. I have seen your wisps and skulls, but no actual bodies. And yet you are telling me there is a whole *army* of dead that got up and congregated in this god-damn desert of all places, just to hamper passersby?"

Navon's face fell at Jikun's rather pathetic image of their qualms. "That is not how the dead work…" he attempted.

But Jikun was chortling now. "And even so, *corporeal* entities can be managed. It's the smoke that is downright impossible." His mind flickered with images of the twisting tendrils flaying Eph'ven citizens. "The Pass would be a *godsend* after Dahel."

Navon's expression lost its mild annoyance and his foot stomped impatiently at the jest. "Just CEASE speaking! We are not simply talking about a *few* rotten corpses. Do you really know so little about magic?!"

"That would explain why I am so bad at mine, would it not?"

Navon was not amused. "And why you have such an absurd prejudice against necromancy," he readily shot back.

Eldaeus rocked onto his heels to observe in a shameless gape.

Jikun loured. "I have gotten by just *fine* without knowing."

"*Barely*, Jikun. And your ineptitude must cease. If you were merely dismissing the Pass, I could possibly overlook your ignorance yet again, but you agreed to Darcarus' ridiculous plan to hunt down an obscenely powerful necromancer! You will need me. You will need *my* magic. And you need to understand what you are going to face. Relstavum will not be like you—casting a few spells and then falling to the ground in a weakened heap. Relstavum can fight *endlessly*. Like I can. *Unlike you. Unlike Darcarus.* Necromancers do not become *tired*. You respected the Beast, and yet my magic was the only force strong enough to seriously harm it. If you do not kill Relstavum as soon as you engage him—if you lose the upper edge—he can defend against your attacks perpetually. You will end up sprawled on your back, begging for him to kill you, or you will accomplish the deed yourself through your inexperience and overexertion."

Jikun's lips drew taut. "And what makes you two so special?"

"Now you sound like an indignant child. That is not what I am inferring. You are unique… you just never did anything with your gift."

"Because I was already the best."

Navon's expression acidified.

"I never had time, Navon! In Darival, every elf was a cyromancer. There was no academy for 'honing your skill.' Magic was innate. *Everyone* had the gift. You started throwing ice beneath the feet of your parents the moment you could run from them. So mastering it was purely a matter of time and effort."

"And you were too busy whoring."

Jikun shot him an incredulous glare. "No, I was steeped in academy books on military strategies and histories—in between hunting thakish and swordplay. Do you think I could have become the general by merely throwing a show of ice before the council?"

"I think, back on Sevrigel, a *dung* beetle could have become the general if he had the right connections to the council."

"...I am too dumbstruck to be offended. And you have about five seconds to articulate your point before I use my better judgment to decide this conversation is over."

Navon hastened to keep the general's attention, though he was forced to elevate his voice as Eldaeus, bored of the direction of their conversation, began howling a painful tune in the ancient elven tongue. "Each magic has a price. Most forms of magic utilize two sources of power." He raised his fingers to signal the two forms, as though Jikun needed such basic mathematical assistance. Perhaps he was suggesting the prince needed it too, but the Sel'ven had already lost interest and was unabashedly examining Eldaeus' trinkets.

He was likely fully aware of the technicalities of magic. He had, after all, summoned a dragon.

"The first is innate ability. It can be likened to... potential muscle mass," Navon continued. "As hard as an elf trains his body, he will never achieve the size of a human who does the equivalent. Each individual's innate level of magic holds the same concept—though it is rarely determined by race, but rather by heritage and favor of the gods. Two innately powerful mages are likely to beget an innately powerful child, as in my case. But sometimes the bestowal of striking magical power is seemingly random—it is just as possible to find an innately powerful mage whose parents are of no note in some little city in the middle of a frozen tundra."

Jikun pursed his lips. *'He means me, doesn't he? Bastard.'*

Darcarus seemed to be listening enough to counter the Helven's insults. "The difference, Jikun, is what you choose to do with that innate gift," the True Blood attempted to reassure him.

Navon glared at the prince. "But even *if* you should decide to utilize it," he continued loudly, "there is a second qualifier to that magical potential: the health of the caster. Magic courses through our bodies—"

"Does *all* of this have to do with what I need to understand about Relstavum?" Jikun barked. "Because I feel like we are sliding into a lesson that I don't give two shits to learn."

"Well try to give at least *one*. You do need to know all of this, 'damn it,'" Navon insisted adamantly. "And it's about time you understood and desisted from berating my magical use. Magic is all around you—it is why you lost the war. It is how we escaped Dahel. It is what Darcarus used to keep the hel'onja from devouring you."

"Yes, and you have yet to praise my magical prowess," Darcarus agreed absentmindedly as he looked up from where he was turning Eldaeus' bracelet about.

Jikun fell silent.

"Now… as I was saying… The health of the caster. Right. Expending magic exhausts your body; like running, jumping, or climbing, spell casting exerts the caster's energy and strains the body. To a caster like you, who simply treats his gift as 'cast-on-whim,' it's the same as a sickly child with no muscle mass attempting to scale a mountain. You expend very little before your strength wears out—your magic becomes sporadic or wild, then eventually dies all together."

Jikun was listening a little more intently now, despite the continued insults. He had always been aware of how quickly his physical strength was drained, but on more than one occasion, such a weakness had nearly caused his death; the thakish in Darival and the Sevilan Marshes came prominently to mind.

"And like training with an ill body, harmful consequences can result. Instead of pulling a muscle, your magic could end up out of control. Just as you berate my magic for threatening me, Jikun, *you* use your untrained magic with the risk that it could severely injure or even *kill* you. Magic must be used, nurtured, and strengthened the same as you train your body," Navon continued. "And as for your body, when it grows weak, as yours has since leaving Sevrigel, every spell is that much more taxing and difficult to complete. You have always had a high innate ability *and* excellent physical form—though I can't say so right *now*—but your magic is like the muscle you never use. A trained mage with half your talent and half your health could best you with hardly any effort."

Jikun bristled. "I would like to—"

"See them try? Really? Do you truly believe you could win?"

Jikun fell silent. Even in excellent form, as he had been in Darival, after a few spells he had tumbled from the back of Nazra and had nearly been devoured by the pursuing thakish.

Kaivervi's visage came suddenly to mind and he shoved it stiffly aside. *'Now of all times?!'* "What else do you have to say?" he insisted swiftly.

Navon paused. "…And now we come to necromancy."

"By Sel'ari's cunt, *finally*," Jikun swore, feeling relief that his lack of knowledge would soon be amended and he could despise necromancy to his fullest potential.

The Helven's indignation flared. "I will stop right here."

Judging by Darcarus' slant away from him, he seemed mutually offended.

Jikun gestured apologetically. *'Not the time to provoke him,'* he chastised himself. "You can't stop here. I cannot have listened to all this and never reached the god-damn point."

It was likely only due to the desire to explain his own talents that Navon continued despite the blasphemy. "All of this was the 'god-damn point,' Jikun." He waited for the Darivalian to fall silent and adopt a superficial mask of regret. "Physical health. Innate ability. These are the requirements for *most* magics. *Necromancy* is an exception. The strength of a necromancer is based partially on innate ability, but *overwhelmingly* on the tenacity of his own soul. Let me use Tiras as an example."

Here was a historical figure every humanoid knew—from the most secluded dwarf to the grimiest of goblins. And every elf knew his story by the age of five. "Go on."

"Tiras is often depicted as a rather gaunt, at times even sickly, Helven who traveled many miles on mercenary work, sleeping on the dirt and eating a rather poor diet. And yet, without question, he was the most powerful necromancer on Aersadore. He certainly had innate ability, but more than that, Tiras' soul was strong. He was extremely self-aware and strong of will, certain in himself and his character, and he disciplined his soul as though it was his very body—utilizing it through spell-training until it far surpassed his physical strength. He could come and go from the Realms as though he were walking in and out of a blacksmith, picking up whatever souls he needed to weaponize his spells. And his strength of character allowed him to not just reach the *First* Gate of the Realms, but the Second, Third, Fifth… even, they say, the *Ninth*."

"I'm a heathen, Navon. I assume these gate numbers should impress me… but they do not."

Navon sighed and Darcarus looked back toward him with an expression that suggested that now, even he found the Darivalian to be an utter fool. Jikun brushed the dusting of grains that coated his flesh, trying to swipe away the prince's expression.

Navon ignored the prince and instead replied, "I could write a book for you, but I will try to be concise: there are Nine Gates in the Realms of the Dead. And I *assume* you actually *know* what the Realms are—the gateway to the gods?"

"...Don't you dare be insolent with me," Jikun warned, raising his hand.

Navon stepped swiftly out of reach as he carried on. "They form what I will call, for your sake, a 'tunnel to Emal'drathar.' Once through the Ninth Gate, your soul rests with your god. Before that, it has to pass through the Gates. The Gate Guardians of each respective Gate force souls through and on toward their god, and the Gates' pull on the souls increases in strength at each new gate—thus only the strongest, most resistant souls can manage to remain in the Ninth Gate long enough to be retrieved."

Nine Gates teeming with the varying strengths of the dead—Jikun could grasp that. But... "*Why* in Emal'drathar would the gods create gates where necromancers could steal their followers' souls? I would think the gods *want* the souls for themselves—not torn apart or obliterated on the surface."

"They did not create the Gateways, Jikun. Tiras did. *Tiras* created the Gates as a way for necromancers to utilize their power. In hopes that one could truly resurrect the dead. Before that, only the Realm existed—a solitary pathway to the gods with a single, powerful pull—the pull of what is now the Ninth Gate. No necromancer could dare enter because the tug would be so instantaneous, so powerful, that their soul would simply be swept onward to Emal'drathar.

"So the only souls a necromancer could utilize were sparse. The Guardian—now the First—was swift to gather the dead into the Realm. All that was left were the souls in Aersadore who had not yet passed to Emal'drathar—brief and fleeting in their presences—and those fragments defiant enough to overpower the pull of the Realms with anger, hatred, duty, loss, or regret. These were souls that felt so deeply on an emotion that a fragment of their being remained and haunted our realm—like what the Lost Infantry Unit in The Pass suggests. But with the creation of the Gates, weaker necromancers could feign death with a fragment of their own soul and still manage—if they were even moderately strong—to return unscathed."

Jikun wondered how long *he* could manage to remain within the Realms of the Dead so that he did not have to grovel before some asinine god for the rest of eternity. He shook his head and refocused.

"Did you hear me, Jikun? A necromancer even *moderately* strong can enter and depart through the gates. I am more than a 'moderately strong' necromancer. I combated the Beast. I kept Relstavum's serpent at bay—"

"Have you ever brought back the dead?"

"I am well aware of the details, but *I have not had to.* ...And that is beyond moderate necromancy."

"You *died* casting a few spells at the hel'onja."

Navon ignored his point. "What Relstavum's skill suggests—merely by the number of souls he has been able to control... by slaughtering an entire *city* at once—is that he is strong. *Very* strong. He will not tire. He will not lose focus. And so we shall have to strike him while his soul is occupied... by surprise. Consider the Beast. The closest Saebellus' creature ever got to killing me was when it attacked me in the Temple of Sel'ari, before the priests and people—when I was unprepared and unsuspecting. *That* is how we must approach Relstavum. And why you will need *me*. What can ice or dragons do against the union of spirits? You cannot freeze them. You cannot burn them. This is why you *have* to allow me to use my magic when—*if*—we fight Relstavum. "

Jikun pursed his lips.

"And if the Eph'vi were right—if there is a regiment of dead trapped on this plane by honor—then you will need me *again.*"

The haunting face of his captain flickered within the memory of smoke. Navon had protected them from Relstavum's spell inside Dahel, but he had died in their brief battle with the hel'onja. Allow Navon to use necromancy?

He did not believe there had been no cost to the male's mistake.

Still, without that assistance, Saebellus' pawn would certainly have killed them all. "I will consider it, Navon."

As though he had not actually expected to win his point, his captain's eyes widened.

Jikun raised a hand staunchly to prevent the male from battling for a certain victory. "But do not ask again." And truly, why should he bother? The Helven would act as he pleased no matter what Jikun said. "So aside from your hope to use your magic against Relstavum... you are stating that these old, duty-bound souls are quite possibly... *realistically*... roaming about our only escape from this god-forsaken desert."

Eldaeus' singing lapsed into a dramatic sigh. "That was his whole explanation!"

"Careful, he doesn't tolerate ridicule," Navon warned with a smirk.

Jikun pointed warningly at the Faraven. "Remember that." He jerked his head toward the prince. "And you are certain there is no other path out of the Aenid?"

Darcarus nodded regrettably, chewing his thumb. "If there was, I would have ended Navon's rambling while we were still young."

Jikun heaved a sigh. "Eldaeus, we will allow you to accompany us, but our journey will be far from safe. We are hunting a very dangerous man. Still, I suppose we were fortunate to find this place." He rubbed a hand over his face. When it came away sticky with blood, he began to question his own sanity. He remembered a prank he and his brethren had pulled back in the army on those who fell asleep during initiation... except they had used ink instead of blood and the symbols had been crude dwarven anatomy instead of the ancient elven tongue.

Eldaeus clutched a hand to his stomach in glee. "Oh, *I* am the lucky one." He grinned. "Now, we have only to wait a few hundred years and the staircase shall be complete and we can leave!"

Jikun stared at him. Good gods, was every plan doomed to regress?! "*What?* A few *hundred* years? *What* staircase??"

Darcarus glanced over his shoulder, as though attempting to discern this invisible path. "Do you mean the stones we climbed down from?"

And as Jikun followed the Sel'ven's gaze, he had to admit that the rocky aggregation did have the vague resemblance of a crudely hewn staircase. For giants.

Eldaeus draped an arm around the prince's broad shoulders and walked his fingers up the golden buttons on his chest. "There it is. Every few hundred years, a chunk of stone falls from the cavern ceiling. You *did* walk down that way."

"Dropped, is a better description," Jikun replied as Darcarus swiftly brushed the mad elf's arm away. "And we do not need to wait for that." He studied the hole in the distance, a mere black smudge on the vast ceiling. "I can build us a staircase of ice. I just need a few days' rest to recover from our recent trials."

Darcarus gave him a warning glare. "More than that. I told you: I need you to be more than half-dead if we are going to fight Relstavum."

Jikun grunted in acknowledgement, but Eldaeus was already eagerly carrying on. "You will also need to scratch out the runic markings on the cavern entrance. I cannot leave so long as they are present."

Jikun paused, a wary tingle running along the breadth of his arms. The sealing runes… so they were indeed for this male.

Navon frowned, daring to ask the question to which Jikun felt he would rather not know the answer. "*What* did you do—*why* could the council not kill you?"

Eldaeus' face fell ashen, his lips pursing into a line as thin as the markings for his symbols. There was a quaver lurking within his voice as he replied in a hushed tone, "I did a terrible crime. And I am very hard to kill. The first executioner tripped on his way up the stairs and cracked his skull open. The second fell into the floor before me and his collar got caught on a nail and he hanged himself."

Jikun's brows raised in astonished disbelief. What in the name of Ishkav…?

"He is hatching dragons from chicken eggs," Darcarus scoffed.

"They switched to beheading but the executioner was assassinated the night before and the replacement fell on his sword."

"How—?"

"They tried Ulasum's Tooth, but I vomited from fatigue and the executioner recoiled. The poison splashed into his eyes and blinded him. The sixth male simply died on the spot. His heart gave out, they said."

Jikun was not so swift to discount the male's tales. There was gravity in his eyes now, something glimpsed past the insanity. He felt the chill slide up his arm and down his spine.

"They tried a volley of arrows, but one of the archers tripped and shot a councilmember through the head. The eighth—"

Jikun stared at him numbly. "Eighth?"

He could hear Eldaeus carrying on, but the inanities seemed to blur together now. What in Ramul, Emal'drathar… all the gods above was this male rambling on about? How had he dodged even a *single* execution? For what crimes were they so determined to kill him? He stared at the suddenly foreboding symbols etched across the elf's body. And why was he covered in such markings? Clearly they must have been etched before he was "imprisoned"—unless a vial of jasebulem ink had dropped from the sky "by luck" for him as well.

"At the end of the twelfth they stopped. I am glad that they did, because the next would have been thirteen. And everyone knows how unlucky thirteen is!" Eldaeus' tone had recovered through the course of his chronicle, and he was now beaming once more in a toothy grin.

"Thir… teen?"

"Yes. Thirteen—ever since the thirteenth son of the human King Rogen of Candoria was born a cripple and infected his family with a plague that drove them all to become insane cannibals."

"The Cadorian Plague. I remember that story," Darcarus announced triumphantly.

Navon latched onto the immediate opportunity for superiority. "Couldn't remember something *useful* from history," he muttered.

"Shall I reflect on those questions of yours?"

Navon crossed his arms, endeavoring to ignore the male. "I don't understand," he directed to Eldaeus. "If they wanted you dead, why would they have locked you in a place like this? This is an oasis. *Clearly* you would have—you *have* had—no problems surviving down here."

"Oh, they did not *know* this was here! They sealed me inside the cave and I clawed and dug my way, trying to escape. When I had dug deep enough, the ground below me suddenly crumbled into little, tiny pieces! I fell and fell and fell and thought it was the end, but no! Lo and behold, I discovered this secret oasis!" And then he began to belt out a tune in ancient elven, glorifying his victory.

Jikun could only blink. What had broken his fall if the great, stone "stairs" had not been present hundreds… or *thousands*… of years ago? "Wouldn't that attempt have been the thirteenth time?"

Darcarus' nostrils flared as he pressed his palms to his ears. "Perhaps they confined him here on account of his voice. I would consider it."

Eldaeus merely grinned as he bounded down the hill. "I have to gather food for our journey!" he sang as he went. "Foooood fooooorrrrr yooouuu!" And then immediately returned to croaking the atrocious ancient elven tune he had been howling during Navon's lecture.

Navon squinted with similar discomfort. "It is almost as bad as Jikun's poetry."

Darcarus' hands fell away, his lips parting in mock surprise. "What did you just say? A Darivalian who writes poetry? Is the concept even possible?"

Navon leaned over with a whisper of amusement in his little secret. "If you read it, you would know the answer to that question is a resounding 'no.'"

Jikun scowled, though he did not respond to the insult. "Maybe if he sang something different… Eldaeus!" he barked. "Sing something else! *The Ballad of The War of Dragons*, *Sel'ari's Blessing*, *Emerol*, or anything, as long as it is not… *that* or *The Ballad of the Seven.*"

"Oh, sing *The Ballad of the Seven,*" Darcarus disagreed. "I despised that song for years, but Hadoream and I sang it near twenty or thirty times on our journey to Dahel. I have grown rather fond of it."

"Do not dare," Jikun reproached.

Eldaeus pivoted, prancing backward as he sang, "I do not know that one!"

Giving the Faraven an amused shake of his head, Darcarus laughed. "*The Ballad of the Seven?* Of course you do. Why count your blessings when men before have lost what they thought they had? Or number your allies in times prewar, when loyalties are not yet bled? Know that the man who stands at your side…" he trailed off as Eldaeus regarded him blankly and paused beneath a fruit tree. "No…?"

Darcarus seemed genuinely perplexed, and Jikun imagined that the True Bloods were reared with even greater indoctrination of Eraydon's tales than the average elf. After all, it was they alone who had remained on Ryekarayn for centuries after their allied humans betrayed the elven kind. Even after the elves' trade crumbled and hostilities rose to tear their kingdom down, they had persisted—all in an attempt to honor the hero's legendary sacrifice.

Darcarus insisted, "With blood they fought the trials north, and with blood they fought to flee, 'til all the dust had settled forth, and seven were left to be?"

A few too many verses had been recited for Jikun's taste, but he graciously forgave the offense. "*Everyone* knows that ballad, Eldaeus," he interrupted before Darcarus could utter the whole ballad. "Unfortunately. …The legend of Eraydon… Tiras, Mesheck, Aura, Riphath, Taine, and Ephraim?"

The Faraven's shoulders rolled dismissively and he reached up to pluck a fattened fruit. "No. I do not know them." He spun round once more, carrying on in ancient elven the terrible melody he had previously been squawking. Except now his mouth was full.

"…Doesn't know who Eraydon is…?" Darcarus mused. "And I thought *I* was a bad student."

The brows of the Helven fixed high. "How can anyone not know the tale? Every dwarf, elf, orc, and human who has ever *lived* knows that story."

The sea green hair bounced faintly with the Faraven's hopping. Jikun drummed his fingers against his lower lip. "Everyone who lived after them, you mean."

With slow realization, Navon's jaw dropped. "What are you suggesting…? That he is *older* than them? Jikun, that would make him well over *nine* thousand. I have only heard of a *handful* of elves enduring past *three* thousand since the elves abandoned Ryekarayn. That would suggest that he is—"

"A True Blood," Darcarus finished. "The Faravi *were* the only race whose bloodline was never polluted by mingling with the elves who abandoned Ryekarayn—you know, given that they were all massacred before Eraydon's war. I suppose, when you consider the extent of that tragedy, he is far more likely a True Blood than a descendant of that night."

Jikun watched Eldaeus frolic once more, the sunlight gleaming down upon his pristine leather armor. Beneath it, the scale armor glittered gold and bronze in equal perfection.

Time seemed to have forgotten the male.

Yet if this bizarre elf had survived that unspeakable night, perhaps some explanation for his insanity was to be had.

Chapter Thirteen

It was well into Jerah's day when the cellar door opened. He pushed up from his stomach and rocked onto his wide heels, watching as the torchlight bobbed into view.

"Jerah?" his master whispered softly into the gloom.

Jerah's eyes shrank to narrow slits as the elf raised the torch above his head.

"Jerah, you are being released," his master spoke softly, setting the torch into the holder.

Hesitantly, Jerah stood. Released? So soon? He had not been allowed out save for once since he had failed to kill that necromancer in the temple… Master's master had been furious and that anger had carried over to swift punishment for Jerah. He cocked his head slightly, absently pulling at his knotted hair with dirty fingers. Blood was still caked beneath his nails. "Today?" he asked slowly.

The ring of keys jingled in the elf's hand as he squinted in the dimness to locate the correct one. "Yes. Now," he replied impatiently, kicking aside a shard of the broken orange stone.

Jerah hardly noticed. The pounding in his chest rose swiftly as the key turned in the locks, first at his ankles, then his wrists. For a moment, Jerah watched the elf struggle to lift them, then he leaned down and plucked the shackles from his master's hand. Jerah tossed them behind him. They struck with a crack through the stone and a booming echo in the tiny room.

His master's brows knit faintly as he glanced at the broken stone. "Jerah, you are to kill Lord Kinraeus of the Noc'olari," he spoke firmly when their eyes met again. "You are to leave no witnesses. You are to speak to absolutely no one. You are to make certain you are not followed. You are to complete this task swiftly and discretely. And, Jerah, you are to return here *immediately* after the task is finished."

Jerah rubbed his raw wrists as he listened. "I am to go to the surface?" *The surface.* He could not hide the eagerness that crossed his face—the expression that raised the corner of his mouth slightly. His jaw flexed at the thought of the smells that would envelop him—the tastes that seemed to ride the twisting air.

"*Yes*, Jerah. The surface. When you leave this place, you will go to the northern bridge—it will be unguarded for a short span of time. You will travel west along the canyon until you reach a great city built into a tree. At the top of the tree is a room with columns of naked bitches at the doors. Kinraeus should be there. If he is not, wait for him to return. He is white-skinned and grey-eyed. His hair is…" He paused, eyes sweeping the cellar until they landed on one of Jerah's stones. He swept it up. "His hair is the color of this stone and pale grey—can you imagine what this color is?"

Jerah tried to embed pale grey into the rich, dark purple of his stone. "Yes…" he replied slowly. He found his mind had simply swirled the two together, but he wished to go to the surface enough to lie.

"What a smart boy," his master praised with a twisted smile. "And you are to kill him. Rip him as you did the others. You must be certain he is dead." His voice soured. "Kinraeus has been plotting with the human king to overthrow Saebellus. We will be attacking their realm soon, but in the chaos of that battle, he might escape. That is why it must be done *tonight*, Jerah. There is no mercy if you fail."

It was a simple enough request and Jerah felt his excitement barely contained. "I will do that," he replied confidently. Then he frowned. "What… are naked bitches?"

His master had opened his mouth to continue, but stopped. His dark brows knit, his eyes rolled, and his thin lips pursed. This expression sent a wave of irritation through Jerah. "Women, Jerah… They look as you and I do, but they are thinner, shorter… they have breasts, here." He gestured to the front of Jerah's chest and stopped as Jerah's blank expression clearly did not inspire confidence. "Like this stone—but larger. Two of them. *Fucking Ramul*, Jerah."

Jerah simply gave a single nod. He had more questions about these women-type columns, and why they were also called bitches, but his master seemed to have run out of patience. Jerah could only deduce that bitches were naked.

"You may go now, Jerah."

Jerah's mind snapped immediately to attention. "Yes, Master," he grinned. He dashed to the stairs, vaulting up the uneven stone and through the large wooden door before his master had even closed his mouth.

Jerah stopped there, vision adjusting to the dimness of the vast world. Stone and wood lay broken about him, and vines twisted through the shattered windows of the crumbling tower. The only sound was of his master slowly climbing the stairs below.

But none of these were Jerah's concern. Beside a pile of shattered rocks there was a door embedded in the ground. Jerah eagerly pulled it up and dropped within.

And here, the darkness was complete.

Jerah paused to inhale deeply, body rippling with excitement. The surrounding stench of dirt, water, and feces welcomed Jerah to its home: Elvorium's sewer system. He silently moved into the increasing stench while rats scattered to avoid his massive boots.

Soon the tunnel ended and there was only murky water, thick with grime and the occasional bloated, floating rodent. Jerah jumped into the murk, pleased that the water rose only to his knees. As he trudged along, the pounding in his chest grew more feverish. His leathery wings trembled with trepidation. Ever present in his mind was the danger that his master had warned him about—the price to remain on the surface.

He had to travel swiftly.

The water level sank lower and lower until only inches remained and then, there was the circle of light. The torch in the sky shone through the grates in the cobblestone as rays of soft, white light. It gave Jerah a peaceful, safe feeling—more even than the cellar.

He waited and he listened.

There was only silence.

Jerah climbed the ladder below the grate and sniffed the air. Dirt, food, stone, and a harsh, rancid smell—but no elves. Jerah pushed the grate open, peering up cautiously.

The surface. It was enchanting—dark, quiet, and dangerous. The black void above him was scattered with thousands of distant torches and a strange, half-circle torch that changed shape every time Jerah surfaced. But unlike the torch in his cell, this torch was always lit—even dimly. Tonight, it left several wisps of smoke around it, blanketing sections of the void above.

Jerah's chest swelled. He forgot the ache in his ankles and wrists as he slipped to the familiar statue beside a great bridge, blending into the shadows. He looked up at it briefly. Many times he had recalled the fierce, elven faces. Even in their state, they still seemed to breathe life. Jerah hoped that, should he ever fail to kill someone and be turned to stone as they had, he looked half as lively.

Jerah sharply turned his head away at the thought. *'Focus!'* he reprimanded himself. *'Unless you too want to be turned to stone!'* And the rebuke propelled him quickly over the great bridge and infinite chasm of darkness that gaped below.

Then Jerah's feet touched the soft, moist earth and he tore off into the darkness. He had traveled many times over great distances when he had hunted General Taemrin and his army, journeying by the light of the white torch and sleeping as it vanished toward the distance.

But that was before Saebellus had defeated them. Jerah alone had never been able to do the deed. They had had a *necromancer.*

Jerah scowled deeply to himself. The evil creatures with their foul magic… Master hated them. Jerah hated them too. He found his forehead had become knit with disgust as he remembered that skeletal elf he had tried so hard to kill at the temple. It was the one creature Jerah had failed against. And, Jerah reasoned, it was undoubtedly why Saebellus had struggled so long against Taemrin.

Still, Saebellus' victory now meant little time on the surface for Jerah… And he missed its wonders dearly. Previously, the most magnificent thing he had ever seen had been General Taemrin. He had seen many things in his travels: wretched smelling plants of varying wild colors, great stones that towered off in the distance, and countless distant torches flickering high up in the void… But General Taemrin had been starkly different than anything he had seen before. Taemrin looked like he had been carved out of stone and attached with long, wild blue hair and fierce eyes of a strange and chilling color. If Jerah had been the one to kill him, he definitely would have kept his eyes.

'But Master never lets me keep trinkets from my killings,' he thought resentfully.

As Jerah moved down the shrinking cliff, after a time breaking to the edge of the forest line, General Taemrin vanished from his mind like the white torch beneath its smoke. Now *this* was the most magnificent thing Jerah had ever seen. He drew to a sharp stop beside a bush, staring wide-eyed in wonder: a white tree reached up so high into the void that it seemed to touch the torches with the tips of its shining grey leaves.

"Lord Kinraeus lives there…" he breathed in awe. *'He must be the greatest of all males!'*

But to get into the tree… Many tents stretched below it, like a scattering of tiny white pebbles, and countless elves moved about between them. Why weren't they sleeping? Elves were supposed to sleep while he was awake! He muttered to himself, irritated that so many were awake. There had never been so many awake before!

But Jerah did not let their presence deter him for long; *he* was cunning. His eyes followed the tree line to the right where the number of tents grew sparse. Swiftly and silently, he darted behind the nearest tent. And the next. He smiled to himself at his rapid stealth: the Noc'olari had no idea that he was there.

Finally, he stepped through a great archway of the magnificent tree. It was all the more awing on the inside. The trunk had been hollowed into winding white staircases and countless levels of buildings.

Jerah suddenly wrinkled his nose, gagging sharply. But gods, what was that smell? Immediately Jerah darted for the very top of the stairs, hoping to escape the wretched scent. Higher and higher Jerah climbed until his legs grew sore and his breath fell short.

Did the elves climb this every day? Why, they must do nothing but wake and climb up and down!

He drew to a stop at the top. There were only two doors here, flanked on either side by the bitch columns that held, what appeared to Jerah, stone reflections of the void.

His eyes dilated and his wings pressed against his back. A drive overcame him at the sight—the pounding entered his head, tuning his ears to the slightest whispers.

Jerah made a single, swift glance about him and grabbed the metal connecting the bolted door to the wooden frame. It popped off with a loud crack and Jerah laid it down silently. Then he darted through the opening.

The rancid smell emanating from inside was stifling. Jerah's eyes watered as he stepped back out of the room, gagging. What *was* that smell?! He growled softly before taking a deep inhale. Holding his breath, he stepped back into the room.

Immediately, Jerah's eyes locked onto two figures lying in the bed. He crept silently beside them, studying the hair of the heads poking out from under the blankets. He cocked his head slightly. They were like the purple of his stone… but lighter. Almost as though grey had been spread over them.

His master had said nothing about two Kinraeuses!

Jerah suddenly found his chest hurting and he remembered that he had to breathe. He inhaled sharply and gagged. Damn that smell! He held his breath again and raised his fist above the head of the male nearest him.

It was a swift, solid blow that sent the skull into itself with a soft crunch. The eyes of the figure beside him flew open and locked onto Jerah, its mouth parting wordlessly. His master had given him this expression before—when Jerah had smashed a rat in front of him.

Disgusting, he had explained. This elf must find him disgusting as well.

The thought angered Jerah and he found his upper lip had raised, revealing his long fangs.

"Ilra save me!" the male cried in a high-pitched tone, scrambling to get out of the bed. "Gods! Kinraeus!" As the covers fell from his chest, Jerah gasped in surprise and wonder.

The male was actually a bitch column… but not made of stone! Jerah forgot about the body of Kinraeus and moved swiftly toward the column. Her body was soft and smooth—she appeared made of the same flesh as elves.

Why, *this* was more magnificent than even the great tree!

He started to ask her how she moved, but then the words of his master rushed back to him. *Speak to absolutely no one*. He closed his mouth again.

'Forget the column, Jerah,' he scolded himself. It did not matter how it could move. He simply had to rip Kinraeus up and be gone.

But the column scrambled toward the unmoving elf. "Kinraeus! Kinraeus!" it screeched. "Run!"

However, the blow, lethal or not, had disabled the elf.

Still, the column would not fall silent. Perhaps the cries would bring the Noc'olari. Jerah would simply shatter it and be done! He stretched out his arm, feeling disappointed that he had to break such a fascinating piece of architecture.

"Back! Back!" it cried, grabbing a nearby box and flinging it at Jerah's head.

But Jerah simply tipped his head down, letting it crack against his horns. Then he picked the statue up. It twisted and flailed, forcing him to tighten his grip… and he found that it bent easily beneath him—not at all as stone should. Its shrieks only grew louder.

"Put me down! Release me, please! PLEASE!"

Wait… his master had said he could not talk to *anyone*… but a column was not an *anyone*. Of course! How foolish of him! "You need to be quiet," he ordered firmly.

Instantly the column whimpered into silence. "Please," it whispered. "Do not kill me..."

Kill? Jerah raised a brow. "I cannot kill what is not alive," he replied. But he felt very foolish explaining this to the column. Although its confused facial expressions were remarkably elven, it could not possibly have a concept of life and death.

Jerah set it beside the bed. "Be silent or I will have to break you," he warned.

It covered its face, trembling. "Did you kill Kinraeus?"

Jerah wondered this himself. He moved back over to the elf and studied him. "I do not know. I will make sure."

But the column grabbed his soaked pant leg and tugged at it feverishly. "Please, please! Please spare him! Please!!" it cried desperately.

Despite its nature, something about it touched Jerah. He found its pleading difficult to hear and his body willed him to let the column have its way. It was such a sad little thing. He put a finger to his lips. "No more sounds," he ordered. "Or I will throw you out the window." He reached forward, sank his claws into Kinraeus' chest, and tore the rib out.

The column seemed to die then—it collapsed against the floor and did not move. Jerah's chest felt tight—he was sorry to see it go. But he forced himself to attend to the elf.

When he finished, he wiped his hands on his shirt. Suddenly his eyes began to sting again and he realized that the terrible smell was unceasingly present. He had just killed someone—he had time before he would turn into stone. But this smell? It had no more time!

He sniffed—it was coming from near the window. He slunk angrily across the room, his growl growing deeper as the rancid smell intensified.

And then he spotted it. There, on the edge of the window, sat a strangely curved cup sprouting brightly colored, vine-like objects. Like the Sel'vi kept.

Jerah picked up the glass and hurled it across the room, feeling satisfied as it shattered into the wall beyond.

Two enemies slain that night.

Task complete, he darted swiftly out of the room and glanced just once, sadly, at the bitch column. He was going to miss it. Perhaps he could find another someday...

And as Jerah stepped through the broken frame of the room, he came to an abrupt stop.

What if he didn't...? What if he wasn't let out of his cell again?

Saebellus no longer had much use for him… Master had told him this. Told him he would not be needed often now…!

Jerah shivered at the thought. The raw skin of his wrists and ankles ached, burning before the shackles even touched them.

He had been released only twice recently. *Twice*. In the past, he had been forced to endure many freezing eras in a cellar. With only the rare visits of his master to keep him company, he had barely clawed through the loneliness.

What if Jerah returned now only to endure *longer* silence?!

He stepped slowly away from the stairs, resistance rising in his belly.

Maybe he *should* have let Kinraeus continue his work with the human king! *Maybe* such a thing would have meant more work for Jerah! His fists clenched. He could *not* sit through another age beneath the earth!

But could he leave his master?

Jerah wrapped his wings around himself. The better question was, could he *survive* without him?

Jerah considered this carefully as his claws dug into the wood for comfort. Master kept him safe. Fed him. Released him. Brought him things to entertain himself. And Master had always warned him of the cost of life on the surface: for every day he lived, another person must die. It was a brutal existence…

He rubbed his forehead across the frame. The cell was safe… the cell was safe…

But when Jerah looked back out to the stairs, he recoiled again. The same hunger that drove him to kill was now refusing to obey. Why could he *not* care for himself? He could take food from mansions—he smelled it everywhere. And he could easily avoid being turned to stone—he had seen no shortage of elves to kill.

Jerah's jaw set.

Yes. *He could be his own master.*

And with that thought, Jerah tore down the stairs and out of the great tree. To *his* surface… *his* freedom. His eyes lifted boldly to the white torch in the sky…

And his gaze faltered. A problem still remained: Elves hunted for *the beast*. They knew he existed. Since Saebellus' war, Jerah had heard the males speak of mercenaries that hunted for him. They would do to him what he did to the elves.

The feeling that rose in Jerah sent him swiftly into the darkness of the trees. What was it like to cease to live…? No waking was… eternal darkness?

Like… being in the cellar day after day with no torch.

But there was one place that he had heard of… Where he *could* be safe.

The realization caused his wings to unfold from his body. "You are smart, Jerah," he reminded himself of his master's recent praise.

His master had spoken of the place often. The place where the dumb and the weak lived—the place of humans and dwarves. In that land, he would be safe. That place.

Ryekarayn.

CHAPTER FOURTEEN

Alvena craned her neck around the archway of one of the twelve entry doors to the magnificent white tree of Galadorium. She stood on the tips of her toes as she peered into the luminescent interior, eyes wide with marvel as she regarded the stunning magnificence of the place. The floor was a smooth, white wood, and all about its reverberating surface rose ornately carved pillars and winding staircases. The buildings inside were innumerable, in shapes and sizes rivaling any the capital had to offer: except that each was carved of the tree itself, seamless with the wall or floor it extended from.

It was an entire city engraved into the ancient tree!

And *this* morning the city was alive with hushed whispers and frantic footsteps. Itirel was gone and she had no one to bother about what had occurred in the night while she had slept. The humans were being questioned and many were being promptly escorted from the city, regardless of their condition. Alvena could only assume that *whatever* had occurred had left the Noc'olari wary of their human guests.

She tiptoed onto the wooden floor, daring to slip in through the archway. She knew she wasn't *supposed* to enter the Noc'olarian city, but no one was around. She closed her eyes and inhaled heavily. It smelled much like Hairem's scribe's room, thick with the scent of old parchment and dust.

And just like in that stiff Sel'ven's abode, she wasn't supposed to touch anything. Hmph!

"What are you doing in here?" a voice berated as it hurried past.

Alvena's eyes shot open in surprise. No one *had* been around.

The female glared reproachfully. "You had best return to your tent."

Alvena donned a sheepish smile as the woman disappeared around a pillar. Ha! *Return to her tent* when such excitement swelled about her? She snorted and strutted to a narrow, winding staircase. She patted the banister, finding it to be as smooth as glass, and followed its trail to study the figures in the distance.

A door above her to the left opened abruptly and two figures stepped onto a wide bridge that swept across the open expanse at the center of the tree. The little white lights that swirled around the railing flickered to life as they briskly passed.

"It's because his wife is so traumatized by what she saw. Mausurem said he saw the creature, too. It was no human, he says. Black-skinned with four arms and massive horns like a dragon," one of the figures spoke.

Alvena hastily pushed away from the banister and scampered along beneath them.

The second figure scoffed. "Mausurem is a drunk and a liar. What he saw was what the ale showed him."

She saw the first figure give a slight shrug of his scanty shoulders. "Maybe his wife will talk in a few weeks."

"Still, that seems like a long while to wait for the iphera."

They strode into the archway leading to a rose-colored door and disappeared into the tumult of noise inside.

Alvena clasped her hands. An iphera was the Noc'olarian burial ritual... Someone *had* died! Four arms and massive horns? *Black* skin? She shivered. Such a beast had been *here?!* It sounded like something out of a nightmare or dragon lore! She was mildly relieved to hear that the male who saw it was a drunk—surely he had completely mis-seen...

But someone had still died.

She placed a foot onto the nearest staircase. *'I wonder who...'* she pondered, eyes dancing up the winding stairs. *'Who died?'*

"Come on, that's enough with you. Out!" came the familiar female voice. "The city is in no mood for visitors today."

Alvena huffed once as the female reappeared around the column, gesturing to the open archway behind her.

"Go on, off with you! It's far too late for this."

'But it's just past dawn! Go to sleep already!' Alvena stuck out her lower lip as she whirled and stalked from the great tree. She just wanted to know what happened! *'Hmph. This is one of those times... What I wouldn't give to speak!'* She struck vengeance upon a little white mushroom and leapt with surprise as its cap popped off in a tiny puff of white smoke and light. She simply wished to see the inside of Galadorium before she left the elven lands!—This was her last day!

She flopped down beside the dead mushroom and crossed her arms. And she *would* see it.

When they were asleep.

Unfortunately, waiting for the Noc'olari to sleep was like waiting for Hairem to clean up a mess. By the time the tree grew silent, the sun was halfway toward its apex and she was near bursting with impatience.

She looked about cautiously, peering around the archway for that pesky female—or any one of her grouchy friends.

Indeed the tree was finally empty.

'Aha!' She took several long and triumphant strides across the floor, spinning once with her arms extended into the great emptiness around her.

Where to go first?!

She stifled her giggle as it echoed through the great chamber, and with a slight hop to her step, took the nearest flight of stairs up into the dimness. With the morning, much of the magical light of the tree had faded.

She climbed the winding staircase and stopped beside the rose-colored door where the two gossipers had entered at dawn. Her small hand ran across the leaves carved into the wood. Each glinted with flecks of silver that highlighted their depths. *'How beautiful!'*

She scuttled across the ground to the window, crouching down low and peering up over the sill. Inside, the tavern was empty, a single blue light circling the room like a sentient watch guard, pausing by the glass as it rounded the bend.

Alvena quickly ducked. *'Oh, don't be silly. It's just a light.'*

She poked her head back up, watching the light stroll on around the room. She had never seen the inside of a tavern in Elvorium, but human drunk houses were often elaborated upon in books: dirty floors, cobwebs, risqué barmaids, a surplus of weary farmers, and, most importantly, burly mercenaries who gathered around large wooden tables to beat their chests and boast of their victories in battle and bed.

This tavern, to Alvena's disappointment, was none of that.

She marched away, regarding the building up the next flight of stairs. *'Stitch in Time...'* she read as her gaze trailed the plaque above a doorway.

Her eyes lit up. That must be a tailor shop!

She bounded up the next staircase and pressed her small, round nose against the glass, her breath creating a little shield of white. She turned and pushed once on the door in disappointment. *'Oh, darn it.'* This was far less exciting than she had thought! Everything was closed and quiet in the daytime. So unlike the Sel'vi!

She folded her arms, glared at the door, and gave it a grudging kick.

With a little creak, it swung open.

Alvena started, dropping her arms to her side in surprise. *'Unlocked!'* she grinned. She glanced around cautiously and then scuttled inside.

The building was empty of people, but orbs of light flickered to life and rose from the floor about her to spread like starlight across the ceiling. She put a finger to her lips in awe and closed the door to relish in her find.

The fabric was smooth and vibrant, gleaming in bold and fearless colors, bright as the summertime flowers in the palace gardens. She ran a hand down a bolt of fabric similar to the dress she wore, then spun to the rack beside it. The Noc'olari wore such daring colors!

'Oh!' She giggled and grabbed the end of a patch of jade, swirling around it once and tossing her long blond hair behind her shoulders as though donning an elegant dress. A dress worthy of a lady. *'Don't be so childish—'* she chastised, but ceased as a shimmering template of blue caught her eye. It lay loose over the lean figure of a mannequin just about her height. She had never seen fabric breathe such life! Even Ilsevel's dresses had been nothing in comparison.

Her fingers itched along the hem, sliding to the lace sleeves as delicate as the cobwebs she had once battled in the palace corners.

A sudden and distant trumpet blast startled her from her wistful thoughts. She jerked upright, ears straining. The sound seemed to resonate from somewhere above her.

She put a hand on the door and abruptly froze. A tumult of noise was growing around her: the clank of armor, the pounding of running feet, the cries of fear and panic…

Alvena staggered away, glancing about the empty shop. Had she drawn such attention?! She dropped below the vision of the window and scrambled behind the counter at the back of the room.

But the noise outside only grew louder.

No, this *couldn't* be for her.

'What is going on…?' She crawled out and surveyed about the room for another egress. Her eyes landed on a second door, opposite the side of the room of the front door. She crawled to it, hoping she remained below the attention of the window.

Then she reached up and cautiously pushed the new door wide.

The front of the shop was forgotten in an instant. She had revealed a considerably sized storage room, and there, along the back wall, was a great window to the world outside.

Alvena scuttled across the smooth wood and pulled herself up by the sill, craning to peer over the edge. Just enough to catch a glimpse of the outside…!

Her heart caught in her throat.

Down below her the white tents lay flattened, thrown to the side, trampled under thousands of feet. Bodies were scattered in their wake, mangled and twisted in the moss. Corpses of countless, defenseless humans.

But it was just a taste of the battle that lay ahead, for before the immense tree stood a swarming mass of troops. The Noc'olarian defenders were pouring from the tree's great arches, racing to meet the enemy with ferocious battle cries and polished steel.

Alvena's legs quaked beneath her and her eyes stung. *'Oh my gods... they've come for me,'* she whispered, pressing her chest against the wall in terror. *'Ilsevel's army... has come for me!'*

She could not tear her gaze away from the carnage below her. The enemies sliced through Galadorium's defenders as though through water. The Noc'olari held little chance for success in the surprise attack from their Sel'varian brethren.

A nearby roar in Noc'olarian jolted Alvena from her paralysis. Her head whipped to the doorway and into the storefront, landing on the looming door.

She had to defend herself!

She hurtled across the two rooms and threw her body into the front door, her fingers fumbling madly to draw the lock. Then she made for the nearest bolts of fabric and flung them as a haphazard barricade against the door.

She spun away, running once more for the window to the outside.

Below her, the yellow banners of Ilsevel's army gleamed with Zephereus' rays, the ship and crown flapping in the winter breeze. Alvena watched as a wave of soldiers washed over the remnants of Galadorium's external defenders before disappearing one by one into the great archways beneath her.

The pounding of feet became the crashing of thunder.

Alvena sank down and drew her legs up to her chest, feeling the parchment crackle beneath.

Was this the end? She pressed her forehead into her knees, rocking forward. This was it? This was as far as she had managed to run from Ilsevel?! *One city*—and she hadn't even managed to do *that* without blunder!

"SURRENDER!" bellowed a clear voice from below, echoing above the roar of battle. "UPON THE ORDERS OF KING SAEBELLUS, THOSE WHO DO NOT RESIST SHALL BE SPARED!"

Alvena heard an ear-splitting scream sharply die as a thud and clank of armor signaled someone had toppled from the stairs.

Yes. *This was the climax of her ill fortune.*

She heard the clatter of footsteps rising up the countless staircases, bearing shouts of "surrender!" She imagined doors kicked in. Elves dragged mercilessly from their homes.

It was only a matter of time before she joined them.

'Hide!' her wit managed to interject.

She scrabbled for another rack of fabrics, grabbing the nearest bolt and unraveling it about herself. Then she hunkered down into the corner and clasped a hand over her mouth. The whole city would hear her panicked breaths!

Yet time fled past and the sounds gradually died into the distance above.

It was a tailor shop... *Perhaps* they would pass it over?! She dared to hope! *'Sel'ari protect me, Sel'ari protect me, Sel'ari protect me!'* she chanted.

She curled up tighter, daring to make the smallest of holes to see out through the storage room doorway to the mound of fabrics still barricading the front door.

There was a sudden thud against its outside surface and an almost inaudible grunt from beyond.

Alvena stifled a cry. They *were* coming for her!

"Lord Adonis, let me," came an immediate request.

There was another thud and the door knocked against the frame.

"It is quite solid, my lord," the voice heaved. "You'll need a mage to—"

"I can take care of it," came a soft, yet commanding, reply.

Alvena's hand tightened on her mouth. *'Don't breathe! Don't breathe!'*

Suddenly, half of the blade of a sword swept through the air before the front door. It had not come *through* the door and there was no wielder behind it; instead, it seemed like half of a disembodied blade simply swiped through mid-air.

Then it withdrew and vanished as it had come.

Alvena's breath slowed slightly in confusion. What was that...?

And then a male stepped promptly through the air and into the shop, materializing as though he had passed through one portal and out another—yet she saw no flicker of magic. No gaping hole. He dropped lightly to his feet from the air just beyond the mound of material, his tight, black leather boots silent as he took a single, terrifying step forward.

Alvena could only assume that this was the soldier Adonis. She found it strange that he wore no helmet—all elven soldiers she had seen wore them, even the mages. He was pretty… *beautiful*, even by Sel'varian standards. As he looked about the room, his blue eyes were unnaturally calm, his lean, unbloodied figure perfectly composed.

He did not *look* like a killer.

But Alvena's eyes fell to his weapon. Its hilt was donned with precious stones and appeared as though it was made of ice. He held it loosely at his side as he glanced back toward the mound at the door.

Alvena quickly regretted her act. *'Now he knows someone is in here!'* She swallowed her breaths and her trembling. *'Maybe he will give up…'* During her thoughts, his body had vanished from her line of sight, but she could hear the faintest footsteps from the other room and the occasional shuffle of fabrics against one another.

He reappeared, standing directly in the storage room doorway to give the room a single, intense scan.

'…He's not going to cease searching!' Alvena breathed, biting her lip. But could she run? Her eyes fell once more to the sword as he switched the blade to his delicate left hand. It freed his right so that he was able to comfortably prod the line of nearby hanging clothes.

Conflict tore at her. Yes, she had to run!

…*No*, he'd slice her before she made it to the door…

She had to try…!

No… he was probably faster than her…

She watched him slowly drop his long fingers from the last dress and his eyes landed on the pile in which she lay.

'No, no, no, no, no…!' she prayed as his boots stopped directly before her.

"Where is Adonis?!" a call rang outside the tailor shop. It was the same clear voice Alvena had heard demanding surrender.

Adonis strode steadily toward the front door.

'Maybe he will leave…!'

And then he halted. "Come out," he commanded in a voice as smooth as his complexion—coaxing, almost.

'He won't leave.' Alvena's teeth tightened on her lip. *'He is bent on killing… These people are murderers… butchers…'*

"ADONIS?!" the voice rang again. The tone had grown almost panic-stricken, as though it had lost something invaluable.

The Sel'ven heaved a sigh. "Vale, Vale, Vale," he muttered below his breath.

'Just leave…!'

But he pivoted unexpectedly, pointing his sword directly at her mound. "Come out."

Alvena froze. He *did* know!

For a moment, she lay there in fear. If she remained, he would be angry and certainly kill her… If she obeyed… then maybe… maybe he would spare her…

With a painful swallow, Alvena slowly uncurled and sat up through a tumble of fabric. She pressed her back up against the wall and waved her hands in desperation to demonstrate that she was unarmed.

The Sel'ven's passive expression immediately flickered with confusion. "What is a Sel'ven doing here?" he asked. But his tone seemed less inquisitive than accusatory. He jabbed a long, narrow finger at her. "What are you doing here?"

Alvena shook her frizzy hair, drawing her legs up against her chest in the most pitiful posture her terrified mind could devise.

"ADONIS?! Gods damn it all! Search the city!" the voice outside bellowed. "Find him! Find him now!!"

"I'm alright, Vale!" Adonis shouted curtly. "I will be right there!" He progressed onward, drawing to a stop several feet away. He bent, extending a slender, un-calloused hand. "Can you speak?"

Alvena winced. That question… Damn that question!

But her silence only set his eyes. "Come," he ordered, flexing his hand. "I'm taking you back to Elvorium."

Elvorium.

Elvorium.

Alvena's fear climaxed and her movement became instinctive. She tore from her passive ball, vaulted to the side, pushed off the wall, and ran like a fox on fire. No! NO! She screamed internally as she barreled for the door. She couldn't go back there! HE COULD NOT MAKE HER!

The elf allowed her to pass into the next room, but stepped briskly in pursuit to seal them within the shop. "This is a rather strange way to go about *coming*. What shall you do?—run your way back to Elvorium? You cannot possibly believe you have any other choice. I am here and you can perceive the soldiers outside this very door." He was calm, his eyes softening as he advanced.

Alvena attempted a further retreat, but found her back pressing into the corner of the room. She was trapped!

He reached out rapidly and caught her wrist.

NO! She felt resistance well up inside her chest and she swung at his pretty face. Kicked at his armored knees. *She would NOT go!*

She saw his jaw instantly tense and he tossed his sword aside; it clanged and tumbled across the floor, knocking a rack of fabrics down across it. He caught her right hand and, with a swift twist, pinned her arms behind her back. She could feel his muscles harden and flex about her as he stabilized his hold, his breath warm on the back of her neck. Then silently and swiftly, in several strong jerks, he dragged her to the front door and stepped toward its unopened state.

Alvena found herself suddenly in a grassy field, the intoxicating smell of wildflowers surrounding her, the sky vividly blue above. Before her, the Noc'olarian hallways and stairways lay as though through the curvature of a glass. But she had no time to make sense of her confusion before he had stepped down onto the white wooden floor outside of the tailor shop.

The field vanished instantly and the door behind her lay closed.

"*Adonis!* Where is your sword?" a breathless Sel'ven charged as he rounded on them. He was slightly taller than Adonis, but just as lean and fair-skinned. "Gods, Adonis. What were you doing?! Emal'drathar knows you would be dead if I didn't keep my eyes pinned on you. What are you doing with that Sel'ven? What is she doing here?"

Adonis turned her to the nearest soldier as the other male rambled his demands. "Tie her with the other prisoners."

The lean Sel'ven behind them continued, sliding his sword into a sable sheath resting against his thick, black-plated armor. Alvena swallowed. There was blood glistening on those matte plates. "The Noc'olari are defeated. While you were…" he looked up at the sign above them. "…Shopping, or whatever you do while the rest of us are fighting." His eyes then widened like those of an owl, round and focused. "Your sword. Where *is* your sword? That was a gift! You can't lose that sword! Is it—"

"Vale, please," Adonis sighed, pushing Alvena ahead.

With the exception of the several soldiers who had converged upon Vale's panicked cries, the enemy troops marched in grim silence along the floor below, leading a train of prisoners in their wake.

The soldier clamped down upon Alvena's wrists. "I will add her to the prisoners. Is that all, my lords?"

Vale elevated his evil, pointed chin. "Yes, that's all."

"My lord, my lord!" came a cry as another of Ilsevel's dogs barreled up the staircase, shoving Alvena and the soldier holding her aside. He put a hand on the wall as he lurched, looking as though he was quite close to vomiting. "A message from His Majesty Saebellus."

Vale's smug brow shot up and he snatched the parchment. His tension faded as his eyes moved further down the page. "By all the gods, does he think me a slave?!" He threw a calloused hand dramatically into the air.

Adonis had vanished and reappeared through the tailor door by this time, his ice-like sword once more in its sheath. Alvena felt the hands tighten on her wrists and a strong push nearly sent her down the flight of stairs. *Back toward Elvorium... toward Ilsevel...*

"Walk," the soldier barked.

Alvena sniffed and took a broad step over a body tangled over the remains of another. One let out a weak groan and Alvena saw a hand twitch slightly in an appeal for help.

"What is it?" she heard Adonis inquire of Vale. "Is something wrong?"

Vale heaved a frustrated sigh. "Jerah never came back last night. And Saebellus wants *me* to take care of it. Like I'm not busy conquering cities as it were. Let's hurry and get these prisoners back to the capital."

Alvena heard a sword slide from its sheath and her heart stopped. He was going to kill her right there! *'Sel'ari, please...!'*

There were several solid footsteps behind her and she whipped her head around, mouth opening in a silent cry of terror.

Vale shoved his sword through the throat of the moaning Noc'olari.

His body jerked once and he stilled.

"*Vale*," Adonis gasped, turning his head away as though in offense.

Alvena's legs threatened to buckle beneath her relief.

"Better to put him out of his misery now," Vale grunted. He slid the sword from the neck, wiping it off briefly on the dead male's cloak. "You should applaud me for my mercy. It's more than these fucking traitors deserve."

CHAPTER FIFTEEN

The air was cold and damp and the floor Jerah lay on was hard like stone: the cellar was growing more uncomfortable as the days passed. He was conscious of the slow and steady drip that pulled him increasingly further from his sleep. He groaned, shutting his lids tighter in an attempt to block out the sound. His master had promised that he would fix that leak…

Palick.

Why hadn't he fixed that damn leak?

Jerah sat up with a start, his eyes going wide and dilating in the darkness. Wait! He had not returned to the cell! His mind swam, his body ached. He was damp and cold, cramped from having rolled into a ball for warmth. His wings peeled away from his stiff torso to stretch, pressing against a stone wall behind him. "Uhhhh," he groaned as he retracted them once more.

The sewer system beneath the city. *'That's right.'* The memories from the previous night crawled back to him as his mind cleared. First there had been Kinraeus' murder and then Jerah had slipped away into the city's sewers. The sewers had gone on for great lengths as inches of cold, dirty water that dragged down his massive boots. There had been no good place for rest or shelter. When Jerah was so disoriented and cold that he could walk no further, he had finally surrendered himself to curling up in a tiny, damp spot on the side of the tunnels.

There Jerah had slept—a deep, solid sleep that had kept him until a rather famished rat started gnawing at his arm.

Jerah looked down then. He had subconsciously crushed the vermin—he was used to their kind. Aside from Master, they were the only company he had.

He knocked it away as he stood. How long had it been? His stomach responded with a low rumble and Jerah could only think of the rich taste of food. He gazed down the tunnel, envisioning a few pounds of raw pork.

And then sudden panic seized him. *'How long had it been?!'* Jerah felt a bubble of fear push away his hunger. He could turn to stone at any moment!—He had to pay the price!

Jerah scrambled frantically over water and stone until rays of light shone down through the grate above. He cocked his head to the sound of movement. How many elves were up there? He had to kill one of them before a day passed outside his cell!

He gripped the iron of the ladder and hauled his massive form swiftly up its length until he could peer from the spaces of the grate. His stomach churned as he met the strangely brilliant light…

And Jerah froze. The churning inside him stopped and grew heavy, feeling like a stone held between his constricting lungs. He could not breathe! And he could barely see—the world was so bright!

The void above was a pale grey-blue and the countless distant twinkling torches he had seen the night before had vanished. In their place—and that of the large, white torch—was a yellow sphere of such brilliance that Jerah could not look at it without his vision fading entirely.

Fear overtook him. Where was he?! How far had he travelled in the day that the void had changed entirely? Was he still on Sevrigel? Or had he somehow crossed into Ryekarayn? His grip on the ladder faltered and he fell to land hard on his leathery wings. Jerah slowly rolled over, staring blankly at the wall before him, strange bright orbs still playing in his vision. His mind felt numb and his heart ached desperately for the safety of the cellar.

How foolish he had been. *How foolish!*

Time blurred together and Jerah lost sense of how long he lay in the muck of the tunnel, staring emotionlessly at algae clinging to the wall. He lay there until he noticed that his vision came more easily—that the orbs were gone—and that the light from the grates had faded.

Jerah turned around slowly. Almost cautiously. Certainly, the light *had* dimmed. He stood and looked warily up through the grate above him.

The void had changed. Indeed, where the grey-blue and fiery orb had lain now rose a deep and more familiar grey.

The sound of the movement had quieted.

With as much courage as Jerah could muster, he pushed aside the feeling in his gut and climbed once more up the slippery ladder. He lifted the grate up and leaned out.

He was between two buildings, in a narrow alley flanked by the creamy, white walls of elven housing. Down to his left was a broad street. There, he could see the occasional elf still moving quietly along, unaware of his presence.

Jerah inhaled sharply, sucking in the cool, damp air through his cracked lips, tasting the sewer water on his tongue as it passed. Where was he? Where was his cellar? And how long did he have before he would turn to stone?!

As panic at the last question once again began to rise, Jerah quickly pulled himself out of the hole.

The other questions would have to wait. For now, he had to kill.

Far above him in the void, he could see the glitter of a single torch. He wondered if, just perhaps, the torches in the black void did go out and only now were returning to light. It was welcome after the brilliance of his last attempt to surface, and his eyes adjusted swiftly to scope the darkness.

A brief hint of meat twisted in the breeze and the low growl of his stomach reminded him of his hunger.

'No, focus Jerah!' he rebuked himself. Perhaps the next black void in the sky would bring with it the cycle of a day. *And that would be his death.*

He crept to the edge of the alleyway and hunkered into stillness. The void grew quite black and was sprinkled with comforting white lights before an elf finally came near. His stride was long and careless as he wandered down the road, but that made Jerah's job easier.

In a sudden, silent movement, Jerah leapt from the alley and seized the elf, dragging him back into the darkness as swiftly as he had left. With practiced efficiency, Jerah crushed the elf's skull between his hands and dismembered him in the fashion he had been told. With the elf's death came the release from fear of his own.

Jerah dragged the body to the side of the alley where it was quickly forgotten and raised his nose in immediate acknowledgement of his fatigue. The killing was done. Now he was finally free to eat.

And then, Jerah determined, he would begin his journey to *Ryekarayn*.

Chapter Sixteen

Saebellus let the door close with a muffled thud behind him, drawing his hand slowly from the handle as though extending the silence into the room. The marble floor was dark at his feet, but across its glistening surface the fire still cackled and belched on the dry wood. He noted that Taemrin's sword, which had once hung above the mantle, was gone.

'Vale,' he muttered to himself. The Sel'ven had been eyeing the blade since they had unearthed it at the Battle of Elarium, trampled and half-buried under debris and corpses. Another token for Adonis, no doubt. Ilsevel would be irritated, but he was relieved to see his bedroom freed of the tackiness of the trophy.

Still, it did little to alleviate his stress. He dropped into the chair before the fireplace, allowing his forehead to rest against his palm. There was not a bone in his body that did not ache. A minute to close his eyes was all he desired.

No sooner had the thought completed than a sharp knock rang out across the room. Of *course* he was not to have that moment.

He heaved a sigh. "Enter."

The door swung open and closed in near silence, but Saebellus did not raise his head. "I hope you bear good news, Adonis?"

The male was beside him before he finished speaking, his delicate footsteps inaudible across the stone. "You look weary," drifted his lieutenant's reproach. "But I do have news."

The omission of "good" made Saebellus cringe internally, but he lifted his face to meet the male's gaze. The corners of the lieutenant's pale eyes were riddled with lines and Saebellus dropped his hand away.

"I am well, Adonis," he assured, gesturing to the chair adjacent to the flames. "Speak."

Adonis made no move to take the seat. Instead, his features hardened and rigidity seized his slender frame. "Relstavum," he began in his soft way, "has acquired a bounty on his head."

Saebellus exhaled. A bounty? He had expected nothing less. "*Good.* Clearly his chaos is having the desired effect. When I spoke with him last, both his bandits and rebellion were closer to fruiti—"

"The bounty is for slaughtering the entire populaces of several cities."

Saebellus jerked upright, wrenched from his languor. The shadows beside the fireplace surged across the wall in a reflection of his disbelief. "*WHAT?!*" he roared, rising to his feet.

Adonis drew himself up in equal measure, disgustingly and haughtily calm. He flicked his hand out, drawing a golden lock behind his ear. "Relstavum has slain three of Ryekarayn's cities using necromancy. Two were of King Joramon's, north of the Makataj. Only a handful of people are reported to have escaped. The last was under the purview of the True Bloods—the Eph'ven city of Dahel."

Saebellus' fingers curled. "*What is that feral human doing?*" he hissed, in a tone so venomous that the lieutenant was wise to take a sharp step back.

Safety achieved, the male goaded him with a crooked smile. His eyes locked in challenge. "Oh? So then, you are outraged?" His tone dropped away from its sickeningly mocking pitch and fell into disdain. "I just returned from Galadorium—I have witnessed firsthand what Ilsevel's plans have wrought. The prisoners will arrive in a few days and then you shall see what is left of our brethren."

Saebellus' gaze did not shift away. He marched forward, daring his lieutenant to remain composed. "This is war," he breathed with cold stoicism. "People die."

"This is *genocide*," Adonis growled. He stepped back once and stumbled, catching his balance on the arm of the chair.

In the brief moment that their gaze was broken, Saebellus closed the distance, bearing down in warning upon his insubordinate soldier.

Still the male dared to breathe his accusation. "Loneliness is more dangerous than the most potent of poisons."

The shadows along the wall flared once. "Get out," Saebellus whispered.

For all his valiant bravery, Adonis failed to conceal the tremble at the sight. His flush cheeks grew grey. "You cannot—!"

Saebellus' chest expanded and he interrupted with elevated volume. "I commanded you to *get out.*"

And whether it was the sudden proximity of the darkness or the tangible bloodlust riding the air, Adonis was swift to obey, shooting the warlord a single scowl before he left the door open at his back.

For a moment, the deafening silence hung about Saebellus—cold and thick, but welcome.

Then the warlord shattered it with a roar. He slammed his fist into his chair and sent it crashing into the murals along the wall. The wood shattered on impact, black fire searing to life upon the covering of silk. The rod above it that held the *War of Dragons* in place snapped, clattering to the tiles and relinquishing the tapestry to the flames.

The act did little to quell Saebellus' fury and so he raised his hand against the last chair before the fireplace.

A sweet voice rose unexpectedly over his rage. "What is troubling you, my love?" There was a quiet click as his wife did what Adonis had not, and he heard the tap of her small feet as she crossed the marble floor.

Saebellus stiffened and the black flames were extinguished with a hiss. From the corner of his eye he could see her sauntering, the golden frame of his crown twirling about her graceful fingers.

"I hope Adonis did not vex you."

Saebellus merely grunted, dropping into the remaining chair.

Ilsevel fell swiftly onto his lap, batting her vibrant eyes in hopes of stirring visible affection. "Quite bold for a mouse, isn't he?" Her fingers extended, the crown sweeping down upon his head. "Now tell me what he did to trouble you, my king."

Saebellus managed no more than a visible twitch of his displeasure, but Ilsevel noted it nonetheless.

"Saebel, why will you not wear this?" she fussed, running one hand to smooth his hair about the circlet.

Saebellus' expression remained indecipherably fixed. "I am wearing it now."

Ilsevel chuckled and tapped his nose with the tip of her polished nail. "*There* is some humor," she smiled, pressing her lips against his ear. Her breath tickled his lobe. "But I should like to see my *king* more often."

Saebellus drew the twisted circlet slowly from his head, letting it hang loose in his calloused hand. "A crown does not make a king." But when her lip jutted out in disapproval, he growled, "You are not asking me to be a king. You are asking me to be a *tyrant*."

Ilsevel recoiled from his chest, her chin tucked downward. "What?" she demanded, making no attempt to moderate her tone. "And how do you reason such an accusation?"

"These planned attacks on the elven cities," he replied, maintaining a level response. "I do not agree with them. In fact, I am staunchly opposed."

Ilsevel's hands fell to rest against her abdomen, and she turned her head aside, the shallow creases of her knit brow emphasized in the flicker of firelight. This was the core of her desires, and his words marred her countenance as though he had personally wounded her. "I see..." she trailed off quietly. She cast her eyes to the other end of the room, even and unblinking.

Where he knew Hairem's body had been found.

Saebellus felt a rumble rise in his breast, and the shadows sibilated in animosity, frenzied by her manipulation.

Yet Ilsevel had never seen him as the banished villain the world had denounced him as. Adonis was right: *loneliness was more dangerous than the most potent of poisons.*

He tried to smooth the lines of her distress by stroking her arm as he spoke. "The humans and Noc'olari were one matter: they knew the price for ignoring the law. But this notion of relocating is forcing these cities to react—we are killing those who might otherwise not act against us. You are ordering us to move with the knowledge that we will slaughter non-Sel'vi by the droves. It is bordering on *genocide*."

"Genocide?" Ilsevel laughed at his words, clasping his hands and meeting his eyes undaunted. "We are not committing genocide, Saebel. We are dividing and relocating the people so they cannot organize rebellions against us. We are not simply entering these cities with the plan to slaughter females and children. *This is war*. If the troops resist, then they die." When Saebellus grimaced, she reminded him, "You may be king now, but what happens when you are dead? The council will rise up in their arrogance and your laws and your image shall be done away with in place of their own selfish desires. The council may be the root of the evil, but all of the elves... *all of the cities* have become equally as debased. Nothing makes this as clear as the day they branded you and my brother traitors."

Saebellus' fingers tightened on the circlet, causing the metal to twist and bend.

"It was not only the council that forsook us, my love" Ilsevel murmured. "The entire world has betrayed us, and so nothing less must be reformed."

Chapter Seventeen

Sellemar glared venomously at the intruding sun, his rancor due in part to the pain of his recent nighttime escapade, and the rest fueled by the hour of the day. *'Where were you when I needed to rise, Zephereus?'* he shot upward resentfully. Between late-night correspondences with his connections in the capital and his own scouting operations, rising at his usual hour—without any assistance—had grown unsustainable!

Now the day was long after the dawn, and here he had just arisen as though he was young and blithe!—Though he supposed he had never *actually* been young or carefree enough to take advantage of such a luxury as *sleep.*

He muttered and scowled to himself as he ascended the large marble steps of the council's hall in long, brisk strides. *Late yet again.* His own lack of punctuality disgusted him and it would surely do the same to the males within. Except that he did not need to hear their haughty rebukes. The lines on his face creased as he thought of Cahsari's beady little eyes staring down at him in their puffed-up, vulture-like folds.

A flicker of white caught his eye and he glanced down. *'What ill fortune is this...?!'* he growled to himself as he poked a slender finger through the bottom of his wine red shirt. *'First the emerald, and now this?'* The war against the rodents of his estate raged on, and he was losing.

But there were priorities!—the fight with the demons, meeting with the members of his Resistance, and most importantly yet: his letter to Sairel for the aid of Hadoream.

The young royal was one elf Sairel *must* spare, as nothing would rally the spirits of the elven nation as the likes of a True Blood.

He gave a sigh of frustration and dropped his shirt, patting it once as though this would conceal his pauper-esque attire and quell his anxieties. What a pitiable state to which he had to lower himself in order to mend Sevrigel's wounds—and what he would not give to adventure in more regal attire once again.

The guards before the Council Hall withdrew at the flick of his wrist, allowing him as usual to push the doors wide for himself and step into the golden chamber of his brethren.

His emerald eyes darted to the bejeweled throne glinting in the morning rays.

It was mercifully unoccupied.

Sellemar exhaled heavily in relief. Yet again he was fortunate that Ilsevel was late. How Sel'ari watched over him. He kissed his thumb where the band of a blue phoenix adorned it and dropped his hand back to his side.

"*El'adorium*," Fildor's scoff instantly assaulted his ears.

"Testing Lady Luck, aren't you?" Cahsari sneered, his eyes twitching in delight as he watched Sellemar hurry up the steps beside the throne. "Too high a position to bother with showing up on the hour," he continued in a pitch that made even the birds outside the windowsills grimace and take flight. "And in. That. State. Of. Garb. It's as if Ilsevel appointed you as dutiful payment for her rescue or some charity as such. I don't believe we've had a *pauper* amongst us before."

Sellemar felt his jaw tense at the conceit. Gods, *if he knew who he was talking to....!* His feet dragged to a stop beside the steps of the Helven's desk. *'Do not do it. It is childish. Do not do it,'* he fought to subdue his irritation, but to no avail. He pivoted, elevating his chin as he stepped lightly before Cahsari's desk. The front was emblazoned with the sigil of a mountain twisted in smoke—or probably, more accurately, tendrils of necromancy. Yet this male reflected nothing of the Helvarian fierceness and independence. He was a groveling, wretched waste of breath even Malranus would have been above shitting out.

And that was quite generous.

"Cahsari," he smiled pleasantly. "You are most certainly correct. Please, teach me from your years of wisdom. Surely no man is wiser."

Cahsari narrowed his eyes suspiciously. "What do you want?" he demanded, cautiously puckering his lips.

"My friends," Mikanum began, waving his pale hand about as though he were clearing the air. "Let us not fall to inane fights and lofty banter." The over-animation of his hand only continued, and Sellemar could hear him carrying on about duty and patience.

But Sellemar focused solidly on the Helven before him. "I speak with all gravity, Cahsari. I—oh, you have something flecked beneath your eye… there. Yes, there."

Cahsari reached a long finger below his eye, brushing his hand across it swiftly. "I don't know—"

"No," Sellemar replied flatly. "Let me."

He reached out.

And flicked him in the eye.

Itirel would have certainly rebuked him for such a childish response and he could almost envision Sairel hanging his head in shame… But it had been *so* satisfying.

His fingers curled into a fist. Of course, he could think of something even *more* satisfying…

Mikanum gasped, his zealous hand falling limp in disbelief. "Her Majesty could be here at any moment, El'adorium!"

Cahsari ignored the room's excited murmurs at the growing conflict and stood with such force that his chair was tipped over onto the floor behind, rattling the windows with its clattering echo. He clenched one hand over his injured eye and thrust the other at Sellemar accusingly. "How dare you, you impertinent swine!"

Sellemar straightened, shrugging the words off like water on an oiled sack, and let his fingers unfurl at his side. Mikanum's words had reached him, even over his temptation to strike far more effectively. "Whether or not my appointment was dutiful payment for the queen's rescue, Cahsari, I *am* the El'adorium. I did not see you risking life and limb for her. But certainly you are a male whose fighting talents are only bested by your bravery." He looked at him challengingly, willing him to attempt to strike so he could lay his vulture-like body across the marble floors.

"The *queen!*" Mikanum hissed. "Stop your bickering this instant!"

Sellemar ignored the Darivalian's cries for pacification and leaned forward, pressing his hands onto the smooth surface of the Helvarian desk. He could see Cahsari recoil, a nervous flicker twitching across his lips. "But a male of your high standing would certainly not subject me to such defeat and subsequent embarrassment *here* before the highest officials of their respective races. I shall *remember my place* as simply the savior of the queen. A male who only rescued her from within Saebellus' army at the fortress of Horiembrig. Donned, I must add, in garb fit only for the privacy of a pauper's hovel."

The door to the chambers swung open abruptly and Sellemar swiftly straightened. He turned from Cahsari with a thin-lipped smile, fully aware that the male was shaken. He would be dense not to be.

Away on his left, he could see Ilsevel glance sidelong at them as she strode to her throne, and Sellemar made swift amends with a gracious bow. He took his seat at the chair of the blue phoenix. Still, even after such a perilous rebuke, Cahsari dared to pass him a scowl.

Ilsevel cleared her throat as she sat, fingers curling about the phoenix hanging near her breasts. "May the goddess smile upon us this morning," she greeted in her sickeningly sweet tone. She inhaled deeply and looked up to the ceiling in a manner fitting of religious respect.

Directly below her gaze, the grout of the tiles was still stained with Valdor's blood, as though she had deliberately refrained from having the servants scrub it clean.

Sellemar fixed his expression in solemnity, averting his eyes from hers as she scrutinized the room. He had avoided the path through the market square that morning, but he was fully aware of the rumors of a lingering stench. A stench emitted by three bloated, headless corpses rotting on pikes and festering with maggots.

Fearing for their lives, Valdor's wife had endeavored to flee the capital with her child. Their attempt to leave was interpreted as complicity with Valdor's treason and they were consequently beheaded and spiked onto the broken statue of their Noc'olarian god.

Sellemar shivered at the imagery.

But such senseless acts would be her downfall. In less than a week, Ilsevel had revealed the demons from the Phantom Isles and the slaughter of a child. She bled the life from her own reign and the Resistance would make certain the world did not look away.

Elvorium's people would see what their compliance had wrought—there was no freedom from her tyranny but by their own hand.

*

Sellemar strolled down the long, narrow hallway below the earth, his mind too preoccupied with the council's—*Ilsevel's*—meeting to sniff and moan about the sad state of the immediate world around him. He would have usually noticed the particularly strong, sour odor of decay—a stench that permeated the hallway due to someone's negligence to change the scented salts beside the lanterns. And he had never *not* observed the peeling green paint and moth-eaten rug, no matter how many times he returned to the secretive place.

But now… He slipped his hand into his pocket, resting it at his side where his latest letter was tucked safely away. His thoughts were not on Sairel or Ryekarayn or the headquarters of the Resistance through which he now strode, but *Itirel*. His letter of warning had not reached his friend in time: Ilsevel had confirmed that Galadorium had been conquered… and if Itirel had been present at the time of the attack…

'He would never turn his back on his people.'

"You cannot change what has happened; you can only move forward," he chastised himself. Danger was his profession. Whatever had happened to Itirel, he would find out with due time. Right now, he had his role to play if he was to save Sevrigel *and* his homeland; he could not leave Elvorium to selfishly seek his brother.

Tonight was yet another step to unraveling the hold of Saebellus and Ilsevel. And the most crucial piece yet.

Nemorium.

He rolled his shoulders and stepped firmly down the hall, determined to internalize his outward confidence. Truly, he was relieved to reach the last doorway. Relieved to have but one scrutinizing pair of eyes upon his barely masked countenance.

He pushed his weight against the stiff door, its weathered wood held snug by the building that had settled over it. But with a low grunt and a strong shove, the old entrance popped open all the same.

He stepped into the room beyond, brushing the imagined mildew from where his shoulder had touched the dirty wood. Once again, to save Sevrigel, he found himself in the most pauperish of situations. Could the goddess never send him to rule a kingdom or, at *least*, to play comfortable nobility?

Blessed too much in his own life, in his own time, he had been.

"You *could* choose to knock every once in a while," the male behind the desk muttered, though he did not avert his gaze from his work.

Sellemar sniffed incredulously at his tone, pushing the door closed with some effort, and strode forward. "Is that how you greet me now?" he jested.

The male behind the desk started, swiftly looking up. "*Sellemar*. I forgot we were meeting today. I thought it was that pigeon-faced Llendril again." The elf reclined against the back of his chair in relief, though he was distracted briefly from continuing in order to straighten the parchment near his arm. "Gods, every hour he's in here asking me how to do this or what to write for that or where to deliver the next package. It's all I can do to not strangle him. You have no idea the idiots I suffer through every day."

"I am on the council, Tilarus," Sellemar replied simply.

Tilarus pointed the end of the quill in his hand toward his friend, grinning at the rare moment of shared humor Sellemar graced him with. "Have a seat. I don't want you just running off the moment I give you the package. The world can wait a moment for us to talk."

Sellemar would, of course, have liked to do just that. There were other matters on his mind, but… *'I suppose there is nothing I can do about them at this time.'* Perhaps it would be good to settle his anxiety. Battles were better fought with a clear mind.

"Go on, *sit*," Tilarus stressed.

Sellemar glanced about the small study. A few nearly empty bookcases. A tattered rug. There was a single cot at the back side of the room, adorned by a mattress plotted with enough holes to rival any of his mouse-plagued shirts. It was grey with dust and unused far before the underground levels of the temple had been surrendered to him and the Resistance. On the right side of the room, a fire crackled and belched smoke up into the chimney, and—*there*. Beside the fireplace was a chair that had fared far more favorably than the bed. Sellemar took hold of it, dragged it to the front of the desk, and dropped stiffly down.

He sank several inches shorter than Tilarus.

The male straightened the stack of parchment Sellemar's movement had shifted. "Tell me, how *did* the council go this morning?"

Sellemar grimaced slightly, recalling his literal poke at Cahsari. Had he really behaved so childishly? He gathered his pride and huffed once. "Better. No one died this time. At least… not directly." He paused, allowing Tilarus yet another moment to obsess over the stack of parchment. "Must you persist? I did not move them."

Tilarus ignored him, indicating for his friend to continue with a spirited gesture of his head.

"Ilsevel replaced Lord Valdor—may Sel'ari grant him safe passage—with Lord Listaria, a *Sel'ven* noble to speak for the Noc'olari. He is young and feverish with adoration. The Noc'olari themselves… It seems Ilsevel has prevailed: they have been defeated. Yet there was one glimpse of hope in Ilsevel's ill news. She mentioned a most curious rumor I had not yet heard. She said that Hadoream has come to Sevrigel. But… that is impossible. Sairel would never allow it…"

Tilarus tapped his chin with the quill. "Mmm." Sellemar could not be certain if the male was agreeing or simply contemplating the possibility.

"Ilsevel also confirmed that Kinraeus is dead—thus ends our opportunity to receive King Joramon's aid. We now rely entirely on a rebellion. Unless, of course, someone manages to kill Relstavum." Here he laughed once—flatly.

Tilarus instantly lurched forward, a grin spreading across his face. "Such dismal words. Come now, I know the queen mentioned your latest venture." He winked, his amusement only growing. "And what a topic of hope it is! The capital is crawling with unrest… with fear of demons and maravian worms and the like, and I very well know the details are enough to put the gods to silence!"

"It seems to have had an effect." On a better day, Sellemar may have allowed himself a smug twitch, but with the uncertain news of Itirel…

When Sellemar did not fuel the flame of his charm further, Tilarus settled his quill into the little ink jar beside the second of its kind—moving them so they each rested back to back. He leaned his elbows forward, careful to not disturb any of the contents on his desk. His obsessive tendencies were at peak performance that day.

Sellemar reached out matter-of-factly and pushed a piece of paper off the stack.

"Malranus fall upon you, Sellemar!" Tilarus blasphemed, snatching the parchment and smacking it back onto the stack—as though the force would prevent further rebellion from the crinkled sheets.

Sellemar's lips twitched. He could not recall any male possessing such a ludicrous desire for spacial perfection.

Other than Sairel, of course.

"But did you have to *sink* the ship?" Tilarus insisted, slapping his palm upon the pile lest Sellemar's childish flare concoct any further trouble. "I must say, a hundred demon bodies floating in Targados is quite the sight, but completely unplanned. *And* you were almost spotted for it. You are lucky the ship was not magically defended. We agreed to tie *one* body to the square."

"These are times where it is fortunate that all elves look relatively the same." Sellemar flicked a golden strand from his brow. "And are you berating me for sinking the ship or for putting the entirety of *The Black Queen's* debasement on display? I *did* still tie a demon to the city square." He shifted impatiently, eyes flicking once more about the room. This talk of his consistent success bored him. He had further plans to address, and the package he sought was nowhere in sight. "Can we discuss this later, Tilarus? Where—"

With his free hand, Tilarus shifted the back of a portrait on his desk subtly toward Sellemar. "I told you—once I give you the package I know you'll just run off to save the world. Give us a moment, oh great hero, won't you?"

Sellemar pursed his lips and glowered, but he remained otherwise still.

Tilarus let out a tsk of disapproval. "Our job would be a lot easier if, instead of sinking ships and slaying demons, you simply slew Ilsevel and Saebellus. They are undoubtedly wicked to the core."

Sellemar did not even consider the suggestion. "We do not embrace Tiras' ideals here. I will not act as a vigilante and subvert the legal process—it is one of the few good establishments that exists beneath the corruption. Besides, the people need to see tradition working if they are to once more respect it. Our world was not always so lost."

Tilarus tossed his snarled hair, his locks as wild and unkempt as a forest sprite's. "Well, then I can only tell you what your overly difficult mission has accomplished—what I assume Ilsevel chose to dismiss," the male continued as he "subtly" angled the frame a little closer toward Sellemar. "The sight and proximity of so many feral beasts has the people frantic. They are demanding tighter security not only in Targados, but all over the country. They want Saebellus and Ilsevel to be merciless with smugglers and their cargo. More importantly, they will tolerate no allowance of demons in Saebellus' military operations. On such fragile ground, Saebellus cannot risk their fury—his army will remain damaged from his wars. No doubt the tyrants can feel the threads of their reign fraying already."

Sellemar noted his friend's creased silk and shadowed eyes. How long had it been since the male had left his study? "Yes, Ilsevel attempted to weave the people's reaction as merely surprise, but I knew it was far more severe. Yet better than that is this: Saebellus will no longer be able to use the Beast in any capacity where its discovery might be perceived by the populace. At least, not without the country's backlash, which he can ill afford. It is a weapon he shall sorely miss. What about—"

Tilarus twitched the frame a bit more toward Sellemar. "*About* that," he interrupted. "Rumor has it that the Beast is already gone. Genuinely and truly gone. And not, surprisingly, due to your efforts. It seems Saebellus is desperate to find it, which tells us that the creature is no longer at his command. He fears retribution enough that I heard he's even bringing in the mercenary pair *Hazamareth and Tsuki*."

Sellemar's brows raised, briefly forgetting about the male's hygiene. "*Them?*"

"He must be serious about destroying the Beast and avoiding public repercussion. Perhaps the creature sensed that its master would turn on it after what happened at the port.

"But forget the Beast. Saebellus will destroy it himself—I just thought you should like to know that your influence has already prohibited the rejuvenation of his forces *and* riled the people against him. Now, *I* want to know the details—how in Emal'drathar above you managed to sink the ship, save the despicable crew, escape, and *still* manage to put on a display in the city square? It's kept me up these last three nights!"

Sellemar smiled, watching as the male flicked the portrait once more. It had made a good ninety-degree turn since his arrival. "With a great deal of slinking about and swimming and freezing. Details another day, Tilarus—after I see that you have taken a bath." He nodded his head toward the frame. "You have something you want to show me, do you not?"

Tilarus reached forward swiftly, the stack of parchment knocked aside as he shoved the frame into Sellemar's hands. "Radiant, isn't she? She just sent that to me. Just had it painted by an exceptional—and exceptionally expensive—artist. Something to keep close to remind me of her."

He did not straighten the stack.

Sellemar looked down at the portrait of the Sel'varian female. Her fair face glowed with amber light and she smiled tenderly through the bright colors about her.

Tilarus wiggled in his seat, but managed to restrain himself from a sprawling grin. Sellemar could not help but wonder if it was sensitivity to his own situation. "My wife is with child."

Sellemar smiled faintly, returning the portrait to the desk. He straightened the stack of parchment absentmindedly before he sat back. Tilarus worried for nothing. How could Sellemar possibly have time to be lonely with the entire of Sevrigel resting on his shoulders? And this was hardly the first—or last—mission that necessitated his entire focus. "That is joyous news indeed. I am happy for you both."

The book had been opened and Tilarus was nearly bursting with excitement. He attempted to add to his news calmly, dictating with a nonchalant wave, "If the child is a boy, I shall lavish him with history books to inspire him to follow the great heroes and if the child is a girl, I shall pinch her cheeks and teach her all the greatest ballads until she is the most famous musician in all the land!"

Sellemar chuckled. How could someone in their profession find the time to do *either?* "A hero or a musician? Come now, Aura was one of the greatest warriors of all the ages and Resil, the best bard. Maybe you should not be so swift to predetermine their futures."

Tilarus narrowed one eye. "Is this the Sellemar I know? The male stuffed full of high-born Sel'varian traditions and stifling formalities?" He pointed accusingly at him. "What have you done with Sellemar?"

Sellemar glared in reproach, knocking his finger down. "They are not just high-born Sel'varian traditions. And hardly stifling formalities. They are absolutely necessary to the preservation of our culture and race and—"

"*There* he is," Tilarus breathed with mock relief. Sellemar stiffened, but his comrade prodded him with a chuckle. Then he sobered, pausing to allow the humor to fade. "Perhaps…" he began. "You will do me the honor of being the haltura?"

Sellemar's offense vanished. He raised his brows in surprise as he stumbled for his words. "What about your brother…?"

With a snort, Tilarus' gaiety returned in force. "Oh please, *that* wiry lout? I wouldn't trust my brother with my child if he and a *dwarf* were the last males on Ryekarayn."

The haltura was a parental guardian and a very serious honor in every elven culture, but Sel'vi in particular gave it more weight: and so Sellemar did as well. He *was* a male of tradition.

But nothing would happen to Tilarus. He was far above the skills of Ilsevel's soldiers and a mere informant of his level had nothing to fear. Sellemar opened his mouth and closed it at his consideration. "I would be honored," he finally spoke with an incline of his head. In this case, it was Tilarus' gesture that mattered. "*But*, now that I have received this news, *can you finally* deliver the package onto me?"

Tilarus leaned off his rump, pulling a small package from his back pocket to set down on the desk before them. "Alright, I have withheld it from you long enough. There you go."

The lilac package was surprisingly small and weightless as Sellemar turned it about. There was a faint slosh as its contents shifted. "Is this *it?*" Sellemar asked rhetorically.

"Yes." Tilarus' voice had grown softer now. Cautious, even. "This is *Nemorium*. And it was far from easy to come by. You must taste it first, and it will bond instantly to the next person to consume it. The effects will begin approximately a month after the bind. You will hear and see frequent thoughts and interactions, as well as be fully subject to the host's emotions—stronger emotions will trigger the Nemorium more frequently. The effects will last six months, though they will come and go on their own accord. There is no way to reverse them once the magic binds. *You have one chance to do this right.* I know you don't need to hear this, but *be careful*."

Sellemar glanced up at him briefly as he exchanged the package for the letter at his breast. He could see the concern etched plainly across Tilarus' face and wondered if the male had interpreted his thoughts. He sniffed dismissively. "Tilarus, this is just another day for me. Do not fret. Ilsevel has already given me far more attention than I desire: it will be easy to gain the opportunity to slip this to her." Tilarus opened his mouth again, his thin lips working to form another warning, but Sellemar cut him off. "This is the beginning, Tilarus. I will be able to see their plans. Unveil them to the people. If Saebellus felt the pressure from merely the recklessness of his dealings, then one can only imagine what the revelation of his plans shall offer."

Tilarus was, most likely, interested in venting a more detailed lecture about the dangers, but he managed to swallow his chastisement. He plucked up the letter, admirably masking his discomfort and concern. "I suppose the rumors of Hadoream have only rekindled your hope? Another request for Ilsevel's so-feared *prince*, is this? I needn't remind you that Saebellus has a plan unfolding on Ryekarayn and his agent will not allow Sairel's family much time to direct their attention over here."

Sellemar slid back his chair. "Send my regards to your family."

Tilarus closed his mouth and stood as well, moving around the desk to place a hand upon his friend's shoulder. His grip tightened briefly. "As you wish, my lord."

It was the same farewell Itirel and he had shared before the male had been lost to him. Sellemar stiffened.

The rise of the rebellion only grew more urgent. Not just for the sake of Sevrigel or Ryekarayn, but before another ally was lost. "Sel'ari guard us both."

Chapter Eighteen

Once a place of beauty and tranquility, Elvorium now seemed to glint before Alvena like a blade, silver and white, sharp as it jutted through the frosty air. She had fled to escape the sight, and yet here she stood but fifteen suns later, grasped once more by the heart of war. She would never see freedom again—no one could achieve *two* harrowing escapes—*especially* if that someone was her.

Whoever it was that Itirel had left to pursue had saved him from her fate.

As she stepped beneath the wide archway of the city gates, a command issued from her right, "Halt!"

Alvena obeyed, shivering in the cold of the shadows while her toes flexed for feeling in her small, scuffed shoes. Her meager movement was practically the only one she saw: Elvorium had never been stiller. For a moment, she glimpsed a face peering out at them from a window, the eyes drooped in pity. And then they too vanished in the darkness.

A voice rose with unexpected proximity. "Alvena, you are to come with me."

Alvena started and whirled, her eyes locking upon the lean, blond-haired male dominant before her. Adonis.

If she had still held any hope, it dimmed: he truly knew who she was. She fixed her fear behind a scowl of brave defiance, but she could feel the sting of the wind on her still-damp tear streaks.

He gave her no reaction. Instead, he bent for her cuffs, unlocking her bindings. Her relief was swiftly disgraced as they thumped heavily against the knees of the Noc'olarian male ahead of her, nearly causing his weakened legs to buckle.

She quickly averted her gaze and rubbed her raw wrists. This time, there was no Itirel to make the throbbing vanish.

"This way," Adonis ordered, clamping his left hand upon her shoulder. His fingers, icy in the cold, steered her sharply away from the line of beaten prisoners. "Stay by me." His tone was tender, but beneath it swam a tangible threat.

She glanced at the blade at his side; it brushed ostentatiously against his thigh as he strode toward the south.

Alvena's growing horror was only beaten by her tears. The south. Toward the palace.

Toward Ilsevel!

Her death was truly coming to pass. She had jeopardized Erallus and Sellemar for nothing! She had anticipated drowning in an unnamed river or being eaten by a frenzied bear, but here, she had failed even her lowest expectations!

And before the tears could spring back to life, a new realization caused her to suck her sorrow in with a single gasp. *Sellemar! 'Sellemar's letter…!'* His parchment was still tucked against her abdomen! By Sel'ari! When they killed her, they would find it. They would find it and Sellemar… Sellemar…

They would kill him!

Her eyes shot wildly around her. There had to be a way to dispose of the letter. There had to be a way to do so before anyone could find it…!

"Alvena, quicken your steps," Adonis beckoned from the frosted lane ahead. "You're lagging behind."

For a brief moment, Alvena considered if she could run. Just far enough and long enough to stash the letter somewhere. *Anywhere.* She glanced down the nearest alleyway, to a stack of crates piled up against a smooth white wall. *'Like there…'*

A hand latched onto her arm and her eyes shot up to find Adonis' pale and perceptive gaze staring intensely back at her. "*Come,*" he ordered. The softness in his voice was gone, and Alvena's ambition vanished.

What madness had she considered? Except for Ilsevel's soldiers, not another soul was in sight. There was no crowd to envelop her—the male would see her flee and snatch her right back.

Yet Adonis was taking no chances. His grip remained like iron as they continued down the streets, through the palace grounds, and to the very doors that had once welcomed her home from errands in the market.

Alvena's stomach sank.

The last time she had entered, Erallus had been beside her. But this was no longer Hairem's palace and there would be no Erallus to ferry her to safety.

Adonis briskly stepped through, out across the wide marbled floor and vaulted ceilings. His pace was so swift that Alvena had only a moment to send a mournful glance to the elaborate murals of Sevrigel's glorious history—now to be forever marred by Saebellus' reign.

"Come," Adonis called again, and Alvena realized his hand had fallen away. He had made a considerable leap ahead in that short disconnect and Alvena felt apprehensively vulnerable outside his presence. There were far greater dangers than he!

The empty thrones on her left glittered menacingly in agreement as Alvena scurried to his side.

A deep voice boomed suddenly from the hallway just beyond. "Have the prisoners arrived? I dare to pray that that girl is not the only survivor of Galadorium, Lieutenant."

Adonis drew to a rigid halt and Alvena instinctively stepped near. A figure was emerging from the darkness and into the grand hall, taller than Adonis and of far stronger build. He was clad in armor so ornate it put Hairem's royal suit to shame—black, flawless, and glossy, and unlike Vale's, embellished in gold instead of blood. The faint jingle of chainmail could be heard above the gently shifting plates. He stopped before them, his long black hair hanging loose about his ghostly face.

And his eyes… black. Blacker than his armor or hair. Round. Black.

And *empty*.

Alvena shrank away. *'Saebellus…!'* she gasped in realization. He wore no crown—no symbol of his kingship—but Alvena had heard the stories of the black-haired, black-eyed male who had once been a Sel'ven.

"She is not," Adonis replied. She noted that he did not bow, nor address the king with a title. Instead, he placed a hand on Alvena as he spoke, as though making certain she did not leave his side. "The prisoners are being escorted below as we speak. This girl, however, is the mute servant Ilsevel seeks. I suppose you wish to silence her as well."

Saebellus' eyes flicked downward in callous regard and Alvena found she had to look away, unable to meet the intensity of his gaze. She felt as though the whole world could once more hear the pounding of her heart.

This was it. *'Don't cry!'* she rebuked herself. *'It is the least you can do!'*

"Keep her away from Ilsevel," Saebellus spoke after a moment. "I will manage the matter."

Alvena saw Adonis' fists slack. *'...What?'* She quickly wiped her tears aside and dared to look up in an attempt to read the king's expression. But his visage was more stoic than the statues in Eraydon's square.

Yet he did not retract his words. Was he going to spare her life?!

He once more raised his ebony eyes to the lieutenant—in his rigidity, they were the only things that moved. "I considered your words from last night. I agree that Relstavum's crimes—and his *alone*—are abominable. However, it is too early in our reign to weaken ourselves with internal conflict. Relstavum was given orders to operate Ryekarayn's distractions and we shall not give him reason to cease. There will be no further discussion on the matter."

Adonis pursed his lips, but displeasure alighted behind his pale gaze. "I agree that you cannot afford to lose Relstavum. I simply pray that his efforts prevail. And that they are worth the cost."

For a moment, curiosity ensnared Alvena and she jutted her lower lip in disdain at their ambiguity.

Saebellus only added further confusion. "They must. The rumors of Hadoream's presence have increased. As we know Jikun has been seen with the True Bloods, his association suggests that they may indeed be involved with our affairs. Relstavum must prevent them from lending the aid of an army at any cost. And we must quench these rumors before we have our own rebellion on hand."

Adonis' face flickered incomprehensibly, but Alvena nearly leapt. General Taemrin was alive and with the True Bloods?! Then there was still hope for the homeland, even with the great ambassador undoubtedly dead!

"For now," Saebellus continued, "I need you to do what you can to root out this 'Resistance.' The people are only just becoming accustomed to our reign, and that demands security. The unknown threat presented by the rebellion's ploy with the Isles is far worse than the familiar concept of war and relocation."

While she had been stumbling through the bitter foliage, the rest of the world was swift in motion. How shameful!—A resistance brewed, and here she had cowardly attempted to flee to the coast!

Yet Adonis' words cut her inspiration short. "Then I take it that you wish for me to continue trailing Sellemar?"

Her head jerked to the lieutenant. *'Sellemar? Why was he still in the capital? What foolish heroics did he think he might achieve?!'* If Saebellus suspected him, he was in danger no less than her own!

And his foolish bravado only highlighted her cowardice. *'Oh, what would you do against the enemy, Alvena?—Brush their hair to death? Clean the palace until it fell?'*

"Come," Adonis' voice cut into her thoughts.

She looked up, surprised to see that Saebellus was gone and Adonis was already standing at the stairs. What had they done, *run* the moment she had spaced out?

"This way." He began the ascent, keeping an eye that Alvena remained at his heels. They had gone no more than several steps when he lurched against the nearest tapestry and out of the path of a figure barreling down with no regard for the surroundings.

"Turlondiel!" Adonis barked in warning, grabbing Alvena's arm and yanking her safely to his side.

The figure caught hold of the banister in order to assist her halt at the bottom of the staircase. Alvena's mouth had widened into a little "o" of surprise at the sight of such impropriety. No one had *ever* behaved in such a manner when Hairem was king!

The transgressor was dressed in cotton and leather armor, with an ornate sword secured to the equally as embellished belt. This was common attire for Saebellus' army, but... Alvena's eyes remained wide. This delinquent was a *female!* Her uniform had clearly been designed for her, as it was cinched tight to fit her small waist, but then let out to accommodate her generous bust and hips. Her blond hair was in disarray from her recent flight, the curls still bouncing about her flushed face and pointed ears.

"Hello Adonis," she hailed as she caught her breath and absorbed the pair gawking down. Why, even the maiden in the tapestry of Emowyn's Mantle seemed to have been struck with offense. The soldier's voice emerged smooth as silk, and she tucked a wayward strand of hair behind her ear. "I am happy to hear that the prisoners have arrived."

Adonis gathered himself and returned a polite nod. "And I assume your mission went well, Turlondiel?"

"It did," she replied succinctly, as though there was no other way it *could* have gone. Her azure eyes slipped to Alvena, who was still clutched tightly in Adonis' slender hand, and her pink lips curled. "Why Adonis," she purred. "I see you are taking a female to your quarters."

Adonis stiffened. "I found the girl in Galadorium. I... I am keeping her safe." His commanding visage was somewhat lost beneath his stammering.

Turlondiel tsked, apparently disappointed that he did not rise to her teasing. "Adonis, you are as gentle a soul as there ever was. It is lucky you are not allowed into the fray of battles or you would take every young one you see. How you came to associate with such a vile and bloodthirsty male will always be beyond me."

"I must take Alvena to my room," he responded, somewhat less red. "We will speak later. Do you not have a report to make?"

"Of course, Adonis," she agreed with a bob of her curls. She released the banister and carried on her rapid pace to the doors of the great hall. Before them, she paused shortly and glanced once from Alvena to Adonis.

She shot the lieutenant a mischievous smile. "Have fun," she cooed before she disappeared into the hall.

Alvena bit her lip sharply. If she had been as beautiful as Ilsevel or this lady, perhaps Hairem would have loved her, and he wouldn't…

Adonis tapped a foot to the stairs. "Come."

'Come come come. Half of what you say is come,*'* Alvena thought with a huff. But she took the remainder of the stairs and hallways at his heels. Even though she was surrounded by familiarity, there lurked an emptiness to the place. It was her old home… but all the faces were different.

Where was Madorana? Lardol? Erallus?

She bumped into Adonis as he stopped before a door, squeaking as she fell onto her rump. Adonis smiled, but she accepted none of his charisma. What reason did he have to offer her such charm?

And then her eyes widened. What if… what if he… was like the human miners?! Her face twisted in horror. He was a wicked soldier in Saebellus' army of butchers! Why *wouldn't* he rape her?!

"What's wrong?" he asked in that clever façade of serenity. He grabbed her by the arm and pulled her to her feet. "Come. We can't have you out here. What if Ilsevel were to see you?"

Alvena found herself scrambling into the room despite herself.

"Now, make yourself at home," he spoke, sealing them inside. "You will have the divan by the fire as your bed."

Alvena stood, sliding her back against the wall as she did so. She was acutely aware of their distance. She would put up a vicious fight if he dared lay a hand upon her!

When he remained so perfectly innocent, she surveyed the room about him. It was as large and brightly lit as her old room, with an ornate chandelier dangling from the high ceiling. The walls were a deep blue and hung with large tapestries depicting romances from the histories she had read as a child: Princess Aura and Prince Mesheck, King Ralaris and Queen Secora, Heroes Dephaera and Mavorn. Even a great rug in the center of the room held a scene of two lovers intertwined.

Alvena raised her brow as the male set his sword down on the paper-strewn desk. She had never really thought that a cold-blooded killer would be so interested in such deep and emotional history.

She scoffed, wondering who he had killed to acquire the room.

Adonis stepped away, drawing back the curtain of the window and tying it to a hook along the wall. Alvena could see the city sweeping out in brilliance and her heart ached to move closer. It was so magnificent that for a moment, she could find no fear or hate of the place. *Elvorium…*

She forced herself to look away. No, this was her *prison.*

She scanned the divan beside the burning fireplace; it was furnished neatly with silk pillows and was separated from the hearth by a thick-furred rug. But its luxury did not negate her state.

And then there was Adonis' bed—bold green and gold sheets accented with threads of deep red silk. She shrank away, sidestepping to the opposite wall. If she did not go near it then maybe he would change his mind…

The door beside her opened suddenly and Alvena leapt back with an internal shriek. *'Him?!'* she raged as Vale flung the door against the wall.

He rolled his shoulders, tossing his long blond hair from side to side. "Ahhh! Prisoners secured!" his voice rang as he slammed the door behind him. He was unaware of Alvena's tiny frame scrunched against the wall beside it. "Gods, a few long days on the road and I have *never wanted you more*," he purred, dropping his sword to the ground and stalking toward Adonis.

Alvena's eyes widened. Did they… both… live in this room?

Adonis put a hand on Vale's chest as he drew near, keeping him an arm's length away as he gestured with his free hand toward Vale's left.

The male turned and Alvena saw his eyes harden, narrowing into thin, angry slits. "What is *she* doing here?" he growled.

Adonis swung from the demand, stepping past him and plucking up the discarded weapon. He elevated it once, gesturing at Vale in unspoken chastisement. Then he set it on the desk beside his own. "Somewhere beneath Ilsevel's talons, Saebellus still exists. He ordered me to keep her near while he addresses the matter."

Alvena saw Vale's jaw slack, his bright green eyes widening in displeasure. "What?! *Adonis!*" he whined, throwing his arms into the air dramatically. "This must be some cruel prank! Why in Ramul do we have to keep her? Let the bitch-queen have her way! She *always* gets her way eventually! *Ugh!*"

Adonis glared at him reproachfully, but Vale dodged the look by swiftly turning his own scowl upon Alvena. He huffed, "Throw her to the bitch-queen and be done with it. *I want to ravage you.*"

"*Vale*," Adonis warned, his gentle voice rising even as his cheeks flushed. There was intensity in his form as he drew himself up. "If you do *anything. Anything* at all to displease me about Alvena, I will never forgive you. *Never*."

Vale flung his belt beside his sword, falling into a high-backed chair. He rubbed his hand against the breastplate of his armor, as though attempting to scratch an itch beneath. "How are we supposed to live with that little rat in our room?" he muttered hotly. "Why doesn't Laeth take her? That damn elf has no one in his room. Make *him* take responsibility for her."

"No," Adonis replied flatly. He opened the chest at the foot of the bed, drawing out a thick, black cloak from the top. "You know she's innocent and we will demonstrate our support of Saebellus' stance by taking on the duty. That is final." Alvena watched his shoulders lax as he threw the heavy fabric about them. He tugged his long hair free. "Now, I have some business I must see to. Watch Alvena. I'll care for her when I return."

'He's going to trail Sellemar...'

Vale's foot stomped and he smacked a hand down onto the surface of the desk, sputtering. "First you deny me and then you go to spend the night with *Sellemar?!* You've gone too far! I have work too, you bastard! Take the brat with *you!*"

Adonis collected his extravagant sword and studied it briefly. Alvena followed his gaze. Its hilt glittered strangely in the light and when she peered closer, she felt as though she were staring across a frozen tundra somehow contained within the narrow, twisting ice. And that every gem was, in fact, a pocket of rare stone embedded into the face of great, grey mountains. She blinked dumbly and looked up to the two elves, expecting their expressions to be struck with similar awe.

Adonis, however, was still managing Vale's complaints. "Here is a thought to keep you occupied," he reproached softly. "Saebel mentioned Hadoream again. He said that the rumors are increasing. If Hadoream is indeed here, you ought to consider what *you* are going to do." He stepped to the door and smiled slightly at Alvena—perhaps as avoidance to Vale's irritated grimaces and glares.

The despicable captain looked like a troll prodded with a hot iron.

And then the door swung wide and Alvena was left confused. What *Vale* was going to do? Why Vale?

Vale merely gave a thin-lipped scowl, refusing to address the meaning of Adonis' words. "Saebellus told me to take care of the beast, and the mercenaries I'm hiring are in town tonight. You need to be back in a few hours. That's when I have to leave, Adonis… Adonis, don't you walk out on me…! Hey!—Did you hear me?! I'm not taking her with!"

*

"Damn it," Vale muttered.

Alvena had not moved from her choice spot along the wall. She had to pee again, but since she had already been forced to relieve herself in her dress while strung together in the prisoner line, she was less willing to try to communicate this with the murderer. He had not even unclothed from his bloodstained armor!

She observed him as he paced before the balcony doors, glancing occasionally at the climbing moon. He had said he wouldn't bring her along… but Adonis had sounded rather sure of himself.

"Damn it, damn it. That damn bastard. When I get my hands on him it won't be where he wants," Vale snarled to himself as he abandoned his post at the doors. He snatched his sword from the desk and fastened it hastily to his waist.

His eyes landed upon Alvena and he stiffened with irritation. "I can't wait any longer. Let's go, bitch."

'Bastard,' she thought in turn as he stalked to the door. He flung it open and Alvena had to dive out of the way to avoid being crunched against the wall. *'Just leave me here, you callous murderer! Tie me up!'* she wanted to balk aloud.

Vale jabbed at the hall, glaring as she scrambled to her feet. "Follow me," he snapped. He paused mid-stride to glower sourly. "And if you try to run, I'll slit your throat."

Alvena drew her cloak tight, a sinking fear settling in her gut even as she flared her nostrils at his threat. She took a long stride after him. He *would* kill her. Of that, she had no doubt.

Vale pivoted and marched swiftly away.

'...He's nothing like Adonis,' she reflected as they wound their way down the long hallways, twisting stairs, and vast halls of the palace. *'He is cold.* Evil, *truly.'* She narrowed her eyes at the back of his head, willing him to croak. *'Why did Adonis leave me with this monster? I would have rather stalked Sellemar!'* She stopped in her thoughts. Adonis though... he wasn't any better! How had he let all those Noc'olari die? She could not cling to him! She had to be strong in herself...! She set her jaw as she stepped out onto the grounds of the palace. And maybe this would be her opportunity to stash Sellemar's letter!

Vale's hollow eyes caught the light of the lanterns strung high above the palace gates. No. She could not take chances with this male. One attempt... one failed attempt to run... and her body would be lying in a pool of its own blood.

As courageous as Sellemar had been to protect her, she felt ashamed that she could not do the same. *'There must be something you can do if you are to be a captive—something you can at least* learn *for the sake of your allies...'*

She drew away from her thoughts, finding the guilt too great to acknowledge. Instead, she focused on the brisk weave through the golden city. To her surprise, it was busier now than it had been at the peak hours of the day. Perhaps now that the army had withdrawn to the barracks and palace, the city's elves felt daring enough to emerge.

"This is the place," Vale yapped as they stepped past a crooked white gate hanging off its last hinge. "Don't say a—" His face twitched. "Just *stay by me*."

He pushed open the large, dirty door of a rundown estate and Alvena's nose wrinkled. The walls were cracked and worn and the interior was even more scandalous. Alvena had never seen *this* side of the city and for a moment she doubted that they could still be within her precious capital. There were tables scattered across the building's dirty floors, liquor spilt across their surfaces. The elf behind the counter was thin, boney, and solemn, with watery eyes that glided across her and Vale as though he did not truly see.

Why was such a place allowed to remain? It was a *human* tavern in a Sel'varian city! She looked about, aghast.

And slightly fascinated.

Vale snagged her elbow, yanking her through the crowd of jovial and heavily armed humans as they shouted and gurgled through their ale. She could only assume that these ruffians were the humans who had served in Saebellus' army, thus pardoned from Ilsevel's rampage.

Vale flung her away at the top of the stairs and turned his barbarism upon a drunken lout who lingered before a door. He lobbed the man away to access the room painted with a small number six.

Who was within?

She retreated, watching as he rapped thrice with the hilt of his blade. Then he warily joined her away as the door opened to a single, dark crack.

Something wavered in the darkness—a rusty, probing eye.

The door snapped closed.

"Damn mercenaries," Vale grumbled, rapping firmly once more. Only silence was returned. "Can't work with them!"

Alvena sidled up to Vale's hip. What was that about?! Now she was determined to see inside!

At her challenging glare, the door swung inward and Alvena found the cautious male beside her promptly forgotten. She gaped. A shirtless man stood in the opening, his chest glistening in the soft candlelight, his two rusty eyes narrowed. He was human, with skin tanned from the sun and darkest upon his broad shoulders and bulging arms. His chest was heavily scarred, but Alvena thought that it, paired with his rather well-toned muscle structure, only helped to emphasize his dangerous physique.

She couldn't help but giggle internally, even as she attempted a well-founded rebuke. She had never seen a handsome human before. The sheer structure of him made Vale look as though he could be crushed beneath his thumb.

And she liked the thought of that.

"You must be Captain Vale," the man finally spoke after a shameless scrutiny of their figures. He gestured into the room behind him and as he turned, Alvena's eyes were drawn to the long scar that ran down his face and split over his cheek. The candlelight from the room behind caught it briefly with shimmering emphasis.

Alvena had been around many soldiers in her time at the palace with Hairem, but no elf she had encountered had borne such scarring. A *real* mercenary! Alvena saw Vale tear his eyes away from the man's chest and realized that he was as taken by the man's physique as she. She grimaced to share even one similarity with the vile killer.

While she was delighted with the human's appearance, entering the room came no easier. The sound of the snapping door sent her leaping like a frightened cat and she nearly plowed headfirst into a mound of dirty clothes.

Fortunately, no one commented on her embarrassment.

"Hello, Captain Vale," a woman breathed from the edge of the bed.

In the process of regaining her composure, Alvena had not noticed the additional figure lounging in the dim light. This one she identified immediately as a half-elf. The woman had ears that drew sharply to a point, but her features were too strong to have come solely from elven heritage. Additionally, she had a tattoo of a black sun on her *neck*, the spiraling and jagged rays creeping toward her jawline.

No self-respecting elf would *ever* mar her body—even with Zephereus' insignia.

'It looks positively ridiculous…' Alvena thought with great indignation, personally affronted by such a mark. Then her haughty regard dwindled at the appearance of a horrid scar she had been at first too distracted to note. It sliced clean across her throat.

If only Hairem had survived his.

"You are Tsuki and Hazamareth, I presume," Vale inquired. He surveyed the woman on the tossed bedsheets with blatant disinterest, despite her nearly exposed breasts.

"I am Tsuki," the human clarified, folding his arms across his thick chest. "You said you had a job for us." Time was clearly money to this man and he certainly did not seem pressed for work enough to be courteous. He did not bother to even offer a seat—grimy though it was. Alvena's eyes flicked across the divan by the fire and the chair by the wall, each tossed carelessly with dirty leather, rumpled clothing, and shaggy towels—the latter of which she had nearly been lost within. There was even a beautiful necklace with a teardrop charm just lying in their pool of filth!

"Yes, of course I have work for you," Vale retorted, as though the man's words were an accusation.

A glint once more captured Alvena's eye. She crouched and subtly swiped the discarded charm for closer admiration. An amethyst glinted from within the teardrop. *'Why would anyone throw such a lovely thing away?—this certainly would give that audacious tattooed neck a stark improvement!'*

No sooner was it in her hands than Vale snapped his fingers at her. She swiftly and obediently straightened, clutching the charm at her side lest he see and throttle her with a physical rebuke.

"And it is of high priority to Saebellus."

The woman—Hazamareth—leaned forward on the bed, her eyes piercing Alvena with discomforting calculation as she snapped back to attention. Alvena's hand tightened. "And is this it?" she demanded.

Vale scoffed, catching Alvena's shoulder as she tried to shrink into the shadows for safety. "Gods, I wish. Unfortunately, however, *no*." Here he paused, his cheeks growing curiously red. "We need you to kill the Beast."

The Beast. Alvena needed no mirror to know that, contrarily, the color had fled her cheeks. Every servant had heard the tales of the massive casualties it had left in its wake. *Thousands*, they said. Why, the Beast had even dared to defile the temple of Sel'ari herself!

There came an inappropriate volley of laughter from the grinning mercenaries. "Ah, the Beast," Tsuki chortled. "This wouldn't happen to be the same little creature you took twenty years ago in exchange for Rel, is it? That 'insignificant, harmless' demon we *warned* you was far more beast than you could control?"

Hazamareth sniggered. "And here they wanted to take the whole damn ship."

The hue of Vale's cheeks could have rivaled a ripened beet. "Yes. Well, it grew up."

"As they all do."

Vale stabbed his finger at the wench, grappling for his pride. "Remember who sent me," he snarled.

Neither mercenary was visibly swayed. Tsuki drummed his fingers along his arm and threw an offhanded rebuke. "Haz, don't be so rude to our employer." And in an instant, Hazamareth's expression straightened, becoming eerily apathetic.

Alvena's hand had curled so tightly that the little charm seemed to throb, and she felt another chill crawl down her spine. There was something strange about that woman. Something outside the mortal realm.

She had little time to consider the possibilities before Tsuki returned to business. "Carry on, *Captain*."

Vale gathered himself despite the tangible insolence. "It was last seen in the city," he grunted. "Bring me back a horn from its head when you've completed the task and you'll receive the rest of your payment." He tossed a bag that jangled loudly as it hit the bed beside the half-elf. Then he gestured toward the silver blades lying beside the nightstand. "A fair word of warning," he added, a slight sneer erupting. "That fancy gear hasn't subdued it yet."

Tsuki seemed undaunted by Vale's underlying threat and lifted the purse in thanks. The half-elf lowered her head in silent agreement and Alvena watched as her bangs fell back into a distasteful V-shape across her forehead. "A pleasure doing business with you, Captain. We will make short work of it."

And as unsettling as their disposition was, Alvena seized upon their fearless stance before the captain. Maybe this was her chance—perhaps Sel'ari had sent a powerful pair to take her underwing. *'Help,'* she mouthed, clasping her hands together.

Her fingers loosened to release the charm, but Vale reached out, jerking her solidly toward the hall. "*Let's go*, bitch."

And as the door snapped shut behind her, the two faces stared after them, staunchly indifferent.

Chapter Nineteen

A sharp rapping caused Sellemar to startle awake. Groggily, he raised his head from his desk and pried free the parchment stuck to his cheek.

Rap. Rap. RAP. RAP.

"What in Ramul…?" he blinked hard, struggling to focus.

Rap. RAP.

He jerked abruptly, his palm dashing to the side and spilling the still-open bottle of ink. "Damn!" he swore, skidding the chair clear before the contents could drip onto his lap. He snatched the nearest parchment and scraped it hastily across his hand. It offered little assistance and he hunted for something of more use.

RAP. RAP. RAP. RAP. The sharp sound cleared his mind in the surrounding silence, echoing across the vast and empty estate like a thunder clap.

"Damn it, have patience!" he muttered, hurling the parchment as he scrambled for his bedroom door. He improvised by sweeping up the maroon-colored shirt draped beside the fire. What was a little ink to the atrocity of the pauperish hole Cahsari had been so gracious to identify?

RAP RAP RAP RAP.

Sellemar flung the ink-stained rag into the smoldering fireplace and wasted no more time. The sleep was gone; his mind was clear. The disturbance warned of no ordinary guest—*someone* had arrived at the end of the True Blood Tunnel.

Sellemar caught the edge of the banister and swung himself over the side, landing softly beside the wall. *'Alvena?'* he wondered, even as it was for Itirel he begged. He ran his blackened fingers down the marble tiles and pressed his hand flat against their base. The magic charged his palm and he spoke the ancient elven words for its compliance. "May I pass?!"

The wall revolved inward at his request and the golden, vaulted ceiling of the tunnel lit with a flicker of gentle, cerulean orb light.

Beneath the glow, the Noc'olari became illuminated.

"*Itirel!*" Sellemar cried in relief, though he restrained himself physically to a refined smile. The male's flesh was unmarred by weapon or blood... He could not have been present when Galadorium was attacked! *'Praise Sel'ari!'*

"What took you so long?" Itirel breathed in rebuke as he ducked past the speechless male.

Sellemar pursed his lips, watching as the male wiped the perspiration from his brow. This was not the characteristic, ambling greeting he had expected after their time apart. Even when the circumstance was most dire, the Noc'olari was habitually, *unnaturally* calm... Had he been informed of Galadorium's fate? "What has happened?"

At Sellemar's detection, Itirel's anxiety melted. His hand extended and dropped staunchly upon his shoulder. "*Hadoream is in the land.*"

Sellemar stood stupefied with disbelief. "Ha... doream...?" he stammered like an imbecile. Sairel had acceded to his plea?—It could not be true! "How do you know this?" he demanded. "If it is merely a rumor, spare me your optimism!"

Itirel discarded his worn sack beside the still-open wall and rested his lance at its side. "Allies in the south," he replied vaguely, his attention fading as he scanned the estate. "Again, which way is your kitchen...?"

Sellemar had hardly begun to indicate down the hallway when the Noc'olari caught sight of the room at its end and hastened past. He vanished into the doorway beyond, leaving Sellemar to scurry in pursuit. "Hadoream on Sevrigel?" he repeated skeptically. "But I never truly presumed that Sairel would permit this... *regardless* of his father's vow. Ilsevel will certainly threaten *war* upon the Sel'varian Realm if she discovers that a True Blood royal has returned!" He trailed off, envisioning the staunchly resistant king scowling at his missive's proposal.

No, *never* Sairel.

Yet Itirel chuckled, flipping the doors of the pantry open one by one, and, as though he had forgotten his manners entirely, leaving each ajar. He snatched the loaf of bread from the lowest shelf, pausing briefly to regard the chunk nibbled from the side. "Sairel? Oh, he did not agree to this. This was entirely of Hadoream's own choosing. It seems he slipped south with the assistance of Darcarus almost two weeks ago. Some of the sailors who trade out of the Eph'ven city of Dahel smuggled him across the channel to Marilore. Since then, he has made himself remarkably scarce…" He laughed and shook his head. "*War?* We have to *find* Hadoream first."

Hope flared within Sellemar's breast. This was a shocking turn of events. He had expected to expose the lies of Saebellus and Ilsevel one by one, and that the discovery of such duplicity would incite a rebellion within the people. Yet even were he able to cripple Saebellus' army, uproot his council, and divulge his heinous plan, the rebellion would remain bereft of a leader.

But a *True Blood!* Not only would the elven world be eradicated of the centuries of corruption, but a true *leader* would then assume the mantle of responsibility.

Sellemar practically grinned. *'I rescind complaints in full. Your plans are invariably grander than I can conceive.'* He was wrenched from his praise as Itirel heaved another door. "So then Darcarus must be here as well," he concluded. "He has long favored the old cities along Dragon Wing—I would reasonably wager that Hadoream resides there."

Itirel cast wide another door and sighed in dismay. "You need to eat more fruits and vegetables. You will suffer from ailments if you—"

"This is not the appropriate time to lecture me," Sellemar interrupted, scraping his black fingers together in a failed attempt to snap. "Have you scoured the coast?"

The chunk of stale, nibbled cheese hung loosely in Itirel's calloused hand. "I am afraid we have no such fortune," he uttered regrettably. "Darcarus did not accompany him."

"You cannot mean that Darcarus *left* Hadoream's side…?" The notion was too preposterous to comprehend.

And yet Itirel nodded his confirmation. "Indeed, yes." He shoved another hardened lump into his sack. "Yinsara is with him, granted, but our sources verify Darcarus was never on the ship. One can only assume that he has determined that he can best aid Hadoream from Ryekarayn."

"From *Ryekarayn?*" The story was becoming increasingly outlandish. "What can he possibly achieve there? The male has no allies—" His expression flattened. "Surely he does not intend to hunt *Relstavum*."

"This *is* Darcarus of whom we speak," Itirel tutted. "He'll attempt *something* ludicrous."

"Fair point," Sellemar muttered. He snatched a molded chunk from the shelf of a nearby cupboard before Itirel's eyes could land upon its decrepit state. "Still, I see no victory in their reckless path. By not contacting you or me, Hadoream certainly cannot expect to ascend the throne."

"I am certain he's made his intentions quite clear by *not* contacting us. You *know* that this is hardly the first time the idea has been suggested to him. But we *are* on Sevrigel and Hadoream does not want to stir further conflict…" Itirel frowned faintly, raising the last bit of cheese for inspection. "Do you have mice?"

Sellemar bristled. "I am going to get a cat."

"Oh? I thought cats hated you."

"Not every cat can hate me."

Itirel shrugged, reaching his hand along the topmost shelf of a pantry in his quest for further provisions. "What color?"

"I was thinking—Damn, the color matters not! We are discussing *Hadoream*." Sellemar slung open the lower pantry and placed a chunk of dried meat atop the Noc'olari's supplies. "That is the last of my food. Now tell me, *what* does Hadoream think he is doing here alone?"

"What does Hadoream *think* he is doing here?" Itirel chortled. "I do not believe Hadoream *thought* about his actions before he plunged headlong into the heart of the war. I imagine that he is *attempting* to help Sevrigel's people. Ilra knows he's probably bandaging some refugee and boiling soup as we speak."

Such naivety! "Hadoream cannot forever evade his lineage! We have witnessed the state to which this country has fallen without his family! If he wants to truly help his people, he *must*—" He cut himself off, clenching his fist. "If Hadoream will not take the throne, so help me, *I* will!"

Itirel was upon him in an instant, catching the front of his collar to rattle him like an infant's toy. His eyes pinned Sellemar with his full attention for the first time since his arrival. "*Don't you dare*," he sibilated. "We have *all* discussed this before. What *is* our decision? *We cannot shelter this world forever*. Do not, *Sellemar*, cross this line."

Sellemar wrested his hand aside and shoved himself away, scowling. "Then Hadoream *must*—"

Itirel interrupted him in a deliberately passive tone. *Hadoream* a pacifist?—*hah*. The True Blood would find no greater rival to that title than this Noc'olarian male. "Hadoream's mere presence is an inspiration to the people. He is giving them hope and ideas of rebellion. Their spirits are stirring, even without Hadoream leading them to war. *But*," he stressed before Sellemar could interject, "you *are* correct. Sevrigel needs his leadership now. You and I can likely convince him to take the throne, but we must find and protect him first." He dropped his sack onto the counter with a grunt. "There. That should be everything we need."

Sellemar blinked. *'WE?'* "What…?" He briskly stepped away, shaking his head. "No, *no*. I cannot accompany you."

Itirel leaned forward, fixing him with narrowed eyes. "And is this decision because of your cat?"

Sellemar mimicked the Noc'olari's expression. "No, this decision is not because of the cat-I-do-not-yet-own," he replied flatly. He pinched the bridge of his nose and leaned against the wall. "I have to stay here," he insisted as his free hand gestured about the drafty interior of the old Rilden Estate. "If we are to change this country, we require more than an improvement in monarchs—the people must comprehend the crimes Saebellus and Ilsevel have wrought. When the people realize what they have caused by their compliance to such horrors, they shall become our rebellion and the strength in Hadoream's army. That is my responsibility to oversee—you can fetch our prince. After all, your skills of persuasion far surpass what I can offer."

"Hah. Your praise is flattering, but—"

Sellemar pressed a palm to the invaluable vial tucked safely into his inner breast pocket. "I just acquired the Nemorium. Once I have administered this to Ilsevel, failing to incite a rebellion will be impossible. We must change the hearts of the people or no army or king will deliver this country from its cycle of self-destruction. You can accomplish your task without me, Itirel—I have complete faith."

Itirel straightened slowly. "Flattery, again. Thank you for your confidence, but I am not a god. And neither, as I apparently must remind you, are *you.* I will refrain from asking *how* in the *Nine Realms* you managed to acquire Nemorium and simply ask how are you going to manage to slip it to Ilsevel? Waving a glass of wine before the queen and tempting her to drink is far greater a challenge than you make it sound. You are talking about being equally as capable of slipping her *poison*. She is hardly *that* inept."

Sellemar pursed his lips, wishing he had a plan to divulge. And in his search for a distraction, an unwelcome thought leapt into his mind. He had been so relieved to see his friend that his initial reason for his anxiety had vanished.

His throat tightened. Even the confidence of the male would surely waver in the wake of the news. "Itirel…" He swallowed his hesitation. He was not gifted with the charisma to ease into such a tragedy. "Galadorium has been destroyed."

What little color Itirel possessed drained. For the briefest moment, his composed expression wavered; his eyes faltered. Yet he did not address the matter. "It is too dangerous for you to stay here," his friend breathed after a moment. "Far too dangerous. Ilsevel is mad with bloodlust. We shall have to manage without the change of heart—surely such a thing can be achieved once we have Hadoream on the throne."

Sellemar shook his head firmly, his lips drawn tight.

"E—"

"*No,*" Sellemar spoke forcefully. "And where will you find an army? Ryekarayn?—Saebellus' plans there have disabled any hope for aid. I will be fi—" He stopped abruptly as a knock rang out from the door to the estate. "*Truly?*" he muttered. He turned to the hallway stretching to the Grand Hall and the estate's front doors. A silhouette lingered behind the clouded panes of glass beside it. "Wait here… Stop venting your frustrations on that bread."

Sellemar stepped quickly to the tattered curtains adorning the front window and peered out through the small crack along the side. If Tilarus had dared to show himself in person here…!

His stomach dropped.

'Ilsevel.'

Sellemar promptly withdrew, hastening across the marble hall and breaking into a sprint within the hallway. "*Go.* Ilsevel is here!" he gasped. He grabbed Itirel by the arm, dragging him and his obscenely heavy sack swiftly toward the open tunnel. "Find Hadoream. All of Sevrigel is depending on you." He picked up the lance, shoving it into the Noc'olari's thick arms.

Itirel hesitated just for a moment, no doubt struggling through a mix of "sage advice" and "necessary warnings," but he finally surrendered himself to Sellemar's push. He took a single stride to fade into the darkness. "Be careful, my friend." His tone of concern was unnervingly blunt. "We are not immortal… If you find yourself in danger, do not count on Sairel's protection. He cannot reach you here."

The shadow behind them shifted and a louder knock spurred the Noc'olari forward. "May Sel'ari bless you," Sellemar replied grimly, running his hand along the tiles. "Thank you."

And the wall closed with a quiet thud.

Sellemar straightened, his breast filling with confidence. Ilsevel had come to see him. Perhaps Sel'ari even now presented encouragement for his choice to remain behind.

"Greetings, Your Majesty. I am honored," he spoke as he swung the great door wide. He dipped into a regal bow.

Ilsevel glanced through her escort of guards, surveying the darkened and dreary home with disdain. "Still quite drafty," she lamented, drawing her heavy silk cloak about her shoulders to ward off the chill in the winter air. She stepped inside and drifted idly toward the kitchen as though she were mistress of the estate. "Where is your dining room? Have your servants prepare us something."

Sellemar frowned. Visions of empty cupboards and recently crumbled bread rose in response to her words. "I am afraid that I have neither servants nor food at this time," he replied awkwardly. And what a shame that a male of *his* stature owned so little in this land, even *before* his comrade had raided his meager stores.

Ilsevel paused at the entrance to his hallway, her hand running along the ancient tiles. Then she whirled and batted her bright eyes. "Will you then take me to dine, Lord Sellemar?" she inquired, flashing a smile so sickeningly sweet that it caused him to roll his shoulders in discomfort.

"I have some important—" he began instinctively as she swept back and wrapped her slender hands about his arm. But he immediately rebuked himself. *'This is Sel'ari's door to you,'* he snapped. He offered what he hoped was some semblance of charm. "But *anything* can wait for your sake," he amended.

*

The establishment Ilsevel had chosen was an extensive, three-story building with a white marbled exterior and countless balconies jutting around the upper floors. Sheer chiffon curtains hung in varying shades of gold behind the closed glass doors, casting a warm array of orange light to fall to the cobblestones outside.

Crystal chandeliers, magically lit orbs, golden dining ware—the presentation possessed all the airs of a grandiose eatery. Still, Sellemar found himself unimpressed and wondered if his distraction was evident. This was an elven establishment otherwise *worthy* of his praise.

"Thank you." Ilsevel's words interrupted his thoughts. The server had pulled her chair aside and she seated herself with a graceful flourish of her skirts. They had stopped on the topmost floor before a table secluded within a vast row of dark, mauve curtains.

Sellemar realized his discourteous behavior too late and muttered a quick apology. For the briefest moment, he had thought that he had seen a familiar face at a table to their left, but the curtain closed and ended his perusal. He dropped into the chair across from the queen, trying to fashion what he perceived to be a charming smile.

Ilsevel raised her glass to the side as the servant elevated the bottle of wine. "El'adorium, you seem troubled," she began, swirling her glass.

Damn Itirel for being correct! How in Sel'ari's name was he to manage to slip the Nemorium to the queen with her sitting a yard away, ogling him with such shamelessly attentive eyes?

In his mild consternation, he had drowned out the inquiries of the servant beside him and only the brief flick of Ilsevel's eyes recalled him to the room. "The El'adorium would like a glass. I'm afraid business has left him absentminded." She gestured to the goblet before him with a sweet, understanding smile.

Sellemar took a long sip. Damn. *Focus*. Ilsevel's eyes lingered on his, her slender hand resting closer to his side of the table than was entirely natural. He slowly lowered his glass. "Server, I would prefer something a bit drier," he requested, maintaining focus on Ilsevel's gaze. "A white wine from the mid to late eighty hundreds, if you can oblige."

The servant nodded quickly in acknowledgement and cleared his throat to begin a rambling inventory of the foods the eatery would provide.

Ilsevel leaned slightly to the right, away from his voice. "That will do," she replied with a crinkle of her nose and a dismissive wave of her hand. She only reclined into her seat as he shuffled away. "I so love dining outside the palace," she began again, as equally sweet and soft as she was outwardly passive. "My brother loved this place. I sometimes come to this balcony alone to reminisce about the time we spent here. It is nice to have a change in scenery… and to be away from prying ears." She smiled and gestured curtly to the guards around her. "If you could wait outside, that proximity will suffice."

Sellemar glanced sidelong as the soldiers filed out, hearing the soft clank of their armor settle outside the wall of curtains. Ilsevel followed his gaze and in that brief absence of all attention, Sellemar slipped the vial from his breast pocket and pressed his hand into his lap. He forced a smile as her gaze returned. "I could not agree more. Nor could my company be enhanced by a more beautiful lady." He offered the words as courtesy dictated, but they left his tongue with a bitter aftertaste.

Ilsevel devoured the compliment. "Last time we spoke, Lord Sellemar, I failed to deduce much outside your charming character," she purred. She dipped the tip of her ring finger into her wine and touched it slowly to her tongue. "But now that you sit on my very council, I should like to remedy that distance."

Sellemar's hand tightened around the vial. If he had found an opportunity to empty the Nemorium within her glass, already the bond would be complete even by that scant taste!

"You are clearly a refined individual," she continued. "Nobility, I would surmise, but you flaunt no titles or heritage. I am left puzzling why you would withhold the information... Unless secrecy is your ploy of attraction." She allowed her eyes to run brazenly down his body. "I do find that... *terribly* attractive." And then she looked away, feigning a self-conscious laugh.

Sellemar's smile drooped. Were males truly weakened by such audacious flirting? "My parents were Lord and Lady Dalaenel Estavorn of Eraydon City. I find the burden of nobility stifling for a male in my profession."

"Well, I see no reason for it to be so. Your work has acquired you great renown on Sevrigel. Why would your nobility be shackling in light of that fortune? Unless you *enjoy* living amongst the mice in squalor." Ilsevel's smile broadened and Sellemar felt his cheeks flush. "And you have no lack of experience with nobility, do you? Tell me," she continued, her eyes flickering with amusement, "what do you think of the True Bloods' third prince, Hadoream?"

'...Prince Hadoream... Does she know....?'

The curtain rustled and the server reappeared, a glass in one hand and a recently half-dusted bottle in the other. "Here is the wine you requested, my lord. Vintage from the summer of eighty-eight hundred, to be precise. Finest vintage of the time." He placed a glass delicately on the table and uncorked the bottle, all the while unaware of Ilsevel's rapidly tapping foot.

When he departed, Ilsevel rose to follow him with hushed rebukes. "Be silent about your work next time," she snapped quietly, clearly hoping Sellemar's exceptional hearing could not detect her rage. "I do not need to know you are here for you to labor. I am in a *very* important engagement."

Thank the *gods* the female's desire for authority extended to seemingly every aspect of her life. Sellemar's hand swept from his lap, subtly uncorking the vial, and in a single flick of his wrist the translucent contents had poured into the soft, golden wine before him. "Why," he exclaimed as he lowered the glass from his lips, wresting Ilsevel's attention from the servant. "This is a *splendid* vintage indeed!"

Ilsevel turned, flashing her smile in all its mendacities. "May I?" she requested brazenly, gliding to their little table and dropping herself once more across from him.

'Ah, you are a natural at this,' Sellemar praised himself as he smugly slid the glass toward her. And Itirel had doubted him! Hah! With one taste, the bond would be complete. Ilsevel's thoughts and actions from the moment the wine touched her lips and forward... he was soon to grasp it all.

Ilsevel met him halfway, her long fingers locking over his. "Foolish servant. Where were we? Ah... I remember. I was asking about your opinion on... Prince Hadoream, was it? Yes." She drew her hand away then, taking the imbued wine with her. "I have seen so many paintings of Hadoream with his brothers, yet he is so oddly nondescript. Vague. Ageless. One must wonder at the inaccuracies of his depiction. ...Dare I venture so far as to suggest," she continued more slowly, "that such an act was deliberate."

Sellemar stiffened. *So she truly did not know.* He rebuked his defensive emotions and forced his attention away from the glass. "Prince Hadoream? I met him. He seemed well-read."

Ilsevel chuckled, raising his glass to her lips. "You're skirting a response. *Come*, El'adorium. A male for whom their king would pledge his life is not a male who merely 'met' his brother. What do you know of Hadoream? Tell me about his character. His wisdom. His personality. *Defining* characteristics, perhaps?" She leaned forward, her eyes wide, the glass departing without a drop against her tongue. "What would he think of our reign?"

For a brief moment, Sellemar forgot the urgency of the Nemorium. The inquiries of Hadoream's nature were worthless... unless she knew more than Itirel had suggested. "Prince Hadoream is a free spirit and is mildly eccentric. He passes much of his time along the coast or causing mischief with His Highness, Darcarus. I dare say the two of them are nigh inseparable. As Darcarus *is* often his totem of inspiration, he can be childishly naïve." He paused, discomforted by her eerily fixed grin. "This naivety might lead him to disagree with the necessity of your methods. He cares very deeply for the people around him; he holds no fear for his own life and will recklessly endanger himself for the wellbeing of others. I think the fact that he is a remarkable embodiment of the gentle core of elven nature is why he is depicted so generally." He took a slow sip from his first glass of wine, lingering it at his mouth in an attempt to redirect her to the more pressing matter at hand. When the intensity of her gaze passed beyond his hint, he dared to question, "Why interest yourself with him? A child's opinion matters not in your reign."

Ilsevel remained fixed. She raised the imbued glass, swirling the golden wine about in a slow, rhythmic fashion. Her tone was indecipherable. "As a close acquaintance with the True Bloods, it surprises me that you do not share their disapproval with our cause."

"Hadoream's disapproval, my queen," he replied carefully. "It was Sairel who vouched for my character. Sairel is wise enough to know better than to intervene in your plans."

"Yet we both know he still disagrees with our methods."

Sellemar felt the dagger pricking beneath her words. Her affection was merely a mask. She did not trust him. *Not for a breath.* "It is a tragedy that the True Bloods reign with such misguided power… While Sairel is dear to me, he possesses flaws—none of which is greater than his blindness to the corruption infesting these lands. Like his father, he is too frightened to assume the necessary stance. While he has remained on Ryekarayn, I have had the wisdom to return. Surely he will warm to you when he beholds the glory of Sevrigel reclaimed." His silver tongue would have put the god of deception to shame.

Ilsevel's gaze broke then, her smile broadening so wide that her face looked ready to split. Yet the careful composition revealed nothing to suggest his words had truly swayed her. "Even so, Saebellus will keep his army nearby… for now."

Sellemar felt his stomach drop. Something was amiss in her eyes… and in her tone. *'Itirel was wrong. She* knows *that Hadoream is here. She suspects my loyalties…'*

"Ah, there we are!" Ilsevel exclaimed abruptly, curbing Sellemar's rising agitation. The curtains beside them drew back to reveal a host of servants filing in from the room beyond. They entered and circled the table, layering it with a vast assortment of foods until nearly every inch was covered in appetizing entrées. Ilsevel lifted Sellemar's glass of white wine as the last dish was placed before her, extending her arm out to offer the glass back to him.

Sellemar's brow knit. No… *She had not taken a drop!* "How did you favor the wine?" he asked quickly, dragging out the unfolding of his napkin into his lap as though unaware of her attempts to return his glass. He summoned all the experiences of his career to offer the most expressive smile he was capable of producing—one that suggested his naivety to her suspicions. Adoration in her charm. *Stupidity* to the danger he faced.

The last servant entered the room and turned to close the curtains behind him.

Ilsevel laughed, drawn once more into the façade that she believed remained unbroken. "I shall try it right now. I'm afraid I was so absorbed in your words that I have not even had a sip!"

"Ah, if it isn't *the queen*."

The curtains closed, but the words reached them even so. Ilsevel's arm remained extended, her body stilling as all her attention seemed captured by the voice. "*Vale*."

The curtains shifted and the Sel'varian captain swept into the room between their folds, darting in as briskly as though they were doors readying a lock to resist his entrance.

Sellemar's lips pursed. He remembered Vale. He remembered him perfectly. From the top of his long, braided blond hair to the bottom of his polished leather boots. He had encountered the bloodthirsty male only once before: during his ill-fated "rescue" of Ilsevel from Saebellus. They had fought, and Sellemar had left the bastard with a knife wound bleeding out his gut.

Yet somehow, he had survived.

Sellemar regarded Vale now, his hatred only having grown since their last encounter. Saebellus' captain had all the appearances of a refined elven military leader. But his swagger was loose and raw, and his eyes unabashedly swept their quiet corner as though he was entirely welcome to join them.

"Gods, and it's the bitch El'adorium too!" Vale exclaimed, eyes locking onto Sellemar with instant animosity. "I'm still wearing a scar from your little stunt, you cunt." He drew two fingers to his side, pressing them against his black, silken shirt as though to remind Sellemar where he had nearly gutted him.

Sellemar had not forgotten. Still, he was above responding. Why even *Saebellus* had lowered himself to deal with the likes of Vale, he could not fathom. He was as crude and human-like as any Sel'ven had ever come.

"What are you doing here, Vale?" Ilsevel demanded. "I did not invite you to dine with me. Don't you have *work* to do? Prisoners to slaughter? A male to desecrate?"

"A male to desecrate," Vale repeated flatly, tearing his seething glare from Sellemar with a little flash of a venomous sneer. "I suppose you're referring to Adonis. Nah. I'm doing the desecrating *after* dinner. And I didn't need an invitation. I dine here *all* the time. Nearly daily, in fact. I heard your delighted voice when your food arrived. It was like the high-pitched cries of an orgasming whore. A male whore, obviously. Haven't heard a female." He paused briefly as though to relish their shock and offense. "I haven't seen you since we got back from Galadorium. Thought I'd drop in to see who was being forced to endure your presence today."

"*How dare you,*" Ilsevel gasped. "If Saebellus did not have a use for you, so help me you'd be joining Valdor beneath the earth! Now you will leave this *instant.* I thought I made it *very* clear that if you have *anything* to say to me, you will have to say it through Saebellus."

Vale paused, regarding her stoically, seeming to debate his options. There was a shift in the armored men beyond the curtain and Sellemar had no doubt they were fully aware of the spat between them. Their lack of response, however, suggested such a clash was not unusual or alarming.

Vale finally seemed to come to a conclusion. "Is that your wine?" he asked abruptly.

"Yes. No. *It doesn't matter—!*"

And to Sellemar's horror, through Ilsevel's gasps of indignation and rage, the Sel'varian captain swept his hand through the air and plucked Sellemar's wine glass from her hands. There was a tipped glass. An unnecessarily loud gulp.

And the Nemorium was gone.

"Pleasant to see you, too," Vale belched, and let the glass fall from his fingers to shatter at his feet.

The curtains flung aside instantly at the sound of splintering glass and the soldiers stood at the ready, weapons drawn.

Ilsevel was practically bursting with rage. Her tiny hands had balled into fists, her mouth hanging open so wide in shock and offense that her chin threatened to touch the marble floors. "Take him from my sight *immediately!*" she stammered.

Vale snorted. He flourished his hand dismissively at the soldiers about him and shoved one aside as he passed. "Next time," he called over his shoulder as he went, "let's try you playing at some level of courtesy with me, shall we? I have to get back to my desecrated lover and that little bitch of yours. *My* wine will have arrived by now."

"*Saebellus will hear of this!*" Ilsevel snarled in reply.

The soldiers exited to their posts, the eatery returned to a hushed murmur, the curtains closed… but Sellemar could only sit in transfixed horror.

"*Captain Vale,*" Ilsevel breathed as she dropped back into her chair.

A server had hurried into the room to sweep the glass away, his eyes downcast for fear of her rebuke at his appearance.

But Ilsevel paid him no heed. "He's furious with me," she continued with a shake of her head. "They picked up the servant girl in Galadorium and, at Saebellus' request, I have ordered Vale and Adonis to watch over her until her execution."

Sellemar hardly gathered her words. Had… had the Nemorium just bound him and…?

"Why Saebellus *ever* settled for a male like him, I shall *never* understand. He is the *first* Sel'ven I would purify this country of!" She picked up her silverware and stabbed angrily at her meat. "And then that lover of his. I swear, all he thinks and talks about and *does* is *vile* intercourse!"

Sellemar's lips parted and his mind urged him to form a response. But he could not. Ilsevel had exclaimed when the food had arrived. Vale had heard her and entered.

A clash had ensued, his wine had been taken, and—

And the Nemorium was gone.

"*By Sel'ari*," he breathed in repulsion.

"My shared feelings, exactly," Ilsevel huffed.

CHAPTER TWENTY

Alvena woke on the divan, finding herself curled tightly into a ball in a subconscious attempt to ward off the chill. The fire had abandoned its hearth, leaving winter to take a delighted patrol about the bedchamber. The little charm she had fastened about her neck was as cold as ice and she curled a hand around it, determined to send it warmth. She sat up stiffly, keeping the silk sheets wrapped tight, and peered over the back of her makeshift bed.

Adonis had returned sometime late the night before—long after Vale had paced the room, thrown Adonis' pillow on the floor, and then fallen asleep. As the brilliant sunlight was barely dimmed by the curtains, she marveled at how it was possible she had slept so late.

Her eyes slid to the two forms curled beneath the covers, dead to the world. If only she could slip out now while they were practically unconscious…

She cautiously hunkered down as a knock rang out from the bedroom door.

"Captain Vale! Lieutenant Adonis! It is nearly noon and the prisoners have not been reassigned. His Majesty has told me to inform you: if you do not get down there this instant he'll…" the guard hesitated before he continued awkwardly, "hang you by your most valuable appendages in the palace courtyard for every hour you delay."

Alvena saw Vale sit bolt upright, his eyes wide. "What…?" he croaked. "Shit. Adonis, it's almost midday! Get your fat ass out of bed!" He swung his legs over the side, nearly tumbling out as the covers braided around his feet.

Adonis' hand rose up and smacked him across the back. "Don't call me fat," he mumbled as he swung himself groggily out from the other side.

Forgetting herself for a moment, Alvena smiled. Then she straightened her face and gave them both a resentful scowl.

"And a pleasant morning for you as well, bitch," Vale grunted, glancing her way as he sauntered to the chest along the far wall. His mouth worked in preparation to spit toward her, but the rug of the lovers intertwined caught his eye and he seemed to consider preserving its unmarred state and swallowed.

Alvena let her lips curl back in a threateningly toothy glower. As though she were capable of harming him at all. *'I hope Sel'ari stuffs your soul in Ramul!'*

"Vale, her name is Alvena. Use it," Adonis grumbled into his hand. He yawned and stretched an arm high above his tousled hair. Then his head drooped once more.

Vale acknowledged Adonis' rebuke by aggressively flipping open the lid of the chest against the far wall. When the noisy gesture won him no response, he dug his way furiously through the mound of clothes.

"Alvena," Adonis began as his feet touched the floor. Remarkably, he had managed to come back awake on his own. He crouched on the floor and slid his sword casually out from underneath the bed.

Alvena promptly noted where he had stored it this time before her attention snapped up, wide-eyed and innocent.

Adonis waved his porcelain hand in her direction. "I brought your chest of clothes from your room. It has not been touched. I am sorry that you were forced to remain in that attire yesterday… I had assumed before you two went out that Vale would care for your needs, but *apparently* he does not understand simple etiquette. …He does not boast good manners."

Alvena dropped the blanket about her and eagerly swept the room. Adonis had wobbled to Vale and stooped to open another chest. But it was not hers. Her trunk was…

'Oh, there it is!' She bounced to the long wooden chest pushed against the back of the divan. Had he fetched this for her in the night, even after he was out so late? Finally she could rid herself of the filthy clothes clinging to her in that abominable grime! *'Thank you,'* she wanted to mouth, but quickly averted her body as Vale flung his night's clothes aside and bent shameless to brandish the moon's less reputable face.

"*Vale*, have some decency!" Adonis barked.

"Psh, *you* have some decency."

"But you—" She heard Adonis give an embellished sigh.

"Stop stammering your offense and get changed. No doubt Laeth tattled on us for being late. Little whiner. When I get down there, I'm going to shove my sword up his ass."

Alvena glanced up in time to see Adonis roll his eyes, snatching up Vale's discarded clothing as he did so. He set them in a neat pile beside Vale's chest.

"I didn't mean my *sword* sword, Adonis. That's just for you. I meant my actual sword."

Alvena grimaced, attempting to ignore Adonis' gasp of indignation and Vale's subsequent remarks as she pulled a simple dress from the chest. She slipped between the fire and the divan for concealment, but neither male was paying any attention to her. Even with the dirty dress off, she hardly felt any cleaner: she reeked of fear and the long march along the canyon.

Alvena sucked in her breath and clamped her jaw. *'Toughen up, Alvena,'* she rebuked herself. At the end, this had to be better than any treatment the prisoners below were to receive.

*

After their hurried meal, Alvena descended into the winding stairwell of the dungeons. Before her, the two Sel'vi squabbled about appropriate decency in the presence of a female, but she caught only fragments of their discussion. The stench below was overpowering all her senses. By the time they had reached the first floor of the prison, Alvena's eyes stung with the putrid odor.

Hairem had *never* allowed his prisons to deteriorate so!

"If *I* want to change and she doesn't look away, I am not at fault," Vale contended. "She probably likes males. And I am a *damn* attractive male."

"With *that* attitude you most certainly are not," Adonis muttered.

Alvena scowled at Vale's stupid grin, but the male was fully enraptured by his lover. He attempted to trail a hand down Adonis' side. "Oh, you *adore* my confidence."

Adonis swatted him away. "*Tell her* before you strip naked."

"That takes the spontaneity right out of it!"

Adonis lifted the crook of his arm, ignoring Vale's protests. Alvena had long since covered her own nose with her palm, though this offered little relief. She couldn't imagine Adonis' arm prevailed in offering any greater respite. "This stench is almost unbearable!" he gagged.

Vale sniffed and shrugged. "That's Alvena."

"Cease being rude. *You* can bathe her when we are through."

Alvena shuffled with embarrassment and set her attention on their path. Webs shimmered from up high while dust bunnies skittered around their feet. The dirt and grime clinging between the bronze tiles had managed to find an equal hold upon the hall's ornate, tawny columns. The dismal state of it all was only accentuated in the bright blue light of the vaulted ceiling's orbs.

Under Saebellus' rule, surely the city would one day follow in the spiraling pattern of decay.

Then her ragged leather touched down upon the ancient tiled mural in the center of the columned hall. Even without the flag billowing boldly behind the male in the image, his identity was clear: he was a True Blood king, exacting judgment upon a criminal. The regal figure stood erect and proud, a gleaming sword in his left hand and the criminal's head clutched triumphantly in his right.

For a moment, she envisioned that it was Vale's.

"We're not on duty for this floor," Adonis interrupted her fantasy, and propelled her gently onward. "This way." He steered her through the rows of pillars and down another staircase to the second floor.

Here, the vaulted ceilings fell away.

"Adonis, Vale!" a voice barked from their right.

Alvena turned, peering around the side of the two males. A Noc'olari stalked toward them from across the hall, his ageless face skewed into creases and tightly drawn lips. He was not as handsome or as kind-looking as Itirel.

The male gestured a grey hand down the old stonework, to the cell doors stretching open in the distance. "Do you know how many prisoners we have had to relocate today? I have been down here for *six* hours already!"

"*We* have been down here for six hours," came another voice from their left. A female stepped out of a cell, wiping her hands on her pants as she approached. Alvena recognized her as Turlondiel, the reckless soldier by whom she and Adonis had nearly been plowed over. Even in the cool air of the lower dungeon level, strands of her flaxen curls were stuck to her brow with sweat. Still, she seemed significantly less wild in her clammy state. "*Six* hours," she stressed as she shook out a dirty cloth.

Vale scoffed. "*Only* six hours."

The Noc'olari shot him a glare. "*Finally*, Turlondiel reported you to Saebellus."

"*You?!*" Vale gasped. He pointed his finger accusingly at the female. "Why you little bitch!"

Turlondiel gave a bored sniff and upturned a dainty chin. "I am sorry to implicate you as well, Adonis," she tsked. "I'm sure you were out late again, but after such a delay, I could not possibly excuse *Vale*."

Adonis swiftly bowed his head. "I apologize, Laethile, Turlondiel. Saebellus did have me on a mission last night and I did not return until dawn. Vale… was also out late."

Alvena made a face. *'No, we got back quite early enough. He just stomped about for hours muttering about how half of Sevrigel would pay to bed him.'*

Whether he accepted the apology or not, Laeth pivoted to the right and surveyed her. His grey eyes creased softly and Alvena imagined a hundred years were tucked into each wrinkle. So that would place him about… He spoke before she could finish counting, but by such standards he was ancient. "And you must be Alvena. This is certainly not the place for a lady, but I suppose you are under the care of Adonis. This may extend a few hours and you will find yourself terribly bored."

Alvena raised her brows. Like Itirel at Galadorium, he spoke tenderly… But if he was *not* a beast, then why did he serve *Saebellus?* She narrowed her eyes at him, refusing to be softened by his glib words.

Vale gave a childish huff. "If *you're* so nice to her, why don't you take her?—Hard to do things to my man with that thing about."

Adonis placed a tempering hand on Vale's arm. "Laeth is correct, Alvena. Why don't you take a seat over there?"

"The wall? The dungeons are not the place to bring the lady to begin with," Turlondiel rebuked, tossing her curly locks behind her shoulders. "Surely there were guards to watch her in your quarters so she might *relax*. I don't know why she must be subjected to Vale *and* the prisons. You would think one punishment is sufficient for having done nothing at all."

Throughout her tirade, Vale's chest had expanded with disdain. "Always siding with the females," he accused.

"And," Turlondiel continued with growing offense, "have you let the poor lady bathe?! By the gods! You're not keeping a dog!—and I needn't remind you what happened the last time you *did* try to keep a pet." She ignored Vale's indignant gasp and gestured to the wall. Her eyes were stern, yet the droop in her lips conveyed compassion. "Well, it cannot be helped now. Sit, Alvena."

Alvena glanced to the right where Turlondiel and Adonis had indicated, watching the torchlight dance upon the bumpy stones. She wrinkled her nose—it was crusted with dirt!—almost as filthy as the room of those two despicable mercenaries! She looked back at the group in dismay.

"Ok, let's just forget you let that bitch sell us out to Saebellus and get to work," came Vale's biting tone.

"*Vale…*"

"What, I can't provoke him? You kill any enjoyment I have in being forced to endure his friendship."

Laeth shoved a scroll into their hands, his voice tolerantly amused. "Although your bickering brightens my day, I must return to the task of caring for the wounded. *Please* manage the relocation of those on your scroll."

Vale muttered a few additional but indistinguishable comments and unfurled his parchment. "I'll take this side, you take that," he grunted before he swung about on his heels, pushed Alvena aside, and marched to the first cell. "Numbers 303, 304, 305, and 306," he called to attention. "Names?"

Alvena shuffled her feet forward and peered cautiously around Vale as the voices inside replied. There were four females huddled in the cell, their right hands shackled to one another with a long, sable chain. Their bodies appeared worn and beaten, their faces hollow and grimy. The waste pail along the left wall emitted a powerful odor despite its emptiness.

Alvena's body reeled away in protest. *'Those poor ladies...'* she put her fingers to her mouth, feeling ashamed that she had even once complained about her own state. They were just four of the numerous Noc'olari who had been ripped from their city and dumped into the overcrowded cells...

Elvorium's prison system was never designed to hold so many people!

Vale pointed to the first victim. "Mistarel." He slid his finger to the second. "Elarium." Then he gestured to the third. He extended a second finger to encompass the fourth female before he scratched something indecipherable on his parchment. "You two may return to Galadorium."

The second and third females instantly clung to each other as their vivid eyes brimmed with agonized tears. "Please, my lord," one begged. "We are sisters. Our husbands are dead. Please place us both—"

But their frantic wails accomplished nothing. Vale could not possibly have a heart. The captain pivoted and marched to the next cell, his face disgustingly apathetic, his eyes appallingly dull. He halted before the next door. "Names."

Alvena lingered beside the first cell, watching the females console one another in tearful Noc'olarian. She could not understand them, but their hushed tones were soothing as they cradled one another. She had never had a sister. Or a brother. But being torn from Lardol and Madorana...

Alvena's hand clenched the charm, her heart aching. It throbbed oddly beneath her hand, but she barely noticed. Why wouldn't that bastard let them go to the same city—back home to Galadorium?! It was the least he could do after what they had endured!

"But I'm pregnant!"

The cry from her left drew Alvena to the cell behind her where Adonis had stepped inside. He was crouched before the females, parchment unrolled against his legs as he scribbled away.

"Oh?" she heard him reply. "Then it would be wiser for you to return to the Noc'olari. Reselph, I will have to change your location to Liasae."

Alvena's hand loosened, the throbbing gone. *'Why... Why is Adonis serving Saebellus? He doesn't seem like the other cold-hearted butchers...'*

Her thoughts trailed off as she heard Laeth exclaim excitedly, "Ilra bless you! I told you that he would be well! That is wonderful. Here, let me help you lie back..."

Her brow furrowed until the muscles in her face hurt. She didn't understand. She *couldn't* understand. What she had seen and heard of Saebellus and his army was, on one hand, vicious and bloodthirsty, yet on the other, starkly... *elven*. She lingered in the middle of the hallway behind Adonis and Vale. Vale never ceased to pass stoically from one cell to the next, inscribing names and assigning cities, while Adonis lingered in each cell, losing himself in conversation or attempting to explain the dynamic of the new location.

Alvena's eyes flicked from one to the other. They were so different! In every way, Vale and Adonis were nothing alike! Vale was everything she expected from Saebellus' savage army, but Adonis...

'No Alvena, do not let him blind you!' She forced her feelings of resentment forward. *'You know they are wrong.'* They *had* to be wrong. *Ilsevel had killed Hairem.*

"Adonis, hurry up!" Vale barked from down the hall. He had made notable progress in the last few hours. "I'm going to have to start doing your work at this rate!"

Alvena turned. Adonis, meanwhile, had disappeared into the very first cell of Vale's endeavor.

"*Adonis!*"

Alvena scuttled aside as Vale stomped in pursuit. He vanished into the cell with Adonis, face drawn in obvious frustration.

"These two women need to be changed to the same location," she heard Adonis calmly begin.

But Vale rejected the request with a laugh. "We're not here to pamper the traitors! These people were attempting to undermine Saebellus. They were *fully aware* of their crimes."

There was silence for a moment.

"I don't think you understand the concept of relocation!" Vale's mocking had fallen away to a growl. "They're related? All the *more* reason to tear them apart!"

But when Adonis' voice came again it was hard and solemn. "Vale. Change their names. *For me*. Now."

The crying in the cell died down and Vale reemerged, looking worn. His eyes passed by Alvena as though he did not notice her.

Adonis appeared next, sighing heavily. "I apologize, Alvena. War can make even the best of us into beasts." He paused to observe Vale, who had halted outside a cell in the distance.

"Name," his voice echoed back to them, softer this time.

"Now, if you will excuse me. Please, have a seat." Adonis beckoned to the side as he drifted past her. "This will all be over soon enough."

Alvena sank against the wall, letting herself slide down to her bottom. *'They serve Ilsevel,'* she repeated to herself. *'Ilsevel killed Hairem.'*

CHAPTER TWENTY-ONE

A loud splash echoed through the tunnels as silver-toed boots clanked against stone hidden within the murky water.

"Hazamareth!" Tsuki barked, flicking drops of sewer water off his hand. *'You should know better,'* he thought with a glower.

His comrade regarded him stoically, quite unfazed by his tone. "My hand slipped," was her flat reply. She shrugged his annoyance away with her lean shoulders and flipped a finger casually toward the darkness ahead.

Tsuki turned, redirecting his attention to the task at hand. "I can smell it," he begrudged with a sniff and wrinkle of his brown nose. "And gods does it reek." He identified the scents easily, even above the putrid odor of the sewer. There was blood—undoubtedly lingering from the beast's victims—and the unique odor of the creature itself… a mix of sewer grime and stone embedded with the sweetly sickening aroma of wet, rancid leather. Gods, nothing he had hunted had ever achieved such a horrid stench. Tsuki blinked back the stinging tears.

"Are you… crying?"

"Yes," Tsuki replied sarcastically. He wiped the back of his hand across his face, forgetting that it was sprinkled in a layer of elven piss. "Damn it, Hazamareth!" he growled. "You know I can't stand the smell of this place!"

They had been combing the city for hours, perhaps remaining too long in tight confinements without respite. Yet Tsuki made no attempt to fight his irritation—this *was* the usual result of their long days together. And there was a sense of relief in it. It disrupted the usual mood in their relationship… A relationship which was normally so pleasant that it unsettled him.

Nothing in life ought to feel so secure.

Hazamareth passed smoothly ahead of him, then turned around and raised her arms with a smirk, displaying the ease with which *she* could traverse the elves' tunnels.

That was the arrogance of the elven blood, for certain. Tsuki swiftly contained the smile tugging at the corner of his lips—but Hazamareth knew that he rather liked when she grew so provocative.

'Damn it,' his irritation broke through once more as he felt the soft squish of something beneath his boot. As of now, the whole *world* was trying to provoke him. And he was not nearly so fond of them.

"You are lagging," Hazamareth hissed from the stone ahead. She, fortunately, had returned to a silent prowl. Aside from the occasional crunch of dried leaves or bones, and the faintest plink from a leaky stone somewhere behind them, the world was now eerily quiet.

Then they rounded the bend.

Tsuki's instincts flared, the hair on his arms rippling over his scars. He caught Hazamareth roughly by the shoulder and jerked her to a stop. His fingers remained locked about her as his eyes swiftly adjusted to the darkness up ahead. A mass of black was curled on the floor where the scents intensified.

The beast?

"Beware the lethal heap of clothes," Hazamareth jested calmly, prying his hand off her shoulder. She sauntered forward, examining the rotting meat and piles of victims' clothes strewn about the long tunnel.

"Damn. It's not here," Tsuki growled. He watched as his comrade's eyes surveyed the crushed breastplate collected without the body of its victim. She need say nothing. Tsuki knew they concluded the same. *'So this is where the beast was staying...'* His face twisted in mild disgust as his comrade poked the corpse of a recently deceased rat that had met its demise like so many of the beast's humanoid victims: with a swift fist to the skull.

Or in this case, the whole body.

Hazamareth prodded it again, watching the maggots slither and roll off. *'He hasn't been here for days,'* her wordless gesture told him. Then she pushed off her knees with a grunt and gazed into the darkness of the adjoining tunnel. "He questioned that woman about the coast." She glanced back, looking to Tsuki for solidarity in the decision.

Tsuki's brow furrowed as he watched the half-elf scratch her nose with the same rat-prodding finger. "Of course he'll go to the coast. Anything to make our job like containing dragon fire in a drought," he muttered in resentful agreement.

*

Over a week had passed since Tsuki had discovered the beast's hideout beneath the sewers. In that time, he had been forced to trail the bodies halfway across the elven lands. He scowled in derision. And that trail had led him *here*.

The Port of Elarium.

The *damn Port of Elarium*.

Tsuki breathed into his hands, rubbing the faint warmth it created over the tips of his calloused fingers. Gusts rolled in with the waves to buffet the crest of the hill where they now sat and waited for the beast's movement. It was a sharp reminder of the admonition he deserved, of that selfish mistake twenty years past—if he had simply refused to trade the little demon for Relstavum's life, then there would be one less of its kind roaming the world.

And then Tsuki would not have found himself here, at the rebuke of the gods. He scowled at the city for good measure. Of all the ports infecting Sevrigel's coast, the beast had uncannily chosen the *one* place where the bounty on its hunter's head was enough to buy a man a sizeable estate and a woman to go along with it.

And thanks to that notoriety, he and Hazamareth were forced to lurk outside, watching the dockyard as their eyes frosted over like those of a cursed Darivalian watchman.

Well, as *his* eyes frosted over.

Hazamareth extended her hand in an offering of warmth, but Tsuki knocked it aside with a glare. Just *looking* at her sent a shiver down his spine—and he certainly was not going to hold her hand for companionship. "You're as cold as death," he rebuffed. He scowled and gazed toward the west across the endless grey waters. "I don't know how the thing is planning to cross the ocean… What is it thinking?"

"Thinking…?" Unfazed by the rejection, Hazamareth returned her arm to its resting place across her left knee, twisting a silver coin across her fingertips. There was a slight burning left in its wake, but due to her years of frequent contact with the poison she hardly seemed to notice. "The beast has left corpses for weeks now all along the main road. If it steals away on a ship there will be a slaughter all the way to Ryekarayn. The sad, little humans could not possibly stop it." She paused, fingers pressing tightly against the coin as she watched a ship vanish into the horizon. "And yet," she continued slowly, flicking the coin back into the bag at her side, "I doubt we'll see it attempt to gain access straight onto any of these vessels. Stowaway, perhaps?" She cocked her head slightly and blinked in consideration. "Wouldn't that be a marked leap of intelligence for the creature."

Tsuki tilted his head at a mirrored angle. *Was* there any other option for the beast? He could not see one. He pressed his hands into his stomach for warmth. Away from the shelter of the trees, the ocean breeze bit into their flesh with animalistic savagery. "So many scents, I can't distinguish him anywhere around this place… Gods only know where he has gotten himself already."

He squinted down the sharply sloping hill. The dockyard was awash in Ryekarian humans and cargo. Thirty-two ships lay docked along the coast, bows creaking as they rocked in the waves. Men making their last daring trips of trade before they fled from Saebellus and his insane, *petty* conquests.

The humans lumbered to and from the ships, hauling goods in and out of the cargo holds, stopping to perch atop unloaded crates for long swigs of rich ale. It was easy to distinguish their elven counterparts—polished, pristinely dressed, and working ceaselessly at their tasks. Yet they too were rugged and scarred, attesting to the illegal activities they participated in with the human-kind.

But worse than the stench of all of them—human and elf alike—was that of rotting fish, olfactible even over the waves of salt and the perfume of city flowers. While the workers below were unbothered, Tsuki grimaced enough for the lot of them. Still, he preferred it to the countryside they had spent the last few weeks gallivanting across. There was something about the bustle of cities, the variety of aromas, the tooth and nail fight for survival that made it so… *civilized.*

Hazamareth had clearly been watching him. "There will still be ale left in Elarium when we are finished," she reassured.

Tsuki's irritation subsided at her endearing attempts to pacify him. She was ever aware of the cause for his surly behavior. He offered a slight smile of apology. "You damn well better," he smirked, finding it impossible to remain resentful. At least, at her. The enduring cold was another matter entirely.

Beside him, Hazamareth's mood was considerably lifted by his smile; her chin elevated to a distasteful observance of the port. Certainly it was too cheerful for her taste. She tapped the side of her jaw thoughtfully. "He's probably in there now," she ventured. "Somehow, he *must* have gotten inside." But her pleasant mood could not mask her skepticism.

Tsuki did not blame her. Hours before, she had ventured alone through the streets, but had unearthed no sign of the beast. Without Tsuki's olfactory perception, such a result was unsurprising. The beast had moved with unnatural speed, sweeping from one poor soul to the next, to keep the victims at an unbroken one-a-day. It was not like the other creatures they had hunted… It was smarter than those driven only to kill. Despite its supposed lack of knowledge of the outside world, it seemed to be learning swiftly. The beast had even begun to drag the bodies off the main road and stash them within the forests. Whether it had a true sense that it was being followed, Tsuki doubted. But that made it all the more dangerous. Preemptive caution—an understanding of its actions.

This was no ordinary demon of Sheolra.

As the beast grew more apt at hiding its trail, they had come to rely on scent as their primary form of tracking.

Tsuki inhaled deeply, suggesting to his comrade that he was doing his part. *'You better not be considering what I think you are,'* he growled to himself. But she was. He could tell she was. *'He's probably in there now,'* Tsuki scoffed as her words echoed in his mind. While Hazamareth's face was smooth and stoic, her tone had been all too suggestive.

But this was one city Tsuki had as much interest in *not* entering as Elarium had interest in keeping him out. Its grand architecture and towering walls could not sway him. Nor its prestige as Sevrigel's capital of the south. Nor even its fame of elven luxuries. He had glimpsed its prison once, and that was more than enough a taste of its hospitality for him.

He scoffed, muttering a curse below his breath. Despite the great number of years that had passed, he could not imagine they had forgotten him. It was certainly fresh in *his* mind… One of the largest infections of bloodthirsters he had ever uncovered.

But the favor he had done for the damn elven city—the *country*—was not recognized by such ignorant elves.

When the elves had found him in Sel'ari's temple, surrounded by those pretty little bodies, they had been more eager to torture him as a murderer and sentence him to die than to understand why such a violent act had been inevitable.

A wave crashed along the hill's crest, spraying them with salt. Tsuki grimaced, howling further misery into his internal recesses.

Hazamareth's elbow caught him sharply in the side, rebuking his visible bitterness. "Alright, that's enough," she barked. "He'll kill again before he attempts to board a ship."

"Yes. And then he'll be easy to find," was Tsuki's matter-of-fact reply. He scowled at the vision of Elarium's citizens. "We can wait for him at the docks after he's made a fresh kill. The scent of blood will cling to him, and he'll be easy to track: the less time inside Elarium, the better." *'Less risk for us.'* He left the last words unspoken.

They could not save everyone.

But the implication was enough to banish any semblance of Hazamareth's patience. "Up," she snapped, and, as it was unlike the half-elf to give orders without Tsuki's full accord, Tsuki stood.

"I want you to know I am not going into those damn sewers," he grumbled. "If you could smell what I smell you wouldn't be so eager to go prancing about in their shit." But he knew that Hazamareth would not buy his excuses. The half-elf gathered exactly what he was thinking. They had travelled too long together for her to *not* know.

"Quit acting like such a Sheolran imp," Hazamareth chided him with her usual disregard for Tsuki's qualms. "I will watch your back." Her hazel eyes flashed with command. "Now let's go. I am not waiting for the beast to murder someone."

Tsuki scowled. Hazamareth's aversion to letting the beast have just *one* more kill was irking. *Understandable*, but irking. Ever the challenging path.

'Damn it, Hazamareth. Strengthen your spine.'

But before Tsuki could cede to her demands, he caught a familiar scent riding the wind. Faint, even to him, but he had grown too accustomed to the sensation to miss its passing.

His nostrils flared. "Blood, Hazamareth. I believe it's too late." Especially being upwind of the city, Tsuki could not deny that he smelled enough fresh, elven blood to warrant a wholly gruesome death.

Hazamareth offered little reaction as she resigned herself to the information. She nodded once more toward Elarium, her mind now clearly focused on the task ahead, and stepped staunchly through the grass. "Well, you got your wish—so let's make this short."

Tsuki fell in beside her, slowing their gait to a casual stroll down the hill. The great walls of the city rose up like a cliff, extending toward the sky in a soft silver-grey that glowed with orange hues in the setting sun. The accenting towers glinted with pale yellow windows and golden balconies. Yet the haughty elven naivety and nauseating grandeur disgusted Tsuki. With all their pretty buildings and fancy artistic scribbles, the elves had much to learn before they realized the world was not made of gold and good fortune. The world was a dark and gritty place, and the elves lived in deliberate ignorance of it all. A human city, with its practical taverns and grounded inhabitants, was far more his preference—especially now in a location where elven ignorance had the entire city guard on the lookout for the very head that was about to offer them salvation.

As they slipped into the throng and passed beside the city watch at the entrance, Tsuki felt, for a brief moment, like the creatures he hunted. He tucked his chin down.

"Watch yourself, half-breed," an elf mumbled below his breath as Hazamareth was jostled into him.

Tsuki let out an external sigh, feeling as though all attempts at discretion were about to be for naught. *'Half-breed?—Damn it. That'll do it.'*

Tsuki tensed, anticipating the furious and violent response of Hazamareth, but to his surprise, his comrade ignored the elf. Perhaps a flicker of wisdom rose above her anger, reminding her that they did not need attention drawn to them right beside the city watch.

"Which way is it?" she asked, sniffing as indignantly as a Sel'ven who had misplaced a polished boot in a pile of horse dung. And then abruptly, wisdom darting away with a mocking laugh, she hurled the elf out of the way with such vehemence that the bastard was flung to the ground.

And *there* was the woman Tsuki had expected. *There* was the human blood that refused to take shit from those god-damn elves. *There* was a good lack of common sense.

"Northeast," he replied with a grunt as he stepped over the cursing elf. He spat as he passed, pushing himself into the crowd. But he enjoyed the ferocity with which his comrade responded to the elf's prejudice. No bowing of the head or inane groveling.

Ah, the good old *human* blood pumping through their veins.

But despite Tsuki's delight, he was swift to step into the nearest dark alleyway and lose the eyes of the unamused. "To business," he grunted, hearing the soft footsteps of Hazamareth on the cobblestones behind him.

He inhaled heavily, the tangy scent of blood filling his lungs. The corpse was not far. When they reached it, the blood clinging to the beast's body would, expectantly, be enough for Tsuki to track it down.

And then they'd kill it. He rested a hand eagerly on the hilt of his sword.

They wound up the city's gentle hills, the trail becoming almost tangible, and finally halted before the back wall of a final alleyway.

'The smell must be strong enough for even Haz, now.' Yet she made no attempt at silence. *'Gods damn it. Always fearlessly clanging around!'*

Tsuki gestured sharply at the woman to cease the arming of her crossbow. This… was not what he had expected. Tsuki raised his hand and flared his nostrils. This smell… this intensity of putrid waste and rotting clothes…!

He stifled a gag; there could be no doubt.

'Still there?' Hazamareth mouthed, hazel eyes widening as she realized the meaning of his gesture.

'Still there,' Tsuki repeated to himself, giving his comrade a cautious nod. Every muscle in his body rippled with tension as he prepared for the inevitable confrontation. Then he dared to expose his face into the alleyway beyond.

But no massive figure came darting for his throat. Instead, a hunkered, still form was visible in the darkness: the beast crouched near its victim, its great shape eerily statuesque.

'It's still there...' This was the first time the beast had remained near a death for so long. But its back was toward them. *'What is it doing...?'*

Tsuki stiffened abruptly. Rose blossoms and recently dyed silks…? *There was someone else present*. Not the corpse, but someone *alive*.

'Is that... a child?' he deduced as he strained his eyes against the dim light.

Yes. A child. Tsuki's lips parted in disbelief.

The beast was hiding from a child.

Tsuki rested his hand on his silver blade, then stopped. A second brat had appeared from around the corner, sidling up to the first.

"What is it?" the first child whispered in a high, little squeak, slinking closer to the body.

Tsuki heard the slight *tink* as Hazamareth resumed the preparation of her crossbow. He swiftly jerked his hand in rebuke.

"Elsaela, d-don't go near it!" the little boy stammered. "Elsaela!"

'Damn it!—Where are your parents, you little street urchins?!' Tsuki swore. At this rate, they were going to have two more bodies on their hands. Worse still, if the beast used them as a shield, Hazamareth would most certainly refuse to take the shot!

Tsuki's fingers curled tightly around the hilt and he began to slide his blade free. *'Before they get too close…!'*

Yet before either he or Hazamareth could blink an eye, the silhouette pivoted, turning and rushing toward them in a single, rapid lunge.

Tsuki's instincts sent him reeling, lurching back into the false safety of his dumbstruck comrade.

The creature was infinitely faster. There was no hesitation, no surprise from the beast—as though it had known all along that the two mercenaries were nearby. It locked eyes with Tsuki, clutching him by the skull and hurling him into Hazamareth with force enough to shatter average bones.

Then, without breaking stride, it tore off into the alleyway behind them.

"*Damn it*," Tsuki moaned, scrambling to his feet and flinching at the pain that speared through his spine. "What was it doing?!" He glanced over his shoulder at the corpse: the children were gone.

"GO! We're losing it!" Hazamareth hollered, sparking his mind into focus. She scrambled for her scattered bolts, spitting a wad of blood from her lips where Tsuki's skull had cracked smartly against her ashen face.

Tsuki lunged into motion. Lose the beast? *Never*. He whirled and dashed down the alleys after the massive creature, grasping for the visage of the beast in that brief contact. Eyes… All he could remember were the piercing, yellow, serpentine eyes.

And fear. Not his own fear. Its fear.

The beast feared him.

He skidded around another corner as the creature's scent changed direction. He caught a glimpse of its heels disappearing around the bend ahead.

'Got it,' he thought smugly. This was not the terrifying beast Saebellus' captain had described it as.

He slowed, hunching slightly as he neared the curve. His fingers trailed along a series of barrels as he passed, tapping softly. The darkness would have been a challenge for any other human, but he could clearly distinguish the broken stones at the back end of the corridor, the fishermen's barrels long left empty to gather dust, and the seamless white marble that veered to the path of his prey.

It was the scent that unnerved Tsuki. The wretched odor remained immobile, warning him that the beast had halted somewhere out of sight.

Tsuki edged forward, leather armor creaking defiantly as he crept. Gods damn it, it was like having Haz right on his heels! With a determined lunge, he swung around the corner of the alleyway, blade drawn back for the blow.

He was met instantly. It was a blur of shadow, a sudden shift in the darkness. Without pause, it caught his sword in its massive, bare hands. Tsuki threw his body urgently backward and out of reach, attempting to slide the blade free. But the beast's hold was like iron. With a savage snarl, its great hand tightened and yanked the sword toward the ground.

Tsuki held on for just a moment too long; his body was whisked off balance with the creature's force. His fingers flew free, grasping desperately for balance.

And then the beast raised the sword by the blade and broke the hilt upon him with terrible force.

Tsuki's lack of stability cost him the ability to dodge: the weapon collided with his shoulder like a pole on a humlid ball, flinging his body into the wall beside him with a booming thud. Agony shot through his torso as bones threatened to shatter beneath his throbbing flesh.

He stifled the pain with a single groan and threw himself frantically away from the oncoming fist. It smashed down where his skull had been and a terrifying crack shot through the stone, forked like lightning.

Inwardly, Tsuki recoiled. *He had seen what the creature was capable of doing to a man.* He rolled onto his side and pushed himself up, his weakened shoulder nearly buckling his arm out from underneath him. He felt the breeze of the second fist pass by his cheek, spraying broken cobbles into his wheezing mouth on its contact with the stone.

The miss offered only a moment's reprieve. Before Tsuki could stagger to his feet, he was wrenched upward by his fractured arm. Even as the inevitable event pounded through his brain, his instincts thrust his clammy hands futilely before his skull.

But the blow did not come. With a screech, the beast lobbed Tsuki away.

Tsuki's arms crept from his face in time to see a second bolt rip through the beast's heart. His stomach leapt and he let out a strangled cry. It was the only pitiful sound he could manage at the sight of his god-damn glorious comrade and her silver bolts.

The beast's yellow eyes tore wide. Its second cry of agony echoed down the alley like a roar of ungodly thunder. Tsuki glimpsed its huge wings silhouetting as it poised for a position of… but he realized too late.

Offense.

The beast hooked Tsuki by the arm and, with a horrific bellow, slung his body once more into Hazamareth.

The crossbow dropped from her thin fingers as she made a valiant attempt to soften the blow. The two tumbled across the cobblestones and into a nearby barrel, the wind thankfully knocked from their lungs as the old fish rot splintered about them.

"What in Ramul was *that?*" Hazamareth rasped as the beast vanished down the alleyway.

Tsuki was already scrabbling to his feet, his shoulder aching in comradery with his spine. "Well, *let's follow it!*" he heaved.

The two half-hobbled, half-sprinted in pursuit, boots flopping against the narrow streets, eyes darting in the pale sunlight that snaked its way to the floor of the city.

'Just wounded?' Tsuki's jaw tightened as the beast yet increased its distance.

Hazamareth gave a similar grimace. "If a crossbolt through the heart won't kill it, we had best start discussing in which catacomb we'd like to be laid."

But what had started out as drops of blood across the stones gradually became extensive paintings across the pristine elven walls. In the adrenaline from its injury, the beast had fled swiftly through Elarium: but its condition was now apparent.

Tsuki slowed, huffing heavily. "Definitely fatal," he breathed, eyeing the large, crimson smear across the white marble beside them.

Hazamareth hooked the crossbow to the iron clasp at her hip, nodding staunchly. "Different or not, they all die the same. Let it be a lesson to us: we do not show mercy for these beasts *again*. Saebellus is just lucky there are people like us around to deal with his stupidity, or one night he'd be liable to wake up with that thing looming over his bedpost. And he would have brought the demise upon himself."

CHAPTER TWENTY-TWO

Jerah's heart was racing. *Damn* it was racing. He felt sluggish as blood rushed from the wounds in fast, rhythmic pumps. He stumbled, trailing a bloody hand along the wall.

The mercenaries Master had warned him about had finally caught up to him. They were not like the elves he had encountered. *These mercenaries were not afraid of him.* Even now, their scent was growing closer. He stumbled and grasped at the shafts protruding from his heart.

Pain.

Such pain.

Jerah had never felt such pain before. It dulled his senses, clouded his mind. For a moment the world spun and darkened.

His body suddenly started, shouting at him to stay awake.

Jerah shook his head violently and seized the first shaft in his heart. With a howl of agony, he tore it furiously out of his chest, spraying the cobbled stones with blood. He slammed his fist into a wall, shattering the exterior stones like glass. As though such violence would bring him some comfort. His fist tightened once on the freed crossbolt and then, with a cry of pain, he threw it aside and raised a hand to his chest. He could feel the skin rapidly closing, but the pain was no less intense.

He tore out the second bolt, throwing it in the opposite direction of the first, gritting his teeth against crying out again. *He had to be strong.* Master had warned him. *Warned him* that it was not safe outside the cellar. And he had not listened. Had not listened…

The thoughts rang out, over and over again in his delusion, and he slumped heavily against the wall.

Outside was free. He was free. Inside the cellar was dark and lonely. *Forever dark and lonely.*

He had been having adventures beyond his imagination since he had left. Experiences he had never fathomed. The cycle of day and night seemed so contrite now, so long ago learned. There were scents, people, cities, trees, animals… so many things that had been beyond his reach within the cellar.

He only had to get to Ryekarayn. *On Ryekarayn he would be safe*.

Jerah fixed his mind on his goal and with that determination, his senses cleared. With a soft grunt, he pushed his massive form off the wall. There was no time to hesitate: the two mercenaries were gaining on him.

He began to move, his thick legs propelling him forward, faster and faster as his strength returned. Twisting and turning, he snaked through the alleyways toward the scent of the ocean. Still *faster and faster* until he pulled himself to a sudden stop at the site of the gate leading out of the city.

Jerah drew swiftly into the shadows. He knew elven soldiers lurked at the entrance to their cities, waiting to snatch their prey.

He glanced down at himself. The two cloaks from the road killings he had draped across his broad shoulders had come loose during his encounter. He took a moment to adjust them, pulling a hood over his horns. The cloaks barely concealed his wings, so he tucked them tighter against his back and drew the fabric over his bloody chest. Yet the meager coverage lessened his anxiety: he had made it into the city before. He could make it out.

Slowly, head lowered, steps steady, he strode toward the gate leading out toward the docks, hunkering his body into the crowd in an attempt to blend in.

Still, Jerah readied himself to be challenged.

Yet, like the city's watch when he had entered the city from the east, these men guarding the western entrance did nothing. They seemed more interested in the humans jostling their way in and out of the gate than even his large, hooded form. He hunkered down lower, his body dipping slightly below the tallest nearby elf.

Finally, with a gasp of relief, he broke free of the crowd and found himself standing at the base of a hill, the towering walls now behind him and freedom at his front.

Freedom at his front.

His breath caught, yellow eyes going wide in awe. Before him stretched water as far as he could see… and then…? The end of the world. He looked to the north and south. Where was Ryekarayn?

He stepped forward slowly, scanning the coast. Perhaps only ships could reach the human lands? There were many of these vessels, just like his master had described them, but more magnificent than he had ever thought. And the humans that sailed them—he was surprised by how elvish they appeared. Despite their pungent scents, they seemed hardly different. Just hairier, fatter elves.

He watched as one such particularly hairy human took a long swig of ale from atop a crate, sniffing as his reddened nose dripped in the chilly ocean breeze.

Jerah wiped his hand across his own nose in instinctive response.

"Off, Jasiid. Get this crate onto the ship." Another human had approached the former, stopping before him with his thin eyebrows tucked together and his lips curled in displeasure. He looked much like his master had often appeared when things were not going his way. "We still have over a dozen more to move before we leave port. Don't backtalk me. Get your ass going. Now."

This language was not elven. And yet he knew it. His brow furrowed, his mind trying to pinpoint where he had learned it. Long ago… a room. A large room… with woven nets between wooden pillars… In a large room…?

Jerah watched the group of men heave the crate up and carry it toward the line of ships bouncing on the ocean waves. His face lit suddenly with an idea, his lips curling beneath the hood. *'Ah, so clever, Jerah.'*

Finding the nearest crate stack, he hunkered down behind it and peered above in a cautious assessment of his surroundings. There were far more humans than he had expected, but they seemed absorbed in their own tasks. He hesitated, trying to find an opening with fewer watchers. He had just a moment to leap inside…!

And he stopped.

The damn crate was full. He scowled furiously, lifting it up above his head to hurl it down toward his feet in his frustration.

"By the gods, what are ya doing?!" A human shouted, his deep voice booming across the cobbled dock.

Jerah paused, crate still hanging above his head. He turned slowly, seeing a group of humans staring back at him, their mouths agape in dumb awe.

Then they seemed to think abruptly as one and moved forward to surround him. Jerah half-dropped the crate in his hurried attempt to retreat.

"Are ya a half-giant or something? Malranus Almighty the *strength* of ya," the same human continued.

Jerah hung his head, pulling his shoulders up around his neck as though tucking himself into the safety of his own skin. What should he do? Talk to it? Master told him to never talk to them.

"Eh, if it is it'll have no wits to be talkin' back," another human spoke. "Cap'ain 'ld love to have one of them on board."

There was something about his tone that grated on Jerah, but he kept his stare downward. Master had always hated when Jerah had raised his eyes in challenge. And there were more humans here than Jerah.

"Cut the sarcasm, Jasiid. Why wouldn't he? More use than yer sorry ass. Can ya talk? Well, giant?"

Jerah raised his head, keeping it just low enough to maintain a shadowy interior. He said nothing, his eyes shifting from one to the other for a way to escape. Could he run for a ship? No, they would certainly see him climb aboard...

"Ya want to make a few silver pieces? Help us finish this load up and the boys here will tip ya."

Jerah was silent, confused as to what behavior was expected of him. He shifted nervously.

"Well? We haven't got all day. Just pick it up."

It seemed a small request. Unsure what to do otherwise, Jerah reached down and raised the crate up over his head, then looked to the humans for confirmation.

They responded with immediate applause.

The first human pointed down to the ships. "See the ship with the purple sails? That's our ship. Go put that on the deck of that ship. Do ya know which one I'm talking about?" He approached Jerah suddenly and before Jerah could decide what to do, the man had dropped a silver coin into his pocket.

Jerah nodded, his body relaxing somewhat. *'Purple. Like my stones,'* he thought to himself, feeling the weight of the coin against his leg. His chest swelled a little with pride at its touch.

A sudden scent snapped him back to the crowd of humans before him.

The city. The mercenaries.

They were very close now.

Without another glance toward the men, he turned and hurried for the ship. He hardly noticed the other humans who struggled beneath the weight of their packages, and he had little time to fear the rickety planks stretched out across the water as his bridge to the deck.

And the ship...? The ship was no more than an expanse of flat wood and steps, old rope and stinking rot.

This was his passage to Ryekarayn?

As Jerah began to lower the crate onto the deck, a man barked at him from a basket above the ship, "Don't just set it there—take it below!"

Jerah glanced up once, but he could only see a flag beating against the stalk of wood growing from the ship's center.

Below deck? He looked around. How did he get below deck?

He smiled as he spotted a set of open double doors to his right. 'That *must be below deck.'* He heaved the crate back into his arms and grunted down the first flight of stairs. And stopped. In the torchlight he could make it out.

A large room with nets between wooden pillars. A ship? Had Jerah been on a ship before? His brow furrowed and he inhaled deeply. The smell. Rat urine, old clothes, grime, and rotting meat that rose up from the floor one level below. Not unlike his cellar.

Silhouettes he could not distinguish and words that he could not make out shifted at the edge of his memory.

Yes… he was sure of it. He *had* been on a ship before. A long time ago…

But he couldn't remember *why*.

Jerah hesitated, wanting to look around the great room further, but the shout of the basket man brought him to attention. He still had his crate job to finish.

He moved forward slowly and down to the final level of the ship. He set the crate beside the others and paused thoughtfully.

"You are clever, Jerah," he told himself with a sudden, crooked smile. Oh so clever.

He could not help feeling rather proud of himself as he stuffed the contents of the crate into the darkness between other crates. Climbing inside the now emptied box, he then pulled its lid over top, shutting himself safely and securely out of the humans' sight.

And on a ship, he did not have to kill. This was an unexpected relief to Jerah. He had not killed the last time he had been on a ship. He could not recall *what* he had done on that ship, but he remembered his first kills clearly.

He nestled into the darkness, blood-loss weighing in, his body aching.

And before he knew it, he had drifted off to sleep.

Chapter Twenty-Three

"Just a little farther…!" Eldaeus' cries of excitement were growing into a terrible crescendo, and no matter how tightly Jikun gritted his teeth, the pitch was no less painful. As the final crackle of ice settled before the cavern's egress, the mad elf crowed again, "There!"

"I know *there—I'm* the one building our staircase," Jikun snapped. In the moonlight that slipped in through the ceiling of the dome, the bottom of the stairway glittered faintly with a blue sheen against the cavern wall. A single memory managed to smuggle its way out of his defenses: a reflection of Darival… an echo of cerulean light that shone off the face of the mountains below Kaivervale.

He scoffed with disgust in himself, but his tone revealed nothing of his inner shame. "Careful," he warned the others as he took step after Navon.

Grunting and teetering followed in his wake.

"Did I pick up a pair of whores?" he barked back to their groans, eyeing Darcarus and Eldaeus struggling with their food-laden cloaks. "You two had better move more swiftly when we get above or Navon and I are going to leave your asses for the snakes."

Darcarus moaned and caught the side of the railing. "Ishkav fuck the both of you," he swore with Darivalian-worthy flare. "How did Eldaeus and I get squired carrying *your* cloaks?"

The two weeks had done wonders for their scrapes and bruises, but broken bones were another matter entirely. Jikun indicated once to his cracked ribs and bandaged chest, then gestured toward the whole of the Helven.

Navon feigned a commendable stagger of weakness.

Darcarus glowered. "Asinine," he muttered before directing his attention to the Faraven, who was, at that moment, challenging the laws of nature with his tilt. "Eldaeus, *stop* leaning backward. I swear to Sel'ari, if you knock me down these steps, I will disembowel your mother."

Eldaeus gasped at once in delight.

Jikun ignored their nettlesome bickering as he rested a hand on the icy railing. "I will go first so we have somewhere to grip on our climb up the shaft." Of course no one was listening, so Jikun snapped sharply beside his captain's ear. "*Move*."

Navon hastily plastered himself against the railing with a white-knuckled hold, allowing Jikun to squeeze past.

'A mountain-born elf with a fear of heights. Once again, he would make a much better Sel'ven,' Jikun smirked as he raised his hands into the darkness. At his command, a series of icy plates jutted from the wall in what he hoped was some semblance of a pattern. "I'm not certain there is any consistency to the handholds," he began, and cut off as Eldaeus bounded past him. "Bird boy, I thought *I* had to go first to scratch out those runes!" He caught the male sharply by the arm and wheeled him toward Navon.

Eldaeus' single-minded enthusiasm was immediately quenched. He instead leaned daringly over the railing, ogling the great distance below as though the shaft was instantly forgotten.

"Now stay here and wait for my call," Jikun ordered, reaching up into the darkness. "And comfort Navon."

"What?!" his captain balked.

Moments after Jikun's ascent, Eldaeus' voice arose as a high-pitched cry from the tunnel, closely accompanied by a fury of painful echoes. "Another good question, very-safe-Navon. See, I fell with a chunk of stone and right before it hit the earth, I PUSHED OFF from it like this—"

"AH! Careful! You will break this! *JIKUN, HURRY UP!*" Navon's voice rose in panic. "By Sel'ari, he is going to bloody kill me! Eldaeus, *stop* rocking—where are you going?!"

"God-damn Faraven!" Darcarus swore. "No wonder you're all extinct!"

Jikun sighed and slid himself into the cold night air. All signs of the serpent were gone. To the south, a darkened line was all that remained of Dahel. Now that Saebellus grasped the throne, the warlord was withholding none of his destruction.

Jikun turned away from the sight, suppressing the discomfort that coiled up his spine. The glowing runes that lay before him, however, offered little reprieve. The fate of Sevrigel had chased him across the Windari Channel, but Eldaeus only offered further uncertainty for the months ahead.

'Yet he has been my best sign of fortune since I arrived... Our only hope out of the desert...' He winced. '...And *I made a foolish promise.'* Before his caution could hold his hand at bay, he drew his knife and sliced through the first rune.

The effect was instantaneous. The frigid air crackled as though lightning tore through the stone, and the knife surged with heat. Jikun dropped the blade with a cry of surprise. Before it even hit the earth, the glow of the runes faded to nothing more than a darkened scrawl on the sandy ridge.

Jikun gathered himself, rubbing his scorched palm vigorously. "It's done!" he called into the darkness. "You can come—!"

"Oh good!" Jikun reeled back as Eldaeus' face popped out of the darkness. "I just got so impatient!" the Faraven exclaimed, wriggling himself out into the sand. He stood, extending his arms and spinning in an extravagant circle. "By all the gods and goddesses still living, *what a blessing!*" he whooped.

"*SHHHHHH!*" Navon snapped as he slid out next, unceremoniously tripping Eldaeus into the sand. His eyes flicked warily across the horizon. "We don't know if Relstavum is still out there!"

"With my god-damn cloak," Darcarus interjected with a furious kick.

While Jikun ignored the expected announcement, he was no less frustrated. Eldaeus, scurrying upwind of the flying sand, became the target for the brunt of his annoyance. "If you are coming with us, you have to behave like any sane elf and *not* get us killed! What we are doing is incredibly dangerous."

Eldaeus clapped a hand abruptly over his own mouth.

"...Is that agreement that you will be quiet?"

Eldaeus' voice rang muffled through his palm. "I just remembered! You could have been counting my teeth! You were not, were you?!"

"I am hardly *that* bored," Jikun replied flatly. "...Why?"

Eldaeus exhaled, letting his hand fall away. "You know... counting teeth robs a year of life for every tooth! You can never be too certain." Then he swung back around toward the endless sands of the north. "Come along, hatchlings," he whispered. "We have a long run before us!"

Navon caught the male swiftly by the back of his pristine leather. "And we are *not* running."

And they did not run. If fact, Jikun was certain Saebellus would rule Emal'drathar by the time they reached the desert's border. But it was their destination that dominated Jikun's mind: the Pass of the Dead remained his constant, haunting vision. Would a horde of slaughtered soldiers truly haunt the land of their defeat in an endless crusade for revenge? *Why* would they do so if they had died with honor for their country—even if their attempt had been in vain?

Yet despite Jikun's attempts to wrest himself from the delusional beliefs of his companions, he could not escape the anxiety of what possibly lay ahead. The imagery grew day by day with almost unnatural speed, as though one with the Aenid Mountains. By the time the three had reached the edge of the massive, grey stone, the peaks seemed lost above them in the stars.

Jikun's eyes swept left and right, struggling in the dark. "So where is this path…?" he challenged. Several small, black shapes hovered near the cliff-faces, but part of him dared not ask what they were.

Eldaeus raised a finger to the east as he sauntered forward. "Just over there. Where the six crows are sitting."

Jikun strained his eyes in disbelief. *'At this time of night…?'* Validating Eldaeus' words, he distinguished several crows perched atop a boulder, almost as still as statues. He shivered reactively as they turned.

"Do you feel that?" Navon whispered, his voice cracking.

"Yes," Darcarus grunted.

"*No*," Jikun lied, locking eyes on the mountain path. "Now desist from infecting me with your childish superstitions." The moonlight's attempt to stretch its rays into the twisting mountains abruptly ceased where the path began—nothing persisted but an endless void into the abyss, sable as the ocean's depths. To his left, a crow abruptly screeched and hopped to face him, its cries rallying the birds around it to frantic bobbings and screams.

Jikun recoiled into the now-comforting familiarity of the sands and drew his cloak snugly about his body. There *was* something unsettling about the darkness—and the fact that the wild crows seemed rallied by his movement only intensified his alarm. "No."

Up ahead, Eldaeus reappeared, his strangely etched face hollow in the moonlight. "Why?" he queried, his voice unnervingly cheerful.

Jikun coughed, flinging his hand boldly at the pass. "*Absolutely* not. We can't see a damn thing in there," he barked. "Whether or not your story about the infantry unit is true—and I have my doubts—we don't know what else could be lurking within. We can wait until the morning."

Eldaeus began hopping with the same intensity as the crows, his eyes like two freakish globes. "Oh no. We *cannot* wait until the morning. The infantry unit sleeps at night. In the morning, they will surely overtake us. We have to travel at night. *Always* at night. I said I could get you through safely... *This* is how we must move!—The path is not long, come!"

Darcarus' fingers danced above his hilt even as he strode to the entrance. "His plan sounds half-sane to me..."

Behind Jikun, his captain had enough instinct to disagree. "I don't know... Eldaeus, it is utterly black in there." His own words reignited his unease and he withdrew, firmly shaking his head as he stepped beside Jikun. "Even if we *wanted* to travel at night, Jikun is right—we cannot see a thing."

Eldaeus cocked his head and spun to face the path. "Really?" He was silent for a moment, then pivoted and snapped his tattooed fingers. "No worries. I have a thought!" Then he flopped abruptly down at the egress in a puff of dust and nestled himself against the stone. "At the first light of dawn, we will *run* through—*really* fast—before everyone wakes up. It is a risk, but it sounds like a reasonable compromise, does it not? You will get a little light and I will not be killed!"

"I would prefer to live, myself," Darcarus seconded.

Finally, some sense from the both of them, even if it was of the most basic kind. "Agreed," Jikun decided, settling down across from Eldaeus. He stared into the darkness a moment longer until concern threatened to overtake his senses. "Wake me when we are ready to move." He rested his head against a stone and closed his eyes, forcing them to remain shut even as every instinct shouted at him to peer once more into the dark.

After a moment, he heard Navon inquire softly, "...So, what exactly *are* the males of this infantry unit now?"

"Well," Eldaeus began, leaning in close, "wraiths, mostly. They still have all their armor and weapons, but they are definitely dead. I suppose... they are like wraiths or lich."

"*Sh!*" Jikun hissed. "I am trying to rest. You two whispering only makes me strain harder to hear you."

"These undead," Eldaeus continued in a normal tone, "are fairly—Ow, why did you kick me?!"

"I said *SH*."

*

"Ok, get up! Up!"

Jikun cracked open his lids and grimaced. His spine was stiff and his cheek throbbed with the effect of an unpleasant brawl. "Did I actually fall asleep?" he groaned, even as his eyes caught the ray of light on the horizon.

"Somehow," Navon replied blearily as he hauled him to his feet. "But it's time to move."

Jikun pushed off of his support and stretched—though it was an action that would afford him little delay. Darcarus already stood at the mouth, tension rippling through his frame. *'He has traveled all across Aersadore and still believes the path is haunted?'*

It was not a comforting thought.

Yet, at the moment, that road was merely dirt and stone, speckled with the occasional weed that struggled for life along the otherwise barren path. The width between the grey stone flanking it on either side was hardly wide enough for two males to walk through side-by-side—like the pass at Turmazel Peak where thakish had often lain in wait.

And then Jikun's eyes swept upward. The sight was little better: endless, sheer faces of the mountains, jagged here and jutting forth there, with sharp ridges like knives looming overhead. Jikun inspected them warily. Rather than thakish, *here* they faced the precarious balance of lurking stones.

'Lurking?' he rebuked himself shamefully. *'Gods, I'm turning into one of those three.'*

Three… His head spun around, realizing that they were one companion short. "Where is Eldaeus…?"

"GOOOOOOD MOOOOORNING LORD SUNSHINE!" Eldaeus crowed from behind him. He was perched atop one of the large boulders that marked the entrance to the pass, extending one hand toward the dawning sun as though he could raise it through sheer force of will. With an elaborate twist of his ancient cloak, he leapt like a spritely winter wolf down the stone, springing to the front of the group. When the momentum of his initial jump had faded, he drew to an abrupt halt and whirled to face Jikun and Navon's flabbergasted expressions.

Darcarus clearly shared their thoughts, rapidly plucking at the gold button centered on his breast. "I think I am more afraid of him than I am of the dead."

But Eldaeus put a dismissive finger swiftly to the prince's lips. "*Shhhh*, we must not wake the infantry!"

And away he went.

Jikun raised a hand to his temple, massaging it as he began to follow the bounding elf. "Good gods." There was a part of him that began to say it was too early for such loud tones and nonsense, but in the case of Eldaeus, Jikun could not think of a time of day he would *ever* find it bearable.

"At least he is not singing," Darcarus muttered.

Navon recovered a second later, striding up to the two and falling into step beside Jikun. He wasted no time in dropping the weight of his conclusions. "I spoke to Eldaeus at length about these mountains and I am ashamed to admit that I truly believe him."

"You should be." Jikun forced a laugh, nearly tripping over a loose stone as he shot his companion a look intent on inflicting greater humiliation. "Have mercy on me. I can only handle one mad member of our group at a time."

"Well that's not really fair then, is it? Eldaeus will always occupy all the time for himself." Navon reached into his cloak, retrieving three fish and swinging them about as he continued, "For a non-necromancer, he has a remarkable understanding of the souls and the Gates."

"Perhaps he simply overheard your lesson."

"...That was a summary for children." When Jikun failed to retort, he persisted, "And the elves who escorted him to imprisonment feared the same tale—all substantially saner than he, I imagine. Not to mention that the 'prince' seems on Eldaeus' side."

Darcarus snatched a fish before Navon's wild gestures lost him his breakfast. He flicked some rotted fruit from its stinking, scaled flesh. "It is hard *not* to believe the tale when an entire culture has structured their lives to avoid the place."

"And the Lithri still believe they are Lithriella's Chosen. You know how elves are—how much stronger is a rumor than the truth?" Jikun rescued a fish as well, biting the head first in deliberate disobedience to the Faraven's warning that such a thing was bad luck. "I have never seen a wraith, a lich... any undead, for that matter, *except* for those which flicker about within necromantic spells. I know Navon said that souls can resist the pull of the gate, but we are not talking about one or two here, we are talking about hundreds... *thousands*."

Navon shrugged faintly, taking, Jikun noted, a bite from the tail. "I read a bit about it in my book... *The book you stole from me.* It has me wondering if perhaps Relstavum can summon something like them... I mean, he obliterated Dahel." When Jikun gave no reaction, he asked, "Can I dump out the fruit yet? It really has gone bad. You should have dried it out like the fish. Now my cloak reeks like excremental waste and—" But his complaints were broken by the sudden reaction of the Faraven ahead.

Eldaeus had spun about, his eyes ripped wide, his jaw swinging low. Jikun felt his heart drop into his gut as the Faraven raised a shaking finger, pointing it into the barely lit chasm at their backs. His cry emerged barely audible through its frenzied quavering. "LOOK!! BEHIND YOU! AN UNDEAD!"

Jikun and Navon reeled about as one, his captain thrusting the kitchen knife high in preparation for Jikun's first assault from the ground. Ice rushed to Jikun's extended palms, crackling across his fingertips. He was flanked by Darcarus, who unleashed a wave of purple smoke that began to take the shape of…

And Jikun stopped, perplexed. The pathway was as empty of the undead as it had been only moments before, a lazy wind winding through its empty passage. A single crow plucked at a weed on their right as a small beetle scuttled its way to safety.

Darcarus' magic fizzled out and the creature he had summoned vanished into the dawn.

Jikun whirled, fear giving rise to a swift temper. "Why, you little *cunt!*" he growled.

With a feverish giggle, Eldaeus pranced several steps ahead. "Oh, you should have *seen* your eyes!—like a troll grabbed you right about the middle. I thought for sure they were going to pop right out of your head!"

"Damn it, do not waste my strength!" Darcarus hissed.

Navon relaxed, letting his hand drop to his side with a chuckle. As though his ashen complexion was actually a rosy-cheeked expression of mirth. "You truly had me there."

"I know, I know," Eldaeus patted himself on the back.

Literally.

Jikun sighed, anger abated by Navon's tolerant humor. He let the ice fall to the ground as he strode forward, crushing it beneath his heel. "What were you saying, Navon?"

Navon sheathed the kitchen knife at his waist, his cloak still gripped white-knuckled in his other hand. "Can I drop this fruit? Even the best of it smells like piss."

Darcarus sniffed and quickly waved a hand before his nose. "I do not care what Jikun says. *Yes*. By Kamora and all things beautiful, yes. I will be eight thousand and still be scraping that stench out of my nasal passageways."

Having obtained all the permission he needed, Navon untied the cloak and let the rotten fruit roll out behind him. The crow at the weeds lifted its head warily, hopping forward several feet to pluck at the fermenting cores.

The fruit was gone, but to Jikun's dismay, the stench remained to creep along behind them. Ahead, the path twisted to the right and rolled into the distance. "For how far does this go on?" he demanded, glaring at the endless cliffs of stone.

Eldaeus glanced over his shoulder. "Oh, for at least a few hours. That is why we have to pick up our pace if we want to make it out before…" he trailed off, stumbling to a halt as he rounded upon them. His gape was locked over their shoulders, his expression frozen as he began to choke on his terrified bellow. "L…look behind you…! AN UNDEAD!"

Darcarus was already in action, his magic swiftly forming a monstrous wolf. Jikun and Navon were at his heels, the kitchen blade extended, a spear of ice preparing to launch from Jikun's fingertips. Jikun's mouth opened to cry out on the offensive…!

A crow squawked in the empty pass, ruffling its feathers in irritation at the intrusive stares. "Keep it up and I am going to start counting your teeth," Jikun growled.

Eldaeus gasped. "That is just spiteful!" came his muffled reply.

Jikun turned back around, but the Faraven had already pranced ahead.

"Come on, we have to keep up," Navon sighed, adrenaline gone as swiftly as it had come. He dragged his dirty, bandaged feet forward.

"Why?" Jikun spoke below his breath. "It's not like we can lose him. Unfortunately. As he said, there is one way in and out." He narrowed his eyes at the back of Eldaeus' sickeningly cheerful hair. "He is going to be useless against Relstavum. I think we should make a pact now that if there *are* undead, we leave the maniacal elf behind as a distraction while we make a run for safety."

"Agreed," the other two replied in unison.

"LOOK BEHIND YOU!" Eldaeus bellowed down the canyon. "AN UNDEAD!"

He *was* determined, Jikun could offer him that much. He heaved dismally. "Is he going to keep this up the entire way?"

"Probably," came his captain's weak reply.

But Jikun had to admire the Faraven for his resolve. Eldaeus did not try it once or twice more: it was at least a dozen more times with increasingly dramatic expressions of terror or tones of shock. At least twice he feigned a fairly believable faint.

"Alright, Eldaeus," Jikun snarled when he finally lost count of how many times he had whipped around, prepared for the ghastly horde. "I now swear that if you utter the word 'undead' one more time, I will run a spear of ice through your skull and may Lithriella wing me if I lie."

Eldaeus' grin faded and his ugly lips twisted into an expression of horror. He elevated a god-damn finger and choked out shamelessly, "L-l-l-ook! BEHIND YOU! UNDEAD!"

Darcarus shot out his fist. "That does it!"

Navon put a tempering palm on the prince's wrist. "At least he is adding variety."

"*How so?*"

"He said *undead* this time, as opposed to *an* undead."

Jikun knocked Navon's hand away from the Sel'ven, readying to assist in the deed. "I swore if he pulled that… Eldaeus, give up!" he roared as the Faraven retreated a step, fright and surprise still audaciously ingrained into his features.

"REALLY!" he choked. "LOOK BEHIND YOU!"

"Can I just put us all out of our misery?" Jikun groaned, glancing over his shoulder to pacify Eldaeus.

Navon dipped his head, finally appearing ready to agree.

Jikun's boots dragged to a stop, his breath frozen in his chest. *'Wait, that was not present before!'* he thought, his mind slow to grasp the sight. He stumbled, instinctively leaping aside in disbelief and alarm. "NAVON!" He swung his hand, magic tearing from his body and erupting through the earth before him.

Framed in the path loomed four men unlike any Jikun had seen, weighing the air with a thick, suffocating aura. They were hardly distinctive from one another: ashen pallor, sunken cavities devoid of eyes, and sparse, stringy hair flowing down beneath their dented helmets. Jikun's ice shattered against their breastplates, but pierced through the leathery flesh inside their boots with a sickening squelch.

As Navon turned, his countenance shifted to panic. "Sel'ari protect us!" he cried.

"I told you! I told you!" Eldaeus shouted. "And you did not believe me!"

"Silence, you crazy bastard!" Darcarus thundered as Jikun formed a spear in his hands.

But as swift as they had come, the wraiths vanished.

Jikun remained locked to the barren path, head swiveling wildly, his breath emerging short and ragged. "Those were dead soldiers," he exhaled. "Did we kill them?!"

Eldaeus shook his head. "No, they will be back. But do not worry. They have to appear before they attack."

"*Attack?!*"

"Those were scouts," Eldaeus spoke rapidly, his face twisted between a smile and a grimace, as though unsure whether to delight in his knowledge or fear it. "They will be back with their infantry brothers. Do you not understand anything about war?!"

Jikun reeled around, his face contorting in anger at the merry grin reflected to him. "How can you smile at this moment?! We have to move!" He forced his legs into a run, kicking up dirt as he caught Navon by the arm. "*Run, Captain!*"

Eldaeus' face grew solemn as the pair dashed past him. Darcarus was at their heels, flinging the Faraven back against the wall as he went. "Hm…" the Faraven mused. "You are right! I do not know how my luck works against an entire infantry unit. Someone is *bound* to kill me."

"*Then imagine those of us without your nonsensical luck!*" Jikun hollered.

Eldaeus' voice broke with surprise. "You are right! Emal'drathar above, we must hurry! I will give you a peapod when we get out of here!"

"*I DON'T WANT A DAMN PEAPOD!*"

Navon let out a shout of panic beside him, and Jikun quickly twisted his head over his shoulder.

His stomach dropped.

Where once the path had contained nothing but their own footprints, now there lay a writhing mass of pallid, surging corpses. They were attired in their ancient, battered armor, burned and scarred by dragon fire. Rust-colored cloaks once drenched in blood twisted about their bodies in the tattered remains of scorched material. The air was so heavy with dread that it seemed to press down upon Jikun's body, slowing his attempts to flee. At the front of the horde clanked a male in shattered plates, the metal held to his form with mere remnants of leather.

A gaping hole was hewn through his breast.

Eldaeus let out a bellow to the north, and Jikun could see yet another swarm of wraiths rising from the earth to obstruct their escape. Jikun's heart lurched, a vision of Elarium flaring. *'We're surrounded!'* And no sooner had he grasped their situation than the undead leader shrieked from behind, echoing like the mother of all thakish across the cliff faces. The pitch reverberated so painfully that Jikun's body crumpled beneath it, the sound overcoming all his years of experience on the battlefront. As his eyes rose to meet the sunken cavity, all dismissal of the Captain Aritos of his aged parchments vanished.

This creature was no illusion. It brandished the tattered remains of its infantry banner, flesh pulling free from yellowed bone as the arm elevated the flag in unison with its shrieks. A substance began to gush from its mouth in ebony waves, flowing down its body to be crushed beneath its armored feet.

'We are dead...' Jikun stared numbly.

There was a flash of movement on his left. Darcarus darted swiftly between the general and Aritos, his eyes hard, his face chillingly calm: as though the aura held no command over him.

"Distract the lich!" Navon yelled from somewhere nearby. "Distract the lich and I will take care of the rest!"

Darcarus had already sprung into action. Purple and black smoke twisted from his fingers and took shapes—great, bestial forms of creatures that Jikun immediately recognized through their ashy hue. At the front stood a three-headed cerebus—snarling and snapping at the spectral creatures as they drew near. To its right was a wolf substantially larger than Nazra, paling only in comparison to the thakish that had materialized beside it. And behind them, a large, sleek cat took form beside the rallying cry of a chimera. The Sel'ven's dragon may have fallen, but the beasts he had conjured were of no dismissive stature or ferocity.

Hope kindled once more in his breast, dampening the oppressive aura—it was foolish, but still better than damnable cowardice!

"ATTACK," the prince bellowed, and instantly the beasts were unleashed upon the surging undead, raking the lich to the floor as the backline leapt and smashed into the mass of troops.

As Jikun struggled to grasp the incredible magic before him, an unfamiliar word whispered in his mind. He pivoted with a roar. "Navon, you cannot use necromancy!"

"There is no other choice! *For once listen to me!*" Navon's hands had risen into the air, wisps forming and snaking about his fingers as an otherworldly cry erupted from the dead behind.

The cry belted Jikun with a physical aura, a feeling he could only liken to the power that had emanated from Darcarus' massive dragon or the great eye of Darival. Jikun's throat constricted and his fingers grasped for a blade. Nothing except a spear of ice graced his fingers. He stumbled, eyes sweeping the line of wraiths. Darcarus' beasts had already been lost—swallowed like

Darivalian pups in an avalanche. The lich had returned to the front line, old teeth clamped together as vengeance seethed from his toothy snarl.

"How do we slay it?!" Jikun croaked, hefting his spear against the lich. Black ooze leaked from recent wounds, and it reeked with the putrid odor of rotting flesh. He thrust his spear swiftly into the flesh exposed by the cavernous hole in the lich's breast, forcing it back a step. The lance stuck with a soft squish, clanking as the tip met the back plate.

The lich merely bared its rancid teeth and elevated its tarnished blade.

Damn it!—these beasts were corporeal and yet Jikun's attacks afforded him *nothing.*

"Sel'ari," Darcarus gasped as a spear swept around Aritos, aimed for his gut. The body of the Kamorian panther reappeared, smashing into the advancing undead and sending it tumbling into the throng behind.

Eldaeus' cry came from deep within the chaos, "Careful! Only the lich's blade is real, but the wraiths' weapons will still wound your soul!"

"Forget their weapons," Jikun shot back. "How do we *kill* them?!" *'And if we cannot kill thousands here, how do we kill the man who already can?'*

The enemy frontline was momentarily broken by Darcarus' panther, and Jikun's mindless wanderings shattered with it. He shot out his hand, struggling to detect water in the dry dawn air. A wall of ice shot from the earth before Darcarus, disgustingly frail. He cursed himself—his magic was nothing outside of Darival!

A second later, the ice shattered, showering them with cold, brittle shards.

No, his magic was nothing like the well-trained True Blood's, and all the experience of war would serve him nothing against a horde of undead—against an army! Darcarus' bravado was no more than a reflection of his stupidity! Even now, the prince was forced to fling the wounded bodies of his beasts as his last defense.

Just as Jikun had flung the bodies of his soldiers to flee Saebellus.

With a final howl the chimera vanished as well, and Darcarus stepped back to Jikun's side with his first flicker of fear. Perhaps he finally realized that they had truly lost.

Jikun erected another wall before the prince, flinging himself back against the mountain as the ice shot from the earth inches before his face. His breath fell short and fast. Was it a new wound? The old? His ribs, perhaps? Damn it! He was as dead as he had been if he had stayed on Sevrigel!

But there was no escape here!

A mocking screech resounded outside his barricade and Jikun tensed, his breath emerging as a cloud of white. For a moment, sickening silence filled the air. Utter, unnatural silence—as though the very world around him had frozen with his walls.

Then the unearthly swords thrust through, undeterred by the material plane, and all of Jikun's thoughts vanished with them. He could see the blades lodged into his chest. He could hear Navon call out. But the pain that tore through his frame was unlike that of any worldly wound he had ever received.

His mouth opened to scream, but no sound emerged.

There existed only a great, iron gate that rushed to meet him, surrounded by the faces of those he had once failed…

Then a howl of material wind roared from outside his wall of ice, and the cries of the wraiths grew shrill and panicked. The spectral blades withdrew from his body and Jikun choked back a cry of pain. He pushed off from the wall, frantic to avoid another blow, and allowed his ice to melt to clear his path of vision.

There stood Navon, his gaze set and his mouth thrown wide. The words he bellowed were ancient and unfamiliar, tearing high into the pale, blue sky. His eyes rolled up into his head as his neck snapped backward. His hands were elevated and his body trembled violently, teeth clanging together as though he had lost control of his jaw. Jikun had never seen the magic rack his friend's body with such brutality, and for a moment the sight before him felt as threatening as the one behind.

A thunderous rumble suddenly reverberated through the canyon and Jikun spun about as a high-pitched keening burst from the center of the wraiths. He clasped his hands over his ears, but it seemed that he felt the piercing sound in his soul rather than heard it on the material plane: his gesture did nothing to subdue the sound that was rising to a terrible cadence. Beside him, Darcarus sank to his knees, wracked with pain.

From the focal point of the resonance, a chasm tore open from the earth, spilling black smoke across the undead horde. When the corpses were blanketed in entirety, they were ripped into the earth, their cries consumed in a blast of wind.

The smoke dissipated; the portal and wraiths had disappeared, leaving a near-empty path behind.

Only the lich remained, banner flung to the ground at Jikun's heels. Aritos' mouth twisted in rage, his long yellow nails scraping the hilt of his blade as he wailed and swung high.

Navon stilled, turning to face them.

From their left, Eldaeus' battle of laughter with the wraiths had ceased. "Navon…" he trailed off, displaying his only hint of alarm since the assault had begun.

Navon laughed once—a cold, empty, unfamiliar laugh. He raised a crooked finger, pointing at Jikun's stiffened breast. "*Vinsare*," he whispered.

Behind Jikun, the lich exploded, showering the path around them in metal and chunks of stretchy flesh. *They had triumphed. 'Navon was right.'*

Jikun had only a fragment of a second to experience relief before he felt his own chest seize. Blood gushed from his nose and mouth. He gurgled out a gasp, fighting the pressure building critically from within. *'He's going to kill me,'* he grasped numbly.

Eldaeus abandoned his extravagant battle with the air and rushed to Jikun's side, catching him as he collapsed. He shoved a glass vial into Jikun's hands as blood frothed from the Darivalian's mouth in foaming waves. "Do not let this go," the Faraven ordered, rounding on Navon.

Darcarus had staggered to his feet, seized with the same bewilderment and horror. His eyes locked onto the Helven and he charged, slamming his body into Navon's to send the necromancer sprawling across the path.

Jikun felt the pain at his sternum grow as his ribs threatened to tear away from one another. He struggled to discern Navon's state: he lay in the earth, inert and sprawling, eyes rolled high into his pallid brow.

Then abruptly the male gasped, as though he had been drowning and could breathe for the first time. His eyes closed tightly.

With that breath, the pressure in Jikun's chest vanished. He coughed and spat, swiping the back of his hand across his nose as his airways cleared.

But his attention never diverted from Navon.

The necromancer's eyes fluttered open and he moaned, pushing himself upright. Dirt and fragments of stone fell away from his chest as his fingers trailed to his breast. "I was at the gates again," the Helven whispered in confusion. "Deeper into the gates than I ever… Second gate? Third? I…" He faltered as his hollow gaze found his general. "…*JIKUN!* By Sel'ari, what happened?!" He scrambled to his feet, stumbling once as his wavering coordination plowed him into the side of the mountain.

Darcarus' hands shot up instantly, but remained still. Unaware of the prince's threat, Navon righted himself and scrambled to Jikun's side. "What happened?!" he panted, extending his hand.

Jikun shoved the arm away with a feeling of unfamiliar terror at the Helven's proximity. "*YOU!*" he snarled.

Eldaeus had crept away, squatting at a considerable distance to observe.

Navon's face twisted, his voice emerging strained and hesitant. His hand extended once more, cautious this time. "What do you mean…?"

Jikun snatched up a piece of the lich's leathery flesh, shoving it into his captain's palm. "Darcarus intervened," he spat with another mouthful of blood on top of the shriveled skin. "The wraiths and lich attacked, you used your necromancy, and then *you turned on me*." He wiped his lips across his cloak, closing his eyes tightly for a moment. "If not for him, you would have killed me."

"I don't remember…"

"Dare tell, what part of necromancy was this that you chose to omit from me in your *lesson?!*" Jikun demanded, eyes flashing open. "The part where you kill us along with Relstavum?!"

"I am sorry," Navon stammered, yet he attempted to draw himself up. "You know it was not my intention to injure you! I lost my soul for but a *moment*—but I have returned and am wiser for it—!"

Jikun's teeth gnashed together. "*Silence!*"

Navon's jaw snapped shut and his determination faltered.

"Endangering yourself was one matter, Navon. But not others… *not* me…!" A controlled fury was rising. "I did not leave Sevrigel for this!"

Navon's head jerked toward Eldaeus as the Faraven pushed off his knees and approached. The captain swiftly attempted to pull Jikun to his feet. "It will not happen a—"

Jikun struck the Helven once more, the slap cracking across his dusty arm. "Do not *dare* to touch me, necromancer," he hissed. He extended his hand to Eldaeus as the male stopped beside him and allowed the mad elf to pull him to his feet.

Eldaeus' fingers fluttered with some sane semblance of urgency. "We have to move—I do not know what has happened to those wraiths."

Darcarus drew away from the mountain face, balancing Jikun from the left. Two gold buttons dropped from his battered cotton to bounce away and hide amongst the pieces of the splattered corpse. "For once, Eldaeus is sound. We cannot endure another encounter."

Jikun gripped onto the leather around the Faraven's shoulders, steadying himself before he stepped away with crippled pride. Gods strike his shame!—

he had shown an utter lack of strength before the horde and now he wobbled like a lame mare!

Navon's eyes scanned the ground... the walls nearby... then finally flicked upward, as though searching once again for something lost.

"Navon," Jikun barked, drawing the Helven's attention. "You swear to Sel'ari that you will not cast again or so help me, I will bind and leave you here in ice."

He saw his companion pale, yet his breast swelled once more in defiance. "I was trying to save us!"

"*By killing us?!* I would rather die to my enemies than by an ally's blade in my back."

Jikun felt Darcarus' coarse hands tighten as the prince growled venomously, "Do you not see what you almost did to us? And still you consider using your magic? You are as great a threat as Relstavum, only *infinitely* more unpredictable. We laughed about Eldaeus' futility, but you... *you* are a true risk!"

Navon's eyes flicked between the prince and Jikun, gathering the severity of their threat. "...I swear this by Sel'ari," he finally exhaled. He shifted to the blade of Aritos still lying amongst the chunks of rotted flesh, lifting it and extending it toward Jikun.

"It is done. Now stop groveling like some god-damn green foot," Jikun snapped, wresting from Darcarus to snatch the blade. "We will not speak of it again. And if any one of you tries to help me along once more, I will smash your brains in with this hilt."

Eldaeus' attention abruptly seemed to lose focus and his face broke into a grin. He sprang forward singing, "Then up up we go-eth! Through the mountains, up the road-eth!"

"Once more, Eldaeus, and I'll freeze you first."

*

The remainder of the mountain path was a blur of grey stone and dirt—solemn, empty, and eerily quiet. And no one, with the exception of Eldaeus, had any intention of breaking that silence.

After Navon had explained necromancy, Jikun could admit that he had *considered* the possibility that the dark magic might contain their only chance against Saebellus' necromancer. But now he rebuked himself for having been as witless as a mountain troll. Navon was ever the ideological, naïve fool and his poor judgment had hurled him into life-threatening dangers on more than one occasion. Yet again, such a reckless act had left him searching, just as he had done after the battle with the hel'onja. As though the captain had *lost* something.

And Jikun doubted he would be so lucky as for it to be the Helven's stupidity.

He wearily glanced toward the sullen face of the Helven. So long as their lives were not in danger, he believed that Navon would keep his word. Yet with their degree of luck, misfortune was likely lurking around the next mountain bend, and Navon would be prepared to use his necromancy to combat it. He would never relinquish the cursed souls, even for Sel'ari.

But he and Navon were not the only ones stinging from the battle; the conflict had taken a significant toll on Darcarus as well. The act of summoning itself was not what had weakened him, he had explained, but rather the state of the creatures he had banished. Their lives now drained his strength for recovery, leaving the Sel'ven pale and hobbling—a dismal visage of his former, cocky little self.

However, their encounter with the undead had not managed to dampen Eldaeus' spirit. He was prancing ahead of them, belting out a painful tune where half the words were forgotten and filled with a language Jikun was fairly certain he had invented. He vanished around a bend in the stone, cackling delightedly. "The egress! The egress!" he shouted suddenly from up ahead.

Navon's face lit up and his footsteps quickened. "If he's deceiving us again, I say you follow through with your threat," his captain suggested, forcing a beseeching smile.

Jikun sighed internally; his temper was fading despite his resolve. How swiftly had Navon forgiven him after he had failed to attend the trail for his practices inside Sel'ari's temple? So Jikun chuckled and, though empty, Navon took it as acceptance of the entreaty.

Comradery over common sense.

"The egress!" Eldaeus belted once more.

Navon tsked. "By Sel'ari, I don't know how we are going to continue enduring his antics."

But as they rounded the bend, the trials of the Makataj were forgotten: there indeed beckoned the end of the mountainous path, and Eldaeus' searing vibrancy was nowhere in sight.

Jikun's boots pressed onto the cold, frosted grass and he shook the unease from his footfalls with the sand. His wounded chest expanded past the pain and he savored the scent of the damp, lush earth that glistened with dewdrops in the morning light.

So this was Ryekarayn. North of the wasteland upon which they had wrecked, the land grappled for more familiarity with the elven nation. Here the trees were smaller, the earth harder, and the grass coarser—like the people it had bred.

"We made it," Darcarus breathed in disbelief.

Navon's unrestrained laugh rang out behind them. "Praise Sel'ari," he cried.

And then Eldaeus dropped by his knees from a nearby tree, swift to shatter their reprieve with his grinning swing. He had put the effort into the climb and fall purely, Jikun imagined, for the satisfaction he received from their expressions. "So… where next on our journey to Relstavum, comrades?"

Relstavum. Merely hunting the man this far had been a trial, but only one end for their struggles existed. Jikun tapped his fist to his lips as he tried to recall the name of the city Darcarus had mentioned weeks ago. Cool, hard glass met his skin and he opened his palm in surprise. His hand still gripped the narrow, long vial. He uncurled it and scowled at the contents. "I told you, I don't want your damn peapod."

"Keep it, keep it! It will bring you good luck. Like you said, I cannot be the *only* one with fortune. Plus, I saw you eating those fish backward. You have to balance the bad luck out *somehow*."

Jikun shook his head in exasperation, but he pocketed the idiotic trinket. *Just* in case the male was not *entirely* insane.

Darcarus passed him the faintest smirk. "Keep it, you unlucky bastard. Nordeep is a few weeks north and our confrontation with Relstavum will follow in quick succession." The Sel'ven glanced sidelong at Navon—the first time Jikun noticed the prince fully regard the Helven since the male's possession. There was an undeniable flicker of distrust in those piercing, blue eyes.

Jikun imagined that, like himself, the True Blood was considering whether the necromancer amongst them would be of assistance or a danger in the battle ahead.

Neither he nor Jikun would allow Navon to jeopardize their cause again.

Chapter Twenty-Four

The journey to Ryekarayn was long. Jerah had few expectations, but nevertheless, the journey was *exceptionally* long. Neither was this helped by the ceaseless rocking of the ship, the darkness of the cargo hold, nor the cramped box in which he was forced to remain for the vast majority of each night and every day.

The crates around him had provided him with food and the barrels with water; the humans seemed to store more than fabric within. He used one such fabric crate for his waste, hiding it between the folds. All throughout the day, he could hear the sound of feet above him and, several times a day, around him. The humans would venture down into the cargo hold not only for their food and water, but at times to talk and shout for long hours about the numbers of "dice" and the fine state of women, all of which Jerah found most fascinating. They talked about cities down the eastern coast of Ryekarayn ripe with "fuckable" women. Jerah made a mental note to see such sights. And then, occasionally late at night, two particular men would venture down to wrestle in an unusual, naked state when Jerah would otherwise enjoy freedom of the cargo hold.

But he remained patient until the last stretch of the journey came: until he knew they were close to shore. He could hear a change in the sailors' voices. He could smell it on the wind. Far less vulgar than the elven lands with their plague of brightly colored, stinking plants, this smell was of dust and wood and stone. Jerah lifted the lid of his crate to inhale deeply, hardly able to contain his excitement.

"*Ryekarayn!*" he dared breathe aloud.

The ship took its time drifting into the dock. Jerah could hear the distant sounds of the human tongue growing louder, and of other ships creaking in the waters around them.

"Drop anchor!" he heard a human above him bellow.

Jerah let the lid snap shut. He waited, anticipation growing. Ryekarayn! This was the land where he was safe! The land where he did not have to hide… where he was not hunted! He felt an overwhelming sense of elation, so powerful that his body trembled.

“Gods I cannot even budge it,” grunted a man suddenly from beside him. “Get over here and help me. *Damn* this one is heavy. We should have brought that half-giant with us!”

There were soon four men around his crate, lifting it up and carrying it out of the ship. Jerah could hear the slosh of water against wood as they moved across the pathway to the shore. There was a gentle thud onto stone and the sound of footsteps walking away.

After waiting for several heartbeats, Jerah popped the lid and peered out.

At first, he was blinded by light—fierce, fiery light from the orange torch in the void. He winced, closing his eyes tightly.

“Look,” he urged himself.

Jerah opened his eyes more slowly. At first he saw only cobbled stone and shadowy figures. Then they clarified, becoming tall and burly humans, large crates, piles of lumber, and even a large, wheeled creation pulled by two powerful creatures. The dock flowed right into a city—one with no wall and no guards. There was a large, long archway that led deeper within, in which buildings towered above and around the tunnel. Low overhangs of buildings to the left and right sheltered two of the four-legged beasts and some cargo, probably protecting them from the water that sometimes fell from the void. But this was all trivial beside what Jerah noted most of all:

There was not an elf in sight!

Jerah slowly raised the lid and stepped out of the crate, a mixture of feelings causing his movement to be slowed with awe. He let his bloody cloaks fall to the stone behind him and dropped the wooden lid beside the tattered heap in a breath of excitement.

Ryekarayn!

He did not immediately notice the hushed voices, the gasps, or the stillness that followed him as he slunk toward the archway. There were other fascinating wonders that caught his attention. What was the object the man beside the archway held that could play such a strange and fluent sound? What was that sour scent? What were the fabric objects hanging across the archway in identical designs?

He passed into the archway, too excited by the mystery that lay beyond to stop and ask his questions. There was no crowd jostling him here—everyone moved aside swiftly, pressing their bodies against the stone wall. Much better than the stifling crowd of elves.

Jerah emerged from the tunnel and gasped as he cast his gaze into the brilliant light beyond. Such a sight! He turned his head slowly, trying to take in everything around him.

There was a vast section of land unburdened by buildings and instead filled with countless canopies of fabric and wooden tables covered with arrays of unknown objects. Here, the city became a bustle of noise and humans, but Jerah found it fairly easy to move between them. He ducked his head below an orange canopy and stopped beside a crowd marveling at an assortment of glowing, round, clear stones.

"Do not touch!" the fat man behind the counter warned the humans before him. "You break it, you buy it, my friend!"

Jerah looked around hesitantly. He just wanted to poke it. Just with his claw. That wasn't *completely* touching it… Just to see what it did. He reached out a hand.

"Ah ah, don't—" began the man, and then stopped. The humans around him hushed as well. Jerah felt space grow around him.

"Oh my gods, what is it?" someone whispered.

But Jerah hardly noticed. He poked the glowing orb, watching the lights inside quiver. He picked it up, turning it slowly in his great hands.

"Take it and go!" the human stammered. "Go!"

Jerah raised his brows and turned, remembering that there were others around him. Well, the human was certainly in a hurry to send him off! He paused, pulling the silver coin from his pocket. He set it down before the jiggling belly. *'Break it, you buy it,'* he reminded himself. He supposed he *had* touched it, after all. Jerah moved away from the table, turning the orb slowly in his hands as he tried to watch the streets and his new possession at the same time.

What a city! Buildings bounced torchlight off stark white sides and caught the red glow of the wooden beams stretched across their grand surfaces. Little panels of wood were lined in neat little rows across the rooftops with the utmost care and precision.

Humans were breathtaking!

He stopped. He had hardly moved away from the table when a nearby figure caught his eyes. He lowered the orb.

"Hello," the little figure stated. "I like your costume."

Jerah looked down at it, smiling slightly. "I like…" he paused. What did he like about the little creature? "Your eyes," he finally determined. He crouched down slowly before it. What was it? It was like the two he had seen on Sevrigel after he had killed his last elf. Much too short for an elf and much too short for a human. This little creature, however, looked remarkably like them. His brow furrowed. A dwarf, perhaps? Not nearly as fat as his master had made them out to be… in fact, this one wasn't fat at all… Boney and sickly, even by elven standards. But it was certainly much, much shorter than the elves or humans.

He supposed he could talk to this one. Master had never said anything about dwarves. "You are a skinny dwarf," he commented to it slowly in its human tongue, the language coming readily to his lips.

The dwarf cocked his head slightly. "I'm not a dwarf," he replied with a series of fast little grunts. Humor, Jerah remembered. They ended abruptly as its beady little eyes fell to the orb. "Can I see that?" It pointed at the ball in Jerah's hands.

Jerah drew the orb back toward himself slightly. "Well, it's mine," he warned the not-dwarf. He had left his stones on Sevrigel, after all. This was all he had.

The not-dwarf stuck out its bottom lip, an expression Jerah had never seen before and was unsure of how to react to.

Jerah slowly held out the orb. "You break it, you buy it," he warned.

The not-dwarf took it, turning it over in its hands. "Why are you dressed like that?" it asked, even as its eyes remained fixed on the quivering light.

Jerah looked down at his dirty, stained clothes. "These are my clothes," he replied slowly. The not-dwarf was just as filthy as he was, skinny, sickly… eyeing the orb like a hungry, homeless animal.

The not-dwarf looked up. "I mean, why do you have those horns and wings strapped to you?"

Jerah scratched his chin, forgetting the wonder he had at the creature's unusual clothes. "They're not strapped to me…" he replied, confused. "They are my wings." He stretched them out to their full extent, casting a great shadow across the street.

The not-dwarf stepped back.

"Why are you so short?" Jerah retorted with a huff.

It hesitated in its reply, eyes still wide, body tense. "…Because I'm just a child."

A child is short, Jerah committed to memory. And is not a dwarf. He had been told nothing about childs before. *'They must be like bitches,'* he determined to himself. Whatever that defined them as.

There was a sudden shriek. "Galway save us!"

Jerah glanced up for a moment to spot the wide-eyed, fearful face of a woman. Why…? He looked back toward the child.

And let out a low growl. With orb in hand, it had turned and fled down the street.

Jerah straightened and took off after it, the rest of the world forgotten.

That was his.

But Jerah had not gone far when he realized that the path left by him was not the same as the path left by the child. He slowed and came to a stop. Before him, humans still cowered in terror. Behind him, bodies shrank away from where he had run, eyes wide, jaws slacked.

And then it came to Jerah: *they all feared him.*

He pulled his wings back tightly against his body, trying to lessen his size. He just wanted his orb back… He glanced up in time to see the smug child vanish into an alley. Jerah looked away. Perhaps chasing a child… was forbidden? He lowered his head slightly.

He just wanted his orb…

Then he heard a sound. A sound he had only heard twice before, but had clung to his instincts with the sharp threat of pain. He jerked his body to the left, but the shaft of wood still pierced through the side of his arm. He turned in time to see a second weapon raised by a man of the city's watch, the human's body locked into a position of offense as it raised the bolt. Jerah raised his hands defensively, trying to demonstrate that he meant no harm.

The guard did not hesitate. The shaft tore through his chest.

Jerah stumbled, hearing the click of the first weapon readying once more. He whirled, scrambling desperately past the nearest human for cover behind a table. He heard the thud of a bolt against the wood.

His chest grew tight with fear and confusion. Why? Why was he being hunted?! Were these men from Sevrigel?! *What had he done?!*

But it did not matter; he had to get away. He had to get out of the city! Jerah's chest seized with pain and he grabbed the table and raised it up. Its shadow swept out across the street and the surrounding humans stumbled back in surprise.

Why?!

Jerah shoved his questions aside and let the table loose. It hurled through the air, slamming into the guards.

And with that, Jerah turned and fled into the crowd.

His heart was racing, his muscles aching from the wood twisted into them. He breathed loudly and heavily, breaking for the first alleyway he could see. He searched frantically for a sewer entrance.

There was none.

Jerah's head jerked back over his shoulder to see several curious humans daring to return his stare, but they quickly vanished as his eyes met with theirs. No, he couldn't go back that way! He clenched his great fist and lurched deep into the alley.

"That way!" he heard someone shout from behind.

But Jerah kept running, twisting around a corner into another bustling street, searching frantically for the exit to the city. He scanned the street once, but saw nothing.

With a cry of frustration, he attempted to retreat back into the darkness of the alley from which he had emerged, but the shouts and screams were only growing louder from within.

And so Jerah pressed forward and ran.

Was his master wrong? *Could* Master be wrong? The idea had never occurred to him! His feet pounded against the stone and when a group of men dared block his way, he knocked them aside like brittle branches. The oblivious crowd that lay beyond them was too dense for his charge!

'Another way...!' Jerah thought as he spun down another street, searching for the nearest alleyway and its comforting darkness. Unlike elven cities, these buildings were closely linked, with hardly more than a few feet of space between their walls and, often times, none at all. But Jerah had to find a place to hide!—even as he barreled his way through the thinning crowds, he could smell the pursuers behind him.

Where could he hide? The city seemed to go on forever!

He could only keep running and running. The pain in his chest began to slow him down, and the weakness in his legs from being cramped in the ship's crate began to take its toll. He stumbled once, barely catching his balance. But the sight ahead remained locked in Jerah's gaze. He had to… keep…

With a sickening snap, a sharp pain shot through his back and embedded into his bone.

Damn… it…

He stumbled again.

Another.

Jerah fell to one knee, pressing his hands into the wet, white earth. His eyes began to close, his head dropping forward toward the ground…

And then his body jolted as it had done on Sevrigel. Another instinct took over, another drive of will. His muscles tightened, his vision sharpened. His fear and distress vanished like the torches in a puff of smoke.

And suddenly Jerah bolted, sprinting with speed and force unmatched by the human guards behind him. They shot him again, but Jerah barely felt it. He slammed his body into the first guard, the curious crowd shrieking and fleeing in horror for the nearest buildings.

The second guard stumbled, his brown eyes peeling wide with terror. Jerah reached out, grabbing his arm and snapping it backward through the metal. He slammed his fist down through the helmet of the first guard, tossing the second to the wayside. When he straightened, he spotted a third guard retreating into the crowd.

Jerah bared his teeth, daring him to raise his weapon, but the man remained frozen in fear.

Jerah turned.

The crowd that had once blocked that side was gone. And now, up ahead, Jerah could see it. He could see the exit of the city. It was so close…

His breaths became wheezes through the pain, but he dragged his feet forward. No one stopped him. And he did not stop. Step after step, he trudged his way beneath a second archway, dragging his hand along the wall for balance. He did not notice the splendid fabrics, the carved statues, the painted vases.

And then he emerged into the light of a wide, frozen street.

Jerah's head rolled up to look around, focusing on the shadows of the land to his right. There. Behind the white-dusted forest, towering up in great splendor and vanishing into the clouds, were enormous pointed stones. He did not know the name of them, but he had seen them in the distance all around Sevrigel. They beckoned him with their familiar shadows against the void.

Jerah moved toward them, body trembling, knees buckling.

Maybe… maybe in those peaks he would be safe. Unhunted. Tucked away into the quiet of that darkness…

Maybe… just once…

But that was unlikely.

CHAPTER TWENTY-FIVE

Sellemar grimaced as the male in his weathered, oaken chair slumped forward, his form shuddering with the pain of several broken fingers. It was truly pathetic. The vulture had sentenced so many to horrific deaths, and yet he could not taste even a little pain without whimpering like a dying pup.

Sellemar had wounded Saebellus' ability to recover militarily. He had aroused the fears of the people. He had *failed* with the Nemorium but *this*—the strike upon the council—would expose the vices of the people's sanctimonious politicians.

He would proceed with the rebellion despite the absence of the knowledge of Saebellus' plans.

Sellemar poked the wretch pointedly in the eye. "Up, Cahsari. I know you will eventually succumb to my demands, so why not surrender the information and save yourself the… pitiful amount of pain that I shall continue to inflict upon you?"

Cahsari sniffed and spat purely out of spite, the wad of clear ooze splattering across the tip of Sellemar's polished boot. He looked up, sunken eyes meeting the El'adorium's with pure detestation. "I'm not going to tell you where it is, *Sellemar.* You'll have to find a way to string up Ilrae without my assistance. I know you won't do anything to me worse than…" he paused briefly to grimace at his broken fingers. He sucked in a painful wheeze. "…This. You've refrained from spilling my blood so far—I don't think you have it in you to really *torture*." He managed to tap his foot on the fur of the thakish rug at his feet. "You have me sitting on a rug of *white*. How much blood would you stain this with, *El'adorium?*"

Sellemar slightly arched his brows. *'Probably not the ideal place for such an untidy affair,'* he considered briefly. He scanned the room thoughtfully, hoping that inspiration would strike him for a creative next blow. "This is true," he ceded after a moment. "I have always traveled with someone who is far better than I at such barbaric methods of retrieving information..." He paused as he strode to the fireplace behind the Helven, raising the poker from beside the fire. *'Messy...'* He pivoted, returning to the councilmember's side. "But you provide me with few options. I cannot '*make a deal*' with you. The formation of such arrangements is what has allowed you to conceal your crimes for so long."

Cahsari's eyes fell on the poker and for a moment, they held a flicker of genuine fear. His confidence was waning and Sellemar's lack of experience in such an art was only instilling further anxiety within the councilmember.

'Perhaps,' he imagined Cahsari thought, *'the otherwise-talented male will deal a mistakenly fatal blow in his attempt to cause sufficient pain.'*

Sellemar sighed, flipping the poker casually. "I am endeavoring to determine how I might make best use of this... instrument. I suppose, if you are rather inclined, we could experiment and discover what loosens your tongue."

Cahsari swallowed audibly. "What do I care? You will kill me when we're through, whether or not I tell you the entirety of the council's business."

Sellemar brandished the device once more, elevating the ash-coated end to the Helven's nose. "No. Worse. I will inject you with a dose of Noctemrian and you shall wake up drooling in the city square with a list of your crimes hanging about your neck. And not a fragment of memory of how you arrived there." Sellemar pressed a little further until the dusty end rested against the male's beak. "But do not suggest that I am not generous—I shall hang the evidence against your fellow council members as well. That way the lot of you dishonored cowards can have company for the next thousand years while you shit in buckets and eat the waste from the palace dining halls."

The imagery was elegance itself, but the vulture merely shuddered. His eyes crossed briefly as he regarded the instrument, which now likely seemed an emblem of good fortune. His voice emerged with a crack. "If I tell you, you will keep my son from this fate."

"Why? Because he is innocent?"

"He *is*—"

"NOT innocent," Sellemar interjected sharply. "I told you I do not offer concessions to *men* like you. If your son has committed crimes—and he has—then he too shall be held responsible. Worse than his sexual exploitation of the human women is his dealings in Ulasum's Tooth. Elvorium is plagued by a generation of vagrants who while away their time drinking poison; they dream of the glorious days that once were beneath the True Bloods instead of seeking splendor for their own generation." His voice dropped into a growl that would have stilled even a lycanthrope. "Certainly this complacency enables you to easily maintain your power." He lowered the poker, careful not to drip ash on the thakish fur.

"Of *course* the people cling to the True Bloods," Cahsari spat. "Before them, they clung to the image of Eraydon. Every several thousand years or so they hoist a new symbol up on a pedestal, perceiving it to represent something greater than their current fortune. No one wants to acknowledge that this shithole we call life is all there ever has been… and all there ever will be. If elves like myself have come to terms with that truth and are ready to grasp what we can in this life, we are being rewarded for our understanding of reality. We are not dreaming of a past that never was or a future that never will be."

Sellemar stiffened. "Sevrigel *was* once a noble nation. Males like *you* and your *son* have torn her down." *'My people* were *once greater than this pacified herd!'* He jabbed at Cahsari's chest, restraining the blow just enough to bruise the flesh. "What did you tell the country when you sentenced the centaurs at the Sevilan Marshes to die? 'We're protecting the emblem of the goddess.' And to the traditionalists: 'the True Bloods counseled us to save the phoenix.' Lies. *You* fabricated that 'reality' in the minds of the people and in Taemrin's army. You create the lie of a perfect world and then fill your coffers with the rewards that the complacency of your subjects bestows. How many elves did Taemrin lose in those marshes?" He jabbed at Cahsari again, striking him beside the first blow. "How many? Do you even comprehend the weight of souls your greed has cost?!"

Cahsari grimaced in silence.

"No wonder Taemrin chose to fight to every male's last breath instead of surrendering. He was likely *relieved* to die after having lost so many of the country's sons festering on a hill in the raging heat—all while *you* procured even greater wealth. Defeat. Depression. Trauma. Do you not see that because of *you* Saebellus sits on this throne?! That he now marches across the country and slaughters your brethren?!"

Sellemar gave a final, solid blow beside the second, watching as the Helven clenched his teeth. "I know Ilrae owned *The Black Queen*. He could not have destroyed *all* of the evidence—not a business male like Ilrae. Papers must exist somewhere. Something he wrote, signed… *I know* you are disgustingly close to that bastard Fildor, and Fildor allowed *The Black Queen* passage through the Windari Channel. And *he* informed me that Ilrae asked you to conceal the papers and money until the uproar over the demon incident subsides."

Cahsari grunted as Sellemar dropped the poker to his side, observing his smudged shirt with dismay. Apparently, he was fully intending to ignore Sellemar's accusations. "Not all of us are so eager to look like paupers," he growled spitefully, eyeing the hem of Sellemar's shirt.

Sellemar did not have to look down to know that another hole undoubtedly graced his clothing. *'I must get myself a damn cat,'* he groaned. But that was a matter for another day. "Ignore what I said, but you shall know when you stand before the gods what evil and destruction your vices have wrought upon our land. But I am wasting my breath discussing politics and *reality* with you, Cahsari. My point remains: no mercy shall be given to those who tear my country down. Not for you. Not for your son. *Not for Ilsevel.* The next time I brandish this—"

"Poker."

Sellemar's eyes narrowed. "—will be the last time we speak pleasantly to one another."

The Helven wiggled, struggling for a climactic display of defiance. But while Sellemar could not boast of his skills in the art of torture, he was damn fine at tying knots.

Finding no leniency in his bonds, Cahsari redoubled his efforts in rambling to delay the next blow. "You are the El'adorium. We have all seen the way that Ilsevel looks at you. And we know what you are paid. You live in a shithole, but it *could* be great. You could have the queen as your mistress. You could have power second only to hers and yet… You throw it all away. You are an ideological *fool.*"

Sellemar raised the poker sharply. "I warned you."

A loud knock rang out from the great hall below, echoing throughout the empty rooms.

Sellemar slapped a hand over the male's mouth. "Whoever that is just saved you," he growled. With a swift flick from his pocket and jab of a needle, the Noctemrian flooded the Helven's veins. He drooped like a wilted plant.

Sellemar withdrew his palm, wiping the drool on the male's hair, and hastened to his balcony. *'Who could it be…? Not* Ilsevel again.*'* But his gut told him otherwise.

"Damn," he muttered, promptly absorbing the scene below. He held the edge of the white glass door as the wind fought to slam it closed behind him.

Four gold-plated soldiers stood ankle-deep in the snow before his entrance, two behind and two in front of the driftwalking queen. Ilsevel was glancing about the exterior of the estate, a look of mild disgust distorting her features. Her gaze began to turn upward and Sellemar stepped swiftly back into his room.

"*Damn it*," he swore again. He sliced Cahsari free from the ropes and crammed him unceremoniously beneath the bed. *'Why has she come?'* He tossed the broken ropes into the drawer of his desk and shoved the chair into its place beside the fire.

Downstairs, he heard the soft creak of the front door swing open.

She certainly wasted no time in intruding.

"Lord Sellemar?" drifted the queen's melodic voice. Her tone was sweet and welcoming—*we have all seen the way Ilsevel looks at you*—but Sellemar knew a more sinister game was afoot.

He slicked back his unruly hair as he strode quickly from the room. Still, he could not fathom what she sought. He swung around the narrow hallway to emerge on the landing above the entryway. "Your Majesty," he greeted, leaning over the railing. "I was not expecting you. What a pleasant surprise." He felt his tone lacked emphasis and so he amended his greeting with a dashing smile. Unfortunately, he suspected this gesture was as weak as his words; he had never possessed a talent for acting. Charisma and discretion: those were Itirel's duty—even *Sairel* had been more adept at them in his youth.

And *that* was remarkable.

Ilsevel looked up from where she ran her hand along the banister of the staircase, her eyes darting briskly across the dark marble hall as though making certain that he was alone. Then she turned her face upward until the torchlight fell across her features in a particular way. The angle was slightly unnatural, but Sellemar could only assume she was trying to achieve a certain appearance in the lantern light.

He smoothed his shirt, finger catching in the atrocious hole Cahsari had so generously identified. Damn, he had not changed. Still, he began to descend the stairs. "Your Majesty—"

"Oh no, remain there," Ilsevel replied, holding up her hand. "I see your home is still as empty as when I visited you last." She drew her snow-dappled shawl about her shoulders and feigned a shiver. "It's terribly drafty in this old place, isn't it? How appalling of my late husband to reward you with such a hovel. But… you must have a warmer room. Somewhere where you… spend your time?"

"Only my office. *My bedroom*, as it were. Sadly the room serves two purposes and—" Sellemar began, but saw the smile grow. "I can light the fires in the sitting room downstairs. The place should warm quickly enough," he began hurriedly, taking another step down.

He could see a dangerous flame light behind her eyes, but it was quenched the moment he perceived it. She flashed a broader smile. "No need. I would love to see your office. It must be quite hospitable if you have not bothered to maintain the rest of your estate. What is it, I wonder, that you do with all the wealth you have earned?"

Sellemar's body stilled. The queen had reached the stairs and was ascending gracefully to his level.

His lips twitched uncontrollably between a smile and a grimace, and his mind tried frantically to recall if any appendage of Cahsari's body was still protruding from beneath his bed. *'His foot. I believe his foot!'*

"Is it this way?" Ilsevel inquired as she reached the hallway. "I see a light…"

Sellemar hurried to lead the way. "Yes. It is. But I am afraid that work has kept me so busy and I am certain that it is terribly messy—a mess. Just everywhere. Things strewn. The floor. I think the *walls*. Probably the ceiling. I would be mortified if your majesty saw—"

But Ilsevel progressed onward even while he stammered his protestations. He gave a sharp intake of breath as her hand rested on the handle.

'If she finds him I will be forced to abscond with her and lock her away.'

Ilsevel threw open the door and stepped inside. "Ah!"

Sellemar hurried past her, nearly knocking her over in his haste. Cahsari's foot was nowhere to be seen.

"The place is spotl—"

Sellemar swiftly snatched the poker from where it still lay on the marble floor. "A mess. Like I said," he explained weakly, leaning it against the fireplace. The rest of the room glistened with dustless perfection.

Ilsevel closed the door softly behind her. She gave a slow wink. "Why, if I did not know better, I would say you didn't want me in your room."

Sellemar's hand slipped off the poker and it clattered to the ground. "Wha—I… Celi—It… You should… I meant…"

Ilsevel giggled, putting her fingers to her lips as she turned to properly investigate his private quarters. "Ah, it is so much warmer up here. I see that this *is* where you spend all of your time. But not your wealth." She raised her fingers to the clasp at her neck and flung the cloak away, revealing a dress Sellemar was quite certain violated a prostitute's understanding of modesty. A high slit in the thigh… a deep V that descended halfway down her torso… *'Good gods, Cahsari was right… That dress could* not *have been fashioned on Sevrigel.'*

He drew his eyes sharply from the thin folds that fell over the curves of her buttocks. "Your Majesty," he stated quickly. "I had no warning you were coming and I am afraid that I have made plans to meet with several delegates. I would not wish for them to arrive and find you here."

Ilsevel feigned deafness to his words. She had glided over to his wardrobe and swung open the polished doors, surveying the clothes inside with a slight cock of her head. "So regal. A true male of nobility," she whispered. She glanced once over her shoulder. "I like that." She left it open as she perused the shelves beside it, fingering the old books and parchments absentmindedly. "From the True Bloods, I assume." She stopped, her finger running down the spine of one of the novels. "*The Legend of Eraydon*. Far more worn than the rest of this collection. Interesting. Is it yours, my lord?"

Sellemar reached his wardrobe in three brisk strides and closed it with a snap.

Where had he spent his wealth, she had asked. And now apparently she was set on a course to discover the answer for herself.

"No. I know the story quite well. I believe Lord Rilden was fond of history. That era in particular."

She smiled, drifting away from the shelves and to his desk. "I am a scholar of history, myself…" He saw her cheeks flush, as though embarrassed by the revelation. "Eraydon and his companions awed me as a child. Prince Mesheck, Princess Aura, Prince Ephraim… They lived in a time when the old kings were not afraid to do the work themselves. Tiras was always my favorite, though, willing to do whatever the end required, regardless of the cost…" She opened a drawer of his papers and shook her head slightly. Sellemar was not certain if she was disparaging the mess inside or lamenting her own words. "Ephraim, on the other hand, was a strict follower of the rules. My least preferred. His actions… I think he was always trying to prove himself as good as his father, Ralaris. Always trying to live up to his name…" She opened another drawer. As she withdrew a handful of sliced rope, her smirk grew with a wild flash of her eyes. "But I don't think you are a male who follows the rules," she whispered.

Sellemar swallowed. "That is… I… …have no idea."

She winked. "I can only imagine what you could do with this rope and this room…" She let the rope fall from her fingers and a soft exhale escaped her parted lips.

A soft moan emerged from Cahsari, breaking that moment of silence.

Sellemar started. "That was not me! …I mean, it *was* me but I… see I have this terrible ache that—"

Ilsevel smiled understandingly, advancing until her body was inches from his own. She blinked slowly, and when her eyes met his again, they were filled with words he could not interpret and certainly did not wish to hear. "Before you revealed your presence to the council, you went by the name of Ralaris, didn't you?" she whispered, her fingers running down the length of his chest.

"Yes. A savant of history." Sellemar choked on his own response and hastily stepped away. "It *is* rather hot in here, is it not? I should open the balcony." He hurried past her to the doors, throwing them open to feel the relief of being enveloped in the frosty winter air. *'Good gods, Sellemar, what have you done? You should have gone with Itirel! Already she envisions your neck in a noose—and she will not stop until she sees you fall.'*

When he turned around, Ilsevel was seated at the edge of his bed. The old mattress sagged slightly, even beneath her light weight, and he imagined Cahsari was finding himself rather cramped beneath it.

And what did she hope to gain from him with her body? "I assure you, the chairs by the fire are far more comfortable."

Ilsevel laughed once, running her tongue over her upper lip. "Maybe I shall find myself in one of those as well."

There was another soft moan. This time, Sellemar could not be certain if it was Ilsevel or Cahsari, but the distinction hardly mattered. He had to extricate the queen. *Now.* "Your Majesty, I am flattered that you should be so concerned about my state of affairs in this manor. I hope that, upon seeing this room for yourself, you can be quite certain that I am well and comfortable." His eyes flicked out the window to ostentatiously gauge the time of day. "Ah, the delegates shall be arriving shortly. What a tragic interruption to our time… Certainly you will permit me to take you to dinner in exchange?" Sellemar gathered the cloak from the thakish rug, noting that Cahsari's foot had found its way outside the darkness of the bed. *'Loedrin's breath upon you! Even unconscious you are a pain in my ass!'*

Ilsevel smiled and blinked, but gave no indication of departing.

Sellemar stepped rapidly to her side, giving Cahsari's foot a sharp kick.

There was a low moan.

“Sellemar,” Ilsevel breathed, and reached swiftly for his shirt.

Sellemar shoved the cloak into her hand, nearly crumpling her arm against her heavily exposed breasts. “There you are, Your Majesty. To keep you warm on the road. If the delegates should arrive to find you here with me, one could only imagine the scandal.”

Ilsevel could ill afford to harm her fragile reputation. She stood, albeit with regret etched into her features, and clasped the cloak across her slender throat. “Do not worry about finding a time to dine with me, Lord Sellemar. I assure you, I shall be back. I have learned *so* much about you… too much, our enemies might say.” She brushed his arm as she turned. “I am certain the delegates shall be as entranced by your charm as I am.” Then she stepped from the room, the train of her silk gliding across the floor behind her.

‘Itirel was right about one thing…’ he groaned, dropping onto the edge of the bed. The Helven let out a soft grunt beneath him.

Every question she posed… every smile she flashed… Each was rife with warning.

If his rebellion was discovered, all the might of his True Blood brethren could not protect him.

Chapter Twenty-Six

"Alright, time to get off this shithole," Hazamareth informed, pushing open the door to the ship's sleeping quarters. She frowned in concern, watching Tsuki dry heave into a barrel beside one of the wooden posts. "Gods, Tsuki. We're docked now," she gibed.

"Well then, tell the damn ship to stop rocking," Tsuki groaned, blearily gripping his wide hand around a pillar for support.

Hazamareth walked forward, stopped beside her comrade, and surveyed him. His sun-tanned skin was pale and clammy. His usually straight and strong frame was hunched over with an arm tucked into his gut.

He was not an attractive sight.

"Alright, let's get you up," she grunted. She lowered her body to put an arm under Tsuki's. "Come on. Up. We'll put some solid ground beneath those weak legs of yours."

Tsuki leaned against her in silence. Damn, he really *was* ill to not even offer a half-formed retort—granted, that was usually all he managed even on a good day. She grunted as he sank against her. And by Malranus was he *heavy!*

"The last time I had to haul your ass like this, you were sprawled out in that tavern… The Cuddly Sprite, was it?" Hazamareth groaned, wishing she had a bit of Tsuki's usual strength. "No more of that disgusting vandrant fat you call *meat*."

Tsuki grunted, staggering forward. "The *Ugly Knight*. Gods, five centuries and you still can't read." He stumbled and clutched at her narrow shoulders. "Don't strain yourself. You haven't eaten much since we set sail. You must be weak, yourself." He rubbed his neck subconsciously.

Hazamareth felt her mouth salivate, but she forced her eyes away from the wound at the base of her companion's collar. "It's you who needs to rest. I am fine."

And that was *partially* true… just light sensitivity and the rapid heartbeats of the ship's crew thundering about in her head.

Tsuki shot her a due reproach and they continued their slow ascent to the ship's deck. When they broke out into the glaring evening sun, Hazamareth found she hardly had the courage to raise her eyes and scan the bustling deck.

Maybe they were *both* a little pathetic after the voyage…

"Fair ye well, lads," the captain hollered from the bow as he gathered his belongings lowered from the foretop. "Always welcome aboard *The Wench*—if you can stomach it!"

There was a chorus of laughter and Hazamareth heard Tsuki let out a low, guttural growl. She pinched her comrade's ribs. "Hush," she rebuked. "Let's try to rise above the scum today, shall we?"

"Lucky I'm still feeling ill or they'd—" Tsuki began.

"Tsuki, *hush*." *'The temper on him…'* Though she had to admit, it was pleasant to see a flame after the simpering of the last few days—but they had already pushed the crew far past their welcome. *'We just need to get out of this rat nest.'* She struggled toward the disembarking plank, moving as briskly as Tsuki would allow.

They had wobbled no more than a few yards before she heard several pairs of boots rushing toward them from the starboard. She shifted her hazel eyes to the side. Three familiar faces were hastening to intercept them. *'Ah, of* course.*'*

"Sorry," Gavin began as Hazamareth made to step around the human. He planted his burly body between the two mercenaries and the shore as Kellam and Aldridge fanned out to block their path. Hazamareth could hear their riled blood even before she looked up to see the stupid sneers plastered across their sun-burnt, peeling faces.

"Don't you think you've given him enough trouble?" Hazamareth began calmly as the ship shuddered in the waves.

Tsuki closed his eyes and began his nervous drumming against her arm.

She shifted her weight, regarding the three of them stoically. It was the elven side of her that now took charge: the side that determined her lack of reaction was more infuriating than the best laid insults. "So he doesn't have sea legs—we have all heard the jab by now. Might you have thought of something new?"

Kellam flicked a boney hand, retaining equal calm. "Naw. Poor pup. We just thought we'd see him off, seein' as how it's his last day with us an' all." He scratched the flaking skin beside one of his dirty ear cuffs and leered.

"How kind of you." Hazamareth narrowed her dark eyes in gentle warning. "And here I thought you were still sore about losing all that coin. How shameful of me. Gentlemen such as yourselves would hardly start a brawl over such trifles."

The humans exchanged stupidity, uncertain if sarcasm laced her tone.

"Now if you'll excuse me, I have to take my friend to—"

Aldridge flapped his arms with a heady laugh from his barreled gut. "Hold your tongue, lady—no need to speak another word. Please, take your man before he stains your pretty leather boots."

Tsuki swallowed back a heave.

Kellam swept aside, allowing a very narrow path between him and the edge of the plank. Even his puny ass would have struggled to squeeze by.

'Well, this isn't going to end well,' Hazamareth resigned. She adjusted Tsuki's balance and prepared for the inevitable. The *notion* that they had *cheated* in the recent acquisition of their wealth was…

Frankly true and entirely deserved.

She gave the sailor a falsely amiable nod and began her slow march forward. Beside her, Tsuki was fixated on the bustling dockyard ahead, but Hazamareth suspected he was readying himself for a fight.

As they came to pass between the men, she saw the muscles along Gavin's flaking shoulders tense—and then the brawny arms flew out to shove them into the frigid sea below.

How disappointingly unoriginal. Hazamareth had seen it so plainly written in the man's body language it was almost a shame to have to respond.

Tsuki sprang into action, ripping from her grasp to catch Gavin's right arm. Hazamareth pivoted, snatching her comrade's left bicep. At that, Tsuki flung himself toward the center of the plank, whipping the stunned human clear off his feet. With calculated efficiency, Tsuki used the momentum of the man's body to swing himself around behind the smuggler.

In a swift kick, Tsuki sent Gavin clear off the plank.

There was the immediate response of feet behind them accompanied by a storm of angry shouts. Hazamareth could expect no less—while wit and talent were certainly lacking, comradery was not.

Tsuki, however, had not broken his movement. Even as Gavin made a resounding splash below, Tsuki carried his energy into a fist square into the nose of Kellam. The wiry lout was sent tumbling into the water on the opposite side of the plank.

Hazamareth looked over her shoulder in time to catch view of the half-dozen approaching bastards before Aldridge seized her wrists and yanked them behind her back. Even worse than her incapacitation was her renewed proximity to his stench of cod liver oil and sea salt.

"We should have dumped you in the waters first," she jabbed before she was forced to stifle a gag.

Aldridge merely gave her a good shake as his comrades crowded before her. "Haven't you two bastards caused enough problems?" one of his shipmates growled.

Two others had managed to wrestle Tsuki's wild swings into submission. He could do no more than watch as one of the smuggling bastards laid Hazamareth squarely in the jaw.

Her head snapped to the side.

"You attack one of us and you attack the lot of us," another smuggler gnarled, drawing a small knife from his dirty linen shirt. "Which one of you wants t' wear a souvenir?"

His shipmates drew their shoddy steel blades to join in the fun, but a stern roar of command bellowed suddenly from the dockyard below. "That's enough!"

The humans' childish jeering ceased as they cast their eyes to the cobbled square. Hazamareth craned her neck to spot two of the city's guard standing at the foot of the plank, eyeing them harshly.

The hands about her loosened. "Just havin' a bit of fun," Aldridge called. "No harm intended."

"Then release them and disperse," the guard barked back. "Or I will have the lot of you taken in for disrupting the peace."

"MEN," hollered a voice behind them. "You heard the gentleman! Back to work!"

"Back to work," Aldridge repeated with a furious huff, shoving Hazamareth down the plank. "God-damn lucky—that's what the two of you are."

Tsuki was quickly at her side, steadying her as hastily as he balanced himself.

The fight dispersed, the city guard spun away and marched down the snow-spattered docks.

"Well, that could have turned ugly," Tsuki muttered, dropping his weight shamelessly against her side. "Hate to be a wanted man here as well." His fingers tapped rapidly against her arm.

"Give us another century or two—we'll manage it," Hazamareth replied as she swung a hand up to signal the ship's captain a final finger salute. Then she patted her comrade's restless fingers still.

A crowd had crammed together near the ship: a mix of burly sailors and wide-eyed townspeople hoping for the fight to rekindle. It was as though nothing in their dry, simple days could be more interesting. She would have given them no regard except that she swore a familiar face had peered out at them from the crowd…

Tsuki groaned, lurching forward unexpectedly. "Damn. Let's get on some solid ground already!" he choked.

Hazamareth corrected his unbalanced gait. "We *are* on solid ground." She loosened her grip. "Any better?" A bead of sweat rolled down his temple. "You do not *look* any better…"

"I'm not," Tsuki grunted in response.

Hazamareth glanced back up toward the dispersing crowd, but there remained no one she recognized. She brushed it aside. There were more important matters at hand—like the beast. What sort of sailors let a nearly horse-sized creature vanish onto a vessel? And for that matter, what idiotic *humans* had let it pass? "I will get us a room at an inn and leave you to rest and clean up. I shall ask around about the beast. The ship that ferried it was supposed to stop by this city. If so, I have no doubt that a murder or two will get us back on its trail."

Tsuki nodded. "Damn world will not stop rocking. To Ramul with ships. Next time our job jumps continents, we let it," he balked, even as the port bustled with the stifling mass of the civilization he so loved.

Hazamareth ignored the meaningless gripe.

They made their way through the crowd, under the long archway beneath the buildings, and into the market square. Here, the populace only intensified. "Keep your eye on your pockets," Hazamareth warned as she inspected a dirty child tossing a storm-orb between his hands. The boy paused to watch them from beneath a low-hanging canopy, his crafty face flickering in the orb's light. "Thieves around… Should be an inn nearby, though." She turned expectantly into a side street. "And as I suspected," she said as she gestured triumphantly to a creaking wooden sign of a fat bird at rest. "The Pigeon's Coop. Always the cleverest of names."

"The Crow's Nest," Tsuki sighed.

Hazamareth swung the door open with her foot and stepped into the tumult of noise. The air was thick with lantern, torch, and candle smoke while the floor maintained a tidy affair of pools of spilt ale. Her brow furrowed. Not clean enough for her taste, but then, she had learned to put up with the shady places Tsuki preferred to bed in. That was, after all, the human way.

She moved to the counter, extending a hand. “A room,” she requested. The rotund bartender scrutinized the two of them for a moment, milky eyes trailing their weaponized garb. *‘Yes. We’re not sailors,’* she thought impatiently. *‘Just give me the damn key.’*

The man finally swung to the back wall. “Two silver. Only have rooms with one bed left. ’Ll get you two.”

Hazamareth dropped the coins and slid them through a puddle of grime toward the innkeeper. “One is fine.”

The man lumbered to the counter, an eye squinted in thought as he dropped the key from the fat rolls of his palm. Whatever thoughts swam about beneath the ample blubber he kept to himself. “Upstairs on your left.”

“My thanks.” And she helped Tsuki up the stairs. She drew to a stop beside the door. “Stay out of trouble for a few minutes.”

Returning downstairs, Hazamareth took a seat on a stool by the counter, leaning one elbow forward in the single dry spot she could find. Bartenders always seemed to know the most about a city; they were the best single, collective source of information in the land.

The man breathed into a mug before he wiped it slowly with a dirty rag. “What d’ya want?”

Hazamareth grimaced at the imagined taste of the bitter liquor. “Anything,” she replied to be polite, setting down an extra coin with her payment. “I just arrived in this city. Perhaps you could inform me of something in particular. Any… exceptionally brutal murders as of late? Anything that stands out?” There was no use in preliminary banter.

The man slid the coins into his free hand as he handed Hazamareth a mug. He began with a strong lilt, leaving off the beginnings and ends of what seemed like a random slew of his words while he hardly dared to put more than half a dozen together. It grated on Hazamareth, and she had to remind herself to not scowl in derision. Despite hundreds of years surrounded by humans, her elven ass still retained some remnants of a stick. “Mercenary type, eh? Aye. There’s been a brutal strin’ o’ murders as o’ late. Hardly a person tha’ll leave their home without ensurin’ there’s at least a dozen other people ’round. Not that it’d help much. House ’r streets. Don’t matter nothin’ to it. ’Nd we know what it is too. Seen it by just a week ’r so back. Terrifyin’, huge creature with horns ’nd wings ’nd yellow eyes. Killed some city guard ’fore takin' off out o' the city. Comes back ev'ry night… if it ain't a new person dead, it's a new person missin'. The body'll show up later. There's a slew o' guards stationed 'round the city. Don't do anyone no good. Somehow it gets in 'nd out. Has to hole up under bridge. Best that can be reckoned is the Yislaval. Yislaval Mountains, that is. They're the mountains just north o' here. Only one way in 'nd out on foot, but if it can fly, then you best be talkin' to Lady Luck, 'cause you won' never find it in that death trap. *Filled* with yislaval."

Yislaval… those damned winged vermin—elvish in appearance but as feral as any wild beast. She had not dealt with their kind in a *very* long time. And yet, she could not help but smile as she stepped lightly off the stool, her mug untouched. Well, her work for information had hardly ever been easier. "Thank you. You told me exactly what I needed to know." She paused. "If I may ask, is there a reward around here for the beast?"

"Mighty large one," the innkeeper replied with a sharp nod of his head. "From the governor."

Hazamareth tapped her head and gestured her thanks, stepping lightly up the stairs. There was nothing like a day when she did not have to drag herself across a filthy city looking for information. This beast was fortunately as consistent and indiscreet as ever.

She reached the top of the stairs and pushed their door open. "Just me," she called in warning.

Inside, Tsuki was seated cross-legged against the headboard, a loaded crossbow in his lap. He settled it onto the nightstand as Hazamareth closed the door behind her. A roaring fire had already significantly warmed the room, and Tsuki's bare chest was glistening slightly in the heat.

Hazamareth surveyed the clutter already expanding across the small chamber. "I thought we discussed keeping things a little tidier? We would not have lost the Amulet of Rohar if you had just put it away."

"*Me?* What I remember is that *you* wore it last."

Hazamareth ignored him—mostly because he was likely right. "The beast is here," she began, plucking up his strewn stockings and boots as she went. "Apparently arrived a week ago and has been killing every night. The general assumption is that he has taken refuge in the mountains. There are plenty of guards around town, but no one has laid a hand on him." She dropped her boots aside and unlaced her shirt. "The humans know only one way in and out of the mountains by foot. Judging by the way the beast has travelled thus far, those wings are likely as useless to him as a woman to a eunuch." She rubbed her lips, her mouth suddenly aching. She could hear Tsuki's heart thudding steadily in his warm chest, pumping blood through his powerful body. "Damn it," she muttered below her breath.

"Hungry, Haz?" Tsuki asked with a smirk and slightly raised chin. "Probably should have stopped to eat. Has to be something you like around here. You know. Something *else*."

Hazamareth leaned down and snatched up her boots. "Yes, I will go get something to eat."

And before the words had fully left her lips, the atmosphere around them changed; with great force, the door to their room flew back against its hinges, crashing into the wall with an echo that resounded high above the tavern's din.

Tsuki and Hazamareth moved as one for the crossbow, but were forced to recoil as a silver dagger shot across the short expanse.

The blade lodged into the bed with a soft thud. "Well, well. If it isn't Hazamareth and Tsuki," the Sel'ven male at the door commented, leaning against the frame with an ostentatious sniff. "Gods, who figured you two would show yourselves here? Causing a scene at the docks is how you two avoid attention, is it? Kisix certainly has delivered revenge to my blade." A slow sneer crept across his chapped lips. "Last time I saw you was… let me see… when you tried to turn me in to the city guard for murder. Some comrades you amounted to. I had heard that the two of you were unscrupulous, but I never imagined you so far as *backstabbers*. Relstavum? Yes. But *not* you."

Hazamareth gave an extravagant yawn. So she *had* seen him: *Vethru*. His slender frame was as boney as ever, and his eyes were sunken and dark beneath his straight brows. As far as the Sel'vi went, he was as ugly and weather-beaten as some crippled, old swamp hag. But she was not soothed by discounting his appearance; Vethru was still an elite mercenary who they were lucky to have avoided for so long.

And he had a new companion.

The male beside the Sel'ven brandished his sword, searching the two mercenaries with the eagerness of any green knave.

Hazamareth spat and pushed herself upright once more. The blade shifted uneasily in the stranger's hands. "I see you picked up a new partner. And some rather expensive armor. Now how would a mercenary in our profession manage such a feat?"

Vethru looked down at his gleaming silver plates. "Brief mining stint outside Elvorium. You would not *believe* what humans will pay for a bag of shiny blue rocks." His eyes shot up, flitting back and forth between her and

Tsuki. The sneer gradually faded, replaced by an even more unbecoming scowl. "What—neither of you two are going to ask?"

"Ask what?" Tsuki emitted a bored sniff. "With the way you're carrying on you'll tell us whatever it is yourself."

Vethru's companion raised his sword and stepped forward, no doubt to defend his employer's prodigious pride, but Vethru raised a hand. "Tythis, what did I tell you?—That won't work on them. They require something a bit more… unique." He leaned back into the hallway where a crowd of hushed voices had gathered. "Make yourselves scarce," he snarled once, then drew fully into the room.

The door snapped shut at his heels and Vethru once more engaged them. "The question you should be asking is, 'Why am I not still rotting in prison?'" When neither Hazamareth nor Tsuki gave any indication of being impressed, he was forced to continue on his own. "First and foremost, I escaped. Unfortunately, the warrant made it impossible to acquire most jobs and I was often forced into menial—"

Hazamareth raised a finger. "Outsider opinion: do you think the sign outside this place looks like it says The Pigeon's Coop or The Crow's Nest?"

Tythis blinked. "It's The Crow's Nest, isn't it? Looks like a crow to—"

"Gods damn it," Vethru snarled again, stomping on his crony's foot. "For three centuries I had skirted the law, but one deceitful accusation by you and my reputation was crippled."

"I think the rest of us have moved past your double-crossing," Tsuki interjected below his breath. "Revealing our secrets certainly wasn't going to obtain any favor from us."

"Double-cross?!" Vethru seethed, practically frothing at the notion. "If you had informed me of your nature before we got involved, the whole matter would have been avoided!"

"Well, we're not likely to take chances like that, are we? Consider yourself fortunate that we didn't just kill you," Tsuki snorted. "Now, did you come here in an attempt to monologue us to death? Good gods, you elves and your theatrics. Let's just get to the stabbing. One of us is bound to end up dead and then this whole conversation will have been pointless."

Vethru's face had flushed from a bold shade of pink to an audacious flare of red. "I am here on behalf of the Brotherhood, whom I now serve, to collect the bount—"

Hazamareth scrambled suddenly for the nightstand, but Tythis was faster. He leapt and swung his blade high at her throat, causing her to reel away in surprise.

Vethru's lips thinned and twisted, his amber eyes narrowing in amusement. At her act of desperation, his outrage had faded to triumph. "Oh, I told him, Hazamareth. There are no secrets kept for backstabbers. The whole god-damn Brotherhood has you on their list. Class A mission."

Hazamareth did not acknowledge his gleeful droning. Eventually the male's monologue would grow dull even for his ego, and he would instead turn to violence. She looked back toward Tsuki, subtly reaching for the dagger he had lodged in their bed. Her comrade met her gaze with a slight shake of his head. He would be of no help. *'Still disoriented.'*

Their lack of response culled Vethru into prompt silence. His eyes landed upon the crossbow they had recently skirmished for, and he calmly strutted forward. "Is this what you were after?" he queried as he lifted the weapon from the nightstand. He made a scene of admiring the weapon, running his boney fingers along the polished sides. "What an extravagant piece of equipment. Cheat it out of someone, I suppose?" He fingered the bolt. "Take note, Tythis: Regardless of strength, all beasts die the same." He raised the weapon slowly. "But—"

Hazamareth had enough of the incessant speech. At this rate, they were likely to be locked in an eternal and pointless banter until someone slit their own god-damn throat. She loosed the blade behind her back before the male had finished gloating. It lodged into Vethru's side. There was an instant click in response as the male staggered back.

Hazamareth felt a surge of unfamiliar pain as the bolt lodged sickeningly deep into her chest. "Ga.... ah..." she breathed. She slumped toward the edge of the bed.

"HAZ!" Tsuki lunged forward with a cry, catching her before she slid to the floor. He tore the bolt from her chest and flung it away across the wooden floor.

But its effects had already set in. Hazamareth could feel the sickening sensation sweeping her body, burning deep within her muscles. "Shit, Tsuki," she breathed. "One... damn... bolt..."

Tsuki laid her down, grabbing the blade at his side and steadying himself against the wall.

'Still... in vertigo...' Hazamareth thought numbly. And at that moment, her own vision doubled briefly.

"Now you're out of bolts," Tsuki growled as Tythis rushed to Vethru's aid. "We each have a woman down. But *do not* test your experience against mine. If Vethru told you anything about us, you should know: I am *far* older than you, *elf*."

Hazamareth tried to focus her eyes, but the haze clouded her perception. Better she be shot than Tsuki; a shot like this would have certainly killed the human.

She could barely distinguish the knit of Tythis' brow as he considered his options. *He could not possibly believe Tsuki's bluff.* It was obvious even to her that her comrade was lucky to be on his feet, let alone fight.

Tsuki drew himself up, undaunted by his own visage. "I'd get your comrade to a healer before the poison kills him," he hissed, pointing his blade at the gasping Sel'ven.

Hazamareth smiled inwardly. Now there was the wit that had kept them alive for so long.

The room darkened suddenly.

*

Hazamareth felt herself shaken slightly before powerful arms cradled her close. "Haz. You still conscious?"

The half-elf weakly opened her eyes. *'What... happened?'* Where were those damn mercenaries? Had she fainted? Her mind felt foggy from the silver, but her senses were oddly sharp. "Are you… bleeding…?" she mumbled.

"Gods be damned. I was worried for a moment," Tsuki breathed. "I thought it struck your heart." His grip tightened and she felt herself lifted and nestled into the comforts of the bed. "Vethru's little lackey had cheap shit. I will be fine," he interrupted before she could open her mouth again.

So he *was* injured. Her eyes were too unfocused to distinguish the wound, but the scent of blood was tangible. *'Cheap weapons my ass...'*

For a short time, she only heard the stitching and binding of their wounds.

Then Tsuki settled down beside her. "It will probably be a few weeks before you're fully healed. We can't take any chances with that creature," he spoke sternly.

Another delay? "Damn them all!" Hazamareth swore in aggravation, her head flopping uselessly in a sad attempt to elevate it. "What about Vethru and his man?"

"Slid the rest of the furniture against the door for tonight. Innkeeper said the damages will be on them. He won't let them back in here. We'll switch rooms in the morning." He paused and Hazamareth could hear his grin. "...We pissed off the wrong Sel'ven, didn't we?"

She grimaced, pain surging once more through her breast. "You know, it was Relstavum who never trusted him. I would have thought there are enough beasts to hunt without Vethru needing to turn his attention on the two of us."

What had Vethru expected? That they would allow him to hunt them down without a decent fight? A man in their business should have been grateful *prison* was the only end they sought for him.

But if he had found a home in the *Brotherhood*...

"Forget about both of them, Hazamareth. Be quiet and rest."

Hazamareth twitched a smile and closed her eyes. Yet she twisted uneasily beneath the sheets. Her mind was not occupied with thoughts of *if* the vindictive bastard would return, but *when*.

How ironic. The hunters had become the hunted. Like some god-damn soulless beasts.

Ryekarayn. How she had missed it.

CHAPTER TWENTY-SEVEN

Throughout his years of study, Jikun had often heard Darivalian scholars speak wistfully of Ryekarayn's mild winters, especially when a sudden tundra blizzard would entrap their citizens for days.

But what was imagined as mild by Darival was hardly mild for the rest of Aersadore, and Jikun quickly gathered that he was not fond of this western interpretation of winter. It was not pleasant like on Sevrigel, where the trees still twisted magnificently in their leafless elegance. It produced no winter blooms to sprout across the hillsides. It offered no Galoom's Touch to fill the otherwise lifeless appearance with leaves of vibrant green.

Jikun looked down upon his bare feet padding softly in the freezing muck.

No. Humanity's domain on the western side of the Windari Channel was dark, wet, and dead. Scraggly, leafless tress. Frost-tipped, brown grass. And an overabundance of mud graced by the occasional vomit of snow. It was merely as though the fall and winter had met and were incapable of deciding which season ought to have its due—so they had dueled until both were groaning and heaving across the hillsides.

But whether the scenery contended with Darival's stark, pristine beauty was irrelevant: the wind chill did, leaving Jikun somberly reminded of the weakness of southern blood. His companions tromped alongside him, eyes squinted painfully against the wind, shaking and chattering and groaning about their frozen limbs. While he had willingly surrendered his boots to Navon to salvage the male's feet, the act had, in turn, saved him from very few of their verbal trials.

He swore once beneath his breath as a hidden stone lodged itself between his toes. He had enough grievances without nature's generous assistance.

Jikun plucked the stone free and flicked it away. If Darcarus had not tossed aside his riches for Relstavum to gather, they would be far closer to acquiring some semblance of decent clothing! "Let's move like the peaks are melting!" he barked, gesturing away from the Faraven as the male paused beside another tree.

Eldaeus had taken no part in the shivering, complaining, or bickering—he possessed no concerns of the sane. As he had within the Pass of the Dead, the maniacal elf had created a game out of their journey, prancing and twisting his way along the line of redbern trees, trying to hold his piss for every three hundred and sixty-second tree, and other such endless nonsense. It was at least somewhat tolerable that *someone* was enjoying their trek—albeit in a less than appealing manner.

"Hurry up, Eldaeus," Jikun barked. He could hear Navon rifling forlornly through the sack, searching for remnants of still-edible food. "And give it up, Captain—we are going to have to hunt and scavenge. Which wouldn't sound so bleak if any one of us knew which of these damn plants won't poison us."

Darcarus immediately bristled with offense. "Pampered little Sevrigelians. I informed you of which bark and needles you can eat."

"I'm not a deer," Jikun retorted flatly. "And those berries you told me were safe were definitely NOT. If I don't get something to eat soon, so help me I will settle for one of you." And then, as though Sel'ari herself had heard his threat upon her precious little True Blood, a fattened meal on wings soared free of the canopy and flew toward them.

A spear of ice formed instantly at Jikun's fingertips.

"Whoa! Wait wait wait!" Darcarus shouted, catching his wrist and sharply jerking his arm down. "That's mine!"

Jikun let out a dangerous growl. "I saw it first you bast—!"

"No, I mean that is my *pet*," Darcarus cut him off. He extended his wrist to the bird and the raven landed, ruffling its feathers affectionately as it sidled farther up the prince's arm and away from Jikun's hungry gaze.

Navon plucked the spear of ice from Jikun's grasp in the event he changed his mind. "Is that the reply to the raven you sent?" he inquired.

"What?" Darcarus cocked his head and angled his body away from them to coo lovingly toward the fat pigeon. If there was a scroll tied to one of its plump legs, the sight of it was lost.

Navon skirted around, attempting to regain view of the bird. "A reply to the raven you sent," he repeated.

"I did not send—"

"I saw you send it the night before we entered The Pass," Navon insisted.

Darcarus turned; the raven had vanished. "OH. Yes, *that*." He laughed, his stoicism shifting to dismissive mirth. "No, no. She was just stretching her wings. She is a bird, Navon, *not* just a little wisp of magic; my soul aches if I do not let her free."

Navon narrowed his eyes, but now that the potential meal was lost, Jikun spun away for better prospects. He had argued enough to know *that* would not quench the gnawing in his gut. He squinted against the glare of the midday sun as it peered from behind a blanket of clouds just long enough to blind him. His patience in waiting for the pissing Faraven was certainly at an end. "Damn it, I am going on ahead, Eldaeus!"

But then he realized that the male was no longer there. Somehow, he had managed to not only hike up his pants, but also to scurry to the top of the hill before them. He perched there now, entirely still, with the vague resemblance of a peacock.

"How did he…?" Navon trailed off in similar amazement from Jikun's right.

"Hurry!" Eldaeus cried.

"That must be it!" Darcarus exclaimed in relief, striding quickly past Jikun toward the eager male. "Just over that hill. *Gods*, I am equally as starving! I would shovel cow dung with my bare hands if it meant a good meal."

Apparently, the surplus of bark and needles had not satisfied him either. Jikun stepped sharply away from the prince lest the male's lack of self-respect infect him as well. He directed his attention to Navon, who had been forced to let his most recent quarrel with the prince die once more.

"What do you think the townsfolk will make of Eldaeus when they see him dancing about the hill decorated like that?" Jikun queried. "Insanity would definitely be a possibility, but *I* think I would first conclude that he is some sort of, I don't know… nomadic tribal shaman, or an alchemist's partially failed attempt to turn a peacock into a man."

Navon nodded his head thoughtfully, puckering his lips to the side as he stroked his chin once in feigned seriousness. "I could see that. I could *definitely* see that."

"Hurry!" Eldaeus was squawking noisily. "Oh, you should see it!"

Something in Eldaeus' tone made Jikun jog a little faster. In his time at the academy, what spittle was spent discussing humans was merely used to attack their word and honor—a hatred no doubt formed by their promise and betrayal to Eraydon in his hour of need, held and cultured by nine thousand years of separation between the races. And once leading the army, Jikun found the situation to be similar: no one wanted to see the land of the plebian and underdeveloped humans, and fewer still cared to speak of it. It was traitors' land, and no elf worth his weight in thakish spit would ever consider setting foot upon the edges of the continent—let alone live there.

But now that he was to save the place from the clutches of Saebellus, Jikun was feeling mildly less critical. Fair-scented whores had enticed him… spoken of vast cities and castles, of great armies and wealth the elves had never imagined humans to possess.

'Relstavum will be dead by the spring. We will be as comfortable as we were on Sevrigel and all those soldiers will rest as easy as babes.'

And so it was with slight hope that Jikun's head rose above the crest of the hill to obtain his first glimpse of a human city—to the wealth and grandeur whispered to him.

He blinked in confusion. "What… what is that?"

Darcarus stepped up beside him, brow knit. "What? Have you never seen a human settlement before?" he laughed and tossed his head, as though shaking off pity for Jikun's naivety. "They are *humans*—they do not share the same luxury or wealth of the elven nation—they are far too engrossed in burying their dead and scrounging for food to be concerned with such extravagances as gleaming towers and radiant silks." His voice was hard and bitter as he spoke next, but he gazed down the hill with visible empathy—as though the prince, with his pretty silk clothes and mounds of gold, could ever relate to them. "Existence must be brutal when the rest of the world turns its back on you—let alone your own kindred."

Jikun shook his head, ogling the little speckle of houses with their clouds of white smoke billowing from thatched roofs. Their homes displayed grey or brown stone at their bases with the upper portions laid in dirty white or tan paneling. Over those crossed beams of russet wood. Large, square windows were set along the faces with tiny triangles of dull glass and broken shutters. As though to lament the state of the world around them, baskets of dead plants hung with forlorn resignation along the dismal sills.

The humans were, as all elves had warned him, living a pathetic existence. He glanced sidelong at the prince, who he swore still had bark between his teeth, and then scowled at the pitiful display of civilization. He had sacrificed his honor, but there still remained enough of it to find abhorrence at the squalor.

Darcarus gave his chest a single, solid smack. "Welcome to the human side of the world, General."

* * *

The human side of the world… A long time had passed since Navon had seen his homeland. Even with the populace of primitive smugglers and Eph'ven inhabitants, the Makataj had felt like an extension of Sevrigel, bound to the rules of the ancient lands.

But north of the Aenid, the world had truly neglected all essence of magic and advancement. In dawn's morning light filtering through the overcast sky, the broken rooftop panels and patched shutters of the village were more befitting an abandoned village than anything believably inhabited. Yet Eldaeus was dancing about in mad delight. There was not a person in all his books that could rival Eldaeus' eccentricities… At least, since the Pass, there was no one he could remember. Still, he could at least conjure a comparison for the village: it was not unlike what Westewod had resembled as Raelanar and Isala used it as a militant base for their last, surprise attack against Destrian and his thugs. Even if their personalities had grown vague, their deeds, at least, remained strong.

"…Where are you?"

Navon blinked as the icy world seemed to rematerialize before him. He glanced sidelong at Jikun. The male was eyeing him irritably, as he had often done since the Pass. "What…?"

"Just standing there blankly while I was talking to you. Where did you drift off to? …Never mind. Nothing new," Jikun muttered, but Navon was aware that the state of their surroundings was the culprit in turning his friend even more stridently against him. The Darivalian was glowering sourly at the rather emaciated cows digging through the snow for remnants of frosted grass, and his fingers curled and uncurled at his side as though relieving tension.

As the providers for the wealthy, villages were the most common form of civilization in the human realms. But as these culturally vacant zones were practically slave farms to their rich overlords, they were largely ignored after their services were rendered. A century before, Navon had given the flea mines a wide berth. But now this world and all its faults was theirs… though the fact did not ease Jikun's acceptance of the situation.

"I smell something cooking… perhaps we can work for a meal," Navon chirped, offering the so-often-needed optimism. Fortunately, frequency of its use had perhaps even made it a characteristic of his own. "We may have some luck finding mercenary work here." Yet unfortunately, he saw no sign of the regional lord he had promised; contrariwise, these poor farmers were unlikely to offer much in the way of food or coin. "Food aside, we need to acquire clothes—and shoes—for the winter." He wrapped himself tighter beneath his thick cloak, but he knew where Jikun's ambitions lay.

Nordeep.

Many centuries past, the human king of Ryekarayn divided his kingdom into regions—possibly out of laziness, possibly as the only way to control such a vast continent of primitive indigents. The lords of each region were charged with the protection and comfort of all cities within their dominions. However, every so often, a settlement would fall outside the efficient structure. Nordeep was undoubtedly one such renegade city.

Housing the criminal empire of the mercenary world, Nordeep had likely followed the patterns of the notorious Comstead during Eraydon's era—growing so vast in power that soon its regional lord feared its strength and influence too immense to dare impose further commands upon it.

He scowled deeply at Darcarus. The male was wholly responsible for Jikun's mad belief that the answer to his purpose lay in Relstavum's death. But the True Blood was too enraptured with the appearance of the crumbling village well to notice the captain's reproach. Even if he had, Navon imagined the prince's response would have been a similarly derisive glare.

Navon was—after his valiant efforts to save them from the Pass—expendable.

Jikun was swift to rebuke Navon's suggestion of labor. "No. Our deviation here is merely to acquire food for the rest of the journey to Nordeep." And he set out in a soft crunch across the field and down onto the snow-laden path—to call it a road would have been too generous, as the way was clearly all but forgotten by the civilized world. "We can't allow Relstavum to destroy another city—every moment he's free, Saebellus is closer to solidifying his grasp on Sevrigel."

Navon was swift on his heels. "General, I am entirely in agreement with defeating Relstavum, but I do not believe for a moment that there are not," he dropped his voice in hopes that only the Darivalian could hear him, "strings attached in working for this Brotherhood. I just don't think we've been told all of the information. What was the prince's plan *before* we fell into his hands? This is work for… I don't know… heroes. Like Eraydon. We are *not* them. This is no 'Goldbeard and the Giant' story that ends well."

"Such a god-damn savant."

"…That is not an insult!"

"You are jealous."

Navon gave a start. "Of *what?!*"

But an alarmed cry prevented further argument. "By Zephereus above!" came a hoarse voice as a door to their right was flung wide. An old man hurried out with an elderly lady at his heels. Navon immediately noted that though both were ineffectually clad for the winter chill, the elves still stood naked by comparison.

"Why, I 'aven't seen elves 'round these parts in thirty years!" the old woman marveled.

The poor old man hushed his wife, his feet padding deep into the snow as he cautiously approached. "What 'appened t' you elves t' bring you so far south? Was it bandits? Or 'ave they gone an' attacked the Realm? You aren't from *Dahel*, are you?! We just 'eard the news! What a tragedy! By Ishkav, Relstavum's surely Death 'imself!"

Darcarus smiled politely, bowing his head in respect and picking up the old woman's wrinkled hand. His charm was deadly. "Why, thank you for your concern, beautiful lady," he cooed, flashing a smile that would have sent the maidens in Elvorium swooning. This was the first glimpse that some semblance of nobility resided beneath his abhorrently crass and irrational behavior. "We have fallen to the most dreadful of misfortunes and our hearts would be humbled to find aid amongst our brethren."

Navon saw Jikun wrinkle his nose at the comparison and jabbed him once in the ribs to warn him against throwing out some of his acidic comments. Though he was not an ally to Darcarus in his plan to defeat Saebellus, he *did* want a good, warm meal: and if he had to use the prince to get one, so be it.

The old man shifted a little closer, prepared to fend off the handsome male from his blushing wife. "There's no need t' be ashamed, my friends," he began, his focus remaining on the elves' condition. "'uman bandits got weapons just the same as you elves. An' prob'ly better than that tarnished ol' sword at yer friend's side. 'ere, let me—"

Navon placed a tempering hand on Jikun's arm. "Do you know of any work?" he swiftly inquired. "Something perhaps to feed or clothe us and we would be more than grateful." Surely one of his heroes would have had something far more elegant to add, but none of their words came to him. He opened and closed his mouth again. *Gods*, how could his own character be so… *empty!*

He straightened his posture, hoping to appear somewhat more dignified. "We are on our way to Geldin Laeris for work."

Darcarus flinched.

"Geldin Laeris' Brotherhood?" the old man clarified, sagging eyes jumping between the four. "Surely you elves aren't that desperate!"

Navon watched Darcarus for a reaction, but the male had smoothed his serpentine features into mere amusement. "They're mercenaries," he soothed the old man.

But the woman broke in insistently, yanking her crinkly hand up to point at him with a stern reprimand. "Mercenaries?! No, they're the worst o' the worst. They've got the largest military force second t' the king! An' 'ow's 'e done it?! Laeris ropes them in when they're young or desperate an' naïve—just like you. Then before you know it, you're in but you can't get out! Laeris 'as a mob o' loyal men who'll make sure o' that. Aside from the royal family itself, there's *no one* Laeris's afraid t' touch! Why, Lord Seamus 'ad a son who joined the Brotherhood, took on too much debt, an' was dead before the third face o' Noctem. Take our sick cow, Feber, t' the temple in Sanae… an' we'll pay *two* silver if it can 'elp you boys stay outta that line o' work."

Darcarus caught the woman's flailing hand and patted it gently. "One silver will do. I assure you, we will be fine, but your concern touches me deeply."

Jikun's disgust could remain silent no longer, and he leapt in to break the genial mood. "Two silver is still a pauper's wage."

But it was not the coin that concerned Navon. Or Jikun's barbarism. There was not an ounce of surprise—or caution—on the prince's face. *'Of course he knows all about Laeris…'*

"If you would excuse me for just a moment…" Navon tugged Jikun through the snow to the edge of the broken well. In his disgruntlement, the general offered little resistance. "Jikun, I cannot *pretend* to support this insanity any longer!" Navon hissed. "The True Bloods are respectable, honorable, and just. But this male… I think it is quite obvious why he's unpopular with his family. He *deliberately* omitted any details on the Brotherhood! We are not selling our souls to a group of thugs." He caught Jikun's wrist as the male attempted to brush his concerns away. "You want to prove your own worth?—Good acts are never justified when joining evil to destroy evil. Just as there is no justification for sacrificing a thousand lives to save ten thousand more."

This was not the path of the heroes in his scrolls, and to not align themselves with a hero's cause would be to pit themselves against Sel'ari. This path was *not* the wisdom of the male he had come to admire!

Jikun sharply jerked his arm free, but even when he had broken from Navon's grasp, he remained stiffly in place, his eyes narrowed in a look Navon could almost interpret as... *pity*.

And yet, he said nothing.

Navon elevated his tone just loud enough to be forceful, but still quiet enough that the Sel'ven down the street could not hear him. "Yet rather than acknowledge this truth, you are determined to follow Darcarus, who clearly cannot return to Sairel because his plan is *madness*. Not only is the end ambition mad, but the path itself is just as foolish! If we fail this Brotherhood—to whom we shall be enslaved—they will flay the skin from our bones and hurl our corpses into a ditch. Yet as a king's son, Darcarus shall remain unharmed. See, Darcarus cares nothing for us. He is bent on securing assistance for Hadoream, and so he needs people like us—desperate enough to agree—to join him on this mad venture. And even then, I don't believe this to be his only plan or he would *never* have sent his beloved brother to Sevrigel in the first place." He shook his head violently. "I know you are wise enough to see the truth, General. Consider the alternative—you were an inspiration to every soldier who has ever been beneath your command. We are *soldiers!* The human armies value individual strength—as males of both strength *and* intelligence, we would rise quickly in their ranks. If you joined the army, *you* could use your military expertise to render Saebellus' forces here worthless. Defeating that power here is Aersadore's greatest hope. As strong as Relstavum may be, a single man cannot conquer the world."

The pitying look in the general's eyes had not vanished, and yet his words once more failed to address that detestable emotion. He sucked in a tempered breath, as stoic and rigid as he had been throughout Navon's plea. "Do not flatter me. I should become one more faceless foot soldier in a battle over which I truly hold no sway? *That* is why I sacrificed my troops at Elarium?! Well I am not oblivious to what is going on, Navon. You are sick with jealousy."

Navon could hear Eldaeus chatting away to the old pair of humans with the unintentional success of keeping them occupied, yet he kept his outrage quiet. "Of *what* do I have to be jealous?" he fumed. "I am the sole reason we have lived this long!"

Jikun's rigidity broke in a single laugh. He reached out, grabbing Navon by the front of his thick cloak and jerking his chin about to face the quartet down the road. "Of Darcarus—that I take his counsel. After what happened in the Pass of the Dead, you know you have become a liability."

Navon watched as the Sel'ven patted the old man playfully on the shoulder. He jerked his head sharply away, smacking at the Darivalian's arms. "I am not jealous," he hissed. "You are bending your strength to wickedness. Only tragedy results from misguided power!" He shoved Jikun forcefully to emphasize his disgust in the male's accusation.

The general stumbled, but he did not raise his arms against him. "Gods, what happened to you?" he lamented. "Where is your ambition when it truly matters? We are on the human side of the world—as you feel the necessity to repeat until my ears bleed. We have *nothing*. And yet you aspire to remain that way."

Fury boiled within Navon's gut. "You do not hear a word I speak! You were not meant to live as a coward beneath the thumb of a politician—*even* a True Blood! Join the war and I promise you I will not let you lose the battle!"

There was a brief flicker of fear then, something Navon was barely able to glimpse beneath Jikun's mask. Then the general's voice emerged unsteadily as he hissed his next retort. "You are an ideological fool."

"And you are broken." Navon's tone softened. "Your strength fractured in the Sevilan Marshes… While I lay there ill and delirious, *you* remained conscious to witness the death you were helpless to stop. Then you consumed it to survive. You have worn a mask as you *always* do to hide the trauma of those months, but the male I served for fifty years would *never* have abandoned his troops before that day… Even if such fidelity meant being executed by Saebellus. He would have accepted that fate if it provided even the *chance* to save his brothers. Now I fear you will do anything to ease that guilt."

During his accusation, Jikun's lips had parted and his breath emerged audible and hoarse, as though his lungs had constricted beneath his fractured ribs. Navon tensed, preparing for another attack of anxiety.

But it did not come. Instead, Jikun's jaw set. "I will win this war. But not by relying on you."

Navon felt himself grow cold—he knew he had lost. "…I will come with you if only to try to save your life," he ceded quietly. "But I beg of you to treat Darcarus with some semblance of caution. He wants something *immensely*. Not all his smooth words are truth." He cast his gaze briefly down the street to find that the Sel'ven was watching him, his face solemn, his eyes cold and perceptive.

There was a warning in them.

Suddenly Eldaeus gave a loud cackle from Darcarus' right as the human spoke. When Navon looked back upon his general, he found that Jikun still faced him, resolute and determined to believe his course. But Navon knew he was looking into the soul of a wounded animal… backed into a corner and desperate to fight on. Yes, clearer than ever before, *he* was seeing Jikun through *his own* eyes.

Navon's gut tightened at the thought. Without the voices of the heroes of his tomes, he could see the world around him so clearly—no longer as events shaped and formed in relation to the deeds of those long past, but through the experiences of his own life. And those of Jikun's.

This pawn of Saebellus' was truly as Darcarus had warned: *a distraction.*

Even across the channel, the warlord had defeated his general.

CHAPTER TWENTY-EIGHT

"Gods, *finally* we're finished!" Vale breathed as he and Adonis retraced their steps along the dungeon hall to reach Alvena's resting place. Vale's steps lacked their usual luster as he drew up before her, and Adonis' bright eyes were vacant and dull. But Alvena was not surprised. Sitting cornered within the prisons for the last two weeks had depleted her as well, and all *she* had been required to do was squat on the floor with her book.

Upon the second day of her captivity, as punishment for his failure to draw Alvena a bath, Adonis had sent Vale to the market to purchase her a novel to occupy the long hours of the prison visits. But while Adonis' intention was to penalize Vale, it was Alvena who suffered the result.

"*A Botanist's Guide to Flowers*? You bought the first item you saw, didn't you? Vale, you could not have chosen a more boring or useless tome! It is the middle of winter *and* Alvena is trapped indoors," Adonis had chastised vehemently.

Vale had shrugged the rebuke away. "She's a girl. It's got flowers. What more can you ask for?"

Certainly not sense from Vale, Alvena had learned.

She lugged her heavy tome into her arms and hastened to the front of their party. If she had to endure the wailing of one more Noc'olari, her frayed nerves were bound to snap entirely.

Adonis smiled and the Noc'olarian cells were pushed instantly from her mind. "Famished, are we?—I believe dinner will be served soon."

A deep, commanding voice upon the stairs snapped Alvena from her hunger. "Adonis, Vale."

She had only needed to hear the voice once to commit the sinister figure to memory. She trembled her way fully behind Adonis. Framed in the stairway was King Saebellus, his armor cast aside for dark, simple silks that only assisted in highlighting his pale complexion and ebony eyes. *'Sel'ari, protect me!'* She gripped onto Adonis' side. *'Has Ilsevel won?! Vale said she always gets her way! Will she kill me herself or will she force me to rot in the dungeon?'* After the last several arduous weeks, she could not determine which, now, was worse.

Saebellus halted at the base of the steps, fixing her with a scrutinizing glare before she melded wholly into the lieutenant's back. "...Still reassigning?" he asked after a brief delay. "Come, let us eat. I am certain you three could use a good meal." Alvena exhaled, even as the warlord's stoic tone dropped sharply with disdain. "I swear to Kamora, *no one* does their damn jobs around here."

To her left, Vale winced. "That was two weeks ago and I had a late night!"

Alvena dared to peer around Adonis' arm in time to see Saebellus whirl and ascend the stairs. "That is not what I am referring to," he stated flatly as they attached promptly to his heels. "The dungeons smell malodorous... of putrid waste and decay. If the prisons are over-filled, I expect Ilsevel's soldiers to work twice as hard. I need not inform you that they are *not*," he growled.

'Why would you expect Ilsevel to do any good?' Alvena thought with a huff. *'Anyone who serves her must be just as wicked.'*

So of course the mess fell on Saebellus' soldiers to rectify. Adonis expeditiously volunteered. "I will attend to the situation after dinner," he announced. "Let me be responsible for the matter."

Saebellus marched across the mural on the first floor, running his hand briefly across a dusty column as he passed. "No, the relocation and scouting is enough responsibility for you. We will leave this work to those currently in charge... and they *shall* be held accountable."

There was no further sound until they emerged free of the dungeons and Alvena's unruly stomach began a conversation of its own. She attempted to quietly sidestep along the hallway's shadows, but the rumbling in her gut was not equally concealed by the darkness. The smell of food was particularly overwhelming, and as they passed the dining hall Alvena spotted why. The room was laden with towering, succulent dishes and goblets filled with wine so cherry red that they seemed a dessert all on their own. The room bore all the necessities to feed high Sel'varian nobility, Saebellus' most prestigious soldiers, and...

Alvena let out a squeak and darted past the archway, finding her movement too fast to gather more than the smug expression, sickeningly sweet smile, and voluptuous figure of *Ilsevel*.

Saebellus glanced at Alvena's scampering figure; he arched one blackened brow. "Keep the girl free of Ilsevel's path. For now, she must remain a prisoner; I did persuade Ilsevel to that concession."

'So he has not let her have her way!' Alvena thought at the same moment that Vale muttered a disgruntled curse. Inside, she could glimpse a private dining chamber.

But just as Alvena's fears subsided, the warlord added, "Be aware that Ilsevel is not likely to let this matter pass. Making an exhibition of the servant's death solidifies Ilsevel's story of Hairem's suicide. And whether or not that story is relevant any longer—"

Vale interjected with a snort. "The bitch just has to be right."

Saebellus' head jerked back and Alvena once more fused with the blameless lieutenant. "In here," he continued as he swung the door to a small room wide.

'The king... holding the door?' Alvena realized for the first time that Saebellus was not escorted by guards as she would have expected. Hairem had always been accompanied by at *least* Erallus, and quite frequently by two soldiers of his personal guard. His lack of defense could only attest to arrogance or great personal strength... and Alvena held the impression that it was the latter.

She swallowed her fearful awe.

"Sit," he commanded, and drew out her high-backed chair.

As Alvena obediently thumped into her seat, her unabashed stomach rumbled once more to life. She pitched her book carelessly under her seat. The small, round table was lavished with heavily spiced meats, colorful fruit, and an assortment of raw, mixed vegetables. At the center was a simple, round, flaky bun that was bursting with white frothy cream.

Saebellus was the first to reach for the food, and he was terribly slow at filling his plate. Alvena wiggled restlessly, tapping her little silver charm against her breast. Did she have to wait until he was done grappling with those berries? Vale and Adonis were dolloping their plates already... but should she wait? She was just a servant girl. Rather, *used* to be a servant girl. Whatever she was now was certainly lower than even *that.*

"Eat," Saebellus instructed.

Alvena started, quickly dropping her charm and snagging the closest vegetable onto her plate.

Saebellus seemed satisfied with the act and his attention returned to his subordinates. "You two were up late. Again."

Alvena stared down at her randomly snatched atrocity. Damn it! Did she have to eat this now? Gods, she *hated* mourifel! It tasted like grass.

Vale, contrarily, had a steaming, golden leg. He waved it about as he replied snappishly, "You had Adonis on Sellemar's ass again, so what do you expect? I can't sleep when he's not around!"

Alvena froze. *'Sellemar!'* Somehow, she had forgotten Adonis' orders to follow the lord the moment she had severed her connection with his generosity: while her watchers had been sleeping, she had hurled Sellemar's invaluable letter into the safety of the fire. The incriminating mandate inscribed therein—instructing any True Blood follower to assist her—was now no more than a pile of ash.

Saebellus dropped the last bit of his food rather forcefully. "That is no excuse, Captain," he barked. "You were late again. The new recruits will not respect me if they do not respect you."

Alvena glanced at Vale, who scoffed so brazenly that she sank a little deeper in her chair. "There are twenty men," the captain stated. "One of them is so god-damn old my father wasn't even yet a seed when this man dropped from his old lady's legs."

Saebellus' napkin cracked in the air as he shook it loose. "His name is *Kevus* and he has experience. He was among Geldin Laeris' most elite mercenaries before he retired."

"He retired," Vale muttered, "because he's so god-damn old."

"Vale," Saebellus reproached through a bite small enough that his words went unhindered. "He is an extremely reputable mage and you will find him useful. You will *utilize* his skills or I will station you as target practice."

Vale shot Alvena a scathing glare as though she was responsible for his rebuke.

'You're the one provoking him,' she thought sourly, and jutted out her bottom lip in disdain.

Vale grunted. "He doesn't say a word."

"And I thought you, of all people, would appreciate that."

Vale slouched dramatically to emphasize his impatience. "*No*. He just stares at me intensely, all day long… as though he wants to snap my neck."

Saebellus cocked his head and needlessly brushed the napkin on his lap. "And this is an uncommon reaction?"

Alvena snickered to herself while Adonis chuckled.

"Oh, hah. You are hilarious. Have your laugh at my misfortune."

Alvena did, but Adonis coughed into his hand and carefully positioned his fingers over his pale lips. The creases about his eyes, however, remained deep. "Perhaps we can put the new recruits to work on locating Cahsari…?—I am assuming the male has not yet been found."

Saebellus' amusement died instantly. "No."

The grim decline in tone sobered Adonis as well, and Alvena felt her delight snuffed out. By Sel'ari this dinner was a bore! "Well, if none of the Watch saw him leave the city, he must still be within."

"That is what we thought about Alvena," Saebellus replied, and six eyes shifted to inspect her briefly.

She feigned obsession with the evil green lump on her plate.

Vale waved the gravity from the air with a casual flick of his turkey leg. Then he took an inappropriately large mouthful and uttered something Alvena could only assume was to be translated as, "It's been four days."

Saebellus was not quite as capable. "What?" he demanded.

Vale's jaws rapidly flexed as he attempted to chew his grotesque mouthful.

"I think what he is saying," Adonis offered gravely, "is that Cahsari is dead."

Vale inclined the turkey leg in Adonis' favor and nodded once. "The Refifthance thrikes againn," he gurgled triumphantly.

Alvena watched a little dribble of brown juice journey down his chin. *'Barbaric. You could have been trying to eat a little this whole time instead of attempting to shove it all down your throat,'* she sniffed. Why, he didn't even have the proper table manners of a palace servant!

"*If* the rebel faction has 'struck again,' it is only because you have failed to find them," Saebellus growled with equal disgust.

"ME?" Vale gave a garish gulp followed by a mildly delayed gasp. "You have suggested that Sellemar is in some way involved—so wouldn't that make this *Adonis'* fault?" He wiped the back of his hand across his chin and thrust the dangling leg at his lover. A little spray of turkey juice flew from the brandished meat and landed next to Adonis' plate.

The lieutenant's pale eyes creased with irritation.

Saebellus ignored the indignation, tapping his wine glass on the gilded tablecloth. "Frankly, I do not care about Cahsari. If the rebels have disposed of him, they will have done me a favor." His eyes met Vale's then, and the captain shrank.

'Oh, what has he done now?' Alvena wondered smugly. Clearly Vale had a whole slew of transgressions against Saebellus!

The king's next words capitalized on the prickling atmosphere. "What," he began in a tone so delicate that Alvena held her breath, "has happened to our *other* missing friend?"

Vale's mouth opened and hung as heavy as a wet bedsheet.

"Vale has it handled," Adonis quickly intervened. He tapped his lover's jaw shut. "Do not worry, Saebel."

The warlord's head tilted ever so slightly and Adonis quickly busied himself with his food. *'You are on your own,'* his actions read.

How Alvena loved to see the captain squirm!

"Adonis is right. I have the situation managed," Vale mumbled, flailing his wine glass about before downing it in full.

There was a clink as Saebellus' knife ruptured through the meat on his plate, but his overall countenance remained unsettlingly still.

"Oh come, Saebel." Vale attempted a weak laugh.

"I have been informed—and *not* by you—that Jerah is now on Ryekarayn. Where the True Bloods are."

"They would never consider allying themselves with the likes of him."

Alvena's nose scrunched. *Who* was an enemy so great to Saebellus and yet so repulsive to the True Bloods?

Saebellus feigned consideration, an expression altogether more terrifying than if he had just let out a roar. "I suppose, now that I have acquired the throne, I ought to *take chances* with such matters."

Vale could stand the pressure no longer and tossed his turkey leg forcefully onto his plate. "Alright, the fucking beast is on Ryekarayn!"

The *Beast?!*

"What of it?" Vale continued. "The mercenaries are there as well. If Jerah isn't already dead, he *will* be. If he falls into the hands of the True Bloods, you can string me up by my genitals—*that's* how god-damn certain I am that this will be dealt with!"

That type of response certainly offered Vale some weight, yet Saebellus was unimpressed. Of course he wanted the Beast disposed of! The creature had crippled General Taemrin's defenses on more than one occasion and the new king could certainly not afford such retaliation. "While I would enjoy holding you to that absurd promise, I cannot afford even the most mundane pleasures. As Jerah is now on Ryekarayn, the only reasonable course is to assign the matter to another."

Sense had now abandoned Vale entirely and he slammed a fist in outrage. "You contacted Relstavum?! That god-damn human was the one who told me to hire Hazamareth and Tsuki to begin with! If this is anyone's fault, it is *his!*"

"Then you should be happy to transfer responsibility of the matter onto him," Saebellus replied coolly.

"Let this go," Adonis murmured.

Vale sat back stiffly with an acknowledging grunt.

"And even dead," Saebellus added softly, as though trying to smooth his captain's disheveled scales, "Relstavum might utilize him."

'No one *should have use of the Beast,'* Alvena thought, but they certainly cared nothing for her qualms. She loured at her plate and reached for a chunk of bread and meat. She would, at least, eat the good things first. Then maybe she could cut up the mourifel and slide it around her plate a bit. Lardol had always yelled at her for that, but he was no longer here to shake admonishment. Her face fell.

"In addition, I have a more pressing matter for you and Adonis to address." Saebellus reclined in his chair, setting his utensils down and lifting the napkin to wipe his lips.

Vale's crossed arms demonstrated that he was still mildly disgruntled, but he nevertheless elevated his gaze. Adonis too had paused from his meal to engage. Now that the room was silent, Alvena was wholly aware of how terribly loud her chewing must sound and reduced herself to merely prodding at her cooling food in contempt.

"In a month," Saebellus began, "you are to travel to the Ruljarian city, Raestra, along the Velhar River. These are the councilmember Ilrae's people."

She heard Adonis' breath catch.

"You are to capture them, kill the resisters, and bring the compliers to Elvorium for relocation. I want the Noc'olari fully transferred before the battle."

Alvena fought down the images of the dead that had haunted her for weeks. *'It was because of the humans that the elves suffered,'* she had told herself. But now that excuse held little weight. What had the Ruljenari done to deserve the same violent fate?

She watched Adonis push his vegetables across his plate, equally as unsettled. "...Saebellus, the humans and the Noc'olari were a verdict I can accept... but *what* are Ilsevel's reasons for the Ruljenari?"

Saebellus' broad chest expanded. "*Our* reasons, Adonis. Ilsevel is my wife. These decisions are made mutually."

Vale scoffed. "Dragon shit. You've made one god-damn call since Ilsevel straddled you and it was about the fucking mute."

The shadows in the room elongated, enveloping the light from the chandelier. Alvena now was sitting straighter, lifting her little shoes free of the floor lest they get her as well. "The reasons given to war the previous races apply as well to the Ruljenari. The elves of this country have become accustomed to moral folly. Relocating the elven races is the most efficient method of disrupting both the rebellious factions and their own self-interests. As they have refused to submit willingly to this act, you shall bring them here by force. Although this method might be harsh, we have risen past the tolerance for inaction."

Alvena looked to Adonis for direction, but the male's lips were drawn and his hands interlocked tightly together.

The mantle for confrontation thus fell to Vale. "...Keep this course and the world will start calling you the Mad King," he muttered in a barely audible tone, suggesting that he half-hoped the warlord would not hear him. "A terrible, terrible, terrible lie, as the mad king lives, his people die."

"*Get out.*"

Alvena saw the shadows engulf those of the chandelier and she recoiled for fear that the great, golden adornment would come crashing down upon them.

Beside the glowering captain, Adonis extended a supplicating hand. "Vale is just expressing his belief that these wars do not adhere to our vision." Alvena doubted this was entirely true—after all, the captain was clearly evil. Still, Adonis continued, "Slaughtering mass numbers of Sevrigel's inhabitants is what turned us *away* from the council. We are now treading down the very road we once despised."

Alvena could see Saebellus' eyes flicker incomprehensibly and she wondered what emotions Adonis had stirred. "This is what I want, Adonis," he finally whispered. "Visions evolve."

"*I think*," Adonis dared to continue, "that this is what *Ilsevel* wants."

The muscles along the pallid jaw popped and Saebellus' lips curled to reveal gritted teeth. "*This is my decision*, Adonis. Ilsevel has helped me to see that my vision was not enough. More than the old government must fall."

"Loneliness is more dangerous than the most potent of poisons."

Saebellus set his glass down with such force that Alvena feared it would shatter. "Do not question me again, Adonis."

Yet, to Alvena's horror, Adonis *continued.* "The ends justify the means?—If they do, why did we not complete our orders to massacre the sirens?"

Saebellus stood, sliding his chair back with a grating scrape. His expression was still indecipherable. "Adonis. Vale. You will address Elvorium's prisoners and those that Turlondiel brings from Tadorwen. Then you will go to Raestra and you will escort the survivors here. That is an *order*, Adonis. If you do not like my methods, you may *leave*."

With a flutter of hope, Alvena's head swiveled. This was his chance to walk away!

But Adonis' face had grown instantly apologetic. His head bowed sharply. "I'm sorry, Saebel. Sit down. Eat with us."

Saebellus flung his napkin across the table. "And keep a close eye on that child. I am clearly too weak to restrain Ilsevel for long." And then he staunchly left the room.

Alvena tensed, recalling the smug, fat lips of the queen just a hall's width away. Would Saebellus truly relinquish her to that witch?

No… he was just furious with his subordinate's attacks… Her gaze drifted back to the two males, but they had leaned in close to grimly whisper without her.

Her eyes slid to her plate, the mourifel chunks swimming about her meal. Even without their presence, her appetite had vanished. She lifted the knife and slid it slowly across her plate. What if Adonis and Vale were right… what if Saebellus *was* weak to the queen's whims…?

Her fingers tightened and she slipped her hand into her lap. How long did she truly have before Ilsevel came for her?

She crossed her legs, letting the folds of her skirt envelop the blade.

*

When the three had finished their meals and returned to the bedroom, Alvena retreated to her divan. A blanket of plush, white fur awaited her there and she reclined herself comfortably within. Adonis had recently purchased the gift for her to nestle beneath when the night's fire would die. She stuffed the knife securely between the cushions, the blade wrapped snuggly in the folds of her cloth napkin, and opened her book upon her lap.

'Aha! I recognize you!' she accused the round, green flowers that blossomed in the picture. *'I picked you for Ilsevel.'* She scanned the

accompanying text, noting the galientris' high level of toxicity. *'If only I had stuffed you down her throat instead of into her hand.'*

The lieutenant stood at her shoulder, observing her with an uncharacteristically somber expression. Words flitted just beyond his silence. He unbelted his sword and slid it beneath the bed with a polished boot, delaying the inevitable.

She turned another page, forcing him to speak first.

Finally, he seemed to gather strength enough to address her. "Alvena, you will need to come with us to Raestra," he ceded.

Upon the bed, Vale had taken a seat nearby, unfastening his boots with suggestive glances toward his partner.

Alvena blew out her cheeks, finishing with a jut of her bottom lip. So they indeed believed Ilsevel might still squash Saebellus' will.

Adonis tried to offer a pitiful sigh. "Alvena, Ilsevel may have given us permission to keep you in our custody, but if we leave you unattended, do you truly think she won't seize you?"

"I'll tell you what *I'd* like to seize," Vale interjected below his breath.

Alvena's fingers curled tightly about the spine of the book. Ilsevel was just waiting for her moment, like a Kamorian panther stalking an innocent little bunny in its hole.

"So this matter is settled. In several weeks, after we finish our affairs here and Turlondiel returns with her prisoners, we shall go to Raestra. The sights of war are terrible indeed, but you must endure such an experience or jeopardize your life."

"I'll tell you what *I'd* give my life for right now," Vale muttered again.

She nodded her head slightly, as though only imparting a partial nod would properly convey her disgruntlement. But she believed Adonis' conjectures were correct.

After all, if she was being honest with herself, her feeble kitchen knife would do her no good against Ilsevel's guards.

Vale finally laid back, gesturing to Adonis to come near. He made no attempt at subtlety this time. "Come here," he purred. "I *need* you. Lately, you have been spending all your nights with that bastard!"

Adonis kicked his boots beneath the bed and tsked. "Please tell me you're not still bitter about Sellemar."

"...I am *more than* still bitter. He splattered poor Kraesin across the floor and nearly had me following him through the Gates!"

Alvena saw Adonis shift a little uncomfortably and smiled to herself. Sellemar had nearly killed Vale? This was the first pleasant news in weeks.

"Speaking of Sellemar, I heard you intruded on his meal with Ilsevel when we were dining a few days ago."

Alvena remembered when Vale had staunchly left their table because he suddenly felt the need to "vomit." Apparently, he had not, in fact, been ill.

Adonis crossed his arms and Alvena mimicked the tightness of his fold. "Ilsevel has not ceased her complaints and that female is *dangerous*," Adonis warned. "Apparently, you were quite rude to the both of them."

Vale's chin tipped up. "My two least favorite elves in my favorite eatery," he replied tartly. "Now *enough* about Sellemar before I lose my desires altogether!"

Adonis' rigidity melted away and he settled onto the other side of the bed. "Vale, Alvena is present. I will not make her uncomfortable."

Alvena glowered at the boorish captain. *'He's doing enough for the both of you,'* she thought resentfully.

Vale rolled onto his side, reaching out languidly to stroke Adonis' leg. "Use your magic…" he persisted. "If you can use it for Saebellus' wars you can *certainly* use it for *us*."

"Speaking of *Saebellus*," Adonis immediately reproached, further deflecting Vale's advances, "you still have not told him about Hadoream. You cannot side with Darcarus on this matter—your loyalty to Saebel should come first. If you do not tell Saebel the truth, you are *betraying* him."

Adonis had chosen the perfect moment to manipulate his partner. Alvena could see Vale's eyes spark, seeking a swift compromise. "You are right, of course. I will tell Saebel… You just have to allow me time to warn Darcarus. I swear."

Tell Saebellus? Warn *Prince* Darcarus? What did Vale know?

Adonis watched the encroaching trail of Vale's fingers and allowed himself a conceding smile. "Alright," he submitted. "I suppose that is fair."

Vale's lips twitched and he sat upright. "You have the disposition and patience of a god," he breathed. He slithered forward, putting a hand to Adonis' chest.

Alvena's eyes widened, their conversation forgotten. The book slipped off her lap and landed with a thunk. Were they going to have relations right in front of her?!

"I am too lucky. Every time I look at Saebel's debacle with Ilsevel, I am reminded of this." His hand frisked down Adonis' chest as though Alvena was not sitting mere yards away, gawking in horror. "Imagine if you had not let those smugglers fuck you. I'd be a lonely—"

With a sudden flash in his eyes, Adonis' relaxed features lost their soft curve and he punched Vale squarely in the jaw.

Alvena nearly clapped, equally shocked and delighted by the blow.

The Sel'ven tumbled across the bed, almost spilling over the side. "That was cold and insensitive," Adonis growled, knocking Vale's grasping hand away.

Vale put the hand to his chin as he crawled back toward the bed's center. "Damn it, Adonis! I was complimenting you! It all worked out for the best!"

Adonis tossed his head, raising his chin in solid indignation. "You can drink a bottle of Ulasum's tonight."

"I'm sorry," Vale cooed in terribly sweet supplication. "You're right. I'm an insensitive bastard and I didn't mean for my words to bite. Let me make it up to you. Please?"

"I believe I told you to poison your tactless tongue."

Vale slid forward, cautiously reaching out a hand and placing it on Adonis' thigh. Alvena watched Adonis smack it sharply and Vale drew back. "I will do whatever you say," he whispered.

She saw Adonis smile faintly, but he kept his expression hidden from Vale.

"*Anything* you say," the captain tried again, replacing his hand on Adonis' leg and drifting it up his thigh.

And suddenly they were gone.

Alvena started, jerking her head from left to right, but only an empty room met her searching eyes.

With a terrible, dawning realization, she remembered how Hairem would grieve in frustration, saying that after every battle, Saebellus' army would simply… *vanish*.

So *this* was the male who had single-handedly allowed Saebellus to win the war.

CHAPTER TWENTY-NINE

The curtain of the tiny room was drawn; only the howls of wind and the tink of ice against the glass signaled the blizzard's presence. Inside, the air was hot and muggy, so thick that Hazamareth felt she could almost drown in it.

She gave a deep, pleasured inhale.

Tsuki was rebinding his wound, his calloused hands snagging on the soft gauze as he wound it around his chest. "Doesn't this room feel chilly to you?" he asked. "Maybe I should throw in another log."

Hazamareth snorted once, the only necessary signal for her disapproval.

"Fine," Tsuki begrudged, and pinned the final edge of his gauze to the rest of his haphazard creation. He dropped back against the headboard, jarring Hazamareth and nearly causing her to drop her book. "Three days and I already feel the beast is lost. If Vethru cost us our bounty, so help me, I'll make an exception to hunt him next!"

"Stop fretting, Tsuki," she remarked, her finger sliding fondly down the old parchment. She turned the next page, admiring the fine sketch on the left. There were not a lot of words, but that was fine by her. She had never cared much for reading. Still was not particularly good at it. "We'll leave this place when we can. The beast has been killing someone every day—when he stops, we'll know he's fled and then be but a day behind. Anyways, our experience with their kind says he is not going to relinquish such easy hunting grounds. *Especially* when he believes he's lost us across the channel."

A knock resonated through the wooden door and Tsuki snatched up the crossbow. "If that is Vethru again I'm going to just land one straight between the eyes. No speech," he growled. He swung his legs out of the bed and stalked stiffly across the room.

Hazamareth gave a crooked smile, amused more by his sauntering gait than his words. She knew Vethru would not be on his feet for some time. Without the ability to regenerate, his recovery might be weeks behind theirs.

Still, Tsuki opened the door a crack, leading the welcome with the tip of his crossbow.

"You haven't changed a bit," a man mused from the other side, and Tsuki was forced to retreat as the door was pushed wide.

Hazamareth dropped her book, ears perking at the familiar voice. "Rel!" she exclaimed, brows rising into her dark hair. "Good gods, it has been many moons! How did you find us? Aren't you about done working for Saebellus? Has he given you that old book yet?"

She noted Tsuki's eyes had brightened and he had lowered his arm, letting it and the crossbow drop loosely to his side. "If you're coming back to hunt with us, you picked a damn good time. The creature we're after is worse than any bloodthirster or lycanthrope you can remember!"

Relstavum stepped deeper into the room, head slowly swiveling about their surroundings. His boot extended backward as he moved, tapping the door closed. His black eyes flicked once—shamelessly—to Hazamareth's breasts, and then down to the weapon swinging slowly at Tsuki's side. A thousand expressions flitted across his rugged face, but before Hazamareth could gather even one, they were gone—replaced with the stoic, indecipherable male they had come to know and respect. Yes, he had abandoned their trade to serve some sniveling warlord, but *he* was no less the formidable warrior. His hand swept into his vest and emerged partially to reveal an old, tattered tome.

Then the book vanished once more.

"Ah, so you've been paid," Tsuki noted. "Then you're done with Saebellus, I assume?"

Hazamareth shook her head in disgust. "A decade of work for a *book*...? Relstavum, you're simply mad."

The man merely inclined his head. "I was on my way to Nordeep when I received a command to convene with the two of you. So I am, in fact, here on business on Saebellus' behalf." He stepped past Tsuki, spun about in a billow of ebony fabric, and dropped into a seat strewn with dirty clothes.

The weathered chair was far from the only disaster. If Hazamareth had known Relstavum was coming, she would have at least gathered the clutter into a single pile.

Or mountain, if she was to be at all accurate.

Yet, even surrounded by that chaos, the chair was flattered by the spectacle of the dark, rugged skin and superbly attractive physique that now resided upon it. Not only was the body clean, but it was practically bathing in wealth. Clearly, Saebellus had offered the man far more than the promised book.

It was moments like these when Hazamareth wondered what it would be like to have work where the reward was tangible gratitude rather than another scar. "So what does your mighty warlord want of us?" she sniffed and tilted her chin away. "We are already working for that prickly little captain of his."

She watched as Relstavum reclined, slipping into their environment as though he were once more one of them. He clasped his hands together, raising only his index fingers to form an arch pressed against his lower lip. "You work for Vale no longer—your employment has been transferred to me." He nudged a mass of clothing aside as he shifted his feet upon their disheveled floor. A cockroach sprang free and made a scurrying dash for Hazamareth's undergarments. There was silence as the three pairs of eyes followed it. "…My request is very simple," Rel continued when the abhorrent little beast vanished within. "I still need Jerah dead, but now I also need his body."

"Jerah? You *named* the creature? What in Ramul do you want with his body?!" Tsuki balked, jerking his gaze from the mound. "You do not trust us to do our job?! We have *never* abandoned a mission, Rel. We're the ones who taught you that principle in the first place! You were with us for over twenty god-damn years and you dare to suggest us dishonest?!"

Hazamareth felt a shiver run down her spine and she shot Tsuki a cautious glance. Relstavum's expression was sharp enough to cut stone. With as great a hunter as Rel had been, she had almost forgotten about the border of madness along which he had always seemed to dance.

Why, he would burn down the whole inn if he was determined to kill the roach. And they no longer had the Amulet of Rohar to protect them from such a rampage.

"It is not I who requires proof, but Saebellus," he replied coolly. "And that is who has employed your services."

Hazamareth laughed once, hard and loud and straight of face. It was a fine show of bravado in the face of the necromancer's glare. "The entire, massive body? You are simply mad, Rel. I just had to half-drag Tsuki through town and I feel as though I broke my spine." She paused, eyes narrowing, tone lowering. "Are you certain it is not *you* who wants the body?"

Her boldness faded as Relstavum's expression remained unnaturally fixed. A chill clouded his gaze—amiability shoved aside. "Tsuki is strong," he replied softly. "I have seen him carry five times his own weight."

And Tsuki, the vain bastard, was too flattered by the exaggeration to deny it.

"Twenty percent will be added to compensate for the inconvenience this addition shall cause you. With the exorbitant coin you were promised already, this should more than extinguish any qualms."

Hazamareth clenched her teeth. "This beast is different, Rel."

The man's long, dark fingers tapped in unison upon the arm of the chair, growing in speed at her words. His eyes had been so very calm, so very *sane* when he had arrived.

But that was gone.

"And what do you always say?" he whispered. "Different or not, they all die the same."

'Maybe not this one.' But she did not voice her doubt aloud.

Tsuki, however, was determined to dismiss their previous failure to slay the beast. "They all die the same," he affirmed, and dropped down once more beside her. "Thirty percent, Rel. Then you can consider the beast already dead."

It was the wise response… Any other would have made them the roach.

CHAPTER THIRTY

The city of Nordeep, where Geldin Laeris' Brotherhood maintained its headquarters, was a week's march north across snow-covered plains and ice-laden trees. *After* Sanae, of course, where they had taken the damn cow.

Fucking Feber.

Despite that Sanae was a deviation from their *true* destination, Jikun had been willing to compromise that much—if nothing else than to pacify Navon's jealousy. The male was growing more unbearable by the day.

"Navon," he barked. "Where is Eldaeus?"

Navon pointed wearily at a drooping redbern tree. "Where do you think, *Jikun?*"

On Sevrigel, such foliage would have been a mere sapling, but here, the towering giant was the largest tree for leagues. There was a brilliant flash of color near the peak, and Eldaeus' head rustled into view. "Jikun! Navon! It is a city! A *small* city, but it *is* a city!"

And then he promptly crashed through the frozen branches to narrowly avoid landing on his head.

Jikun hardly spared a moment of flat regard before he found his legs propelling him past the groaning Faraven and up the small crest of the hill.

"*Nordeep*," Darcarus spoke with satisfaction as Jikun inhaled the sight.

"Beautiful," Jikun instantly approved. A strong stench of human waste and burning wood wafted to the sky, but by all the gods, it was better than anything they had encountered yet.

He had learned to lower his expectations.

The walls of the city shone like silver-tipped marble in the evening light, glinting, Jikun imagined, from the ample number of soldiers manning the walls. There was a beauty to the order of military presence. "Now this is far more promising, Navon. And you wanted to go shit in trenches with a band of farmer boys." He snorted his disdain at the Helven's sad attempt to keep him occupied and stepped briskly down the hill and across the tree-speckled field.

"Ouch-ch-ch-ch! Wait for me!" Eldaeus called from somewhere behind.

But Jikun paid him no heed—gone were the pathetic expanses of thatched huts they had traversed through along their way. This was the first city they had encountered with *genuine* potential to lead them to Relstavum. Although this prime settlement was not elven, it was a testament to what heights of power one man could achieve.

And evidence of how much he had to offer.

Navon reached his side as they passed through Nordeep's southern gate—a massive, iron portcullis drawn up into the thick, pale stone. The guards on either side of the short tunnel acknowledged their passage with no more than a brief flick of their eyes, and in a few short steps the four elves emerged onto the cobbled roads.

"Eldaeus, stay close. Navon, watch him."

Although the Helven's physique was stiff with disapproval, his pale hand caught Eldaeus by the back of his leather jerkin, restraining him from an inevitable prance down the bustling street. "This is not what Sel'ari would want."

"I do not answer to Sel'ari," Jikun replied coolly.

Darcarus tutted, exchanging a brief roll of the eyes with Jikun, and then stepped casually to the front of their company.

Since the Pass, respect for Navon's opinions had befittingly dwindled.

Darcarus smoothed down his half-opened shirt—two more buttons had freed themselves from the now-tattered cotton. If his rakish attitude persisted, soon he would meld seamlessly into the humans' squalor. "Excuse me, my lord," the prince called to a tattooed, barrel-chested man lingering near the city gates.

Jikun was quite certain the man was not even the shit a lord scraped off the sole of his boot. But he refrained from correction.

"Could you be so generous as to point me in the direction of the Brotherhood?"

Information in hand, Darcarus sauntered once more to their sides. "What is the disdainful look for this time, Navon?" He spun toward the bustling street, his question rhetorical. After all, a disapproving expression had become the permanent state of Navon's face. "The Brotherhood is this way."

As they progressed farther into the city, the truth of the old woman's words became apparent; Laeris' control had leeched from north to south.

Soldiers and mercenaries were intermingled with the commoners, wandering about the market stalls and popping in and out of buildings at every turn. The most prominent of these were men dressed in black leather armor with tattoos running the breadths of their right arms.

'Laeris' insignia?' Jikun wondered briefly. Like the barrel-chested man at the city gates. Marking them as property. He felt a slight recoil at the notion that he would soon be one of them. *'A small price to pay for the necessary deed. Freedom* after *retribution. Strength first.'*

And Laeris certainly had both. The old man had mentioned Laeris' tower, and no matter down which street they turned, the blood-hued monument stood like a beacon in the center of the city, proclaiming Laeris' control. His pockets were lined by this city's every endeavor—legal and otherwise. And the tower itself... It was more impressive than any human structure Jikun had seen—although the competition was paltry at best. Standing fifty meters tall, it was composed of rough, cherry stone and surrounded by white, wooden buildings that only emphasized its impenetrability.

It was an impressive show of force. Elves were far more subtle in their flaunting, but *this* building, with its bloody hue, was steeped in threat.

"I think this is a good idea," Eldaeus chimed in response to what Jikun could only imagine was a muttered comment from Navon. "I have good armor." He tapped the thick leather on his chest and smiled. "It has held up all these years. Best there was! Is. Was?" He carried on thoughtfully as they ambled down another street.

"Oh good. *Eldaeus* thinks this is a good idea. I hope you two imbeciles feel confident now," Navon growled.

Jikun prickled, but he followed Darcarus around the final bend and into a relatively empty side street. At the end was a building as equally red as Laeris' tower. Human males crowded the rooftop terrace, their raucous voices punctuated by the sharp rap of dice knocking together and rattling across a wooden surface. But they were only partially enwrapped in their game—even as another set of dice bounced between them, their heads turned to follow Jikun and his companions.

The vigilance of Laeris' men was not exclusive to the last building—the whole of the street was crawling with the poorly disguised lot. *'Excellent facade,'* Jikun scoffed as he eyed the bulging muscles of the supposed baker who repeatedly swept the same clean step. And to the alleyway on Jikun's left, only a human could have missed the soft rasping of someone lying in wait behind a stack of dusty crates.

"It is that building directly ahead," Eldaeus informed them excitedly. "It is red, just like Laeris' tower!"

Jikun yanked the Faraven to a halt. "Our names are Cizael, Ardwen, and Nevae," he growled sternly. "Eldaeus, do *not* forget."

"I still loathe that name," Darcarus muttered as he tapped his signet ring several times in quick succession. He removed it and dropped it hesitantly into his inner breast pocket. As displeased as the prince was, their identities would only last so long as Eldaeus' memory remained intact. "I am rather certain that is a female Farvian name."

Eldaeus snorted and waved his hand with a reassuring smile, as though the suggestion was absurd.

But he did not verbally deny it.

"Use the names," Jikun ordered, and released the Faraven's leather with a gentle shove. He marched forward up the remainder of the street. Every pair of eyes had fallen to them. *'In a city of well-armed mercenaries and thugs, we paint an exceptional sight…'* He glanced sidelong at Navon, who had managed to wither somewhat back into a wraith-like state after the recent lack of food. And his sour expression did not help matters. *'…Yes. Impressively pathetic.'* He gave his captain's heels a tap to urge him to pick up his feet, then peeled a clump of mud from his dirty sash. When neither of the hulking humans before the red building's door moved to admit them, he pushed it open and stepped inside.

Eldaeus let out an immediate choking gag and Jikun cuffed him sharply into silence. Now *this* was a familiar scent—just a bit more… *human*. Sweat and old leather. The lingering odor of wet dogs. Dried manure that likely clung to some brigand's shoes. Jikun hated and loved it at the same time—it was the stench of battled men… Pungent, but familiar. And after weeks of wandering the land, he imagined he did not smell much better.

His nose wrinkled at the thought.

"At least we can make faces," he heard Eldaeus mutter indignantly.

Jikun blinked back the dots of light that still danced before his eyes, disabling him from spotting who may have seen his brief lapse of stoicism. When his vision began to return, he first noted the dim light spreading out over the spacious, circular room, emanating from an improvised chandelier designed from a wagon wheel. Even the gaudy elven contraptions that had dangled about the palace with abhorrent frequency were preferable to this primitive composition.

"Well, well, what have we got ourselves here? Dare I believe it? *Elves?*" a silky voice, raw with malice, drifted across the smoke.

"Calm your raging affections," the prince instantly retorted.

Jikun's vision cleared and he noted for the first time shapes of men seated in a ring of benches along the wall. Most of these men were unbranded. At least half were well-armed. And even through the rising tension, he could not help but marvel at their diversity. Elves were consistently tall, fair, and toned. But here... *here*... Bulging, wrinkled, thin... old enough to be his father, young enough to be his son, and three whose skin was as black as the mud in the Sevilan Marshes.

Humankind held little consistency in its creations—and Jikun had to admit, after the duplicated faces he had seen every day in his own army, the variety was somewhat relieving.

In a hideous and appalling sort of way.

"Mayhap the naked, little vagrant doesn't know who he's talking to, sir," one of the humans along the wall whispered, soft enough that a distant human could not hear. But to Jikun, his voice carried like a trumpet blast.

Jikun glanced sidelong to spot the original speaker and found the weathered face of a middle-aged human—almond-eyed and square-jowled, like some white-skinned orc from his academy books' paintings. The golden emblem on the man's chest glinted softly, a testament to at least relative success in the mercenary field.

Jikun swiftly caught Darcarus by the arm as the prince rallied his next impetuous response. "Sit," he growled, shoving Darcarus down beside Navon. His captain narrowed his eyes, as though demanding to know what he had done to deserve equal punishment.

Having seen the brief, unruly display, the human's lips twisted into a crooked smile, revealing blackened teeth. He scratched his hooked nose. "I *was* talking to you, elf," he sniffed deeply, gesturing to Jikun. "What a cliff you must have fallen from to find yourselves here, asking *humans* for help. There is no order—no list of meetings. The Brotherhood will call you in as it amuses them—and judging from your *fascinating* appearance, I imagine you'll be next."

There was a chorus of snickers.

Jikun's toes curled and he realized then that he was still standing, the floor cold beneath his bare feet. He could hear muffled speech through the door on the right of the room—too faint to define but elevated enough to imply that the current meeting was not progressing well. He dropped down onto the nearest cushion, careful to avoid a spatter of blood on the stone nearby. "I heard you the first time, *human*," he intoned. "I can hear you *breathing*."

But Jikun's caustic retort only emboldened the prince, who raised his finger in warning and then slid the crude gesture across his groin. Here, more than ever, the prince's overly candid behavior shone.

The humans nearby exchanged uncertain glances, clearly wondering if the sign was worthy of a brawl.

Their leader decided upon a wide show of teeth. "I am Makados. This is Keb, Kei, Coe, Harbesh, and Thamos." Makados leaned forward as he spoke, gesturing to each man on his right and left in turn, as though he too wished to see their faces upon their most recent introduction. Though Jikun could not imagine why, as they were each as equally hideous as the next.

Keb, Kei, and Coe appeared to be related—they wore the same vividly-colored clothing that contrasted brazenly against their ebony skin, and each displayed enough earrings in one ear to forge a small blade. Their noses were similarly broad and flared, and their neatly rounded heads were as smooth and polished as a mirror.

Harbesh scowled beside them, so red of face and hair that Jikun imagined he had baked too long in the summer sun. One abnormally lengthened arm scratched at his ankle while the other poked and prodded at a gap in his teeth.

And then there was Thamos, scrunched between the four in a form so massive he threatened to crack the stone bench on which he sat. His body bulged beneath his leather… but of sheer muscle rather than fat. Jikun was certain that nothing less than giant's blood pulsated through his purple veins.

"From the company of the Black Helm," Makados added as Jikun's lip curled. "What brings the four of you men here? Are you *aspiring* mercenaries?"

Jikun did not react to the man's taunting. "Cizael, Nevae, Ardwen, Eldaeus," he replied calmly, alleviating his eyes from the sight of the man's hulking crew by finding that the ghastly chandelier had starkly improved.

Darcarus smacked him on the chest, causing his old wound to ripple with pain. "Don't tell the bastard my name," he growled as Jikun clutched a hand to his breast.

"Ahhh," Makados cooed, his pink tongue flicking across his sable smirk. He reclined against the wall, snapping his long, rough fingers at Jikun. They were too dry to make more than a scraping sound. "So you are the head of this ragged band. I don't believe in all my travels I've seen worse results from a leader."

Jikun let out a growl, but Navon interjected before he could speak. "Keep your witless tongue to yourself, human. Your assumption is shockingly naïve."

Makados' tone was mockingly sympathetic. "Oh, aren't you the perfect military dog?"

Navon's mouth had shot open with a readily prepared retort, but at those words he paused. "*What?*"

"Aw, you look offended. Nevae, was it? You've been silent since you arrived—noting the cushions where you were to sit, the door where you would have your meeting, the reaction of your leader… And now, at his offense, you leap to his aid."

The captain stiffened.

"Even now, you are boiling to fight—but since you're weaponless, I assume you are a mage? Well, I'm afraid you couldn't harm us." With a thrust of his square chin, he smacked a hand to his chest. "This here is armor from the Karkadose Region—forged by the dwarves—where we recently crushed a rebellion fueled by Lord Hugo's son, the Whelp of Tendosmere. We'll use it again in the next war. I suppose that's where the four of you are headed. That is the only type of work that would take the likes of you. There are many equipped as well as us and against them, your magic would hardly make a *scratch*."

"Shall we find out how *deep* a scratch?" Navon hissed as his fingers unfurled.

Even Darcarus had lurched forward in his seat, hand on his hilt, eyes dancing eagerly in the dim light.

But Jikun was wise enough to realize that if they were to paint Laeris' personal ass-kissers' entrails across the walls, he was not likely to welcome their visitation. He pressed a hand solidly to Navon's chest as the male began to rise, noting the pounding of his captain's blood. Despite his warning grip, Jikun could feel Navon's chest expanding for a scathing rejoinder. And then suddenly, the voices behind the door escalated into frantic shouts. The men in waiting stilled, the spar between the humans and elves forgotten.

They were all one people as they listened now: locked with anxiety, hushed in fear.

Still louder the shouting rose until there was a sharp, definite cry. It then became a strangled, suffocating gurgle that slowly—unhurriedly—sputtered out.

Both rooms were as frozen as the ice clinging to the window panes. Jikun could imagine what had transpired. He recalled the blood behind him and stiffened. He had only a moment to wonder at the accuracy of Navon's qualms before the door to the right opened with a soft, moaning hiss.

It was a wonder that the one little sound could hold an entire room of born fighters at bay, and yet the trepidation intensified.

A large, bearded man emerged to recline against the frame, and Jikun's keen eyesight immediately detected a faint spray of blood staining his bulging forearm.

"Well… he is dead," Eldaeus commented matter-of-factly.

The man in the doorway pivoted as the Faraven's voice unexpectedly splintered the quiet. His round, heavily-lidded eyes surveyed the four elves with unrivaled intensity.

They had taken his interest, as Makados had foreseen. For once, Eldaeus' yammering had benefited them.

'This is *what we wanted,'* Jikun reminded himself through the discomfort of the man's gaze.

Then the human raised a meaty hand into the air and gave a single, solid nod. "The Brotherhood will see you now," he rumbled, and waved the four toward the open door.

There was no feigned formidability here: every inch of the man's being quivered with the unmistakable lust for violence.

If Navon was Jikun's sword, then *this* was Laeris'. And it seemed quite probable that he could snap Navon in half like a pile of old bones.

'By Malranus Almighty, these creatures are huge…' Jikun thought briefly before he took long, purposeful strides across the room, hiding all visible signs of doubt.

Behind him, he could hear Darcarus toss an inappropriately casual, "You have a little smear there on your arm."

But Jikun focused on his own bearing as he stepped into the room beyond. The smell of blood was tangible in the vast space, but wherever the Brotherhood had executed the poor fool—and however they had done it—remained a mystery.

"*Elves*," stated a voice down the length of the polished wooden floor, in a tone not unlike that which Makados had spat upon their arrival.

'The humans speak the same way about us as we do about them,' Jikun realized. And then wondered what in Aersadore a human could possibly find at fault with an *elf*. He raised his chin slightly at the tone, regarding the speaker with distaste. He was eyeing them with a similar expression, seated at a long desk of what Jikun guessed to be obsidian—a rare and fragile stone used to

hunt demons. Which was ironic, as Jikun was fairly certain that the man who sat behind it was a demon in his own right.

The shelves of humanoid skulls lining the wall attested to his theory.

Cutthroats, just as the old lady had warned. But he did not glance sidelong at Navon, already fully sensing his pointed scowl. This was not a *distraction.* This was their path.

"Come, take a seat," the man continued as the echo receded, and he gestured to the sagging chair before his desk. "Always a *story* with elves." The door creaked shut behind them and the blood-spattered sword took his station beside the speaker.

'Always a story...' Jikun repeated with a grimace. Not one he wanted to tell. His eyes fell upon the seat and he found himself hesitating for the briefest moment. It was not a lack of confidence in his decision, nor the shelves of skulls that encircled them, *nor* the blood-red chandelier swinging softly from the rafters that caused him unease: these were merely theatrics designed to test the nerves of the visitors to the Brotherhood.

A child's game.

Instead, Jikun's body was urging him to recoil from the scent of real blood in the air—the stench of iron—and the lingering taste of magic: a sour odor that sparked at the tip of his tongue and slithered across the scars on his arms, poking and prodding for a way inside his body. Suffice to say, he felt mildly violated. But he was extracted from his own discomfort as Darcarus seized control of the room.

"Your previous supplicant appears to have not fared so well," the prince stated as he strode to the chair. He dropped onto its worn cushion, sinking deep within its folds.

The human stroked the end of his thinning eyebrow rapidly, and Jikun surmised that he was mildly irritated. "If you have come to the Brotherhood, you must know that we do not tolerate men who fail to deliver. Unfortunately, he was one such man," Mikael said. He gestured to a second chair that Jikun felt quite certain was not there a moment before.

"I will stand," Jikun replied, glancing down to the filthy square of green fabric frayed over the peeping feathers.

The man looked up from his parchment. Even in the soft candlelight, Jikun could discern the maze of scars and toughened flesh, weathered by days on the road; but now, his fingers and nails were stained black from the ink of endless hours behind a desk. "I advise you to sit," the human spoke softly. And before Jikun could debate how much of his pride would be wounded by his compliance, he felt two iron hands grip his shoulders and force him into the chair.

Yet no one had touched him.

'This man is a mage,' Jikun realized with a grunt, fighting the urge to reach up and rub the bruises from his naked skin. Was this the man he was about to serve? Gods damn the prince to Ramul for losing his money outside Eldaeus' cavern! "...Are you Geldin Laeris?"

The man etched a missive across the parchment before him, but Jikun's ability to read Common was poor at best. "No. I am not Geldin Laeris. I am Archmage Mikael and Lord Laeris' second-in-command. Master Laeris is occupied on far more valuable matters. Of which a defeated general and his dogs are not one."

Jikun felt the warmth rush from his cheeks.

The archmage continued impassively. "Personally, I would like to question your state of affairs further, but the Brotherhood does not require your sniveling story, just your success." He looked up, eyes locking with Darcarus. "What is it that you would like to request of the Brotherhood, *Ardwen Elesmore?*"

'They are even aware of our falsified names?!'

Eldaeus inappropriately leapt in, excitement rising even above the chill and Navon's imminent thrashing. He stretched his arms wide, wiggling his fingers eagerly as the archmage shrank away. "Grand work. Slaying dragons. Slaying evil-doers. Slaying trolls. Slaying wereboars. Slaying orcs. Slaying—"

"What is a wereboar?" Navon interrupted. "I do not believe those exist."

Eldaeus looked aghast. "Of course they exist. Wereboars. Big boars with claws and fangs. Sneak into your window at night and suck your blood. Then, at the full moon you transform and fall into a bestial rage."

Navon shook his head slowly. "I think you are confusing two other creatures..." he trailed off.

Jikun spun and shot them both the mouthed warning, *'I will kill you.'*

Navon cuffed Eldaeus upside the head and Jikun whirled back around. Fortunately, Darcarus had regained his senses and had refocused the archmage on him.

"Firstly, my lord, we require soldiers' gear," Darcarus had begun, inclining his head in supplication. "We need three full sets of light armor, three sets of clothes, three cloaks, two long swords—"

"Three," Eldaeus whispered. "I need two."

"—*three* long swords, four long bows, a score of arrows each, four horses, basic medical supplies, four bedrolls, flint and steel, four oiled canvases and sacks, a week's worth of rations a piece, two hooded lanterns with four pints of oil, four waterskins, four whetstones, fifty yards of spider-thread rope, a dagger, a map of the region, and a map of Ryekarayn."

The disheveled prince was clearly familiar with gallivanting across the countryside.

The archmage appeared less impressed. His watery eyes shifted from one elf to the next and his tone remained flat. "Is the Realm without even the most basic necessities?"

Darcarus started. So the Brotherhood had even identified the prince. *'Of course they would...'* But the fact that Laeris' men still treated them with such nonchalance only proved how powerless they soon would be.

Darcarus forced a smile. "Sometimes the Realm does indeed feel bereft."

The archmage tapped his black fingers once. "Is there anything *else* you demand?" he continued with a sniff. "Perhaps a sprawling estate, or a castle or two?"

Darcarus chortled in what he feigned as genuine amusement. "You are full of wit, my lord."

Mikael stroked his brow once more, grimacing slightly as he regarded the four elves. Still, the compliment seemed to pacify him. "You are requesting at least twenty thousand bronze in debt to Geldin Laeris. And what, pray tell, do you plan to offer the Brotherhood should you fail to *repay* this loan? You have asked for *quite* the ludicrous sum. Clearly the Sel'varian Realm is not supporting the expeditions of the unfavored son and his band of war criminals."

Behind him, Jikun felt Navon clutch the back of his chair. Based on Mikael's tone, the Brotherhood had no fear of subjecting even the prince to their methods of punishment.

Darcarus merely smiled. "You are most correct, Archmage—the Realm will have no association with our mission. As such, we have nothing to barter with."

The archmage laughed once. "I had heard you were practically disinherited, but the proof still takes me by surprise," he spoke flatly. When the Sel'ven did not respond, the archmage slid his fat tongue along his lower lip, leaving a glistening trail in its wake.

Jikun had the terrible imagery of a slug sliding across a dried leaf.

"*Most* people," Mikael began dryly, "come to Geldin Laeris with collateral: land, buildings, rare artifacts… Even the royal line and non-human regions have beseeched us before. But *you* four offer him nothing." He set the quill into a little glass jar and crossed his thick, blackened fingers against his chest. "And the loan you ask for is no small sum. While the Brotherhood does not deny even outlandish requests, our position is very clear." He reached out one hand, slowly, and pointed to one of the skulls on the shelf to Jikun's right—a particular, glistening heap of bones whose grin seemed even more hideous than the next. "As you have nothing to offer, your collateral will be your lives. You have three months to repay this loan *in full*. Then we shall come hunting for you. We will retrieve the gear you will have stolen and we will add your skulls to the collection. In simple terms, prince, we shall ransom you and kill your companions as slowly and painfully as our creativity devises." His eyes locked sharply with Jikun's. "You will not scream loud or long enough to satisfy us. Cooking alive, disembowelment, rotting in your own excrement, impalement… these will seem like pleasures when we are through with you."

But Jikun remained unfazed. He was about to confront Saebellus' greatest beast—what threat could the Brotherhood hold over him now? "Yes, *and?*"

The archmage's brows fluttered. "Still here, elf?" He chuckled, eyes rising to Navon beside him. "This is more courage than you must have shown at Elarium, where the world thought you dead. I admit—we are surprised to see the elves' celebrated general alive… and *here*." A slow smirk engulfed his face, and Jikun could only imagine Navon's visible discomfort. His watery eyes fell once more upon Darcarus. "If this is what the four of you *truly* desire, it is not within my power to deny your request.

"As your collateral is your lives, your bodies shall be marked as property of Geldin Laeris. Your right arms shall be branded with the marking of the Brotherhood. This will avoid any uncertainty when we are forced to hunt you down and kill you. The brand will not fade *nor* can it be removed. If you should fail to return here in three months, the brand will radiate a glow as blue as cobalt and remain so *indefinitely*: all mercenaries of the Brotherhood—and for that matter, *all mercenaries on Ryekarayn*—will know a bounty rests upon your head. I would say such unfortunate people have not survived more than a few weeks under the activated brand."

The thought of being even temporarily branded was revolting, but the alternative was far worse. "We will pay off the debt—the consequences of our failure mean nothing to us," Jikun replied coolly. There was no arrogance in his confidence—he had been a general for thrice as long as the archmage had even lived.

Darcarus nodded sidelong at him, blond locks freeing from the braid to cling to his perspiring throat.

The archmage unclasped his hands, but he did not reach for his quill. "To the second matter of the loan, then." He paused to tap the parchment on his left. "There is a list of missions of varying class levels. A quarter of all your profit on such ventures is given to the Brotherhood directly by your employers. Each class offers a range of payments for the work. I will provide you with a list of Class D and C missions, but given your lack of history with our organization, the highest I can offer you is a single Class B mission."

"Our debt is our own affair, is it not?" Darcarus balked. "We are only interested in what information you have on the necromancer known as Relstavum—and any bounty therein."

Navon grunted, but the male was wise enough to remain otherwise silent.

The archmage's weathered brow creased. "So you attempt to confront Saebellus even now." He glanced once at Navon and back to Darcarus, tutting softly. "The agent, Relstavum, is an Elite Class mercenary venture. Borin here handles those, but I *assure* you: the Brotherhood cannot and *will* not risk its investment by sending the likes of you four on such an excursion, regardless of your history with the man's employer. You are an investment, now. And your failure with an army under your command leaves us with little confidence that you can succeed against this force—single entity that he is."

Jikun slammed his palms against the sable stone, his stomach knotting at the rebuke. "Relstavum is the only reason we are here!" he declared furiously.

Mikael merely dipped his quill twice and scrawled illegibly across the page. "If Laeris wanted to dump his money down the sewer, he would give it to charity."

Jikun's eyes landed on the hulking human beside the archmage, whose nostrils flared with condescension. Borin grunted. "*If* you pay off your debt, elves, we can consider such an advancement of trust. But I'm sure I'll be sending someone to crush your throats in by the end of winter."

'Is that what happened to the last man?' Jikun's eyes flicked across the room in search of a visible sign, but whatever mess had been made had also been admirably swept away.

There was a soft creak as Darcarus settled beside him, his eyes dancing, his lips curled.

'What is he thinking...?' Jikun wondered. *'Why is he demanding nothing? This is why we are here...!'*

Navon could sense the tension in Darcarus' silence and interjected before Borin could devise a venomous retort. "Mikael, what about the war to quell the rebellion?"

Jikun bit his tongue.

Fortunately, Navon's request pacified the archmage, and the man ceased the rapid stroking of his eyebrow. He smacked his dried lips idly together. "It is the Class B mission I referred to previously: the king's war against Lord Barister in the Karkadose region."

Jikun let out a soft hiss of disapproval.

"...Though I suppose you elves are probably unfamiliar with *human* trivialities." The archmage grimaced and disdain was once more plain in his tone. "While we were already expecting a famine, the recent political upheaval of your elven nation has cost Ryekarayn a vast amount of trade and assistance. And it seems that your warlord-king has been putting his newly acquired royal treasury to use. Against us. Lord Barister, thane of the Karkadose region, has been paid a ludicrous sum by Relstavum—on behalf of Saebellus—to amass a force to overthrow the king. The country's dissenters are certainly lending him strength—bandits, mercenaries, soldiers, farmers... even the tribal dwarves of the Yinwel have joined him." He shook his head, as though that fact was more unbelievable when spoken aloud.

"The king is offering generous pay for every able-bodied man who volunteers to fight against the lord. Two thousand bronze a soldier. Between the four of you, the sum would amount—after our share—to nearly a third of your debt. For a few weeks and a single battle, that is no small achievement, *especially* in these times. Why, most farmers are leaping at the chance... Of course, they'll merely be fodder for Barister's front line." His eyes landed on Jikun's dirty sash. Though he added no comment, Jikun could feel the implication snaking across the distance. "After the battle, assuming you survive, and if you fill the next two months with Class C missions *and* you are moderately lucky, you *may* just be able to pay off your debt. Then, we can discuss Relstavum."

But Jikun knew that by then, action would be too late. He fixed his gaze upon Borin, and the sudden realization of Darcarus' countenance persuaded his muscles to ease.

Fortunately, they had other means by which to find Relstavum.

Navon stepped forward, swift to grasp what hope the archmage offered in an alternative course. “We will take these missions you speak of, Mikael. What do you require of us?”

The archmage finally plucked his quill from the ink. “We will brand you, provide your gear, assign your missions, and dispatch you. And may Lady Luck guide you—you will need her bounty. Welcome,” he announced, “to the Brotherhood.”

CHAPTER THIRTY-ONE

Since landing upon Ryekarayn—battered, beaten, but alive—Navon should have known that such a reckoning was coming. Such predictability should have been apparent to even the most ignorant of individuals:

The hero, traumatized and fallen, irrevocably seeks validation of his own self-worth, to make internal amends for all the wrongs he has committed.

Tiras had done so after the death of his family. As had Konavas after the murder of his brother. Yet somehow Navon had grown so blinded by his champion's success that he had ignored the weight of his failures.

But since the Pass, his mind was clearer. Now he could see.

Jikun was no different than those legends he so admired; he fit so perfectly into the role it was as though he had stepped from the pages of a tragic scroll himself. But Sel'ari had given the general the chance to redeem himself from his selfishness: by delivering him to a military path where he could make amends for the cowardice that had cost the lives of thousands.

Now she tested her pawn, waiting to see whether he would become the hero or remain the thief.

As Navon's eyes slid down the shafts of light to the tattoo branding his arm, a wave of unease assaulted him. Success was never won by impatience. Never by evil deeds. And yet, here he was, in bondage to the Brotherhood.

'Our servitude is solely to win the war,' he told himself. After all, who in history could he possibly mimic to dissuade Jikun from his decided course? No clear personalities remained to him but his own… And that felt unfamiliar. Unused.

Navon heaved a sigh and returned his gaze to the orderly interior of the armory. While Nordeep was despicable in most regards, this building was yet another example of the city's unquestionable success in its depravity. The interior was a blur of polished armor, cotton clothing, heavy steel weapons, and tough leather gear. After the second armory, those that followed had simply melded together into a muddled experience of expensive equipment and human stench. But this was the mercenary capital of Aersadore. Apparently, even Sevrigel's elven mercenaries were known to cross the channel to purchase from one of the city's *thirteen* armories, as he had been informed by every blacksmith along the way.

Navon was only so certain that they had arrived at the final shop by Eldaeus' distant calls of concern: "We really should not purchase anything here! Do not spend a single coin! Ohhhhh you are going to be *so* unlucky! Ah! I feel unlucky just standing in here!" A deafening clatter resounded throughout the small room. "AH! See? What did I tell you?! That suit of armor just launched itself at my innocently cherubical face!"

"Eldaeus, cease your childish behavior and go wait by Navon!" the Helven heard Jikun snap. "If you bother me one more time, I am going to test the bite of this sword on your exposed flesh."

There was an offended gasp strangled off by a mad cackle, as though the Faraven was uncertain which reaction to display. "That did not work out for you the last time!"

"You did *not* best me in that duel of sticks!"

"Eldaeus! Come here!" Navon barked sharply. "Leave the general in peace."

There was a flourish of brilliant color from around the side row of shelves and Eldaeus sidled to Navon's side. "He is impossible," he tsked.

"All great men are," Navon replied, pressing his fingers to his temple.

Jikun emerged from around a row of shelves a moment later, waving about a red, voluminous shirt. Darcarus was at his right hand. "Look at this damn waste of fabric," he was growling before his eyes had even located the pair. "It's a sack. Look at these massive *sleeves*. If I purchased this, it could double as a tent. How greatly would that diminish our debt?"

"I agree," Darcarus lamented, tossing a hand. "You need something far more befitting of your station. Surely they have silver or gold around here…"

"Are your theatrics quite finished?" Navon chastised, tapping his foot. The prince was shameless! "Darcarus, Jikun, I thought you said there is a task we *have* to accomplish this evening before we depart?—At this rate we will never leave Nordeep. Just pick a shirt—any shirt. Or I will pick one for you."

Jikun snagged Eldaeus from where he was attempting to slide away along the wall and held the blood-red shirt against the Faraven's torso. "If we are to be taken seriously, we have to dress with respect for ourselves," he barked militaristically, not deigning to spare Navon a glance. "You have the coin of a high-end mercenary and yet you chose to dress like a grunt."

Navon glanced down to survey the simplicity of his black cotton and russet leather. "We told the Brotherhood we would join the warfront. And until we actually *complete* the mission we *are* grunts! I am not going to pretend otherwise."

Jikun dropped the shirt and Darcarus kicked it beneath a nearby shelf.

Navon's lips tightened. "Our priority is survival. Dress accordingly, *General.* Don't make me deliver your ass again."

Jikun's shoulders rolled; his chest expanded. He said nothing and instead whirled sharply away into the nearest row of shelves, Darcarus whispering as they went.

Eldaeus exhaled in relief. "I thought surely he was going to pin that tunic to me with daggers. Hideous tunic. Would have clashed something awful with my pale complexion."

Navon could only manage a grimace as he sidled along the side of the wall in an attempt to get closer to the two whispering elves. "That is terrible," he replied absentmindedly.

Eldaeus rambled a few more forlorn comments before his lean, tattooed arm extended and dropped abruptly about Navon's shoulders, yanking him just out of sight of where Jikun and Darcarus were now pouring over a map. Despite their days on the road, somehow the Faraven still smelled cleanly like wet grass and smoky leather.

Navon glanced sidelong at the tattooed arm and shied away, trying to get the Darivalian back into view. "What are you—"

Eldaeus leaned in close. "Can I confide in you?"

Navon met the elf's bold stare with sarcasm. "This isn't a confession of affections, is it?"

"I fancy the ladies, Navon. You are quite homely by comparison."

Navon grimaced and shrugged the arm fully away. "I'm trying to eavesdrop, Eldaeus, and you are making it quite impossible!"

Eldaeus' eyes brightened and he dared speak yet again. "That is what I am trying to confide," he insisted, voice rising. "I heard Jikun and Darcarus mention Borin."

Navon ceased his attempt to creep along the shelves and rounded on the Faraven, cutting him off. "Jikun did not obtain any information about Relstavum, so we are not pursuing the necromancer. There is—"

"—You are blind."

Navon's jaw fell agape. The Faraven's lips had twisted down, his teeth tight. And then the next moment, the grimly determined demeanor had faded to be replaced by a maniacal grin.

Still, the insane elf was right. Navon had thought his consideration of the general unhazed, and yet he had just attempted to deny damning evidence of the male's intentions. His shoulders stiffened and he forced his mouth to form the words, "What did Jikun say about Borin?"

The male hopped forward once and his eyes widened into two wildly dancing emeralds. "He said that he wants answers. I heard them mention Borin. What answers is he looking for? How will he acquire them? Why are we lingering in Nordeep? Why are we in the thirteenth armory?"

Those were all questions Navon should have asked himself—well, except for the last one—and he cursed his hesitation to doubt the general. His eyes shifted—though his head was slow to follow—to survey where Jikun was now tapping his fingers impatiently on the long, weathered counter of the armory's proprietor. The cold, icy eyes were glaring occasionally at the plump shopkeeper, who was stroking the newly signed parchment of their agreement with the Brotherhood.

Inwardly, Navon sighed with resigned admiration. Even in Jikun's bruised and battered state, he still managed to maintain a proud and commanding posture. By Ramul, it was highly probable that the male could be naked as the day he dropped from his mother's womb and still command a room. Yet…

"Jikun is not the one we need to watch, Eldaeus," Navon muttered softly. His eyes fell to the tattoo along Darcarus' arm as the male leaned on the counter beside his general.

"This is quite the figure you're looking at acquiring," the shopkeeper ventured as Navon joined the pair at the counter. "You must be considerable warriors. What sort of work are you elves in that you should request such a hefty sum?"

Jikun lifted his breastplate and turned it over with a deliberately slow smile, as though he enjoyed the look of awe the merchant produced.

Navon's gaze met him steely, quickly subduing his friend's enjoyment. *'What sort of work are you elves in?'* he repeated the human's question to himself, finding he bore an uncertain answer. "Joining the king's men," he tested.

The human seemed unimpressed and Jikun laughed once—a hollow, dismissive laugh.

Navon let his mouth close obediently. Makados was right. Beneath his mask of heroes and legends, *he* was just another military dog.

* * *

Tension rippled through Jikun's muscles as he flattened his body against the coarse alley wall, his chiseled frame becoming but one more unobtrusive shadow in the passageway's stone. Borin, Laeris' sword, was even more massive in the open cobbled streets than he had been in the Brotherhood's poorly lit chambers. A god-damn half-giant of a man; a hulking silhouette in the moonlit darkness.

"I am so cold!" Eldaeus whispered, a little cloud of warm breath skirting the nape of Jikun's neck.

Jikun grimaced, the hair on the back of his neck rising. He did not turn around. *'Too close,'* he muttered to himself, and firmly pushed the Faraven back into the night. "Be silent, Eldaeus. He is almost here," he hissed.

The male clamped his mouth shut and obediently retreated as soundlessly as though he had never been.

Jikun drew his hood over his head and lifted the wooly fabric to mask the lower half of his face. Behind him, he heard a rustle as both elves made likewise to conceal their identities, their disguises clean and crisp from the day's fortune.

Darcarus leaned into the shade across from him, nodding his creaseless brow once in unspoken attention.

The human drew closer, his body growing to fill the empty street with his every step. His breath was audible, heavy and thick, as though his lungs strained to expand within his hulking chest. Another boot thudded across the frozen earth—to Jikun's tensed ears, it fell like a distant toll of thunder, heralding the coming of a treacherous storm.

Jikun hovered one hand above the hilt of his sword while he lifted his other slightly in the air. He felt the faint tingle of ice, dull and throbbing, as it flitted across his fingertips.

A whisper of fabric grazed his skin, and he was abruptly aware of Navon's presence at his side. The Helven's pale face was shrouded in shadows, hollow and sunken in the dim moonlight. "Jikun, turn away from this," he pleaded. "It is not too late—we can join the war and stop Saebellus! *Do not let your pride destroy you!*"

Darcarus seized Navon by the shoulder, shoving the coward back into the darkness.

"*Silence!*" Jikun hissed again. The brand marking him as *cattle* seared across his arm in a reminder of the degradation of his current path. *Pathetic.*

The time for speech was at an end. Borin had reached the alley.

Jikun's fingers spread above the barren earth and a shaft of ice erupted from beneath, raining dirt and stone as it slammed into Borin's side and hurled the half-giant into the alleyway. Despite the speed and force with which he had been thrown, the man emitted no more than a grunt as he careened into Eldaeus' ill-placed body. The elf's arms spiraled wildly to maintain his balance, and the mercenary sprawled into the dust.

There was the briefest stillness in the massive man's form, as though he had been dazed by the blow; then his enormous hand flew from the dirt and snared Eldaeus with an iron grip. Before the Faraven could cry out in alarm, his body was flung into the earth with a resounding thud, leaving the male still and silent.

"*Be still!*" Jikun snarled, sprinting forward. Cold water pulled from the soil and hardened, piercing the air to halt a hair's width from Borin's chest. Here, in the shadows of the alley, they were nigh-invisible daggers—poised to strike at the human's slightest movement.

As though grasping his situation for the first time, Borin's head jerked wildly up and around, absorbing the three elves surrounding him. His broad hand fell slowly to his side. "…What is this?" he growled as the silence settled. "An ambush?"

Navon darted to Eldaeus' side, pulling him free of the human's range. "Gods show mercy," he seethed. "*We should walk away from this!*"

Jikun stiffened and threw his shoulders back.

"Yes, this is an ambush," Darcarus interjected smoothly.

Jikun dislodged his captain's admonishment with a defiant strut forward; a crackle of ice glittered into being, forming a short barrier between the immense arms and Jikun's polished boots. "I want the information you hold concerning Relstavum. And if I should find it less than I desire…" The ice lengthened and caressed the weathered leather strapped across the giant's breast.

Borin's nostrils flared. With startling speed, his fist flew outward, shattering the ice as though it were merely glass. He snagged the hem of Jikun's cloak, tearing it from his tall, lean frame.

"*WHO?!*" Then Borin's eyes widened with incredulous recognition. "I know who you are," he spat, flinging the cloak aside as Jikun hastened to restore his dominance upon the man. "You're the greedy elves from earlier today—the war criminals who figured they'd poke Balior with a stick. Twenty thousand in debt, aren't you? *Malranus' fire could not have burned you more thoroughly.*" He laughed then, a mocking, hollow laugh, as though the bodily threat to him—gleaming a mere fraction away—was gone. "You failed to defeat Saebellus with an army and now you want to face his forces without one? Relstavum is the man's *beast.*" His laugh intensified, threatening to reach Emal'drathar to mock Jikun with the gods.

But Relstavum was not Saebellus' Beast.

He was far worse.

"Silence!" Jikun snarled, the spears of ice diving through the man's rich clothes to prod beneath his bronze-hued flesh. He snatched his cloak from the earth, aware of the soft, white rays that exposed his unique features. It was too late to withdraw—he was too deep along his path. "I won't ask kindly again, human," he growled.

Darcarus gave a sharp, encouraging nod. *Do not forget what brought us to this place,* it said. He leaned forward, flicking a piece of rubble casually from Borin's shaven crown. "Answer the question, Borin," he repeated. The smooth nail left a streak across the silver stubble.

"You're fucking mad," the man swore, and the ice crackled once in warning. "Mad—!" But Borin's howls subsided, his chest quavering as it attempted to retract from the perilous daggers. "Your warlord has created an army within a single man: Relstavum is soul harnessing, though I'm certain none of you god-damn fools has any idea what in the Nine Realms that is. But you *should* know who *Tiras* is; Relstavum has *Tiras'* necromantic writings from Vise and he can *use* them. You can't have the mission because it's beyond your fucking abilities. Laeris has invested too much money in you to throw you to Saebellus' dog! Right now, there isn't a mercenary company alive that can contend with his might—and the man is only growing more dangerous. *This* is a matter for kings and armies! By Malranus Almighty, Relstavum levels *god-damn cities.*"

Darcarus lurched forward without warning, slamming his foot against the slick ice bearing down upon the giant's shoulder. His hair had unraveled from its elegant braid, the strands swirling about his contorted lips. "And if this man continues to breathe, he will cost my brother his life and Aersadore her freedom. So *I'll ask you one more time, human!*"

The ice prickled as Jikun adjured, "Now, Borin!"

The half-giant bared his massive, grey teeth, etching a meager show of defiance across his insolent face. "You want to get yourself killed?—fine, *elf*," he jeered. "Relstavum was in Ironwatch two days ago, heading north. But you'd better vanish into the nearest god-damn mountains, because when I'm free of this, the Brotherhood will send mercenaries to hang you by your entrails whether or not you succeed. Who in the Brotherhood did you think you were questioning?" His voice was rising in fury and Jikun could almost feel the sound penetrating the nearby walls. "I'm not a god-damn commoner. I'm not a god-damn mercenary. I'm—"

'Laeris' Sword...' Jikun stilled, mind whirling at these new threats. His feet felt leaden, weighing him inescapably to the frosty earth. He had considered the torture. The necessity of using force to extract the withheld information. Even how the gargantuan man might retaliate with his own might. But Jikun had not reflected upon the *others* that existed beneath Borin's whip. How could he have forgotten that?

'You're slipping, Jikun.'

Borin's voice was mounting to a roar, now. "—Geldin Laeris' elite. I control every damn mercenary you could ever *think* to know. I have seen your face. *I know your kind.* If you think Relstavum is your enemy... You just opened the god-damn Gates. You won't get two cities from here before the Brotherhood will have blades in your back!"

Jikun's knees threatened to betray him and he clutched at the cloak in his pale hands.

"Even without our brand, your appearance is blood in the snow! If you think we won't find you before dawn, you—"

Navon interrupted with a vociferous cry. "Jikun, I advised you against this! *Soul-harnessing?!* Join the king's war—by Ramul, you are a soldier! Release him now and perhaps we can bart—"

Borin laughed, the sound a cavernous boom that rattled the icicles dangling from the nearby wooden eaves. "*Barter?* There is no bartering, elf! You will be *lucky* to die by Relstavum! The Brotherhood will hunt you down and we will *rip* retribution from your *bones until your screams deafen the god*—" His voice strangled off with a soft gurgle.

There was a suffocating silence. Navon uttered a choking gasp.

From the midst of the chunks of ice and earthen debris, the man's fist tightened once and then fell limp.

Jikun stared blankly at the daggers that had ruptured through the hulking human… that had pierced through his vital organs and crushed his burly throat.

Jikun's palm opened and the ice melted away, leaving the man sprawled across the earth.

With a casual hop, Darcarus freed himself from the proximity of the encroaching sludge. "…Well done. We have what we need."

"*Jikun, by Sel'ari, WHAT HAVE YOU DONE?!*" Navon finally managed to scream, his azure eyes wide with horror. He sprinted toward the corpse, as though there remained some hope that the human had endured. That he might yet be saved.

But Borin was dead.

His sacrifice was necessary.

This was Jikun's last chance to abolish Saebellus' tyranny before Ryekarayn was lost. And Sevrigel forever with her.

Navon leapt from the corpse, mouth twitching with unparalleled fury—an anger that Jikun had never before seen the Helven bear. It was untamed—not at all the careful vault of emotions Navon had filtered through before—and it was powerful enough to cause the male's body to shake like the Turmazel peaks before a potent avalanche. "YOU SHOULD NEVER HAVE BEEN IN THIS SITUATION. Jikun, by *Sel'ari*—!" He thrust a trembling finger toward Darcarus. "You should *never* have been looking for Relstavum. You should *never* have gone to the Brotherhood. You should *NEVER* have hunted Borin down! You have been under Darcarus' whip since the Makataj! We had our chance to do things right! We had our missions! Even after all of your mistakes, we still had a chance to pay off this *ludicrous* debt and regain our footing in the war, but *that* was not enough for you! You have to defy even the Brotherhood to PROVE your life is worth more than THOUSANDS. But your life, Jikun, *your life* will NEVER be worth thousands! It will NEVER be worth every soldier who fought and died for us! You fled Elarium because you were *afraid. And you have killed because you are desperate to believe otherwise*. You couldn't defeat Saebellus then, and you cannot defeat him now!"

The spread of blood had reached Jikun's boot, but he did not step away. Instead, he gazed down upon it, numb to its meaning and its cause. Darcarus had stepped forward, pressing a hand to Navon's breast and forcing him to retreat. Jikun welcomed the distance, finding his breath catching in his throat. "How can your opinion mean *anything* to me?" he whispered. "Aside from necromancy, Navon, you just repeat what you hear. You do what I say. You don't have enough sense of self to know what to do if we had to break the law of these lands in order to make amends." He looked up then, his face smoothed in a reflection of his resolve. "This is my chance to prove that what I do here, the lives I save here... the *difference* I make here, were all *necessary* to win the war!"

But Navon was not swayed by sense; his sharp chin tilted back as he crowed with indifference. "Relstavum is malevolence itself and you are closing that gap in character! At least I have enough self-awareness now to know that the male I admired died in those swamps along with everyone else! Even after Borin told you that Relstavum is *soul-harnessing*, you remain determined to hunt him! I don't care to hear your excuses, Jikun. You have gone *too far*. You have passed reason and justice. You are no better than the man you wish to hunt." Then he pivoted, lurching forward and flinging Darcarus into Jikun as he went.

"Where in Ramul are you going?!" Jikun demanded furiously, wrenching himself upright. "We have to leave for Ironwatch tonight!"

Navon reached the end of the alleyway before he whirled. "*YOU* are god-damn going," he spat in a warbling cry. "With Eldaeus so that someone can TRY to keep you safe from Darcarus' self-centered machinations! As I have *always* done, but to no god-damn appreciation! But I will not sacrifice what character I have left and the chances I have been given. I will not squander them in your desperate attempt to 'make things right' through further wrongs. I am not god-damn going!" He raised his cloak sharply. "See this?" He smacked his leather once. "And *this?!* I am going to pay off *YOUR* god-damn debt! *I* am going to defeat Saebellus. You can join me, or you can chase his god-damn human pawn across Aersadore until he slays you!"

Jikun felt Eldaeus slide up to his hip. "That is more god-damning than you do in a *week*," he breathed in awe.

Jikun stiffened, breast expanding in commanding assertion. Navon would not leave him. Navon had no direction without him. *He lived to serve*—he always had. He felt Darcarus slowly straighten on his left. Even his hatred for the prince could not drive Navon away. Jikun trailed a hand painfully to his side to remind his former captain of his condition. "Navon—!"

"Oh, and one, *tiny* detail for you to consider in your venture," Navon interrupted, waving his hand as he uttered a scourging laugh. "Soul-harnessing is the same rare magic that necromancers believe the Mad King used to slaughter the entire Farvian Realm. Every slain victim's soul remains *here* on the *mortal* plane; thus, the more souls the necromancer gathers, the stronger he becomes. Darcarus was kind enough to inform us that this man had slaughtered *how many* cities prior to Dahel? If Relstavum knows that lost necromancy, then he does not have to visit the Gates to acquire souls: he suffers no risk in being trapped within the Realms. And without risk, he has no limitations. Relstavum would truly be an *army* contained within a *single man*."

Jikun felt his skin blanch. "Navon, we will need—"

"After the war, I will wait in Sanae for a few days," Navon stated, challenging Jikun's resolve with utter apathy. "To see if you have experienced a change of heart. Then, General Jikun Taemrin, you shall have to *pray to the gods* to find me again."

Chapter Thirty-Two

Jerah awoke with a start, eyes snapping toward the faint light hovering at the entrance before him. What had stirred him?

His ears twitched under their strain.

…Nothing?

When only silence answered, Jerah decided it must be so. Slowly, the pounding of his heart faded and his body eased. He paused a moment to stretch and yawn before he surveyed his surroundings.

His home was tucked into the side of one of the rocks that touched the void. Mountains, they were called. He had learned this from the city where he went to kill each day. Inside his particular mountain there was nothing but a pool of water in the back and the stench of waste from the strange winged creatures hanging upside down above him. Jerah had let them stay *since* they had arrived first. They seemed somewhat accepting about sharing their hole. And, since none of them nibbled on him while he slept, they were far better company than the rats in his old cellar.

Jerah rose to his feet. Above him, the creatures hung still. Whatever had roused him moments before—if something had—was gone. He stepped around his pile of goods taken from the city and walked to the entrance of his home. He crouched down before the light, letting his vision adjust before he cast his gaze outward.

He had not climbed very high in the mountains—perhaps about as high as Kinraeus' ceiling had been tall. Narrow ledges had helped him make his way up, but his long, slightly hooked nails had been his most useful tool for the ascent. Despite his relatively low position, the scene around him was quite nice. The view was rock and tree extending all the way to the horizon. Occasionally, Jerah would see large and small winged creatures swoop and soar around and through the mountains' alleys before they vanished into small crevices in the rocks around him.

But now, his hole was eerily still. He rubbed the wounds on his chest nervously. Had the city's guard found him?

He withdrew a little in fear. He wanted nothing more than to stay in the mountains in peace!

A tiny creature with spindly, scaled legs was clinging to the opening of his cave. It popped its head out and looked about. Jerah inched a little closer. *'Is it safe, little freewing?'* he thought to the creature he had named. It offered a little toss of its head and then hopped out to the side of the mountain to stretch its wings. Another freewing confidently followed it.

"You're just overreacting, Jerah," he told himself. Emboldened, Jerah stepped out into the light, stretching his cramped wings. The torchlight in the blue void above warmed his bare chest and the ache of his muscles faded. He would have to get new clothes one day. He smiled, watching the little freewings take flight toward the ground below.

Jerah suddenly noted that the warmth had left his flesh. His instincts stirred, driving him swiftly back into the mountain.

It was not smoke that blocked the torch, but a winged creature far greater in size than the freewings. It swooped low in the void, dipping between the peaks of stone. Jerah had seen them before, but never so close. Elven in shape, and yet covered in the strange fur that likewise covered the little freewings. A woman in the city had worn some of the fluff sticking out of a stiff piece of clothing upon her head, and Jerah had overheard them called *feathers*. They protruded as great wings along the base of the creature's arms.

The creature landed on the face of the mountain not far away, screeching loudly. Talons curled into the stone from its long, scaled fingers and toes, while beady, yellow eyes flicked up and down the mountain's alleys. Its long tail thumped against the stone in a steady drumming.

Jerah pressed a hand to his naked chest. Like him, the creature wore no upper clothes. Instead, feathers crept from its scaled legs and invaded its torso.

Another screech, a chilling shadow, and a second of its kind landed sharply beside the first. This one was a bitch—as naked and round-breasted as elven and human women.

The two screeched in unison, regarding the mountain's floor with what Jerah thought were distinct expressions of frustration.

What were they looking for?

Jerah crouched down, hoping the darkness of his home sheltered him from their sight. Yet he didn't withdraw completely: curiosity held him near. What *were* they? Were they dangerous? Could he kill them? Could *they* kill him?

Then a distant screech echoed through the mountains and they let go. With a flap of their long wings, their bodies twisted behind the stone and they were gone.

Jerah straightened, slowly stepping back into the light. "What shall I call them?" he pondered as he gripped the side of the mountain. He began to move alongside it in the direction they had gone, tugged into pursuit by his thoughts. He could hear the distant echoes of screeches around him.

They were certainly quite loud. Loudwings? Hm. That *did* define them well. "Loudwings." His brow knit. What a ridiculous sounding name when spoken out loud. "Not clever, Jerah," he reprimanded himself.

He dug his talons into the stone as he stepped wide over a gap in the ledge. "Brownwings?" After all, most of them *did* have brown wings.

He slid further along the mountain, crossing the wide gaps and clambering up small ridges. He paused along a long, unbroken ledge to cock his head in the observance of a great shadow that swooped up the face of the mountain without a source.

Jerah shook his head and refocused upon his march along the ledge. He followed it for some time as he considered his options. "Largewings? Longwings? Darkwings?" He frowned. Maybe he should remove the wings entirely.

He stepped around a bend and into a wide canyon. His eyes were drawn instantly to the sea of shadows swarming across the distance. Several of the… *nameless*… creatures were flitting and sitting about a very large ledge that jutted out of the mountain.

But it was the darkness behind them that made Jerah's blood pump and his eyes dilate. Behind their frenzy rose a hole in the stone, far, far greater in size than Jerah's home. *Something* twisted and writhed inside the darkness.

Jerah hunkered down, watching as the creatures swept in and out of that mass, shrieking as they went, pointed faces jerking back and forth across the canyon.

He swiftly retreated into the safety of the narrow alleys. There were far too many for his liking.

Still, Jerah found them, at least for now, preferable to elves *and* humans.

They had never tried to kill him.

*

Jerah woke quite late the following day. It had been a long night. Not only had he made his kill, but he had found an entire building *filled* with clothes. A building filled with clothes! Now *that* was a good reward for pushing those useless, nameless creatures out of his mind.

With great eagerness, Jerah had bounded across the shop, gathering everything in sight.

Unfortunately, Jerah had given little thought to how he was going to haul his prizes up the mountain. He had been forced to spend a great many hours attempting to create a sack from one of the billowy black shirts. This had been somewhat successful and the losses during his climb were few.

Now rested from his adventure, Jerah carefully inspected his earnings.

What should he wear? There was such a variety! Master had always worn many different clothes and sometimes he had talked about buying his wife something nice to wear for the night. Should he likewise change once or even *twice* a day?

Jerah frowned. No. That seemed like too much work. He scratched the stone beside him thoughtfully. "This shall be my shirt," he decided, picking up a wide, green piece. He paused as it jingled softly.

He shook it again. The same sound came from within.

Promptly, Jerah scooted closer to the light of the void torch and looked toward the bottom of the shirt. How fascinating! Small metal rings protruded from beneath the fabric. He quickly peered into the shirt. And inside! In his hurried gatherings the night before, he had not noticed this!

Jerah beamed proudly. What a magnificent shirt! Wouldn't his master envy him!

He smiled to himself as he pulled it on. Fortunately, humans were much fatter than their elven counterparts. It was certainly too large for an elf, but Jerah found it a little tight; it pinched a bit on his skin. Still, it was such a magnificent shirt that Jerah was certain he could stand the mild discomfort.

He looked toward the other clothes piled in a careful heap. "Ah… those… mercenaries wore something like this…" he spoke softly, picking up a large piece of short leather. He pulled his arms through and wiggled it down over his head. Only, that was as far as it would go.

"Doesn't fit! Doesn't fit!" Jerah grunted as he fell backward in his struggle to escape. After he had finally managed to toss it aside, he was far more careful about selecting a larger piece.

What he found only covered the upper portion of his torso, but Jerah gave it a sharp and satisfied prod with his nail. Perhaps it would help protect him from more shafts of wood in his heart.

He shivered at the thought.

Then a loud screech jolted his body rigid. He peered out into the evening light. Already the cycle of the bright torch had faded. How fast it sometimes seemed to move—and always when he was enjoying himself!

Jerah grudgingly dropped his treasures and scurried for the city.

*

As Jerah twisted his way along the mountain floor in his return for home, he found himself attempting to imitate one of the melodious objects he had seen a man playing. The human had been seated before a window, strumming away, and Jerah thought it was a nice and happy sound escorting him from his successful kill.

How did the object make such a sound without a mouth?

He strained his voice to imitate its pitches. Damn, it was so difficult!

He put a claw into the mountainside and ceased his poor attempts at mimicry. He had noticed something dark on the ground beside him.

'What is that…?'

He reached down and picked up a lump of fur. *The feathers the nameless had.* He turned it slowly in his hand, excitement building in his gut as his fingers ran over the stiff, weightless fluff—it was nothing like rat fur!

He raised it to his face and sniffed. And it was covered in blood!

Jerah looked around himself quickly.

Why, there was more of it! He excitedly picked up another few pieces, moving away from the mountainside to follow the slowly growing trail. Had one of the nameless been killed? It would relieve him to know that was possible. He picked up another patch and dropped it into the pile wobbling in the crook of his large arm.

The trail continued for some time, taking Jerah quite a distance off his usual path and into a place within the mountains where he had not been before. His collection was growing quite large!

…Though he hadn't figured out what he was going to do with the feathers once he had collected all of them.

Finally, the source of the wondrous collection became visible and Jerah's attention snapped up to the mountain sides, cautiously alert. For the first time, he realized that he was far from his home and covered in bloody feathers.

Still, Jerah took a step forward. Up ahead, the body of the creature was easy to distinguish. Jerah could see the side of it, sprawled out in the dirt, surrounded by more blood and more feathers.

He sniffed the air. It smelled oddly smoky, but he could detect nothing else unusual.

'Is it dead?' he wondered warily, inching closer. Even if it wasn't dead, Jerah figured it could hardly be a threat in its tattered condition. He slipped a little closer and stopped beside it.

With an intake of breath, he crouched down to examine his find.

"What was it?" he breathed aloud, head cocked. It wasn't an elf or a human or a nameless… and yet it embodied much of their qualities. The first thing he noticed was that it was naked. He had never seen anything naked so clearly before. Well, except, of course, for himself. This creature was much like him in body—with all the arms and legs and things in-between.

'Is this what elves look like naked?' he wondered, raising his brow. It had pointed ears like the elves. And no talons or scaled feet.

But then he noted its wounds. Its dark-skinned body was covered in them—scratches and small holes and black marks. But many more were oddly red and bubbly.

Jerah cocked his head to the other side, wondering what made such wounds and if it was what happened to elves or humans when they did not immediately die. Still, if it was healing, it wasn't doing so very quickly… Far, far slower than Jerah.

Strange.

And what did the face look like? He leaned forward eagerly, but from his position he could only see the side of the creature's body. He scooted his feet through the dirt, slowly circling around its body, until he came to face the front of the creature.

And grimaced. What was wrong with it?

He poked its face with a long talon. The hair was black and orange and red, vivid as the color of elven clothes, and cut in an oddly jagged fashion. The face was covered in the red bubbliness of the rest of the body where gashes had once been. The tongue lolled slightly to the side where several of its sharp, pointed teeth were missing. It had no lips, the skin was torn, and a gaping hole resided where a nose should be. The bone of its chin was exposed and stained red.

Jerah looked down, following the little trail of blood leading from its mouth. He gasped in delight. A tooth! He picked it up and placed it in his pocket.

Oh. Right. He had been distracted again. Looking back at the body, Jerah reached out and prodded the exposed bone once.

The creature gave a slight jerk.

With a shout, Jerah tumbled back through a cloud of feathers, taloned fingers flexing in preparation. But the creature did not move again.

Jerah righted himself. "Are you alive?" he asked, and daringly poked it in the chest.

It did not move.

Jerah brushed the feathers from his head and looked around the mountain alley. Was this what the other nameless were looking for…? They had seemed so desperate. So angry…

A soft thud caused Jerah to sit up straighter, his eyes wide. The heartbeat of the creature!

It *was* alive. Alive!

…What should he do? He stared at it, jaw slacked, head cocked.

Then slowly, he put a hand to the place of his own wounds—now but little red dots. He felt a heaviness on his chest; it made it difficult to breathe. His chest *hurt* for the creature.

Perhaps… perhaps this thing was like him. Perhaps something *had* hunted it. Perhaps it had almost died. Perhaps it had barely gotten away.

Perhaps… it needed him.

The scattered feathers were forgotten. Jerah reached down, picked the creature up, and pulled it close. "I will take you to my home," he told it in the chance that it could hear him. "You will be safe there."

With the creature slung over his shoulder, the path back up the mountain was very difficult for Jerah. The creature's weight, though little, was enough to cause pain in Jerah's nails. By the time he reached the top, his entire body groaned in rebellion.

Jerah clambered into the hole and laid the creature down gently at the pool in the back. Then he chose a shirt and dipped it into the water to slowly wipe the dirt and blood from the creature's dark skin. Yet no matter how intensely Jerah scrubbed, the strange, red, bubbly flesh remained. He ignored it and moved down the body, making sure to scrub every place on the creature until it was as clean as any elf Jerah had ever seen.

Lastly, Jerah reached the fingernails—his least favorite part. He raised the creature's hand and paused. He leaned forward and sniffed. *'What?'* His lips parted dumbly, his eyes squinting. Its own flesh and blood were embedded beneath each of its nails.

'But why?' Jerah could not think of a time he had ever had his own flesh and blood on his talons.

Were its wounds… self-inflicted?

Jerah lowered the hand. "Well… it does not matter," he told himself firmly. The creature was still in need of his care. He diligently cleaned the creature's nails with the cloth, as he had once done to his own talons in the cellar of his master so very many nights ago.

After he had cleaned them, he reached over for his next favorite shirt and pants and pulled them onto the naked body. With the remaining treasure of clothes, Jerah lined a section of the stone floor, away from his hanging winged companions, and then laid the new creature upon it.

With a sigh and a tired groan, Jerah sank to the earth. Exhaustion buffeted him. When was it? He looked out of the cave, catching the faintest hint of light from the rising of the day torch. So late… He yawned, leaning against the wall of the cave with a grunt. He would just close his eyes for a minute…

'Have to... keep a... watch... on... it......'

*

Palink.

In the pool at the back of Jerah's home, the slow drip of water sounded with a soft tink, just like in his old cell. He raised his head, stretching and yawning and breathing in the fresh scent left by the damp world outside. The void must have leaked again.

He leaned forward with a weary grunt.

"Oh!" He had almost forgotten about the furless creature! He quickly looked over, relieved to find that it had not moved from where he had laid it the night before. But it was shaking slightly.

Jerah's chest tightened and he scooted forward. "Aw, you are cold," he noted, looking for more clothes. Hm. He had used them all for it to lie on. "I will have to get you some more." He stood, peering out of his hole. *'But if I leave it here, the nameless might find it... Maybe they will eat it?'* He looked back at the creature.

Damn it! What to do?

Jerah paced along the length of his home, considering his options. He *was* going to have to kill, so the creature would have to be left alone. The nameless seemed sparse at night, so he would wait until dark to leave. Then perhaps the creature would be safe.

He felt quite proud at his reached conclusion.

Yet, worry followed him out to the city and back, the creature ever present on his mind. Was it still sleeping? Was it too cold? Had the nameless found it?

But when he returned, he found it just as he had left it.

Jerah smiled, dropping the pile of clothes beside the creature. Then he laid piece by piece across its body in a thick and careful pattern.

'I wonder if it is hungry...' Jerah's brow knit. *'At least thirsty?'* He pooled some water into one hand and carried it to the creature. He sat it up and put its face against the pool.

"That doesn't work," he concluded after a moment. He raised the face out of his hand and laid it back down. It was still breathing deep in sleep, so Jerah drank the water and sat back to watch.

Suddenly, its thin body jerked and with a brief shudder, its eyelids peeled wide.

Jerah lurched forward eagerly, wondering what color eyes it would have.

Yellow! It had yellow eyes just like his own!

Jerah opened his mouth to exclaim his delight, and stopped as its gaze shifted toward him.

It gave a venomous hiss.

"You are safe here," he tried to reassure it.

It responded with a growl.

"Are you hungry?" He questioned once again in the human tongue.

When it merely bared its teeth, Jerah attempted to pacify it. He reached over and picked up a piece of meat. It watched Jerah silently for a moment as he moved it onto the floor in front of him. He cut off a small piece with his talon. "Here," he offered.

It responded with a sudden, ear-splitting screech that trailed off into a guttural growl.

Jerah dropped the piece and leaned away. "My ears hurt when you do that," he rebuked.

It let out a second, ear-splitting screech.

With ears ringing, Jerah angrily bared his fangs, raising his shoulders up to demonstrate his massive form. The snarl that left his lips shook free the loose drops hanging above the pool.

The creature's eyes widened in fear and it shrank away. Its intense stare locked onto Jerah's leg, as though willing him to collapse.

There was a sudden tingle and Jerah looked down.

He choked out a gasp. Fire!

Jerah quickly put his hand over the little flame, snuffing it out. When he looked back to the creature, it had subsided once more into unconsciousness.

Jerah slowly removed his hand, revealing the stain of a little scorch mark upon his pants leg.

"What, Master, was *that?*"

CHAPTER THIRTY-THREE

"I explicitly stated a *red* swatch, Tilarus—the color that we strive with great airs to maintain so staunchly vibrant. The color of the ancient royal line. The hue of our blood. The champion of the military front. And yet you managed to fail *utterly*. You are lucky I found you at all," Sellemar criticized as he watched the elf perch himself atop a barrel.

Tilarus scoffed, his pale green eyes creasing at the corners. Noctem's moon was dim, even for a winter's eve, and his expression was almost lost in the darkness of the alleyway. Still, Sellemar could see him wave a hand facetiously. "Oh, just admit that this time I hid it quite effectively and even *you* could not find it. It is certainly red." He stiffened his shoulders beneath his thick, cotton tunic.

Sellemar waved the swatch in the chilly air to diffuse the stench of fish that breezed in intrusively from the docks. "How can you argue that this is red? *This* is pink. The swatch is most *certainly* the pinkest fabric I have ever had the misfortune of laying my eyes upon."

"No, definitely red."

"Now you are just being stubborn."

"They were out."

Sellemar regarded him flatly. "Material Possessions was out of red fabric."

"Yes."

"And Fabric Tales? Mages and Bolts? That one at the corner of Silengar and Nuvae?"

Tilarus raised a hand. "There is a shop at Silengar and Nuvae?"

"Yes," Sellemar sighed. "With the wooden sign of that veritable *mountain* of fabric."

Tilarus regarded him blankly.

"On a golden platter?"

"*Oh!* You know I always thought it was a hat... Wide brim... a little pointy?"

"...Do you know what the color *red* looks like, at least?"

Tilarus snatched the swatch from him and stuffed it deep into his pocket. "We should just do away with pictures entirely. It isn't as though we are on Ryekarayn—I dare say every elf has been taught to read for at least ten or twenty millennia." He sniffed, wiping his nose across the back of his hand. It had grown several shades more scarlet than his swatch. "*Anyway*," the male stated, gesturing to the wall as though offering Sellemar a fine place upon which to lean his back. "Why could we not simply meet at the headquarters?"

Sellemar's lips drew tight, remembering the pretty face of the young male Sel'ven he had observed lingering about the place. "No... This is the second time I have seen one of Saebellus' lieutenants hovering near me this week, and I am fairly certain he is a mage—one moment he is lurking in some nearby flowerbed, and the next, he has vanished."

Tilarus bit his lip. "Have care, Sellemar. A male like that could equally appear behind you and put a knife in your back."

Sellemar ignored the comment. "For now, I am avoiding that area... They may hold the temple suspect. If we lose the Resistance before the rebellion has sparked, there will be no source with which to set the tyrants aflame."

Tilarus shrugged. "We are so close to rebellion... do you honestly believe Saebellus can still prevent his fall?"

"We have weakened his army and kindled distrust, but Saebellus is far from defeated. Once we reveal the genocide to the people, I will strip Cahsari and lay the council's crimes bare for all to see. When the people truly comprehend what their complacency has wrought, they will seek a new leader. We must be present until Hadoream's forces arrive. When all this has come to pass, *then* Saebellus will fall."

"Well, this is why you are the leader. You make the plan sound *easy*," Tilarus snorted. Then he paused, letting the corners of his lips dance. "You mentioned nothing of revealing Saebellus' plans... Nothing of the Nemorium. And I notice that you have quite a number of scratches. I do hope the two are related. Another exciting tale?"

Sellemar slipped his hands casually beneath his cloak. *The Nemorium.* That was the subject he was most fervently attempting to banish from his mind. Tilarus had warned him the effects would begin thirty days after binding... and tomorrow would mark the thirtieth.

Damn the cursed bond he was soon to endure! "Oh, the scratches are nothing," he coughed faintly. "Just a cat."

"...A *cat?*"

Sellemar glared.

"I'm just trying to say," Tilarus began, throwing his hands up in defense, "that the response was not nearly as glorious as I expected." When Sellemar's scowl grew withering, he choked back a barely disguised laugh; it departed his nose as a gauche snort. "Gods, why would you get a cat? Dabbling in Ulasum's Tooth, are we?"

Sellemar remained stoically unamused.

"You never did get along with Sorsa *or* Pexan."

Sellemar scoffed. "That is because *your* cats were despicable creatures."

The creases at the corners of Tilarus' eyes faded. "And on the contrary, *your* cat seems delightful."

Sellemar's hands dove deeper into his soft, cotton pockets. The Nemorium was beginning to sound like an inviting topic. "Have you any news?"

"About my wife?" Tilarus leapt to the topic, though he had to be aware that it was *not* the information to which Sellemar had been referring. "She is doing magnificently. Radiating like the sun. Healthy as a goddess. Sel'ari bless her!"

"...And here on *Sevrigel?*"

With a huff, Tilarus' face grew grim and he anxiously adjusted the cuffs of his sleeves before speaking, as though there was some way they could have fallen out of order. "I have word from Sairel. Ilsevel and Saebellus are making fairly severe threats upon the Sel'varian Realm for Hadoream's presence in the—"

"This is unbelievable."

Sellemar blinked. "What?"

Tilarus paused, releasing hold of his wrist. "I said that Ilsevel and Saebellus are making fairly severe—"

"Don't you dare try to pacify me now!"

Sellemar closed his eyes tightly. A drumming was resonating within the recesses of his mind. It was intensifying, rising to consume the world around him. What...?!

"Sellemar?"

"Saebellus..."

A high-pitched whining swallowed his words. Darkness engulfed him.

"Sellemar, are you alr—"

"SAEBELLUS!"

Sellemar felt himself stiffen, his body drawing away from where his hands had pressed against the cold, weathered wood of the ancient table before him.

The pounding ceased. The whining dimmed.

The darkness had abated and he found himself in the vast, stone hall of Elvorium's palace. A single chandelier swayed as though whirling from a storm, the little flames of its score of candles flickering in the wind it created for itself. Unnatural shadows scraped and clawed their way up the wall, illuminated as light landed directly upon them.

Saebellus stood before him, dressed in silk so black that even his hair seemed muted beside it. No light reflected off the rigid composure of his body; instead, it scattered about him as though fearful of his mere presence. His long, pale face had contorted in rage, his eyes a challenging void to the other emotions stirring in the room.

Ilsevel shifted in her chair against the far wall, a glass of wine gripped so firmly in her tiny hand that the stem threatened to snap beneath her force.

Vale finished straightening from the table, his eyes flicking once over the little pawns scattered across the map of Sevrigel. *'Burn it all,'* he thought with a scowl, running a hand down his scarlet tunic. He cleared his throat, eyes rising once more to Saebellus. "Hadoream is nothing. Sairel would never be so stupid as to allow—"

Saebellus whirled, his teeth baring like the fangs of a serpent, ready to strike at Vale's attempt to pacify him once again. "No? NO? *How do you know this*, Vale?! Has the goddess granted you some vision of the future?! DO share your wisdom!"

Vale pursed his lips, eyes shifting toward the door of the chamber hall. *Gods* did he wish he had gone to scout in Adonis' stead and sent *him* to deal with Saebellus' rage today.

"LOOK AT ME, VALE!"

The shadows along the wall rose sharply and flickered like talons above the room, veering haphazardly each time the chandelier light scurried across their forms.

Vale allowed his gaze to meet Saebellus'. "Sairel has... fifty thousand civilians? How many soldiers, in that lot? To be sure, the Sel'varian Stronghold at their west may bend beneath his demands to supply him troops, but with Relstavum creating every kind of threat outside their doors, neither Sairel nor the Stronghold can possibly spare the soldiers without fear of being laid utterly to waste. And *even if he could*, at best he could acquire thirty-five thousand: and that *includes* the arming of some civilians. Twenty thousand is all—"

Saebellus roared in frustration, and his hand slammed against the underside of the large wooden table. As though it were made of straw, it flipped high into the air, sending the pawns scattering across the marble floor. A thunderous echo resonated through the chamber as it smashed into the tiles at the captain's feet. "Twenty thousand is *all?* Is *ALL*, VALE?! I was the unchallenged king of this land for mere DAYS before Kinraeus attempted to usurp my power through the human king. No sooner was he killed than some rebels crippled my attempts to recover my military force. And now, with the threat of a rebellion at our gates, the *True Bloods* have forced their way back onto this continent! My grip on this throne is weakening every *DAY* Hadoream remains alive! *And you attempt to pacify me with*, 'Should you kill his brother, Sairel only has twenty thousand to send to war!' KILL Hadoream? I CAN'T EVEN FIND HADOREAM!"

Vale swallowed audibly. He knew why. Adonis' words echoed in his mind. *'You are betraying Saebel...'* He could see that even Ilsevel had pressed her body away, eyes wide in fear as she regarded the king.

Saebellus' temper...

Still, Darcarus deserved a chance to save Hadoream. Vale owed him that much. He raised his chin, steadying his voice as he met the lifeless gaze of his general. "If you choose not to kill Hadoream—and merely imprison him instead—the rebellion will vanish and you will have nothing to fear from Sairel. *Even if* you choose to kill the little prince, I doubt Sairel would attack the continent. What good would it do if his brother is already dead? Sairel and Darcarus will be the last of their line: with Darcarus practically disowned, if Sairel were to lose the war, the True Bloods would be at an end. Sairel would not risk their family line to wage war for his dead brother's sake."

Saebel's face remained fixed in anger, but he raised his hand to the bridge of his nose and pinched. "Mm," was the only vague response he offered.

Vale grimaced, gaze shifting toward the bitch-queen.

She scowled at his obviously hostile thoughts. "Saebellus," she began softly, fully aware of how daring it was to attempt to change the topic. "Since we have Vale here, perhaps we can discuss that matter I mentioned to you again the other night. Your captain came into the Fel'ruan and humiliated me before the El'adorium. *Simply* because I *agreed* with your request to leave Alvena in his care. I believe killing her would settle this matter more effectively and I—"

Saebel's hand dropped from his face and Ilsevel choked back her words. "*Humiliated you? Alvena?* Do you think *I GIVE A DAMN?!* Alvena is a little servant girl who saw you murder Hairem: a deed long past and THE LEAST OF OUR PROBLEMS. *Hadoream, who is still alive*, is in the south, stirring my kingdom against me. And *ALL YOU CAN THINK ABOUT IS THAT LITTLE CUNT!*" The ancient table burst into black flames, devouring the wood with insatiable lust. "*SO HELP ME—!*"

"Saebel, your map," Vale swiftly interjected. "Ilsevel was just attempting to pacify you. Foolishly, but she meant no harm." His gaze shifted to her and his eyes narrowed. *'You owe me,'* it read with a hidden sneer.

The flames were extinguished in a puff of thick smoke. As Ilsevel let out a breath, her glass abruptly slipped from her fingers, shattering across the briefly silent room like a wail in a catacomb.

Saebellus started, face softening faintly as though his sense of self had been reestablished through his rage. He turned and focused on the bitch-queen, waiting for her to speak.

Ilsevel's hands trembled slightly as she placed them into her lap and stifled her uneven voice. "Even if a rebellion takes hold here, they shall crumple without a king. I will send my best male to find Hadoream, my love."

Saebellus remained still, but his tone was dangerous in its query. "And who is that?"

Ilsevel drew herself up, elevating her chin as though she was fully aware of Vale's amused regard. Clearly, she did not want to appear frightened before him. But they were all terrified of Saebellus. Gods, the male was a maniac in his rage.

Stupid bitch had nearly pushed him over the edge.

"Well?" Saebellus demanded, angling his body fully toward her. "Who?"

Ilsevel's eyes darted to the shadows behind the king and Vale followed her gaze.

'No, not—'

"Ra'vonis," she exhaled deeply.

Saebellus remained unnaturally still, his words the only suggestion of his displeasure in her response. "That *murderer?*"

Vale stifled a snicker of mutual contempt. "I always thought Ra'vonis was *pathetic*."

The shadows where Ilsevel's gaze had fallen altered abruptly and a figure seemed to materialize from the darkness. His weather-beaten face was twisted, his cracked lips curled; his eyebrows contorted to consume his grey-rimmed eyes. But Vale could still glimpse them, blue-black and as empty as Saebellus'. They swept up Vale's slack torso and pierced into his dumbstruck gape. "Call me pathetic again, little damsel," a low growl emerged.

Vale's hand darted to his hilt on instinct. His gut churned. "Were you in here the whole fucking time?"

"Why not? You're Saebellus' dog. I'm Ilsevel's." The man raised a scarred hand to flick a lock of long, black hair from his broad shoulders.

Vale watched the strand of hair fall beside the half-elf's crooked nose. Vale had helped improve its garish state with a swift punch several months ago, but it still dipped unpleasantly toward the silver stubble of his wide, flat chin. He drew himself up; he would *not* look weak before Saebellus.

Ra'vonis calmly stepped forward, aware that the room had gone silent.

"I said," Vale began evenly, casually running his finger down his very straight, decidedly more attractive nose, "that from the moment you butchered the captains, I knew that you were *pathetic*."

Ra'vonis promptly darted forward and Vale had little time to gather that the man had even moved.

Gods was he fast!

Ra'vonis caught Vale's wrist where it lay at his hilt, twisting it fluidly behind the elf's back. He swept a blade from his thick belt and pressed it against Vale's groin. "I'd threaten your throat or your gut, but we all know what you value most." He gave an abrupt shove to release the captain, pushing him headfirst into the stone wall. "Pick your battles, little damsel."

Vale gripped an old tapestry for balance, his lips twitching into a snarl. "*Damn you!*" He drew his blade as he pivoted, parrying the thrust of Ra'vonis' waiting dagger, and threw his weight into the man's chest.

Ra'vonis' footing faltered, causing him to stumble and drop to a knee. Even as he fell, his fat calf swept beneath Vale's legs, toppling him into the smoldering table.

"Fuck!" Vale swore, and before he could free himself from the debris, Ra'vonis scrambled forward and threw his repulsive body down upon him. "Get your ugly ass off of me, you god-damn, bitch-queen pandering coward," Vale swore between grunts as he caught Ra'vonis' greasy hair and forced himself on top. He snapped the man's head back and, where he usually enjoyed the pain and gasp of the body beneath him, Ra'vonis was trash even *he* would not fuck. He slammed his fist into Ra'vonis' stubbled throat and the man coughed and gagged.

There was a flash of steel and Vale caught too late the sight of Ra'vonis' blade piercing for his groin…!

An explosion of fire tore between them and Vale let out a cry as the flames licked his hands and face. Ra'vonis scrambled away, stifling his own agony beneath a muted whimper.

But his general was far from through with them. Vale felt the pain even before the pale hand clutched his throat. It dug its fingers around his trachea and crushed down until he could not breathe. He saw the other hand dart out and catch Ra'vonis by the back of his head, slamming his face into the marble floor with the same force previously exerted upon the table.

"Sellemar?! Breathe!"

Saebellus' voice came to them in a dangerous whisper through the pain. "If I have to intervene again, *I will kill you both*."

The fingers around his neck released and Vale let out a choking gasp for air. Orbs of discolored light flickered before his eyes as he attempted to focus on the surrounding room.

"Sellemar!"

Saebellus continued the previous conversation as though the fight between the two soldiers had not interrupted him. He turned his back to the scrambling heaps. "I will grant you the privilege of assembling a mission, my love."

'…Didn't want to look weak… Damn it!'

Clarity reformed on Ilsevel's triumphant face. "I assure you, you will not be disappointed. We will turn the tides of this fight back upon the rebellion—*they* will take responsibility for Hadoream's death."

"SELLEMAR!"

Sellemar gasped, a white marble wall appearing unexpectedly before his eyes.

"By Sel'ari, my lord. Was that the Nemorium? You lost consciousness… You seemed to be struggling to breathe!"

Sellemar was suddenly aware that he was no longer upright. Strong arms were wrapped around his torso, supporting him in a half-sitting position. Tilarus was crouched over his chest, the grey of his winter cloak shielding him from any passerby who might peer down the alley.

A tumult of emotions assaulted him, frustration at the forefront. *Gods* it was bad enough to appear weak before Saebellus—now he appeared weak before Tilarus as well! He wanted to wrench Tilarus off of him and shove him into the alley wall. He wanted to fuck him—to subdue Tilarus until the male was *begging* for his own release and the furthest thing from his mind was that he was *weak*.

"You didn't tell me you were successful!"

Tilarus' wide, concerned eyes swam into his vision. Sellemar shuddered, revulsion beating back his conflicting emotions, rushing clarity past the fog of the Nemorium's grasp.

This was Tilarus. His companion.

He emitted a long exhale. "I was not successful." He straightened and Tilarus' support fell away.

"You weren't? What do you mean? Whose thoughts then were you sharing?"

Sellemar's cheeks grew hot. "Captain Vale's."

Tilarus paused, as though unsure that he had heard correctly. "Captain… Vale's?"

"Save your amusement for another day," Sellemar muttered gruffly. "This is the first time I have experienced his decrepit mind. He was in a meeting with Saebellus and Ilsevel. They agreed that Hadoream's presence is fomenting rebellion, but they cannot locate Hadoream…" Tilarus chuckled, but Sellemar was not so ready to share in his amusement. "Vale *knows*," he added grimly. "…And yet Saebellus does not."

Tilarus' grin died. "How and *why?*"

Sellemar slowly rubbed his brow. "Out of loyalty, it seems, to *Darcarus*…"

Tilarus could only stare in an utter lack of comprehension.

"But for now," Sellemar continued, "they are searching for the young prince aged past the palace paintings. They were discussing what to do with him when found—the consequences of killing or imprisoning him." He abruptly recalled the black-haired half-elf with the broken nose and the smug sneer. "The last I grasped was that they intend to *kill* him and frame the Resistance."

Tilarus started. "*Kill* Hadoream?! Have they no fear of Sairel?!"

"They fear Sevrigel's people more." Sellemar's brow creased deeply. "And… Alvena…"

"What?"

Sellemar shook his head as he struggled to grasp what the enemy had said. "Alvena… that little girl who witnessed Hairem's murder… They have her…" He gritted his teeth. "She is just an inexperienced child… I should not have expected her to be capable of reaching the coast! Now I have her to be responsible for yet again."

"Sellemar, what in Emal'drathar are you rambling about? Forget the servant girl. Leave her to me—I will ensure her safety. You have *far* more pressing matters at hand!"

Sellemar's head snapped up curtly. Tilarus was right. "We need to expedite the people's mistrust. It is time to reveal the extent of the genocide… How does the Resistance feel about digging up the dead?"

CHAPTER THIRTY-FOUR

The skewered, broken body of Borin was seared into Navon's mind's eye—stiff and bloody, the belly gorged as though sheared by the tusks of a wild boar.

Disbelief. Shock. Horror. They were all understatements to the abhorrence Navon experienced. His *own* genuine, unmasked disgust. All their little group had known of Borin's morality were conjectures based on his membership to the Brotherhood. And Sel'ari would *never* justify killing a man on *conjectures*.

But Darcarus and Jikun… *Damn* Darcarus! *Damn* Jikun! The Darivalian had been so desperate to ignore his guilt… to believe he had chosen rightly at Elarium… to believe he was *necessary* to the downfall of Saebellus, that killing Borin had been *justified!*

Saebellus had wholly and truly won—he had not only stolen the lives of the soldiers Navon had loved, but now the soul of his general as well.

'I should have intervened before we even questioned Borin. I knew Darcarus was a drake! And yet I was too afraid that Jikun would rebuke *me! Coward! The fault is mine as well.'* Any given legend from his tales would have done so.

But without their guidance, he was a lost fool.

He glanced once, shamefully, over his shoulder, but the alleyway was long since lost behind Nordeep's wall. He sat atop his mount and watched the emptiness of the city's gates, half-hoping that Jikun would emerge from within their clutches and give him reason to second guess his decision.

Why could not his general have been driven with some mad desire to make amends or serve a god or even fling himself into the alcohol-ridden despairs of guilt his anxiety attacks surely offered?

But his gaze fell. *No*. Instead, the role Jikun asked of him had passed the realms of the heroes in his tomes… *twisted* to the design of thieves. Darcarus' hold and Jikun's desolation were an inseparable pair.

And he could no longer follow Jikun's path. Now… now the goddess was demanding he weave a story of his own. Not as the champions he tried to emulate or the hero he wanted to be.

'As who…?' he wondered. But the loss of his heroic foundations made the answer clear. As the person he was. *'As Navon.'*

Navon's life outside books and scrolls had limitations. His attempts to ignore this had already cost him dearly; he could not afford to be reckless with his soul again. The military offensive was his best opportunity to deal a blow against Saebellus.

The role was not glorious, it was not legendary, but it was necessary. It would be a single ripple of change, but what more could one pebble do against the sea? His path was the first time in a century—since he had last been in these lands—that he was alone. That no one needed him. No one needed his patience, his insight, his encouragement… And now, the time had come for Navon to infuse his own self with the lessons he had once imitated for Jikun's sake.

The call of necromancy… to explore his *own* capabilities, had never been clearer.

The journey north was long and bitter, and it was only through Jikun's headstrong act that he had all the necessary gear to survive the winter trek. What extra coin he had saved through his frugal purchases was spent on the care of his horse. Navon was left to consume stale rations.

The road, if it could be called such a thing, was a winding path of mounds of snow and chiseled ice, glowing by the moonlight and blinding in the sun. It was empty until he arrived within a two day ride from the army's encampment. There, a drivel of poorly armed farmers from regions all over Ryekarayn began to trickle in toward the valley of green tents.

'Fodder for the front lines,' he recalled the archmage's words. The king would be more than willing to accept the swords of the least of these men, but how many would die so that a well-armed soldier like Navon might live long enough to deal a solid blow to Barister's defenses?

And deal a solid blow he would. The time had come to seize a victory of his own.

'War is the action taken to determine who has strength enough to live, and who has strength enough to die. Death can be the gateway to victory, but not all men are brave enough to face this truth.'

If there was one truth that necromancy had shaped, one truth Sel'ari and Jikun and all the Sel'vi did not know, it was that.

Death can be the gateway to victory.

But Navon knew it. And it would shape him.

*

"The front line? You will have to forgive me, elf, but the *front* line, let me clarify, is at the *front* of our army. *At* the face. Where Barister's men will first collide with ours. I'm running out of ways to say this, so let me put it in a way you might be capable of understanding: the front lines have a high mortality rate. It means you will very probably die."

Navon watched the human lieutenant totter through his response. He certainly bore no similarities to an elven military commander, but rather, he was as animated as any green foot that had first stumbled into Navon's care. His long, dirty finger poked the table at which they sat several times to emphasize his point, stabbing into the weathered wood with dirt-crusted fingernails. The fingers withdrew for a moment and Navon admired their remarkably crooked state, imagining that they had been broken on more than one occasion.

"I understand the front line, Lieutenant Joceus," he finally replied as the man paused to breathe. He understood it—but certainly had no experience. The front line of the elven army was not doomed to slaughter.

Human military operations sounded far less reassuring.

"I don't need another man to shield me. As you have pointed out, I am equipped well enough to defend myself. It would be a crime for me to allow some farmer with a pitchfork to fight my battle."

"It's not *your* battle, it's the *king's* battle," Joceus countered with exasperation. "And the king is looking for good soldiers to engage after the front lines meet. What additional pay is offered to the front line is hardly worth the risk."

Navon raised his chin and squared his shoulders. He would have stood, if he had not felt that a physical display of his resolve would offend the human's pride. "Lieutenant, I wish to be on the front line. It is the only place you will find my sword."

The human settled into his seat and rubbed the tangle of curly brown hair gathering about his chin. There was a dramatic pause, an exaggerated sigh, and then he scribbled a brief missive onto the parchment before him. "As you wish, Nevae. You will be in Division One. And may Zephereus protect you in your reckless desires." He stood and waited until Navon was at his side before he raised the sun-bleached cotton of the olive tent flap. "That's the region of red tents to the west. You'll be under the supervision of Lieutenant Pearse. Oh, and take this." Lieutenant Joceus shoved a swatch of fabric into his hand. It was an unadorned, courteous red, as though already prepared for the bloodbath its wearer would receive. "Wear it at your waist. It lets the rest of the men know your regiment."

Navon ducked beneath the frosted fabric and slid past the line of waiting humans. Not a moment passed after the tent flap closed before it was flung open once again by a scraggly farmer boy, eager to add his name to the king's list. *'Cotton and wool. A scythe. The child is undoubtedly front line fodder.'*

In the far distance, a splash of deep red lit the horizon, foretelling the soldiers' deaths to come.

"By Zephereus above, would you look at that," a crisp voice carried across the bustling field. "I didn't know they let women join the army. You there! With the black hair. Division One. *Miss*."

"Oooh Zane, I don't believe it's a woman."

There was a brief fit of self-amusement and low-tuned whistling.

Navon rolled his eyes internally. *'Let it go, Navon. They could be talking about anyone...'*

"HEY, ELF. Yes you, eunuch! There is only one of your god-damn kind around here."

Against his better judgment, Navon glanced over his shoulder to scrutinize the line of weather-worn and shivering recruits, then past their crooked row. Just beyond were six humans lounging upon a stack of unmarked crates. All were fat—practically bursting with the arrogance so common in the human race. Their polished armor, emblazoned with the emblem of the army, barely managed to contain their rolls of well-fed blubber. Golden cuts of fabric hung from their belts, and Navon required no knowledge of the army to postulate that this lot was of the king's own militia—neither mercenary nor recruit nor high lord's guard, but of the royal army itself.

And they were itching to flaunt themselves before the line of hopeful recruits.

"I guess you found that it takes more than some fancy equipment to move off the front lines, eh?" one of the men snorted, gesturing across Navon's body to the red cloth dangling from his belt. "Not a mark upon you. Your old man sell his farm for your equipment?"

The men about him laughed, but the line of aspiring recruits looked on dismally. They did not have the coin to buy such gear, and the envy in their eyes was tangible. If even *Navon* had been placed on the front lines, surely they were doomed.

Navon responded with a falsely amused smile and a single nod of generosity to their insolence. He turned back toward the red tents and set his pace at a brisk walk. *'First Makados and his men, and now* these *humans. It is as they say—those of slow wit are fast to fight. And humans are rich with idiocy.'*

"Hold up. Don't scuttle off," one of the humans beckoned in a sweet façade. "We didn't mean nothing by it. We need men like you. Gives the enemies false hope. And climbing over the mound of bodies makes them that much easier to cut down!"

Something thumped heavily against Navon's back, and he let out a grunt as the force against his torso tilted him into a stumble. *'Navon, remember: patience bears the fruit of success,'* he warned himself as he turned slowly about. There was a soft plop as the remnants of snow slid off his spine and dropped behind him. "Can I… assist you in some way?" he asked, his lips twitching in and out of a strained smile.

"Whoa there, eunuch. Don't get too friendly: we don't fancy a tumble with your kind." There was a brief volley of snickers and the largest of the men continued, rising to his feet. He was neatly kept and a beacon of polished steel; the emblem on his chest, the ring on his finger, and his glib tongue told Navon he was a lord's son. "Show us what you can do. We want to put on a show for the lads here. Show them what it's like to be on the front line. Inspire them with your indisputable skill."

A sea of faces in the line of recruits had turned to watch—farmers and non-farmers alike. Navon breathed softly into his hands and rubbed them together absentmindedly, willing warmth to return to his fingers. Half his mind *was* listening, but it was the juvenile half. The side that enjoyed nosing through Jikun's belongs and gossiping about his poetry.

The side no longer reined in by the wisdom of males that had gone before. *'Well, you cannot just stand here and let them* all *think you bloody weak,'* it argued.

And that was a sound enough argument for his other half as well.

Navon locked eyes with the largest of the fattened men. It had been weeks since he had felt comfortable casting necromancy—his attempts to be greater than himself had too often wrenched him past his limitations. *'Cast only within your own talents.'* He exhaled quietly and raised his chin. "I give to you, your front line," he spoke softly, raising his arms in a slow, dramatic pose.

Everything was better with theatrics.

The king's men watched him for a moment, their gazes slightly hopeful that he might exhibit some flare before he fizzled out in a dramatic display of failure. When his arms reached their zenith and the winter earth lay unchanged, the soldiers finally opened their mouths in broad grins, readying a flow of mockery.

And then their joy was sucked into the abyss with the sudden roar of unearthly screams that bellowed and snarled in a swirl of icy wind. The ground below the men erupted in a pillar of black smoke, sending their bodies careering into the air to arch beautifully over the sea of sun-bleached olives… before they crashed climactically into the stack of unmarked crates they had enthroned themselves upon moments before.

Navon was sure to flourish a bow to the pained faces of the sprawled men. "Although I do not usually fancy a tumble with your kind," he finished haughtily, "I believe you have just been *fucked*."

"By Zephereus, what in Emal'drathar is going on?!" shouted Lieutenant Joceus as he rushed from an entanglement with the flap of his tent. His eyes flitted down the line of gasping and awestruck recruits as he searched for the source of the disturbance.

Navon straightened swiftly, jerking his hand to his side as he ordered the magic to dissipate. The voices hissed once in complaints of ingratitude, then seeped into the ground to leave the six bodies groaning in their wake.

Applause burst from several men in the line, and Lieutenant Joceus' eyes landed upon Navon in fixed disapproval and unquestionable dislike. "You there! Soldier!"

Navon shifted sheepishly and attempted one of his more charming smiles. It had saved him from a gauntlet or two on more than one occasion.

Lieutenant Joceus' eyes narrowed. "You, soldier, are being court-martialed to the general. *Now*."

'Excellent entrance, Navon. I can see you are bound to make many a friend. Can't have Jikun for a companion?—why have any.'

*

The tent of General Bardolph was as immense in size as the man it was required to house. The floor was laden with numerous hides and littered with cheap but ample furnishings. A generous fire warmed the interior, but its purpose seemed nullified by the open flap to the outside. Lieutenant Joceus closed it as he departed, securing Navon inside to face the general's full wrath.

Suddenly, the cold air seemed far more inviting.

Bardolph waited until a heavy silence had settled over the room, as though he was brewing over his options for the Helven's punishment. Then he pounded the desk between them once, causing Navon to jolt sharply in his chair. "So, *Nevae*, was it? You sent Bertelemy and his men up to visit Emal'drathar and back down, did you?"

Navon straightened, watching the plague of wrinkles on the man's brow fight to fold over one another. "Not *that* high, sir."

The general smacked the desk again and a wide grin split across his face. "I've been waiting for someone to beat those pompous city boys down. Dyryke's men arrived from Eraydon City two weeks ago and they've overrun the place with their damned arrogance. And Bertelemy is the worst of them. You can hardly breathe through the thick of it. Making the new recruits feel like a general pile of dragon shit." He pointed a thick, dry finger in Navon's direction. "But not you."

Navon remained rigid and attentive, uncertain how to react to the general's sudden candor. "No, not me, sir."

Bardolph reclined in his chair, resting one arm over his great gut while the other rifled furiously through his desk drawer. "Let me pour you a drink. It *was* Nevae, wasn't it?"

"Yes, that's it."

The man set two glasses down upon the unpolished surface and filled them promptly. It was a messy affair, but he did not seem to notice. "Here you are, Nahvae," he grunted, sliding the glass across the surface.

Navon was quick to seize it before it could sail over the edge. "Thank you, General."

Bardolph raised his glass in a wordless toast and sucked down half the liquor in an obstreperous gulp. "So what did you use on them? Black wind and strange voices, Joceus said. I've never known much about magic. What was it? Illusions? I knew a girl in my youth from the Galestram region who did illusions. She was much prettier that way."

Navon opened his mouth and closed it. *'Is this a ruse...? Some sort of trick...?'* He lifted the glass of liquor uncertainly. On Sevrigel, a court-martial was a serious offense—not a date with the general. Jikun would have personally beaten the shit—in colloquial terms—out of any soldier brought before him.

After a few such displays, no one was stupid enough to transgress that far.

"It was necromancy," he finally admitted, and took a sip in the event that this bolstered their comradery. Immediately, he choked back a gag and swiftly wiped his nose on the back of his hand.

Bardolph let out a roar of laughter. "Don't have Black Blood where you come from? They say The Vein dwarves first brewed it as a poison, but as it turned out, it became a coveted tavern pint instead! That's a real man's drink, there. It'll put hair on your chest. Even an elf's chest."

Navon set the glass down. Faced with that prospect, he would rather err on being cautious. "General Bardolph, am I… being disciplined?"

The general snorted into his liquor and then finished the glass, wiping his mustache with his sleeve. "Bwhaha! *Disciplined?* I've been waiting for someone to come along and do me the favor. No, Navie, you are not."

The rapid transformation of his name was certainly becoming reprehensible. *'Since you have arrived, being Navon has worked out thus far…'* "Navon. Just call me Navon."

The general paused and then gave a considering nod. "Navon. That's a bit easier." He poured himself another glass. "Let me give you a little advice, Navon. Necromancy is a bit of a volatile topic right now, what with the disappearance of Tiras' book from the king's archives in Vise. Rumor has it that the new elven king of Sevrigel had it stolen. I wouldn't go flaunting that skill right now. Not saying you can't use it—we can *certainly* use a mage of your caliber—but let's try to save such a thing for the enemies from here on out, shall we? Dyryke's men are a rather sizable collection of bastards and you certainly don't want to piss them *all* off. I have no doubt some backstabbing goes around on the field. You don't want to give them another reason to hate you."

Navon smiled weakly. "I'm an elf—I'm fairly certain they will only need the one."

Bardolph chuckled through a mild belch. "That reason being that you tossed them to the sky like daisies, or whatever they took issue with to begin with?"

"Both, I suppose."

Bardolph leaned forward, lifting his arm from his belly and resting it upon the desk. He did not seem to mind that his leather was swimming in his spilled liquor—or that it had the acidity level to melt dragon scales. "About that... A frontlinesman. How did a man like you end up on the front line? Lieutenant Joceus is clearly doing a piss poor job—you can never trust these city boys. They strut their way into these expensive academies and never grasp practical application. I'll get you moved right damn fast."

Navon firmly shook his head, his amusement swiftly turning to severity. "No, sir. I'd rather not."

Bardolph blinked. "Well, you may be the first god-damn man to ever say that. Why in Ramul would you want to stay there? Do you know what the front line *is?*"

"Yes, sir. I know what the front line is."

"And you want to stay."

"Yes, sir. I want to stay."

Bardolph smacked his lips in admiration and gave his tousled head a slow shake. "And by Zephereus above, can you tell me *why?* It's not the money, is it? Because men on the front line don't live to collect the money. That's why we 'pay them' like we do."

Navon folded his hands calmly across his lap. It was a wise general that cared about the safety of one man. "I have experience with war, General. And I don't need a farmer's son playing shield for me. If I can't hold my own ground, I don't deserve to be out there. If there was a genuinely strategic reason for me to be in another position, certainly. But disrupting the enemy front line most certainly takes precedence. And so, there I will be."

Bardolph's mouth opened and closed. He tugged at the end of his beard in visible contemplation. "A soldier's words, if I ever heard them. What brings an elven soldier to a *human* army?"

'Lie, Navon. As you always do. Even here, you can't be all *of you.'*

But Navon's lips had no more than parted when Bardolph's eyes flickered, as though he had formed a theory of his own. "Bah. Never mind that, Navon." He raised his glass and Navon's jaw fell closed. "Prove your skill in the next battle and I may just have a real place for you."

CHAPTER THIRTY-FIVE

The Black Blood rippled toward the bottom of Jikun's mug, catching the chandelier's light in waves as the liquid bounced against the polished sides. Something floated at the top, dipping and rising with the crests, twisting in the little storm brewing inside the glass. Jikun flicked the cup against the side again, watching as a sloshing wave engulfed the entity. *'Good riddance, Navon,'* he glowered at it.

There was a sudden, sharp knock against his skull, and the offending tankard bounced away. Jikun swore, spilling his ale across the table as his hand jerked to the growing lump.

Eldaeus' mad cackle grated against his ear, but before Jikun could disembowel him, the Faraven was once more consumed by the bustling throng of tavern patrons.

Adjacent to him, Darcarus leapt to his feet too late, failing to evade the trickle of ale that spilled into his lap. He elevated his own mug high to safety. "That is what happens when you let your mind drift," he rebuked. "Now I surely look as though I pissed myself." He patted his groin once, but in the dim firelight the measly spot was inconspicuous. He shifted his chair and quickly composed his posture, grasping for some semblance of nobility. "Do you think she witnessed that?"

Jikun pulled his palm away from his throbbing head. He leaned around the male to catch sight of the brunette barmaid fondling the wiry beard hairs of a nearby human. "No, she is still enraptured with that atrocity over the—"

"The *blonde*," Darcarus interrupted him, jerking around to catch sight of the hefty brunette. "*What?* You thought I fancied *that* broad? Malranus Almighty. She looks like she wants to eat him." He shivered. "She would suck the True Blood line dry."

It was a comment that would have sent the Helven reeling with abhorrence. In his absence, Jikun felt it appropriate to offer a minor grimace.

"Oh *come now*, General—you speak equally as crass!" Darcarus barked as he gave the table a firm, chastising slap. "I thought for certain you would laugh, or at least break a smile across those icy lips." He took one of his too-polished fingernails and prodded Jikun's shoulder affably.

Jikun's lips drew tight at the unwanted comradery. At the beginning, he had lingered near Nordeep, half expecting the Helven to come crawling back with simpering apologies. "He hasn't been off on his own like this in decades," he had said. "He will return. Give him a day. Two at most. He will come crawling back." And a week later, after a hundred of Eldaeus' "do you still believe he is coming backs," Jikun had ceded that perhaps he *had* crossed a line and Navon was not, in fact, going to return.

Gods damn that Helven!—already Jikun missed the unquestioning nature of the Sel'vi that Navon had once aspired to be! The thought made his boot tap rapidly on the wooden floor of Ironwatch's shoddy inn. "I hope he takes a lance through the foot when he steps out onto that battlefield and lies cold and alone for the rest of the damn war."

"Aw. That is terribly sweet. I hope he stays safe, too," Eldaeus chimed as he rematerialized from the crowd, two mugs in hand. He flopped into the empty chair on Jikun's right and took a swig from both, leaving behind an unbecoming mustache. "What are we discussing?"

Darcarus tipped his mug, draining it. "Navon. *Apparently*." He clapped the tankard down forcefully, but the effect of the clatter was lost in the tumult of noise. "By Sel'ari, Jikun. Navon chose to abandon *us*. We do not need him for this task. In fact, we already know he is a liability—both to us and himself. You might be an inexperienced mage, but you know your limits. We cannot say the same for your former captain. You cannot have forgotten what occurred at the Pass."

The line of Jikun's lips grew tighter. Of course he had not forgotten. Necromancy… the bane of Navon's existence. In that moment within the Pass, all their years of familiarity had been lost. What remained in his captain's azure eyes had been raw, unadulterated malice… and *greed*.

Yet now he was not at Navon's side to make certain the fool did not hurl himself back into those Gates! He was like a god-damn petulant child determined to test common sense for himself no matter how many times it slapped him in the face!

Darcarus cleared his throat forcefully. "*He* left *us*, General."

That, at least, was true. Jikun grunted.

Darcarus tousled his mane and reclined in his chair. "The only reason the male even has the equipment to join the war is through *our* assistance. The fates of Sevrigel and Ryekarayn are in peril and yet he chose such a safe, and dare I add *cowardly*, path." He tossed his shoulders with disgust.

Feigned disgust, Jikun was aware. Slander devised to ensure the general's fury with his former captain. Now that they were so close to confrontation with Relstavum, the prince had begun to ease and his silver tongue was slipping. Certainly Navon deserved every berating word, but that Darcarus should think him thick enough to not perceive his intent made Jikun's skin crawl.

They were *both* fools.

He was starting to believe Eldaeus to be his wisest companion.

A gust of frigid night air billowed across the room and Jikun's eyes lifted, glancing briefly at the open doorway. He was surprised to see not the entrance of a farmer or shopkeeper—or the Brotherhood mercenaries he now feared to be on their tail—but Darcarus' midnight raven. The prince's face immediately alighted like a Darivalian toddler in his first spring. The raven swooped low over the heads of the oblivious farmers to land lightly on the crook of his extended arm.

This time, Jikun noted the scroll tied to her leg. "Another raven stretching her wings?"

Darcarus glanced away from where he had been smothering the creature with affection. "Your tone?" The muscles in Jikun's jaw tightened and the prince's expression shifted. "Ahh… You are brooding about Navon again." His fingers ceased their incessant scratching of the raven's puffed head. "Jikun, release him from your mind. He is nothing but pois—"

Jikun slammed his fist against the table, causing the bird to rustle nervously. Darcarus quickly cupped a calming hand over its back.

"Not another word about Navon," Jikun retorted stiffly. "And answer me this—what message does that scroll contain?"

Darcarus' mouth remained open. Jikun could see the passage of a dozen thoughts behind his piercing eyes before one settled. "I have been conversing with contacts about the state of Sevrigel. Shall I indulge you further?"

Whether or not the male was telling the truth was obsolete. A breath escaped between Jikun's teeth. He slammed his mug down sharply, causing the spilt liquor to ripple nervously once more. "Navon is managing to soil a good evening from a hundred leagues away, and to Ramul if I let his asinine decision spoil this place!" A human tavern was as good as any: the rich smell of leather and sweat, the heavy smoke of a roaring fire, and women saddled with more curves than an elven city street. He lifted his mug high, bellowing, "BARMAID! REFILL!"

Darcarus broke into a grin and the raven vanished with an affectionate peck. He let out a whoop that would have sent the hair on most Sel'vi bristling. "That is far better!" But the grin was short-lived as a tall, rosy-cheeked blonde turned to answer his summons. "Damn, that is the maiden!" He quickly confirmed that his groin was obscured beneath the table before he donned a rakish smile.

Jikun swept the woman's sandy curls, rosy cheeks, and ample display of cleavage. "Gods, sate my lust," he inhaled, passing her curiosity a slow wink.

"*You are fully aware I have had my eyes on her since we arrived,*" Darcarus reproached out of the corner of his mouth.

"Don't you lose your long life if you fraternize with infidels? I thought you had your virginity to maintain, *prince*," Jikun rejoined.

The barmaid halted before their table, fluttering her dark lashes and flashing teeth relatively well-kept for the west side of the Windari Channel. "I have been watching you all night," she purred, "hoping I'd catch the eye of one of you stunning stags." Her eyes lingered on Darcarus' fine features… on Jikun's broad chest…

And then died as they made the final round to Eldaeus. Who was blowing bubbles into his ale.

"…What's wrong with him?"

Jikun jammed his elbow sharply into the Faraven's side. "I have no idea."

Darcarus swiftly tossed Eldaeus' mug aside. It skittered across a few balding heads before disappearing into the crowd. "But who needs ale when your beauty is sure to whisk away all the troubles of this world." He slathered his charm on so thickly that Eldaeus' antics were plainly forgotten. "Gold as she rises over the darkness of the land, warm as her light strokes, blue as her gaze wanders… Lo, it is not the sun that melts the coldest night of winter, but the maiden I see before me."

The woman flushed. "You *siren*," she replied, batting her lashes in feigned timidity.

Unlike Darcarus, Jikun could not flit from candor to poetry on a whim, and thus he knew the battle was undeniably lost. In addition, he would not have been able to continue the conversation without pointing out that sirens were invariably women.

First Esra and now the barmaid. Maybe he *was* more fortunate with the prostitutes. Kaivervi flitted at the corners of his mind and he sharply rebuffed her advances. Instead, he begrudged his own lack of charm and took consolation in his last swig of liquor. He raised his mug once more. "Black Blood."

Darcarus glowered disapprovingly, but Eldaeus swiftly joined in, having retrieved his first mug from somewhere off the dirty floor. "I also need a refill of whatever was in this mug!" He brushed away a few hairs clinging to the wooden lip.

The prince was momentarily distracted with bemusement. "I must ask, *how* in Ramul did you get something to drink? We did not buy you anything."

The barmaid plucked the tankards from their extended hands, her expression growing sour as she regarded the two males whose untimely interference had robbed her of an admirer. "I'll fill these up," she spoke stiffly. And to Darcarus' visible dismay, she sauntered away to another table, her large bottom swinging easily with her steps.

Eldaeus merely grinned. "That man over there said that I could have his mead if I licked his boots."

Jikun followed the male's finger to the floor, where a barrel-chested human lay in an unconscious heap. A squat, dwarfed little human was using his generous belly as a rather respectable drum. "And…?"

"Well, he lied and so I took it. He tried to punch me but he slipped and knocked himself out on the edge of the table."

"…Of course he did," Darcarus muttered with a huff. "And what about the other one?"

Eldaeus raised his second mug. "Oh this one? I traded a necklace for it."

Jikun's brow knit. "You traded a *what* for it?" he demanded.

"A necklace."

Jikun's expression grew flat at the grinning response. "…Yes, those were the words I thought you uttered. Where in the Nine Realms did you pick up *jewelry?*"

Eldaeus stuck his bottom lip out, squinting his emerald eyes. "I did not steal it. I found it. In my oasis. And a human said he would trade me his mead for the charm."

Jikun's body grew cold, a trickle of fear ebbing down his spine. "You found a necklace in your *oasis?!*" He distinctly remembered chucking Relstavum's "amulet of protection" over the edge of the cliff shortly after their fall. He had assumed that the cursed twist of metal had been safely abandoned in the grass and stones. But of *course* Eldaeus had recovered it.

Eldaeus nodded triumphantly, oblivious to his transgression. "Oh yes. It was Farvian, too! Farvian tracking! They used to use the amulet on royalty or great lords' daughters—so they always knew where they were. Or where their bodies were. But it was not mine! I wonder how it got—"

Jikun caught the Faraven by the front of his shirt, nearly upending their table as he wrenched the male out of his rambling. "Eldaeus, did you say *tracking?!* Have you had that damn thing with us the whole time?!"

Eldaeus' blew out his cheeks. "Well... obviously. How could I have left it somewhere and returned for it...?" he trailed off and instead addressed what he seemed to believe was the problem. "I do not know why you are so agitated—we could not have sold it for even a rabbit's foot! I definitely swindled that man for his mead."

"I don't care about its value! I care that Relstavum could know our location and *worse*, be tracking us!"

"*Oh...!*" Eldaeus trailed off. "Well..." he paused briefly and then offered an inappropriate clap. "Then I definitely made a most excellent trade!"

Jikun dropped the male and lurched to his feet. He felt as though the barreled gut now pounded for him. "We need to leave. Distance ourselves from this place. We do not know who Relstavum might have on our trail and how close they might be!"

Eldaeus hugged his second mug and muttered derisively into its interior.

Darcarus knocked it from the Faraven's hands and stood as well, his chair clattering against the dusty floor. "He has been in possession of that charm since the Makataj?! We were never approaching our adversary in secret!" His hand gestured wildly at Eldaeus. "As I have said before, he is a liability!"

Jikun stiffened at the accusation. "Enough." He reached for his cloak as another blast of frigid air gusted into the room. "On your feet, Eldaeus. We leave now. Saebellus' every pawn likely knows our location."

But Eldaeus remained, gawking at the door, mouthing some inaudible irrelevance.

"What?" Darcarus barked, leaning forward. His fingers snatched at the feathers protruding from Eldaeus' hair. "What are you saying, you stupid bastard?—I cannot hear a thing in this din if you do not holler."

Jikun followed Eldaeus' gape. "Damn it. Where is your apparent luck now, Eldaeus?!" Although he had not bothered to remember the six, well-armored humans filing into the room—that had been *Navon's* responsibility—

the words the Faraven was mouthing were undoubtedly the names of Laeris' haughty mercenaries from a week ago. *'Makados,'* he read. *'Keb. Kei. Coe. Harbesh. Thamos.'*

After the revelation of the Farvian charm, their appearance was far too coincidental for Jikun's taste.

'Mercenary work for Laeris, or for...?' He smacked Darcarus' wrist before the prince could draw the attention of the entire room with his raucous behavior. "By the door," he hissed. "Look who—"

Darcarus uttered a single curse and spared Eldaeus' garish adornments from further harassment.

Across the spatter of tables, Makados' almond eyes slid past Jikun, flicking between the three and then out over the jostling room—searching, he imagined, for the missing player in their quartet. An image of the mangled corpse of Borin flashed instantly before Jikun's eyes and his lungs constricted to a painful gasp.

"I need the charm back!—it was lucky!" Eldaeus wailed, breaking him from his trance.

"*What?!*"

"The moment I cast it aside, this occurred!"

Darcarus shoved a swift fist into the Faraven's gut and the male's irrational cries fell silent. "*Now let us leave*." He fetched his cloak and jerked his head toward the old wooden stairs that ascended into the gloom of the inn above.

Eldaeus managed a single, choking sputter of defiance. "This is what happens when you buy armor at the thirteenth blacksmith! I warned you that even my luck cannot combat thirteen!"

Jikun ignored the Faraven entirely. *'Out through a window,'* he thought. Unlike Navon, Darcarus did not require permission to take initiative. They would lose fifty feet of spider-thread rope, but it was a small fee to skirt a confrontation with Laeris' men…

And Relstavum's hired dogs.

"Wait right there," Makados' deep voice boomed from a mere yard away. His thugs had rammed their way through the clamorous crowd and now stood flanking the elves on their left and right. "What a surprise, meeting the likes of you here. We surely thought you'd be off doing grand things… After all, it looks like the Brotherhood spared no expense in equipping you."

"But they spent it on thirteen," Eldaeus broke in mournfully.

Jikun stretched for his cloak draped over the back of his chair, but Makados' wide, calloused hand shot down and clenched about his wrist.

Jikun felt his magic shiver through his breast in disdain. "And I thought the six of you had affairs in the war against Lord Barister," he grunted through gritted teeth. "You are terribly far from that… Could the army not even use you for front line fodder?"

Eldaeus sniggered, but Makados did not share his easy humor. His hand tightened like a vise. "I did say we were going to join the war," the quivering jowls spat. "But I never said it was for the human king. The Brotherhood has jobs for all types. You just have to pick the winning side."

Jikun's muscles writhed. "So you serve Saebellus."

"We serve *Relstavum*. Who he serves is of no concern to us. But if you boys want to strip down naked and hand over all that new gear, we'll give you a head start."

Jikun struggled to mask his discomfort, but the moment his mouth opened to retort, Makados leaned into his weight, throwing Jikun against the side of the table. Something at his hip cracked.

The Darivalian's humor was spent. A chill emanated from his hand, flooding magic through Makados' smooth black gloves to the pasty white flesh beneath—enough cold to turn the mercenary's blood to ice. Yet to Jikun's consternation, the man did not even utter an amused grunt. *'It's that damn magic resistant armor he boasted about,'* he realized with a groan.

Still, such a triviality was easily countered. His eyes landed upon a nearby mug that was flailing about in an old, sun-dappled hand. Jikun kicked outward, catching the mug underneath and sending the ale sailing high into the air. A spear of ice ruptured forcefully from the liquid, racing through the air and straight into Makados' cheek. The great jaws flew wide, bellowing in astonishment and pain. Yet the short, yellow spear ultimately had no more effect than to dislodge a few blackened molars.

"An elemental mage?!" Makados hollered, his eyes wide and wild.

They were offensively bulbous. Jikun caught the human's hair, slamming his ugly face sharply into his knee. "I see that expensive armor assists you very little. Send Relstavum my regards." And he snatched the icy tankard from the stunned patron's hands to bash the mercenary solidly to the ground.

The makeshift weapon would have to suffice. His more effective, Eph'ven weaponry was currently festering in a particular Helven's boot.

All the while, Eldaeus was dancing along the far wall, cackling with delight in the chase.

But Darcarus… Darcarus had managed to accomplish utterly nothing and was now held pinned in the arms of the powerful Thamos.

Keb and Coe flexed before him, their blades eager to bite.

'Damn it!' Jikun growled, leaping over Makados' mildly improved features. He caught Keb by the roots of his wiry black hair, jerking him safely away from Darcarus. Unbalanced, the human collided with the edge of the table and crashed into the groaning body of his leader.

"Against a throng of the living you suddenly become useless?!" Jikun accused, the waver in his voice barely contained.

Coe swung about to face him, his dark lips peeling back to reveal a pearlescent sneer.

"I can't summon one of my creatures inside this place!" Darcarus grunted. He leapt off his feet, forcing Thamos to hold him upright. The leverage allowed the prince to slam his freed heels into the lower back of Coe. With a sharp snap of his head, the man careened wildly past Jikun's salute and into a group of startled farmers beyond.

Thamos swiftly redoubled his efforts to restrain the prince. "They would destroy the place," were the last words Darcarus managed before he was folded over and his athletic escapades ceased. The burly man flared his nostrils warningly. Then his eyes flickered ever so slightly to the right, out into the room behind the general.

Jikun instinctively erected a wall of frozen water at his back and heard the immediate clang of steel. "Almost," he mused softly as he forced his fury into the puddle of ale between them.

A stalagmite punctured instantly from the center and straight through Thamos' calf.

"GAHHHH!" the huge man screeched, flinging himself into the busty blond who pummeled him sharply with her empty tray.

Darcarus scrambled safely to Jikun's side. The clamor of the tavern had hushed. The entirety of the room had united to watch the fight unfolding in the corner.

Makados' voice rang out in a gargled squall. "He's an elemental mage! Watch yourselves!" But as Thamos clutched the great spear of ice jutting from his thigh, the warning seemed rather unnecessary—if not subtly insulting.

Darcarus snatched Jikun's cloak and gave him a thrust toward the stairs. His gloating would have to be postponed. "Well done, now let's *go!*"

Eldaeus had already reached the staircase and was beckoning them excitedly to his side. Harbesh and Kei lay in a tangled heap, one apparently bleeding from a self-inflicted wound.

Jikun sprinted past, catching the Faraven by the leather as he went. The stairs behind them grew slick and wet with ice. There was a crash as the pursuing Coe was sent tumbling down into his ally. A well-placed shaft of ice prevented any further attempts to rise.

Or bear children.

"Damn it! Around! Go around the building!" Harbesh swore as he staggered upon the first step.

An immediate sheet of ice expanded across the floor around them, transforming their attempts to retreat into comical collisions with half-full mugs and clattering chairs.

"Your bow—use your bow!" Makados countered in desperation, but Jikun and his allies were already lost beyond the hall.

Eldaeus slammed the door behind them, dancing madly from foot to foot, screaming for the enemies below to come and engage in a bitter duel to the death. Jikun and Darcarus made for their belongings and secured a rope swiftly to the leg of the wooden cot. A moment later—to Eldaeus' great disappointment—they descended into the thick snow outside their window.

"Our horses," Darcarus barked as he raced for their stalled mounts.

Jikun's grey hand pressed against his hip where a small, glass vial had shattered. He swore quietly in agreement. Relstavum's useless lackeys had only spurred him onward.

Icy wind tore by them, sweeping in great gusts of snow. That was their path—northward, away from the wretched inn and into the heart of winter.

Chapter Thirty-Six

Water fell from the void in a steady shower. It ran along the crevices of the rocks and poured steadily into the little pool at the back of Jerah's hole in the mountain. In its trail it left the rich scent of the forest, as though it had picked up the leaves and dirt and sprinkled them like water across the canyons.

Jerah drew his tattered wings around his body, shifting away from the grey and dismal void to stop by the side of the strange creature he had taken in. It was deeply asleep, curled tightly into a ball on one of the only remaining dry patches.

Jerah crouched down beside it, wondering if it would remain awake for even longer that day. It *had* been staying awake for longer and longer each time it awoke, but its angry and cautious behavior had remained unchanged.

Jerah scratched the base of his right horn and wiped the rain off the tip of his nose. "You are scared," he reasoned, patting it on the head. He paused, warily watching its eyelids for the deepness of its sleep. When they shifted once, he excitedly moved his hand down the creature's head to the display of colorful locks spread across the ground.

Jerah raised a red clump up and slid it across his hand. It was red all the way to its head! How did it get it to be red? He dropped the lock and raised a short chunk of orange hair, pulling slightly at the creature's head in wonder. The orange, too, grew straight from its head!

Then Jerah dropped it in mild disappointment. Why did it get such wonderful colors in its black hair, but all Jerah got was brown everywhere? He reached for his own long and tangled hair, glaring at it resentfully. "Boring," he rebuked it. He extracted a twig from a tangle before he let it drop heavily against his shoulder.

Ah well, it could not be changed. At least Jerah had nicer skin. He ran a hand down his arm with a proud nod and raised his chin in defiance to the creature's superior hair. "You have ugly skin," he told it with a huff.

And then he gasped, recalling his master's response to such behavior. *'You asshole, Jerah!'* he growled at himself. He dropped his hand from his own arm and hesitantly reached out to touch the creature in a gesture of apology. He stopped. No, the creature would be far angrier if he tried to touch it.

He looked at his half-burned pant leg. It seemed to him that when the creature was frightened or angry, fire would light on Jerah's pants. And not just the red ones he had tossed away. Apparently, on *any* pants. And touching was one of the creature's firm "noes."

Jerah put a hand to his groin subconsciously and slid slightly away. This fire seemed like a rather dangerous power to have.

"You mustn't get so wrathful," he rebuked the sleeping creature, imitating the tone of his master. "Patience, my dear…" he trailed off. My dear what? Master had always said Jerah. But *he* was Jerah. "You need… a name." His eyes widened. Not just a race. *A name*. Jerah excitedly scooted closer. Why, he had never gotten to name anything before!

How had Master chosen his name? What was Jerah? It was not a word he had heard before. Nor a collection of words. Did it mean something? Was it a good name? He frowned, perplexed at how little he knew about his own name.

The creature's yellow eyes fluttered open and Jerah quickly scooted farther away. Better not get too close. It didn't like that.

"Are you hungry?" he asked, offering up a thin piece of meat. It had torched the food Jerah had given it the day before, so Jerah could only assume it preferred its food to be cooked. He raised the stolen meat a little higher to make sure the creature could see that this was a fine piece of meat. "This is another cooked one from town," he informed the creature, just in case this fact was not apparent. He set it down on the cold ground. "Oh, see how delicious that looks. Mmm. Mmm. Eat it up before someone else gets it first!"

The creature narrowed its yellow eyes and reached over cautiously, watching Jerah all the while as its thin fingers locked onto the meat and slid the chunk away. When it seemed to determine Jerah would remain where he was, it ripped off a soft, tiny piece and put it deep into its mouth.

"It must be difficult to chew with those teeth missing," Jerah said, getting comfortable. "Oh. I don't know if you want this back, but I found one of your teeth when I met you…" He fidgeted with his pockets and paused. "Oh…

Never mind. They were in the red pants. But you torched those so I threw them off the mountain."

The creature hissed in response and Jerah retreated farther in an attempt to pacify it. The creature seemed somewhat more comfortable with this distance and even took a moment to look away. It examined a wound on its wrist, studying it with what appeared to be an almost thoughtful expression.

"I was thinking," Jerah spoke, carrying on as the creature once more began to eat, "that instead of figuring out what you are, I shall give you a name." He tapped his chest proudly. "I am Jerah."

The creature hissed again, taking a bite of its food in what Jerah thought seemed like a rather irritable way. It lowered its head, black hair falling to shade its face.

Jerah lifted a strand of his own hair with a frown. The creature's hair was so… smooth and soft. Like his master's. But Jerah's hair… was rough and knotted. Could his hair also be as theirs was? He ran a talon slowly along the ends, pulling at it gently.

The creature paused its eating, meaty juices dribbling down its narrow, broken chin. It raised a brow, head cocked slightly to the left.

Jerah could see its focused gaze from the corner of his vision. *'It likes watching this,'* he thought, marveling at how simple it was. He gave his hair another tug to amuse the creature.

It snorted and looked away.

Jerah frowned, dropping his hair. Right, he was going to name it. He scratched his chin, pondering the creature's nature.

"You are very… wrathful," he spoke after a moment.

The creature licked all about its fingers with a sharp, red tongue, seemingly ignoring him. Jerah cocked his head in interest.

"As I was saying," he clapped his hands together to refocus. "Wrathful. But that is not special. That is not a special name. So I shall call you…" He slowly turned the word over in his mind. What names did he know? Kinraeus, Sairel, Jerah, Master, Hairem, Ilsevel, Saebellus… "Wrath…er…us. Wratherus." He leaned forward in his excitement. "You are Wratherus!"

The creature's eyes shrank to narrow, black slits, and it let out an ear-splitting screech.

Jerah felt a familiar warmth tingle his skin. Without looking down, he smacked a hand upon his pant leg. "I am Jerah. You are Wratherus."

The creature let out another screech and dug its nails into the meat clutched tightly in its dark, thin hands.

"Wratherus, that is enough screeching. You are hurting my ears," he spoke firmly.

The creature rubbed the tip of its pointed ear and then let out a soft hiss. Then, with a soft jut of its lower jaw, it took a slow bite.

Jerah's face lit up at the obedient silence and he smiled. "That's a good Wratherus."

CHAPTER THIRTY-SEVEN

'I should not be here...' Navon thought as he watched the line of men creep along beneath the overhanging icicles.

At least, they fancied themselves creeping. They were hunkered into the shadows, smashed together at the shoulders… but they were also muttering and bickering as they trampled toes and breathed white clouds over each other's ears.

The night was still and cold, the type of night on Sevrigel fit for slipping out of one's tent to practice death spells on unsuspecting forest creatures.

But that was not the way of these humans. A league to the west of the bustling city of Danesland, the king's army was still sorting through new recruits. The only sneaking about after curfew that was warranted in the book of such men was for a drink and a luscious woman.

The escapade was straight out of Jikun's tome on how to tempt the gods of death when *not* engaged on the battlefield. Navon's eyes swept upward, eyeing Noctem's face as it slipped out from behind the blanket of clouds to wash their little company of curfew-breakers in a soft, white glow. Jikun would certainly be proud of this game, but what was *Navon* doing here?

Months ago, Jikun would have had to drag him away from the civilized world, but now… He had to admit that he was having a little fun. And there were no heroic personalities remaining to berate his childishness.

The war was almost over and, gods willing, Saebellus' defeat was nigh.

"Fendrel, get back into the shadows, you fat clod!" someone hissed.

Down the road, the two hulking forms of milling military men wandered along the empty street. If they had been of Elvorium's Night's Watch, Bryce's words would have sang to their ears like trumpet blasts.

"We are going to get court-martialed!" Walter cackled. "I've never done this! Don't you feel *alive?!*"

'Court-martialed... again.' Navon glanced once more to the night sky, but now in search of hours and minutes. "We don't have long before the lieutenant makes his rounds. If they catch us out of the camp—"

There was an indignant snort from up ahead. "Well, if they didn't have such ridiculous regulations, we wouldn't be havin' to do this. All for a god-damn drink," the voice of Crewe begrudged. "General Bardolph can rub water hemlock on my cock. But not before I get me a woman. I'm not fightin' the king's war without tastin' a little salt."

Navon winced. *'By Sel'ari, he resonates like an uneducated version of Jikun.'*

The man at the head of the line gave the street a quick survey and then sprang across a patch of lantern light for the door. "Welcome to the Drunken Hyena, boys!" he crowed. "Prepare yourselves for a night of drinks and merriment!"

The rest of the men forgot their need for secrecy—what little they had possessed at the start—and rushed to join him. Navon brought up the rear—just to give Sel'ari one last chance at having him court-martialed before he fell to the wiling hours of intoxicated human play. But there would be no such luck; the large wooden door clamped shut behind him.

The Drunken Hyena was, objectively, a disagreeable dwelling. On the way over, Crewe—who seemed to be as familiar with taverns as the others were with "fine" ale—informed him that the building had once flaunted white wood, polished glass, and little boxes of flowers to don the windowsills. Possibly with enough sophistication to not make a Sel'ven gag at the mere sight of it.

But all such niceties had long since fallen to decay. Now, the two-story home had been renovated into a tavern, and with this transformation came the neglect of innumerable human guests: the outer walls were stained, the windows had dulled, and the rafters inside flaked off as tiny bits of wood dust to flavor the drinks below.

A respectable elf would never be caught within a league of such a pinnacle of human decay.

'I'm glad there are no Sel'vi to see me here,' Navon mused to himself.

"Come on, Navon. You're staring off again. Get your boney ass inside. All the way. You look half-a-mind to bolt. I'll buy you a drink to settle you in," Galter offered good-naturedly, nearly shouting to be heard over the din.

It seemed they were not the only group of the kingsmen to slip away for better prospects. The assemblage of Navon's own human crowd was gathered about Galter, waving sheepishly at their fellow units across the room. When they had finished their salutes, they turned every which way in hopes of finding that choice table at which to spill their own liquor and shout out creative profanities.

Navon slunk slowly after his party, aware that Galter's eyes had remained fixed upon his face.

The man's nostrils flared. "Crewe, look how tight his lips are. Bet you a copper you couldn't poke a needle between them." He smacked a massive hand onto Navon's shoulder and jerked him to the front of their little group. "*Two* drinks, if you can make your lips *any* tighter, elf."

Navon's lips faltered into a smile. "This place would not mark the first of my choices. *Three* drinks, if you want me to enjoy myself."

Crewe was still engrossed with the offer of a copper and Navon could see him rustling hurriedly about his pockets.

"Three it is!" Galter agreed, ambling away to shove Fendrel toward a table beside the wall. The others followed suit, sliding along the benches encircling the precariously tilted stand. They crammed in shoulder to shoulder.

Navon was the second to last to settle in, finding himself pasted between body odor and a heap of protruding bones.

"What *is* your sort of place, elf?" Galter taunted as he waved for the attention of a barmaid. "The archives?"

Navon hesitated. *'Do not admit to that,* savant.*'* "I enjoy…" But he trailed off for lack of any suggestion that did not involve large piles of books or statues of the goddess.

"Well, that settles that—the sorry soul can't think of a single place!"

"Nothin' beats a tavern!" Crewe chimed in. "Liquor and breasts!"

Navon's eyes were quick to follow Crewe's to the redhead by the barkeep. *There* was certainly the pinnacle of liquor *and* breasts. "I *have* missed the sight of a pretty female. *Woman.*"

The men about him seemed suddenly at ease, as though those words had incorporated him instantly into their unspoken brotherhood. "Navon is going to get a necking, boys. Redhead by the counter. Look at him blush."

Navon felt a flush inflame his cheeks, but supposed it only assisted in his guise of sharing their barbaric interests. "If she will have me!" he agreed with matched enthusiasm.

But Galter was not ready to let this opportunity pass Navon by. "Hey barmaid!" he hollered with an impressive boom, and waved a calloused hand avidly about to gain her favor.

Admittedly, there was a flicker of disappointment in Navon when it was *not* the large-breasted vixen that responded to Galter's call. Instead, the Helven grimaced as a rather thicker and heavier woman approached: the kind fit only for the human race. A poor elf, finding himself beneath her, was likely to remain there indefinitely.

Navon heaved an open sigh and the men about him cooed in commiserating chagrin. "Ah, such is fate! It seems that tonight does wish me ill," he dramatized.

Walter gave a painful squint of his eyes.

Crewe cackled gleefully. "We all came here for a little romp, and there's enough woman there for all of us!"

Navon gave an involuntary convulsion at the thought.

"Here she comes! Hush hush!" Galter hissed over his comrades' heckling.

The heavyset woman sauntered over, swinging her hips to and fro as though she was unbalanced by the sheer size of her buttocks; the men on either side of her were forced to part lest they be trampled beneath her insuppressible gait. She drew up before the table and Navon found the sweet odor of elven meads and the sour tang of dwarven ales swiftly muted by the scent of rose petals and mint leaves. Even the heavy burning of the fireplace nearby could not quench her rather intoxicating perfume.

And Darcarus had claimed that Ryekarian women possessed a horrifying stench.

"What can I do you men for?" She leaned forward, placing a hand on the edge of the table to let the loose cotton of her shirt drape dangerously close to exposure.

Several men leaned forward to give her a good sniff. And glimpse beneath the supple folds.

Navon, on the contrary, was enveloped in the observation of how the table had snapped away from the wall and became, for a moment, properly balanced. "Black ale," he replied absentmindedly. "Three pints for myself. On this man, here."

Several of the men managed to look away long enough to admire his audacity.

"Make it four. I think this man is going to need a bit more of a prod to get upstairs, if you know what I mean," Galter said in a lowered voice, giving the woman a valiant wink.

But it didn't take two, three, *or* four pints to drown the common sense in Navon. By Ramul, if he was being honest, it had not even taken one back when Jikun had faced him with the prospects of his last night on Aersadore. But that was a long time ago. *Scarletta*... Navon pushed his first mug between his hands; by the time he drained its sweet contents, he had eased into the boisterous comradery. "I would take a woman like that, boys," he ceded over their own conversation. "One wrong move and she'd flatten me like… But you know what? I think that would serve Jikun a well driven point. Leaving with *Darcarus*. I am constantly at his service and yet he tosses me aside like a used leather sheath." Disgruntled, his hand clamped about his mug.

"…Who is Jikun?"

"Darcarus' new lover…?"

"Isn't there some prince named Darcarus?"

"I have no idea."

"Did he just say '*used leather sheath*'…?"

"Well he said Jikun is a man."

"…I don't think he fancies the ladies…"

Navon paused and snapped his fingers once or twice, attempting to spark his mind to clarity. "What was that male's name—the one in *Velemere's Tale*," he continued his ambling thoughts. "The one that got crushed like felsin bread by the troll. Thedofurn… Themodees… Thenuren…?"

The soldiers blinked and exchanged cautious glances. "Are you drunk already…?" one ventured in amazed disbelief.

"*Jace*. That was it." Navon raised his mug and took several rewarding swallows. "You should *all* read more. I read all the time. The archives…! I would take a book over a fuck on any given day! Who smells like cow shit? Gods, I don't know how you have missed such a story. *Everyone* knows that story."

"…By Zephereus…! That *is* his first one, ain't it?" Walter blinked, leaning forward to peer over the tops of Navon's remaining mugs. He tugged at the end of his charcoal mustache eagerly. "What's he drinking? I want me some of that."

Navon threw his hands into the air before striking down across his own face to push the frayed edges of Walter's mustache back down. "What a cultural pity," he bemoaned. When Walter's mustache remained indifferent, the Helven began to empty his second pint. "Before anyone else," he began decidedly, "I'm going to have a romp with her. Right—"

"You men! The table with the eunuch!"

Navon directed his attention to the unmistakable address from several yards over. "Why…? That's the second time since I enlisted…"

Galter and the others swapped a glance, but Navon was too engaged with his insulters to translate the exchange. The beckoning men were seated at a small table much like their own little slab, albeit straighter and cleaner, and not crowded by so many stinking bodies.

One was gesturing vigorously. "We want to play a game of fosmel. We need a pair. How about it? Wager a few coins? Drinks, perhaps?"

The men around Navon hunkered in low to hiss across the table, but the captain remained fascinated by the two challengers' appearances. The speaker was the larger of the two—a good head taller than Navon and twice as thick. His arms looked like massive twists of uncooked dough—round and bulging, yet strangely soft, with pockets of skin dipping away here and there as though his flesh had been severely seared.

The man beside him was smaller than Navon by a hand and far leaner. He displayed a complexion as dark as the elves of the southern desert, but with far less appealing features—the most prominent being an enormous nose that threatened to block what limited vision his squinting, little eyes offered to him.

'Why, Jikun couldn't have described them any less gracefully himself!' he applauded.

"Fosmel—that's the game with the stones, ain't it?"

"Yeah, that's the one. I was village champion."

"No you weren't."

"Hey Navon, have you played?"

It took Navon a moment to realize that the hushed voices were addressing him. "Me?" he trailed off indignantly. "I know how to play—when your father leaves you with *nothing* you learn pretty fast how to make a coin in unsavory fashions. Jikun and I used to play whenever we'd camp outside a city. I taught him *all he knows* about gambling. Ungrateful bastard. He is probably winning coin right now without me…!" He cuffed the table in offense. "And is he using it to pay off his damn debt?! *I think not!*"

Crewe elbowed Walter suggestively. "…There's that Jikun fellow again…"

"We got it," Galter announced, swiftly drawing their attention. He pivoted to face their challengers. "Navon and I will face the two of you! Five silver and nothing less!" He leaned over and elbowed Navon sharply in the side. "Stop drinking so you can play, son."

Navon stiffened resentfully. "*You* could be my grandson."

"*If* you fancied women," someone sniggered.

Navon whirled, but Galter and the others were already filing free of the benches to drag him off to the far side of the tavern.

*

The game was substantially longer than Navon had previously had the displeasure of experiencing. Their human adversaries did not play like the men of Sevrigel. Five silver—or whatever trivial bet had been made—seemed akin to a battle to the death for the prize, with each shot meticulously nurtured and considered. Contrariwise, Galter thought that it was best to "just let her go." He was a doer, and his doing was significantly worse than his thinking. Fifteen minutes later, he and Navon were *still* in the process of losing miserably in the crudely scribbled lines with their vaguely oval-shaped stone. With the assistance of Navon's double vision, these imperfections did not help.

"Don't get cocky," Navon bolstered some rounds later as Galter skirted the edge of the field once again. He eyed the well-thrown stones of their opponents, Bronwen and Hayes, venomously. *He* might have been the gambler, but *Jikun* had always ensured their victories… Always been the cheater. Navon raised his stone in futile determination. And stilled.

A wry smile slipped across his lips. He did, after all, have magic of his own. And, having consumed a few pints, Navon felt that a slight edge was entirely justified. He was incredulous about being bested by the supercilious dough boy and his underling. …And wherever Jikun was gambling, he *certainly* was not going to win more than *he*.

Galter did not catch the glint of victory flashing in his partner's eyes and had begun to respond ruefully to the men about their own abysmal skills when Navon's stone left his hand along with a few guiding wisps of necromancy.

Hayes' mocking grin faded and Bronwen gave a contemplative shrug as Navon's stone slid into place beside their own, smooth as the grey tendrils that had carried it. "Bound to happen eventually," Hayes consoled his comrade.

"As I said before, boys, my friend and I have just begun." Galter intoned smugly.

And through his new and revised method, Navon found the gap between the pairs rapidly diminishing.

"Look at that. By Galway we're losing now!" Hayes cried in dismay, a dozen painful minutes later. "Straight up the middle, he does. Every time. Straight up the middle! Unnatural, it is!"

Navon gave a casual, boasting flick of his necromancy-wrapped stone as he prepared another toss. An intellectual response had tempted his tongue, but this haughty display was decidedly more satisfying: his stone sailed up into the dim yellow lights near the tavern rafters and down toward his hand, all the while leaving Hayes and Bronwen to scowl contemptuously as he delayed his throw.

"I won't keep you ladies waiting," Navon cooed smugly, and gave a casual flick of his wrist.

Abruptly, Hayes' skinny little hand shot forward, snatching the stone from the air.

In a *normal* match, where Navon was *not* cheating, this would not have been a problem.

But that was not the case.

The wisps of necromancy wrapped wildly around Hayes' hand before Navon could draw them away, howling at the unfamiliar master that dared disturb them.

The stone dropped heavily to the inn floor.

There was a definite moment of silence as Galter's eyes widened and the soldiers about them stiffened. Bronwen and Hayes stood stupefied at the scene.

Then slowly, a fat, flaking finger rose accusingly to Navon's breast. "You're *CHEATING!*"

Galter patted Navon sharply on the shoulder as the wisps dissipated. "Well, technically you never *did* say that wasn't allowed."

"He has an excellent point," Navon chimed in agreement.

Bronwen took a menacing step forward and flexed his bulging, doughy arms. A little vein popped up and slithered to his elbow. "We win," he growled his implied threat.

Navon glanced down once at the stone and then to the hulking human. "Well, now *you* are cheating," he remarked calmly, inching slightly away. If he had reasoned the bursting barmaid could flatten him, then Bronwen could certainly do far worse. Out of the corner of his eyes, he could see Hayes sidle off to the left, but Navon dared not take his attention from the massive form ahead of him. "You said twenty rounds. Highest points win. Seems a bit—" Navon let out a bark of surprise as two spindly arms caught him around the shoulders, bending him backward. His heart flipped as Bronwen slung his arm back. "Galter, where in Ramul is your help?!"

"I said I agreed with you," the human replied indignantly, and out of the corner of his eye, the Helven saw the man give a deliberate nod to endorse his point—to which the other soldiers quickly agreed.

Navon slammed his feet into the ground and pushed backward, swiftly forcing Hayes toward the door of the tavern, but Bronwen was prompt to pursue. "Oh no you don't. We finish this here, coward!" And his massive, pudgy fist rose sharply in the air.

Navon grunted resentfully as he pulled his legs tightly toward his chest. "Intelligence is not akin to cowardice," he huffed. He kicked out, slamming his heels against the bulky chest. With the force of his thrust, Navon careened backward with the scrawny Hayes, sailing into the door of the tavern. Hayes croaked out the breath in his lungs as he slammed into the door and, as though the hinges were made of goblin iron, the great wooden door popped off its bolts and knocked outward. A tray of golden buns flew to the floor from the startled barmaid and slipped beneath the men, flattening with a squirt of frothy white cream.

"Damn it, this armor is new," Navon grunted resentfully as his elbow dropped into the cream.

The ruckus fell dead. The barmaid bemoaned her loss. Navon twisted free of Hayes as the scrawny little man hacked for breath.

And then a furious roar broke the silence. "This eunuch was *CHEATING!*" Bronwen pointed fiercely at Navon's wide-eyed, innocent gape.

There was a slow shift of feet and chairs as the seething mass of humans turned to stare.

"Cheating?!" another human rallied in offended accord.

"Eunuch?!" Navon cried with outrage.

"No, no, it just *looked* like cheating," Galter attempted in pitiful defense.

Navon sighed inwardly as the inevitable coming event struck him. *'It's like being out with Jikun again.'* "Told you we should have skipped the tavern," Navon jibed.

And with that, the room erupted. Bronwen hurled the first punch, but Navon dodged his bulky body with the nimbleness graced to even the most ungainly of elves. A flurry of adjoining fists followed. Somewhere nearby, the Helven's division of farmer boys had stepped in to defend their comrade.

Navon felt a blow skim his shoulder and dropped swiftly to crouch beside a table. He rose in response with a liquor-stained stool, clubbing a red-faced human in the shoulder and another square in his beak of a nose. *'Oh damn it. That was Crewe...'*

His human companion stumbled in a daze and then snapped once more into focus. His eyes widened and he quickly skirted to the safety of Navon's side.

"Where have you been?! I had nearly a dozen men on my ass before our comrades pulled some attention off of me!" Navon scolded, raising the stool to block a blow. "This lot nearly had me hanging by my ankles in the rafters!"

Crewe blinked in confusion, still uncertain about what had struck him, but he wove a lie Navon could be proud of. "What do you mean, where was I?! I punched out at least three hulkin', half-giants of men and nearly lost my arm!"

"Ah, the drama," Navon lamented, and slipped beneath a limb to punch Bronwen squarely across his jaw. He saw a puff of dead skin flakes rise from the man's nose and then he tilted and faltered, hurtling down to crush poor Hayes beneath him.

"We should probably leave," Galter ventured in a panicked shout above the clamor. "We're outnumbered!"

"Five to one. Nothing I haven't done before," Navon quipped. *'Wouldn't have been a night out with Jikun otherwise.'*

But he agreed. The time had come to leave. Ale was sailing high now, showering down like rain as mugs sailed to and fro across the room to clobber unsuspecting foes with their fall. Navon skidded across a nearby table as a human crashed past him, vaulting nimbly across Bronwen's sprawled body. A pudgy hand swept by him to snatch at his leg, but a good kick from Navon's steel-toed boot deterred further attempts.

With another leap and a scramble, they broke out into the open street and scurried away across the cobblestones and into the alley beyond. They sank against the stone to catch their breath.

"*This* is how we celebrate going to war?" Navon panted, placing a hand against the wall for support. He shook his head in amused disbelief. "A little bar fight to test your skills for the battlefield, I suppose?"

Galter did not seem to hear him. "Damn it all. Now I can't get a woman. Oh don't look so smug, elf. No romp for you, either."

Navon straightened with a chuckle. The adrenaline had faded and an uncomfortable throbbing was gnawing at his shoulder. He rubbed it gingerly, valuing the sting in light of the good time he had just had. With Jikun, he could not possibly make full use of the night without waking up a bit battered and bruised, or without the likes of a thousand mountain dwarves pounding about his head.

His face fell a bit. *'To Ramul with Jikun. We are apart and yet it is still him I am serving!'*

The sting at his shoulder began to throb far less pleasantly. Somehow, across the leagues, the general could still sour a fine mood.

CHAPTER THIRTY-EIGHT

"Hm. We are all out of food today…" Jerah spoke with a frown, spinning slowly in a circle to survey the empty cave. "You eat too much."

Wratherus snorted, tossing its head slightly. Then its furious glare fixed on a little bug that scuttled toward its bed.

Jerah, too, paused to watch it for a moment. It was a cute, little brown bug with a hard shell and tiny back legs. Far better looking than a cockroach. What should he call it…? It rolled over a small rock and bounced once as it landed beside Wratherus' bed.

And then, in a sudden burst of flame, it was gone.

Jerah clasped his hand to his chest. The poor thing! "Bad Wratherus!" he rebuked as the flames died. He sighed. He couldn't blame the creature. It simply did not understand. "Now, we are out of food," he repeated. "Tonight I will have to go to town and bring us back more."

Wratherus looked up sharply.

Jerah frowned. "I go to town *every* night, Wratherus," he reminded it. "And you can wait to eat until then. Sometimes, I would go many, many days and nights without food. You can too… I think…" He paused. Hm, maybe he should make sure to have food around for it. Perhaps it was not as strong as he was. Jerah thoughtfully eyed its skinny body.

Wratherus stood up slowly, making its way gingerly toward the pool of water. It seemed mostly healed, but Jerah could not be certain. It had not allowed him to check on it after it had become fully conscious. *And* Jerah had only one pants left: he didn't want to take chances with making it angry.

Wratherus crouched down to fill its slender hands with water. The hole in its face would not close, so drinking was a messy activity. Jerah watched as water dribbled from its jagged jaw, tinkling softly onto its bare feet.

"I know what would take your mind off of everything," Jerah began. "We can practice more words. My master used to do this with me."

Wratherus looked back at him and wiped a hand across its boney chin. It hissed.

"No words right now? How about just three. Let's just learn three new words." He raised his tone into one of excitement, attempting to instill the same feelings in the creature.

Wratherus regarded him in an annoyed manner for a moment, then pushed off its knees to stand. It turned to face him attentively. It had little patience, but sometimes it would become submissive.

Jerah smiled proudly. He was becoming good at understanding it. *'I must be patient with it,'* he would tell himself.

The creature tapped its foot.

Jerah quickly pointed to it. "Foot," he began in the Common Tongue. He always used the Common Tongue around it. The human language just seemed so much simpler to Jerah. Each day he had tried to teach the creature new words. He didn't know how to put many numbers together, but he did know that they had spent seven days learning words. It seemed to understand many body parts, injuries, when he had to leave, food, yeses, and noes, but sentences seemed beyond it.

And it seemed to know its name. Jerah was quite proud of this.

The creature put a hand to the mountain wall.

"Wall," he said. "That is a wall."

And lastly, Wratherus sat.

"Sit," Jerah said, standing and then sitting again to emphasize his point. "Sit. I just sat down."

The creature cocked its head.

Jerah frowned. "Uh… in the elven language it is only one word… I don't know why the humans use two. Sat is sit. Sit. Sat."

The creature stood and then sat back down.

"You sat. Now you are sitting." Some words seemed harder for it to grasp. Jerah didn't blame it. He was finding himself becoming perplexed. He rubbed his forehead. Maybe he should have just taught it the elven tongue?

While Jerah contemplated this, he saw Wratherus slide its body about, presenting Jerah with its back in the attempt to find some privacy. Jerah saw it raise its black shirt over its stomach.

'It must be looking at its wounds again,' he thought, trying to turn his gaze away so that only the corners of his eyes could see.

Wratherus looked at its wounds often—at least twice a day. Once, to Jerah's horror, it had even lit its own flesh on fire. What was left behind was the same bubbly flesh Jerah had seen when he had first found it. Whether it was burning itself from internal rage or for some other reason, Jerah could not know, but it seemed determined to do so despite Jerah's warnings.

Yet even the old bubbly flesh had gone away with time. Jerah caught glimpses of the creature's brown skin beginning to return around smooth, white and red patches that had come to replace the burned skin.

Maybe it healed well after all.

It dropped its shirt suddenly and wrapped its arms around itself, letting out a violent shake. Determination settled into its features as it abruptly began to inspect their quarters. Jerah knew that look—it was searching for something to burn.

And then a realization came to Jerah. "Are you cold?" he asked sympathetically. He remembered how cold it had gotten for many days in the cellar. And over the days since Jerah had found the creature, the mountains had grown bitterer as a chill wind swept in from the ocean with hints of salt and frozen water.

Jerah sniffed, raising his chin slightly to inhale the scent that hovered in the canyon outside their hole. He had not smelled that frozen water scent since he had fought General Taemrin by the swamps. It brought back such memories… For a moment, his heart ached for Sevrigel.

"I can get you more clothes, too," he spoke, loud enough to force his attention back to the creature. He scooted a little closer and stretched out a wing. "These make me warmer," he offered cautiously.

Wratherus' eyes narrowed as the large wing crept closer around its back.

Jerah paused, waiting for a hiss. It had made it clear before that such a sound was equivalent to a firm "no."

But there was no hiss. Jerah slowly put his tattered wing across the creature's back and wrapped it around its sides, creating a little blanket of warmth about them.

For hours they sat in silence and, even when his wing grew tired, Jerah held it there.

Finally, when the torch in the void began to go out, Jerah stood, drawing his wings tightly against his own back. He felt a little bad to leave it cold again, but he was going to find it more clothes. "It is time, Wratherus. I must go to town now. While I am gone, you can use your bed for warmth. I know it's a bit dirty…" He turned toward the entrance and stopped, hearing the sound of feet padding along behind him. He looked over his shoulder curiously.

Wratherus was standing a short distance behind him, its yellow gaze intensely set.

This was the first time the creature had made it to its feet so steadily since Jerah had found it. *'It must be feeling a lot better!'* Jerah thought with relief. He took another step toward the entrance, watching as Wratherus slid its foot across the ground after him.

Jerah stopped, spinning around. "Wratherus, you can't come," he insisted, even as he felt elated at its attachment to him. "The town is dangerous. There are many creatures there that try to kill me. They may try to kill you, too. They are afraid of things like us. Things not like them."

Wratherus tossed its wild hair and turned its head away. Jerah felt a pain in his heart.

"Well… Wratherus, if you come you have to listen to me," he insisted.

Wratherus turned its head back toward him, yellow eyes widening as though with excitement.

Jerah found himself smiling. "Alright then, let's go."

Wratherus picked up a shirt from the ground and ripped a large piece from it. It tied the fabric around the bottom half of its face, concealing the broken state of its jaw. With the disfigurement hidden, Wratherus looked almost elven. Jerah wondered if perhaps it felt and understood a little more than he had assumed.

The two emerged carefully onto the side of the mountain. The darkness of the void surrounded their small forms, and the white torch flickered at half-light behind a cloud of smoke. The mountains were washed with a faint, white glow across their grey surfaces.

Jerah glanced back at Wratherus and held out a hand to help it along the broken path. The creature made a sound Jerah had never heard before: fierce and resistant, rejecting Jerah's offer of help with what he could only assume was a scowl.

Jerah withdrew his hand. *'It doesn't want me to help it?'* he pondered as he began to move along the path, nervously glancing behind him to make sure Wratherus was alright.

He was surprised to find the creature moving easily along, steadying itself by pushing its slender fingers into cracks along the mountain face. It glanced once at Jerah with its firm gaze, and then continued to place its narrow feet confidently across the stone.

As one they descended to the mountain floor.

"You did very well," Jerah complimented it, impressed with its mobility. Even without talons, the creature could climb and move just like him. In fact, its balance seemed, perhaps, even superior.

The creature's expression was difficult to read without seeing its lips, but Jerah thought it looked at him with at least a little bit of pride.

He wanted to pat it, but resisted the urge. *'One pants left, Jerah,'* he reminded himself. "This path leads us right out of the mountains to the town," Jerah informed with a sniff to their surroundings. "Food and clothes and humans are there."

Wratherus gave no reaction, but took silent step behind him.

Jerah smiled to himself, thinking of the little, feathered creatures that hopped along his home in the mountain. He glanced once over his shoulder, taking a moment to watch Wratherus angrily light a small, flying bug on fire before the creature hopped over a large stone to continue its pursuit.

Jerah felt quite proud—he was caring for it all by himself! He walked a little straighter, leading it along through the dark mountain pathways and out into the expanse of trees that lay before the town.

"These are called trees," he informed Wratherus as he patted the trunk of the closest one. "Through these trees is the city!"

Wratherus stared at him stoically, not mirroring the enthusiasm.

Jerah nonetheless continued cheerfully on, stepping over the twisted branches of the tree that grew in the dirt. As they reached the end of the forest, Jerah stopped, raising his hands.

"And that, Wratherus, is named a *house!*"

He gestured to the small stone building in their path. Jerah had first seen it a week before, but had discovered its interior was empty. He liked to imagine himself living in it like the elves and humans did in theirs: not having to flee from anything, but just being able to eat and rest in comfort. He thought he should like it to be white like the dark void's torch, with a doorway large enough for him to not duck beneath.

"No one lives inside it," he continued as Wratherus stepped warily toward it, eyes narrowed.

It let out a soft growl.

Jerah opened his mouth to question its disapproval and stopped. He cocked his head. "Wratherus, humans don't live alone in houses. They live in cities. This house here is all alone so there are no humans—" He stopped abruptly.

What was that smell?

Wratherus' growl deepened and its body shifted lower to the earth.

No… that smell… *Jerah knew that smell.*

He swung around, his heart pounding in his chest.

There was nothing but the darkness of trees.

It couldn't be. Impossible. He had crossed the ocean!

He froze, his heart beating violently. He found his body urging him to flee, but he remained still. If it was *them* he could not run. *He could not run again.*

Two figures gradually became visible, their tall bodies spotted with light as it shone down through the branches. The long clothes of one creature billowed out behind him. The glint of metal shone off the side of the other.

Jerah took a step back, face contorting with fear at the confirmation of who they were. *The mercenaries!*

'No!! Why did they follow?! How did they find me?!'

"The beast," one of the mercenaries breathed, drawing his sword. It glinted slightly as he turned it toward Jerah. The white torch lit the brown-haired man's narrowed eyes and highlighted the scars running down his dark face. He strode forward, the dirt of the forest floor scraping under the bottom of his thick-soled boots.

Even though he looked only human, Jerah could not help but feel another wave of fear wash over him. He knew this human was strong. *Very* strong.

His black-haired comrade reached for the weapon at her side, stepping into the large shadow of the nearest tree on her left, her eyes reflecting silent agreement as though they had conferred without speaking.

This column was deadly. Jerah's gaze flicked down the length of the lean, black-haired woman, following the path of her hand.

She was reaching for the weapon that fired the metal-tipped wood!

Jerah lowered his muscular body and snarled. "Get behind me, Wratherus," he whispered.

"What is beside him?" the man asked, as though he had not realized that Jerah was not alone.

"Looks like… an elf?" the column spoke in reply, pausing briefly from the loading of her weapon to glance up.

There was no more time to listen. Jerah shoved Wratherus behind him and into the shadows of the towering trees. "I SAID GET BEHIND ME!" he roared.

Jerah's foot pushed off from the ground, propelling his body forward with joint-aching speed. He could see the mercenaries' faces light with surprise and twist in horror.

No, this time he would not be caught first. *He would not be hurt again.*

Instinct and adrenaline tore through Jerah as he ran, only the sound of the bitter wind whipping past him.

The column quickly raised her weapon, but Jerah's speed was superior. There was a click. He pushed off the nearest tree, away from the anticipated path of the wood, and lurched forward. The brown-haired man's expression flickered in fear.

Yes, they should fear him. They were not the only creatures that hunted in the night.

Jerah leapt at the man, slamming him to the ground with his legs as his bare hands bent the blade away. Small stones bounced with the force of the man's impact, and his body spasmed as breath was torn from his lungs.

But Jerah vaulted immediately away, knowing that the column aimed another of the deadly shafts.

No. Not this time!

He lurched forward across the dark earth and slammed his fist into the column's chest, hearing the sound of stone breaking beneath his fingers. He hurled her into the tree beside him, a crack ripping through the length of the wood, showering him with fragments of the branches.

"HAZAMARETH!" the man screamed from directly behind him. He had moved *fast.*

Jerah dodged, but too slowly. The power that swept with the blade was unlike that of any human—

It swept clean through Jerah's throat. A glitter of blood sprayed toward the void torch.

Jerah jerked away, grabbing the blade as he went. But then he stumbled, his legs feeling suddenly weak. He fell to a knee, grasping a hand to his throat as he realized he could no longer breathe.

The mercenary's blade clattered from his hands.

What was this…? An injury like this… Did it mean…?

He felt spurts of blood and an abrupt surge of dizziness.

The man did not hesitate: his own swords lay in a mangled heap, but he drew the metal of his fallen comrade and swung at Jerah's neck again.

"YOU DIE HERE!" the mercenary shouted.

There was a sudden flare of heat before Jerah, rising in intensity with a roar of ferocious wind. Jerah fought through the pain, struggling to see the source…!

Fire.

Fire had engulfed the powerful human.

With a scream, the brown-haired man reeled away, dropping the sword. He fell to the ground to roll desperately across the dirt. "Damn you!" he cried in agony.

But the flames burned on.

"Come, Jerah," a voice behind him suddenly spoke in the elven tongue, smooth and lightly accented.

Who…? "Wratherus?" Jerah mumbled his shock, and found that his blood had slowed. He could breathe once more.

He looked back at the fierce eyes that watched the body rolling and burning in the dirt. The man was not yet dead. He could not leave.

Jerah pushed off his feet. "Wait," he commanded. "Now that you are with me, they might hurt you, too."

And before the brown-haired man had struggled fully to his feet, Jerah slammed his fist into the human's skull, watching the body fly back against the walls of the abandoned house. The stones shattered with the force of the impact and in a terrible groan, the building collapsed, burying the crushed mercenary within.

Then Jerah turned to the column still lying by the tree beyond. Her eyes had opened.

And Jerah halted, perplexed. Wratherus was already beside her. It was crouched by her head, speaking too softly for Jerah to hear.

What was it saying…?

But by the time Jerah had moved close enough, it had finished. Its yellow eyes were narrowed and its sharp fingers clutched about her throat.

When its hands came away, a scorch mark remained about her neck.

Maybe the creature could not kill her. Jerah would do it instead.

He reached out to rip his talons across her chest, but Wratherus hissed. "No," it ordered.

Jerah's fingers flexed. "But—"

"No." There was quiet authority in Wratherus' voice.

The building beside Jerah burst suddenly into flames and his mind immediately cleared. Almost as quickly as the flames had sprung to life, the heart of the fire died to merely gnaw at the kindling across the roof—the only wood left on the building to burn.

But his instincts were gone. He could think as himself again, and he knew danger still lurked. Someone may have heard the fight. And certainly someone from the town would see the fire! He couldn't take his chances. His heart rate sped up, the wound at his throat aching painfully. "We have to go. *Now*. Someone may come looking for these mercenaries. Come!"

He stumbled away from the black-haired column that had gone motionless beneath the tree, and Wratherus stepped behind him. There was a purposeful distance to its silent stance, but its eyes told Jerah it was listening.

With a final glance at the destruction behind him and Wratherus at his heels, Jerah fled in search of another city.

CHAPTER THIRTY-NINE

"Tsuki. Up."

The words drifted to him as though from a vast and hollow distance.

The tunnel of a catacomb, perhaps?

Yes. Gods damn it, he must finally be dead.

"*Tsuki.*"

Tsuki tilted his head against the ground, feeling an immense stiffness in his neck. It caused his breath to wheeze out from his throat. Ashes and fragments of stone and wood slid off his face as he shifted; they rolled away across his cheeks to the floor beneath. He coughed and gasped, exhaling a lungful of ash.

Then his eyelids fluttered open in the darkness. "Uhhh…" he groaned. Pain seared his body, demanding his complete immobility.

If he was not dead, he wanted to be.

Still, his vision adjusted swiftly to the night. The light of the moon was generous through the canopy of trees, repelling the shadows to reveal the smoking landscape around him.

Beside him, Hazamareth's pale and dirty face was fixed in concern. Black hair clung to his companion's cheek, plastered by blood, and her hazel eyes were tinted with mutual discomfort. There was a wound upon her that had not been present before he had been buried alive: a scorch mark of a hand gripped about her throat.

"*Damn it,*" Tsuki heaved as the memories of the fight swept through his consciousness. Their first encounter with the creature had left him with some daft notion that they could actually best it. But they had been beaten horribly. So undeniably outmatched.

Hazamareth heaved a stone off of his legs and extended a hand. "Judging by Noctem, I think we have been unconscious for a few hours. Gods, you look dreadful. You are fortunate that building had very little to sustain that fire or you'd be dead, my friend."

Tsuki heaved himself to his feet, noting the large stones that fell away beside him. The tingle from a recently shattered spine admonished his movement. "My head feels like someone took a boulder to it." He paused, distracted by the moonlight that cascaded down his ash-smudged flesh. "…And I'm naked."

"Fire will do that," Hazamareth tsked simply and reached around to the nape of his neck. A chill nipped at the base and as she drew her fingers away, a dark liquid glinted softly in the moonlight. "The damn beast is as sturdy as you are." Her fingers danced idly before she raised them to her lips.

"Gods, not that. You're like an animal."

"Waste not," she denied. As the blood touched her lips, the scorch mark began to fade.

Tsuki's body was tugged away through the remaining damage, following the soft drift of snow as it began to mask the remnants of battle. The beast and its pet were long gone, lost within the folds of winter. How in the Nine Realms were they going to contend with its strength a third time? They had nearly decapitated the damn creature, and yet it had snapped them like they were mere fragments of ice!

He stumbled slightly as he extracted himself fully from the rubble, an old, stone sign cracking beneath his heel. "Used to be an inn. Lucky they abandoned this place before the beast arrived."

Hazamareth found his boot and her brow contorted briefly. "The Dead Wolf. Why, isn't that fitting?"

"It would be if that's what was actually displayed," he sighed. "The Feral Hound, Haz." He bent down with a wince, ferrying his mangled sword from the smattering of the beast's blood.

A dead wolf was nearly what they had earned for their efforts. They needed a *real* plan—one not solely based upon their brute strength and expensive weaponry. His fingers drummed along the twisted silver. "Come, Haz. We need to scour the archives. If we have to rely on sheer decapitation to kill this creature, we are likely to be ripped to pieces before we can drive a blade that close. Especially with that Malraven at his side." He assessed his scorched flesh. "As if the beast alone wasn't already like a small army! I have half a mind to let this one go in hopes it turns around and teaches that arrogant warlord a well-deserved lesson." He wobbled forward and snapped his fingers at his silent comrade. "*Come*."

For once, Hazamareth did not grin at his predicament. "Tsuki, I don't believe this creature is like the others."

"Did you just realize that? I'm not even certain it's a demon!" he retorted, slamming his boot into the sludge of blood and snow. It rebuked him with a jarring pain. "Talk while you walk, my friend."

Hazamareth's sable bangs split, pasting on either side of her perspiring brow as she shook her pallid head. She made no attempt at pursuit. "That is not what I refer to. I think that *he* might be like *us*."

'Like us…' Tsuki snorted, feeling his ribs crack against the force. "It's murdering people," he growled in disdain. "It is *not* like us."

"You saw it defend that Malraven, same as I," she countered again, prying her hair back down. The "v" of her bangs pointed sharply down her nose, where a spatter of blood still caked from the internal hemorrhaging the massive fist had caused.

Tsuki's lips drew tight, noting that her chest had not yet corrected its cave. "So we let people die in exchange for its life lesson? Surely the beast would have shown no more hesitation if the inn had been filled with swaddled infants!"

"And we were once no different! Yet look at us now. This is no unintelligent beast as Vale suggested. This creature is… *human.* We hunt beasts because they fall outside the law. This *man* falls within it. He is not our responsibility. And if we attempt to hunt him again, he *will* kill us."

Tsuki sucked in a breath, remnants of his rampages threatening to shake him with their haunting images. *'Like us?'* "…What are you trying to tell me?"

"What you very well know in your gut," she replied, her voice steeling. "That we are no dogs of war—no servants of Saebellus. No pawns of the gods. We work by our own hand as we always have."

Tsuki felt all the pains in his body rallying at her words. Whether he was feeling defiance or rage, he was not yet sure. "We never break a contract!"

"*And we never hunt men.*"

Tsuki let out a venomous hiss, but he could see the fierce glint in her eye. *'This creature is more than a beast,'* his mind whispered. True demons never failed to serve themselves first… Yet this… *man* had thrown the elf to safety before engaging in self-defense.

"Once, I showed you the same mercy I suggest we now show him." She extended a soft hand. In the bitterness of winter's night, her fingers were as cold as ice, reminding him how inhuman they were. "Now I ask you to extend the same. We do not steal lives for coin."

"Then what, Haz?" he began, the tapping of his free fingers so rapid upon his bare thigh that his joints stung. "Do we simply forget Rel's fury and how he'll retaliate, or ignore the scourging of our good name? Are you telling me that we let this beast roam free to murder?!"

"*Man*," Hazamareth corrected. Then she offered a solution offensive in its simplicity, her hand growing tight. Yet centuries before, her compassion had been all that had stayed his destruction. "We will trail him. I need to make certain the truth of the Malraven's words. He said that he has the beast within his control."

Tsuki eyed her neck where the elf had attempted to brand his warning. If that Malraven was the *man's* reasoning… his "*Hazamareth*"…

In the growing flurry of snow, the smoldering embers hissed in warning. "*Nothing*," he growled firmly, "can subdue that beast."

CHAPTER FORTY

The white torchlight was shining directly above Jerah in a brilliant sphere of light. He slunk out of the shelter of the forest and stepped into the small expanse of white, cold fluff beyond. The field stretched across the land between the trees and his target city, long blades of grass that crunched beneath his heavy boots barely poking free. The land was frozen from the cold that had spread across it from the ocean: Jerah could smell the salt hovering lightly in the air.

Wratherus and he had traveled swiftly away from the mountains since the night before, hardly stopping to either eat or rest, and even when they had, Jerah did it only for Wratherus' sake. It seemed that the creature was not as sturdy as himself and required a more delicate balance of care and travel. But he felt proud to care for it, as it had shown him protection and devotion when the mercenaries had come to kill him.

Jerah marveled at the feeling that he had developed for it… It was a new feeling: a feeling of being closer than he had ever felt to Master. A devotion built not out of need, but out of trust.

He did wonder what it had said to the column, but it would not tell him. In fact, the creature had not spoken to him in the human or elven tongue since they had fled, despite Jerah's persistent attempts to converse with it.

And now they had come to Jerah's next target: another city. He could distinguish it clearly once freed from the obscurity of the forest line. This city was stretched across the length of the tree-studded field, not surrounded by the walls or guards Jerah was accustomed to. It was significantly smaller than the other cities he had encountered, with wooden towering buildings and soft, yellow light flickering from the occasional glass-paned window. The direct torchlight above made the shadows short and tucked tight against their sources.

He paused behind the shadow of a tree, peering out at the city cautiously. He could hear Wratherus come to a distant halt behind him, still ever wary of their proximity.

"This city is very quiet," Jerah spoke after a moment, using the elven tongue in hopes that the creature would be swayed to converse. His eyes dilated against the darkness, ears straining in the silence. There was no music, no bolstering ruckus from some bustling building, no merchants or guards. He watched a few frost-speckled leaves roll slowly across the dirt street and vanish beneath the wooden overhang of the nearest building.

Jerah slowly pushed away from the tree. "It shall be easy to make a kill in this place!" he spoke, his voice rising in cheerfulness. It had been a long time since he had been able to kill without having to fight for it. Even the last city had become gradually more difficult to enter and leave.

He glanced back at Wratherus. "Come, Wratherus. I must make a kill here. Then, we can finally sleep."

Wratherus' composure was ever straight and unruffled. Half of its face had remained hidden beneath the torn, red fabric, but its voice was clear as it offered a single, firm word. "No."

Jerah began to smile at its first word spoken to him since the mercenaries, but then blinked as its meaning reached him. He cocked his head slightly. No? No, what? "You can stay here if you like. I will return when I have made my kill," he finally responded.

Poor Wratherus, he determined—it must be exhausted.

"No," Wratherus replied steadily.

Jerah pursed his lips, but held his patience. "Wratherus, I make a kill every night. I must make one now. You can either come with me or stay here, but I must make my kill. Will you come with me or will you stay?"

"*No*," Wratherus' voice rose more forcefully.

Jerah heaved a sigh, much like his master had done when Jerah asked too many questions. His patience was now thinning. What did it not understand? He paid for his life every night. Did the creature not understand that his actions must continue, even freed from the mountains?

"Wratherus—"

"You do not kill," Wratherus cut him off, eyes hard. Jerah could almost see a fire burning behind them, fierce and dangerous.

Jerah swung his legs about, turning his back to it even as instinct warned him against doing so. "Wratherus, I must go. I will return soon." He stepped forward.

A sudden explosion of flames engulfed the frozen grass before him with a ferocious hiss, and Jerah leapt away. He watched as the flames twisted and licked the dark air in an attempt to threaten him further.

Jerah turned his head, narrowing his yellow eyes into dangerous slits. "Wratherus, you cannot stop me from this. If you try…" he trailed off, stomach knotting tightly.

Wratherus said nothing, but lifted its chin in calm defiance.

Jerah watched the creature closely as he raised a heavy boot, pressing it slowly into the charred earth. Flames instantly ignited the ground, blasting his leg with heat and sending him reeling in pain.

Jerah snarled, turning sharply. "Wratherus, I must kill!" Then he pushed off the frozen earth and darted toward the city.

A fierce sound split the air, like that of the void when water fell, and he was tossed like the frost-covered leaves of the city, tumbling across the grass and landing on his chest. He pushed himself off the ground slowly, body aching, head spinning from the tremendous force. "Wratherus," he growled, "I have to—" But his words were cut off again as another explosion of fire knocked him toward the tree where the creature stood. "Wratherus—" The next explosion tossed him several feet to the side to land with a thud and jingle of chainmail into the earth.

Jerah felt his heart pounding as instinct began to rise. He raised a hand defensively. "Wait. Listen," he began desperately. "If I do not kill one person a day, I will turn into stone like a woman column, and I will cease to be." He lowered his hand to the frozen ground. "So… I must go."

Wratherus advanced to stop a short distance from him. It looked down at him for a moment, its eyes expressionless, its chin raised. Then it crouched, letting its head fall slowly to the side. Its black and red hair slipped over its shoulder as a strand of orange passed in front of its right eye. It studied him stoically for a long moment, then spoke in a gentle voice, as though it understood him entirely. "You do not need to kill."

Jerah shook his head, pushing off the ground. It *didn't* understand. He would have to go to the city by force… He had to! He moved at the creature suddenly, reaching a taloned hand for Wratherus' throat, heart seared with pain at what he had to do.

But a blast of fire slammed into his face and shoulders, knocking him to the earth, singeing his flesh and hair. He leapt up again, swinging out a wing to block the expected onslaught of flame. This time the earth erupted beneath him, tossing him high above Wratherus.

Jerah twisted his body in the air and landed on his feet. With a terrible roar that made Wratherus retreat a step, Jerah pushed off the ground once more with all his force.

And then a tremble seemed to shake the air around him. His entire body burst into flame and with it, the creature vanished from view. Jerah collapsed to his knees, dropping his hands to catch his weight. The flames instantly extinguished, but he could smell the fumes of charred flesh and see the smoke rising off his chainmail-covered chest. Pain rippled through his body and Jerah let himself fall forward, rolling once onto his back.

There he lay sprawled, eyes staring blankly up at the void above. *This was it...* "If I do not kill tonight… I die," he begged.

"You do not kill again. You will not die," came Wratherus' calm reply. The creature was close, its voice soft and consoling.

Jerah clenched his fist slowly to stop his trembling. He would die. He would cease to be. An endless cycle of nights locked within the cellar would engulf him, but he would never be free of it. He would never rise to see the torch in the void again.

And yet, a calmness began to settle over him. The pain his chest felt when he saw the breath die in the sleeping males in their beds or the elves passing quietly on the streets…

That would die with him.

He would not kill tonight. And tonight, neither would he feel that pain that made his stomach knot and his chest hurt. He blinked back the stinging in his eyes as relief settled over him.

Perhaps, this was a good death.

He bit his lip hard to fight back his fear.

Yes, this was a good death.

He felt a warm hand come to rest upon his clenched fist. Wratherus did not speak, but its touch brought peace to Jerah at the end. Jerah turned his head slowly, eyes locking with the steady gaze of the creature. Where before they had remained vacant of emotion, now they were filled with compassion and strength. Jerah's fist loosened and the creature's fingers wrapped into his palm.

There were no words spoken between them. Jerah watched as the white torch made its journey into the west while the yellow torch began to glimmer from the east. Higher and higher it rose, vibrant orange and red rays filling the void, banishing the darkness as it came.

And soon it rose above them, beaming in all its brilliance and fire.

And Jerah lived.

'How can this be...?' Jerah sat up slowly, eyes widening in wonder as he regarded the melting frost around him. He turned his head toward Wratherus, lips parted in confusion.

He could see a faint crease at the corners of the creature's eyes, and it drew its hand away. With a soft grunt, it pushed off its knees and twisted its head to the side with a loud crack.

Jerah rose to his feet beside it, inhaling heavily. "I am alive...?" he breathed. He put a hand to his chest, feeling the steady beating of his heart beneath it. *'I do not need to kill to live...'* A pain twisted his stomach as his mind flashed to those he had already killed. *'If I do not need to kill on the surface... then Master... then Master lied to me...'* The thought made his chest tighten, his muscles stiffen. *'Master wanted me to kill... and told me I had to so that I would fear this place... and return to him. He wanted me to fear the surface...'*

But he didn't. No, Jerah did not fear the surface any longer.

He threw his arms up, letting out the sound he had once heard his master and his company make so long ago. Jerah did not know what it was, but his chest was filled with strength and excitement. He ran forward a few steps, turning in circles as he went. He inhaled heavily, taking in the salty scent of the sea blowing in from his left and the icy forest behind him. "Wratherus, we can go *anywhere!*" he spoke, turning toward the creature. "We do not need to travel by city—we can see the whole world of Ryekarayn!"

The creature's gaze had been fixed to the distant forest line, but Jerah's words seemed to recall it from its sudden gravity. The corners of the creature's eyes creased then, its body otherwise rigid and carefully composed. "Yes," it replied simply.

Jerah spun around toward the distant mountains of the south, those pale gray shadows against the blue void, and took long strides forward.

Ryekarayn was waiting for him.

CHAPTER FORTY-ONE

The sun was brilliant in his midday zenith; he had shoved the clouds aside and sat enthroned in the great blue canvas, eager to see the bloodshed of his enemies and the triumph of his heroes. All across the battlefield, the humans cried out to him, "FOR ZEPHEREUS!" while it was the king they fought and died for.

And died they did. When Zephereus had stretched above the midday sky, the armies surged through the thawing snow and clashed in a clatter of metal and the soft squish of steel through exposed flesh. The ill-equipped front line dropped in scores, but a raging sea waited at its flank.

Even the finest of Lord Barister's rebels could not repress the waves. As the front line shattered, the king's main force swept in, slicing through the kinks in the defenses and plowing toward the middle where Barister hid entrenched amongst his own men. There was no doubt in Navon's mind that the rebel's chest was swollen with regret. He possessed Saebellus' wealth, but not his military genius. Every rebel Barister had managed to scrape together with gold—the farmers, the bandits, and the mercenaries—all fell the same to the king's forces. Soon Barister would join the dead.

But not Navon. Through the chaos of battle, his necromancy writhed at the forefront, a wild, twisting cloud of black smoke that devoured the enemies with screams of delight.

If the army was the sea, then Navon was the kraken.

Not far to his right, Galter was stumbling about in the fray, his large body protected by a dented breastplate he had managed to scavenge from a newly fallen corpse. His thick hand clenched the hilt of his sword while he hacked furiously at the enemies surrounding him. It was a pathetic sight, but Navon had little attention to spare.

He raised his hand, fingers creaking in the cold, and a wisp tightened on the ankle of Galter's opponent, sending him toppling into the snow. Galter lunged and chopped haphazardly at the man's exposed flesh.

Then Navon spun away, azure eyes falling to the sprawl of Barister's forces. All those corpses that still needed counting. A delighted grin slipped across his pale face. *'Better equipped but so few in number…'* it was hardly an entertaining fight. His hand flicked forward, a twisting chimney of black spiraling up from the ground. Armor and men scattered, screaming in their struggle to free themselves from the clawing hands.

Navon's eyes narrowed, his grin fading into a cold and calculating grimace. They would not escape him. He jerked his hand backward, and as though one with him, the grasping, smoky hands latched onto the nearest foes and dragged them inward, bashing their bodies together and plunging for weaknesses.

And it felt *so good.* Navon could feel a swirl of delight in his gut with every spell he cast, joined as one with the clash of voices—a freedom that laughed and screamed to taste the fresh winter air. There was an ache too, an ache through every fiber of his soul as he sliced off a portion and sent it to the gates, disguised for death. But once within, those slivers returned, traveling to and from the Realms of the Dead, yanking souls out to cluster and grovel at his command.

It was a good ache—like working a muscle that was weak. And Navon felt stronger the deeper the ache grew.

This was what it meant to throw those legends and heroes aside. *This* was what it meant to be Navon. *Navon* was not a static, hardened personality, but a collection of all those souls that vied for his favor.

Navon was one of them, joining and twisting in their ecstasy!

He let out a cry of laughter that echoed over the battlefield as he raked the boney, skeletal fingers of his magic across the hands of an enemy soldier. He watched as the man flailed in agony and dropped his weapon at his feet. The king's men fell upon him, thrusting blades wildly into his body.

Their vigor impressed him. These humans in their haphazard gear… *THEY* knew how to fight!

Navon watched as his victim stilled and the tendrils plunged into the body, feeling the release of the soul. The spirits about him cackled in delight and their glee sent a shiver down Navon's spine. He felt them fill the crevices of his empty personality with their rich pain and ample greed.

There was a sudden wave of heat on his left and Navon instinctively vaulted backward and away into the icy field. Still, the oncoming fire seared him, scorching his arm in a mix of burning flesh and leather.

The smell was so sweet and familiar that Navon felt another rapturous thrill… He could *feel* the saliva building in his mouth and he spun in search of this new opponent.

'I'll have your soul as well,' he whispered gleefully as his eyes landed upon his foe.

The man was dressed in unmarked gear, black leather armor, and polished steel gauntlets—too well equipped to be a farmer and not well enough to be one of Barister's own men.

'A mercenary, like me,' he thought, and the personal challenge returned his grin in all its force.

The human's dark eyes faltered, his lips—tinted purple in the cold—curled with focus.

And fear. Navon could *taste* his fear—sweet and tangy—like the bile the man withheld against a lurch of terror.

The mage raised his hands again and Navon felt the tendrils of smoke curl and twist to defend him. There was a buzz through the air, like the prickle from a bolt of lightn—

Navon's eyes widened in a split second of realization and he rapidly attempted to shield himself with the nearest corpse; it failed to leap forward in time to absorb the blow. Navon was jolted from the ground, thrown into the air like a child's rag-doll. He smashed into a row of soldiers behind him. His insides trembled and moaned, his mind flashing through a thousand conflicting thoughts and feelings as disorientation left him sprawling.

"Navon!" came Galter's shocked call of concern. "Are you—?!"

Navon's mind steeled as he felt a threatening tremor course through the ground. The call of the next Gate beckoned to him, compelled him to reach deeper for his defense… But Navon ripped himself away, sweeping what souls he could safely gather. The tendrils lashed out and grabbed the nearest enemy soldier, throwing him into the earth before the Helven. The lightning caught the human, causing his body to leap and dance in an amusing caper of his last living moments.

Then the corpse dropped in a sweet smoldering of cooked flesh.

Navon scrambled to the side, free of the mage's most recent attack, and readied his souls for the next defense. He knew what to do now—he was ready for another bolt.

Across the short battlefield, the human's hand extended outward.

'This is different!' he had time to realize before a spear of ice punctured through the snow to drive up into his gut.

He sneered, contemptuous. *'And too easy!'* The tendrils beneath twined lazily around his legs, shoving the ice aside as it grew, leaving it to angle wildly to the west.

And then Navon unleashed the Gates upon his foe. They were his. Opened to him. The second. The third. But he dared no further than the fourth. A dozen fragments of his soul lay ready to ferry souls out and down upon the living world. A red glow burst from his cloud of smoke, hissing in ancient words that Navon did not recognize and yet seemed to comprehend. There was a form twisting in its mass, weathered and old, like the mangled remains of the wraith they had battled in the Pass. A sliver of red swept forward and for the briefest moment, it had the shape of a sword. It plunged through the horrified mercenary, cutting the soul clean in two.

As the souls were swept into the gate, Navon screamed in triumph. There was no surprise magic in this battle—no reinforcements to materialize from thin air. They did not need such tricks to defeat the rebel: Saebellus' forces here were no more than a *distraction.*

There was a sudden blast of trumpets across the battlefield and as though Navon had been standing in a haze, his vision abruptly cleared. He felt the fragments of his soul fleeing from the Third Gate to return to his body, clawing frantically to slip out before the Guardians realized the fragility of his focus. A soft gasp he recognized as his own escaped his lips as pain erupted and enveloped his arm. It dropped to his side and he clutched at it painfully. The Gates slammed shut. "By Sel'ari, what in Ramul…?!" he cried in confusion.

The trumpets blew again and Navon saw a flicker of white fabric flutter from somewhere within Barister's ranks. Or rather, what was left of them. The rebel remnants were stumbling toward the banner, to stand in that last moment as one before they were led off to whatever consequences the human king would devise.

And Barister himself… he would no doubt be executed for his treason.

'They are surrendering... We won!' He exhaled in relief, eyes sweeping the battlefield. *'By Sel'ari... ...We didn't just win... ...I annihilated them...!'* It was then that the number of dead about him solidified. Relstavum's human army lay in heaps across the earth, sprinkled with countless bodies from the king's first division.

Away from Jikun… away from the necessity of any other role to play… he had been Navon. And Navon… Navon was… He stared numbly at the soft wisps of necromancy that still lingered near the surface of the snow.

Navon was victorious.

Then his head swung back across the field to the crumpled body of the elemental mage. He could still feel the chill of the ice as his necromancy had forced it aside. How *easily* the experienced human had fallen to the twisted tendrils… His hand tightened over his wound as concern ripped through him.

"Navon."

Navon started, eyes shooting up from the earth to meet the deep, brown gaze of General Bardolph. There was a smile on his face, broad and greedy as it looked down from his mount to the pale, shaking elf before him. "I said if you did well, I'd have a place for you." The smile twitched once. "And you did well."

CHAPTER FORTY-TWO

The night was clear and crisp, and the starless sky above was unruffled by even the most meager of winds. For the first evening in weeks, the snow and ice beneath Jikun's boots was hard and dry. Jikun sucked in a deep breath of air in the frosted forest as he tied the reins of his horse to the low branch beside him. The weeks had been fair—no blizzards, no unbearably bitter nights, and no sign of the Brotherhood.

And now Saebellus' crowned pawn was but a thakish leap away.

He allowed himself a smile as Eldaeus pranced in beside him, flinging his reins into Jikun's hands before dancing off once more into the snow. Not too long ago, the Faraven would have received a good cuffing for his annoyance, but now…

All his trials were nearly at an end.

Jikun tied Eldaeus' reins beside his own and heaved the Faraven's sack of collected acorns off the rump. "You almost forgot this," he called to Eldaeus as he dropped the bag beside a tree. "Wouldn't want you to end up eaten by a werebear… or whatever it is."

Eldaeus blew the bag an affectionate kiss from across the clearing and went back to digging in the snow.

Jikun's smile remained forcibly fixed. "What are you doing *now?* I think you have all the acorns you need."

The Faraven waved a hand dismissively before hurriedly returning to his inane task. "I am not looking for an acorn right now—oh! I found one anyway!—I am burying my broken fingernail. You know, so druids and shamans cannot find it and put a curse on me."

Jikun grunted, his amusement short-lived. "Eldaeus, go get more wood for the fire. And don't wander too far. If you make us hunt you down again, I am eating that peapod you gave me. *And* your rations."

Eldaeus gasped in horror. "I told you, a wereboar chased me down! I had to run! That is why I need the protection of those acorns!" the maniacal elf denied, waving his arms about his head as though Jikun's attention was not already fully upon him. He pointed sharply at Jikun's pocket. "And when you go to sleep tonight, I am taking that back!"

"*Eldaeus.*"

The male swiftly drew his body into an obedient salute and marched off to duty lest Jikun be forced to prematurely follow through with his threat. The Faraven was fortunately unaware of its destruction at the hands of Makados.

"Crazy elf," Jikun muttered as he ducked below the branch and into the clearing beyond. He kicked the sack of acorns aside. "I am willing to wager a few hundred that Eldaeus runs off again. And I *just* reminded him to take this with."

Darcarus did not appear to hear his jests. He had already lit a fire, the little circle of orange glowing brightly in the night to cast warm rays against the trunks of nearby trees. Task completed, he stood preoccupied at the far end of the clearing. His gauntleted hand was extended to the leafless canopy and moments later, his raven dropped from the branches to perch upon his forearm.

Jikun watched the male stroke her ruffled head and then untie the little scroll upon her leg. He seemed so engrossed by her arrival that he did not notice the Darivalian make his way to the flames or hear him drop their sack of rations beside it.

"Did you hear what I said before?" Jikun demanded.

The missive was opened, read, and pocketed, and all the while Darcarus offered no reaction.

Jikun rolled his eyes and stooped low to pack together a ball of snow. "I asked if you are listening to me, Prince." He straightened with a smirk and hurled the snow at Darcarus' back, watching with satisfaction as it splattered against his spine.

The prince merely offered an absentminded shake of his head.

'What occupies his thoughts?' Jikun let out a mild growl. "Eldaeus is still carrying on about that wereboar nonsense." He withdrew three neatly bound meals and assessed the shadowed face of the Sel'ven, trying to interpret his grave expression. "You want the dried fish or the dried pork? ...I will give you the fish."

Darcarus loathed the seasoned fish, and yet he did no more than pivot to face him, his expression uncharacteristically bland. The raven vanished in a cloud of purple and grey wisps.

"Alright… be so god-damn strange… Eldaeus needs a companion in his insanity." He tossed a package of pork at Darcarus' feet and watched as the male took a single, solemn step over it. But it could not be that he was not starving; their last meal had been when the sun shone from its apex—and that was many hours before.

Jikun pushed off his knees, marching to face the prince directly, chin rising in challenge. "I already tire of this new disposition, so tell me: what is the reason for your gravity? We are only a few days away from Rustall! I would expect you to be as giddy as Eldaeus. Our task is almost over—in a few days' time, you will have an army and Saebellus' grip on both continents will be broken."

Darcarus met his gaze with sharp and attentive eyes. And then they suddenly faltered and swept in search of the package of dried pork. He hastily bent down to retrieve it, but made no rush to return upright.

"So what is it?" Jikun demanded. "Are you *frightened?*"

At those words, Darcarus let out an audible sigh and turned the package over until he had inspected every angle. "In regards to that, Jikun…" he began, sweeping a hand through his hair as he stood.

Jikun felt his gut tighten with the tone of address. At those five words, the calm of the night and hopeful optimism of the morning vanished like Noctem's face behind a sudden cloud. They were left in darkness, with only the flickering glow of the fire to light the clearing. Jikun sucked in a breath. "Answer me or I swear to the gods, I will be the first one to put a scar on that pretty little face," he demanded, his voice emerging in the dark, cynical growl that had merely been waiting to be loosed.

Darcarus met his eyes once more, but this time his jaw was set, his chin raised in the solidity of his frame of mind. Even the threat of Jikun's temper did not daunt him. "I am not leaving with you tomorrow morning."

Jikun felt the muscles of his jaw give way entirely.

"I said," Darcarus repeated slowly, "that I am not leaving with you tomorrow."

And as the repetition settled, Jikun's shock gave way to rage. He felt his blood run hot, his lips curling into a toothy, furious snarl. "You god-damn lying son of a Sel'ari-whoring cunt," he hissed, a barrage of the Helven's warnings rushing in to mock him from within the crackle of flames.

But even as he spewed venom at the prince, Darcarus drew himself up, shoulders snapping back in unshakeable determination. "Jikun, this mad venture to kill Relstavum was about my brother. It was *always* about my brother. And I would not have sent him to Sevrigel if this insane plan was my only choice! Acquiring Sairel's army was my last resort—*my* desperation. I mean, us… the three… *two* of us, killing Saebellus' necromancer? Gods know I prayed it would not come to that. I had other paths… paths I tried to bring to fruition, but all of them failed… Until tonight. An offer has been made."

For the first time since the prince had deigned to face him, Jikun noticed that the tiny scroll was still clutched in his white-knuckled grip.

"So all along… when you said she was… 'stretching her wings' or you were 'learning news from Sevrigel'… you were conversing with your 'paths.' I am a fool…" He laughed shamefully. "A fool. Navon swore you would do this the first moment some 'better' opportunity presented itself. What loyalty do you have to us?" He laughed again, but the sound was empty and filled with disgust.

Darcarus' chin retained its height, his voice level. "Apparently, Lord Barister was defeated seven nights ago, and this has allowed the human king to open negotiations with myself. He has agreed to meet me… To offer me aid in the form of troops." He lifted his hand sharply as Jikun stepped forward. "*Relstavum remains free*—if left alive, he will simply concoct another distraction. Everything I promised you still holds! I simply *cannot* be there to assist! My first duty is to my brother and I must attempt to barter for military assistance before Relstavum regroups here."

"Why you god-damn—!"

"This venture has *always* been about my brother!" Darcarus' voice elevated as he took a sharp step forward, *toward* the temper that threatened him. "I have never hidden that, you damn fool! Hadoream is why I was out here in this forsaken land, and why I was hunting Saebellus' force to begin with! A better door has opened and I am *taking it*."

Jikun threw his arms into the air, attempting to vent skyward every ounce of his body that desired to strike the prince. "I cannot believe your audacity! We are less than a *week's* journey away from severing Saebellus' hold on Ryekarayn entirely and you turn tail and *flee!*"

"I HAVE ANOTHER DOOR!" Darcarus roared. There was a screech from a bird nearby as the frightened creature took flight. "But it is *not*," he hissed, "another door for *you*." He made a wide gesture that encompassed the horses, the rations, and the gear strapped unmarred to Jikun's body. "I have a better path to aid my brother *now*, and protecting him is my first priority—*not* defeating Saebellus. Navon saw his escape to find his so-called atonement and he took it; Saebellus is now weakened, but he is *not* defeated. Now *you* remain: Relstavum will create more chaos—slaughter more innocents, reassemble after his losses. You stand here, capable of severing Saebellus' ties entirely and opening the doors to even greater military assistance for Sevrigel. Here you can justify the loss of your army… those *thousands* that died… But you must do so yourself. Otherwise, what value does your life hold over those of your soldiers? You either join Navon in believing their slaughter by your hand was in vain, or you accept that slaying Relstavum… *saving* this country and crippling Saebellus… was always the only door for you… was always *your* fate."

White tents erupted into blackened flames and something crackled and popped beneath the helmet of a dying soldier… haunting echoes Jikun had barely kept at bay. The walls cracked as the force of his emotions pressed outward, straining to escape the confinements in which they had been bound for too long.

Darcarus' words came softer now, offering him refuge from the bursting dam. "You claim you fled Elarium to prove that you were destined for a greater purpose. Navon… Eldaeus… myself? This is not our trial. This is your justification. *Now prove that all those soldiers did not die in vain, General.*"

Jikun inhaled shakily. But the prince was right. This was his only path. This was *always* his only path. It was why he had crashed in the Makataj. Why he had found Dahel… encountered Relstavum. Why he had sold himself out to the Brotherhood… Killed Borin… Journeyed this far. He had thousands of lives to justify—only by destroying Saebellus' power would he fulfill his role. "…So are you leaving now?" he asked, his voice tight with anger.

Darcarus nodded slowly. "Yes, I have a long ride ahead of me."

Jikun stepped forward once and before the prince could react, he had snatched the package of pork from his skinny fingers. "Then I will be keeping this."

Darcarus blinked once in surprise. "Excuse me?"

"You heard me," Jikun grunted, sweeping up the sack of rations. "These were to hunt down Relstavum."

Darcarus opened and closed his mouth in obvious amazement. "I…"

"Go eat your god-damn needles and bark. Or go crawling back to Sairel." He stalked toward Eldaeus' acorns, dropping the food safely beside the bundle of supposed luck.

Darcarus let out a single laugh. "You know, in better times, I think we would have made fairly decent companions." He passed by the scowling

Darivalian and swung himself upon his mount. “It is unfortunate which paths fate chose for us.”

But Jikun refused to be melted by the prince’s attempted charisma. “You chose this on your own, you viper. Now get out.”

Darcarus gave no reaction to the insult. “If you truly feel the need to replace me, one of my contacts informed me that Saebellus’ Beast abandoned its master and is now on Ryekarayn. It has always been a dangerous force—even against necromancy.”

Jikun’s mouth could not have slacked lower. “And now you have the audacity to suggest *that?* Get your god-damn ass out of my sight!”

And Darcarus whirled his horse about and trotted quietly into the forest line.

“Good riddance,” Jikun muttered vengefully.

There was a sudden rustle in the branches above and Eldaeus dropped by his knees beside him.

“Gods damn it!” Jikun shrieked, nearly swinging out to knock the Faraven fully from the tree.

Eldaeus grinned crookedly as he rocked, watching the prince fade into the darkness. “And then,” he spoke solemnly, “there were two.”

Chapter Forty-Three

Sellemar turned the little porcelain figure in his hands, admiring the detail. The hair, the face… this was assuredly the most carefully crafted one yet—and that was to be expected. He had spared no expense for the figures of his shrine. He probably could have bought a dining room table or half a new wardrobe. Or perhaps hired someone to clean the uninhabitable lower level of his estate.

But here, in this room… the small shrine to Sel'ari was far more valuable to him than any such trivialities.

Sellemar ran his thumb affectionately over the carving before he placed the statue of Aura beside that of her betrothed, Mesheck. She settled there unsteadily and he moved Tiras aside in the event she decided to lurch forward and knock him from the shelf.

Above the little huddle of statues, in the candles that bobbed against his breath, the face of Sel'ari flickered with amused compassion.

"Eraydon. Riphath…" he shifted them to the left of her outstretched marble hands before lifting the last figure before her. He prayed briefly that she would protect him as she had protected the six heroes so many years ago. Sellemar too needed shelter and guidance for the trials ahead. What he had witnessed through Vale's eyes boded ill for Hadoream and more importantly, Sevrigel.

Saebellus' determination to retain his throne had reached a climax—even the death of a True Blood was justified. His mind throbbed as he recalled the warlord's acceptance of Ilsevel's plan to slay Hadoream and frame his Resistance. The rebellion would never survive such an accusation. Not yet.

But it would soon. Cahsari had finally broken to Sellemar's interrogation, and tonight he would lay the councilmember before the city square with the crimes of his brethren.

The instigation would be complete. The rebellion would truly begin. And the Resistance would lead it to fruition.

That, of course, made the True Blood essential to the restoration of Sevrigel. But where *was* Hadoream? *'What is delaying Itirel...?'* He reached up to rub his temple. The pain was increasing now. *'Damn Hadoream for hiding away!'*

There was a sudden crack of thunder that seemed to pierce from the center of Sellemar's mind. He started, his hand jerking up, narrowly missing the little shelf.

His breath caught. It was late. The night was dark. And yet, in the silence he could hear no rain. The sky outside his balcony doors was cloudless.

'Then what?'

There was a crackle of thick fabric being pushed aside. He knew the sound well.

'A tent flap...'

His eyes snapped open, his breath emerging fast and hard from the abrupt awakening. His heart pounded in his chest like the drums of battle.

A boom of thunder ripped again, closer now, bearing down to consume his tent.

"Vale, get up!"

The unexpected voice that closed the distance in the dark was hoarse and frantic. Fear cleared Vale's mind. He fumbled in the dark, igniting his lantern and brandishing it before his breast.

Second General Saebellus. The Sel'ven was garishly distorted in the shaking light, the shadows of his face pocketing and elongating his striking features. He was soaked to the bone, his blond hair plastered against the sides of his pale face like a hood. His blue eyes were bloodshot, hollow with the reflection of Vale's own fright.

And his hands. The palms of his hands were sealed in fresh, glistening blood.

"What happened?" Vale demanded in a hoarse whisper. But he knew the truth. He had seen this all before!

Yet he clung to Saebellus' words.

The lips parted to a black slit, hanging frozen. Then they twisted, emitting a response so soft, so vacant, that Vale was forced to draw near. "I..." the second general's voice dipped and was lost.

Vale's lungs constricted. *'Say it...'* his mind dared to demand.

Saebellus spoke again. His words snaked across the distance with force. "I killed General Angrenor."

The color drained from Vale's face; he could *feel* it leave him, rush away to his gut. It wanted to pass further, but he collected himself. He had known. He had known that this would come to pass. *'The general brought this upon himself,'* he flayed his qualms. *'He pushed us too far. Asked too much!'*

Yes. *The time had come for the meek to be silent no longer!* "What is the plan, General?" he whispered.

Saebellus stood and Vale realized then that the male had been supplicating on his knees. Now he was tall. Strong. Courage had risen above the fear. His words emerged rapidly, forceful and direct. He was at once the general Vale knew. "We must rally the rest of our supporters. We must leave the army. We will participate in this genocide no longer! The capital will see that we will not slaughter the innocent—not for them. Not for anyone!"

And then Vale was racing at Saebellus' command. The tent flap echoed behind him, battering violently in the wind. Faster. *Faster.* He had to bring Adonis. Thunder was bellowing once more like the furious cries of the goddess herself. *'Tonight of all nights!'*

His feet pelted across the puddles.

Soon, it was mud. Bloody mud, as though the blood of General Angrenor had seeped through the earth to engulf him.

'Why is the earth red?

'...For rebellion. We cannot turn back!'

His hand stretched to the tent that suddenly rose before him, but it seemed distant. Surreal.

Something was amiss.

Terror was bubbling up inside him once more. *Dread.*

He lunged forward desperately, again and again, and yet his fingers could only brush the coarse side. *'Adonis... I have to bring Adonis!'* And then abruptly his fingers closed around the fabric. He wrenched the covering aside and the tent collapsed about him, exposing the scene within.

Sprawled across the earth, sickly white and riddled with holes... Adonis lay dead. It was then that Vale realized. *'The blood at my feet... it is his!'* "WHY?!" he screamed.

The assassin emerged from the shadows. *'Ilsevel? No... she was not there that night!'*

And even as his mind struggled to make sense of the heartache before him, Adonis' body began to convulse. His lips croaked his name in growing desperation, as though he could still be saved. "Vale… Vale. Vale! VALE!"

"*I will purify the races of their depravities*," the wraith hissed, *"for I own the king."* And her hand plunged into Adonis' breast—

"Vale. Vale!"

Vale's eyes flashed open, his chest heaving from the pain of labored breaths. He felt a hand upon his shoulder, shaking him firmly. But the voice was soft and calm. *Safe. Alive.* They were sitting in a field of short, wispy grass, Noctem's moon illuminating Adonis' solacing features.

"Adonis," he wheezed and shuddered, pushing himself up unsteadily. He smacked his bare chest once, the abrupt sensation helping to clear his mind. "A nightmare…"

Adonis pressed close to his trembling arm, keeping a hand upon his shoulder to reassure him of his presence. As he was *always* there to reassure him. "Which one?"

Vale exhaled heavily and wiped his palm across his face, sliding the beads of sweat away. In the coolness of the night air, it was a wonder he had managed to perspire. He shrugged his shoulders slightly, hoping that the hand would fall away.

It did not.

"The night Saebellus killed Angrenor," he ceded. "But you… were already dead when I came for you."

Adonis' fingers tightened and he leaned his head gently against his shoulder, pale eyes meeting his empathetically. "But that's not what happened."

'I will purify the races of their depravities,' the bitch-queen had said.

Under the rule of the council, their lives had been perpetually in peril. But after all their sacrifice… was he… was *Adonis*… any safer? "No… But if we lose this war, it will."

The world was sideways—he was tilted, knocked askew. On the marble floor. How…? *'Gods, my head…'*

And then he was once more in the field; Adonis was consoling him, pushing his anxieties aside. "It is Saebellus who is king. He will not let death be the penalty of our differences."

No… he was on the marble floor again. A blurred outline lay several inches away, glinting softly in the firelight.

"He will keep us safe. That will *not* happen to us."

The Nemorium faded entirely and Sellemar's vision cleared, revealing a scene of disarray and shattered glass. He shifted his neck with a pained groan, his head throbbing where he had struck the floor upon his collapse. He had fallen against the shrine, knocking the curtain from its hanging to land precariously close to the burning candles.

"Would not that have been the epitome of pathetic deaths," he muttered resentfully as he pushed himself gingerly upright. "Sel'ari's shrine burns to the ground with myself entrapped, all while I dream of another male coddling me—*SHIT!*" A sharp pain sliced through his palm and he jerked his hand reflexively from the floor. Bright droplets fell in its wake.

The remains of the figure of Ephraim lay on the marble, scattered in a dozen fragments. Now stained red with his blood.

CHAPTER FORTY-FOUR

"The sun ascends toward its zenith and yet night is gaining on us!" Eldaeus crowed, his wild, green eyes watching the unnatural cloud of darkness forming in the west. "We are getting close. *I can feel them.*"

Jikun's lips twisted into a grimace of agreement. He could feel it too—a disturbing heaviness that weighed upon his soul. The air was clear but for a few unruly flurries, and yet something else was tangible. In his experience, there was but one taste that matched this bitterness… this weight. *'Death.'*

"What I wouldn't give to have a god-damn necromancer right now," Jikun hissed with resentment.

"You mean Navon?"

"…Yeah. That's the one," Jikun spat.

Eldaeus shrugged. "I would personally rather have a skilled hunter."

Jikun turned enough in his saddle to catch the calculating contemplation of his last remaining companion. "…Why a hunter…?"

"Well, because wereboars are extremely dangerous prey."

"…You know we're hunting Relstavum, right…? That darkness is from *Relstavum*. I told you, wereboars do *not* exist."

Eldaeus had learned better than to disagree with him. "Well, I do not think we are going to get Navon either way," he huffed with an air of indignation.

Jikun threw him an exasperated glare. *'At least I have Eldaeus,'* he boasted sarcastically. And if he had listened to Navon—listened that Darcarus had been using him—he might have had his captain as well.

'No you wouldn't, you fool,' he rebuked himself, reminding his delusional affections that his captain had made himself very clear. Even if he had listened to the male, this outcome would likely have been the same.

As Darcarus had stated, they had walked different paths since Elarium.

Jikun briefly wondered where the two now were. Navon possibly remained on the war front, reverting into the same game they had spent a century playing. It was familiar to him and offered some semblance of unity to allay his fear of being alone. And the prince? He scoffed in derision. The prince was probably sailing to Sevrigel to rush to his brother's side, Ryekarayn's woes entirely forgotten.

Gods damn them both.

Eldaeus had more than proven his value as a companion—he, at least, was still beside him for the final task.

The silhouette of a town was materializing beneath an expanding sable cloud. *'We have managed to stay on Relstavum's trail through every trial.'* His gut tightened painfully. *'And we are close, now.'*

Their mares pawed restlessly on the cart-chiseled snow as they neared the unmanned gate. Darkness had settled over the land, a thick blanket that blocked the sun with such detestation that no light could penetrate through its shroud. Instead, the sky around them glowed orange, casting the town in an amber hue like the dying embers of a fire. The portcullis had been raised wide, but only a dusting of snow scuttled in to coat the desolate street.

The town was as still and silent as the frozen tundra.

Jikun felt a chill slither down his spine, but it was not the winter air that had caused it. He pulled the reins taut, drawing the mare to a stop before the walls.

"You may be right, Jikun," Eldaeus spoke after a moment. "Wereboars cannot write."

But the male's insanity could not weaken the tangible fear that hung leaden in the air. Etched across the grey, stone walls were the familiar markings that had marred Dahel—black, chilling circles that were scrawled with precision across the surfaces. Jikun could almost pray for such a mental ailment that would deaden the dread that threatened to overtake his senses.

"YOU THERE!" a shout burst from the leftmost tower. A human had appeared, partially obscured beneath the remains of a parapet.

Jikun started at the unexpected living being. *'They're not dead yet?!'*

"By Zephereus, are you all they sent?!" the soldier wailed in disbelief. "You won't be enough. The man is mad! I said we need an ar—!"

But he never finished. A roar of otherworldly howls surged like a storm from the necromantic symbols below him, erupting with a flash of blood-red light. They reduced his booming voice to the pitiful cries of a child as they submerged the town of Rustall in a grey, hissing haze.

"*Gods, it's happening!*" Jikun hollered as his mare reared. He clenched his thighs tightly as he fought from being flung from the saddle. Memories of hungry, clawing wisps and splayed bodies rushed across desert sands. "Like Dahel! Eldaeus, these people are going to die!"

There was an internal crack of thunder that shrieked its way to the town's core and the necromancy flared to life. Black tendrils erupted like a nest of angry serpents, pouring from the visible symbols in droves, slithering their way into the streets and buildings in a ravenous quest for living creatures.

Eldaeus was out of the saddle in seconds. There was startling life in his eyes—not like the wild innocence that drove him to reckless trivialities, but a clarity of genuine comprehension.

The lucidity passed as quickly as it had come, but a fragment of sanity seemed to remain. "Give me the reins!" he cried. "Dismount!"

And without sensible reason, Jikun obeyed. The screams were escalating now, horrible, twisted shrieks that emanated not from the necromancy, but from the souls it tore from the living hosts. "What are you doing?!"

Howls… hideous howls! He could not hear himself above their gleeful keening! He felt as though his mind was slipping… sliding… rushing away from him…!

Eldaeus' hand was upon his forearm, the horses gone. *'Where?'* And then there was blood.

His blood?

No, Eldaeus' blood. It wove a mark upon his frigid hand, intricate and unknown.

The keening dulled.

"What is this?" Jikun gasped, the voices whispering like distant thunder across his brain. He winced as he glimpsed the smoke spiraling through the town beyond. *'Dying... they are all dying in there...!'*

Eldaeus drew his blades. "*Real* Farvian protection magic!" And before Jikun could reply, the male sprinted for the city's gate with a maniacal bellow that could rival the howl of any Darivalian wolf. "We must stop Relstavum and save the people!"

Jikun's boots anchored him to the snow, like shackles binding him to the safety of the field outside. "This is—!"

"Our chance!" Eldaeus cried, and he halted a step before the town's gate, turning and beaming with triumph. It was optimism that would have put Navon to shame.

And then he turned and leapt inside.

Jikun put a hand to his chest, feeling the terror inside expand. *'Damn it!'* he growled to himself. *'He is right! I cannot fight Relstavum directly, but while he's distracted, I can sure as I god-damn breathe drive a blade through his back!'*

Suppressing his fear, he crossed the border of the living and into Death's domain.

The effect was instantaneous. A chill coiled into his lungs upon his first inhale, searing his insides with such cold that it burned as keenly as fire. Eldaeus had stopped several yards ahead, his blades hanging loosely in his hands as though the reality of his course had abruptly caught up to him.

"Do not break the seal," Eldaeus uttered in an agonized whisper. His voice lilted oddly to Jikun as though from across a great distance, warped by the souls through which it passed.

Jikun gritted his teeth and advanced, pausing only briefly at the Faraven's side. "Come, Eldaeus. *We have to move!*" He walked past the male, feet stirring the thick fog about their calves in a twist of shimmering silver. There was a soft squish beneath the heel of his boot and his mind leapt with images of raw, torn tissue. He steeled his resolve. "We have retribution to pay!"

The steps behind him immediately quickened. Even Eldaeus understood.

Yet they had not advanced far before the bodies began to litter the streets—twitching corpses of things that had once been.

At first, there were merely one or two, shoved into the alleyways and mounds of snow at haphazard angles, as though mangled by some great beast. They twitched and flailed, but their eyes were glazed and the mouths hung loose and dry.

Jikun had seen enough dead to identify them easily—moving or not. His feet hastened until his accelerated breaths shredded his lungs with the baleful chill.

"We are getting closer," Eldaeus gasped in mutual affliction, head flitting from terrace to terrace as though the stalactites were poised to rain down upon them.

Jikun's breath wheezed painfully through cracked lips. "Not fast enough," he replied, feeling his sense of self struggling arduously to remain within its corporeal structure.

But the Farvian warding endured, dulling the voices of the necromancy. Still, they tore at his core. Faster and louder now, as though the force of magic was congregating in the town's center, beckoning them to join.

Nearby, a hand slammed into the frosted glass of a window pane. It slid away and a yowl of delight erupted from within.

"Faster!" Jikun urged. "Relstavum is harvesting the last of the living from this region of town—his magic is moving toward the center!"

He was running, now. The buildings were rushing by in blurs of brown and white, imprinted with corpses that littered their stairs and pressed against the windows. The magic had grown swifter since Dahel—where once the necromantic chaos had sent the people fleeing for refuge, now they appeared to escape no further than the steps outside their homes.

He skidded around the icy bend in the street and jerked to a stop. Eldaeus rammed solidly into his shoulder, but Jikun hardly noticed. His body had stilled, his breath so imperceptible that it created no more than a tiny puff of white before his lips. Something stood silhouetted in the supernatural glow.

"What is that ahead…?" Eldaeus murmured with an audible swallow.

For the briefest moment, Darcarus' beasts conjured in great forms across Jikun's mind. *'He came back?'* His eyes strained into the darkness, speculating how far the prince had run before empathy had hastened his return.

But when the street ahead remained quiet, Jikun's guard rose once more. "Like the serpent near Dahel…" he trailed off quietly. *'The hel'onja is not the only undead beast Relstavum can summon…!'*

In the unnatural darkness of the streets up ahead, two shapes were silhouetted against the amber glow—hulking, bent shapes, unnaturally suspended in time. The larger of the two stood on four legs, its posture as rigid as stone, but with fur rippling across its massive body in the whipping breeze. *A vandrant*, a territorial beast of Arisfare, the region in which many of the True Blood Sel'vi had resided before Eraydon's death. And the other, Jikun recognized from Dahel—the creature that had flattened its body to unnatural thinness. An agretha, Esra had said. *'Her favorite.'* He felt a prickle run across his skull, causing his hair to rise. Even across the distance, Jikun recognized the unmistakable glistening of scales and the spikes that jutted along its back and hindquarters in lethal spires.

But the creatures did not so much as glance his way.

"I do not believe they know we are here," Eldaeus exhaled in almost tearful relief.

The adrenaline fled Jikun's body in a rush. "We will avoid them," he whispered, hardly audible even to himself. "Step into the alleyway."

But the dark magic around them seemed to feed off of his alarm. The soft whisper he had spoken intensified, echoing across the distance, louder and louder until he screamed his command in the face of the tremendous beasts. "STEP INTO THE ALLEYWAY!"

The two forms abruptly quivered, as though awoken from a deep sleep. Jikun could hear the cracking of bones, the popping in sockets where tendons snapped in place like the stiff, dried string of a bow.

"*They know,*" Eldaeus croaked.

Jikun's hand flew to the hilt of his blade and the movement evoked a chain reaction from the necromantic monstrosities. The vandrant crouched onto its haunches and then launched high across the cobbled stones to land with an earth-shattering thud before Eldaeus. The tremor sent the Faraven staggering backward in a flurry of snow.

There was a flicker of movement in the distance where the beasts had stood sentinel.

The agretha had vanished.

"Eldaeus, watch out!" Jikun shouted, frantically scanning the landscape for some sign of the creature.

Silver fog swirled in web-like strands and the Darivalian leapt to the side, crashing into a booth of abandoned leather. He raised his hand against a churning pool of black that broke from the concealment and flowed rapidly toward his feet. Damn it, this was a delay he could not afford!

He threw his frustration into his magic; ice ruptured powerfully from the earth in a disarray of stalagmites, puncturing through the black liquid as uselessly as a sword through water. A few shards of ice careened from his control to pierce through nearby windows and puncture writhing corpses.

The agretha retreated into the darkness and Jikun used the momentary reprieve to glance for Eldaeus. Perhaps they could yet devise a swift escape…!

No sooner did he allow himself to be distracted than the pool of black rematerialized at Jikun's breast, erupting with spines. Three deflected off his breastplate to leave behind a massive dent, two gouged clean through the scale mail along his arm, and the last tore his ear in two, spraying his hair with blood.

'It's fast!' There was no fleeing this beast. Instinct gripped Jikun coherently above his pain; he scrambled for the opposite end of the booth.

Across the street, Eldaeus had daringly scaled to the upper story of the nearby building and was hanging precariously by the ice-coated balcony rails. He swung at the pursuing beast as it leapt and embedded its talons into the stone.

Jikun pressed his hilt to his bleeding arm. *'At this pace, Relstavum will finish the spell before I return them to the earth!'* He rolled around the booth, ice crawling at his fingertips.

The beast had vanished once again.

'Shit!' Jikun swore, leaping to his feet. He stumbled once more into the open expanse of the street, scouring the road and walls for the black pool.

There was a soft ripple in the shadows and, on instinct, Jikun drew the snow into a wall of ice, sucking the moisture from the air and intensifying the already dry atmosphere.

A thud of spines smashed against his barricade.

He was making no progress on the offensive! Was Navon truly so necessary to his magical success?! At the Pass, the male had almost killed him! While Jikun had never honed his magic, his lack of experience had never endangered anyone but himself. He could feel the memory of the pain Navon had inflicted expanding in his chest… one rib threatening to tear apart from the other…

And a thought pushed past his resentment.

The instant the volley ceased, Jikun countered. He spun free of his protection, causing the snow to melt and reform as great spears of ice that ripped through the creature's legs. As the agretha's pinned body quivered to liquid once more, its form bulged, flexed, writhed…

And then exploded in an internal mass of expanding ice.

"Fuck you, Navon," Jikun exhaled heavily through the tinkling of icy shards. He spun around the frosty street.

The Faraven was standing calmly in a bank of snow, the headless body of the vandrant pumping blood out at his feet.

Jikun had no time to wonder at Eldaeus' miraculous success. "Are you alright?" he grunted, sheathing his blade.

Eldaeus' grin spread and he nodded triumphantly. "Not a scratch on me, but my boots are stained." He looked down and turned out his heel. "And I am not certain if I can scrub this out."

Jikun's concern dulled to be replaced by a familiar exasperation. "Focus, you half-wit! Relstavum is still—!"

His words were terminated as a keening shattered through the protective barrier on his mind. The taste of iron filled his mouth and he whirled around. From the town's walls beyond came a rushing, twisting cloud of black, as though the shroud over the sky had dipped down and now roiled and careened its way to them. Instinct seized hold of Jikun and he sprinted forward, grabbing his companion as he went. "RUN!" He looked down at his hand frantically, but the Farvian protection was still intact. *'Maybe this is it—the culmination of the spell!'* "Faster, Eldaeus! This might be our only chance!"

The Faraven let out a squawk as he glanced over his shoulder. "You do not have to warn me! The proximity of that sea is enough motivation for me!" He paused and then grinned. "I just made a rhyme, did you hear that? Sea, me?"

Jikun willed himself to run faster. *'Ice. You can still barricade yourself in ice,'* he told himself, but he was plagued with doubts of whether his magic could protect him from such a sinister force.

The hazy forms of buildings ahead were taking shape now, growing in size and prestige. A statue loomed amongst them, brandishing a stone sword to the raging heavens. *'The town square!'* If Relstavum controlled his souls at the center of Rustall, then these were the man's final moments…!

And then Jikun's body lurched, invisible talons ripping at him from the inside. He tottered, regaining his balance through pain-filled gasps.

Beside him, the Faraven's eyes bulged and his mouth opened in a silent cry of agony. "I do not think," he rasped, "that the Farvian protection can hold if we move much closer!"

Jikun felt the ground beneath his feet shift and a thousand hands, as faint and delicate as cobwebs, reached from the teeming ocean of silver beneath them. The Farvian symbol on Jikun's skin burned with fury. "We can't stop here!" he shouted, and dove behind a nearby empty booth. "We have to move closer—I cannot control enough magic to cross the distance and we cannot afford to miss…!"

The thick smoke, churning with the consumption of the city, was advancing. They were running out of time! Jikun leaned sharply from the booth, straining to discern the shapes through the mist at the town's square. A wailing of souls ripped past him from a nearby building, blowing the glass clear from the windows to shower them with tiny shards. And then the mist ahead dimmed and a silhouette of a man became emblazoned against the reddening sky, tall and weathered, wearing a thick cloak that billowed in the howling wind. He emanated raw power as he raised his arms to Emal'drathar, commanding the otherworldly storm to do his bidding.

Jikun's heart dropped into his gut even as magic leapt to summon the snow about him. *'Relstavum!'*

"JIKUN! LOOK OUT!" Eldaeus screeched.

Jikun rounded and was enveloped by his companion's horror. In the span of two heartbeats, the cloud had closed the distance to them and was now a mere fraction of a yard from crashing down upon them like an avalanche. Twisting coils of black smoke reached out greedily, red wisps like veins pulsing deep within. The symbol on Jikun's hand split his flesh, breaking through the strain of protection and leaving him defenseless.

'This... is it,' he whispered to himself.

Eldaeus' voice resounded from nearby, the final rallying cry to defend himself, to *fight!* "JIKUN! HELP!"

Ice crackled through the mist, forming an orb of protection around the pair. *'It's not enough!'* his mind screamed. And then darkness immersed them.

Utter, silent darkness.

Jikun felt a gentle tug on his vitality, then a jerk. Then his strength was being whisked away, sapping from his body like blood from a gaping wound. He could hear the ice around them crack. Why had he never honed his skill?! Now it would cost him everything! His nails tore into his palm in painful concentration, recalling the barrier he had erected to protect himself from Saebellus' avalanche at Widow's Peak. It felt like a millennium had passed since then. *'This is your last chance to defeat him. Hold. HOLD!'*

The darkness faded behind a flicker of red spots dancing in his eyelids. Weakness... A surge of such god-damn weakness...! "I can't do it, Eldaeus!" he gasped.

"You do not have to," the Faraven whispered calmly.

Jikun's eyes opened and found that the darkness was gone. The last slivers of silver haze were vanishing into the earth, and even the furious clouds were beginning to dissipate. Sunlight was slipping in now, genuine rays of winter light dropping a pale, blue glow upon the ground beneath them.

The ice fell to water. All signs of necromancy had vanished.

They had survived, but so had Relstavum.

Jikun pressed a clenched fist against the wall of the booth beside them. "Relstavum...!"

"There is still a human there," Eldaeus hissed with stark coherency. He was crouched on the balls of his feet, vivid hair and wide eyes peering up over the top of the booth. "He is just... standing there...!"

Jikun shoved the male down, pushing his face into the snow. "What are you doing, you imbecile?! You're a damn hyaline in the tundra! Stay down!"

Eldaeus grunted. "At least I am not a peacock."

Jikun shifted silently and dared to peer around the side of the weathered booth. There was a human, as Eldaeus had said. Relstavum stood at the center of Rustall, his hair whipped to disarray by the force of the wind. But he was not alone; since Jikun had seen him last, he had acquired an ally—a hulking form of a man dressed in black, and a…

Jikun's gut dropped. And at Relstavum's feet was a blood-red drake.

Both the human and the beast waited attentively, watching the necromancer as he took his first steps away from a fading necromantic circle—unsteadily at first, tugging the cloak about his legs free from the gnarled fabric it had become in the surges of wind.

Relstavum, even after expending so much power into a spell that had ripped the very life from the town, still stood. Unsteadily, but still, *he stood.*

Jikun flexed his own fingers. He could feel the weakness aching in his bones. *'If you don't strike a necromancer while he is vulnerable… if you lose the upper ground… you will die,'* Jikun repeated Navon's warning in his mind.

Like any war. Like his loss at Elarium.

This was it. This was his last chance.

Jikun gave a long exhale. The man was hunched slightly, his steps slow. *'Weak…* Distracted… *'* His eyes swept the expanse between them. The distance was too great after the energy he had already exerted.

His mind flicked rapidly to his own gear and he reached swiftly behind him to pull his bow free. The bowstring hung severed from the top. *'The fight with the agretha?'* "Damn it! Eldaeus, give me your bow!" He reached over swiftly and freed the weapon from the male's back.

Eldaeus instantly yanked it away. "No. You broke yours. This one is mine. You cannot ruin mine as well!"

"What in—give me the damn bow, you fool!" Jikun hissed, trying to wrestle the bow as quietly and subtly as he could manage behind the small, wooden shelter. "I will shoot Relstavum!" His hand landed on Eldaeus' arm, but his attempt to freeze the male's skin only caused his own hand to stiffen. *'Damn, focus!'*

Eldaeus clung to his weapon tightly, entirely unaware that Jikun had endeavored to strip the bow by force. His eyes were feral with irrationality. "No! I will do it! It is my bow! I can do it! You never trust me!"

Jikun clenched his teeth and narrowed his gaze, shooting the town square a swift glance. The humans were still prowling about the area. The drake had a half-eaten corpse dragging by entangled entrails on its toes. He looked back at the Faraven, his words rife with warning. "*Do not miss.*"

Eldaeus huffed, raising his bow. His movement was swift and smooth as he drew the arrow from his quiver and notched it in the string. "You have seen my hunting. I never miss." And with the speed and precision of unparalleled luck, the male's arrow loosed, hissed through the air, and punctured straight through the middle of the human's skull.

The *other* human's skull.

"Fucking Sel'ari's cunt!" Jikun swore, watching as the massive man toppled to the snow at Relstavum's feet. "What in Ramul are you doing?!"

Eldaeus looked affronted, clutching his bow in indignation. "What do you mean?! You said to shoot him so I did!"

"*You cunt!* It was *that* man!"

And as one, Relstavum and the drake turned toward their street.

"I feel encroaching death…" Eldaeus whispered. "Let me fight him!"

'If you fail to take him unaware…'

Jikun's shoulders jerked straight. He lifted his hand, preparing the water in the air for his command. *'Navon is wrong. This is my fate.'* He forced a soft exhale. Ice rushed to leave his fingertips.

Relstavum's voice came suddenly across the distance, strong and certain, striking the magic from Jikun's body with a single phrase. "General Jikun," his voice called with confidence. "I recognize your soul from Dahel."

The color drained from Jikun's face. If he had held some notion that he could succeed, it had vanished.

"What a chance that we should meet yet again. I admit: that was a terribly clever ploy to slip the tracking charm onto some worthless cutthroat. My men have not been able to locate you since. I did not expect such perception of the charm's functionality. Tell me, how did you know what it was?" The human laughed, then glanced about with wry expectation. "Ah, it does not matter. It seems the end is you and I after all, General, but the result for you will be the same. Saebellus will be *most* disappointed to hear of your failure. He admires your… *persistence*… even if the others in your company failed to find the trait so *charming*."

Jikun's body tensed. He could not fail. He did not need Navon or that traitorous prince to do what he was fated to accomplish. As Darcarus had said, this was not their battle. This was *his*.

The necromancer's laugh escalated across the cobbled streets, ricocheting from stone to stone. "But I must ask… where *is* your captain? And *where* is that cocky little True Blood? I expected at least *one* to stand by your side. How… *disappointing*. I could have slain three enemies of the empire at once.

Had I known that your captain was bored of the challenge, I would have exerted greater efforts into assuring the Beast was constrained and here to entertain him. Alas, it yet roams free, gallivanting across the human lands, murdering and thieving in hapless villages." He paused briefly, as though offering Jikun an opportunity to respond. When he did not, the human continued. "Your captain always enjoyed such confrontations, did he not?"

"He is stalling," Eldaeus whispered, breaking the hold of the conversation. "He is weak. He had to travel deep into the gates to cast that spell. Not all of his soul has yet returned."

"And I won't let it," Jikun growled solidly, drawing his blade. He stood briskly and saw the flicker of recognition in the human's eyes just before he let his magic loose. The ice shot from the ground, a blur of pale blue that sucked the strength from Jikun in a wave of nausea.

As though toying with a small child, the necromancer's hand extended and waved casually, tossing the drake before him as an armored shield. The ice shattered against its scales with a clang that echoed through the streets while other shards tore through the soft flesh of its belly. The final blow pierced straight through its neck and out its mouth to shower the snow in a splash of blood.

Jikun's fingers curled. "*Go!*" he roared.

Eldaeus had vaulted across the ice before the word had fully left Jikun's lips, sprinting toward the human's haggard form with balance worthy of a Darivalian.

Relstavum let out a cry of wonder at the sight, the veins on his neck bulging with unrivaled greed. "*You are them! Who are you?!*"

Jikun did not pause to wonder at those words. He rushed forward, raising his hands as he did so and targeting his focus on the man's skull, aiming for that final, solid blow that would seal both their fates. But before his magic could burst free, a tendril ripped his legs out from underneath him, slamming him backward into the stone. Jikun felt the smack of his skull against the icy cobbles, the strange dance of lights once more before his eyes. His spears sailed through the air off course and shattered uselessly into the branches of a nearby tree. The ice that was lodged in the drake's throat—so *close* to Relstavum—splintered away harmlessly toward the empty sky.

Jikun shook his head dumbly, trying to push upright, but the sheer attempt to move caused his body to flop uselessly in the snow. His eyes swiveled, attempting to locate the human. And he felt the briefest flicker of hope.

Eldaeus—the persistent and maniacal Faraven—was undaunted by the power of the necromancer or the souls at his command. He dove past the drake, past the writhing wisps of necromancy. Then he was before Relstavum, slicing at the man's massive arms and darting away like a coiled viper, ready to strike once more. Relstavum's face had contorted in rage, the emotion greater even than his visible greed, and his mouth curled and cried out with dark and frantic words. Tendrils, still weakened from his previous spell, lashed out haphazardly for the Faraven.

Again Eldaeus danced across the necromancer's vision, watching the flow of Relstavum's balance as he struggled to command every spell.

The last of the haze from Relstavum's blow was clearing from Jikun's mind, and he heaved himself shakily to his feet. He could still feel the unnatural chill of the ice beneath his fingertips, weaker now than ever, but raw with desperation. Relstavum was distracted—he could ask for no more.

A black hand shot suddenly from the writhing smoke as Eldaeus darted in. The smoky fist curled about the flashing blades, seizing hold of the weapons and master long enough to strike. The tendrils exploded, slamming into Eldaeus' chest.

Pain washed over the bright green eyes—an audible croak of air tore free of his lungs. His hands weakened from the swords and he flew backward from the blow, narrowly dodging the stone of a building nearby to shatter through its frost-painted window. The stalactites along the roof shook and fell free, cracking along the bank of snow.

Jikun found his voice. "Eldaeus!" he cried, but his mind recalled immediate attention to the opportunity.

Rallying his remaining strength, he felt the prickle of magic on his fingers grow into a tingling surge. Something inside him seemed to snap as the final bit of that strength rushed from him and poured into the earth, willed into a material force. A crackle resounded through the clearing as ice formed and pierced into the air…

Relstavum whirled back to Jikun in alarm, realizing too late that the Darivalian still remained. And then he froze, blinking in confusion as their eyes met.

He laughed, a single, mocking laugh. "Your soul isn't even worth harvesting."

Light erupted from the building where Eldaeus had sailed. Without hesitation, Relstavum pivoted from Jikun, tearing through the snow toward the Faraven beyond.

Why was he running?! Why hadn't his magic pierced the human?!

He opened his mouth to shout and felt a gush of warmth spill down his chin. His knees buckled and he slid toward the snow, becoming abruptly aware of an excruciating pain sweeping through his chest. He looked down, pale eyes flying wide.

A spear of ice had erupted from the earth and ripped through his heart.

The sword in his hands slid from his fingertips as his head dropped to the side.

So Navon was right. *'One soul pales beside thousands…'*

If the gods had divined his survival—his place in their greater plan—he had chosen the wrong path to Saebellus' end.

From the corner of his vision he saw Eldaeus rise from behind the glass, the symbols on his body glowing with terrifying brilliance even as the darkness of the necromantic cloud washed over him. As Relstavum stole yet another soul.

As Saebellus secured yet another victory.

The faint images of war flickered to Jikun's mind. The burning tents. The soldiers flinging themselves before him. The screams of pain as they were cut down. Those who had died to protect their country, their families, their homes…

He was no different than Relstavum. All those lives he had stolen to save his own. He was no hero.

Jikun stared numbly ahead as he exhaled his last breath.

And after all his running, what had he died for…?

Chapter Forty-Five

The door burst open with a clang, smashing into the marble of the wall behind it. The density of the stone was all that prevented the tremor from quaking through the walls to reach the occupants inside. An admirable force—dangerously so—from the female that had flung it. A testament to her rage.

Ilsevel. Soft, sweet, and yet treacherously volatile.

The shadows on the wall leapt toward the intruder, their long talons reaching out as though to rip her down in their lust. "Now the rioters have attacked Lord Listaria's home—it has gone too far! Too far!!" she cried. "How *dare* the rebellion make a display of my council. MY COUNCIL!"

Saebellus shifted his weight forward onto his hands, eyes rising from the male spread before him to meet those of his wife. They were as wild as her hair, as though she had just been out in the windy streets, possibly to ferry the terrified lord to safety within the palace walls. Still, as much as her beauty captivated him, Saebellus had work to finish and, once again, Ilsevel was more than ready to waste his time with the trivialities of politics.

The shadows flickered and faded once more into the darkness, keen to skirt his gaze. The darkness was still… and yet, he could feel that chill from their proximity, ever a reminder of the curse.

But it was Vale who responded to the intrusion first, his hatred for the queen an irresistible prompt toward a venomous attack. "HAH!" his captain roared. "You think *that* is bad?! We have a dozen rebelling cities within a few leagues of us, smashing shit every time one of our soldiers so much as looks at them! Take your complaints to your mewling City Watch. Have *them* deal with it… and with *you*." He poked the face of the male before him, causing the bound figure to moan pitifully.

Saebellus shot Vale a sharp, warning glare, his black eyes growing as hard and cold as the marble walls that surrounded them. His captain was free to speak at will outside her presence, but he had *warned* the male about riling his queen.

Vale took immediate notice of the darkest corners of the room and his jaw snapped closed.

Saebellus straightened slowly, drawing himself up to a calm and collected stance, masking the emotions roiling below the surface: his temper buffeted his gut and ribs like a living thing trapped within the cage of his breast. How many cities would rise up against him due to the meddling of the anarchists in his capital's square?! His fist tightened, pressing into the pool of blood at the splayed male's feet. "Do you understand why this has happened? Your rage is not going to end this uprising, Ilsevel. The Sel'vi of our nation demand that the corrupted council members be removed. The *other* races believe Cahsari and the council's crimes are a ploy by the monarchy… by you… by *us*—to remove their racial representation—their voices. Their belief is only extenuated by the fact that the two, and only, *Sel'vi* of the council were noticeably absent from the list of crimes. And this includes Listaria." He revealed only the slightest tightening of his lips as an outward gesture of his displeasure. "As long as Hadoream is free to stir dissention, these resistors of our reign will always believe they have another choice!"

But his calm exterior only launched Ilsevel into a greater fit of rage. She thundered across the marble with her tightly bound feet, her lips curled into a snarl of pure hatred. "I don't care what they want, Saebellus! They can't act as they please against my reign! Make an example of them!" She stopped when she reached the table and raised her hand, prepared to pound it violently against the bound male's chest, heedless of the gaping hole in its center. "I do not care that we cannot find Hadoream! *WE* are the monarchy, Saebellus!!!"

Saebellus' hand grasped her wrist in an instant. The chandelier above them began to rock, as though a breeze had penetrated the windowless room. And his fingers… his fingers applied just enough pressure to cause her to still—for the color to drain from her face in a moment of considerable fear. "You cannot kill whomever angers you, Ilsevel," he whispered. "Hadoream's power is balanced on the people's fear—do they fear more what we shall do to them if they join the True Bloods, or do they fear what we shall do to them *without* the True Bloods? If you strike the rioters now—while no other entity exists to blame for their discontent—the whole *country* shall turn on us. We have no choice but to pacify them as best as we can manage until we have found the source of this rebellion—then we shall crush it and end their opposition. We find ourselves nearing the cliff… Whoever planned this has executed it *quite* effectively. Jikun may be dead. Relstavum may eliminate Silandrus and his Realm. But if we do not locate Hadoream soon, we will indeed lose everything to this spirit of resistance."

Ilsevel's breath sucked in sharply as he loosened his grip and set her free. Her hand dropped against her abdomen, where she clutched her own wrist in a self-comforting gesture. But she was calmer now. Finally, she seemed to grasp the presence of the tattered body of the bound male spread across the table. Her eyes lingered on the soft tapping of blood as it dropped onto the marble floor to graze the end of her silk dress.

She took a sharp step back. But she was listening.

Vale was attentive as well. He had paused from his work, his sharp features twisted into tangible distress. "Saebel," he began slowly, running his tongue across his cracked lips, "perhaps you've been too focused on Hadoream's demise. If Relstavum overthrows the True Bloods and we kill the Resistance, what does Hadoream matter? The people will become complacent without their rebellious leaders."

Saebellus felt a slight twitch at the corner of his lips. He did not respond to the wholly idiotic response, for beneath his captain's words he knew lay another message. "What is it, Vale?" he demanded softly.

The shadows stilled. The candles flicked and dimmed. Ilsevel retreated hastily to the doorframe.

Vale did not look up. His hands made themselves busy, quickly locating the bloody tools scattered across the stone. "It is because I truly do not believe Hadoream will ever seize the throne that I have felt that this… *tiny* detail… was unnecessary. I'm only mentioning this now since… you truly seem to feel that finding the princ… essisabsolutelynecessary. But I know that if we kill the rebels and blame them for the discontent, everything will fall back in your favor."

Saebellus grimaced slightly at the rapid change in Vale's speech. He paused a moment, dissecting the mangled words.

Ilsevel had not noticed. "We *will* find Prince Hadoream—Ra'vonis' ability to track is second to *none*."

"Princess."

Ilsevel blinked. "What?"

"Princess," Saebellus repeated calmly. "I believe Vale just informed us that the reason we have been unable to locate the dear True Blood is because Hadoream is not a prince. Hadoream is a *princess*."

Ilsevel's thick lips hung mid-gape and he saw her struggle to grasp what vital fragment of Vale's words she had missed. Her eyes widened suddenly. "*Princess?!*"

And with that, Saebellus' fist slammed down. The table before him cracked as though it were as dry and weak as driftwood, folding in on the cleric. The wood and priest collapsed to the marble floor with a crash, the moan choked out by his final breath. The shadows twisted, writhing as though in identical pain. "*YES*," the king hissed with such venom that Vale reeled away in terror. "A *woman*. Hadoream is a *woman*." He stepped forward, the damaged bones of the cleric's hand crunching beneath his heel. "And here we have crawled and clawed and strangled information from this land, but the answer to our *failures* lay but a *whisper* away." His hand shot out, catching Vale by the throat and driving him into the ebony wall. "*TELL ME WHY!*" he roared.

The chandelier spun, lights flickering wildly in the wind and sputtering out one by one. Only the candle Ilsevel had set beside the door remained, its flame squirming and elongating in the rush of darkness.

"Saebel, I'm sorry," Vale sputtered, hand flailing to grasp his arm. "I was only privy to the truth because of my comradery with Darcarus! I swore I would tell no one!"

"But you told Adonis, did you not?" Saebellus sibilated. The darkness grasped for Vale, crawling down his hand. The captain's skin grew grey as death and caved.

Vale wheezed as Saebellus' vise briefly tightened. "No!"

Another lie. Yet the shadows withdrew abruptly. Saebellus' expression revealed nothing at Vale's response, but his chest seared with pain. His hand released and he stepped back. "Why?" he asked once more, his voice nearly inaudible even in the silence.

Vale gasped and coughed, slumping against the wall and clutching his wounded hand. "Silandrus wanted Hadoream to be treated with impartiality. He wanted her political voice heard, her military talents obeyed, her freedom respected… The council and the society it infected would allow none of that!"

"How dare you keep this from Saebel!" Ilsevel shouted.

Vale ignored her, swiftly continuing, as though his torrent of information would nullify his disloyalty. "Hadoream was yet one more motivation for Silandrus to leave—to forge a Realm where she would be held equal. When Darcarus whispered the truth to me, I swore I would tell no one—his people may now know, but Sevrigel does not!"

Saebellus' lips twisted into a snarl. "You have *crippled* my empire, Vale," he hissed. "We have chased the god-damn phantom of a *prince* across this land! Every day that Hadoream has been free she has strengthened the rebellion against me!"

Vale paled, but his words emerged fiercely. "I broke my vow *now*—that's more than you should *ever* dare ask for!"

Ilsevel let out a laugh, but Saebellus swiftly raised his hand, cutting her off. He dipped his head, meeting his captain's pained gaze. "Thank you."

Ilsevel choked back her amusement with an indignant yelp. "*What?!* Saebellus, it is because of Vale that—!"

"It is *because* of Vale that we know at all." Saebellus let Ilsevel's jaw hang in the silence as he extended his hand and waited for his captain to accept. "I apologize, Vale. You would have been right to deny me the information indefinitely."

"Not indefinitely," Vale muttered, grasping his palm and allowing Saebellus to pull him to his feet. "I ought to have told you sooner. My loyalty is *first* yours."

Ilsevel's jaw closed, opened, and then snapped shut once more. She crossed the room in long, brisk strides, planting her body sharply between them. "The *princess* is nowhere close to being found because we must begin anew! Do you realize how long it will take to inform all of our contacts that they are looking for a *female* and *not* a male? The *Resistance* is working *now*. We cannot wait to stop them—they are destroying the peace—undermining our reign! *We cannot wait for Hadoream to fall!* I need not remind you why I came into this very room to begin with!—*The riots are ripping this city apart!*"

Saebellus reached for the scrap of clean fabric on the floor beside him, wiping his hands across it. "Ilsevel, to change this country you must weave what you wish for them to see and hear. Relocation is a slow and challenging process. But slaughtering those who are questioning our methods only makes their wails greater *still*."

Ilsevel's venomous eyes narrowed and shot toward his captain—he could plainly see that she desired Vale's lean corpse on the crumbled table instead of the weathered cleric's.

Saebellus tossed the blood-stained cloth to Vale, watching briefly as the male struggled to clean his tools with his crippled hand. The mark from the shadows had darkened upon his skin and his fingers moved stiffly. Still, his captain did not complain. "The rebellion has shown the people what it wishes them to see and *how*. I will now return the favor." The shadows sank low, fleeing his sweeping vision. "We shall rip the 'Resistance' from our city and frame them for the unrest. The Sel'vi are a proud people—we shall use that pride against them."

Little could curb Vale's hate for long. Color had returned to his cheeks, and he could not resist a jab. "They would rather accept another source as the cause of their strife than admit to their own fucking corruption."

The captain's boldness returned Ilsevel's courage. "But *how*, Saebel?" she insisted, stomping her tiny foot. She placed a hand hesitantly upon his arm and her sudden trust sent a shiver down his spine. "How do we push these riots onto the rebellion when we cannot find them?"

Saebellus' fingers extended gently over hers and he allowed the corner of his lip to elevate.

"We have now," Vale interjected triumphantly. "What do you think we do out there all day while you're playing politics for the masses? We aren't just killing farmers and their sons."

Ilsevel's eyes widened, her soft lips parting greedily. Her sky-blue gaze darted across the splayed cleric, hungering for his story, and then found its way back to Vale's smug expression. "You know where the rebels are?" she whispered.

Saebellus' nostrils quivered. "Indeed. Adonis' tracking of Sellemar has come to fruition. While his discoveries do not offer us enough evidence to imprison the Ryekarian, you are to place him under constant watch—he is to go *nowhere* without his escort."

"Sellemar..." Ilsevel started. "In his close relations with Silandrus' family, he *must* have known about Hadoream's identity! He *must* be with the enemy!"

"It would seem. Yet as you planned, leaving him free has had value—he has led us to the heart of the rebellion—and we will gather evidence of his involvement tonight." He gestured to the man she had nearly dispatched to the Realms herself. "The lower level of the temple where Sellemar has been seen has been given to non-religious purposes. This priest has confirmed its use by the insurgents."

"To think, even the people of our goddess betray us now!" Ilsevel snarled.

Saebellus' mood swiftly darkened. "I think Sel'ari has betrayed the interests of her people for some time, Ilsevel—too eager to see herself grow in popularity and station to risk inciting the notion that her people may not be as pure as she would have the world believe." He *felt* the color of his hair... of his *eyes* as he spoke. "And this shall be the last day her city riots against *us*."

Chapter Forty-Six

A knock rang out from the hall below and Sellemar groaned. With the display of the council's deception in Elvorium's square, the rebellion had truly commenced. Could he not enjoy his crucial victory in peace?

He set his glass of wine aside and scowled venomously at the window.

He need not wonder who had interrupted his rest—he knew.

'It was only a matter of time before she tried again...'

"Feign illness. Vomit a few times," he muttered to himself as he descended the stairs. But he doubted even that would dissuade her.

He swung the door wide for the queen and readied himself to utter some falsified greeting. Yet Ilsevel pushed past without even a flash of charm or a bat of her pretty eyes.

She whirled, her eyes pinning him with an intrusive gaze. And then she smiled.

The alteration in tone was chilling.

'What now...?'

"How are you, Sellemar?" she spoke softly, running a hand shamelessly down his chest. "Are you as troubled as I am of late, or has the world done right by your design?"

Sellemar stood rigid, carefully displaying only an expression of detachment. There lay a threat beneath her words. He watched her fingers curl. "While the world threatens your reign, you know I cannot find rest."

"Do I?" she openly challenged. As though only in jest, her smile grew. "We have tried to extinguish the terrible lies, but it seems they have triumphed. What a vicious plot this 'Resistance' weaves." She reached out unexpectedly and slammed the old door against its frame.

The chandelier above them quivered.

Sellemar attempted to remain at ease. "You... seem terribly vexed, my queen. Tell me—what can I do for the crown?"

Ilsevel laughed at his words, catching his arm to spin about him. She ended on his left, clutching his shoulder with unnerving proximity. "I need to find another source to blame for the city's unrest," she lamented. Her nails skidded up his arm to his chin, then slowly walked their way up his carefully composed face. "Now tell me: Who. Can. I. Blame?"

Sellemar's head ached sharply, but it was not from the fingers that jabbed him. "What can I do for the crown?" he repeated calmly.

How could she know?

Ilsevel heaved a dramatic sigh. "I am certain you help every day. After all, you visit Sel'ari's temple often—surely you have said more prayers than the whole of this kingdom combined!"

Sellemar attempted to smile, but his lips faltered. The pounding was growing to a warring drum. "If you seek an enemy, then allow me to assist you. What can I do?" With the repetition he was beginning to sound like one of the Mythowood's sprites.

"Oh Sellemar," she simply sighed, and lifted a hand to squeeze his chin. This time, her nails dug in like talons. "How noble of you to offer yourself. But do not fret over my fate. We have a solution to our problems. I instead have come to keep you safe. At least, that is how you can view it." She gestured to two of the soldiers lingering at the frame. "Think of them as protection from the rioters... And *not* as an escort designed to observe your *every* move."

Her fingers departed with a jerk and it took every bit of Sellemar's will to remain unmoved. He knew his smile had long since dissipated. "I am flattered," he intoned.

Internally he reeled, his heart beating to the cadence of the pounding in his head. His time had passed. *'She suspects,'* he thought grimly. He had led the country to rebellion, but he could not see it through the end. *'Damn it. What led her to...?'* He recalled the lieutenant lingering about the temple weeks before. *'Him.'* He pressed a hand to his head, assiduously fighting the growing roar.

"I have personally selected two of the best mages Saebellus could offer. You are in the *best* of care."

'Mages. Damn mages.' But his residence contained the True Blood Tunnel. Mages now were nothing more than an inconvenience to his doorstep. Still, he would give her nothing more against him. "I am honored by your generosity," he spoke, but his composure faltered beneath a blinding glare of light outside his own eyes.

Ilsevel did not appear to note his growing confusion. She snapped her fingers once, briefly recapturing his attention. "Let us depart," she demanded to her remaining escort. She pivoted toward the door and drew her head into her hood to rebuff the evening chill. Her face disappeared within, becoming one with a dark blur of stone, lost in the evening light.

But her soldiers vanished entirely.

Sellemar started and blinked, trying to differentiate the divide between the Nemorium and his own reality. Damn it, he had to stay conscious until she was gone!

Ilsevel was talking, but he only caught the last of her ramblings as his futile resistance intensified the volume of the Nemorium's whine. "—they shall remain guard outside your doors, there whenever you need to depart—"

But it was not that he was prisoner in his own home that vexed him. The damn uneven streets were to blame! *'Ouch-ch-ch. Damn cobblestones. Fucking...'* Vale hopped once on his left foot and rubbed the toes of his right. "Move it—while they're still ignorant!" He gave the expanse of cobblestones that led from the palace behind him a menacing glare before his scowl returned to the glinting gates before him. A tumult of voices arose from outside as the rioters glimpsed the throng of soldiers approaching—

"Sellemar, are you—?"

The humming swelled fiercely within his mind, as though he had been dragged to the raging bellows of a dwarven smith. Damn the bitch-queen for interrupting his thoughts! Sellemar slid his feet forward furiously and tossed his head. *'Focus!'* he chastised himself, wrenching his mind once more from the revelation of the Nemorium. "I am humbled by your graciousness to leave soldiers where I have none," he managed to speak, even as he clutched the railing for balance.

Ilsevel inspected him warily, but he had no gaze for her. He watched the golden gates part to the throng outside. Then he stepped through, lifting his blade against the rioters in warning. He had better things to do than slaughter these fools. *Tonight the rebellion would fall!*

"Do not be frightened," Ilsevel merely cooed. "As long as you stay within, no harm shall come to you."

Sellemar strenuously managed a moment of balance. "I am afraid I had Black Blood before you arrived." He uttered a pitiful laugh before he found himself at the front doors of his estate. He had no recollection of passing the distance. "Thank you. Let me waste no more of your sacred time." His hand was swiftly turning the ancient knob before she could reply. "Have a pleasant evening, Your Majesty."

"Yes, and you as well. My soldiers shall make sure of th—"

"Yes yes, farewell, Your Majesty."

And with an unruly shove and a swift farewell, the door clanged loudly at her back, as though warning them to return victoriously. *'And I will. Beneath the watch of the bitch-goddess, I'll slaughter her mewling herd,'* Vale growled inwardly.

The rioters surged about him and only Saebellus' warning kept him from driving a blade through the nearest male's gut.

Sellemar's eyes flew open, his breathing ragged as he struggled from the spell. "*No*… DAMN IT, Sellemar! Not now!" he hissed. He could not escape through the True Blood tunnel tonight; prisoner or no, he would not remain inside while Vale slaughtered his allies! He stumbled to the kitchen, managing to seize his cloak from the counter, and knocked a rioter flat. He made certain to step squarely on the bitch's breasts as he carried forward.

'Saebellus said not to kill *them,'* he thought smugly.

A blast of cold air snapped Sellemar back to reality and he realized he had flung wide the west window to his estate.

He did not bother to close it.

Down the shadowed land, Ilsevel and her guards were traveling south, out onto the icy street to make their way back to Saebellus…

'We have a solution to our problems.'

The death of his Resistance…! By Sel'ari, Tilarus would be there as well! Sellemar whirled toward the west. Far in the distance, past the gleaming white marble of the sprawling city, he knew the temple of his goddess sat, oblivious to the impending raid!

His feet pounded across the snow, too torn between speed and confusion for driftwalking to erase his mark. *'Ilsevel suspects you!—You are supposed to be a prisoner! Leave no trail!'* he swore at himself, and his feet pulled free of the white blanket so that his next steps barely brushed the surface.

At least the streets were clear. It made it far easier for his soldiers to move. Fifty of them—more than sufficient to empty the bitch-goddess' halls of resistors and clerics alike. *'It's what happens when you cross Saebellus,'* Vale thought.

But it was hard to hear himself think over the cries of the rioters pushing themselves up his ass. They were tight behind his soldiers, crying for fucking justice.

Justice was exactly what he was about to serve!

Sellemar shook his head violently. *'This is not justice!'* he cried to himself as he broke free of the old Rilden Estate's grounds, his feet racing down the path to the inner city. *'Sel'ari protect them!'*

The bitch-goddess? In his gut he knew she didn't care!

Sellemar shook his head again, his vision flickering wildly between the market street outside his estate and that which Vale occupied in the south. The fucking civilians were just getting in his way!

But he ran, stumbling and then running again... no, damn it, he was walking! What did it matter if he moved more quickly? The fucking temple would have no idea what was approaching.

'RUN!' Sellemar roared to himself, once more forcing his legs into a burst of speed. He clipped a booth as he moved, sending the contents on the edge scattering out into the road.

He felt no pity for the female as she scrambled to gather her wares. He had never cared for them. None of them. They were all the same—selfish. Mewling. Hateful... They all despised him. All the same. All of them.

Sellemar gritted his teeth against the venom. Against the pain. Vale's emotions were strong and his mind was clear. Every fiber of his being struggled to not collapse beneath the weight of the captain's loathing. With every step he took the pressure only increased.

He hastily reached up as something cool trickled down his lip. He swiped the blood away from his nose, sucking in a painful breath of chilled air.

And he ran. Who was closer?!—He or Vale?! He had covered a great distance, but there was still an expanse before those damn resistors met their end!

"In my way... in my way!" he snarled as a male strolled idly in his path. Sellemar reached out, snatching the male by the arm, and hurled him into the alley beside him. He heard the crack of something as it broke beneath the male's fall, but he did not slow. *The bitch-goddess!* He had to reach her in time!

"Are you alright?"

"What's going on?!"

Sellemar could not distinguish if the voices that besieged him were nearby or halfway across the city. Were they his or Vale's eyes he saw from?! Were they his ears or that cursed male's?!

He began to round the clear lane of the bend before him and realized too late that it was Vale's eyes that saw the road. Sellemar collided solidly with the edge of a cart near the market square, knocking the wind solidly from his lungs. He tumbled over the snow and ice to lie sprawled before the blacksmith's door.

"What's going on, Captain?"

"Are you alright?"

'Do not slow me down...!' Sellemar's arm flew down to the hidden blade in his boot and back up again, the hilt of the dagger cracking against the skull of the male that reached down to assist him to his feet. "Get out of my way!" he roared, lurching to his feet. His eyes peeled wide and wild as he watched the male clutch his skull and fall back. "You are fortunate you are not one of them or I would finish you off!" he snarled.

And with painful breaths Sellemar managed to extract himself from the elves that rushed to the victim's aid. His hands were trembling now, his legs nearly buckling beneath him. So... close...

No. He was there. He was at the temple of the bitch-goddess. He sucked in a breath of cold air. Fresh. Clean. Ah. This was what victory smelt like.

"Move out. Surround the perimeter. Kill every cleric on the temple grounds. Attempt to take all non-clerics alive... but inflict whatever wounds necessary to do so. If they draw a weapon against you, do not hesitate to slit their throats."

'Tilarus, too. I need to take Tilarus alive. He will know much. I will bring him before Saebellus and everything shall come to light!'

Sellemar's eyes cleared as urgent voices reached him.

"You're on holy grounds!" someone shouted over the tumult of voices.

A throng of rioters was gathered nearby, restrained only by the threat of the weapons held in the hands of Vale's soldiers.

The captain was nowhere to be seen.

Sellemar's eyes widened, rising away from the rioters and scattered soldiers that held the perimeter.

Away to the Temple of Sel'ari.

They were already inside.

Chapter Forty-Seven

A cry ripped through the raw night air, issuing from within the temple of Sel'ari. It wrenched Sellemar's consciousness fully from the Nemorium, piercing the veil of his confusion by the grace of the goddess herself. The thunder dissipated from his mind like the echoing scream, Vale's feelings of hate, triumph, and confidence vanishing with it.

That cry… the first cleric of his goddess had fallen!

His eyes swept the frosted earth, up the steps still slick with ice, to the door barred against the riled crowd. His mind hastened to formulate a plan. He should have held one by now, but the Nemorium had dulled his own cunning. Vale's bloodlust was a poor replacement to calculation and planning.

A dozen guards were scattered across the grounds of the temple and its perimeter. Two were at the doors of the temple, and one male, armed with a spear, held the rioters before the steps at bay.

"Defilers!" a voice roared from somewhere within the furious mass, and the cries grew all the louder, drowning the screams from the temple within.

Sellemar gritted his teeth at his own languorous wit. *'You must act! Better plans have had better days to form!'* He threw his cloak over his shoulders, twisting it around his neck in a thick, makeshift scarf to cover the lower half of his face, then drew his head into the shadows of his hood. The pitiful disguise would have to suffice to conceal his identity—even if he was to escape the city through the True Blood tunnel tonight, it was far safer to leave no trace of his involvement.

Gathering his resolve, he ran. Soon Vale would be upon his Resistance and there would be no one left to lead the city's rebellion.

The elves in the crowd were pressed tightly against one another, creating a near-solid barricade between Sellemar and the temple. Cursing, he cut through their ranks with sharp jabs from his elbows and several violent thrusts. As he shoved the last protestor aside, he carried his momentum toward the nearest guard. His hands shot out, grasping the swinging spear and wrenching it to the side.

"What—?!"

The shaft tore free of the soldier's grip, and the male's cry of surprise was cut short as Sellemar's foot sent him sailing down the marble steps to crash into an unconscious heap.

The crowd behind him roared with vicious approval, and in several swift thrusts of Sellemar's appropriated spear, the two soldiers before the temple doors were hurled with equal prowess into the angry mob.

'Keep them,' he breathed beneath the victorious cries of the elves latching onto their prey. He flung wide the temple doors and praised Sel'ari that he had not lapsed into the Nemorium's dreams during the brief skirmish.

The door thudded shut behind him and Sellemar's heart clenched grimly. The interior of the temple was in chaos, bodies of the slain clerics splayed across the floor and, in their final pleas to the goddess for salvation, draped grotesquely over the feet of statues. The floor was puddled with blood that lapped against the boots of the soldiers who were now ransacking the temple in search of any hidden offenders.

Across the room, away from the density of their search, a flash of movement caught the remaining candlelight—a lone cleric scrambled from the dark and dashed for the temple doors, fleeing from behind a small, golden statue along the wall.

An enemy soldier spotted him, whirling from his furious blows upon the flowers at Sel'ari's feet, and lurched triumphantly into the terrified priest's path.

Sellemar's arm flew back, his aim straight and strong. The newly acquired spear was shoddier than his own, but it swept true, striking Vale's dog clean through the back. A moment later, the wild-eyed cleric burst past him and through the temple doors to safety.

His freedom did little to alleviate Sellemar's distress; the male was the sole survivor of Elvorium's most holy order.

He steeled his emotions as the temple doors thudded closed. He could spare no sympathies now; their souls were already cupped in the hands of the goddess.

"Who are you?!" one of Vale's soldiers demanded, rising from Sellemar's victim. He brandished his sword in wide, extravagant arcs. "How did you get in here?!"

Sellemar locked eyes briefly.

And then he ran.

He bolted past the smooth white pews, the rows of pearlescent candles, the murals of mythologies and glorious deeds. He vanished through the doorway at the far northwestern end, onward toward the clerical dormitories and the headquarters of the Resistance below.

Through the Nemorium, he had seen Vale lead his throng to the temple's rear—where Saebellus' lieutenant had scouted weeks before. It was the faster of the two routes… avoiding the maze of halls that Sellemar would be forced to navigate… But he steeled his hope that their search would delay them. *'There still may be time to save the others!'*

"Wait!" the soldier cried. "Stop!" But when Sellemar paid him no heed, a fury of footsteps pursued. "Seize him!"

Sellemar skidded around the corner and into a jade statue of his goddess, pushing off her shaking form and lurching around the bend. A shatter of stone resounded behind him, followed by the violent tongues of the soldiers who stumbled in its wake. Sel'ari would give him what aid she could.

He crossed the final expanse of polished tile that adorned the doors of the cleric's living quarters and vaulted down the winding staircase.

Down the steps to the storage level of their dormitories.

To the headquarters of his Resistance.

He spun around the bend and was met with a wail of alarm.

"Hush, it is me: Sellemar!" he sibilated through the concealment of his cloak.

"*Sellemar!* Praise the goddess—what has happened?!" Seferia pushed from the crowd, her features pulled tight, her lips contorted in a ghastly grimace few fair faces could manage. "Gelradis, Sunae, and Voremel went above to find answers, but they have not returned!"

A throng of faces flickered in the shadows of the lantern light, sunken, ashen… filled with olfacible fear. They huddled at the bottom of the stairway, the great length of hallway stretched out behind them. At the opposing end, cloaked in the shadows, was the second and last egress from the headquarters.

The point where Vale and his butchers would descend.

They would soon be surrounded.

Sellemar regarded the small crowd of comrades, accounting for each of the frightened faces. Most were present.

Denwen raised a sword in the dim lantern light. He was no more a fighter than half the members present. Spies. Scribes. Informants. That was the majority of his allies. "They may have found us, but surely we can fight our way free!" he shouted fearlessly.

Sellemar's lips grew tight and he gestured with his hand to sweep the group aside. They parted before him. At his back, shouts and the pounding of feet warned him pursuers were not far behind.

Surrounded.

"To fight our way free is indeed our only solution. Vale's soldiers are fewest in number in the temple proper, and a crowd of rioters below Sel'ari's steps will offer us concealment as we flee."

The group remained silent, clinging to his every word, knowing their lives well and truly depended on his experience. He selected several from his small, ashen following. "Equel. Nurae. Liadoren. You will—" he paused as his eyes finished their final lap about the group. His chest constricted. "Where is Tilarus?"

Liadoren strained to gaze down the great length of hall, where the gloom nearly swallowed the end beyond. His eyes were those of a spy, keen and unrivaled in their perception. "Tilarus is still watching the rear stairs."

As though on cue, the male's familiar voice rang out from beyond the shadows, a shrieking echo across the tense quiet. "They are coming! By Sel'ari, *they are coming!*"

His warning ceased and an audible *twang* whisked across the distance. There was the sound of flesh colliding with stone—a resounding thud and a clatter—and then Tilarus' body rolled out from the stairs.

He sprawled across the floor in death-like stillness.

Sellemar cried out in panic, his mask of calm before his followers lost. "TILAR—!"

"I'm well!" the male's groan interrupted his cry, and Sellemar could just distinguish the struggle of a figure rising to his feet.

The tightness in Sellemar's gut receded, and he was swift to recollect his wit. He could not afford to give way to partiality. He addressed the others, pointing urgently up the winding stairs behind him. "The temple. Go! Equel, Nurae, Liadoren—take to the front. Disable Vale's soldiers and break for the temple doors."

As they hastened to obey, he rushed down the length of hall toward his friend, blood pounding in his ears. Had Tilarus been shot?! He could not afford to carry the male to safety! Admonishments rushed to his mind. *'Damn Tilarus! Damn Vale! No, I should have trained him for combat!'*

There was the sudden hiss of a distant voice and the shift of armored plates sliding softly against one another. "This way, Captain!" Though their footsteps were yet inaudible on the stone, Sellemar knew Vale's soldiers were dangerously close.

At the base of the stairway, Tilarus had managed no more than to rise and limp a yard forward. Sellemar skidded to a halt at his side. *'No arrow!'* "You are too slow," he rebuked, catching the male's elbow and jerking him swiftly to the safety of the south end.

"*You're* too damn fast," Tilarus retorted with a grimace, fingers clasped solidly to Sellemar's arm. The sound of footsteps had grown loud. "I thought we were dead! *How did you know?!*"

But as the last words left his mouth, Vale's commanding visage appeared at the bottom of the stairs, a dozen males crowding into the narrow confines behind him. Their armor was smooth, polished, and spotless—they had not yet tasted blood.

Sellemar's hand rushed instantly to the cloak about his neck, making certain that it obscured the details of his face. *Vale*. This was not the first time since the Halls of Horiembrig that he had been forced to endure the wretch, and yet better here than in the captain's despicable mind.

A sudden glint caught his eye and he ducked, flinging Tilarus as he dove. *'Damn!'* he swore at himself as the arrow sailed away into the darkness. Saebellus' men were not idle, slow, or hesitant. They found no reason to question their commander. There was a soft tink as the metal tip struck the stone behind and, for the first time since he had rushed to Tilarus' aid, Sellemar realized that the soldiers who had pursued him from the temple now battled with his Resistance at the stairs.

There was another glint and Sellemar's attention returned to the bow. His arm flashed with deadly precision; before the second arrow was loosed, his knife whisked through the air, severing the bowstring and lodging deep within the archer's throat.

Vale's soldiers leapt aside with shouts of surprise as the marksman fell in a clatter of arrows.

"He only had one god-damn knife you cowards!" Vale admonished in a roar. Yet the captain held his blade tensely before his breast, wise enough to maintain a cautious defense even when Sellemar's only visible weapon was spent. "Surrender now and we will let you live—those pages you sent upstairs to fend us off are long dead. You are surrounded." His eyes flicked down Sellemar's body and his smile grew.

Sellemar only uttered a single word: a command to Tilarus. "*Run.*"

Tilarus immediately obeyed, bolting down the hallway toward the side of his brethren.

"What a champion," Vale cooed with a sneer. "Pity your brain isn't as sharp as your aim!" And then Vale's group surged onward with newfound confidence.

Sellemar swiftly leapt backward. His eyes shot along the hall, searching for an item of defense, and spied an old lantern. It was laced in cobwebs, dangling beside the scented salts. He wrenched it from its hook, shielding against the swift thrust of a blade. The glass between the iron shattered at the vigorous blow, and Sellemar used the change in structure to catch the second thrust through the iron frame. He twisted it clear of his body and kicked outward, slamming his heel into the male's nose.

It met the same fate as the glass.

Vale let out a roar of rage. "What in Ramul?!" And he shoved his howling soldier aside to plunge for Sellemar's exposed gut. A slight change in the muscles of Vale's neck warned Sellemar of the captain's true target, but the feeble lantern could not impede a well-thrust blade. The force of the blow knocked the lantern aside and the sword cut clean through his thigh.

There was a surge of pain and a gush of blood, but Sellemar sucked it down in a single breath. *'This lantern is not going to stop Vale,'* he ceded. But it would serve one final, satisfying purpose.

He slammed it against the wall, the hot oil spraying out to scour the stunned throng. Then Sellemar spun on heel and ran.

"Gods damn it! Fuck him!" Vale roared as the males beside him cursed and leapt aside, their reflexive actions doing nothing to save them from their scalding welts.

Down the hall, there was a shout of triumph and his companions ascended the southern steps. The bodies of the temple pursuers lay trampled beneath their fleeing feet and Sellemar rushed to join them, gritting his teeth against the throbbing pain in his leg.

But Vale and his dogs had swiftly recovered, snapping at his heels.

'If I do not slow them, the others will never escape,' Sellemar realized. But he could do nothing more without a weapon!

He vaulted from the ground, kicked off the wall, and caught the edge of the ceiling's chandelier. The force of his momentum pitched him forward and he dropped, considerably ahead of Vale and his soldiers.

The Resistance had now disappeared up the steps and Sellemar snatched a blade from a fallen guard as he ran. Too many long hours in the Nemorium had given Sellemar more knowledge of Vale's emotions than he had ever wanted to possess—temperamental irrationality when he was losing, and audacious overconfidence when he was winning. Sellemar would have loved nothing more than to grind Vale's inexperienced face into the moth-eaten rug, but there were more pressing matters at hand. While the Resistance remained in danger, he had a responsibility to ferry them to safety.

Sellemar mounted the stairs, pursuing his allies to the marble halls of the clerical dormitory and the temple beyond. If they could just reach the crowd of rioters outside, the Resistance would yet live.

He saw the last of his allies vanish into the temple's interior, but an immediate cry warned him that the temple was no longer empty. He hurdled over the last several yards and caught the engraved frame, swinging himself into the sanctuary.

His heart sank at the sight.

Two guards had stationed themselves near the door, barricading freedom from his comrades. At the moment the Resistance drew near, they leapt on the offensive. A surge of heat and light burst forth from one of the soldiers, enveloping the body of Denwen and blazing past Sellemar in a bellow of turbulent wind.

Sellemar had no time to feel shock or grief. *'Another mage?!'* he swore as he identified the aged caster to the right of the doors.

His face hardened and he spun around, preparing to face Vale's emergence from the hall beyond. He elevated his blade and shifted his stance. His Resistance could not possibly repel both forces.

The sound of footsteps in the hall increased and Vale and his soldiers tore into the room. The captain's eyes landed briefly on Sellemar before they swept to the far larger quarry of the Resistance beyond.

"Go around," Vale shouted to his soldiers, dismissing Sellemar's presence. "I'll take care of this cunt!"

But Sellemar knew he now remained as the only inhibitor between the convergence of the two forces. He darted to the side, skidding to a stop before four of the males who advanced to fulfill Vale's command. He swung his blade, diving past their inexperience and slicing into kinks between their steel plates. In a swift series of blows, they fell in a heap before Vale's stunned visage.

Yet near a half-dozen more had managed to circumvent Sellemar's range.

If they reached his allies, the Resistance would never survive. He raised his hand to his scarf grimly. Another method, then.

Fortunately, months inside the male's head presented him his solution.

It was not the most grand of deaths. It was hardly what he had envisioned for himself. But Sel'ari had offered him a generous and noble course.

Some wars were only won through sacrifice.

"Are you certain you want to try this alone again?" Sellemar challenged, and tore the scarf free of his face.

He could practically hear Vale's core tremble with enmity. The captain's eyes bulged, his nostrils flared. Somewhere within the deepest recesses of his throat, a choking cry emitted. "Kevus, to me!" he shouted, even as he took a swift step back.

A clatter of metal hit the floor as one of Vale's soldiers before the temple doors fell, yet the mage broke aside and rounded toward his captain's command. The Resistance's battle breathed new life, but the grey eyes of the mage were now upon Sellemar.

Inwardly, he grimaced.

"Kevus, this is the only one I want. This is the only one we need!" Vale cried frantically, even as another of his soldiers fell to the Resistance's blades. He raised his sword in challenge. "*Sellemar*—how terribly unsurprising," he hissed. "What stupidity led you to this point in your life?"

"I would ask the same of you," Sellemar replied, and lunged.

Vale reeled away, but a flash of light from Sellemar's left caused him to swiftly change course.

He rolled, feeling the jolt of energy rip by.

Behind him, another clang of metal resounded. *They were almost free. 'Sel'ari!'* He just had to live long enough for that!

But Vale cared nothing for the remaining Resistance, nor for the soldiers that died to them. His pride had sustained a blow only revenge would fill.

Sellemar lurched to his feet, scrambling to clear the swipe of Vale's vengeful blade. He darted to the left, prepared to move to the offensive, when his direction was wholly lost to him. Something slammed into his back, knocking him askance and directly into Vale's grasp.

Vale's fingers snaked out, catching Sellemar by the hair… and his blade drove swiftly into his gut. A triumphant sneer lit the captain's features as he drew Sellemar's head back. "I think it went something like this, didn't it?" he whispered, voice quivering in glee.

Sellemar's adrenaline forced the pain aside and he swung pointedly for Vale's throat. *The Resistance was not yet free! Not yet free…!*

The blow never connected. A scarlet flare smashed into his forearm and his bones snapped like twigs beneath the force. The sword flew from his limp fingers, resounding as one with the clatter of the captain's last soldier at the temple doors.

Vale's face leaned in close, his breath hot on Sellemar's pallid skin. "And this, you cunt, is fate. Did you *truly* think you could best me twice?"

Sellemar spat, a spurt of blood spraying across the captain's face. "Not all action will effect change, but change is not possible without action." Were those truly his final words? *'Damn…'* There was the sudden scrape of metal against marble and a blast of winter air billowed into the temple room.

Vale's victorious sneer faltered and his eyes flicked up toward the temple doors.

"Thank you, Vale, for loathing me so intensely," Sellemar heaved through gritted teeth. "The Resistance lives to fight another day. I can only pray Saebellus understands why you only have bodies to show for your efforts today."

Realization swiftly transformed Vale's triumph to horror. "Healer…! We need a god-damn cleric!" he panicked.

What an irony—they had killed them all.

Perhaps Vale looked up in time to see Tilarus' cloak tails before he vanished out the temple doors, but by the time the captain ran screaming in fury to the stairs, the Resistance was gone.

Even Noctem had concealed his eyes from the innocent blood that had been spilt inside the goddess' walls, leaving the captain and his soldiers in a blanket of winter's darkness.

CHAPTER FORTY-EIGHT

The weeks of overseeing prisoners had passed by with a deadening, draining tedium. Alvena did not care about the stench or squalor as long as she did not have to sit on the filthy, stony floor. Adonis and Vale had adopted similar hollow-eyed expressions whenever they descended to the prisons, but Saebellus' command that the Noc'olari be relocated had to be obeyed.

Yet hardly after the cells were finally emptied, Turlondiel returned from Tadorwen and promptly refilled them. Tadorwen's inhabitants, like those of so many other cities, had refused to acknowledge Saebellus' reign. The prisons were still half-full by the time Vale was ordered to gather his forces to attack the Ruljarian city of Raestra on the Velhar River.

Alvena had not wanted to leave the comforts of the palace for the war-torn road, but company with Adonis was certainly preferable to the chaos in the capital. Her fingers tightened on the mane of Adonis' mare and she lost her braided strands into the mass.

Of course the disorder was Vale's fault. He had raided Sel'ari's temple and left only the bodies of Sel'ari's priests and unidentified followers in his wake. Night after night, the rioters had cried for vengeance, and when it did not come, they had taken it upon themselves to act. They had rioted, attacking Saebellus' soldiers in the city streets and demolishing the Council Hall.

She could not imagine what madness had overcome the people, but Saebellus had swiftly ended the insurrection. While weeks had passed since then, she knew peace would not last—Vale had crippled the capital!

"You have been very silent," Adonis finally spoke, leaning slightly around her in the saddle. "Are you bored? Are you tired of reading? What are you pondering?"

'Silent? Of course I am silent,' Alvena huffed. And obviously she was bored *and* tired of reading—by now she had read her only book half a dozen

times. Still, she held it firmly against her breast. Her knife was tucked safely inside; in the heart of war, it might be her only protection from the justifiable rage the Ruljenari would feel when Saebellus dared to infiltrate their city. She looked away from the chunks of silver mane she had just rediscovered in order to glare at him reproachfully.

Adonis only smiled and Alvena felt her tension ebb away. She was being unfair—he had intended no offense by his words. "Are you thinking about the cold?" he asked. "It is terribly bitter!"

Well now that he mentioned the weather, she *was* thinking about it. Snow blanketed everything in her vision except for the countless tall, armored soldiers marching relentlessly eastward.

"Are you worried about the war?" Adonis tried again, daring to ask such a question as they rode amidst the horde of polished helms. "You should not be. You will be at my side the whole time—and I do not engage in battle."

Alvena's eyes shifted down to his side and she cocked her head in question. At his hip lay the icy hilt, encrusted with its gems, snug in an ill-matching, simple silver sheath. Inside, the once-great tundra she had glimpsed upon their meeting now seemed broken and dull. Yet this did not dampen the weapon's lively bounce against his hip.

Her arm hugged the book tighter.

'I remember you had that in Galadorium, too.'

Adonis followed her gaze and tapped the hilt affectionately. "Ah. This was General Taemrin's. Darivalian craftsmanship. Vale presented it to me… as a gift. We both respected the late general—may Sel'ari grant him safe passage. He was a great leader and a highly regarded tactician. It is most unfortunate that he found himself on the wrong side. We would have been honored to have him."

Alvena regarded him quizzically. *'Well that's a silly thing to say. I think the general was very clear that he did not agree with you.'* He had been Hairem's general and Hairem certainly had stood staunchly opposed to their movement. She remembered her king's cry when he had heard Elarium was lost… *'Simply the wrong side…'* she scoffed bitterly. But as Adonis smiled back at her, she briefly wondered why.

Then she froze, her eyes widening in disbelief.

Why?

Why?

How could she even ponder *why* Hairem and his army had opposed Saebellus?! Somewhere in Emal'drathar, she imagined an emotional slap struck her beloved king.

She leaned so sharply from Adonis that the weight of her tome nearly sent her toppling from the mare. The lieutenant swiftly caught her by the shoulders, holding her fast.

Alvena glowered. How dare he be so kind! Taemrin had been her general as well!

Adonis' fingers loosened as he gave a slight shake and, while Alvena could not see his face, she swore it was laughter that moved him. "I suppose you still think us the bloodthirsty, power-hungry libertines—but if not for the council's deception, I believe *many* of your allies would have fought by our side."

Alvena's attempted scowl faltered and she found herself turning to meet those pale blue eyes. There was only kindness reflected back to her. Why could he think that?

They were enemies.

'Enemies,' she reminded herself. After all, that's why she had brought the knife—it wasn't like Adonis would truly risk his own life to protect her.

And she made no attempt to hide her demand for an explanation. In their months together, he knew exactly what her squinty-eyed reproach meant.

"Of course," he agreed, and his lips pursed briefly. "I never held great talent as a fighter," he began. "Once I merely held a station as a scout. Now, I am a lieutenant, but my skills with weaponry remain abysmal at best." He paused for a moment and chuckled to himself. "That *has* to be the highest rank someone in my position has achieved."

Alvena let one of her eyes nearly close in admonishment. Why, if his skills with the sword were half as abysmal as his storytelling, he ought not to even have the weapon!

But he continued, oblivious to his error. "Vale was on the front line. Every battle, General Angrenor would send him into the forefront of the carnage." His eyes flicked north briefly and Alvena knew they were searching for the captain. "Other soldiers advanced in rank and left the lines, but year after year after year, there Vale remained. I think the general knew about him—his sexual relations. And even if the general did not have proof…" he trailed off grimly. "At least, that was Vale's theory."

'That wasn't right,' she thought, then scolded herself. Sympathy for Vale? She flicked a piece of ice from the mare's hair apathetically, and Adonis knew better than to linger.

"At that time, Saebellus was the Second General. Until he was dishonorably discharged, the Second General was appointed by the General to succeed him if he should fall, on or off the battlefield. Now, as matters stand after the *incident*, the council has become too anxious to relinquish that much control." He paused, perhaps seeing Alvena's expression erode to confusion. He was only getting worse!—A jumble of disconnected facts! Had his parents never read to him?!

"...I am digressing and speaking vaguely..." The creases had abandoned the corners of Adonis' eyes, even as his lips remained curled. His voice became a somber whisper, barely heard over the whistle of winter's wind through the scraggly trees. "Let me... speak again... Alvena, I *want* for you to understand why it is that Saebellus warred against the empire. It is not you and I who are enemies."

Alvena leaned a little closer, her hands slacking from the hair. *'Yes...'* she thought. Adonis was far too kind... Saebellus too merciful... to be the wickedness whispered to her in the night.

Someone had *lied* to her, to Hairem... there was surely someone else to blame!

"Just over three-hundred years ago, the reigning True Blood—King Silandrus—was caught in a terrible feud with Elvorium's council. They were at odds over their dealings with the sirens. It was an impassioned debate. The sirens had long been snatching travelers from the woods or small vessels upon the waters to ferry them to their underwater cities. Presumably to mate and... eat them."

The wind seemed to howl in amusement, but Alvena's eyes grew wide in horror. 'Eat *them?'*

"There were not a great number of disappearances... but when a band of mercenaries stole several siren maidens for their carnivals on Ryekarayn, the attacks grossly multiplied. Then, it came to pass that Fildor's brother and his crew were captured on a voyage down the Velhar; this rallied the council to argue that *war* was necessary. Despite Silandrus' valiant attempts to persuade them to less excessive methods, the council refused. When the war erupted, steep casualties were incurred on both sides. We possessed far superior numbers and weapons, but the power of the siren call caused many of our soldiers to simply throw their bodies into the depths of the river, never to be seen again." The pink hues of his gentle face had become tainted with grey. An emptiness occupied his eyes, so strong and deep that Alvena was afraid to look within for fear that something darker lurked inside.

She tried to dismiss the small flinch she saw his muscles make. Death by drowning sounded far less brutal than the bloodshed she had witnessed in Galadorium… Yet the longer she looked at the pretty elf, the more her opinion changed. To see one's comrades and friends willingly plunge themselves into an icy grave… Alvena had seen paintings of the watery beauties in books, but the enchanting persuasion they held over males had never really seemed that frightening…

Until now.

Adonis inhaled deeply, his hands clenching and unclenching upon the leathery reins. "When the capital received news of the mass casualties, Silandrus reached the end of his tolerance. As he refused to forcefully overthrow the people's elected council, within months, he and his children left."

'But he should have stayed... fought the council!' Alvena thought in frustration. *'Now look what has happened!'*

Adonis' grimace was a reflection of her own. "Saebellus was not bound to the political traditions. He was furious that the council had driven the True Bloods out, and he spoke against it—against *them*. The council punished him for insubordination and stripped him of his rank for more than a century." Adonis regarded her enraptured expression and the grey of his pale skin faded to be replaced with a fiery red. "This is where the council began to weave its own history of events."

Alvena found her breath growing soft. Even the winter air had grown still, as though it too was keen not to miss a word.

"The transition of the True Blood departure was disastrous. There was a rebellion against the council and their supporters, scattered across Sevrigel, but nonetheless powerful. The council was forced to spend *one hundred and fifty years* quelling the people. The moment a whisper arose of resistance, we were there and the rebels were slain. But each instance was disposed of quietly—the council did not want to instill notions of further uprising. So every town. Every city… until no one dared breathe the *words* 'True Blood' lest they find the council's army at their gates in the morning."

Alvena shivered. Just one hundred and fifty years ago? No one had ever mentioned the uprisings to her. And she had never read even the briefest passage of them in her books.

Had the council truly concealed such a historical backlash for their corruption? Hidden such a desire of the people?

She wanted to believe his words were a lie, but she knew that was not true. She had witnessed what the council members' selfishness had wrought upon Taemrin's army in the Sevilan Marshes—*nothing* withstood their greed.

"And of course, the council did not forget the sirens. The ongoing skirmishes with the race were small during the rebellion—Sevrigel's army could not spare many of our soldiers to combat their aggression. But when the True Blood uprisings finally settled… the council ordered a complete massacre of the siren race." The unrelenting tone of his voice finally quavered; pain lanced his pretty face. Beneath his amber gloves, his grip on the reins had grown so tight that the leather between them was pulled taught. "And we marched to their waters to obey."

Alvena swallowed. Genocide… even if the sirens *had* been in the wrong, to wipe out an *entire* people…

Adonis seemed to know exactly what she thought. She felt his chest stiffen against her back. "Yes, Alvena. All of them. Age mattered not. Involvement in the original kidnappings was irrelevant. If you were a siren, then by Malranus Almighty, you were sentenced to die." He paused, letting her eyes widen until Alvena was quite certain they would all but fall from her head. "It *was* terrible. Horrific. The first week of battle… the murders we saw… the murders we *committed.* Against a true military operation, they were powerless. We poisoned their waters. Burned the surface when they tried to escape. We swept them into nets. Cut them down while entangled. And at the end of that first week, Saebellus refused to comply any longer. He killed General Angrenor."

Alvena stilled, but no pity for the dead male reached her heart.

"That night, Saebellus rallied our allies in the army. It was a long, bloody struggle; we could not desert without a fight. We vanished deep into the forests where we hid with help, no less, from the sirens." He paused to smile fondly at the soldiers around him. "That's where your late general comes in—Jikun Taemrin. The council summoned him from the north—he had been too far secluded to know the details of Saebellus' military history or his reasons for rebelling. And he was too militaristically obedient to question the council. For fifty years, we hid and grew in number. But we tasted battle. Fifty years of skirmishes with General Taemrin. At that time, I am certain he did not consider us a true threat. In his opinion, we must merely have been a group of outlawed rebels, hiding in the woods, causing him a minor inconvenience. But when those fifty years ended and we emerged in our accumulated force, he thought differently." His chest expanded in what could be nothing short of admiration and pride.

Alvena made no attempt to interrupt him now. She was enthralled.

"For the last century, Alvena, we have been fighting to reclaim this country from its corrupted leaders and compliant followers. To reclaim it for every decedent's voice that has been silenced. We are fighting for the very reason the True Bloods would not. Tell me, is your side *truly* so just?"

Alvena felt her stomach knot. No. The answer was *no*. But she straightened her spine, elevating her chin to his hardened gaze.

Her side *had* become complacent to injustice. *As she had lately grown to share.*

'But neither,' she thought firmly, *'is justice found in you. What Saebellus has ordered is murder no less than what you said the council has done.'*

The wind began to howl again as though siding with her, demanding answers. It roared through the polished ranks about them, flinging ice as it went, tossing Adonis' hair askew to hide all but remnants of his face. "...Ilsevel is queen now," he spoke after a moment, his voice a bitter concession. "We find ourselves on a different road than that envisioned by Saebellus alone... but as long as we have him, the end will be the same. That is what we are fighting for. If you want to exact change, you do not always have the luxury of walking a paved path. Sometimes... that way is barred. When you thus find yourself at the crossroads of morality, is it better to choose the lesser of two evils but, in such a path, never reach your destination? Or, is it at times better to choose the darker road, if such a course means you will find the light at its end? There are times when you must play the role of the thief in order to rise still greater as the hero."

And then the earth itself seemed to agree, quelling its howling wind to an amenable murmur.

But Alvena's lips pursed. She understood now how Saebellus and his supporters had pulled her in. They were not the faceless, soulless males that had distressed Hairem and now haunted her nightmares. They had felt pain. Loss. Desire. Hope. *They were elven*. But any kindness they had was not synonymous with goodness.

Using evil to combat evil made them no better than the wickedness they fought to oppose.

'And I,' Alvena determined, *'will not accept evil as our only path. If the middle road is barred, I shall find a way to break through it.* I *will be complacent no longer!'*

She had heard how, across the channel, the former general had made one last stand against Saebellus—and how he had finally met the end he had managed to evade for so long. Here within her own country, the Resistance had lit the fire of truth and hope within her people. But now they too were gone.

Yet one road remained. The middle path. Unused by the last three centuries of separation. It was a force Saebellus had once fought for. A force he beheld for himself. A force capable of rallying the world against him.

And Saebellus' victories on both continents had not damaged its viability.

Someone had only to tear the barrier down.

The True Bloods who had once refused to stop the corruption could remain silent no longer.

It was time for them to come home.

It was time for the people to rise with them.

...But if even she understood their threat... their *power*... this last, untrodden road to Aersadore's salvation... then Saebellus did too. And to keep the way barred, she knew he would strike them from the earth—Silandrus, Sairel, Darcarus, Hadoream—there would be no heroes left to raise the strength for Sevrigel's last battle.

Chapter Forty-Nine

Alvena wiggled in the lush grass, shying away from the clusters of long and seeded blades. Despite the wide, open air, they determinedly drooped toward her, invading her winter garb with unwelcome tickles along her throat. She snatched several of the offenders with a sweaty palm and uprooted them viciously from the earth. But even as she crossed her arms in triumph, a new score taunted her neck from behind.

She huffed, waving one hand before her face. She had dozed for just a moment during the ride to Raestra—yet somehow when she had reawakened, the wintery slopes of Sevrigel's eastlands had entirely vanished. Adonis had given her no explanation before he and the mare had abandoned her in a valley's weeds with the rest of the army. *'Where are we?—What an awful place to rest!'*

The sun reappeared from behind the single cloud, and Alvena increased the vigor of her hand. The wind was a capricious stalker—it had wailed and moaned at her for their entire trek east from Elvorium, but now, the moment that she desired it, the frosty current was nowhere to be found! The humid air hung so heavily she was liable to drown in it!

Suffering in solidarity with her, thousands of silver lumps were scattered across the jade field as far south, west, and east as she could see. The winter air they had so meticulously prepared for was gone. How—in their silks and wool and heavy metal suits—were Saebellus' troops not simply keeling over from the swelter?

Their resolve certainly made her own seem woefully feeble.

She elevated her gaze longingly above their glinting helms to the shadowy north. While the sky above her shone as blue as the kisacaela gemstones, she had but to follow its expanse for a hundred yards before darkness swallowed it in a grey, dense, wintery gloom. As though she was gazing onto a wholly different plane. There the clouds hung above the abrupt beginnings of a forest, whose towering branches were bent low in their sheaths of ice. Yet not a single one protruded so much as a twig into the summery air.

'How strange!' Had they entered some grand expanse of magic?

"So, do you have to work hard to maintain such an excellent physique?"

Ugh. Vale had returned.

She glanced surreptitiously askance and located his lean, sweaty frame sitting cross-legged nearby. He was bent forward suggestively, engaged in a sad attempt to woo a striking Sel'varian soldier.

Alvena rolled her eyes, lifting her heavy tome and fluttering the pages before her face. The few loose strands of hair not stuck to her cheeks with perspiration flew back to bat her ears.

The ill-fated Sel'ven fended Vale off with polite disinterest. "No, Captain," he replied.

Something slipped from the last pages of her book and Alvena quickly stuffed the object into her boot. She stiffened, shooting the captain another glance. To her luck—and the soldier's misfortune—Vale's eyes retained their blatant perusal of his well-toned figure.

"By Kamora's hand, you have the prettiest eyes—after Adonis, of course," he blundered again, and Alvena could almost *hear* the elf's revulsion.

She plucked at a remaining clump of impudent grass and turned away. *'Is this how Galadorium began?—This doesn't seem like the beginning of a battle,'* she thought as the horde about her slumped and yawned. The humans in their ranks had taken to chewing on long stalks of grass like some furless and distastefully bearded form of cattle.

"After Raestra, how would you like to step into a tavern with me and Adonis? He may not openly display this adorable trait, but he *loves* a second pair of hands," Vale cooed softly.

'A second pair of hands for what?*'* Alvena pondered briefly. She pinched herself as his vulgarity formed an obscene image. *'That's what you get for eavesdropping!'*

"...While the offer is generous, I must decline, Captain."

A distant laugh followed the sarcastic rejection, and Alvena jerked her head around.

Her scrunched nose relaxed. Adonis was wading through the grass, as majestic as a prince in an assemblage of white silks and grey leather. Two tall men flanked him on either side, one round-chinned and thick of frame while the other possessed an old face besieged by a ghastly goatee. Alvena wondered if Vale had not selected the men in part for their homeliness—insurance that his lover would never be tempted to stray. Regardless, the vibrant purplish red of their noses and ears—attesting to their voyage outside the field's warm boundary—only worsened their garish appearances. The larger of the two humans quickly masked his toothy grin as Adonis ripped the seeded heads off of several lofty stalks.

Adonis halted behind Vale, his stance dangerously austere.

'Oh, punch him again!' Alvena urged. While there was no bed for Vale to topple from, a good sprawl in the grass would still do well to lift her mood.

Vale carried on, fully unaware of the peril. "I prefer to be on top myself, but if you change your mind, I might even extend you the honors."

Adonis cleared his throat with impressively loud sonority, sliding to the west until his shadow towered menacingly over Vale. "*Captain*," he began sternly.

Vale jolted with a wince. "Y-yes, Lieutenant?" He collected himself swiftly. "What did you see?"

Adonis gave him the faintest of reproachful glares before he struck a pose of militaristic rigidity. Alvena pushed out her bottom lip in disappointment. "Everything is as we expected, Captain. The docks are quiet and the commoners appear to have retired for their evening meals. What city guards we found stand at ease."

Vale relaxed, as though the divulging of such information had spared him from Adonis' forthcoming punishment. But Alvena expected a rowdy spat would follow the battle.

She smiled smugly. Vale always lost such scuffles.

The captain pushed off his knees with a grunt and for the first time, the meaning of Adonis' words registered in Alvena's mind.

Adonis had left her in the grass to scout. He had *finished* scouting.

Battle was upon them!

"ON YOUR FEET!" Vale bellowed across the lazy expanse. Instantly, the inertia fell away. The only sound that dared reply was that of the soldiers' tinking armor as they rose at his command. The captain thrust his long fingers unceremoniously into the windless sky and gave a twist.

No words were needed to spur the soldiers to further action—their polished ranks reformed in perfect, orderly rows to march in Vale's wake. Adonis turned his attention immediately upon Alvena and drew her close, shielding her from the thousands of feet that increased their pace into a northern-bound stampede.

"Come," he finally issued as he whirled to follow the army's flank.

Alvena's clammy hands closed about her tome. *'This is it? No speech? No rally?'* She should not have expected anything different from Vale, who had the poetic sense of a tifrat, but she would have welcomed a delay of any kind! How the spirits of his troops held fast without even a restorative word astounded her!

Adonis was not deterred by her hesitation. He clamped a hand about her elbow to direct her after the two soldiers that served as his unsightly escort. They crossed the distance to the border of ice-laden trees, where Adonis' alabaster mare, Ethwen, was flicking the last remnants of Alvena's braid from her tail.

'I'd much rather remain here while you fight!' she thought as her eyes trailed the crisp line between peace and war. On one side of the invisible boundary, the jade field rolled across a serene valley. On the other, where the arching roots and massive branches soared, the russet earth was a tangle of autumn leaves and winter frost.

The thick man on Adonis' right extended a calloused hand, coarse black hair springing between the gap in his bracer and glove. "Give the soldiers a moment to clear the way, my lord," he instructed.

Adonis pushed the hefty arm aside. "I know the process, Ronan. Before Vale appointed you, I had done this successfully a hundred times." When the older of the two opened his cracked lips to interject, Adonis rebuffed him sternly. "You are here for Vale's sake, Kevus, not mine." He stiffly swung himself atop his mount.

Alvena surveyed the bulging hulk of the plate-armored human and the strong, leathered stalk that was the older man. The more soldiers to guard Adonis, the safer she was as well! *'But I suppose even he has pride...'* she thought as she clambered into the saddle before him. *She* could afford none.

Adonis' voice suddenly rent the air, and Alvena let out an internal squeak as the horse plunged forward, smacking her body backward against his armored chest. *'Ouch-ch!'* she grunted as her head tested the solidity of his breastplate.

The pain was swiftly forgotten as they lurched across the final patch of sunny grass and into the shadow of the arching root of a massive tree. Instantly, the world changed. Cold assaulted them, penetrating through Alvena's defenses to find the sweat that had once made her heavy clothes cling. Thick, cinereous clouds swirled overhead while billowing flakes prodded for any kink in her winter gear. She glanced once behind her for the desirable shield of warmth and light, but only the bleak sky stretched beyond.

As they broke from the shelter of the trees, Kevus' voice strained against the violent gusts of wind. "Stay close," he bellowed, pulling ahead with Ronan. They galloped down the frosted grass, their horses' hooves pounding against the hard earth of the valley's gentle slope.

Alvena clutched Ethwen's mane for comfort. They galloped across an auburn valley that was bisected by a river of breathtaking width. Marring the stunning landscape was an impregnable fortress of grey stone, its walls so high that its interior buildings were fully obscured. Elvorium boasted of its canyons and lakes, but these elven-made walls put such trifles to shame! A hundred mages could hurl spells at the stonework for days, yet Alvena felt certain the defenses would remain unscathed. Before it, Saebellus' troops surged, seeming no more than a colony of silver-backed ants.

The Ruljarian city of Raestra!

And yet, *Adonis rode toward such a fortress!* She squinted her eyes, putting the assemblage of Saebellus' forces into focus. They were gathering near the four black steel gates that served as the egress into the city. Gleaming shields hung above them, protecting the ranks from the hail of arrows that descended by the thousands.

Unlike Galadorium, the river city would not fall easily. While Alvena had no prior battle experience, it was clear to her—as it must be to even *Vale*—that Saebellus' troops had challenged too great a target.

Her eyes snapped away in search of a safer point of entry, falling upon the frothing crests of the Velhar River. It twisted along the valley, wild and untamed as it flowed from the center of the city. Bobbing along its eddies floated a fleet of sleek ships, each vessel fluttering a deep blue banner in the evening light. Saebellus had no ships, and he would never dare face the Ruljenari in their field of military proficiency. Over the expansive waters she beheld a pair of tremendous female statues who extended their arms to form a mighty bridge between Raestra's northern and southern walls.

Those indomitable females offered but two options: drown within their waters or shatter against their walls.

"Hold fast," Adonis' voice whispered against her ear.

Alvena returned her attention to the gate, letting out a cry as a shadow engulfed them. A volley of arrows cascaded from the heavens, the mass so thick that the evening's rays could not penetrate their shroud. Kevus' hand elevated, and with a grand sweep across the bitter air, the attack sailed clear of Adonis' vicinity to clatter harmlessly in the tall red grass.

"They are ready, Lieutenant!" Ronan bellowed as they burst into the midst of Saebellus' waiting horde and closed in on the looming gate.

When the lieutenant did not reply, Alvena dared a single glance away from the danger. A canopy of shields had arisen to protect them and Adonis' face was shrouded in the darkness. She spun back round, the gate suddenly a goblin's nose from Ethwen! Her mouth flew wide and then…!

One moment the gates were before her, threatening to shatter her tiny frame like glass, and the next she was galloping through the trampled field in which the soldiers had leisured moments before.

'Where…?!' She swiveled her head: behind them, the warm grass ended abruptly at the muddy boots of Saebellus' cheering force. To her left and right, stone and steel was cut clean through the center to arch high above in a striking frame.

Alvena gaped, swinging her head once more to the north. There stood the heart of Raestra itself: homes of slated grey. Cobbled streets laced in colorful river stones. Glorious statues that were dwarfed only by the spires of an ancient, blue-stoned palace.

It was as she had dared not believe: through Adonis' magic, he had created a plane of passage straight through the impenetrable walls of Raestra!

She could hear the roar of the troops as they marched to join them across the plain. A screeching trumpet blasted from the city wall and Alvena imagined the sight below as Saebellus' troops seemed to vanish before the Ruljenari's eyes.

But Alvena knew where they would soon appear.

'General Taemrin never had a chance,' she whispered to herself, leaning into Adonis in shameless awe as he jerked to a halt. She watched the swarm pour past to flood Raestra's pomerium.

Another trumpet blast tore into the evening sky, but the Ruljenari could have little hope for salvation now. Vale's voice boomed above the chaos, bold and brazen even as a volley of arrows sailed down upon him. "RAZE RAESTRA TO THE GROUND!"

A mage near Vale's right snapped his fingers and the hail of arrows flew away, revealing the captain's triumphant sneer.

Alvena's stomach churned. *'You let them in—don't let this be like Galadorium!'* she cried to Adonis, searching his face for direction.

He gave her no acknowledgement, instead bending forward, jostling her into Ethwen's neck. There was the solid thump of his heel against the mare's flank and they tore out behind the last soldier, hooves clattering upon the cobbled streets to the fringe of battle.

The mass of dead and the stench of blood ripped Alvena's breath away. Bodies scattered the stones like clumps of snow, spilling over one another in lumps and mounds like grotesque snowbanks. Their eyes seemed to find hers, bloodshot and hollow, paralyzing in their fear. But she dared not look away. This was what was wrought by the use of evil as the path to victory—and she could not let herself remain naïve! *She* would remember them.

A sharp glint in Alvena's peripheral vision jolted her upright. A mace swung high and smashed into a Ruljen nearby, splattering Alvena's leg with blood. She shrieked, throwing her book before her face as though it could possibly deflect so much as the shaft of a spear. Ronan dropped his mace, kicking the body free of Adonis' vicinity.

The sun dipped and fell, and the dead around Alvena grew. It was only when the fighting had dispersed across the streets and faded deep within their wide, icy lanes that Adonis too nudged his mare onward. She waded through the corpses and scattered weaponry, then down a narrow road. A section of troops had already made swift work of the vicinity, and the dim sheen on the river stones suggested the way to be bereft of bodies or even excessive blood. In fact, the darkness swallowed almost all of the carnage, feigning a sense of peace that only made Alvena's heart beat faster.

Her eyes darted across the dark windows of an abandoned home, the panes of glass glinting eerily down upon her like too many sinister eyes. The curve of the balconies below adorned the building with an unnerving grin.

Something shifted in the darkness and Alvena let out a yelp.

"It's alright," Adonis soothed, his arms nestling her within.

"Just some prisoners," Damon grunted.

Alvena dared to look again, but the forms of the victims were indistinguishable in Noctem's shadows.

A soft creak sounded from their right and Alvena leapt once more. Why, she'd rather be standing amongst the dead than the unknown! A nearby door had swung wide, preceding the fiery glow of a bobbing torch. Through the narrow opening, Alvena could glimpse disarrayed furniture, a broken vase, a toppled table, and a thick, lush blanket of baby blue. But then the silhouette of a Sel'varian soldier blocked such sights from view; the male emerged in the doorway, huffing beneath the weight of the Ruljen he dragged.

Ethwen slowed to a walk, and Adonis locked eyes upon the limp victim. Alvena forced herself to do the same. *'You may be able to do nothing, but do not dare look away,'* she ordered herself sternly.

Orange and white light mixed across the Ruljen's unarmed frame, pulling greys and whites from his pallid flesh. Locks of dark hair were plastered to his temple, spilling over a swollen eye.

Alvena's assessment shifted downward, to the abundance of liquid flowing from his chest.

Her stomach heaved.

"Lieutenant Adonis, this section of the town has not yet been secured," the puffing soldier grunted, nodding his insistence to Adonis' escort. "There could be any number of enemies unaccounted for. Captain Vale has forbidden your presence here until such a time when he has deemed it—"

Before he had finished his sentence, Adonis had dismounted.

"Lieutenant Adonis," Ronan immediately barked. "You heard the male. Return to your mount immediately."

"Captain Vale will not be pleased," the mage muttered below his breath, stroking the appalling silver fuzz upon his chin.

Adonis shot them both a scathing glare and extended a white-gloved hand. "I *command* you to remain there." While the escort exchanged uncertain glances, the lieutenant hurried to the wounded male's side. "Lay him down," he bade the breathless soldier. When the soldier obeyed, Adonis dropped to his knees, sweeping off his thick fur cloak to wrap the dying male in his warmth.

To Alvena's surprise, it was not Adonis' compassion that moved her.

Ronan stiffly dismounted, slicking back his wiry hair with the blood that dashed his forehead. "I ask you again, Lieutenant, to return willingly to your mount."

Adonis' fingers only tightened upon the Ruljen's hands, staining his gloves red as he helped the weakened fingers grasp the ebony shroud.

Alvena's own hand curled about the charm around her neck. It was by *his* magic that the fall of Raestra had occurred. That this male lay here now. She felt a twinge in her chest and the cold familiarity in her boot. Had she held the responsibility to stop him?

When she forced herself to meet the Ruljen's eyes once more, they had glazed over, becoming no more than mirrors to the sliver that hung in the cold night sky.

A roar erupted from down the road. "Adonis—*Lieutenant*—what the fuck are you doing out here?! Ronan, Kevus, were my orders not fucking explicit?!"

As one, they turned to the vicious chastisement: Vale stalked down the center of the road, eyes ablaze with disapproval.

"Of all the ill timing," Adonis grimaced, and Alvena imagined that he could no longer rebuke the captain for his prior flirting. He gently released the dead hands and straightened to respond—though his defense was unlikely to quell the captain's fury.

There was a crash from inside the Ruljarian home. A voice cried out unexpectedly from the still-open door, drowning out Adonis' reply. "Ninsar!" it wailed, the tone swiftly morphing into rage. "Loedrin's breath upon you!" A broad elf burst from the darkness, a male and female flanked at his back.

Alvena choked in surprise. She leaned back on the saddle sharply, but Ethwen would not budge without Adonis' command—even at the sight of the three enraged Ruljenari. They were donned in half-plate, dark eyes wide, long hair pulled back. Each of their scimitars was elevated, prepared to drive into the gut of Saebellus' stupefied soldier.

A sudden flare of purple light whisked through the air, singeing the Sel'varian soldier's helm as it passed. The light illuminated the stricken face of the first Ruljen for just a breath before it struck with a bone-shattering crunch. The face exploded in a wash of blood and soft pink flesh, obliterating the skull like an egg dropped on stone.

Alvena wobbled on the mare, hurling what little contents her stomach still contained.

The showering blood spurred the soldier into action. His blade swept free of its hilt, meeting the thrust of the second attacker.

"STAND DOWN!" Adonis roared as the soldier plunged his blade into the breast of the second male Ruljen. "I said *stand down!*"

The female leapt past her dying comrade, driving her scimitar inexorably at Adonis' gut.

With a swift parry, the lieutenant forced the blade away. "Please lower your weapon or my guards will have no choice but to—!"

Vale was running now, bellowing a dozen curses at the Ruljarian female who dared strike at his lieutenant.

Ronan's bow swept up and launched twice. In an instant, the final attacker dropped to one knee. With one of the two vibrant, plumed shafts protruding from her forearm, her scimitar clattered to the ground.

Alvena dared a single breath.

"Enough!" Adonis' shouted. His boot flew, catching the leather-wrapped hilt to send it skidding across the cobblestones.

The female leapt at the opportunity forged by his compromised balance. Her hand snagged his ankle and with a swift yank, she swept Adonis' leg out from under him and flung it high into the air.

There was a crack as Adonis' skull smacked against the icy stones.

"ADONIS!"

But Alvena could not echo Vale's scream. Even when her lungs howled for air, she could not find it. For a moment, the world seemed to slow. She could see the rise of Ronan's bow for the Ruljen's heart. She could feel Vale's anguished cry vibrate through the swirling air. She could see another figure rushing from the home's still-swinging door.

When the world seemed to move again, she was standing beside Adonis, uncertain how she had arrived. His fair face had turned ashen in the moonlight, the pinks of his once-alabaster cheeks lost within the hue.

"ADONIS!" Vale bellowed again, and then he was upon her. His elbow struck her ribs, hurling her into a snowbank. Without a second spared, he tore his glove free, pressing his long fingers against Adonis' wrist. Only the faintest puff of white before Vale's lips let Alvena know that Adonis was still alive. "Kevus, Ronan, get him to Laeth *immediately!* East quadrant! NOW!"

As Alvena gingerly returned to her feet, the two guards rushed to Adonis' side. *'He is alright!'* Yet a prickle of guilt accompanied her joy. No fountain of his empathy for one dying soldier could restore the lives of the elves that adorned the bloody streets—or reverse Saebellus' success.

Vale vaulted upright, rounding upon the wounded female. His foot kicked out, catching an arm raised in swift defense. "You fucking cunt! You could have killed him!"

The female winced, but her arm remained.

Alvena mindlessly shuffled closer until she could see the details of the buttons lining her thick wool sleeves. A Ruljarian boy was held in that good arm. He was tall and scrappy, with riverweed hair and muddy eyes. By his still-round face, Alvena guessed he had seen no more than a dozen winters.

Her eyes fell to the dead Ruljen in the sable cloak. It was he the boy resembled.

But Vale would not have noticed such a detail. His eyes were wild with rage, and the female's union with the boy only furthered his fury. "I swear to the gods you'll never see this river rat again," he snarled, seizing the youth by the arm and wrenching violently against her hold.

Alvena took an instinctive step forward before sense drew her still.

"No, Galway, no!" the female shouted. When her grip tightened, Vale's foot raised again, slamming down onto the arrow's shaft. It jerked and twisted in the bloody wound, the agony lending the female a howl that rose high above the city's din. Her grip faltered and Vale swept in to rip the shrieking boy free.

The tome tumbled from Alvena's arms. *'ENOUGH!'* she wanted to scream, but Adonis was not there to echo her distress.

Vale lobbed the youth at the soldier on his right, who had wrenched his blade free of his Ruljarian victim and now waited attentively for further direction.

The boy's guardian reached out too late, catching only the fall of Vale's wrist. She yanked herself to her feet and her knee slammed solidly into Vale's leg in a foolish attempt to mar his balance.

Vale stumbled away. His fingers curled around his hilt as he barked to the soldier behind him, "Take the child to the prisoners and add some scars if he resists!" The female stumbled forward in a desperate attempt to intervene, but Vale whipped his sword free of its crimson sheath and swiped viciously at the air between them. "I can tell Adonis with a clear conscience that you're a resistor," he snarled, swinging his blade high for the fatal blow.

At the sight of the glinting steel, a voice inside Alvena leapt to command. She did not allow herself to think—no doubt, no hesitation, no cowardice to stay her blade. Her hand wrenched the dinner knife free into the dim moonlight and she lunged, closing the remaining distance between them. The ebony hilt was nearly swallowed in her hand, so small a weapon against the powerful figure.

But she did not seek his gut or chest: it was the chink beneath his arm that caught Alvena's eye.

As Vale's arm rose into the clouded sky, she drove her knife home.

A thunderous cry erupted from the captain and reverberated down the hilt. Alvena released it as she scrambled away across the stones. Her whole body trembled, alive with the warmth that soaked her glove.

Vale's arm dropped toward his back to clear the deeply plunged hilt. Yet his arm was rapidly growing weak; it knocked against the blade, tearing a cry from his lungs that caused Alvena's heart to stop. He clutched frantically at the rush of blood, staggering away as his wild eyes blinked in rapid succession.

The Ruljen stood immobile, her lips parted, her eyes blank. Alvena thrust a wild hand. *'RUN!'* she screamed internally.

Down the road, the soldier with the youth let out a yelp of surprise. "Captain!" he hollered, and she could hear the thud of his feet as he rushed to aid. At a blur of movement from her peripheral, she knew his charge had bolted free.

'RUN!' she screamed again, thrusting her hand hysterically down the road. *'Just run!'*

Vale had managed to switch his sword to his free arm, and in a delusional rage, he haphazardly lurched for the Ruljen's gut.

The pathetic act was enough to restore the female's wit. With a single whisper of the river tongue, she spun and fled, her wounds hardly inhibiting the speed with which she vanished down the nearest alley.

Vale's sword clattered at his feet. "Gods that's a lot of blood..." he choked, staggering against the nearest building. "You... fucking cunt...!"

A cacophony of shouts penetrated Alvena's stupor. From the north and south, a dozen soldiers rushed to the source of Raestra's commotion.

Alvena's hands dropped limply to her side, but her jaw was set.

For the first time in months, she felt certain of her course.

She had no regrets.

CHAPTER FIFTY

Navon pushed his mug across the table, watching as it skidded through the puddle of spilt ale. There was no one around the small table at which he sat. No company. No one with whom to share a drink. He eyed the two empty mugs placed expectantly before two empty seats, then slid his mug back to his other hand. It made a soft scraping, but at that hour of night, the noise was lost within the din.

"Finally finished the drinks, 'ave we?" a sultry voice inquired as the barmaid sidled over. She cocked her hip, resting her tarnished, bronze tray casually against it. "You've been nursin' those all day, Navon. You stayin' *another* night in 'ere? You need me to fill the other mugs again?"

Navon quickly looked up, shaking away his unease. He smiled. "Yes, thank you, Alessandra. The usual. Still waiting on those friends." He pushed the three empty mugs toward her, glancing toward the dingy window on his right. The night was dark and the usual glow of snow was lost beneath the flurry of blizzard flakes. "It's the damn weather. I don't remember a late winter so bleak!"

He noted a brief pause in her response, but when he returned his gaze, she merely tossed her chestnut curls and donned her rosy dimples. "...I fancy you've got it figured out," she finally spoke, and swung off into the crowd.

She passed through, barely noticed. Across the inn, several bodies slumped in their weathered chairs, their faces steeped in puddles of their own vomit or mutually spilt brew. The rest chattered and sang with enough vigor to rattle the rafters. With Sanae's rich temple traffic, the Painted Stallion was flush with coined men.

Of which Navon was not one, but would be soon. He felt the corners of his lips widen as he recalled General Bardolph's admiration. His praise. His offer.

A twinge of guilt pulled his grin away. *'Humble me, Sel'ari,'* he chastised himself, clenching his jaw. The seat beside him was empty, and yet he had the audacity to consider his fortune!

He forced his teeth apart, but it did little to ease the tension. *'He'll be here. Defeated, pride shaken, but he will come. And as we're a few thousand closer to rising from our debt, he might even dare to show a little gratitude.'*

Navon nearly laughed at the thought. He would have to settle for a begrudging rebuke for his desertion. Perhaps a few comments of, "If you had been there we could have slain him!" and other such nonsense intended to salvage his general's pride.

Navon swiped his hand through the puddle, flinging the amber drops across the muddy floor. He dried his fingers slowly down his leg.

"You a'right?" the sweet voice rang out, and Navon became aware of a throbbing in his thigh.

He released his vise-like grip. "Yes, of course."

Alessandra dropped each mug onto the tabletop with muttered sympathies, extending a hand toward his shoulder. Navon recoiled, rejecting her pessimism through gritted teeth, and the woman hastily departed to answer some vociferous call from across the room.

Damn them if he was forced to finish their ales yet again, but it was just like Jikun to make him wait! If there was any truth to General Bardolph's jest about Black Blood, he would be hairier than a mountain dwarf by the time his companions arrived.

He chugged his liquor vehemently and reached for the second mug. And in that large room bursting with pilgrims and successful men, he was suddenly, entirely…

Alone.

There was an abrupt crash against the tavern wall as the door flew back against its hinges. Cold billowed in with a flurry of twisting snow, enveloping the men nearest in winter's embrace. The din died somewhat as a portion of the crowd turned to glare at the uncouth arrival who dared leave the door wide.

But Navon forgot the cold. His hand dropped from his tankard in relief and elation. "Eldaeus!" he exclaimed.

The Farvian male managed one stumbling, faltering step before he pressed his ragged body against the doorframe. He was coated in white flakes, his hair was laden with ice, and his purple lips trembled violently in the cold.

As Navon's eyes swept over the male, his elation began to fade.

He was alone.

The whites of Eldaeus' eyes engulfed his wild gaze as it flicked about the room. Three long, tattooed fingers pressed hard against his bandaged gut, hardly masking the vibrant stain of red.

And then their eyes met and Navon felt his surge of hope quenched within his breast.

"*Jikun*," Eldaeus rasped, "*Jikun is dead!*"

www.ingramcontent.com/pod-product-compliance
Lightning Source LLC
Chambersburg PA
CBHW030822310726
48980CB00006B/603/J
9780986287756